14/9

'
in

'O
for

's

is item by the last date shown.
ww.hants.gov.uk/library

1

Also by Connie Willis

NOVELS

Water Witch (with Cynthia Felice) (1982)

Lincoln's Dreams (1987)

Light Raid (with Cynthia Felice) (1989)

Doomsday Book (1992)

Remake (1994)

Bellwether (1996)

Promised Land (with Cynthia Felice) (1997)

To Say Nothing of the Dog (1998)

Passage (2001)

Blackout (2010)

All Clear (2010)

SHORT STORY COLLECTIONS

Fire Watch (1985)

Impossible Things (1994)

Uncharted Territory (1994)

Even the Queen and Other Stories (1998)

Miracle and Other Christmas Stories (1999)

The Winds of Marble Arch and Other Stories (2007)

SF MASTERWORKS

Doomsday Book

CONNIE WILLIS

Text copyright © Connie Willis 1992
Introduction copyright © Adam Roberts 2012
All rights reserved

The right of Connie Willis to be identified as the author of this work, and
the right of Adam Roberts to be identified as the author of the
introduction, has been asserted by them in accordance with the
Copyright, Designs and Patents Act 1988.

This edition first published in Great Britain in 2012 by
Gollancz
An imprint of the Orion Publishing Group
Orion House, 5 Upper St Martin's Lane, London WC2H 9EA
An Hachette UK Company

1 3 5 7 9 10 8 6 4 2

A CIP catalogue record for this book
is available from the British Library

ISBN 978 0 575 13109 5

Typeset at The Spartan Press Ltd,
Lymington, Hants

Printed in Great Britain by
Clays Ltd, St Ives plc

The Orion Publishing Group's policy is to use papers that
are natural, renewable and recyclable products and made
from wood grown in sustainable forests. The logging and
manufacturing processes are expected to conform to the
environmental regulations of the country of origin.

www.orionbooks.co.uk

To Laura Cordelia –
my Kivrins

'And lest things which should be remembered perish with time and vanish from the memory of those who are to come after us, I, seeing so many evils and the whole world, as it were, placed within the grasp of the Evil One, being myself as if among the dead, I, waiting for death, have put into writing all the things that I have witnessed.

'And, lest the writing should perish with the writer and the work fail with the labourer, I leave parchment to continue this work, if perchance any man survive and any of the race of Adam escape this pestilence and carry on the work which I have begun . . .'

Brother John Clyn
1349

ACKNOWLEDGMENTS

My special thanks to Head Librarian Jamie LaRue and the rest of the staff of the Greeley Public library for their endless and invaluable assistance.

And my undying gratitude to Sheila and Kelly and Frazier and Cee, and especially to Marta – the friends I love.

INTRODUCTION

Though she has published fewer solo-authored novels than any of them, Connie Willis has won more major SF awards than Philip K. Dick, Arthur C. Clarke and Isaac Asimov combined. If we want to explain that striking fact we might wonder if it's because, whilst she has (like those venerable masters of genre) a copious imagination, prodigious writerly skills and canny way with a novum, she also has something they mostly lack. She makes you *care*. The characters she creates and the worlds she builds – especially the historical worlds of her time travel novels – do more than get under the reader's skin; they seep all the way down to the heart.

There is no better example of this than *Doomsday Book*, Willis' fourth published novel but her first big breakthrough title. The novel sends a 21st-century historian back to the 14th-century to research the period; but though this traveller thinks she is prepared, in fact real life overwhelms her preparations; and though she is supposed to have been sent back to the relative safety of the 1320s in fact an error has resulted her being pitched two decades later, right into the middle of the Black Death. Meanwhile a new strain of influenza is ravaging the 21st-century. The parallel is, in a sense, one of the main points of this novel: that the present, the future and the past are all intimately connected to one another. Put like that perhaps it looks banal, but one of the remarkable things about this novel is the way it makes you feel the truth of it on your pulse.

It's a truth particularly well suited to the 'time travel' story, of course; although, perhaps oddly, it's rarely captured by the very many time travel stories and novels the genre produces and has produced more-or-less continuously since H.G. Wells set the sub-genre in motion with *The Time Machine* (1896). This may be because many writers become fascinated with the question of temporal paradoxes – if I go back in time and kill my grandfather, then I will never be born and so won't be able to go back in time and kill my grandfather, so he will not die and I *will* be born and *will* be able to go back in time and kill my grandfather . . . and so on. Willis is, broadly, uninterested in this sterile 'logic-puzzle' aspect of time travel. What fascinates her is not the (when you think about it) rather callous attitude to life and death implicit in that celebrated paradox. On the contrary, she is interested in the way the past *lives*. She knows that a more than individual memory connects past to present, and a more than individual hopefulness connects the present to the future; but she also knows that the idiom of the past is dying, and that moving into the future is about coming to terms with that bereavement.

Willis has written a wide variety of sorts of SF, particularly in her short fiction (and won awards for a lot of it); but it is increasingly clear that her time travel novels are her major achievement. In her first solo-authored full-length novel, *Lincoln's Dreams* (1987), the mechanism of time travel back to nineteenth-century America is the dream; in *Passage* (2001) her characters are propelled back in time to the last voyage of the *Titanic* via the unusual device of near-death experiences. Both novels tell accessible absorbing stories that also, with considerable aplomb, explore the ways in which the past manifests in the present – or vice versa – in ways that are potent if not quite real; in ways that bring us to the limits of life. This meditation is continued in the loosely-linked series of tales and novels to which *Doomsday Book* belongs, centred on a near-future 'time travel institute' at Oxford University that embeds historians in various historical periods. This series began with the Nebula- and Hugo-winning short story 'Fire Watch' (1982), which is set during a vividly recreated Blitz. *Doomsday Book* – also a Hugo and Nebula winner – styles England at the time of the Black Death as a richly humane tragedy. The Hugo-winning *To Say Nothing of the Dog; Or, How We Found the Bishop's Bird Stump at Last* (1998) takes its characters back to the late Victorian England of Jerome K. Jerome's comic masterpiece *Three*

Men and A Boat. To Say Nothing of the Dog is often funny and charming, although arguably its frivolity undermines its effectiveness, and its considerable length feels diffuse. To be clear: I am not suggesting that Willis cannot write comedy. On the contrary, she often displays a beautifully light touch with the comedy of manners of her epochs. But her comedy works best when it leavens a graver tone. In particular, Willis is unusually astute and moving on the emotional impact of bereavement and mortality. A case in point is the capstone of the 'Time Travel Institute' novels, the Hugo-winning *Blackout/All Clear* – a massive, two part, 1200-page novel that returns to the territory of 'Fire Watch' by depositing a group of historians in Blitz-struck London. As with *Doomsday Book*, what lifts this novel out of the run-of-the-mill historical fiction is its bone-deep understanding of the ways death interpenetrates life.

This resonates in Willis' work in two, connected ways. One is the brute fact of bereavement. In *Doomsday Book*, we come to care for Kivrin, and for many of the medieval villagers (Agnes, Eliwys and Father Roche especially). When characters we care about die it hurts us, and Willis' treatment of death in this novel is never sentimental, and genuinely moving. The other way in which death interpenetrates life has to do with its inevitability. We are all going to die, after all; this is our fate. Part of the way the later sections of this novel achieve their effect is precisely by creating a sense of horrible inexorableness about the spread of the plague. But there's a larger context. The 'Doom' in 'Doomsday' means precisely 'fate'; and one way of defining fate is as a mode of temporal perspective. Julius Caesar has already *been* assassinated; his fate is sealed. *I* feel differently, sitting here in the present; it seems to me like *my* fate is open. But a historian looking back at my life from the vantage point of Christmas 2054 will know what happened to me. From *her* point of view, my fate is as sealed as Caesar's. Fate, in other words, is actually just another word for time.

Now, Willis' Time Travel Institute novels all play cannily, and to good dramatic effect, with this problematic. Her historians go back in time secure in the knowledge that they cannot contaminate the time-lines; but in each of her big novels the past shifts in disorienting ways, opening up the possibility that their meddling might be having deleterious effects upon the flow of history itself after all. This is subtly but effectively worked out in terms of the internal logic of the story in *Doomsday Book* (and is an even more important feature of the later *Blackout* and *All Clear*). But it is more than a plot point. It reflects centrally upon Willis own praxis as a writer, and indeed upon writing itself. After all, when we pick it off a bookshop's shelves to read it, a story has already been told, written down and printed. Yet as we work our way through its pages we are caught up in the moment of the narrative as if its ending were somehow still open. Any novel is a 'doomsday book', an iteration of its own simulated relationship between fate and free will.

To dilate upon this a little: it is striking that the (unnamed) protagonist of the novel that inaugurated 'time travel' as a sub-genre of SF, Wells' *The Time Machine*, has such a frankly contemptuous attitude to the past. He is interested only in travelling into the far future. Willis takes the opposite view. Her fascination with time travel is not speculation about how things will develop in the future: her portrait of Oxford in the 2050s feels more 1950s than anything futuristic, something I take to be a deliberate textual strategy. She is interested, rather, with the relationship between the past and the present. That the present (or her near future) of *Doomsday Book* feels thinner than the richly evoked past is a feature of the novel, not a bug; because of course the past informs life more forcefully than the present. The 2054 historians who confidently assert that 'attitudes to death in the 1300s differed greatly from ours; death was a common and accepted part of life and the contemps were incapable of feeling loss or grief' are shown to be wrong in a way that would be laughable if it weren't so tragic.

There is the question of historical errors. Willis' sense of historical period, though it is the product of years of research, is not flawless (there were many diseases in 14th-century England that produced mass-death, but cholera was not one of them; clerks did not wear silk shirts – silk, in the 13th-century, cost more weight for weight than gold; and, absent twentieth-century snow ploughs, roads would not stand out as 'a straight black line, bisecting the snowy plain' as they do in this novel). But I do not think sunspots like these are of any consequence. Shakespeare's historical plays are full of anachronisms – chiming clocks in *Julius Caesar*'s Rome, a character actually called 'Pistol' during the strictly arrows-and-crossbows warfare of *Henry V* – but these don't matter. Or we can be more precise, and say: they matter only to pedants. Pedantry is not the best frame of mind in which to enjoy a novel like *Doomsday Book*; because, like Shakespeare, she captures the mood of a time, the *feel* of medieval England, and she does so with remarkable vividness. To read *Doomsday Book* is to be drawn immersively into a world that is defined by its difference, both to the present and to the present's ideas of how the past was. And because it feels real, we care about the people in it.

Doomsday Book is a long novel, and it starts slowly; but it is length is not egregious. On the contrary, it embodies in textual form that fundamental physics truth: momentum is mass times velocity. It builds inexorably, and the emotional heft of the final third depends upon the larger sense of world and character that Willis builds in the first two books. You don't want to skip them; not if you want to appreciate the genuinely moving potency of the book's final scenes.

Adam Roberts

BOOK ONE

'What a ringer needs most is not strength but the ability to keep time . . . You must bring these two things together in your mind and let them rest there forever – bells and time, bells and time.'

RONALD BLYTHE
Akenfield

CHAPTER ONE

Mr Dunworthy opened the door to the laboratory and his spectacles promptly steamed up.

'Am I too late?' he said, yanking them off and squinting at Mary.

'Shut the door,' she said. 'I can't hear you over the sound of those ghastly carols.'

Dunworthy closed the door, but it didn't completely shut out the sound of 'O Come, All Ye Faithful' wafting in from the quad. 'Am I too late?' he said again.

Mary shook her head. 'All you've missed is Gilchrist's speech.' She leaned back in her chair to let Dunworthy squeeze past her into the narrow observation area. She had taken off her coat and wool hat and set them on the only other chair, along with a large shopping bag full of parcels. Her grey hair was in disarray, as if she had tried to fluff it up after taking her hat off. 'A very long speech about Mediaeval's maiden voyage in time,' she said, 'and the college of Brasenose taking its rightful place as the jewel in history's crown. Is it still raining?'

'Yes,' he said, wiping his spectacles on his muffler. He hooked the wire rims over his ears and went up to the thin-glass partition to look at the net. In the centre of the laboratory was a smashed-up wagon surrounded by overturned trunks and wooden boxes. Above them hung the protective shields of the net, draped like a gauzy parachute.

Kivrin's tutor, Latimer, looking older and even more infirm than usual, was standing next to one of the trunks. Montoya was standing over by the console wearing jeans and a terrorist jacket and looking impatiently at the digital on her wrist. Badri was sitting in front of the console, typing something in and frowning at the display screens.

'Where's Kivrin?' Dunworthy said.

'I haven't seen her,' Mary said. 'Do come and sit down. The drop isn't scheduled till noon, and I doubt very much that they'll get her off by then. Particularly if Gilchrist makes another speech.'

She draped her coat over the back of her own chair and set the shopping bag full of parcels on the floor by her feet. 'I *do* hope this doesn't go on all day. I must pick up my great-nephew, Colin, at the Underground station at three. He's coming in on the tube.'

She rummaged in her shopping bag. 'My niece, Deirdre, is off to Kent for the holidays and asked me to look after him. I do hope it doesn't rain the entire time he's here,' she said, still rummaging. 'He's thirteen, a nice boy, very bright, though he has the most wretched vocabulary. Everything is either necrotic or apocalyptic. And Deirdre allows him entirely too many sweets.'

She continued to dig through the contents of the shopping bag. 'I got this for him for Christmas.' She hauled up a narrow red-and-green-striped box. 'I'd hoped to get the rest of my shopping done before I came here, but it was pouring rain, and I can only tolerate that ghastly digital carillon music on the High Street for brief intervals.'

She opened the box and folded back the tissue. 'I've no idea what thirteen-year-old boys are wearing these days, but mufflers are timeless, don't you think, James? James?'

He turned from where he had been staring blindly at the display screens. 'What?'

'I said, mufflers are always an appropriate Christmas gift for boys, don't you think?'

He looked at the muffler she was holding up for his inspection. It was of dark grey plaid wool. He would not have been caught dead in it when he was a boy, and that had been fifty years ago. 'Yes,' he said, and turned back to the thin-glass.

'What is it, James? Is something wrong?'

Latimer picked up a small brass-bound casket, and then looked vaguely around, as if he had forgotten what he intended to do with it. Montoya glanced impatiently at her digital.

'Where's Gilchrist?' Dunworthy said.

'He went through there,' Mary said, pointing at a door on the far side of the net. 'He orated on Mediaeval's place in history, talked to Kivrin for a bit, the tech ran some tests, and then Gilchrist and Kivrin went through that door. I assume he's still in there with her, getting her ready.'

'Getting her ready,' Dunworthy muttered.

'James, do come and sit down, and tell me what's wrong,' she said, jamming the muffler back in its box and stuffing it into the shopping bag, 'and where you've been. I expected you to be here when I arrived. After all, Kivrin's your favourite pupil.'

'I was trying to reach the Head of the History Faculty,' Dunworthy said, looking at the display screens.

'Basingame? I thought he was off somewhere on Christmas vac.'

'He is, and Gilchrist manoeuvred to be appointed Acting Head in his absence so he could get the Middle Ages opened to time travel. He rescinded the blanket ranking of ten and arbitrarily assigned rankings to each century. Do you know what he assigned the 1300s? A six. A six! If Basingame had been here, he'd never have allowed it. But the man's nowhere to be found.' He looked hopefully at Mary. 'You don't know where he is, do you?'

'No,' she said. 'Somewhere in Scotland, I think.'

'Somewhere in Scotland,' he said bitterly. 'And meanwhile, Gilchrist is sending Kivrin into a century which is clearly a ten, a century which had scrofula and the plague and burned heretics at the stake.'

He looked at Badri, who was speaking into the console's ear now. 'You said Badri ran tests. What were they? A coordinates check? A field projection?'

'I don't know.' She waved vaguely at the screens, with their constantly changing matrices and columns of figures. 'I'm only a doctor, not a net technician. I *thought* I recognised the technician. He's from Balliol, isn't he?'

Dunworthy nodded. 'He's the best tech Balliol has,' he said, watching Badri, who was tapping the console's keys one at a time, his eyes on the changing readouts. 'All of New College's techs were gone for the vac. Gilchrist was planning to use a first-year apprentice who'd never run a manned drop. A first-year apprentice for a remote! I talked him into using Badri. If I can't stop this drop, at least I can see that it's run by a competent tech.'

Badri frowned at the screen, pulled a meter out of his pocket and started towards the wagon.

'Badri!' Dunworthy called.

Badri gave no indication he'd heard. He walked around the perimeter of the boxes and trunks, looking at the meter. He moved one of the boxes slightly to the left.

'He can't hear you,' Mary said.

'Badri!' he shouted. 'I need to speak to you.'

Mary had stood up. 'He can't hear you, James,' she said. 'The partition's soundproofed.'

Badri said something to Latimer, who was still holding the brass-bound casket. Latimer looked bewildered. Badri took the casket from him and set it down on the chalked mark.

Dunworthy looked around for a microphone. He couldn't see one. 'How were you able to hear Gilchrist's speech?' he asked Mary.

'Gilchrist pressed a button on the inside there,' she said, pointing at a wall panel next to the net.

Badri had sat down in front of the console again and was speaking into the ear. The net shields began to lower into place. Badri said something else and they rose to where they'd been.

'I told Badri to recheck everything, the net, the apprentice's calculations, everything,' he said, 'and to abort the drop immediately if he found any errors, no matter what Gilchrist said.'

'But surely Gilchrist wouldn't jeopardise Kivrin's safety,' Mary protested. 'He told me he'd taken every precaution—'

'Every precaution! He hasn't run recon tests or parameter checks. We did two years of unmanneds in Twentieth Century before we sent anyone through. He hasn't done any. Badri told him he should delay the drop until he could do at least one, and instead he moved the drop up two days. The man's a complete incompetent.'

'But he explained why the drop had to be today,' Mary said. 'In his speech. He said the contemps in the 1300s paid no attention to dates, except planting and harvesting times and church holy days. He said the concentration of holy days was greatest around

6

Christmas, and that was why Mediaeval had decided to send Kivrin now, so she could use the Advent holy days to determine her temporal location and ensure her being at the drop site on the twenty-eighth of December.'

'His sending her now has nothing to do with Advent or holy days,' he said, watching Badri. He was back to tapping one key at a time and frowning. 'He could send her next week and use Epiphany for the rendezvous date. He could run unmanneds for six months and then send her lapse-time. Gilchrist is sending her now because Basingame's off on holiday and isn't here to stop him.'

'Oh, dear,' Mary said. 'I rather thought he was rushing it myself. When I told him how long I needed Kivrin in Infirmary, he tried to talk me out of it. I had to explain that her inoculations needed time to take effect.'

'A rendezvous on the twenty-eighth of December,' Dunworthy said bitterly. 'Do you realise what holy day that is? The Feast of the Slaughter of the Innocents. Which, in light of how this drop is being run, may be entirely appropriate.'

'Why can't you stop it?' Mary said. 'You can forbid Kivrin to go, can't you? You're her tutor.'

'No,' he said. 'I'm not. She's a student at Brasenose. *Latimer*'s her tutor.' He waved his hand in the direction of Latimer, who had picked up the brass-bound casket again and was peering absentmindedly into it. 'She came to Balliol and asked me to tutor her unofficially.'

He turned and stared blindly at the thin-glass. 'I told her then that she couldn't go.'

Kivrin had come to see him when she was a first-year student. 'I want to go to the Middle Ages,' she had said. She wasn't even a metre and a half tall, and her fair hair was in braids. She hadn't looked old enough to cross the street by herself.

'You can't,' he had said, his first mistake. He should have sent her back to Mediaeval, told her she would have to take the matter up with her tutor. 'The Middle Ages are closed. They have a ranking of ten.'

'A blanket ten,' Kivrin said, 'which Mr Gilchrist says they don't deserve. He says that ranking would never hold up under a year-by-year analysis. It's based on the contemps' mortality rate, which was largely due to bad nutrition and no med support. The ranking wouldn't be nearly as high for an historian who'd been inoculated against disease. Mr Gilchrist plans to ask the History Faculty to reevaluate the ranking and open part of the fourteenth century.'

'I cannot conceive of the History Faculty opening a century that had not only the Black Death and cholera, but also the Hundred Years War,' Dunworthy said.

'But they might, and if they do, I want to go.'

'It's impossible,' he said. 'Even if it were opened, Mediaeval wouldn't send a woman. An unaccompanied woman was unheard of in the fourteenth century. Only women of the lowest class went about alone, and they were fair game for any man or beast who happened along. Women of the nobility and even the emerging middle class were constantly attended by their fathers or their husbands or their servants, usually all three, and even if you weren't a woman, you're a student. The fourteenth century is far too dangerous for Mediaeval to consider sending a student. They would send an experienced historian.'

'It's no more dangerous than the twentieth century,' Kivrin said. 'Mustard gas and car crashes and pinpoints. At least no one's going to drop a bomb on me. And who's an experienced mediaeval historian? Nobody has on-site experience, and your twentieth-century historians here at Balliol don't know anything about the Middle Ages. Nobody knows anything. There are scarcely any records, except for parish registers and tax rolls, and nobody knows what their lives were like at all. That's why I want to go. I want to find out about them, how they lived, what they were like. Won't you please help me?'

He finally said, 'I'm afraid you'll have to speak with Mediaeval about that,' but it was too late.

'I've already talked to them,' she said. 'They don't know anything about the Middle Ages either. I mean, anything practical. Mr Latimer's teaching me Middle English, but it's all pronomial inflections and vowel shifts. He hasn't taught me to say anything.

'I need to know the language and the customs,' she said,

leaning over Dunworthy's desk, 'and the money and table manners and things. Did you know they didn't use plates? They used flat loaves of bread called *manchets*, and when they finished eating their meat, they broke them into pieces and ate them. I need someone to teach me things like that, so I won't make mistakes.'

'I'm a twentieth-century historian, not a mediaevalist. I haven't studied the Middle Ages in forty years.'

'But you know the *sorts* of things I need to know. I can look them up and learn them, if you'll just tell me what they are.'

'What about Gilchrist?' he said, even though he considered Gilchrist a self-important fool.

'He's working on the reranking and hasn't any time.'

And what good will the reranking do if he has no historians to send? Dunworthy thought. 'What about the visiting American professor, Montoya? She's working on a mediaeval dig out near Witney, isn't she? She should know something about the customs.'

'Ms Montoya hasn't any time either; she's so busy trying to recruit people to work on the Skendgate dig. Don't you see? They're all useless. You're the only one who can help me.'

He should have said, 'Nevertheless, they are members of Brasenose's faculty, and I am not,' but instead he had been maliciously delighted to hear her tell him what he had thought all along: that Latimer was a doddering old man and Montoya a frustrated archaeologist, that Gilchrist was incapable of training historians. He had been eager to use her to show Mediaeval how it should be done.

'We'll have you augmented with an interpreter,' he had said. 'And I want you to learn Church Latin, Norman French and Old German, in addition to Mr Latimer's Middle English,' and she had immediately pulled a pencil and an exercise book from her pocket and begun making a list.

'You'll need practical experience in farming – milking a cow, gathering eggs, vegetable gardening,' he'd said, ticking them off on his fingers. 'Your hair isn't long enough. You'll need to take cortixidils. You'll need to learn to spin, with a spindle, not a spinning wheel. The spinning wheel wasn't invented yet. And you'll need to learn to ride a horse.'

He had stopped, finally coming to his senses. 'Do you know

what you need to learn?' he had said, watching her, earnestly bent over the list she was scribbling, her braids dangling over her shoulders. 'How to treat open sores and infected wounds, how to prepare a child's body for burial, how to dig a grave. The mortality rate will still be worth a ten, even if Gilchrist somehow succeeds in getting the ranking changed. The average life expectancy in 1300 was thirty-eight. You have no business going there.'

Kivrin had looked up, her pencil poised above the paper. 'Where should I go to look at dead bodies?' she had said earnestly. 'The morgue? Or should I ask Dr Ahrens in Infirmary?'

'I told her she couldn't go,' Dunworthy said, still staring unseeing at the glass, 'but she wouldn't listen.'

'I know,' Mary said. 'She wouldn't listen to me either.'

Dunworthy sat down stiffly next to her. The rain and all the chasing after Basingame had aggravated his arthritis. He still had his overcoat on. He struggled out of it and unwound the muffler from around his neck.

'I wanted to cauterise her nose for her,' Mary said. 'I told her the smells of the fourteenth century could be completely incapacitating, that we're simply not used to excrement and bad meat and decomposition in this day and age. I told her nausea would interfere significantly with her ability to function.'

'But she wouldn't listen,' Dunworthy said.

'No.'

'I tried to explain to her that the Middle Ages were dangerous and Gilchrist wasn't taking sufficient precautions, and she told me I was worrying over nothing.'

'Perhaps we are,' Mary said. 'After all, it's Badri who's running the drop, not Gilchrist, and you said he'd abort if there was any problem.'

'Yes,' he said, watching Badri through the glass. He was typing again, one key at a time, his eyes on the screens. Badri was not only Balliol's best tech, but also the University's. And he had run dozens of remotes.

'And Kivrin's well prepared. You've tutored her, and I've spent the last month in Infirmary getting her physically ready. She's protected against cholera and typhoid and anything else that was extant in 1320, which, by the way, the plague you are so worried about wasn't. There were no cases in England until the Black Death reached here in 1348. I've removed her appendix and augmented her immune system. I've given her full-spectrum anti-virals and a short course in mediaeval medicine. And she's done a good deal of work on her own. She was studying medicinal herbs while she was in Infirmary.'

'I know,' Dunworthy said. She had spent the last Christmas vac memorising masses in Latin and learning to weave and embroider, and he had taught her everything he could think of. But was it enough to protect her from being trampled by a horse, or raped by a drunken knight on his way home from the Crusades? They were still burning people at the stake in 1320. There was no inoculation to protect her from that or from someone seeing her come through and deciding she was a witch.

He looked back through the thin-glass. Latimer picked the trunk up for the third time and set it back down. Montoya looked at her digital again. The tech punched the keys and frowned.

'I should have refused to tutor her,' he said. 'I only did it to show Gilchrist up for the incompetent he is.'

'Nonsense,' Mary said. 'You did it because she's Kivrin. She's you all over again – bright, resourceful, determined.'

'I was never that foolhardy.'

'Of course you were. I can remember a time when you couldn't wait to rush off to the Blitz and have bombs dropped on your head. And I seem to remember a certain incident involving the old Bodleian—'

The prep-room door flared open and Kivrin and Gilchrist came into the room, Kivrin holding her long skirts up as she stepped over the scattered boxes. She was wearing the white rabbit-fur-lined cloak and the bright blue kirtle she had come to show him yesterday. She had told him the cloak was handwoven. It looked like an old wool blanket someone had draped over her shoulders, and the kirtle's sleeves were too long. They nearly covered her hands. Her long fair hair was held back by a fillet and fell loosely on to her shoulders. She still didn't look old enough to cross the street by herself.

Dunworthy stood up, ready to pound on the glass again as soon as she looked in his direction, but she stopped midway into the clutter, her face still half-averted from him, looked down at the marks on the floor, stepped forward a little and arranged her dragging skirts around her.

Gilchrist went over to Badri, said something to him and picked up a carryboard that was lying on top of the console. He began checking items off with a brisk poke of the light pen.

Kivrin said something to him and pointed at the brass-bound casket. Montoya straightened impatiently up from leaning over Badri's shoulders and came over to where Kivrin was standing, shaking her head. Kivrin said something else, more firmly, and Montoya knelt down and moved the trunk over next to the wagon.

Gilchrist checked another item off his list. He said something to Latimer, and Latimer went and got a flat metal box and handed it to Gilchrist. Gilchrist said something to Kivrin, and she brought her flattened hands together in front of her chest. She bent her head over them and began speaking.

'Is he having her practise praying?' Dunworthy said. 'That will be useful, since God's help may be the only help she gets on this drop.'

Mary blew her nose again. 'They're checking the implant.'

'What implant?'

'A special chip corder so she can record her field work. Most of the contemps can't read or write, so I implanted an ear and an A-to-D in one wrist and a memory in the other. She activates it by pressing the pads of her palms together. When she's speaking into it, it looks like she's praying. The chips have a 2.5-gigabyte capacity, so she'll be able to record her observations for the full two and a half weeks.'

'You should have implanted a locator as well so she could call for help.'

Gilchrist was messing with the flat metal box. He shook his head and then moved Kivrin's folded hands up a little higher. The too-long sleeve fell back. Her hand was cut. A thin brown line of dried blood ran down the cut.

'Something's wrong,' Dunworthy said, turning towards Mary. 'She's hurt.'

Kivrin was talking into her hands again. Gilchrist nodded.

Kivrin looked at him, saw Dunworthy and flashed him a delighted smile. Her temple was bloody, too. Her hair under the fillet was matted with it. Gilchrist looked up, saw Dunworthy and hurried towards the thin-glass partition, looking irritated.

'She hasn't even gone yet, and they've already let her be injured!' Dunworthy pounded on the glass.

Gilchrist walked over to the wall panel, pressed a key, and then came over and stood in front of Dunworthy. 'Mr Dunworthy,' he said. He nodded at Mary. 'Dr Ahrens. I'm so pleased you decided to come *see Kivrin off.*' He put the faintest emphasis on the last three words, so that they sounded like a threat.

'What's happened to Kivrin?' Dunworthy said.

'Happened?' Gilchrist said, sounding surprised. 'I don't know what you mean.'

Kivrin had started over to the partition, holding up the skirt of her kirtle with a bloody hand. There was a reddish bruise on her cheek.

'I want to speak to her,' Dunworthy said.

'I'm afraid there isn't time,' Gilchrist said. 'We have a schedule to keep to.'

'I demand to speak to her.'

Gilchrist pursed his lips and two white lines appeared on either side of his nose. 'May I remind you, Mr Dunworthy,' he said coldly, 'that this drop is Brasenose's, not Balliol's? I of course appreciate the assistance you have given in loaning us your tech, and I respect your many years of experience as an historian, but I assure you I have everything well in hand.'

'Then why is your historian injured before she's even left?'

'Oh, Mr Dunworthy, I'm so glad you came,' Kivrin said, coming up to the glass. 'I was afraid I wouldn't be able to say goodbye to you. Isn't this exciting?'

Exciting. 'You're bleeding,' Dunworthy said. 'What's gone wrong?'

'Nothing,' Kivrin said, touching her temple gingerly and then looking at her fingers. 'It's part of the costume.' She looked past him at Mary. 'Dr Ahrens, you came, too. I'm so glad.'

Mary had stood up, still holding her shopping bag. 'I want to

13

see your antiviral inoculation,' she said. 'Have you had any other reaction besides the swelling? Any itching?'

'It's all right, Dr Ahrens,' Kivrin said. She held the sleeve back and then let it fall again before Mary could possibly have had a good look at the underside of her arm. There was another reddish bruise on Kivrin's forearm, already beginning to turn black and blue.

'It would seem to be more to the point to ask her why she's bleeding,' Dunworthy said.

'It's part of the costume. I told you, I'm Isabel de Beauvrier, and I'm supposed to have been waylaid by robbers while travelling,' Kivrin said. She turned and gestured at the boxes and smashed wagon. 'My things were stolen, and I was left for dead. I got the idea from you, Mr Dunworthy,' she said reproachfully.

'I certainly never suggested that you start out bloody and beaten,' Dunworthy said angrily.

'Stage blood was impractical,' Gilchrist said. 'Probability couldn't give us statistically significant odds that no one would tend her wound.'

'And it never occurred to you to fake a realistic wound? You knocked her on the head instead?' Dunworthy said angrily.

'Mr Dunworthy, may I remind you—'

'That this is Brasenose's project, not Balliol's? You're bloody right, it isn't. If it were Twentieth Century's, we'd be trying to protect the historian from injury, not inflicting it on her ourselves. I want to speak to Badri. I want to know if he's rechecked the apprentice's calculations.'

Gilchrist's lips pursed. 'Mr Dunworthy, Mr Chaudhuri may be your net technician, but this is *my* drop. I assure you we have considered every possible contingency—'

'It's just a nick,' Kivrin said. 'It doesn't even hurt. I'm all right, really. Please don't get upset, Mr Dunworthy. The idea of being injured was mine. I remembered what you said about how a woman in the Middle Ages was so vulnerable, and I thought it would be a good idea if I looked more vulnerable than I was.'

It would be impossible for you to look more vulnerable than you are, Dunworthy thought.

'If I pretend to be unconscious, then I can overhear what

people are saying about me, and they won't ask a lot of questions about who I am because it will be obvious that—'

'It's time for you to get into position,' Gilchrist said, moving threateningly over to the wall panel.

'I'm coming,' Kivrin said, not budging.

'We're ready to set the net.'

'I know,' she said firmly. 'I'll be there as soon as I've said goodbye to Mr Dunworthy and Dr Ahrens.'

Gilchrist nodded curtly and walked back into the debris. Latimer asked him something and he snapped an answer.

'What does getting into position entail?' Dunworthy asked. 'Having him take a cosh to you because Probability's told him there's a statistical possibility someone won't believe you're truly unconscious?'

'It involves lying down and closing my eyes,' Kivrin said, grinning. 'Don't *worry*.'

'There's no reason you can't wait until tomorrow and at least give Badri time to run a parameter check,' Dunworthy said.

'I want to see that inoculation again,' Mary said.

'Will you two stop fretting?' Kivrin said. 'My inoculation doesn't itch, the cut doesn't hurt, Badri's spent all morning running checks. I know you're worried about me, but please don't be. The drop's on the main road from Oxford to Bath only two miles from Skendgate. If no one comes along, I'll walk into the village and tell them I've been attacked by robbers. After I've determined my location so I can find the drop again.' She put her hand up to the glass. 'I just want to thank you both for everything you've done. I've wanted to go to the Middle Ages more than anything, and now I'm actually going.'

'You're likely to experience headache and fatigue after the drop,' Mary said. 'They're a normal side effect of the time lag.'

Gilchrist came back over to the thin-glass. 'It's time for you to get into position,' he said.

'I've got to go,' she said, gathering up her heavy skirts. 'Thank you both so much. I wouldn't be going if it weren't for you two helping me.'

'Goodbye,' Mary said.

'Be careful,' Dunworthy said.

'I will,' Kivrin said, but Gilchrist had already pressed the wall panel, and Dunworthy couldn't hear her. She smiled, held up her hand in a little wave and went over to the smashed wagon.

Mary sat back down and began rummaging through the shopping bag for a handkerchief. Gilchrist was reading off items from the carryboard. Kivrin nodded at each one, and he ticked them off with the light pen.

'What if she gets blood poisoning from that cut on her temple?' Dunworthy said, still standing at the glass.

'She won't get blood poisoning,' Mary said. 'I enhanced her immune system.' She blew her nose.

Kivrin was arguing with Gilchrist about something. The white lines along his nose were sharply defined. She shook her head, and after a minute he checked off the next item with an abrupt, angry motion.

Gilchrist and the rest of Mediaeval might be incompetent but Kivrin wasn't. She had learned Middle English and Church Latin and Anglo-Saxon. She had memorised the Latin masses and taught herself to embroider and milk a cow. She had come up with an identity and a rationale for being alone on the road between Oxford and Bath, and she had the interpreter and augmented stem cells and no appendix.

'She'll do swimmingly,' Dunworthy said, 'which will only serve to convince Gilchrist Mediaeval's methods aren't slipshod and dangerous.'

Gilchrist walked over to the console and handed the carryboard to Badri. Kivrin folded her hands again, closer to her face this time, her mouth nearly touching them, and began to speak into them.

Mary came closer and stood beside Dunworthy, clutching her handkerchief. 'When I was nineteen – which was, oh, Lord, forty years ago, it doesn't seem that long – my sister and I travelled all over Egypt,' she said. 'It was during the Pandemic. Quarantines were being slapped on all about us, and the Israelis were shooting Americans on sight, but we didn't care. I don't think it even occurred to us that we might be in danger, that we might catch it or be mistaken for Americans. We wanted to see the Pyramids.'

Kivrin had stopped praying. Badri left his console and came over to where she was standing. He spoke to her for several minutes, the frown never leaving his face. She knelt and then lay down on her side next to the wagon, turning so she was on her back with one arm flung over her head and her skirts tangled about her legs. The tech arranged her skirts, pulled out the light measure and paced round her, walked back to the console and spoke into the ear. Kivrin lay quite still, the blood on her forehead almost black under the light.

'Oh, dear, she looks so young,' Mary said.

Badri spoke into the ear, glared at the results on the screen, went back to Kivrin. He stepped over her, straddling her legs, and bent down to adjust her sleeve. He took a measurement, moved her arm so it was across her face as if warding off a blow from her attackers, measured again.

'Did you see the Pyramids?' Dunworthy said.

'What?' Mary said.

'When you were in Egypt. When you went tearing about the Middle East oblivious to danger. Did you manage to see the Pyramids?'

'No. Cairo was put under quarantine the day we landed.' She looked at Kivrin, lying there on the floor. 'But we saw the Valley of the Kings.'

Badri moved Kivrin's arm a fraction of an inch, stood frowning at her for a moment and then went back to the console. Gilchrist and Latimer followed him. Montoya stepped back to make room for all of them round the screen. Badri spoke into the console's ear, and the semitransparent shields began to lower into place, covering Kivrin like a veil.

'We were glad we went,' Mary said. 'We came home without a scratch.'

The shields touched the ground, draped a little like Kivrin's too-long skirts, stopped.

'Be careful,' Dunworthy whispered. Mary took hold of his hand.

Latimer and Gilchrist huddled in front of the screen, watching the sudden explosion of numbers. Montoya glanced at her digital.

Badri leaned forward and opened the net. The air inside the shields glittered with sudden condensation.

'Don't go,' Dunworthy said.

───◦◦◦───

Transcript from the Domesday Book
(000008–000242)

First entry, 22 December, 2054. Oxford. This will be a record of my historical observations of life in Oxfordshire, England, 13 December, 1320, to 28 December, 1320 (Old Style).

(Break)

Mr Dunworthy, I'm calling this the Domesday Book because it's supposed to be a record of life in the Middle Ages, which is what William the Conqueror's survey turned out to be, even though he intended it as a method of making sure he got every pound of gold and tax his tenants owed him.

I am also calling it the Domesday Book because I would imagine that's what you'd like to call it, you are so convinced something awful's going to happen to me. I'm watching you in the observation area right now, telling poor Dr Ahrens all the dreadful dangers of the 1300s. You needn't bother. She's already warned me about time lag and every single mediaeval disease in gruesome detail, even though I'm supposed to be immune to all of them. *And* warned me about the prevalence of rape in the 1300s. And when I tell her I'll be perfectly all right she doesn't listen to me either. I will be perfectly all right, Mr Dunworthy.

Of course you will already know that, and that I made it back in one piece and all according to schedule, by the time you get to hear this, so you won't mind my teasing you a little. I know you are only concerned for me, and I know very well that without all your help and preparation I wouldn't make it back in one piece, or at all.

I am therefore dedicating the Domesday Book to you, Mr Dunworthy. If it weren't for you, I wouldn't be standing

18

here in kirtle and cloak, talking into this corder, waiting for Badri and Mr Gilchrist to finish their endless calculations and wishing they would hurry so I can *go*.

(Break)

I'm here.

—— ∞∞∞ ——

CHAPTER TWO

'Well,' Mary said on a long, drawn-out breath. 'I could do with a drink.'

'I thought you had to go fetch your great-nephew,' Dunworthy said, still watching the place where Kivrin had been. The air glittered with ice particles inside the veil of shields. Near the floor, frost had formed on the inside of the thin-glass.

The unholy three of Mediaeval were still watching the screens, even though they showed nothing but the flat line of arrival. 'I needn't fetch Colin until three,' Mary said. 'You look as though you could use a bit of bracing up yourself, and the Lamb and Cross is just down the street.'

'I want to wait until he has the fix,' Dunworthy said, watching the tech.

There was still no data on the screens. Badri was frowning. Montoya looked at her digital and said something to Gilchrist. Gilchrist nodded and she scooped up a bag that had been lying half under the console, waved goodbye to Latimer and went out through the side door.

'Unlike Montoya, who obviously cannot wait to return to her dig, I would like to stay until I'm certain Kivrin got through without incident,' Dunworthy said.

'I'm not suggesting you go back to Balliol,' Mary said, wrestling her way into her coat, 'but the fix will take at least an hour, if not two, and in the meantime, your standing here won't hurry it along. Watched pot and all that. The pub's just across the way. It's very small and quite nice, the sort of place that doesn't put up Christmas decorations or play artificial bell music.' She held his overcoat out to him. 'We'll have a drink and something to eat, and then you can come back here and pace holes in the floor until the fix comes in.'

'I want to wait here,' he said, still looking at the empty net. 'Why didn't Basingame have a locator implanted in *his* wrist? The Head of the History Faculty has no business going off on holiday and not even a number where he can be reached.'

Gilchrist straightened himself up from the still-unchanging screen and clapped Badri on the shoulders. Latimer blinked as if he wasn't sure where he was. Gilchrist shook his hand, smiling expansively. He started across the floor towards the wall-panel partition, looking smug.

'Let's go,' Dunworthy said, snatching his overcoat from Mary and opening the door. A blast of 'While Shepherds Watched Their Flocks by Night' hit them. Mary darted through the door as though she were escaping, and Dunworthy pulled it to behind them and followed Mary through the quad and out through Brasenose's gate.

It was bitter cold, but it wasn't raining. It looked as though it might at any moment, though, and the crush of shoppers on the pavement in front of Brasenose had apparently decided it would. At least half of them had umbrellas already opened. A woman with a large red one and both arms full of parcels bumped into Dunworthy. 'Watch where you're going, can't you?' she said, and hurried on.

'The Christmas spirit,' Mary said, buttoning her coat with one hand and hanging on to her shopping bag with the other. 'The pub's just down there past the chemist's,' she said, nodding her head at the opposite side of the street. 'It's these ghastly bells, I think. They'd ruin anyone's mood.'

She started off down the pavement through the maze of umbrellas. Dunworthy debated putting his coat on and then decided it wasn't worth the struggle for so short a distance. He plunged after her, trying to keep clear of the deadly umbrellas and to determine what carol was being slaughtered now. It sounded like a cross between a call to arms and a dirge, but it was most probably 'Jingle Bells'.

Mary was standing at the curb opposite the chemist's, digging in her shopping bag again. 'What is that ghastly din supposed to be?' she said, coming up with a collapsible umbrella. ' "O Little Town of Bethlehem"?'

' "Jingle Bells",' Dunworthy said and stepped out into the street.

'James!' Mary said and grabbed hold of his sleeve.

The bicycle's front tyre missed him by centimetres, and the near pedal caught him on the leg. The rider swerved, shouting, 'Don't you know how to cross a bleeding street?'

Dunworthy stepped backward and crashed into a six-year-old holding a plush Santa. The child's mother glared.

'Do be careful, James,' Mary said.

They crossed the street, Mary leading the way. Halfway across, it began to rain. Mary ducked under the chemist's overhang and tried to get her umbrella open. The chemist's window was draped in green and gold tinsel and had a sign posted in among the perfumes that said, 'Save the Marston Parish Church Bells. Give to the Restoration Fund'.

The carillon had finished obliterating 'Jingle Bells' or 'O Little Town of Bethlehem' and was now working on 'We Three Kings of Orient Are'. Dunworthy recognised the minor key.

Mary still couldn't get her umbrella up. She shoved it back in the bag and took off down the pavement again. Dunworthy followed, trying to avoid collisions, past a stationer's and a tobacconist's hung with blinking red and green lights, through the door Mary was holding open for him.

His spectacles steamed up immediately. He took them off to wipe at them with the collar of his overcoat. Mary shut the door and plunged them into a blur of brown and blissful silence.

'Oh, dear,' Mary said. 'I told you they were the sort that wouldn't put up decorations.'

Dunworthy put his spectacles back on. The shelves behind the bar were strung with blinking lights in pale green, pink, and an anaemic blue. On the corner of the bar was a large fiber-op Christmas tree on a revolving stand.

There was no one else in the narrow pub except a beefy-looking man behind the bar. Mary squeezed between two empty tables and into the corner.

'At least we can't hear those wretched bells in here,' she said, putting her bag down on the settle. 'No, I'll get the drinks. You sit down. That cyclist nearly put you out.'

She excavated some mangled notes out of the shopping bag and went up to the bar. 'Two pints of bitter,' she told the barman. 'Do you want something to eat?' she asked Dunworthy. 'They've sandwiches and cheese rolls.'

'Did you see Gilchrist staring at the console and grinning like the Cheshire cat? He didn't even look to see whether Kivrin had gone or whether she was still lying there, half-dead.'

'Make that two pints and a good stiff whisky,' Mary said.

Dunworthy sat down. There was a crib on the table complete with tiny plastic sheep and a half-naked baby in a manger. 'Gilchrist should have sent her from the dig,' he said. 'The calculations for a remote are exponentially more complicated than for an on-site. I suppose I should be grateful he didn't send her lapse-time as well. The first-year apprentice couldn't do the calculations. I was afraid when I loaned him Badri, Gilchrist would decide he wanted a lapse-time drop instead of a real-time.'

He moved one of the plastic sheep closer to the shepherd. 'If he's aware there's a difference,' he said. 'Do you know what he said when I told him he should run at least one unmanned? He said, "If something unfortunate does happen, we can go back in time and pull Ms Engle out before it happens, can't we?" The man has no notion of how the net works, no notion of the paradoxes, no notion that Kivrin is *there*, and what happens to her is real and irrevocable.'

Mary manoeuvred her way between the tables, carrying the whisky in one hand, the two pints awkwardly in the other. She set the whisky down in front of him. 'It's my standard prescription for cycling victims and overprotective fathers. Did it catch you in the leg?'

'No,' Dunworthy said.

'I had a bicycle accident in last week. One of your Twentieth Centuries. Just back from a World War I drop. Two weeks unscathed at Belleau Wood and then walked into a high-wheeler on the Broad.' She went back to the bar to fetch her cheese roll.

'I hate parables,' Dunworthy said. He picked up the plastic Virgin. She was dressed in blue with a white cloak. 'If he *had* sent her lapse-time, at least she wouldn't have been in danger of freezing to death. She should have had something warmer than a rabbit-fur lining, or didn't it occur to Gilchrist that 1320 was the beginning of the Little Ice Age?'

'I've just thought who you remind me of,' Mary said, setting down her plate and a napkin. 'William Gaddson's mother.'

That was a truly unfair remark. William Gaddson was one of his first-year students. His mother had been up six times this term, the first time to bring William a pair of earmuffs.

'He catches a chill if he doesn't wear them,' she had told Dunworthy. 'Willy's always been susceptible to chill, and now he's so far away from home and all. His tutor isn't taking proper care of him, even though I've spoken to him repeatedly.'

Willy was the size of an oak tree and looked as susceptible to chill as one. 'I'm certain he can take care of himself,' he had told Mrs Gaddson, which was a mistake. She had promptly added Dunworthy to the list of people who refused to take proper care of Willy, but it hadn't stopped her coming up every two weeks to deliver vitamins to Dunworthy and insist that Willy be taken off the rowing team because he was overexerting himself.

'I would hardly put my concern for Kivrin in the same category as Mrs Gaddson's overprotectiveness,' Dunworthy said. 'The 1300s are full of cut-throats and thieves. And worse.'

'That's what Mrs Gaddson said about Oxford,' Mary said placidly, sipping her pint of ale. 'I told her she couldn't protect Willy from life. And you can't protect Kivrin. You didn't become an historian by staying safely at home. You've got to let her go, even if it is dangerous. Every century's a ten, James.'

'This century doesn't have the Black Death.'

'It had the Pandemic, which killed sixty-five million people. And the Black Death wasn't in England in 1320,' she said. 'It didn't reach there till 1348.' She put her mug down on the table and the figurine of Mary fell over. 'But even if it had, Kivrin couldn't get it. I immunised her against bubonic plague.' She smiled ruefully at Dunworthy. 'I have my own moments of Mrs Gaddsonitis. Besides, she would never get the plague because we're both worrying over it. None of the things one frets about ever happen. Something one's never thought of does.'

24

'Very comforting.' He placed the blue-and-white Mary next to the figure of Joseph. It fell over. He set it carefully back up.

'It should be comforting, James,' she said briskly. 'Because it's obvious you've thought of every possible dreadful thing that could happen to Kivrin. Which means she's perfectly fine. She's probably already sitting in a castle having peacock pie for lunch, although I suppose it isn't the same time of day there.'

He shook his head. 'There will have been slippage – God only knows how much, since Gilchrist didn't do parameter checks. Badri thought it would be several days.'

Or several weeks, he thought, and if it were the middle of January, there wouldn't be any holy days for Kivrin to determine the date by. Even a discrepancy of several hours could put her on the Oxford-Bath road in the middle of the night.

'I do hope the slippage won't mean she'll miss Christmas,' Mary said. 'She was terribly keen to observe a mediaeval Christmas mass.'

'It's two weeks till Christmas there,' he said. 'They're still using the Julian calendar. The Gregorian calendar wasn't adopted till 1752.'

'I know. Mr Gilchrist orated on the subject of the Julian calendar in his speech. He went on at considerable length about the history of calendar reform and the discrepancy in dates between the Old Style and Gregorian calendars. At one point I thought he was going to draw a diagram. What day is it there?'

'The thirteenth of December.'

'Perhaps it's just as well we don't know the exact time. Deirdre and Colin were in the States for a year, and I was worried sick about them, but out of synch. I was always imagining Colin being run over on the way to school when it was actually the middle of the night. Fretting doesn't work properly unless one can visualise disasters in all their particulars, including the weather and the time of day. For a time I worried about not knowing what to worry about and then I didn't worry at all. Perhaps it will be the same with Kivrin.'

It was true. He had been visualising Kivrin as he last saw her, lying amid the wreckage with her temple bloody, but that was probably all wrong. She had gone through nearly an hour ago.

25

Even if no traveller had come along yet, the road would get cold and he couldn't imagine Kivrin lying there docilely in the Middle Ages with her eyes closed.

The first time he had gone through to the past he had been doing there-and-backs while they calibrated the fix. They had sent him through in the middle of the quad in the middle of the night, and he was supposed to stand there while they did the calculations on the fix and picked him up again. But he was in Oxford in 1956, and the check was bound to take at least ten minutes. He had sprinted four blocks down the Broad to see the old Bodleian and nearly given the tech heart failure when she opened the net and couldn't find him.

Kivrin would not still be lying there with her eyes shut not with the mediaeval world spread out before her. He could see her suddenly, standing there in that ridiculous white cloak, scanning the Oxford-Bath road for unwary travellers, ready to fling herself back on the ground at a moment's notice, and in the meantime taking it all in, her implanted hands clasped together in a prayer of impatience and delight, and he felt suddenly reassured.

She would be perfectly all right. She would step back through the net in two weeks' time, her white cloak grubby beyond belief, full of stories about harrowing adventures and hairbreadth escapes, tales to curdle the blood, no doubt, things that would give him nightmares for weeks after her telling him about them.

'She'll be all right, you know, James,' Mary said, frowning at him.

'I know,' he said. He went and got them another half pint apiece. 'When did you say your great-nephew was getting in?'

'At three. Colin's staying a week, and I've no idea what to do with him. Except worry, of course. I suppose I could take him to the Ashmolean. Children always like museums, don't they? Pocahontas' robe and all that?'

Dunworthy remembered Pocahontas' robe as being a completely uninteresting scrap of stiff greyish material much like Colin's intended muffler. 'I'd suggest the Natural History Museum.'

There was a rattle of tinsel and some 'Ding Dong, Merrily on High' and Dunworthy looked anxiously over at the door. His secretary was standing in the threshold, squinting blindly into the pub.

'Perhaps I should send Colin up Carfax Tower to vandalise the carillon,' Mary said.

'It's Finch,' Dunworthy said, and put his hand up so he could see them, but Finch had already started for their table. 'I've been looking for you everywhere, sir,' he said. 'Something's gone wrong.'

'With the fix?'

His secretary looked blank. 'The fix? No, sir. It's the Americans. They've arrived early.'

'What Americans?'

'The bell ringers. From Colorado. The Western States Women's Guild of Change and Handbell Ringers.'

'Don't tell me you've imported *more* Christmas bells,' Mary said.

'I thought they were supposed to arrive on the twenty-second,' Dunworthy said to Finch.

'This is the twenty-second,' Finch said. 'They were to arrive this afternoon but their concert at Exeter was cancelled, so they're ahead of schedule. I called Mediaeval, and Mr Gilchrist told me he thought you'd gone out to celebrate.' He looked at Dunworthy's empty mug.

'I'm not celebrating,' Dunworthy said. 'I'm waiting for the fix on one of my undergraduates.' He looked at his watch. 'It will take at least another hour.'

'You promised you'd take them on a tour of the local bells, sir.'

'There's really no reason why you need to be here,' Mary said. 'I can ring you at Balliol as soon as the fix is in.'

'I'll come when we have the fix,' Dunworthy said, glaring at Mary. 'Show them round the college and then give them lunch. That should take an hour.'

Finch looked unhappy. 'They're only here until four o'clock. They have a handbell concert tonight in Ely and they're extremely eager to see Christ Church's bells.'

'Then take them to Christ Church. Show them Great Tom. Take them up in St Martin's tower. Or take them round to New College. I will be there as soon as I can.'

Finch looked like he was going to ask something else and then changed his mind. 'I'll tell them you'll be there within the hour, sir,' he said and started for the door. Halfway there he stopped and came back. 'I almost forgot, sir. The vicar called to ask if you'd be willing to read the Scripture for the Christmas Eve interchurch service. It's to be at St Mary the Virgin's this year.'

'Tell him yes,' Dunworthy said, thankful that he'd given up on the change ringers. 'And tell him we'll need to get into the belfry this afternoon so I can show these Americans the bells.'

'Yes, sir,' he said. 'What about Iffley? Do you think I should take them out to Iffley? They've a very nice eleventh century.'

'By all means,' Dunworthy said. 'Take them to Iffley. *I will be back as soon as I can.*'

Finch opened his mouth and closed it again. 'Yes, sir,' he said, and went out the door to the accompaniment of 'The Holly and the Ivy'.

'You were a bit hard on him, don't you think?' Mary asked. 'After all, Americans can be terrifying.'

'He'll be back in five minutes asking me whether he should take them to Christ Church first,' Dunworthy said. 'The boy has absolutely no initiative.'

'I thought you admired that in young people,' Mary said wryly. 'At any rate, he won't go running off to the Middle Ages.'

The door opened and 'The Holly and the Ivy' started up again. 'That'll be him wanting to know what he should give them for lunch.'

'Boiled beef and overcooked vegetables,' Mary said, 'Americans love to tell stories about our dreadful cooking. Oh, dear.'

Dunworthy looked towards the door. Gilchrist and Latimer stood there, haloed in the grey light from outside, Gilchrist was smiling broadly and saying something over the bells. Latimer struggled to collapse a large black umbrella.

'I suppose we've got to be civil and invite them to join us,' Mary said.

Dunworthy reached for his coat. 'Be civil if you like. I have no intention of listening to those two congratulating each other for having sent an inexperienced young girl into danger.'

'You're sounding like you-know-who again,' Mary said. 'They

wouldn't be here if anything had gone wrong. Perhaps Badri's got the fix.'

'It's too soon for that,' he said, but he sat back down again. 'More likely he threw them out so he could get on with it.'

Gilchrist had apparently caught sight of him as he stood up. He half turned, as if to walk back out again, but Latimer was already nearly to the table. Gilchrist followed, no longer smiling.

'Is the fix in?' Dunworthy asked.

'The fix?' Gilchrist said vaguely.

'The *fix*,' Dunworthy said. 'The determination of where and when Kivrin is that makes it possible to pull her out again.'

'Your tech said it would take at least an hour to determine the coordinates,' Gilchrist said stuffily. 'Does it always take him that long? He said he would come tell us when it was completed, but that the preliminary readings indicate that the drop went perfectly and that there was minimal slippage.'

'What good news!' Mary said, sounding relieved. 'Do come sit down. We've been waiting for the fix, too, and having a pint. Will you have something to drink?' she asked Latimer, who had got the umbrella down and was fastening the strap.

'Why, I believe I shall,' Latimer said. 'This is, after all, a great day. A drop of brandy, I think. *Strong was the wyn, and wel to drinke us leste.*' He fumbled with the strap, getting it tangled in the ribs of the umbrella. 'At last we have the chance to observe the loss of adjectival inflection and the shift to the nominative singular at first-hand.'

A great day, Dunworthy thought, but he felt relieved in spite of himself. The slippage had been his greatest worry. It was the most unpredictable part of a drop, even with parameter checks.

The theory was that it was the net's own safety and abort mechanism, Time's way of protecting itself from continuum paradoxes. The shift forward in time was supposed to prevent collisions or meetings or actions that would affect history, sliding the historian neatly past the critical moment when he might shoot Hitler or rescue the drowning child.

But net theory had never been able to determine what those critical moments were or how much slippage any given drop might produce. The parameter checks gave probabilities, but

Gilchrist hadn't done any. Kivrin's drop might have been off by two weeks or a month. For all Gilchrist knew, she might have come through in April, in her fur-lined cloak and winter kirtle.

But Badri had said minimal slippage. That meant Kivrin was off by no more than a few days, with plenty of time to find out the date and make the rendezvous.

'Mr Gilchrist?' Mary was saying. 'Can I get you a brandy?'

'No, thank you,' he said.

Mary rummaged for another crumpled note and went over to the bar.

'Your tech seems to have done a passable job,' Gilchrist said, turning to Dunworthy. 'Mediaeval would like to arrange to borrow him for our next drop. We'll be sending Ms Engle to 1355 to observe the effects of the Black Death. Contemporary accounts are completely unreliable, particularly in the area of mortality rates. The accepted figure of fifty million deaths is clearly inaccurate, and estimates that it killed one third to one half of Europe are obvious exaggerations. I'm eager to have Ms Engle make trained observations.'

'Aren't you being rather premature?' Dunworthy said. 'Perhaps you should wait to see if Kivrin manages to survive *this* drop, or at the very least gets through to 1320 safely.'

Gilchrist's face took on its pinched look. 'It strikes *me* as some-what unjust that you constantly assume Mediaeval is incapable of carrying out a successful drop,' he said. 'I assure you we have carefully thought out its every aspect. The method of Kivrin's arrival has been researched in every detail.

'Probability puts the frequency of travellers on the Oxford-Bath road as one every 1.6 hours, and it indicates a 92 per cent chance of her story of an assault being believed, due to the frequency of such assaults. A wayfarer in Oxfordshire had a 42.5 per cent chance of being robbed in winter, 58.6 per cent in summer. That's an average, of course. The chances were greatly increased in parts of Otmoor and the Wychwood and on the smaller roads.'

Dunworthy wondered how on earth Probability had arrived at those figures. The *Domesday Book* didn't list thieves, with the possible exception of the king's census takers, who sometimes took more than the census, and the cut-throats of the time surely hadn't kept records of whom they had robbed and murdered, the locations marked neatly on a map. Proofs of deaths away from home had been entirely *de facto*: the person had failed to come back. And how many bodies had lain in the woods, undiscovered and unmarked by anyone?

'I assure you we have taken every precaution possible to protect Kivrin,' Gilchrist said.

'Such as parameter checks?' Dunworthy said. 'And unmanneds and symmetry tests?'

Mary came back, 'Here we are, Mr Latimer,' she said, putting a glass of brandy down in front of him. She hooked Latimer's wet umbrella over the back of the settle and sat down beside him.

'I was just assuring Mr Dunworthy that every aspect of this drop was exhaustively researched,' Gilchrist said. He picked up the plastic figurine of a wise man carrying a gilt box. 'The brass-bound casket in her equipage is an exact reproduction of a jewel casket in the Ashmolean.' He set the wise man down. 'Even her name was painstakingly researched. Isabel is the woman's name listed most frequently in the Assize Rolls and the Regista Regum from 1295 through to 1320.'

'It is actually a corrupted form of Elizabeth,' Latimer said, as if it were one of his lectures. 'Its widespread use in England from the twelfth century is thought to trace its origin to Isavel of Angoulême, wife of King John.'

'Kivrin told me she'd been given an actual identity, that Isabel de Beauvrier was one of the daughters of a Yorkshire nobleman,' Dunworthy said.

'She was,' Gilchrist said. 'Gilbert de Beauvrier had four daughters in the appropriate age range, but their Christian names were not listed in the rolls. That was a common practice. Women were frequently listed only by surname and relationship, even in parish registers and on tombstones.'

Mary put a restraining hand on Dunworthy's arm. 'Why did you choose Yorkshire?' she asked quickly. 'Won't that put her a long way from home?'

She's seven hundred years from home, Dunworthy thought, in

a century that didn't value women enough even to list their names when they died.

'Ms Engle was the one who suggested that,' Gilchrist said. 'She felt having the estate so distant would ensure that no attempt would be made to contact the family.'

Or to cart her back to them, miles from the drop. Kivrin had suggested it. She had probably suggested the whole thing, searching through exchequer rolls and church registers for a family with a daughter the right age and no court connections, a family far enough up into the East Riding that the snow and the impassable roads would make it impossible for a messenger to ride and tell the family a missing daughter had been found.

'Mediaeval has given the same careful attention to every detail of this drop,' Gilchrist said, 'even to the pretext for her journey, her brother's illness. We were careful to ascertain that there had been an outbreak of influenza in that section of Gloucestershire in 1319, even though illness was abundant during the Middle Ages, and he could just as easily have contracted cholera or blood poisoning.'

'James,' Mary said warningly.

'Ms Engle's costume was hand-sewn. The blue cloth for her dress was hand-dyed with woad using a mediaeval recipe. And Ms Montoya has exhaustively researched the village of Skendgate where Kivrin will spend the two weeks.'

'If she makes it there,' Dunworthy said.

'James,' Mary said.

'What precautions have you taken to ensure that the friendly traveller who happens along every 1.6 hours doesn't decide to cart her off to the convent at Godstow or a brothel in London, or see her come through and decide she's a witch? What precautions have you taken to ensure that the friendly traveller is in fact friendly and not one of the cutthroats who waylay 42.5 per cent of all passers-by?'

'Probability indicated there was no more than a 0.04 per cent chance of someone being at the location at the time of the drop.'

'Oh, look, here's Badri already,' Mary said, standing up and putting herself between Dunworthy and Gilchrist. 'That was quick work, Badri. Did you get the fix all right.'

Badri had come away without his coat. His lab uniform was wet and his face was pinched with cold. 'You look half-frozen,' Mary said. 'Come and sit down.' She motioned to the empty place on the settle next to Latimer. 'I'll fetch you a brandy.'

'Did you get the fix?' Dunworthy said.

Badri was not only wet, he was drenched. 'Yes,' he said, and his teeth started to chatter.

'Good man,' Gilchrist said, standing up and clapping him on the shoulder. 'I thought you said it would take an hour. This calls for a toast. Have you any champagne?' he called out to the barman, clapped Badri on the shoulder again and went over to the bar.

Badri stood looking after him, rubbing his arms and shivering. He seemed inattentive, almost dazed.

'You definitely got the fix?' Dunworthy asked.

'Yes,' he said, still looking after Gilchrist.

Mary came back to the table, carrying the brandy. 'This should warm you up a bit,' she said, handing it to him. 'There. Drink it down. Doctor's orders.'

He frowned at the glass as if he didn't know what it was. His teeth were still chattering.

'What is it?' Dunworthy said. 'Kivrin's all right, isn't she?'

'Kivrin,' he said, still staring at the glass, and then seemed suddenly to come to himself. He set the glass down. 'I need you to come,' he said, and started to push his way back through the tables to the door.

'What's happened?' Dunworthy said, standing up. The crib figures fell over and one of the sheep rolled across the table and fell off.

Badri opened the door on the carillon's clanging of 'Good Christian Men, Rejoice'.

'Badri, wait, we're to have a toast,' Gilchrist said, coming back to the table with a bottle and a tangle of glasses.

Dunworthy reached for his coat.

'What is it?' Mary said, reaching for her shopping bag. 'Didn't he get the fix?'

Dunworthy didn't answer. He grabbed up his overcoat and took off after Badri. The tech was already hallway down the street, pushing his way through the Christmas shoppers as if they weren't even there. It was raining hard, but Badri seemed oblivious to that, too. Dunworthy pulled his overcoat more or less on and shoved into the crowd.

Something had gone wrong. There had been slippage after all, or the first-year apprentice had made an error in the calculations. Perhaps something had gone wrong with the net itself. But it had safeties and layereds and aborts. If anything had gone wrong with the net, Kivrin simply couldn't have gone through. And Badri had said he'd got the fix.

It had to be the slippage. It was the only thing that could have gone wrong and the drop still take place.

Ahead Badri crossed the street, narrowly avoiding a bicycle. Dunworthy barged between two women carrying shopping bags even larger than Mary's, and over a white terrier on a leash, and caught sight of him again two doors up.

'Badri!' he called. The tech half-turned and crashed straight into a middle-aged woman with a large flowered umbrella.

The woman was bent against the rain, holding the umbrella nearly in front of her, and she obviously didn't see Badri either. The umbrella, which was covered with lavender violets, seemed to explode upward, and then fell top down on to the pavement. Badri, still plunging blindly ahead, nearly fell over it.

'Watch where you're going, won't you?' the woman said angrily, grabbing at the edge of the umbrella. 'This is hardly the place to run, then, is it?'

Badri looked at her and then at the umbrella with the same dazed look he had had in the pub. 'Sorry,' Dunworthy could see him say and bend to pick it up. The two of them seemed to wrestle over the expanse of violets for a moment before Badri got hold of the handle and righted the umbrella. He handed it to the woman, whose heavy face was red with rage or the cold rain or both.

'Sorry?' she said, raising the handle over her head as if she were going to strike him with it. 'Is that all you've got to say?'

He put his hand uncertainly up to his forehead and then, as he had in the pub, seemed to remember where he was and took off again, practically running. He turned in at Brasenose's gate and Dunworthy followed, across the quad, in a side door to the laboratory, down a passage and into the net area. Badri was already at the console, bending over it and frowning at the screen.

Dunworthy had been afraid it would be awash with garbage, or worse, blank, but it showed the orderly columns of figures and matrices of a fix.

'You got the fix?' Dunworthy said, panting.

'Yes,' Badri said. He turned and looked at Dunworthy. He had stopped frowning, but there was an odd, abstracted look on his face, as if he were trying hard to concentrate.

'When was . . .' he said and began to shiver. His voice trailed off as if he had forgotten what he was going to say.

The thin-glass door banged, and Gilchrist and Mary came in, with Latimer at their heels, fumbling with his umbrella. 'What is it? What's happened?' Mary said.

'When was what Badri?' Dunworthy demanded.

'I got the fix,' Badri said. He turned and looked at the screen.

'Is this it?' Gilchrist said, leaning over his shoulder. 'What do all these symbols mean? You'll need to translate for us laymen.'

'When was what?' Dunworthy repeated.

Badri put his hand up to his forehead. 'There's something wrong,' he said.

'*What?*' Dunworthy shouted. 'Slippage? Is it the slippage?'

'Slippage?' Badri said, shivering so hard he could hardly get the word out.

'Badri,' Mary said. 'Are you all right?'

Badri got the odd, abstracted look again, as if he were considering the answer.

'No,' he said, and pitched forward across the console.

CHAPTER THREE

She heard the bell as she came through. It sounded thin and tinny, like the piped bell music they were playing in the High for Christmas. The control room was supposed to be soundproof, but every time someone opened the anteroom door from outside she had been able to hear the faint, ghostly sound of Christmas carols.

Dr Ahrens had come in first, and then Mr Dunworthy, and both times Kivrin had been convinced they were there to tell her she wasn't going after all. Dr Ahrens had nearly cancelled the drop in hospital when Kivrin's antiviral inoculation had swelled up into a giant red welt on the underside of her arm. 'You're not going anywhere until the swelling goes down,' Dr Ahrens had said, and refused to discharge her from hospital. Kivrin's arm still itched, but she wasn't about to tell Dr Ahrens that because she might tell Mr Dunworthy, who had been acting horrified ever since he found out she was going.

I told him two years ago I wanted to go, Kivrin thought. Two years ago, and when she'd gone to show him her costume yesterday, he was still trying to talk her out of it.

'I don't like the way Mediaeval's running this drop,' he'd said. 'And even if they were taking the proper precautions, a young woman has no business going to the Middle Ages alone.'

'It's all worked out,' she'd told him. 'I'm Isabel de Beauvrier, daughter of Gilbert de Beauvrier, a nobleman who lived in the East Riding from 1276 to 1332.'

'And what was the daughter of a Yorkshire nobleman doing on the Oxford-Bath road alone?'

'I wasn't. I was with all my servants, travelling to Evesham to

36

fetch my brother, who's lying ill in the monastery there, and we were set upon by robbers.'

'By robbers,' he said, blinking at her through his spectacles.

'I got the idea from you. You said young women didn't travel anywhere alone in the Middle Ages, that they were always attended. So I was attended, but my servants bolted when we were attacked, and the robbers took the horses and all my goods. Mr Gilchrist thinks it's a plausible story. He said the probability of—'

'It's a plausible story because the Middle Ages were full of cutthroats and thieves.'

'I know,' she said impatiently, 'and disease carriers and marauding knights and other dangerous types. Weren't there any *nice* people in the Middle Ages?'

'They were all busy burning witches at the stake.'

She had decided she'd better change the subject. 'I came to show you my costume,' she'd said, turning slowly so he could see her blue kirtle and white fur-lined cloak. 'My hair will be down for the drop.'

'You have no business wearing white to the Middle Ages,' he'd said. 'It will only get dirty.'

He hadn't been any better this morning. He had paced the narrow observation area like an expectant father. She had worried the whole morning that he would suddenly try to call a halt to the whole proceeding.

There had been delays and more delays. Mr Gilchrist had had to tell her all over again how the corder worked, as if she were a first-year student. Not one of them had any faith in her, except possibly Badri, and even he had been maddeningly careful, measuring and remeasuring the net area and once erasing an entire series of coordinates and entering it again.

She had thought the time would never come for her to get into position, and after she had, it was even worse, lying there with her eyes closed, wondering what was going on. Latimer told Gilchrist he was worried about the spelling of Isabel they had chosen, as if anyone back then had known how to read, let alone spell. Montoya came and stood over her and told her the way to identify

Skendgate was by its church's frescoes of the Last Judgment, something she had told Kivrin at least a dozen times before.

Someone, she thought Badri because he was the only one who didn't have any instructions for her, bent and moved her arm a little in towards her body and tugged at the skirt of her kirtle. The floor was hard and something was digging into her side just below her ribs. Mr Gilchrist said something and the bell started up again.

Please, Kivrin thought, please, wondering if Dr Ahrens had suddenly decided Kivrin needed another inoculation or if Dunworthy had raced off to the History Faculty and got them to change the rating back to a ten.

Whoever it was must be holding the door open – she could still hear the bell, though she couldn't make out the tune. It wasn't a tune. It was a slow, steady tolling that paused and then went on, and Kivrin thought, I'm through.

She was lying on her left side, her legs sprawled awkwardly as if she had been knocked down by the men who had robbed her, and her arm half-flung over her face to ward off the blow that had sent the blood trickling down the side of her face. The position of her arm should make it possible for her to open her eyes without being seen, but she didn't open them yet. She lay still, trying to listen.

Except for the bell, there was no sound at all. If she were lying on a fourteenth-century roadside, there should be birds and squirrels at least. They had probably been shocked into silence by her sudden appearance or by the net's halo, which left shimmering frostlike particles in the air for several minutes.

After a long minute a bird twittered, and then another one. Something rustled nearby, then stopped and rustled again. A fourteenth-century squirrel or a wood mouse. There was a thinner rustle that was probably wind in the branches of the trees, though she couldn't feel any breeze on her face, and above it, from very far away, the distant sound of the bell.

She wondered why it was tolling. It could be ringing vespers. Or matins. Badri had told her he didn't have any idea how much slippage there would be. He had wanted to postpone the drop while he ran a series of checks, but Mr Gilchrist had said Probability had predicted an average slippage of 6.4 hours.

She didn't know what time she had come through. It had been

a quarter to eleven when she came out of prep – she had seen Ms Montoya looking at her digital and asked her what time it was – but she had no idea how long it had taken after that. It had seemed like hours.

The drop had been scheduled for noon. If she had come through on time and Probability was right about the slippage, it would be six o'clock in the evening, which was too late for vespers. And if it were vespers, why did the bell go on tolling?

It could be tolling for mass, or for a funeral or a wedding. Bells had rung almost constantly in the Middle Ages – to warn of invasions or fires, to help a lost child find its way back to the village, even to ward off thunderstorms. It could be ringing for any reason at all.

If Mr Dunworthy were here, he'd be convinced it was a funeral. 'Life expectancy in 1300 was thirty-eight years,' he had told her when she first said she wanted to go to the Middle Ages, 'and you only lived that long if you survived cholera and smallpox and blood poisoning, and if you didn't eat rotten meat or drink polluted water or get trampled by a horse. Or get burned at the stake for witchcraft.'

Or freeze to death, Kivrin thought. She was beginning to feel stiff with cold though she had been lying there only a little while. Whatever was poking her in the side felt like it had gone through her rib cage and was puncturing her lung. Mr Gilchrist had told her to lie there for several minutes and then stagger to her feet, as if coming out of unconsciousness. Kivrin had thought several minutes was hardly enough, considering Probability's assessment of the number of people on the road. It would surely be more than several minutes before a traveller happened along, and she was unwilling to give up the advantage her appearing to be unconscious gave her.

And it was an advantage, in spite of Mr Dunworthy's idea that half of England would converge on an unconscious woman to rape her while the other half waited nearby with the stake they intended to burn her at. If she was conscious, her rescuers would ask her questions. If she was out cold, they would discuss her and other things besides. They would talk about where to take her and speculate on who she might be and where she might have come from, speculations with a good deal more information in them than 'Who are you?' had.

But now she felt an overwhelming urge to do what Mr Gilchrist had suggested – get up and look around. The ground was cold, her side hurt and her head was starting to throb in time with the bell. Dr Ahrens had told her that would happen. Travelling this far into the past would give her symptoms of time lag – headache, insomnia and a general botch-up of the Circadian rhythms. She felt so cold. Was that a symptom of the time lag, too, or was the ground she was lying on cold enough to penetrate her fur-lined cloak this quickly? Or was the slippage worse than the tech had thought and it was really the middle of the night?

She wondered if she was lying in the road. If she was, she should certainly not stay there. A fast horse or the wagon that had made the ruts might roll right over her in the dark.

Bells don't ring in the middle of the night, she told herself, and there was too much light filtering through her closed eyelids for it to be dark. But if the bell she could hear was a vespers bell, that would mean it was getting dark, and she had better get up and look round before night fell.

She listened all over again to the birds, to the wind in the branches, to a steady scraping sound. The bell stopped, the echo of it ringing in the air, and there was a little sound, like an intaken breath or the shuffle of a foot on soft dirt very close.

Kivrin tensed, hoping the involuntary movement didn't show through her concealing cloak, and waited, but there were no footsteps or voices. And no birds. There was someone, or something, standing over her. She was sure of it. She could hear its breathing, feel its breath on her. It stood there for a long time, not moving. After what seemed like an endless space of time, Kivrin realised she was holding her own breath and let it out slowly. She listened, but now she couldn't hear anything over the throbbing of her own pulse. She took a deep, sighing breath, and moaned.

Nothing. Whatever it was didn't move, didn't make a sound, and Mr Dunworthy had been right: pretending to be unconscious was no way to come into a century where wolves still prowled the forests. And bears. The birds abruptly began to sing again, which meant either it was not a wolf or the wolf had gone away. Kivrin went through the ritual of listening again, and opened her eyes.

She couldn't see anything but her sleeve, which was against her nose, but just the act of opening her eyes made her head ache worse. She closed her eyes, whimpered, and stirred, moving her arm enough so that when she opened her eyes again she would be able to see something. She moaned again and fluttered her eyes open.

There was no one standing over her and it wasn't the middle of the night. The sky overhead through the tangled branches of the trees was a pale greyish-blue. She sat up and looked round.

Almost the first thing Mr Dunworthy had said to her that first time she had told him she wanted to go to the Middle Ages was, 'They were filthy and disease-ridden, the muck hole of history, and the sooner you get rid of any fairy-tale notions you have about them, the better.'

And he was right. Of course he was right. But here she was, in a fairy wood. She and the wagon and all the rest of it had come through in a little open space too small and shadowed to be called a glade. Tall, thick trees arched above and over it.

She was lying under an oak tree. She could see a few scalloped leaves in the bare branches high above. The oak was full of nests, though the birds had stopped again, traumatised by her movement. The undergrowth was thick, a mat of dead leaves and dry weeds that should have been soft but wasn't. The hard thing Kivrin had been lying on was the cap of an acorn. White mushrooms spotted with red clustered near the gnarled roots of the oak tree. They, and everything else in the little glade – the tree trunks, the wagon, the ivy – glittered with the frosty condensation of the halo.

It was obvious that no one had been here, had ever been here, and equally obvious that this wasn't the Oxford-Bath road and that no traveller was going to come along in 1.6 hours. Or ever. The mediaeval maps they'd used to determine the site of the drop had apparently been as inaccurate as Mr Dunworthy had said they were. The road was obviously further north than the maps had indicated, and she was south of it, in Wychwood Forest.

'Ascertain your exact spatial and temporal location immediately,' Mr Gilchrist had said. She wondered how she was supposed to do that – ask the birds? They were too far above her for her to see what species they were, and the mass extinctions hadn't started until the 1970s. Short of them being passenger pigeons or dodoes, their presence wouldn't point to any particular time or place, anyway.

She started to sit up, and the birds exploded into a wild flurry of flapping wings. She stayed still until the noise subsided and then rose to her knees. The flapping started all over again. She clasped her hands, pressing the flesh of her palms together and closing her eyes so that if the traveller who was supposed to find her came past, it would look like she was praying.

'I'm here,' she said and then stopped. If she reported that she had landed in the middle of a wood, instead of on the Oxford-Bath road, it would just confirm what Mr Dunworthy was thinking, that Mr Gilchrist hadn't known what he was doing and that she couldn't take care of herself, and then she remembered that it wouldn't make any difference, and that he would never hear her report until she was safely back.

If she got safely back, which she wouldn't if she was still in this wood when night fell. She stood up and looked round. It was either late afternoon or very early morning, she couldn't tell in the woods, and she might not be able to tell by the sun's position even when she got where she could see the sky. Mr Dunworthy had told her that people sometimes stayed hopelessly turned round for their entire stay in the past. He had made her learn to sight using shadows, but she had to know what time it was to do that, and there was no time to waste on wondering which direction was which. She had to find her way out of here. The forest was almost entirely in shadow.

There was no sign of a road or even a path. Kivrin circled the wagon and boxes, looking for an opening in the trees. The woods seemed thinner to what felt like the west, but when she went that way, looking back every few steps to make sure she could still see the weathered blue of the wagon's cloth covering, it was only a stand of birches, their white trunks giving an illusion of space. She went back to the wagon and started out again in the opposite direction, even though the woods looked darker that way.

The road was only a hundred yards away. Kivrin clambered over a fallen log and through a thicket of drooping willows and looked out on to the road. A highway, Probability had called it. It didn't look like a highway. It didn't even look like a road. It looked more like a footpath. Or a cow path. So these were the wonderful highways of fourteenth-century England, the highways that were opening trade and broadening horizons.

The road was barely wide enough for a wagon, though it was obvious that wagons had used it or at least *a* wagon. The road was rutted into deep grooves and leaves had drifted across and into the ruts. Black water stood in some of them and along the road's edge, and a skin of ice had formed on some of the puddles.

Kivrin was standing at the bottom of a depression. The road climbed steadily up in both directions from where she was and, to what felt like the north, the trees stopped halfway up the hill. She turned round to look back. It was possible to catch a glimpse of the wagon from here – the merest patch of blue – but no one would. The road dived here into woods on either side, and narrowed, making it a perfect spot in which to be waylaid by cut-throats and thieves.

It was just the place to lend credibility to her story, but they would never see her, hurrying through the narrow stretch of road, or if they did catch sight of the barely visible corner of blue, they would think it was someone lying in wait and spur their horses into flight.

It came to Kivrin suddenly that lurking there in the thicket, she looked more like one of those cut-throats than like an innocent maiden who'd been recently coshed on the head.

She stepped out on to the road and put her hand up to her temple. '*O holpen me, for I am ful sore in drede!*' she cried.

The interpreter was supposed automatically to translate what she said into Middle English, but Mr Dunworthy had insisted she memorise her first speeches. She and Mr Latimer had worked on the pronunciation all yesterday afternoon.

'*Holpen me, for I haf been y-robbed by fel thefes,*' she said.

She considered falling down on the road, but now that she was out in the open she could see it was even later than she'd guessed, nearly sunset, and if she was going to see what lay at the top of the hill, she had better do it now. First, though, she needed to mark the rendezvous with some kind of sign.

There was nothing distinctive about any of the willows along the road. She looked for a rock to lay at the spot where she could still glimpse the wagon, but there wasn't a sign of one in the rough weeds at the edge of the road. Finally she clambered back through the thicket, catching her hair and her cloak on the willow branches, got the little brass-bound casket that was a copy of one in the Ashmolean, and carried it back to the side of the road.

It wasn't perfect – it was small enough for someone passing by to carry off – but she was only going as far as the top of the hill. If she decided to walk to the nearest village, she'd come back and make a more permanent sign. And there weren't going to be any passers-by any time soon. The steep sides of the ruts were frozen hard, the leaves were undisturbed, and the skin of ice on the puddles was unbroken. Nobody had been on the road all day, all week maybe.

She straightened the grass up round the chest and then started up the hill. The road, except for the frozen mudhole at the bottom, was smoother than Kivrin had expected, and pounded flat, which meant horses used it a good deal in spite of its empty look.

It was an easy climb, but Kivrin felt tired before she had gone even a few steps, and her temple began to throb again. She hoped her time lag symptoms wouldn't get worse – she could already see that she was a long way from anywhere. Or maybe that was just an illusion. She still hadn't 'ascertained her exact temporal location', and this lane, this wood, had nothing about them that said positively 1320.

The only signs of civilisation at all were those ruts, which meant she could be in any time after the invention of the wheel and before paved roads, and not even definitely then. There were still lanes exactly like this not five miles from Oxford lovingly preserved by the National Trust for the Japanese and American tourists.

She might not have gone anywhere at all, and on the other side of this hill she would find the M40 or Ms Montoya's dig, or an

SDI installation. I would hate to ascertain my temporal location by being struck by a bicycle or a car, she thought, and stepped gingerly to the side of the road. But if I haven't gone anywhere, why do I have this wretched headache and feel like I can't walk another step?

She reached the top of the hill and stopped, out of breath. There was no need to have got out of the road. No car had been driven along it as yet. Or horse and cart either. And she was, as she had thought, a long way from anywhere. There weren't any trees here, and she could see for miles. The wood the wagon was in came halfway up the hill and then straggled south and west for a long way. If she had come through further into the trees, she *would* have been lost.

There were trees far to the east, too, following a river that she could catch occasional silver-blue glimpses of – the Thames? the Cherwell? – and little clumps and lines and blobs of trees dotting all the country between, more trees than she could imagine ever having been in England. The *Domesday Book* in 1086 had reported no more than 15 per cent of the land wooded, and Probability had estimated that lands cleared for fields and settlements would have reduced that to 12 per cent by the 1300s. They, or the men who had written the *Domesday Book*, had underestimated the numbers badly. There were trees everywhere.

Kivrin couldn't see any villages. The woods were bare, their branches grey-black in the late-afternoon light, and she should be able to see the churches and manor houses through them, but she couldn't see anything that looked like a settlement.

There had to be settlements, though, because there were fields, and they were narrow strip fields that were definitely mediaeval. There were sheep in one of the fields and that was mediaeval too, but she couldn't see anyone tending them. Far off to the east there was a square grey blur that had to be Oxford. Squinting, she was almost able to make out the walls and the squat shape of Carfax Tower, though she couldn't see any sign of the towers of St Frideswide's or Osney in the fading light.

The light was definitely fading. The sky up here was a pale bluish-lavender with a hint of pink near the western horizon, and she wasn't turned round because even while she had stood here, it had grown darker.

Kivrin crossed herself and then folded her hands in prayer, bringing her steepled fingers close to her face. 'Well, Mr Dunworthy, I'm here. I seem to be in the right place, more or less. I'm not right on the Oxford-Bath road. I'm about five hundred yards south of it on a side road. I can see Oxford. It looks like it's ten miles away.'

She gave her estimate of what season and time of day it was, and described what she thought she could see, and then stopped and pressed her face against her hands. She should tell the Domesday Book what she intended to do, but she didn't know what that was. There should be a dozen villages on the rolling plain west of Oxford, but she couldn't see any of them, even though the cultivated fields that belonged to them were there, and the road.

There was no one on the road. It curved down the other side of the hill and disappeared immediately into a thick copse, but half a mile further on was the highway where the drop should have landed her, wide and flat and pale green, and where this road obviously led. There was no one on the highway for as far as she could see.

Off to her left and halfway across the plain towards Oxford she caught a glimpse of distant movement, but it was only a line of cows heading home to a huddle of trees that must hide a village. It wasn't the village Ms Montoya had wanted her to look for – Skendgate was south of the highway.

Unless she was in the wrong place altogether, and she wasn't. That was definitely Oxford there to the east, and the Thames curving away south of it down to the brownish-grey haze that had to be London, but none of that told her where the village was. It might be between here and the highway, just out of sight, or it might be back the other way, or on another side road or path altogether. There was no time to go and see.

It was rapidly getting darker. In another half hour there might be lights to go by, but she couldn't afford to wait. The pink had already darkened to lavender in the west, and the blue overhead was almost purple. And it was getting colder. The wind was picking up. The folds of her cloak flapped behind her and she pulled it tighter around her. She didn't want to spend a December night in a forest with a splitting headache and a pack of wolves, but she didn't want to spend it lying out on the cold-looking highway either, hoping for someone to come along.

She could start for Oxford, but there was no way she could reach it before dark. If she could just see a village, any village, she could spend the night there and look for Ms Montoya's village later. She looked back down the road she had come up, trying to catch a glimpse of light or smoke from a hearth or something, but there wasn't anything. Her teeth began to chatter.

And the bells began to ring. The Carfax bell first, sounding just like it always had even though it must have been recast at least three times since 1300, and then, before the first stroke had died away, the others, as if they had been waiting for a signal from Oxford. They were ringing vespers, of course, calling the people in from the fields, beckoning them to stop work and come to prayers.

And telling her where the villages were. The bells were chiming almost in unison, yet she could hear each one separately, some so distant only the final, deeper echo reached her. There, along that line of trees, and there, and there. The village the cows were heading to was there, behind that low ridge. The cows began to walk faster at the sound of the bell.

There were two villages practically under her nose – one just the other side of the highway, the other several fields away, next to the little tree-lined stream. Skendgate, Ms Montoya's village, lay where she thought it did, back the way she had come, past the frozen ruts and over the low hill not more than two miles.

Kivrin clasped her hands. 'I just found out where the village is,' she said, wondering if the sounds of the bells would make it on to the Domesday Book. 'It's on this side road. I'm going to go fetch the wagon and drag it out on to the road, and then I'm going to stagger into the village before it gets dark and collapse on somebody's doorstep.'

One of the bells was far away to the south-west and so faint she could scarcely hear it. She wondered if it was the bell she had heard earlier, and why it had been ringing. Maybe Dunworthy was right, and it was a funeral. 'I'm fine, Mr Dunworthy,' she said into her hands. 'Don't worry about me. I've been here over an hour and nothing bad has happened so far.'

The bells died away slowly, the bell from Oxford leading the way again, though, impossibly, its sound hung longer on the air than any of the others. The sky turned violet-blue, and a star came out in the south-east. Kivrin's hands were still folded in prayer. 'It's beautiful here.'

<hr />

Transcript from the Domesday Book
(000249–000614)

Well, Mr Dunworthy, I'm here. I seem to be in the right place, more or less. I'm not right on the Oxford-Bath road. I'm about five hundred yards south of it on a side road. I can see Oxford. It's about ten miles away.

I don't know exactly when I came through, but if it was noon as scheduled, there's been about four hours' slippage. It's the right time of year. The leaves are mostly off the trees, but the ones on the ground are still more or less intact, and only about a third of the fields have been ploughed. I won't be able to tell my exact temporal location until I reach the village and can ask someone what day it is. You probably know more about where and when I am than I do, or at least you will after you've done the fix.

But I know I'm in the right century I can see fields from the little hill I'm on. They're classic mediaeval stop fields, with the rounded ends where the oxen turn. The pastures are bounded with hedges, and about a third of them are Saxon dead hedges, while the rest are Norman hawthorn. Probability put the ratio in 1300 at 25 to 75 per cent, but that was based on Suffolk, which is further east.

To the south and west is forest – Wychwood? – all deciduous as far as I can tell. To the east I can see the Thames. I can almost see London, even though I know that's impossible. In 1320 it would have been over fifty miles away, wouldn't it, instead of only twenty? I still think I can see it. I can definitely see the city walls of Oxford, and Carfax Tower.

It's beautiful here. It doesn't feel as though I were seven hundred years away from you. Oxford is right there, within walking distance, and I cannot get the idea out of my head that if I walked down this hill and into town I would find all of you still standing there in the lab at Brasenose waiting for the fix, Badri frowning at the displays and Ms Montoya fretting to get back to her dig, and you, Mr Dunworthy, clucking like an old mother hen. I don't feel separated from you at all, or even very far away.

———∞———

CHAPTER FOUR

Badri's hand came away from his forehead as he fell, and his elbow hit the console and broke his fall for a second, and Dunworthy glanced anxiously at the screen, afraid he might have hit one of the keys and scrambled the display. Badri crumpled to the floor.

Latimer and Gilchrist didn't try to grab him either. Latimer didn't even seem to realise anything had gone wrong. Mary grabbed for Badri immediately, but she was standing behind the others and only caught a fold of his sleeve. She was instantly on her knees beside him, straightening him out on to his back and jamming an earphone into her ear.

She rummaged in her shopping bag, came up with a bleeper and held the call button down for a full five seconds. 'Badri?' she said loudly, and it was only then that Dunworthy realised how deathly silent it was in the room. Gilchrist was standing where he had been when Badri fell. He looked furious. *I assure you we've considered every possible contingency*. He obviously hadn't considered this one.

Mary let go of the bleeper button and shook Badri's shoulders gently. There was no response. She tilted his head far back and bent over his face, her ear practically in his open mouth and her head turned so she could see his chest. He hadn't stopped breathing. Dunworthy could see his chest rising and falling, and Mary obviously could, too. She raised her head immediately, already pressing on the bleeper, and pressed two fingers against the side of his neck, held them there for what seemed an endless time and then raised the bleeper to her mouth.

'We're at Brasenose. In the history laboratory,' she said into the bleeper. 'Five-two. Collapse. Syncope. No evidence of seizure.' She took her hand off the call button and pulled Badri's eyelids up.

'Syncope?' Gilchrist said. 'What's that? What's happened?'

She glanced irritably at him. 'He's fainted,' she said. 'Get me my kit,' she said to Dunworthy. 'In the shopping bag.'

She had knocked the bag over getting the bleeper out. It lay on its side. Dunworthy fumbled through the boxes and parcels, found a hard plastic box that looked the right size and snapped it open. It was full of red and green foil Christmas crackers. He jammed it back in the bag.

'Come along,' Mary said unbuttoning Badri's lab shirt. 'I haven't got all day.'

'I can't find—' Dunworthy began.

She snatched the bag away and upended it. The crackers rolled everywhere. The box with the muffler came open and the muffler fell out. Mary grabbed up her handbag, zipped it open and pulled out a large flat kit. She opened it and took out a tach bracelet. She fastened the bracelet around Badri's wrist and turned to look at the blood pressure reads on the kit's monitor.

The wave form didn't tell Dunworthy anything and he couldn't tell from Mary's reaction what she thought it meant. Badri hadn't stopped breathing, his heart hadn't stopped beating and he wasn't bleeding anywhere that Dunworthy could see. Perhaps he had only fainted. But people didn't simply fall over, except in books or the vids. He must be injured or ill. He had seemed to be almost in shock when he came into the pub. Could he have been struck by a bicycle like the one that had just missed hitting Dunworthy, and not realised at first that he was injured? That would account for his disconnected manner, his peculiar agitation.

But not for the fact that he had come away without his coat that he had said, 'I need you to come,' that he had said, 'There's something wrong.'

Dunworthy turned and looked at the console screen. It still showed the matrices it had when the tech collapsed. He couldn't read them, but it looked like a normal fix and Badri had said Kivrin had gone through all right. *There's something wrong*.

With her hands flat, Mary was patting Badri's arms, the sides of his chest, down his legs. Badri's eyelids fluttered, and then his eyes closed again.

'Do you know if Badri had any health problems?'

'He's Mr Dunworthy's tech,' Gilchrist said accusingly. 'From Balliol. He was on loan to us,' he added, making it sound like Dunworthy was somehow responsible for this, had arranged the tech's collapse to sabotage the project.

'I don't know of any health problems,' Dunworthy said. 'He'd have had a full screen and seasonals at the start of term.'

Mary looked dissatisfied. She put on her stethoscope and listened to his heart for a long minute, rechecked the blood pressure reads, took his pulse again. 'And you don't know anything of a history of epilepsy? Diabetes?'

'No,' Dunworthy said.

'Has he ever used drugs or illegal endorphins?' She didn't wait for him to answer. She pressed the button on her bleeper again. 'Ahrens here. Pulse 110. BP 100 over 60. I'm doing a blood screen.' She tore open a gauze wipe, swabbed at the arm without the bracelet, tore open another packet.

Drugs or illegal endorphins. That would account for his agitated manner, his disconnected speech. But if he used, it would have shown up on the beginning-of-term screen, and he couldn't possibly have worked the elaborate calculations of the net if he was using. *There's something wrong.*

Mary swabbed at the arm again and slid a cannula under the skin. Badri's eyes fluttered open.

'Badri,' Mary said. 'Can you hear me?' She reached in her coat pocket and produced a bright red capsule. 'I need to give you your temp,' she said and held it to his lips, but he didn't give any indication he'd heard.

She put the capsule back in her pocket and began rummaging in the kit. 'Tell me when the reads come up on that cannula,' she said to Dunworthy, taking everything out of the kit and then putting it back in. She laid the kit down and started through her handbag. 'I thought I had a skin-temp thermometer with me,' she said.

'The reads are up,' Dunworthy said.

Mary picked her bleeper up and began reading the numbers into it.

Badri opened his eyes. 'You have to . . .' he said, and closed them again. 'So cold,' he murmured.

Dunworthy took off his overcoat, but it was too wet to lay over him. He looked helplessly round the room for something to cover him with. If this had happened before Kivrin left they could have used that blanket of a cloak she'd been wearing. Badri's jacket was wadded underneath the console. Dunworthy laid it sideways over him.

'Freezing,' Badri murmured, and began to shiver.

Mary, still reciting reads into the bleeper, looked sharply across at him. 'What did he say?'

Badri murmured something else and then said clearly, 'Headache.'

'Headache,' Mary said. 'Do you feel nauseated?'

He moved his head a little to indicate no. 'When was—' he said and clutched at her arm.

She put her hand over his, frowned and pressed her other hand to his forehead.

'He's got a fever,' she said.

'There's something wrong,' Badri said, and closed his eyes. His hand let go of her arm and dropped back to the floor.

Mary picked his limp arm up, looked at the reads, and felt his forehead again. 'Where is that damned skin-temp?' she said, and began rummaging through the kit again.

The bleeper chimed. 'They're here,' she said. 'Somebody go show them the way in.' She patted Badri's chest. 'Just lie still.'

They were already at the door when Dunworthy opened it. Two medics from Infirmary pushed through carrying kits the size of steamer trunks.

'Immediate transport,' Mary said before they could get the trunks open. She got up off her knees. 'Fetch the stretcher,' she said to the female medic. 'And get me a skin-temp and a sucrose drip.'

'I assumed Twentieth Century's personnel had been screened for dorphs and drugs,' Gilchrist said.

One of the medics knocked past him with a pump feed.

'Mediaeval would never allow—' He stepped out of the way as the other one came in with the stretcher.

'Is this a drugover?' the male medic said, glancing at Gilchrist.

'No,' Mary said. 'Did you bring the skin-temp?'

'We don't have one,' he said, plugging the feed into the cannula. 'Just a thermistor and temps. We'll have to wait till we get him in.' He held the plastic bag above his head for a minute till the grav feed kicked the motor on and then taped the bag to Badri's chest.

The female medic took the jacket off Badri and covered him with a grey blanket. 'Cold,' Badri said. 'You have to—'

'What do I have to do?' Dunworthy said.

'The fix—'

'One, two,' the medics said in unison, and rolled him on to the stretcher.

'James, Mr Gilchrist, I'll need you to come to hospital with me to fill out his admission forms,' Mary said. 'And I'll need his medical history. One of you can come in the ambulance, and the other follow.'

Dunworthy didn't wait to argue with Gilchrist over which of them should ride in the ambulance. He clambered in and up next to Badri, who was breathing hard, as if being carried on the stretcher had been too much exertion.

'Badri,' he said urgently, 'you said something was wrong. Did you mean something went wrong with the fix?'

'I got the fix,' Badri said, frowning.

The male medic, attaching Badri to a daunting array of displays, looked irritated.

'Did the apprentice get the coordinates wrong? It's important, Badri. Did he make an error in the remote coordinates?'

Mary climbed into the ambulance.

'As Acting Head, I feel I should be the one to accompany the patient in the ambulance,' Dunworthy heard Gilchrist say.

'Meet us in Casualties at Infirmary,' Mary said and pulled the doors to. 'Have you got a temp yet?' she asked the medic.

'Yes,' he said, '39.5 C, BP 90 over 55, pulse 115.'

'Was there an error in the coordinates?' Dunworthy said to Badri.

54

'Are you set back there?' the driver said over the intercom.

'Yes,' Mary said. 'Code one.'

'Did Puhalski make an error in the locational coordinates for the remote?'

'No,' Badri said. He grabbed at the lapel of Dunworthy's coat.

'Is it the slippage then?'

'I must have—' Badri said. 'So worried.'

The sirens blared, drowning out the rest of what he said. 'You must have what?' Dunworthy shouted over their up-and-down klaxon.

'Something wrong,' Badri said, and fainted again.

Something wrong. It had to be the slippage. Except for the coordinates, it was the only thing that could go wrong with a drop that wouldn't abort it, and he had said the locational coordinates were right. How much slippage, though? Badri had told him it might be as much as two weeks, and he wouldn't have run all the way to the pub in the pouring rain without his coat unless it were much more than that. How much more? A month? Three months? But he'd told Gilchrist the preliminaries showed minimal slippage.

Mary elbowed past him and put her hand on Badri's forehead again. 'Add sodium thiosalicylate to the drip,' she said. 'And start a WBC screen. James, get out of the way.'

Dunworthy edged past Mary and sat down on the bench near the back of the ambulance.

Mary picked up her bleeper again. 'Stand by for a full CBC and serotyping.'

'Pyelonephritis?' the medic said, watching the reads change. BP 96 over 60, pulse 120, temp 39.5.

'I don't think so,' Mary said. 'There's no apparent abdominal pain, but it's obviously an infection of some sort, with that temp.'

The sirens dived suddenly down in frequency and stopped. The medic began pulling wires out of the wall hookups.

'We're here, Badri,' Mary said, patting his chest again. 'We'll soon have you right as rain.'

He gave no indication he had heard. Mary pulled the blanket up to his neck and arranged the dangling wires on top of it. The driver yanked the door open and they slid the stretcher out. 'I want a full blood workup,' Mary said, holding on to the door as she climbed down. 'CF, HI, and antigenic ID.' Dunworthy clambered down after her and followed her into the Casualties Department.

'I need a med hist,' she was already telling the registrar. 'On Badri – what's his last name, James?'

'Chaudhuri,' he said.

'National Health Service number?' the registrar asked.

'I don't know,' he said. 'He works at Balliol.'

'Would you be so good as to spell the name for me, please?'

'C-H-A—' he said. Mary was disappearing into Casualties. He started after her.

'I'm sorry, sir,' the registrar said, darting up from her console to block his way. 'If you'll just be seated—'

'I must talk to the patient you just admitted,' he said.

'Are you a relative?'

'No,' he said. 'I'm his employer. It's very important.'

'He's in an examining cubicle just now,' she said. 'I'll ask for permission for you to see him as soon as the examination is completed.' She sat gingerly back down at the console, as if ready to leap up again at the slightest movement on his part.

Dunworthy thought of simply barging in on the examination, but he didn't want to risk being barred from hospital altogether and, at any rate, Badri was in no condition to talk. He had been clearly unconscious when they took him out of the ambulance. Unconscious and with a fever of 39.5. Something wrong.

The registrar was looking suspiciously up at him. 'Would you mind terribly giving me that spelling again?'

He spelled Chaudhuri for her and then asked where he could find a telephone.

'Just down the corridor,' she said. 'Age?'

'I don't know,' he said. 'Twenty-five? He's been at Balliol for four years.'

He answered the rest of her questions as best he could and then looked out the door to see if Gilchrist had come and went down the corridor to the telephones and rang up Brasenose. He got the porter, who was decorating an artificial Christmas tree that stood on the lodge counter.

'I need to speak to Puhalski,' Dunworthy said, hoping that was the name of the first-year tech.

'He's not here,' the porter said, draping a silver garland over the branches with his free hand.

'Well, as soon as he returns, please tell him I need to speak with him. It's very important. I need him to read a fix for me. I'm at—' Dunworthy waited pointedly for the porter to finish arranging the garland and write the number of the call box down, which he finally did, scribbling it on the lid of a box of ornaments. 'If he can't reach me at this number, have him ring the Casualties Department at Infirmary. How soon will he return, do you think?'

'That's difficult to say,' the porter said, unwrapping an angel. 'Some of them come back a few days early, but most of them don't show up until the first day of term.'

'What do you mean? Isn't he staying in college?'

'He was. He was going to run the net for Mediaeval, but when he found he wasn't needed, he went home.'

'I need his home address, then, and his telephone number.'

'It's somewhere in Wales, I believe, but you'd have to talk to the college secretary for that, and she's not here just now either.'

'When will *she* be back?'

'I can't say, sir. She went to London to do a bit of Christmas shopping.'

Dunworthy gave another message while the porter straightened the angel's wings, and then rang off and tried to think if there were any other techs in Oxford for Christmas. Clearly not, or Gilchrist wouldn't have used a first-year apprentice in the first place.

He put a call through to Magdalen anyway, but got no answer. He rang off, thought a minute, and then rang up Balliol. There was no answer there either. Finch must still be out showing the American bell ringers the bells at Great Tom. He looked at his digital. It was only half past two. It seemed much later. They might only be at lunch.

He rang up the phone in Balliol's hall, but still got no answer. He went back into the waiting area, expecting Gilchrist to be there. He wasn't, but the two medics were, talking to a staff nurse. Gilchrist had probably gone back to Brasenose to plot his next drop or the one after that. Perhaps he'd send Kivrin straight into the Black Death the third time round for direct observation.

'There you are,' the staff nurse said. 'I was afraid you'd left. If you'll just come with me.'

Dunworthy had assumed she was speaking to him, but the medics followed her out the door, too, and down a corridor.

'Here we are, then,' she said, holding a door open for them. The medics filed through. 'There's tea on the trolley, and a WC just through there.'

'When will I be able to see Badri Chaudhuri?' Dunworthy asked, holding the door so she couldn't shut it.

'Dr Ahrens will be with you directly,' she said and shut the door in spite of him.

The female medic had already slouched down in a chair, her hands in her pockets. The man was over by the tea trolley, plugging in the electric kettle. Neither of them had asked the registrar any questions on the way down the corridor, so perhaps this was routine, though Dunworthy couldn't imagine why they would want to see Badri. Or why they had all been brought here.

This waiting-room was in an entirely different wing from the Casualties Ward. It had the same spine-destroying chairs as the waiting-room in Casualties, the same tables with inspirational pamphlets fanned out on them, the same foil garland draped over the tea trolley and secured with bunches of plastene holly. There were no windows, though, not even in the door. It was self-contained and private, the sort of room where people waited for bad news.

Dunworthy sat down, suddenly tired. Bad news. An infection of some sort. BP 96, pulse 120, temp 39.5. The only other tech in Oxford off in Wales and Basingame's secretary out doing her Christmas shopping. And Kivrin somewhere in 1320, days or even weeks from where she was supposed to be. Or months.

The male medic poured milk and sugar into a cup and stirred it, waiting for the electric kettle to heat. The woman appeared to have gone to sleep.

Dunworthy stared at her, thinking about the slippage. Badri had said the preliminary calculations indicated minimal slippage, but they were only preliminary. Badri had told him he thought two weeks' slippage was likely, and that made sense.

The further back the historian was sent, the greater the average slippage. Twentieth Century's drops usually had only a few minutes, Eighteenth Century's a few hours. Magdalen, which was still running unmanneds to the Renaissance, was getting slippage of from three to six days.

But those were only averages. The slippage varied from person to person, and it was impossible to predict for any given drop. Nineteenth Century had had one off by forty-eight days, and in uninhabited areas there was often no slippage at all

And often the amount seemed arbitrary, whimsical. When they'd run the first slippage checks for Twentieth Century back in the twenties, he'd stood in Balliol's empty quad and been sent through to two a.m. on the fourteenth of September, 1956, with only three minutes' slippage. But when they sent him through again at 2.08 there had been nearly two hours' and he'd come through nearly on top of an undergraduate sneaking in after a night out.

Kivrin might be six months from where she was supposed to be, with no idea of when the rendezvous was. And Badri had come running to the pub to tell him to pull her out.

Mary came in, still wearing her coat. Dunworthy stood up. 'Is it Badri?' he asked, afraid of the answer.

'He's still in Casualties,' she said. 'We need his NHS number, and we can't find his records in Balliol's file.'

Her grey hair was mussed again, but otherwise she seemed as businesslike as she was when she discussed Dunworthy's students with him.

'He's not a member of the college,' Dunworthy said, feeling relieved. 'Techs are assigned to the individual colleges, but they're officially employed by the University.'

'Then his records would be in the Registrar's Office. Good. Do you know if he's travelled outside England in the past month?'

'He did an on-site for Nineteenth Century in Hungary two weeks ago. He's been in England since then.'

'Has he had any relations visit him from Pakistan?'

'He hasn't any. He's third-generation. Have you found out what he's got?'

She wasn't listening. 'Where are Gilchrist and Montoya?' she said.

'You told Gilchrist to meet us here, but he hadn't come in yet when I was brought in here.'

'And Montoya?'

'She left as soon as the drop was completed,' Dunworthy said.

'Have you any idea where she might have gone?'

No more than you have, Dunworthy thought. You watched her leave, too. 'I assume she went back to Witney to her dig. She spends the majority of her time there.'

'Her dig?' Mary said, as if she'd never heard of it.

What is it? he thought. What's wrong? 'In Witney,' he said. 'The National Trust farm. She's excavating a mediaeval village.'

'Witney?' she said, looking unhappy. 'She'll have to come in immediately.'

'Shall I try to ring her up?' Dunworthy said but Mary had already gone over to the medic standing by the tea trolley.

'I need you to fetch someone in from Witney,' she said to him. He put down his cup and saucer and shrugged on his jacket. 'From the National Trust site. Lupe Montoya.' She went out the door with him.

He expected her to come back as soon as she'd finished giving him the directions to Witney. When she didn't, he started after her. She wasn't in the corridor. Neither was the medic, but the nurse from Casualties was.

'I'm sorry, sir,' she said, barring his path the way the registrar in Casualties had. 'Dr Ahrens asked that you wait for her here.'

'I'm not leaving the Infirmary. I need to put a call through to my secretary.'

'I'll be glad to fetch you a phone, sir,' she said firmly. She turned and looked down the corridor.

Gilchrist and Latimer were coming. '. . . hope Ms Engle has the opportunity to observe a death,' Gilchrist was saying. 'Attitudes towards death in the 1300s differed greatly from ours. Death was a common and accepted part of life, and the contemps were incapable of feeling loss or grief.'

'Mr Dunworthy,' the nurse said, tugging at his arm, 'if you'll just wait inside, I'll bring you a telephone.'

She went to meet Gilchrist and Latimer. 'If you'll come with me, please,' she said, and ushered them into the waiting-room.

'I'm Acting Head of the History Faculty,' Gilchrist said, glaring at Dunworthy. 'Badri Chaudhuri is my responsibility.'

'Yes, sir,' the nurse said, shutting the door. 'Dr Ahrens will be with you directly.'

Latimer set his umbrella on one of the chairs and Mary's shopping bag on the one next to it. He had apparently retrieved all the parcels Mary had dumped on the floor. Dunworthy could see the muffler box and one of the Christmas crackers sticking out of the top. 'We couldn't find a taxi,' he said, breathing hard. He sat down next to his burdens. 'We had to take the tube.'

'Where is the apprentice tech you were going to use on the drop – Puhalski – from?' Dunworthy said. 'I need to speak with him.'

'Concerning what, *if* I may ask? Or have you taken over Mediaeval entirely in my absence?'

'It's essential that someone read the fix and make sure it's all right.'

'You'd be delighted if something were to go wrong, wouldn't you? You've been attempting to obstruct this drop from the beginning.'

'Were to go wrong?' Dunworthy said disbelievingly. 'It's already gone wrong. Badri is lying in hospital unconscious and we don't have any idea if Kivrin is when or where she's supposed to be. You heard Badri. He said something was wrong with the fix. We've got to get a tech here to find out what it is.'

'I should hardly put any credence in what someone says under the influence of drugs or dorphs or whatever it is he's been taking,' Gilchrist said. 'And may I remind you, Mr Dunworthy, that the only thing to have gone wrong on this drop is Twentieth Century's part in it. Mr Puhalski was doing a perfectly adequate job. However, at your insistence, I allowed your tech to replace him. It's obvious I shouldn't have.'

The door opened and they all turned and looked at it. The

sister brought in a portable telephone, handed it to Dunworthy and ducked out again.

'I must ring up Brasenose and tell them where I am,' Gilchrist said.

Dunworthy ignored him, flipped up the phone's visual screen and rang up Jesus. 'I need the names and home telephone numbers of your techs,' he told the Acting Principal's secretary when she appeared on the screen. 'None of them are here over vac, are they?'

None of them were there. He wrote down the names and numbers on one of the inspirational pamphlets, thanked the senior tutor, hung up and started on the list of numbers.

The first number he punched was engaged. The others got him an engaged tone before he'd even finished punching in the town exchanges, and on the last a computer voice broke in and said, 'All lines are engaged Please attempt your call later.'

He rang Balliol, both the hall and his own office. He didn't get an answer at either number, Finch must have taken the Americans to London to hear Big Ben.

Gilchrist was still standing next to him, waiting to use the phone, Latimer had wandered over to the tea cart and was trying to plug in the electric kettle. The medic came out of her drowse to assist him. 'Have you finished with the telephone?' Gilchrist said stiffly.

'No,' Dunworthy said and tried Finch again. There was still no answer.

He rang off. 'I want you to get your tech back to Oxford and pull Kivrin out. Now. Before she's left the drop site.'

'*You* want?' Gilchrist said. 'Might I remind you that this is Mediaeval's drop, not yours?'

'It doesn't matter whose it is,' Dunworthy said, trying to keep his temper. 'It's University policy to abort a drop if there's any sort of problem.'

'May I also remind you that the only problem we've encountered on this drop is that you failed to screen your tech for dorphs.' He reached for the phone. '*I* will decide if and when this drop needs to be aborted.'

The phone rang.

'Gilchrist here,' Gilchrist said. 'Just a moment, please.' He handed the telephone to Dunworthy.

'Mr Dunworthy,' Finch said, looking harried. 'Thank goodness. I've been calling round everywhere. You won't believe the difficulties I've had.'

'I've been detained,' Dunworthy said before Finch could launch into an account of his difficulties. 'Now listen carefully. I need you to go and fetch Badri Chaudhuri's employment file from the bursar's office. Dr Ahrens needs it. Ring her up. She's here at Infirmary. Insist on speaking directly to her. She'll tell you what information she wants from the file.'

'Yes, sir,' Finch said, taking up a pad and pencil and taking rapid notes.

'As soon as you've done that, I want you to go straight to New College and see the Senior Tutor. Tell him I must speak with him immediately and give him this telephone number. Tell him it's an emergency, that it's essential that we locate Basingame. He must come back to Oxford immediately.'

'Do you think he'll be able to, sir?'

'What do you mean? Has there been a message from Basingame? Has something happened to him?'

'Not that I know of, sir.'

'Well, then, of course he'll be able to come back. He's only on a fishing trip. It's not as if he's on a schedule. After you've spoken to the Senior Tutor, ask any staff and students you can find. Perhaps one of them has an idea as to where Basingame is. And while you're there, find out whether any of their techs are here in Oxford.'

'Yes, sir,' Finch said. 'But what should I do with the Americans?'

'You'll have to tell them I'm sorry to have missed them, but that I was unavoidably detained. They're supposed to leave for Ely at four, aren't they?'

'They were, but—'

'But what?'

'Well, sir, I took them round to see Great Tom and Old Marston Church and all, but when I tried to take them out to Iffley, we were stopped.'

'Stopped?' Dunworthy said. 'By whom?'

'The police, sir. They had barricades up. The thing is, the Americans are very upset about their handbell concert.'

'Barricades?' Dunworthy said.

'Yes, sir. On the A4158. Should I put the Americans up in Salvin, sir? William Gaddson and Tom Gailey are on the north staircase, but Basevi's being painted.'

'I don't understand,' Dunworthy said. 'Why were you stopped?'

'The quarantine,' Finch said, looking surprised. 'I could put them in Fisher's. The heat's been turned off for vac, but they could use the fireplaces.'

Transcript from the Domesday Book
(000618–000735)

I'm back at the drop site. It's some distance from the road. I'm going to drag the wagon out on to the road so that my chances of being seen are better, but if no one happens along in the next half hour I intend to walk to Skendgate, which I have located thanks to the bells of evening vespers.

I am experiencing considerable time lag. My head aches pretty badly and I keep having chills. The symptoms are worse than I understood them to be from Badri and Dr Ahrens. The headache particularly. I'm glad the village isn't far.

CHAPTER FIVE

Quarantine. Of course, Dunworthy thought. The medic sent to fetch Montoya, and Mary's questions about Pakistan, and all of them put here in this isolated, self-contained room with a ward sister guarding the door. Of course.

'Will Salvin do, then? For the Americans?' Finch was asking.

'Did the police say why a quar—' He stopped. Gilchrist was watching him, but Dunworthy didn't think he could see the screen from where he was, Latimer was fussing over the tea trolley, trying to open a sugar packet. The female medic was asleep. 'Did the police say why these precautions had been taken?'

'No, sir. Only that it was Oxford and immediate environs, and to contact the National Health for instructions.'

'Did you contact them?'

'No, sir. I've been trying. I can't get through. All the trunk lines have been engaged as well. The Americans have been trying to reach Ely to cancel their concert, but the lines are jammed.'

Oxford and environs. That meant they had stopped the tube as well, and the bullet train to London, as well as blocking all the roads. No wonder the lines were jammed. 'How long ago was this? When you went out to Iffley?'

'It was a bit after three, sir. I've been phoning round since then, trying to find you, and then I thought: perhaps he knows about it already. I rang up Infirmary and then started calling round to all the hospitals.'

I didn't know about it already, Dunworthy thought. He tried to recall the conditions required for calling a quarantine. The original regulations had required it in every case of 'unidentified disease or suspicion of contagion', but those had been passed in

65

the first hysteria after the Pandemic, and they had been amended and watered down every few years since then till Dunworthy had no idea what they were now.

He did know that a few years ago they'd been 'absolute identification of dangerous infectious disease' because there'd been a fuss in the papers when Lassa fever had raged unchecked for three weeks in a town in Spain. The local doctors hadn't done viral typing, and the whole mess had resulted in a push to put teeth in the regulations, but he had no idea if they had gone through.

'Should I assign them rooms in Salvin then, sir?' Finch asked again.

'Yes. No. Put them in the junior common room for now. They can practise their changes or whatever it is they do. Get Badri's file and phone it in. If the lines are all engaged, you'd best phone it in to this number. I'll be here even if Dr Ahrens isn't. And then find out about Basingame. It's more important than ever that we locate him. You can assign the Americans rooms later.'

'They're very upset, sir.'

So am I, Dunworthy thought. 'Tell the Americans I'll find out what I can about the situation and ring you back.' He watched the screen go grey.

'You can't wait to inform Basingame of what you perceive to be Mediaeval's failure, can you?' Gilchrist said. 'In spite of the fact that it was *your* tech who has jeopardised this drop by using drugs, a fact of which you may be sure I will inform Mr Basingame on his return.'

Dunworthy looked at his digital. It was half past four. Finch had said they'd been stopped at a bit after three. An hour and a half, Oxford had only had two temp quarantines in recent years. One had turned out to be an allergic reaction to an injection, and the other one had turned out to be nothing at all, a schoolgirl prank. Both had been called off as soon as they had the results of the blood tests, and those hadn't taken even a quarter of an hour. Mary had taken blood in the ambulance. Dunworthy had seen the medic hand the vials to the house officer when they came into Casualties. There had been ample time for them to obtain the results.

'I'm certain Mr *Basingame* will also be interested in hearing that it was your failure to have your tech screened that's resulted in this drop being jeopardised,' Gilchrist said.

Dunworthy should have recognised the symptoms as those of an infection: Badri's low blood pressure, his laboured breathing, his elevated temp. Mary had even said in the ambulance that it had to be an infection of some kind with his temp that high, but he had assumed she meant a localised infection, staph or an inflamed appendix. And what disease could it be? Smallpox and typhoid had been eradicated back in the twentieth century and polio in this one. Bacterials didn't have a chance against antibody specification, and the antivirals worked so well nobody even had colds any more.

'It seems distinctly odd that after being so concerned about the precautions Mediaeval was taking that you wouldn't take the obvious precaution of screening your tech for drugs,' Gilchrist said.

It must be a thirdworld disease. Mary had asked all those questions about whether Badri had been out of the Community, about his Pakistani relatives. But Pakistan wasn't thirdworld, and Badri couldn't have gone out of the Community without a whole series of inoculations. And he hadn't gone outside the EC. Except for the Hungarian on-site, he'd been in England all term.

'I would like to use the telephone,' Gilchrist was saying. 'I quite agree that we need Basingame here to take matters in hand.'

Dunworthy was still holding the phone. He blinked at it, surprised.

'Do you mean to prevent me from phoning Basingame?' Gilchrist said.

Latimer stood up. 'What is it?' he said, his arms held out as if he thought Dunworthy might pitch forward into them. 'What's wrong?'

'Badri isn't using,' Dunworthy said to Gilchrist. 'He's ill.'

'I fail to see how you can claim to know that without having run a screen,' Gilchrist said, looking pointedly at the phone.

'We're under quarantine,' Dunworthy said. 'It's some sort of infectious disease.'

'It's a virus,' Mary said from the door. 'We don't have it

sequenced yet, but the preliminary results ID it as a viral infection.'

She had unbuttoned her coat and it flapped behind her like Kivrin's cloak as she hurried into the room. She was carrying a lab tray by the handle. It was piled high with equipment and paper packets.

'The tests indicate that it's probably a myxovirus,' she said, setting the tray down on one of the end tables, 'Badri's symptoms are compatible with that: high fever, disorientation, headache. It's definitely not a retrovirus or a picorna-virus, which is good news, but it will be some time yet before we have a complete ID.'

She pulled two chairs up next to the table and sat down on one. 'We've notified the World Influenza Centre in London and sent them samples for ident and sequencing. Until we have a positive ID, a temp quarantine has been called as required by NHS regulations in cases of possible epidemic conditions.' She pulled on a pair of imperm gloves.

'Epidemic!' Gilchrist said, shooting a furious glance at Dunworthy as if accusing him of engineering the quarantine to discredit Mediaeval.

'Possible epidemic conditions,' Mary corrected, tearing open paper packets. 'There is no epidemic as yet. Badri's is the only case so far. We've run a Community computer check, and there have been no other cases with Badri's profile, which is also good news.'

'How can he have a viral infection?' Gilchrist said, still glaring at Dunworthy. 'I suppose Mr Dunworthy didn't bother to check for that either.'

'Badri's an employee of the University,' Mary said. 'He should have had the usual start-of-term physical and antivirals.'

'You don't *know*?' Gilchrist said.

'The Registrar's office is closed for Christmas,' she said. 'I haven't been able to reach the Registrar, and I can't call up Badri's files without his NHS number.'

'I've sent my secretary to our bursar's office to see if we have hard copies of the University's files,' Dunworthy said. 'We should at the least have his number.'

'Good,' Mary said. 'We'll be able to tell a good deal more

about the sort of virus we're dealing with when we know what antivirals Badri's had and how recently. He may have a history of anomalous reactions, and there's also a chance he's missed a seasonal. Do you happen to know his religion, Mr Dunworthy? Is he New Hindu?'

Dunworthy shook his head. 'He's Church of England,' he said, knowing what Mary was getting at. The New Hindus believed that all life was sacred, including killed viruses, if killed was the right word. They refused to have any inoculations or vaccines. The University gave them waivers on religious grounds but didn't allow them to live in college. 'Badri's had his start-of-term clearance. He'd never have been allowed to work the net without it.'

Mary nodded as if she had already come to that conclusion. 'As I said, this is very likely an anomaly.'

Gilchrist started to say something, but stopped when the door opened. The nurse who had been guarding the door came in, wearing a mask and gown and carrying pencils and a sheaf of papers in her imperm-gloved hands.

'As a precaution, we need to test those people who have been in contact with the patient for antibodies. We'll need bloods and temps, and we need each of you to list all of your contacts and those of Mr Chaudhuri.'

The nurse handed several sheets of paper and a pencil to Dunworthy. The top sheet was an hospital admissions form. The one underneath was headed 'Primaries' and divided into columns marked 'Name, location, time'. The bottom sheet was just the same except that it was headed 'Secondaries'.

'Since Badri is our only case,' Mary said, 'we are considering him the index case. We do not have a positive mode of transmission yet, so you must list anyone who's had any contact with Badri, however momentary. Anyone he spoke to, touched, has had any contact with.'

Dunworthy had a sudden image of Badri leaning over Kivrin, adjusting her sleeve, moving her arm.

'Anyone at all who may have been exposed,' Mary said.

'Including all of us,' the medic said.

'Yes,' Mary said.

'And Kivrin,' Dunworthy said.

For a moment she looked like she had no idea at all who Kivrin was.

'Ms Engle has had full-spectrum antivirals and T-cell enhancement,' Gilchrist said. 'She would not be at risk, would she?'

Dr Ahrens hesitated only a second. 'No. She didn't have any contact with Badri before this morning, did she?'

'Mr Dunworthy only offered me the use of his tech two days ago,' Gilchrist said, practically snatching the papers and pencil the nurse was offering him out of her hands. 'I, of course, assumed that Mr Dunworthy had taken the same precautions with his techs which Mediaeval had. It has become apparent, however, that he didn't, and you may be sure I will inform Basingame of your negligence, Mr Dunworthy.'

'If Kivrin's first contact with Badri was this morning, she was fully protected,' Mary said. 'Mr Gilchrist, if you'd be so good.' She indicated the chair and he came and sat down.

Mary took one of the sets of papers from the nurse and held up the sheet marked 'Primaries'. 'Any person Badri had contact with is a primary contact. Any person you have had contact with is a secondary. On this sheet I would like you to list all contacts you have had with Badri Chaudhuri over the last three days, and any contacts of his that you know of. On *this* sheet—' she held up the sheet marked 'Secondaries' – 'list all your contacts with the time you had them. Begin with the present and work backwards.'

She popped a temp into Gilchrist's mouth, peeled a portable monitor off its paper strip and stuck it on his wrist. The nurse passed the papers out to Latimer and the medic. Dunworthy sat down and began filling in his own.

The Infirmary form asked for his name, National Health Service number, and a complete medical history, which the NHS number could no doubt call up in better detail than he could remember it. Illnesses. Surgeries. Inoculations. If Mary didn't have Badri's NHS number that meant he was still unconscious.

Dunworthy had no idea what date his last start-of-term antivirals had been. He put question marks next to them, turned to the Primaries sheet and wrote his own name at the top of the column. Latimer, Gilchrist, the two medics. He didn't know their names, and the female medic was asleep again. She held her papers bunched in one hand, her arms folded across her chest. Dunworthy wondered if he needed to list the doctors and nurses who had worked on Badri when he came in. He wrote 'Casualties Department staff' and then put a question mark after it. Montoya.

And Kivrin, who, according to Mary, was fully protected. 'Something's wrong,' Badri had said. Had he meant this infection? Had he realised he was getting ill while he was trying to get the fix and come running to the pub to tell them he had exposed Kivrin?

The pub. There hadn't been anyone in the pub except the barman. And Finch, but he'd gone before Badri got there. Dunworthy lifted up the sheet and wrote Finch's name under 'Secondaries', and then turned back to the first sheet and wrote 'Barman, Lamb and Cross'. The pub had been empty, but the streets hadn't been. He could see Badri in his mind's eye, pushing his way through the Christmas crowd, barging into the woman with the lavender-flowered umbrella and elbowing his way past the old man and the little boy with the white terrier. 'Anyone he's had any contact with,' Mary had said.

He looked across at Mary, who was holding Gilchrist's wrist and making careful entries in a chart. Was she going to try to get bloods and temps from everyone on these lists? It was impossible. Badri had touched or brushed past or breathed on dozens of people in his headlong flight back to Brasenose, none of whom Dunworthy, or Badri, would recognise again. Doubtless he had come in contact with as many or more on his way to the pub, and each of them had come in contact with how many others in the busy shops?

He wrote down 'Large number of shoppers and pedestrians, High Street(?)' drew a line, and tried to remember the other occasions on which he'd seen Badri. He hadn't asked him to run the net until two days ago, when he'd found out from Kivrin that Gilchrist was intending to use a first-year apprentice.

Badri had just come back from London when Dunworthy telephoned. Kivrin had been in hospital that day for her final examination, which was good. She couldn't have had any contact with him then, and he'd been in London before that.

On Tuesday Badri had come to see Dunworthy to tell him he'd

checked the first-year student's coordinates and done a full systems check. Dunworthy hadn't been there, so he'd left a note. Kivrin had come to Balliol on Tuesday as well, to show him her costume, but that had been in the morning. Badri had said in his note that he'd spent all morning at the net. And Kivrin had said she was going to see Latimer at the Bodleian in the afternoon. But she might have gone back to the net after that, or have been there before she came to show him her costume.

The door opened and the nurse ushered Montoya in. Her terrorist jacket and jeans were wet. It must still be raining. 'What's going on?' she said to Mary, who was labelling a vial of Gilchrist's blood.

'It *seems*,' Gilchrist said, pressing a wad of cotton wool to the inside of his arm and standing up, 'that Mr Dunworthy failed to have his tech properly checked for inoculations before he ran the net, and now he is in hospital with a temperature of 39.5. He apparently has some sort of exotic fever.'

'Fever?' Montoya said, looking bewildered. 'Isn't 39.5 low?'

'It's 103 degrees in Fahrenheit,' Mary said, sliding the vial into its carrier. 'Badri's infection is possibly contagious. I need to run some tests and you'll need to write down all of your contacts and Badri's.'

'Okay,' Montoya said. She sat down in the chair Gilchrist had vacated and shrugged off her jacket. Mary swabbed the inside of her arm and clipped a new vial and disposable punch together. 'Let's get it over with. I've got to get back to my dig.'

'You can't go back,' Gilchrist said. 'Haven't you heard? We're under quarantine, thanks to Mr Dunworthy's carelessness.'

'Quarantine?' she said and jerked so the punch missed her arm completely. The idea of a disease she might contract had not affected her at all, but the mention of a quarantine did. 'I have to get back,' she said, appealing to Mary. 'You mean I have to stay here?'

'Until we have the blood test results,' Mary said, trying to find a vein for the punch.

'How long will that be?' Montoya said, trying to look at her digital with the arm Mary was working on. 'The guy who brought me in didn't even let me cover up the site or turn off the heaters,

72

and it's raining like crazy out there. I've got a dig that's going to be full of water if I don't get out there.'

'As long as it takes to get blood samples from all of you and run an antibodies count on them,' Mary said, and Montoya must have got the message because she straightened out her arm and held it still. Mary filled a vial with her blood, gave her her temp, and slid a tach bracelet on. Dunworthy watched her, wondering if she had been telling the truth. She hadn't said Montoya could leave after they had the test results, only that she had to stay here until they were in. And what then? Would they be taken to an isolation ward together or separately? Or given some sort of medication? Or more tests?

Mary took Montoya's tach bracelet off and handed her the last set of papers. 'Mr Latimer? You're next.'

Latimer stood up, holding his papers. He looked at them confusedly, then set them down on the chair he'd been sitting on, and started over to Mary. Halfway there, he turned and went back for Mary's shopping bag. 'You left this at Brasenose,' he said, holding it out to Mary.

'Oh, thank you,' she said. 'Just set it next to the table, won't you? These gloves are sterile.'

Latimer set the bag down, tipping it slightly. The end of the muffler trailed out on the floor. He methodically tucked it back in.

'I'd completely forgotten I left it there,' Mary said, watching him. 'In all the excitement, I—' She clapped her gloved hand over her mouth. 'Oh, my Lord! Colin! I'd forgotten all about him. What time is it?'

'Four-oh-eight,' Montoya said without looking at her digital.

'He was supposed to come in at three,' Mary said, standing up and clattering the vials of blood in their carrier.

'Perhaps when you weren't there he went round to your rooms,' Dunworthy said.

She shook her head. 'This is the first time he's been to Oxford. That's why I told him I'd be there to meet him. I never even gave him a thought until now,' she said, almost to herself.

'Well, then, he'll still be at the Underground station,' Dunworthy said. 'Shall I go and fetch him?'

'No,' she said. 'You've been exposed.'

'I'll phone the station, then. You can tell him to take a taxi here. Where was he coming in? Cornmarket?'

'Yes, Cornmarket.'

Dunworthy rang up information, got through on the third try, got the number off the screen and rang the station. The line was engaged. He hit disconnect and punched the number in again.

'Is Colin your grandson?' Montoya said. She had put aside her papers. The others didn't seem to be paying any attention to this latest development. Gilchrist was filling in his forms and glaring, as if this were one more example of negligence and incompetence. Latimer was sitting patiently by the tray, his sleeve rolled up. The medic was still asleep.

'Colin's my great-nephew,' Mary said. 'He was coming up on the tube to spend Christmas with me.'

'What time was the quarantine called?'

'Ten past three,' Mary said.

Dunworthy held up his hand to indicate he'd got through. 'Is that Cornmarket Underground Station?' he said. It obviously was. He could see the gates and a lot of people behind an irritated-looking stationmaster. 'I'm phoning about a boy who came in on the tube at three o'clock. He's twelve. He would have come in from London.' Dunworthy held his hand over the receiver and asked Mary, 'What does he look like?'

'He's blond and has blue eyes. He's tall for his age.'

'Tall,' Dunworthy said loudly over the sound of the crowd. 'His name is Colin—'

'Templer,' Mary said. 'Deirdre said he'd take the tube from Marble Arch at one.'

'Colin Templer. Have you seen him?'

'What the bloody hell do you mean have I seen him?' the stationmaster shouted. 'I've got five hundred people in this station and you want to know if I've seen a little boy. Look at this mess.'

The visual abruptly showed a milling crowd. Dunworthy scanned it, looking for a tallish boy with blond hair and blue eyes. It switched back to the stationmaster.

'There's just been a temp quarantine,' he shouted over the roar that seemed to get louder by the minute, 'and I've got a station full of people who want to know why the trains have stopped and why don't I do something about it. I've got all I can do to keep them from tearing the place apart. I can't bother about a boy.'

'His name is Colin Templer,' Dunworthy shouted. 'His great-aunt was supposed to meet him.'

'Well, why didn't she then and make one less problem for me to deal with? I've got a crowd of angry people here who want to know how long the quarantine's going to last and why don't I do something about *that*—' He cut off suddenly. Dunworthy wondered if he'd hung up or had the phone snatched out of his hand by an angry shopper.

'Had the stationmaster seen him?' Mary said.

'No,' Dunworthy said. 'You'll have to send someone after him.'

'Yes, all right. I'll send one of the staff,' she said and started out.

'The quarantine was called at three-ten, and he wasn't supposed to get here till three,' Montoya said. 'Maybe he was late.'

That hadn't occurred to Dunworthy. If the quarantine had been called before his train reached Oxford, it would have been stopped at the nearest station and the passengers rerouted or sent back to London.

'Ring the station back,' he said, handing her the phone. He told her the number. 'Tell them his train left Marble Arch at one. I'll have Mary phone her niece. Perhaps Colin's back already.'

He went out in the corridor, intending to ask the nurse to fetch Mary, but she wasn't there. Mary must have sent her to the station.

There was no one in the corridor. He looked down it at the call box he had used before and then walked rapidly down to it and punched in Balliol's number. There was an off-chance that Colin had gone to Mary's rooms after all. He would send Finch round and, if Colin wasn't there, down to the station. It would very likely take more than one person looking to find Colin in that mess.

'Hi,' a woman said.

Dunworthy frowned at the number in the inset, but he hadn't misdialled. 'I'm trying to reach Mr Finch at Balliol College.'

'He's not here right now,' the woman, obviously American, said. 'I'm Ms Taylor. Can I take a message?'

This must be one of the bell ringers. She was younger than he'd expected not much over thirty, and she looked rather delicate to

75

be a bell ringer. 'Would you have him call Mr Dunworthy at Infirmary as soon as he returns, please?'

'Mr Dunworthy.' She wrote it down, and then looked up sharply. 'Mr *Dun*worthy,' she said in an entirely different tone of voice, 'are you the person responsible for our being held prisoner here?'

There was no good answer to that. He should never have phoned the junior common room. He had sent Finch to the bursar's office.

'The National Health Service issues temp quarantines in cases of an unidentified disease. It's a precautionary measure. I'm sorry for any inconvenience it's caused you. I've instructed my secretary to make your stay comfortable, and if there's anything I can do for you—'

'Do? Do? You can get us to Ely, that's what you can do. My ringers were supposed to give a handbell concert at the cathedral at eight o'clock, and tomorrow we have to be in Norwich. We're ringing a peal on Christmas Eve.'

He was not about to be the one to tell her they were not going to be in Norwich tomorrow. 'I'm sure that Ely is already aware of the situation, but I will be more than happy to phone the cathedral and explain—'

'Explain! Perhaps you'd like to explain it to me, too. I'm not used to having my civil liberties taken away like this. In America, nobody would dream of telling you where you can or can't go.'

And over thirty million Americans died during the Pandemic as a result of that sort of thinking, he thought. 'I assure you, madam, that the quarantine is solely for your protection and that all of your concert dates will be more than willing to reschedule. In the meantime, Balliol is delighted to have you as our guests. I am looking forward to meeting you in person. Your reputation precedes you.'

And if that were true, he thought, I would have told you Oxford was under quarantine when you wrote for permission to come.

'There is no way to reschedule a Christmas Eve peal. We were to have rung a new peal, the Chicago Surprise Minor. The Norwich Chapter is counting on us to be there and we intend—'

He hit the disconnect button. Finch was probably in the bursar's office, looking for Badri's medical records, but Dunworthy wasn't going to risk getting another bell ringer. He looked up Regional Transport's number instead and started to punch it in.

The door at the end of the corridor opened and Mary came through it.

'I'm trying Regional Transport,' Dunworthy said, punching in the rest of the number and passing her the receiver.

She waved it away, smiling. 'It's all right. I've just spoken to Deirdre. Colin's train was stopped at Barton. The passengers were put on the tube back to London. She's going down to Marble Arch to meet him.' She sighed. 'Deirdre didn't sound very glad that he's coming home. She planned to spend Christmas with her new live-in's family, and I think she rather wanted him out of the way, but it can't be helped I'm simply glad he's out of this.'

He could hear the relief in her voice. He put the receiver back. 'Is it that bad?'

'We just got the preliminary ident back. It's definitely a Type A myxovirus. Influenza.'

He had been expecting something worse, some thirdworld fever or a retrovirus. He had had the flu back in the days before antivirals. He had felt terrible, congested, feverish and achy for a few days and then got over it without anything but bedrest and fluids.

'Will they call the quarantine off then?'

'Not until we get Badri's medical records,' she said. 'I keep hoping he skipped his last course of antivirals. If not, then we'll have to wait till we locate the source.'

'But it's only the flu.'

'If there's a small antigenic shift, a point or two, it's only the flu,' she corrected him. 'If there's a large shift, it's influenza, which is an entirely different matter. The Spanish Flu pandemic of 1918 was a myxovirus. It killed twenty million people. Viruses mutate every few months. The antigens on their surface change so that they're unrecognisable to the immune system. That's why seasonals are necessary. But they can't protect against a large point shift.'

'And that's what this is?'

'I doubt it. Major mutations only happen every ten years or so. I think it's more likely that Badri failed to get his seasonals. Do you know if he was running an on-site at the beginning of term?'

'No. He may have been.'

'If he was, he may simply have forgotten to go in for them, in which case all he has is this winter's flu.'

'What about Kivrin? Has she had her seasonals?'

'Yes, and full-spectrum antivirals and T-cell enhancement. She's fully protected.'

'Even if it's influenza?'

She hesitated a fraction of a second. 'If she was exposed to the virus through Badri this morning, she's fully protected.'

'And if she saw him before then?'

'If I tell you this, you'll only worry, and I'm certain there's no need to.' She took a breath. 'The enhancement and the antivirals were given so that she would have peak immunity at the beginning of the drop.'

'And Gilchrist moved the drop up by two days,' Dunworthy said bitterly.

'I wouldn't have allowed her to go through if I hadn't thought it was all right.'

'But you hadn't counted on her being exposed to an influenza virus before she even left.'

'No, but it doesn't change anything. She has partial immunity and we're not certain she was even exposed. Badri scarcely went near her.'

'And what if she was exposed earlier?'

'I knew I shouldn't have told you,' Mary said. She sighed. 'Most myxoviruses have an incubation period of from twelve to forty-eight hours. Even if Kivrin was exposed two days ago, she'd have had enough immunity to prevent the virus from replicating sufficiently to cause anything but minor symptoms. But it's not influenza.' She patted his arm. 'And you're forgetting the paradoxes. If she'd been exposed, she'd have been highly contagious. The net would never have let her through.'

She was right. Diseases couldn't go through the net if there was any possibility of the contemps contracting them. The paradoxes wouldn't allow it. The net wouldn't have opened.

'What are the chances of the population in 1320 being immune?' he asked.

'To a modern-day virus? Almost none. There are eighteen hundred possible mutation points. The contemps would have all had to have had the exact virus, or they'd be vulnerable.'

Vulnerable. 'I want to see Badri,' he said. 'When he came to the pub, he said there was something wrong. He kept repeating it in the ambulance on the way to the hospital.'

'Something *is* wrong,' Mary said. 'He has a serious viral infection.'

'Or he knows he exposed Kivrin. Or he didn't get the fix.'

'He said he got the fix.' She looked sympathetically at him. 'I suppose it's useless to tell you not to worry about Kivrin. You saw how I've just acted over Colin. But I meant it when I said they're both safer out of this. Kivrin's much better off where she is than she would be here, even among those cut-throats and thieves you persist in imagining. At least she won't have to deal with NHS quarantine regulations.'

He smiled. 'Or American change ringers. America hadn't been discovered yet.' He reached for the door handle.

The door at the end of the corridor banged open and a large woman carrying a suitcase barged through it. 'There you are, Mr Dunworthy,' she shouted the length of the corridor. 'I've been looking everywhere for you.'

'Is that one of your bell ringers?' Mary said, turning to look down the corridor at her.

'Worse,' Dunworthy said. 'It's Mrs Gaddson.'

CHAPTER SIX

It was growing dark under the trees and at the bottom of the hill. Kivrin's head began to ache before she had even reached the frozen wagon ruts, as if it had something to do with microscopic changes in altitude or light.

She couldn't see the wagon at all, even standing directly in front of the little chest, and squinting into the darkness past the thicket made her head feel even worse. If this was one of the 'minor symptoms' of time lag, she wondered what a major one would be like.

When I get back, she thought, struggling through the thicket, I intend to have a little talk with Dr Ahrens on the subject. I think they are underestimating the debilitating effects these minor symptoms can have on an historian. Walking down the hill had left her more out of breath than climbing it had, and she was so *cold*.

Her cloak and then her hair caught on the willows as she pushed her way through the thicket, and she got a long scratch on her arm that immediately began to ache, too. She tripped once and nearly fell flat, and the effect on her headache was to jolt it so that it stopped hurting and then returned with redoubled force.

It was almost completely dark in the clearing, though what little she could see was still very clear, the colours not so much fading as deepening towards black – black-green and black-brown and black-grey. The birds were settling in for the night. They must have got used to her. They didn't so much as pause in their pre-bedtime twitterings and settlings down.

Kivrin hastily grabbed up the scattered boxes and splintered kegs and flung them into the tilting wagon. She took hold of the wagon's tongue and began to pull it towards the road. The wagon scraped a few inches, slid easily across a patch of leaves and stuck. Kivrin braced her foot and pulled again. It scraped a few more inches and tilted even more. One of the boxes fell out.

Kivrin put it back in and walked around the wagon, trying to see where it was stuck. The right wheel was jammed against a tree root, but it could be pushed up and over, if only she could get a decent purchase. She couldn't on this side – Mediaeval had taken an axe to the side so that it would look like the wagon had been smashed when it overturned, and they had done a good job. It was nothing but splinters. I told Mr Gilchrist he should have let me have gloves, she thought.

She came round to the other side, took hold of the wheel and shoved. It didn't budge. She pulled her skirts and cloak out of the way and knelt beside the wheel so she could put her shoulder to it.

The footprint was in front of the wheel, in a little space swept bare of leaves and only as wide as the foot. The leaves had drifted up against the roots of the oaks on either side. The leaves did not hold any print that she could see in the greying light, but the print in the earth was perfectly clear.

It can't be a footprint, Kivrin thought. The ground is frozen. She reached out to put her hand in the indentation, thinking it might be some trick of shadow or the failing light. The frozen ruts out in the road would not have taken any print at all. But the earth gave easily under her hand, and the print was deep enough to feel.

It had been made by a soft-soled shoe with no heel, and the foot that had made it was large, larger even than hers. A man's foot, but men in the 1300s had been smaller, shorter, with feet not even as big as hers. And this was a giant's foot.

Maybe it's an old footprint she thought wildly. Maybe it's the footprint of a woodcutter, or a peasant looking for a lost sheep. Maybe this is one of the king's woodlands, and they've been through here hunting. But it wasn't the footprint of someone chasing a deer. It was the print of someone who had stood there for a long time, watching her. I heard him, she thought, and a little flutter of panic forced itself up into her throat. I heard him standing there.

She was still kneeling, holding on to the wheel for balance. If the man, whoever it was, and it had to be a man, a giant, were still here in this glade, watching, he must know that she had found the footprint. She stood up. 'Hello!' she called, and frightened the birds to death again. They flapped and squawked themselves into hushed silence. 'Is someone there?'

She waited, listening, and it seemed to her that in the silence she could hear the breathing again. '*Speke.*' she said. '*I am in distresse an my servauntes fled.*'

Lovely, she thought even as she said it. Tell him you're helpless and all alone.

'Halloo!' she called again and began a cautious circuit of the glade, peering out into the trees. If he was still standing there, it was so dark she wouldn't be able to see him. She couldn't make out anything past the edges of the glade. She couldn't even tell for sure which way the thicket and the road lay. If she waited any longer, it would be completely dark, and she would never be able to get the wagon to the road.

But she couldn't move the wagon. Whoever had stood there between the two trees, watching her, knew that the wagon was here. Maybe he had even seen it come through, bursting on the sparkling air like something conjured by an alchemist. If that were the case, he had probably run off to get the stake Dunworthy was so sure the populace kept in readiness. But surely if that were the case, he would have said something, even if it was only 'Yoicks!' or 'Heavenly Father!' and she would have heard him crashing through the underbrush as he ran away.

He hadn't run away, though, which meant he hadn't seen her come through. He had come upon her afterwards, lying inexplicably in the middle of the woods beside a smashed wagon, and thought what? That she had been attacked on the road and then dragged here to hide the evidence?

Then why hadn't he tried to help her? Why had he stood there, silent as an oak, long enough to leave a deep footprint, and then gone away again? Maybe he had thought she was dead. He would have been frightened of her unshriven body. People as late as the fifteenth century had believed that evil spirits took immediate possession of any body not properly buried.

Or maybe he *had* gone for help, to one of those villages that

Kivrin had heard, maybe even Skendgate, and was even now on his way back with half the town, all of them carrying lanterns.

In that case, she should stay where she was and wait for him to come back. She should even lie down again. When the townspeople arrived, they could speculate about her and then bear her to the village, giving her examples of the language, the way her plan had been intended to work in the first place. But what if he came back alone, or with friends who had no intention of helping her?

She couldn't think. Her headache had spread out from her temple to behind her eyes. As she rubbed her forehead, it began to throb. And she was so cold! This cloak, in spite of its rabbit-fur lining, wasn't warm at all. How had people survived the Little Ice Age dressed only in cloaks like this? How had the rabbits survived?

At least she could do something about the cold. She could gather some wood and start a fire, and then if the footprint person came back with evil intentions, she could hold him off with a flaming brand. And if he had gone off for help and not been able to find his way back in the dark, the fire would lead him to her.

She made the circuit of the glade again, looking for wood. Dunworthy had insisted she learn to build a fire without tinder or flint. 'Gilchrist expects you to wander around the Middle Ages in the dead of winter without knowing how to build a fire?' he had said, outraged, and she had defended him, told him Mediaeval didn't expect her to spend that much time out-of-doors. But they should have realised how cold it could get.

The sticks made her hands cold, and every time she bent over to pick up a stick, her head hurt. Eventually she stopped bending over altogether and simply stooped and grabbed for the broken-off twigs, keeping her head straight. That helped a little, but not much. Maybe she was feeling this way because she was so cold. Maybe the headache, the breathlessness, were coming from being so cold. She had to get the fire started.

The wood felt icy cold and wet. It would never burn. And the leaves would be damp too, far too damp to use for tinder. She had to have dry kindling and a sharp stick to start a fire. She laid the wood down in a little bundle by the roots of a tree, careful to keep her head straight, and went back to the wagon.

The bashed-in side of the wagon had several broken pieces of wood she could use for kindling. She got two splinters in her hand before she managed to pull the pieces free, but the wood at least felt dry, though it was cold too. There was a large, sharp spur of wood just above the wheel. She bent over to grab it and nearly fell, gasping with the sudden nauseating dizziness.

'You'd better lie down,' she said out loud.

She eased herself to sitting, holding on to the ribs of the wagon for support. 'Dr Ahrens,' she said a little breathlessly, 'you ought to come up with something to prevent time lag. This is awful.'

If she could just lie down for a bit, perhaps the dizziness would go away and she could build the fire. She couldn't do it without bending over, though, and just the thought of doing that brought the nausea back.

She pulled her hood up over her head and closed her eyes, and even that hurt, the action seeming to focus the pain in her head. Something was wrong. This could not possibly be a reaction to time lag. She was supposed to have a few minor symptoms that would fade within an hour or two of her arrival, not get worse. A little headache, Dr Ahrens had said, some fatigue. She hadn't said anything about nausea, about being racked with cold.

She was so cold. She pulled the skirts of her cloak around her like a blanket, but the action seemed to make her even colder. Her teeth began to chatter, the way they had up on the hill, and great, convulsive shudders shook her shoulders.

I'm going to freeze to death, she thought. But it can't be helped. I can't get up and start the fire. I can't. I'm too cold. It's too bad you were wrong about the contemps, Mr Dunworthy, she thought and even the thought was dizzy. Being burned at the stake sounds lovely.

She would not have believed that she could have fallen asleep, huddled there on the cold ground. She had not noticed any spreading warmth, and if she had she would have been afraid it was the creeping numbness of hypothermia and tried to fight it. But she must have slept because when she opened her eyes again it was night in the glade, full night with frosty stars in the net of branches overhead, and she was on the ground looking up at them.

She had slid down as she slept, so that the top of her head was against the wheel. She was still shivering with cold, though her teeth had stopped chattering. Her head had begun to throb, tolling like a bell, and her whole body ached, especially her chest, where she had held the wood against her while she gathered sticks for the fire.

Something's *wrong*, she thought, and this time there was real panic in the thought. Maybe she was having some kind of allergic reaction to time travel. Was there even such a thing? Dunworthy had never said anything about an allergic reaction, and he had warned her about everything: rape and cholera and typhoid and the plague.

She twisted her hand around inside the cloak and felt under her arm for the place where she had had the welt from the antiviral inoculation. The welt was still there, though it didn't hurt to touch it, and it had stopped itching. Maybe that was a bad sign, she thought. Maybe the fact that it had stopped itching meant that it had stopped working.

She tried to lift her head. The dizziness came back instantly. She laid her head back down and disentangled her hands from the cloak, carefully and slowly, the nausea cutting across every movement. She folded her hands and pressed them against her face. 'Mr Dunworthy,' she said. 'I think you'd better come and get me.'

She slept again, and when she woke up she could hear the faint, jangling sound of the piped Christmas music. Oh, good, she thought, they've got the net open, and tried to pull herself to sitting against the wheel.

'Oh, Mr Dunworthy, I'm so glad you came back,' she said, fighting the nausea. 'I was afraid you wouldn't get my message.'

The jangling sound became louder, and she could see a wavering light. She pulled herself up a little further. 'You got the fire started,' she said. 'You were right about it getting cold.' The wagon's wheel felt icy through her cloak. Her teeth started to chatter again. 'Dr Ahrens was right. I should have waited till the swelling went down. I didn't know the reaction would be this bad.'

It wasn't a fire, after all. It was a lantern. Dunworthy was carrying it as he walked towards her.

'This doesn't mean I'm getting a virus, does it? Or the plague?'

She was having trouble getting the words out, her teeth were chattering so hard. 'Wouldn't that be awful? Having the plague in the Middle Ages? At least I'd fit right in.'

She laughed, a high-pitched almost-hysterical laugh that would probably frighten Mr Dunworthy to death. 'It's all right,' she said, and she could hardly understand her own words. 'I know you were worried but I'll be fine. I just—'

He stopped in front of her, the lantern lighting a wobbling circle on the ground. She could see Dunworthy's feet. He was wearing shapeless leather shoes, the kind that had made the footprint. She tried to say something about the shoes, to ask him whether Mr Gilchrist had made him put on authentic mediaeval dress just to come and fetch her, but the light's movement was making her dizzy again.

She closed her eyes, and when she opened them again he was kneeling in front of her. He had set the lantern down, and the light lit the hood of his cloak and folded hands.

'It's all right,' she said. 'I know you were worried, but I'm fine. Truly, I just felt a little ill.'

He raised his head. '*Certes, it been derlostub dayes forgott foreto getest hissahntes im aller,*' he said.

He had a hard, lined face, a cruel face, a cut-throat's face. He had watched her lying there and then he had gone away and waited for it to get dark, and now he had come back.

Kivrin tried to put up a hand to fend him off, but her hands had got tangled somehow in the cloak. 'Go away,' she said, her teeth chattering so hard she couldn't get the words out. 'Go away.'

He said something else, with a rising inflection this time, a question. She couldn't understand what he was saying. It's Middle English, she thought. I studied it for three years, and Mr Latimer taught me everything there is to know about adjectival inflection. I should be able to understand it. It's the fever, she thought. That's why I can't make out what he's saying.

He repeated the question or asked some other question, she couldn't even tell that much.

It's because I'm ill, she thought. I can't understand him because I'm ill. 'Kind sir,' she began, but she could not remember the rest of the speech. 'Help me,' she said, and tried to think how to say that in Middle English, but she couldn't remember anything but the Church Latin. '*Domine, ad adjuvandum me festina,*' she said.

He bowed his head over his hands and began to murmur so low she could not hear, and then she must have lost consciousness again because he had picked her up and was carrying her. She could still hear the jangling sound of the bells from the open net, and she tried to tell what direction they were coming from, but her teeth were chattering so hard she couldn't hear.

'I'm ill,' she said as he set her on the white horse. She fell forward, clutching at the horse's mane to keep from falling off. He put his hand up to her side and held her there. 'I don't know how this happened. I had all my inoculations.'

He led the donkey off slowly. The bells on its bridle jingled tinnily.

Transcript from the Domesday Book
(000740–000751)

Mr Dunworthy, I think you'd better come and get me.

CHAPTER SEVEN

'I *knew* it,' Mrs Gaddson said, steaming down the corridor towards them. 'He's contracted some horrible disease, hasn't he? It's all that rowing.'

Mary stepped forward. 'You can't come in here,' she said. 'This is an isolation area.'

Mrs Gaddson kept coming. The transparent poncho she was wearing over her coat threw off large, spattering drops as she walked towards them, swinging the suitcase like a weapon. 'You can't put me off like that. I'm his mother. I demand to see him.'

Mary put up her hand like a policeman. 'Stop,' she said in her best ward sister voice.

Amazingly, Mrs Gaddson stopped. 'A mother has a right to see her son,' she said. Her expression softened. 'Is he very ill?'

'If you mean your son William, he's not ill at all,' Mary said, 'at least so far as I know.' She put her hand up again. 'Please don't come any closer. Why do you think William's ill?'

'I knew it the minute I heard about the quarantine. A sharp pain went through me when the stationmaster said "temp quarantine".' She set down the suitcase so she could indicate the location of the sharp pain. 'It's because he didn't take his vitamins. I asked the college to be sure to give them to him,' she said, shooting a glance at Dunworthy that was the rival of any of Gilchrist's, 'and *they* said he was able to take care of himself. Well, obviously, they were wrong.'

'William is not the reason the temp quarantine was called. One of the University techs has come down with a viral infection,' Mary said.

Dunworthy noticed gratefully that she didn't say 'Balliol's tech'. 'The tech is the only case, and there is no indication that there will be any others,' Mary said. 'The quarantine is a purely precautionary measure, I assure you.'

Mrs Gaddson didn't look convinced. 'My Willy's always been sickly, and he simply will not take care of himself. He studies far too hard in that draughty room of his,' she said with another dark look at Dunworthy. 'I'm surprised he hasn't come down with a viral infection before this.'

Mary took her hand down and put it in the pocket she carried her bleeper in. I do hope she's calling for help, Dunworthy thought.

'By the end of *one* term at Balliol, Willy's health was completely broken down, and then his tutor *forced* him to stay up over Christmas and read Petrarch,' Mrs Gaddson said. 'That's why I came up. The thought of him all alone in this horrid place for Christmas, eating heaven knows what and doing all sorts of things to endanger his health, was something this mother's heart could simply not bear.'

She pointed to the place where the pain had gone through her at the words 'temp quarantine'. 'And it is positively providential that I came when I did. Positively providential. I nearly missed the train, my suitcase was so cumbersome, and I almost thought ah, well, there'll be another along, but I wanted to get to my Willy, so I shouted at them to hold the doors and I hadn't so much as stepped off at Cornmarket when the stationmaster said, "Temp quarantine. Train service is temporarily suspended." Only just think, if I'd missed that train and taken the next one, I would have been stopped by the quarantine.'

Only just think. 'I'm sure William will be surprised to see you,' Dunworthy said, hoping she would go find him.

'Yes,' she said grimly. 'He's probably sitting there without even his muffler on. He'll get this viral infection, I know it. He gets everything. He used to break out in horrible rashes when he was little. He's bound to come down with it. At least his mother is here to nurse him through it.'

The door was flung open and two people wearing masks, gowns, gloves, and some sort of paper covering over their shoes came racing through it. They slowed to a walk when they saw there was no one collapsed on the floor.

'I need this area cordoned off and an isolation ward sign

posted,' Mary said. She turned to Mrs Gaddson. 'I'm afraid there's a possibility you've been exposed to the virus. We do not have a positive mode of transmission yet, and we can't rule out the possibility of its being airborne,' she said, and for one horrible moment Dunworthy thought she meant to put Mrs Gaddson in the waiting-room with them.

'Would you escort Mrs Gaddson to an isolation cubicle?' she asked one of the masked-and-gowneds. 'We'll need to run blood tests and get a list of your contacts. Mr Dunworthy, if you'll just come with me,' she said and led him into the waiting-room and shut the door before Mrs Gaddson could protest. 'They can keep her a while and give poor Willy a few last hours of freedom.'

'That woman would make anyone break out in a rash,' he said.

Everyone except the medic had looked up at their entrance. Latimer was sitting patiently by the tray, his sleeve rolled up. Montoya was still using the phone.

'Colin's train was turned back,' Mary said. 'He's safely at home by now.'

'Oh, good,' Montoya said and put the phone down. Gilchrist leaped for it.

'Mr Latimer, I'm sorry to keep you waiting,' Mary said. She broke open a pair of imperm gloves, put them on and began assembling a punch.

'Gilchrist here. I wish to speak with the Senior Tutor,' Gilchrist said into the telephone. 'Yes. I'm trying to reach Mr Basingame. Yes, I'll wait.'

The Senior Tutor has no idea where he is, Dunworthy thought, and neither has the secretary. He'd already spoken to them when he was trying to stop the drop. The secretary hadn't even known he was in Scotland.

'I'm glad they found the kid,' Montoya said, looking at her digital. 'How long do you think they'll keep us here? I've got to get back to my dig before it turns into a swamp. We're excavating Skendgate's churchyard right now. Most of the graves date from the 1400s, but we've got some Black Deaths and a few pre-William the Conquerors. Last week we found a knight's tomb. Beautiful condition. I wonder if Kivrin's there yet?'

Dunworthy assumed she meant at the village and not in one of the graves. 'I hope so,' he said.

'I told her to start recording her observations of Skendgate immediately, the village and the church. Especially the tomb. The inscription's partly worn off, and some of the carving. The date's readable, though – 1318.'

'It's an emergency,' Gilchrist said. He fumed through a long pause. 'I know he's fishing in Scotland. I want to know *where*.'

Mary put a plaster on Latimer's arm and motioned to Gilchrist. He shook his head at her. She went over to the medic and shook her awake. She followed her over to the tray, blinking sleepily.

'There are so many things only direct observation can tell us,' Montoya said. 'I told Kivrin to record every detail. I hope there's room on the corder. It's so small.' She looked at her watch again. 'Of course it had to be. Did you get a chance to see it before they implanted it? It really does look like a bone spur.'

'Bone spur?' Dunworthy said, watching the medic's blood spurt into the vial.

'That's so it can't cause an anachronism even if it's discovered. It fits right against the palmar surface of the scaphoid bone.' She rubbed the wrist bone above the thumb.

Mary motioned to Dunworthy and the medic stood up, rolling down her sleeve. Dunworthy took her place in the chair. Mary peeled the back from a monitor, stuck it to the inside of Dunworthy's wrist, and handed him a temp to swallow.

'Have the bursar call me at this number as soon as he returns,' Gilchrist said, and hung up.

Montoya snatched up the phone, punched in a number, and said, 'Hi. Can you tell me the quarantine perimeter? I need to know if Witney's inside it. My dig's there.' Whoever she was talking to apparently told her no. 'Then who can I talk to about getting the perimeter changed? It's an emergency.'

They're worried about their 'emergencies', Dunworthy thought, and neither of them's even given a thought to worrying about Kivrin. Well, what was there to worry about? Her corder had been disguised to look like a bone spur so it wouldn't cause an anachronism when the contemps decided to chop off her hands before they burned her at the stake.

Mary took his blood pressure and then jabbed him with the punch. 'If the phone ever becomes available,' she said, slapping on the plaster and motioning to Gilchrist, who was standing next to Montoya, looking impatient, 'you might ring up William Gaddson and warn him that his mother's coming.'

Montoya said, 'Yes. The number for the National Trust,' hung up the phone and scribbled a number on one of the brochures.

The phone trilled. Gilchrist, halfway to Mary, launched himself at it, grabbing it before Montoya could reach it. 'No,' he said and handed it grudgingly over to Dunworthy.

It was Finch. He was in the bursar's office. 'Have you got Badri's medical records?' Dunworthy said.

'Yes, sir. The police are here, sir. They're looking for places to put all the detainees who don't live in Oxford.'

'And they want us to put them up at Balliol,' Dunworthy said.

'Yes, sir. How many shall I tell them we can take?'

Mary had stood up, Gilchrist's vial of blood in hand, and was signalling to Dunworthy.

'Wait a minute, please,' he said, and punched hold on the mouthpiece.

'Are they asking you to board detainees?' Mary asked.

'Yes,' he said.

'Don't commit to filling all your rooms,' she said. 'We may need infirmary space.'

Dunworthy took his hand away and said, 'Tell them we can put them in Fisher and whatever rooms are left in Salvin. If you haven't assigned rooms to the bell ringers, double them up. Tell the police Infirmary has asked for Bulkeley-Johnson as an emergency ward. Did you say you'd found Badri's medical records?'

'Yes, sir. I had the very devil of a time finding them. The bursar had filed them under Badri comma Chaudhuri, and the Americans—'

'Did you find his NHS number?'

'Yes, sir.'

'I'm putting Dr Ahrens on,' he said before Finch could launch into tales of the bell ringers. He motioned to Mary. 'You can give her the information directly.'

Mary attached a plaster to Gilchrist's arm and a temp monitor to the back of his hand.

'I got through to Ely, sir,' Finch said. 'I informed them of the handbell concert cancellation and they were quite pleasant, but the Americans are still very unhappy.'

Mary finished entering Latimer's reads, stripped off the gloves and came over to take the phone from Dunworthy.

'Finch? Dr Ahrens here. Read me Badri's NHS number.'

Dunworthy handed her his Secondaries sheet and a pencil, and she wrote it down and then asked for Badri's inoculation records and made a number of notations Dunworthy couldn't decipher.

'Any reactions or allergies?' There was a pause, and then she said, 'All right, no. I can get the rest off the computer. I'll ring you back if I need additional information.' She handed the phone back to Dunworthy. 'He wants to speak with you again,' she said and left, taking the paper with her.

'They're most unhappy at being kept here,' Finch said. 'Ms Taylor is threatening to sue for involuntary breach of contract.'

'When was Badri's last course of antivirals?'

Finch took a considerable time looking through the sheaf of papers. 'Here it is, sir. September fourteenth.'

'Did he have the full course?'

'Yes, sir. Receptor analogues, MPA booster and seasonals.'

'Has he ever had a reaction to an antiviral?'

'No, sir. There's nothing under allergies in the history. I already told Dr Ahrens that.'

Badri had had all his antivirals. He had no history of reactions.

'Have you been to New College yet?' Dunworthy asked.

'No, sir, I'm just on my way. What should I do about supplies, sir? We've adequate stores of soap, but we're very low on lavatory paper.'

The door opened, but it wasn't Mary. It was the medic who had been sent to fetch Montoya. He went over to the tea trolley and plugged in the electric kettle.

'Should I ration the lavatory paper, do you think, sir,' Finch said, 'or put up notices asking everyone to conserve?'

'Whatever you think best,' Dunworthy said and rang off.

It must still be raining. The medic's uniform was wet and when the kettle boiled he put his red hands over the steam, as if trying to warm them.

'Are you quite finished using the telephone?' Gilchrist said.

Dunworthy handed it to him. He wondered what the weather was like where Kivrin was, and whether Gilchrist had had Probability compute the chances of her coming through in the rain. Her cloak had not looked especially waterproof, and that friendly traveller who was supposed to come along within 1.6 hours would have holed up in a hostelry or a hayrick till the roads dried enough to be passable.

Dunworthy had taught Kivrin how to make a fire, but she could hardly do so with wet kindling and numb hands. Winters in the 1300s had been cold. It might even be snowing. The little Ice Age had just begun in 1320, the weather eventually getting so cold that the Thames froze over. The lower temps and erratic weather had played such havoc with the crops that some historians blamed the Black Death's horrors on the malnourished state of the peasants. The weather had certainly been bad. In the autumn of 1348, it had rained in one part of Oxfordshire every day from Michaelmas to Christmas. Kivrin was probably lying there on the wet road, half-dead from hypothermia.

And broken out in a rash, he thought, from her overdoting tutor worrying too much about her. Mary was right. He did sound like Mrs Gaddson. The next thing he knew he'd be plunging off into 1320, forcing the doors of the net open like Mrs Gaddson on the tube, and Kivrin would be as glad to see him as William was going to be to see his mother. And as in need of help.

Kivrin was the brightest and most resourceful student he had ever had. She surely knew enough to get in out of the rain. For all he knew, she had spent her last vac with the Eskimos, learning to build an igloo.

She had certainly thought of everything else, even down to her fingernails. When she had come in to show him her costume, she had held up her hands. Her nails had been broken off, and there were traces of dirt in the cuticles. 'I know I'm supposed to be nobility, but rural nobility, and they did a lot of farm chores in between Bayeaux Tapestries, and East Riding ladies didn't have scissors till the 1600s, so I spent Sunday afternoon in Montoya's dig, grubbing among the dead bodies, to get this effect.' Her nails had looked dreadful, and utterly authentic. There was obviously no reason to worry about a minor detail like snow.

But he couldn't help it. If he could speak to Badri, ask him what he'd meant when he said, 'Something wrong,' make certain the drop had gone properly and that there hadn't been too much slippage, he might be able to stop worrying. But Mary had not been able even to get Badri's NHS number till Finch phoned with it. He wondered if Badri were still unconscious. Or worse.

He got up and went over to the tea trolley and made himself a cup of tea. Gilchrist was on the phone again, apparently speaking to the porter. The porter didn't know where Basingame was either. When Dunworthy had talked to him, he had told him he thought Basingame had mentioned Loch Balkillan, a lake that turned out not to exist.

Dunworthy drank his tea. Gilchrist rang up the bursar and the deputy warden, neither of whom knew where Basingame had gone. The nurse who had guarded the door earlier came in and finished the blood tests. The male medic picked up one of the inspirational brochures and began to read it.

Montoya filled out her admissions form and her lists of contacts. 'What am I supposed to do?' she asked Dunworthy. 'Write down the people I've been in contact with today?'

'The past three days,' he said.

They continued to wait. Dunworthy drank another cup of tea. Montoya rang up the NHS and tried to persuade them to give her a quarantine exemption so she could go back to the dig. The female medic went back to sleep.

The nurse wheeled in a trolley with supper on it. ' "*Greet chère made our hoste us everichon, And to the soper sette us anon,*" ' Latimer said, the only remark he had made all afternoon.

While they ate, Gilchrist regaled Latimer with his plans for sending Kivrin to the aftermath of the Black Death. 'The accepted historical view is that it completely destroyed mediaeval society,' he told Latimer as he cut his roast beef, 'but my research indicates it was purgative rather than catastrophic.'

From whose point of view? Dunworthy thought, wondering what was taking so long. He wondered if they were truly processing the blood tests or if they were simply waiting for one or all of them to collapse across the tea trolley so they could get a fix on the incubation period.

Gilchrist rang up New College again and asked for Basingame's secretary.

'She's not there,' Dunworthy said. 'She's in Devonshire with her daughter for Christmas.'

Gilchrist ignored him. 'Yes. I need to get a message through to her. I'm trying to reach Mr Basingame. It's an emergency. We've just sent an historian to the 1300s, and Balliol failed to properly screen the tech who ran the net. As a result, he's contracted a contagious virus.' He put the phone down. 'If Mr Chaudhuri failed to have any of the necessary antivirals, I'm holding you personally responsible, Mr Dunworthy.'

'He had the full course in September,' Dunworthy said.

'Have you proof of that?' Gilchrist said.

'Did it come through?' the medic asked.

They all, even Latimer, turned to look at her in surprise. Until she'd spoken, she'd seemed fast asleep, her head far forward on her chest and her arms folded holding the contacts lists.

'You said you sent somebody back to the Middle Ages,' she said belligerently. 'Did it?'

'I'm afraid I don't—' Gilchrist said.

'This virus,' she said. 'Could it have come through the time machine?'

Gilchrist looked nervously at Dunworthy. 'That isn't possible, is it?'

'No,' Dunworthy said. It was obvious Gilchrist knew nothing about the continuum paradoxes or string theory. The man had no business being Acting Head. He didn't even know how the net he had so blithely sent Kivrin through worked. 'The virus couldn't have come through the net.'

'Dr Ahrens said the Indian was the only case,' the medic said. 'And *you* said' – she pointed at Dunworthy – 'that he'd had the full course. If he's had his antivirals, he couldn't catch a virus unless it was a disease from somewhere else. And the Middle Ages was full of diseases, wasn't it? Smallpox and the plague?'

Gilchrist said, 'I'm certain that Mediaeval has taken steps to protect against that possibility—'

'There *is* no possibility of a virus coming through the net,' Dunworthy said angrily. 'The space-time continuum does not allow it to happen.'

'You send people through,' she persisted, 'and a virus is smaller than a person.'

Dunworthy hadn't heard that argument since the early years of the nets, when the theory was only partially understood.

'I assure you we've taken every precaution,' Gilchrist said.

'Nothing that would affect the course of history can go through a net,' Dunworthy explained, glaring at Gilchrist. The man was simply encouraging her with this talk of precautions and probabilities. 'Radiation, toxins, microbes, none of them has ever passed through a net. If they're present the net simply won't open.'

The medic looked unconvinced.

'I assure you —' Gilchrist said, and Mary came in.

She was carrying a sheaf of variously coloured papers. Gilchrist stood up immediately. 'Dr Ahrens, is there a possibility that this viral infection Mr Chaudhuri has contracted might have come through the net?'

'Of course not,' she said, frowning as if the whole idea were ridiculous. 'In the first place, diseases can't come through the net. It would violate the paradoxes. In the second place, if it had, *which it can't*, Badri would have caught it less than an hour after it came through, which would mean the virus had an incubation period of an hour, an utter impossibility. But if it did, *which it can't*, you all would be ill already' – she looked at her digital – 'since it's been over three hours since you were exposed to it.' She began collecting the contacts lists.

Gilchrist looked irritated. 'As Acting Head of the History Faculty I have responsibilities I must attend to,' he said. 'How long do you intend to keep us here?'

'Only long enough to collect your contacts lists,' she said. 'And to give you your instructions. Perhaps five minutes.'

She took Latimer's list from him. Montoya grabbed hers up from the end table and began writing hastily.

'Five minutes?' the medic who had asked about the virus coming through the net said. 'Do you mean we're free to go?'

'On medical probation,' she said. She put the lists at the bottom of her sheaf of papers and began passing the top sheets, which were a virulent pink, round to everyone. They appeared to be a release form of some sort, absolving the Infirmary of any and all responsibility.

'We've completed your blood tests,' she went on, 'and none of them show an increased level of antibodies.'

She handed Dunworthy a blue sheet which absolved the NHS of any and all responsibility and confirmed willingness to pay any and all charges not covered by the NHS in full and within thirty days.

'I've been in touch with the WIC, and their recommendation is controlled observation, with continuous febrile monitoring and blood samples at twelve-hour intervals.'

The sheet she was distributing now was green and headed 'Instructions for Primary Contacts'. Number one was 'Avoid contact with others'.

Dunworthy thought of Finch and the bell ringers waiting, no doubt, at the gate of Balliol with summons and Scriptures, and of all those Christmas shoppers and detainees between here and there.

'Record your temp at half-hour intervals,' she said, passing round a yellow form. 'Come in immediately if your monitor' – she tapped at her own – 'shows a marked increase in temp. Some fluctuation is normal. Temps tend to rise in the late afternoon and evening. Any temp between 36 and 37.4 is normal. Come in immediately if your temp exceeds 37.4 or rises suddenly, or if you begin to feel any symptoms – headache, tightness in the chest, mental confusion, or dizziness.'

Everyone looked at his or her monitor and, no doubt, began to feel a headache coming on. Dunworthy had had a headache all afternoon.

'Avoid contact with others as much as possible,' Mary said. 'Keep careful track of any contacts you do have. We're still uncertain of the mode of transmission, but most myxoviruses spread by droplet and direct contact. Wash your hands with soap and water frequently.'

She handed Dunworthy another pink sheet. She was running

out of colours. This one was a log, headed 'Contacts', and under it, 'Name, Address, Type of Contact, Time'.

It was unfortunate that Badri's virus had not had to deal with the CDC, the NHS and the WIC. It would never have got in the door.

'You must report back here at seven tomorrow morning. In the meantime, I'd recommend a good supper and then bed. Rest is the best defence against any virus. You are off-duty,' she said, looking at the medics, 'for the duration of the temp quarantine.' She passed out several more rainbow-hued papers and then asked brightly, 'Any questions?'

Dunworthy looked at the medic, waiting for her to ask Mary if smallpox had come through the net but she was looking uninterestedly at her clutch of papers.

'Can I go back to my dig?' Montoya asked.

'Not unless it's inside the quarantine perimeter,' Mary said.

'Well, great,' she said, jamming her papers angrily into the pockets of her terrorist jacket. 'The whole village will have washed away while I'm stuck here.' She stomped out.

'Are there any other questions?' Mary said imperturbably. 'Very well, then, I'll see you all at seven o'clock.'

The medics ambled out, the one who had asked about the virus yawning and stretching as if she were preparing for another nap. Latimer was still sitting down, watching his temp monitor. Gilchrist said something snappish to him and he got up and put his coat on and collected his umbrella and his stack of papers.

'I expect to be kept informed of every development,' Gilchrist said. 'I am contacting Basingame and telling him it's essential that he return and take charge of this matter.' He swept out and then had to wait, holding the door open, for Latimer to pick up two papers he had dropped.

'Go round in the morning and collect Latimer, won't you?' Mary said, looking through the contacts lists. 'He'll never remember he's to be here at seven.'

'I want to see Badri,' Dunworthy said.

'Laboratory, Brasenose,' she said, reading from the sheets. 'Dean's office, Brasenose. Laboratory, Brasenose. Didn't anyone see Badri except in the net?'

'In the ambulance on the way here he said, "Something

wrong",' Dunworthy said. 'There could have been slippage. If she's more than a week off, she'll have no idea when to rendezvous.'

She didn't answer. She sorted through the sheets again, frowning.

'I need to make certain there weren't any problems with the fix,' he said insistently.

She looked up. 'Very well,' she said. 'These contact sheets are hopeless. There are great gaps in Badri's whereabouts for the past three days. He's the only person who can tell us where he was and with whom he came in contact.' She led the way back down the corridor. 'I've had a nurse with him, asking him questions, but he's very disorientated and fearful of her. Perhaps he won't be as frightened of you.'

She led the way down the corridor to the lift and said, 'Ground floor, please,' into its ear. 'Badri's only conscious for a few moments at a time,' she said to Dunworthy. 'It may be most of the night.'

'That's all right,' Dunworthy said. 'I won't be able to rest till I'm sure Kivrin is safely through.'

They went up two flights in the lift, down another corridor and through a door marked 'NO ENTRANCE. ISOLATED WARD'. Inside the door, a grim-looking ward sister was sitting at a desk watching a monitor.

'I'm taking Mr Dunworthy in to see Mr Chaudhuri,' Mary said. 'We'll need SPGs. How is he?'

'His fever's up again – 39.8,' the sister said, handing them the SPGs, which were plastene-sealed bundles of paper clothing gowns that stripped up the back, caps, imperm masks that were impossible to get on over the caps, bootee-like snugs that went on over their shoes, and imperm gloves. Dunworthy made the mistake of putting his gloves on first and took what seemed like hours attempting to unfold the gown and affix the mask.

'You'll need to ask very specific questions,' Mary said. 'Ask him what he did when he got up this morning, if he'd stayed the night with anyone, where he ate breakfast, who was there, that sort of thing. His high fever means that he's very disorientated. You may have to ask your questions several times.' She opened the door to the room.

It wasn't really a room – there was only space for the bed and a narrow campstool, not even a chair. The wall behind the bed was covered with displays and equipment. The far wall had a curtained window and more equipment. Mary glanced briefly at Badri and then began scanning the displays.

Dunworthy looked at the screens. The one nearest him was full of numbers and letters. The bottom line read 'ICU 14320691–22–12–54 1803 200/RPT 1800CRS IMJPCLN 200MG/q6h NHS40–211–7 M AHRENS'. Apparently the doctor's orders.

The other screens showed spiking lines and columns of figures. None of them made any sense except for a number in the middle of the small display second from the right. It read 'Temp: 39.9'. Dear God.

He looked at Badri. He was lying with his arms outside the bedclothes, his arms both connected to drips that hung from stanchions. One of the drips had at least five bags feeding into the main tube. His eyes were closed and his face looked thin and drawn, as if he had lost weight since this morning. His dark skin had a strange purplish cast to it.

'Badri,' Mary said, leaning over him, 'can you hear us?'

He opened his eyes and looked at them without recognition, which was probably due less to the virus than to the fact that they were covered from head to foot in paper.

'It's Mr Dunworthy,' Mary said helpfully. 'He's come to see you.' Her bleeper started up.

'Mr Dunworthy?' he said hoarsely and tried to sit up.

Mary pushed him gently down into the pillow. 'Mr Dunworthy has some questions for you,' she said, patting his chest gently the way she had in the laboratory at Brasenose. She straightened up, watching the displays on the wall behind him. 'Lie still. I need to leave now, but Mr Dunworthy will stay with you. Rest and try to answer Mr Dunworthy's questions.' She left.

'Mr Dunworthy?' Badri said again as if he were trying to make sense of the words.

'Yes,' Dunworthy said. He sat down on the campstool. 'How are you feeling?'

'When do you expect him back?' Badri said, and his voice sounded weak and strained. He tried to sit up again. Dunworthy put out his hand to stop him.

'Have to find him,' he said. 'There's something wrong.'

CHAPTER EIGHT

They were burning her at the stake. She could feel the flames. They must already have tied her to the stake, though she could not remember that. She remembered them lighting the fire. She had fallen off the white horse, and the cut-throat had picked her up and carried her over to it.

'We must go back to the drop,' she had told him.

He had leaned over her, and she could see his cruel face in the flickering firelight.

'Mr Dunworthy will open the net as soon as he realises something's wrong,' she had told him. She shouldn't have told him that. He had thought she was a witch and had brought her here to be burned.

'I'm not a witch,' she said, and immediately a hand came out of nowhere and rested coolly on her forehead.

'Shh,' a voice said.

'I am *not* a witch,' she said, trying to speak slowly so they would understand her. The cut-throat hadn't understood her. She had tried to tell him they shouldn't leave the drop, but he had paid no attention to her. He had put her on his white horse and led it out of the clearing and through the stand of white-trunked birches, into the thickest part of the forest.

She had tried to pay attention to which way they were going so she could find her way back, but the man's swinging lantern had lit only a few inches of ground at their feet and the light had hurt her eyes. She had closed them, and that was a mistake because the horse's awkward gait made her dizzy, and she had fallen off the horse on to the ground.

'I am not a witch,' she said. 'I'm an historian.'

'*Hawey fond enyowuh thissla dey?*' the woman's voice said, far away. She must have come forward to put a faggot on the fire and then stepped back again, away from the heat.

'*Enwodes fillenun gleydund sore destrayste,*' a man's voice said, and the voice sounded like Mr Dunworthy's. '*Ayeen mynarmehs hoor ale op hider ybar.*'

'*Sweltes shay dumorte blauen?*' the woman said.

'Mr Dunworthy,' Kivrin said, holding out her arms to him, 'I've fallen among cut-throats!' but she couldn't see him through the smothering smoke.

'Shh,' the woman said and Kivrin knew that it was later, that she had, impossibly, slept. How long does it take to burn? she wondered. The fire was so hot she should be ashes by now, but when she held her hand up, it looked untouched, though little red flames flickered along the edges of the fingers. The light from the flames hurt her eyes. She closed them.

I hope I don't fall off the horse again, she thought. She had been clinging to the horse, both arms around its neck, though its uneven walk made her head ache even worse, and she had not let go, but she had fallen off, even though Mr Dunworthy had insisted she learn how to ride, had arranged for her to have lessons at a riding stable near Woodstock. Mr Dunworthy had told her this would happen. He had told her they would burn her at the stake.

The woman put a cup to her lips. It must be vinegar in a sponge, Kivrin thought, they gave that to martyrs. But it wasn't. It was a warm, bitter liquid. The woman had to tilt Kivrin's head forward to drink it, and it came to Kivrin for the first time that she was lying down.

I'll have to tell Mr Dunworthy, she thought, they burned people at the stake lying down. She tried to bring her hands up to her lips in the position of prayer to activate the corder, but the weight of the flames dragged them down again.

I'm ill, Kivrin thought, and knew that the warm liquid had been a medicinal potion of some kind, and that it had brought her fever down a little. She was not lying on the ground after all, but in a bed in a dark room, and the woman who had hushed her and given her the liquid was there beside her. She could hear her breathing. Kivrin tried to move her head to see her, but the effort made it hurt again. The woman must be asleep. Her breathing was even and loud, almost like snoring. It hurt Kivrin's head to listen to it.

I must be in the village, she thought. The redheaded man must have brought me here.

She had fallen off the horse, and the cut-throat had helped her back on, but when she looked into his face he hadn't looked like a cut-throat at all. He was young, with red hair and a kind expression, and he had leaned over her where she was sitting against the wagon wheel, kneeling on one knee beside her, and said, 'Who are you?'

She had understood him perfectly.

'*Canstawd ranken derwyn?*' the woman said and tilted Kivrin's head forward for more of the bitter liquid Kivrin could barely swallow. The fire was inside her throat now. She could feel the little orange flames, though the liquid should have put them out. She wondered if he had taken her to some foreign land, Spain or Greece, where the people spoke a language they hadn't put into the interpreter.

She had understood the redheaded man perfectly. 'Who are you?' he had asked, and she had thought that the other man must be a slave he'd brought back from the Crusades, a slave who spoke Turkish or Arabic, and that was why she couldn't understand him.

'I'm an historian,' she had said, but when she looked up into his kind face it wasn't him. It was the cut-throat.

She looked wildly around her for the redheaded man, but he wasn't there. The cut-throat picked up sticks and laid them on some stones for a fire.

'Mr Dunworthy!' Kivrin called out desperately, and the cut-throat came and knelt in front of her, the light from his lantern flickering on his face.

'Fear not,' he said. 'He will return soon.'

'Mr Dunworthy!' she screamed, and the redheaded man came and knelt beside her again.

'I shouldn't have left the drop,' she told him, watching his face so he wouldn't turn into the cut-throat. 'Something must have gone wrong with the fix. You must take me back there.'

He unfastened the cloak he was wearing, swinging it easily off his shoulders, and laid it over her, and she knew he understood.

'I need to go home,' she said to him as he bent over her. He had a lantern with him, and it lit his kind face and flickered on his red hair like flames.

'*Godufadur*,' he called out, and she thought, that's the slave's name. *Gauddefaudre.* He will ask the slave to tell him where he found me, and then he'll take me back to the drop. And Mr Dunworthy. Mr Dunworthy would be frantic that she wasn't there when he opened the net. It's all right, Mr Dunworthy, she had said silently. I'm coming.

'*Dreede nawmaydde*,' the redheaded man had said and lifted her up in his arms. '*Fawrthah Galwinnath coam.*'

'I'm ill,' Kivrin said to the woman, 'so I can't understand you,' but this time no one leaned forward out of the darkness to quiet her. Maybe they had tired of watching her burn and had gone away. It was certainly taking a long time, though the fire seemed to be growing hotter now.

The redheaded man had set her on the white horse before him and ridden into the woods, and she had thought he must be taking her back to the drop. The horse had a saddle now, and bells, and the bells jangled as they rode, playing a tune. It was 'O Come All Ye Faithful', and the bells grew louder and louder with each verse, till they sounded like the bells of St Mary the Virgin's.

They rode a long way, and she thought they must surely be near the drop by now.

'How far is the drop?' she asked the redheaded man. 'Mr Dunworthy will be so worried,' but he didn't answer her. He rode out of the woods and down a hill. The moon was up, shining palely in the branches of a stand of narrow, leafless trees, and on the church at the bottom of the hill.

'This isn't the drop,' she said, and tried to pull on the horse's reins to turn it back the way they had come, but she did not dare take her arms from around the redheaded man's neck for fear she might fall. And then they were at a door, and it opened, and opened again, and there was a fire and light and the sound of bells, and she knew they had brought her back to the drop after all.

'*Shay boyen syke nighonn tdeeth*,' the woman said. Her hands were wrinkled and rough on Kivrin's skin. She pulled the bed coverings up round Kivrin. Fur, Kivrin could feel soft fur against her face, or maybe it was her hair.

'Where have you brought me to?' Kivrin asked. The woman leaned forward a little, as if she couldn't hear her, and Kivrin realised she must have spoken in English. Her interpreter wasn't working. She was supposed to be able to think her words in English and speak them in Middle English. Perhaps that was why she couldn't understand them, because her interpreter wasn't working.

She tried to think how to say it in Middle English. '*Where hast thou bringen me to?*' The construction was wrong. She must ask, 'What is this place?' but she could not remember the Middle English for place.

She could not think. The woman kept piling on blankets and the more furs she laid over her, the colder Kivrin got, as if the woman were somehow putting out the fire.

They would not understand what she meant if she asked, 'What is this place?' She was in a village. The redheaded man had brought her to a village. They had ridden past a church and up to a large house. She must ask, 'What is the name of this village?'

The word for 'place' was *demain*, but the construction was still wrong. They would use the French construction, wouldn't they?

'*Quelle demeure avez vous m'apporte?*' she said aloud, but the woman had gone away, and that was not right. They had not been French for two hundred years. She must ask the question in English. 'Where is the village you have brought me to?' But what was the word for village?

Mr Dunworthy had told her she might not be able to depend on the interpreter, that she had to take lessons in Middle English and Norman French and German to counterbalance discrepancies in pronunciation. He had made her memorise pages and pages of Chaucer. '*Soun ye nought but eyr ybroken. And every speche that ye spoken.*' No. No. 'Where is this village you have brought me to?' What was the word for village?

He had brought her to a village and knocked on a door. A big man had come to the door, carrying an axe. To cut the wood for the fire, of course. A big man and then a woman, and they had both spoken words Kivrin couldn't understand and the door had shut, and they had been outside in the darkness.

'Mr Dunworthy! Dr Ahrens!' she had cried, and her chest hurt too much to get the words out. 'You mustn't let them close the drop,' she had said to the redheaded man, but he had changed again into a cut-throat, a thief.

'Nay,' he had said. 'She is but injured,' and then the door had opened again, and he had carried her in to be burnt.

She was so hot.

'*Thawmot goonawt plersoun roshundt prayenum comth ithre,*' the woman said, and Kivrin tried to raise her head to drink, but the woman wasn't holding a cup. She was holding a candle close to Kivrin's face. Too close. Her hair would catch fire.

'*Der maydemot nedes dya,*' the woman said.

The candle flickered close to her cheek. Her hair was on fire. Orange and red flames burned along the edges of her hair, catching stray wisps and twisting them into ash.

'Shh,' the woman said, and tried to capture Kivrin's hands, but Kivrin struggled against her until her hands were free. She struck at her hair, trying to put the flames out. Her hands caught fire.

'Shh,' the woman said, and held her hands still. It was not the woman. The hands were too strong. Kivrin tossed her head from side to side, trying to escape the flames, but they were holding her head still, too. Her hair blazed up in a cloud of fire.

It was smoky in the room when she woke up. The fire must have gone out while she slept. That had happened to one of the martyrs when they had burned him at the stake. His friends had piled green faggots on the fire so he would die of the smoke before the fire reached him, but it had put the fire nearly out instead, and he had smouldered for hours.

The woman leaned over her. It was so smoky Kivrin couldn't see whether she was young or old. The redheaded man must have put out the fire. He had spread his cloak over her and then gone over to the fire and put it out kicking it apart with his boots, and the smoke had come up and blinded her.

The woman dripped water on her, and the drops sizzled on her skin. '*Hauccaym anchi towoem denswile?*' the woman said.

'I am Isabel de Beauvrier,' Kivrin said. 'My brother lies ill at Evesham.' She could not think of any of the words. *Quelle demeure. Perced to the rote.* 'Where am I?' she said in English.

A face leaned close to hers. *'Hau hightes towe?'* it said. It was the cut-throat face of the enchanted woods. She pulled back from it, frightened.

'Go away!' she said. 'What do you want?'

'In nomine Patris, et Filii, et Spiritus sancti,' he said.

Latin, she thought thankfully. There must be a priest here. She tried to raise her head to see past the cut-throat to the priest, but she could not. It was too smoky in the room. I can speak Latin, she thought. Mr Dunworthy made me learn it.

'You shouldn't have let him in here!' she said in Latin. 'He's a cut-throat!' Her throat hurt, and she seemed to have no breath to put behind the words, but from the way the cut-throat drew back in surprise, she knew they had heard her.

'You must not be afraid,' the priest said, and she understood him perfectly. 'You do but go home again.'

'To the drop?' Kivrin said. 'Are you taking me to the drop?'

'Asperges me, Domine, hyssope et mundabor,' the priest said. Thou shalt sprinkle me with hyssop, O Lord, and I shall be cleansed. She could understand him perfectly.

'Help me,' she said in Latin. 'I must return to the place from which I came.'

'. . . *nominus* ...' the priest said, so softly she couldn't hear him. Name. Something about her name. She raised her head It felt curiously light, as though all her hair had burned away.

'My name?' she said.

'Can you tell me your name?' he said in Latin.

She was supposed to tell them she was Isabel de Beauvrier, daughter of Gilbert de Beauvrier, from the East Riding, but her throat hurt so she didn't think she could get it out.

'I have to go back,' she said. 'They won't know where I've gone.'

'Confiteor deo omnipotenti,' the priest said from very far away. She couldn't see him. When she tried to look past the cut-throat all she could see were flames. They must have lit the fire again. *'Beatae Mariae semper Virgini . . .'*

He's saying the Confiteor Deo, she thought, the prayer of confession. The cut-throat shouldn't be here. There shouldn't be anyone else in the room during a confession.

It was her turn. She tried to fold her hands in prayer and couldn't, but the priest helped her, and when she couldn't remember the words, he recited them with her. 'Forgive me, Father, for I have sinned. I confess to Almighty God, and to you, Father, that I have sinned exceedingly in thought word, deed, and omission, through my fault.'

'*Mea culpa*,' she whispered, '*mea culpa, mea maxima culpa*.' Through my fault, through my fault, through my most grievous fault but that wasn't right, that wasn't what she was supposed to say.

'How have you sinned?' the priest said.

'Sinned?' she said blankly.

'Yes,' he said gently, leaning so close he was practically whispering in her ear. 'That you may confess your sins and have God's forgiveness, and enter into the kingdom eternal.'

All I wanted to do was go to the Middle Ages, she thought. I worked so hard, learning the languages and the customs and doing everything Mr Dunworthy told me. All I wanted to do was to be an historian.

She swallowed, a feeling like flame. 'I have not sinned.'

The priest drew back then, and she thought he had gone away angry because she wouldn't confess her sins.

'I should have listened to Mr Dunworthy,' she said. 'I shouldn't have left the drop.'

'*In nomine Patris, et Filii, et Spiritus sancti. Amen*,' the priest said. His voice was gentle, comforting. She felt his cool, cool touch on her forehead.

'*Quid quid deliquisti*,' the priest murmured. 'Through this holy unction and His own most tender mercy . . .' He touched her eyes, her ears, her nostrils, so lightly she couldn't feel his hand at all, but only the cool touch of the oil.

That isn't part of the sacrament of penance, Kivrin thought. That's the ritual for extreme unction. He's saying the last rites.

'Don't—' Kivrin said.

'Be not afraid,' he said. 'May the Lord pardon thee whatever offences thou has committed by walking,' he said and put out the fire that was burning the soles of her feet.

'Why are you giving me the last rites?' Kivrin said and then remembered they were burning her at the stake. I'm going to die here, she thought, and Mr Dunworthy will never know what happened to me.

'My name is Kivrin,' she said. 'Tell Mr Dunworthy—'

'May you behold your Redeemer face-to-face,' the priest said, only it was the cut-throat speaking. 'And standing before Him may you gaze with blessed eyes on the truth made manifest.'

'I'm dying, aren't I?' she asked the priest.

'There is naught to fear,' he said, and took her hand.

'Don't leave me,' she said, and clutched his hand.

'I will not,' he said, but she couldn't see him for all the smoke. 'May Almighty God have mercy upon thee, and forgive thee thy sins, and bring thee unto life everlasting,' he said.

'Please come and get me, Mr Dunworthy,' she said, and the flames roared up between them.

———

Transcript from the Domesday Book
(000806–000882)

Domine, mittere digneris sanctum Angelum tuum de caelis, qui custodiat, foveat, protegat, visitet, atque defendat omnes babitantes in hoc habitaculo.

(Break)

Exaudi orationim meam et clamor mens ad te veniat.*

———

* *Translation*: O Lord vouchsafe to send Thy holy angel from heaven, to guard, cherish, protect, visit and defend all those that are assembled together in this house.

(Break)

Hear my prayer, and let my cry come unto Thee.

CHAPTER NINE

'What is it, Badri? What's wrong?' Dunworthy asked.

'Cold,' Badri said. Dunworthy leaned across him and pulled the sheet and blanket up over his shoulders. The blanket seemed pitifully inadequate, as thin as the paper gown Badri was wearing. No wonder he was cold.

'Thank you,' Badri murmured. He pulled his hand out from under the bedclothes and took hold of Dunworthy's. He closed his eyes.

Dunworthy glanced anxiously at the displays, but they were as inscrutable as ever. The temp still read 39.9. Badri's hand felt very hot, even through the imperm glove, and the fingernails looked odd, almost a dark blue. Badri's skin seemed darker too, and his face looked somehow thinner even than when they had brought him in.

The ward sister, whose outline under her paper robe looked uncomfortably like Mrs Gaddson's, came in and said gruffly, 'The list of primary contacts is on the chart.' No wonder Badri was afraid of her. 'CH1,' she said, pointing to the keyboard under the first display on the left.

A chart divided into hour-long blocks came up on the screen. His own name, Mary's and the ward sister's were at the top of the chart with the letters SPG after them, in parentheses, presumably to indicate that they were wearing protective garments when they came into contact with him.

'Scroll,' Dunworthy said and the chart moved up over the screen through the arrival at the hospital, the ambulance medics, the net, the last two days. Badri had been in London on Monday morning setting up an on-site for Jesus College. He had come up to Oxford on the tube at noon.

He had come to see Dunworthy at half past two and was there until four. Dunworthy entered the times on the chart. Badri had told him he'd gone to London on Sunday, though he couldn't remember what time. He entered, 'London – phone Jesus for time of arrival.'

'He drifts in and out a good bit,' the sister said disapprovingly. 'It's the fever.' She checked the drips, gave a yank to the bed-clothes, and went out.

The door's shutting seemed to wake Badri up. His eyes fluttered open.

'I need to ask you some questions, Badri,' he said. 'We need to find out who you've seen and talked to. We don't want them to come down with this, and we need you to tell us who they are.'

'Kivrin,' he said. His voice was soft, almost a whisper, but his hand was holding tightly to Dunworthy's. 'In the laboratory.'

'This morning?' Dunworthy said. 'Did you see Kivrin before this morning? Did you see her yesterday?'

'No.'

'What did you do yesterday?'

'I checked the net,' he said weakly, and his hand clung to Dunworthy's.

'Were you there all day?'

He shook his head, the effort producing a whole series of bleeps and climbs on the displays. 'I went to see you.'

Dunworthy nodded. 'You left me a note. What did you do after that? Did you see Kivrin?'

'Kivrin,' he said. 'I checked Puhalski's coordinates.'

'Were they correct?'

He frowned. 'Yes.'

'Are you certain?'

'Yes. I verified them twice.' He stopped to catch his breath. 'I ran an internal check and a comparator.'

Dunworthy felt a rush of relief. There hadn't been a mistake in the coordinates. 'What about the slippage? How much slippage was there?'

'Headache,' he murmured. 'This morning. Must have drunk too much at the dance.'

'What dance?'

'Tired,' he murmured.

'What dance did you go to?' Dunworthy persisted, feeling like an Inquisition torturer. 'When was it? Monday?'

'Tuesday,' Badri said. 'Drank too much.' He turned his head away on the pillow.

'You rest now,' Dunworthy said. He gently disengaged his hand from Badri's. 'Try to get some sleep.'

'Glad you came,' Badri said, and reached for it again.

Dunworthy held it, watching Badri and the displays by turns as he slept. It was raining. He could hear the patter of drops behind the closed curtains.

He had not realised how ill Badri really was. He had been too worried about Kivrin even to think about him. Perhaps he shouldn't be so angry with Montoya and the rest of them. They had their preoccupations too, and none of them had stopped to think what Badri's illness meant except in terms of the difficulties and inconvenience it caused. Even Mary, talking about needing Bulkeley-Johnson for an infirmary and the possibilities of an epidemic, hadn't brought home the reality of Badri's illness and what it meant. He had had his antivirals, and yet he lay here with a fever of 39.9.

The evening passed Dunworthy listened to the rain and the chiming of the quarter hours at St Hilda's and, more distantly, Christ Church. The ward sister informed Dunworthy grimly that she was going off-duty, and a much smaller and more cheerful blonde nurse, wearing the insignia of a student came in to check the drips and look at the displays.

Badri struggled in and out of consciousness with an effort Dunworthy would hardly have described as 'drifting.' He seemed more and more exhausted each time he fought his way back to consciousness, and less and less able to answer Dunworthy's questions.

Dunworthy kept at it mercilessly. The Christmas dance had been in Headington. Badri had gone to a pub afterwards. He couldn't remember the name of it. Monday night he had worked alone in the laboratory, checking Puhalski's coordinates. He had come up at noon from London. On the tube. This was impossible. Tube passengers and partygoers, and everyone he'd had contact with in London. They would never be able to trace and test all of them, even if Badri knew who they were.

'How did you get to Brasenose this morning?' Dunworthy asked the next time Badri 'drifted' awake again.

'Morning?' Badri said, looking at the curtained window as if he thought it were morning already. 'How long have I been asleep?'

Dunworthy didn't know how to answer that. He'd been asleep off and on all evening. 'It's ten,' he said, looking at his digital. 'We brought you in to hospital at half past one. You ran the net this morning. You sent Kivrin through. Do you remember when you began feeling ill?'

'What's the date?' Badri said suddenly.

'December the twenty-second. You've only been here part of one day.'

'The year,' Badri said, attempting to sit up. 'What's the year?'

Dunworthy glanced anxiously at the displays. His temp was nearly 40.0. 'The year is 2054,' he said, bending over him to calm him. 'It's December the twenty-second.'

'Back up,' Badri said.

Dunworthy straightened and stepped back from the bed.

'Back up,' he said again. He pushed himself up further and looked round the room. 'Where's Mr Dunworthy? I need to speak to him.'

'I'm right here, Badri.' Dunworthy took a step towards the bed and then stopped, afraid of upsetting him. 'What did you want to tell me?'

'Do you know where he might be then?' Badri said. 'Would you give him this note?'

He handed him an imaginary sheet of paper, and Dunworthy realised he must be reliving Tuesday afternoon when he had come to Balliol.

'I have to get back to the net.' He looked at an imaginary digital. 'Is the laboratory open?'

'What did you want to talk to Mr Dunworthy about?' Dunworthy asked. 'Was it the slippage?'

'No. Back up! You're going to drop it. The lid!' He looked straight at Dunworthy, his eyes bright with fever. 'What are you waiting for? Go and fetch him.'

The student nurse came in.

'He's delirious,' Dunworthy said.

She gave Badri a cursory glance and then looked up at the displays. They seemed ominous to Dunworthy, feeding numbers frantically across the screens and zigzagging in three dimensions, but the student nurse didn't seem particularly concerned. She looked at each of the displays in turn and calmly began adjusting the flow on the drips.

'Let's lie down, all right?' she said, still without looking at Badri, and amazingly he did.

'I thought you'd gone,' he said to her, lying back against the pillow. 'Thank goodness you're here,' he said and seemed to collapse all over again, though this time there was nowhere to fall.

The student nurse hadn't noticed. She was still adjusting the drips.

'He's fainted,' Dunworthy said.

She nodded and began calling reads on to the display. She didn't so much as glance at Badri, who looked deathly pale under his dark skin.

'Don't you think you should call a doctor?' Dunworthy said, and the door opened and a tall woman in SPGs came in.

She didn't look at Badri either. She read the monitors one by one, and then asked, 'Indications of pleural involvement?'

'Cyanosis and chills,' the nurse said.

'What's he getting?'

'Myxabravine,' she said.

The doctor took a stethoscope down from the wall, untangling the chestpiece from the connecting cord. 'Any hemoptysis?'

She shook her head.

'Cold,' Badri said from the bed. Neither of them paid the slightest attention. Badri began to shiver. 'Don't drop it. It was china, wasn't it?'

'I want fifty cc's of acqueous penicillin and an ASA pack,' the doctor said. She sat Badri, shivering harder than ever, up in bed and peeled the velcro strips of his paper nightgown open. She pressed the stethoscope's chestpiece against Badri's back in what seemed to Dunworthy to be a cruel and unusual punishment.

'Take a deep breath,' the doctor said, her eyes on the display. Badri did, his teeth chattering.

'Minor pleural consolidation lower left,' the doctor said cryptically and moved the chestpiece over a centimetre. 'Another.' She moved the chestpiece several more times and then said, 'Do we have an ident yet?'

'Myxovirus,' the nurse said, filling a syringe. 'Type A.'

'Sequencing?'

'Not yet.' She fitted the syringe into the cannula and pushed the plunger down. Somewhere outside a telephone rang.

The doctor velcroed the top of Badri's nightgown together, lowered him back to the bed again and flipped the sheet carelessly over his legs.

'Give me a gram stain,' she said, and left. The phone was still ringing.

Dunworthy longed to pull the blanket up over Badri properly, but the student nurse was hooking another drip on to the stanchion. He waited till she had finished with the drip and gone out, and then straightened the sheet and pulled the blanket carefully up over Badri's shoulders and tucked it in at the side of the bed.

'Is that better?' he said, but Badri had already stopped shivering and gone to sleep. Dunworthy looked at the displays. His temp was already down to 39.2, and the previously frantic lines on the other screens were steady and strong.

'Mr Dunworthy,' the student nurse's voice came from somewhere on the wall, 'there's a telephone call for you. It's a Mr Finch.'

Dunworthy opened the door. The student nurse, out of her SPGs, motioned to him to take off his gown. He did, dumping the garments in the large cloth hamper she indicated. 'Your spectacles, please,' she said. He handed them to her and she began spritzing disinfectant on them. He picked up the phone, squinting at the screen.

'Mr Dunworthy, I've been looking for you everywhere,' Finch said. 'The most dreadful thing's happened.'

'What is it?' Dunworthy said. He glanced at his digital. It was ten o'clock. Too early for someone to have come down with the virus if the incubation period was twelve hours. 'Is someone ill?'

'No, sir. It's worse than that. It's Mrs Gaddson. She's in Oxford. She got through the quarantine perimeter somehow.'

'I know. The last train. She made them hold the doors.'

'Yes, well, she called from hospital. She insists on staying at Balliol, and she accused me of not taking proper care of William because I was the one who typed out the tutor assignments, and apparently his tutor's made him stay up over vac to read Petrarch.'

'Tell her we haven't any room. Tell her the dormitories are being sterilized.'

'I did sir, but she said in that case she would room with William. I don't like to do that to him, sir.'

'No,' Dunworthy said. 'There are some things one shouldn't have to endure, even in an epidemic. Have you told William his mother's coming?'

'No, sir. I tried, but he's not in college. Tom Gailey told me Mr Gaddson was visiting a young lady at Shrewsbury, so I rang her up, but there was no answer.'

'No doubt they're out reading Petrarch somewhere,' Dunworthy said, wondering what would happen if Mrs Gaddson should come upon the unwary couple on her way to Balliol.

'I don't see why he should be doing that, sir,' Finch said, sounding troubled. 'Or why his tutor should have assigned Petrarch at all. He's reading for mods.'

'Yes, well, when Mrs Gaddson arrives, put her in Warren.' The nurse looked up sharply from polishing his spectacles. 'It's across the quad, at any rate. Give her a room that doesn't look out on anything. And check our supply of rash ointment.'

'Yes, sir,' Finch said. 'I spoke with the bursar at New College. She said Mr Basingame told her before he left that he wanted to be "free of distractions", but she said she assumed he'd told *someone* where he was going and that she'd try to phone his wife as soon as the lines settled down.'

'Did you ask about their techs?'

'Yes, sir,' Finch said. 'All of them have gone home for the holidays.'

'Which of our techs lives the closest to Oxford?'

Finch thought for a moment. 'That would be Andrews. In Reading. Would you like his number?'

'Yes, and make me up a list of the others' numbers and addresses.'

Finch recited Andrews' number. 'I've taken steps to remedy the lavatory paper situation. I've put up notices with the motto: Waste Leads to Want.'

'Wonderful,' Dunworthy said. He rang off and tried Andrews' number. It was engaged.

The student nurse handed him back his spectacles and a new bundle of SPGs, and he put them on, taking care this time to put the mask on before the cap and to leave the gloves till last. It still took an unconscionable amount of time to array himself. He hoped the nurse would be significantly faster if Badri rang the bell for help.

He went back in. Badri was still restlessly asleep. He glanced at the display. His temp read 39.4.

His head ached. He took off his spectacles and rubbed at the space between his eyes. Then he sat down on the campstool and looked at the chart of contacts he had pieced together thus far. It could scarcely be called a chart, there were so many gaps in it. The name of the pub Badri had gone to after the dance. Where Badri had been Monday evening. And Monday afternoon. He had come up from London on the tube at noon, and Dunworthy had phoned him to ask him to run the net at half past two. Where had he been those two and a half hours?

And where had he gone on Tuesday afternoon after he came to Balliol and left the note saying he'd run a systems check on the net? Back to the laboratory? Or to another pub? He wondered if perhaps someone at Balliol had spoken to Badri while he was there. When Finch called back to inform him of the latest developments in American bell ringers and lavatory paper, he would tell him to ask everyone who'd been in college if they'd seen Badri.

The door opened and the student nurse, swathed in SPGs, came in. Dunworthy looked automatically at the displays, but he couldn't see any dramatic changes. Badri was still asleep. The nurse entered some figures on the display, checked the drip and tugged at a corner of the bedclothes. She opened the curtain and then stood there, twisting the cord in her hands.

'I couldn't help overhearing you on the telephone,' she said. 'You mentioned a Mrs Gaddson. I know it's terribly rude of me to ask, but might that have been William Gaddson's mother you were speaking of?'

'Yes,' he said, surprised. 'William's an undergraduate at Balliol. Do you know him?'

'He's a friend of mine,' she said, flushing such a bright pink he could see it through her imperm mask.

'Ah,' he said, wondering when William had time to read Petrarch. 'William's mother is here in hospital,' he said, feeling he should warn her but unclear as to whom to warn her about. 'It seems she's come to visit him for Christmas.'

'She's here?' the nurse said, flushing an even brighter pink. 'I thought we were under quarantine.'

'Hers was the last train up from London,' Dunworthy said wistfully.

'Does William know?'

'My secretary is attempting to notify him,' he said, omitting the bit about the young lady at Shrewsbury.

'He's at the Bodleian,' she said, 'reading Petrarch.' She unwrapped the curtain cord from her hand and went out, no doubt to telephone the Bodleian.

Badri stirred and murmured something Dunworthy could not make out. He looked flushed, and his breathing seemed more labored.

'Badri?' he said.

Badri opened his eyes. 'Where am I?' he said.

Dunworthy glanced at the monitors. His fever was down a half a point and he seemed more alert than before.

'In Infirmary,' he said. 'You collapsed in the lab at Brasenose while you were working the net. Do you remember?'

'I remember feeling odd,' he said. 'Cold I came to the pub to tell you I'd got the fix . . .' A strange, frightened look came over his face.

119

'You told me there was something wrong,' Dunworthy said. 'What was it? Was it the slippage?'

'Something wrong,' Badri repeated. He tried to raise himself on his elbow. 'What's wrong with me?'

'You're ill,' Dunworthy said. 'You have the flu.'

'Ill? I've never been ill.' He struggled to sit up. 'They died, didn't they?'

'Who died?'

'It killed them all.'

'Did you see someone, Badri? This is important. Did someone else have the virus?'

'Virus?' he said, and there was obvious relief in his voice. 'Do I have a virus?'

'Yes. A type of flu. It's not fatal. They've been giving you antimicrobials, and an analogue's on the way. You'll be recovered in no time. Do you know who you caught it from? Did someone else have the virus?'

'No.' He eased himself back down on to the pillow. 'I thought – Oh!' He looked up in alarm at Dunworthy. 'There's something wrong,' he said desperately.

'What is it?' He reached for the bell. 'What's wrong?'

His eyes were wide with fright. 'It hurts!'

Dunworthy pushed the bell. The nurse and a house officer came in immediately and went through their routine again, prodding him with the icy stethoscope.

'He complained of being cold,' Dunworthy said. 'And of something hurting.'

'Where does it hurt?' the house officer said looking at a display.

'Here,' Badri said. He pressed his hand to the right side of his chest. He began to shiver again.

'Lower right pleurisy,' the house officer said.

'Hurts when I breathe,' Badri said through chattering teeth. 'There's something wrong.'

Something wrong. He had not meant the fix. He had meant that something was wrong with him. He was how old? Kivrin's age? They had begun giving routine rhinovirus antivirals nearly twenty years ago. It was entirely possible that when he'd said he'd never been ill, he meant he'd never had so much as a cold.

'Oxygen?' the nurse said.

'Not yet,' the house officer said on his way out. 'Start him on two hundred units of chloramphenicol.'

The nurse laid Badri back down, attached a piggyback to the drip, watched Badri's temp drop for a minute and went out.

Dunworthy looked out of the window at the rainy night. 'I remember feeling odd,' he had said. Not ill. Odd. Someone who'd never had a cold wouldn't know what to make of a fever or chills. He would only have known something was wrong and would have left the net and hurried to the pub to tell someone. Have to tell Dunworthy. Something wrong.

Dunworthy took off his spectacles and rubbed his eyes. The disinfectant made them smart. He felt exhausted. He had said he couldn't relax until he knew Kivrin was all right. Badri was asleep, the harshness of his breathing taken away by the impersonal magic of the doctors. And Kivrin was asleep too, in a flea-ridden bed seven hundred years away. Or wide awake, impressing the contemps with her table manners and her dirty fingernails, or kneeling on a filthy stone floor, telling her adventures into her hands.

He must have dozed off. He dreamed he heard a telephone ringing. It was Finch. He told him the Americans were threatening to sue for insufficient supplies of lavatory paper and that the vicar had called with the Scripture. 'It's Matthew 2:11,' Finch said. 'Waste leads to want,' and at that point the nurse opened the door and told him Mary needed him to meet her in Casualties.

He looked at his digital. It was twenty past four. Badri was still asleep, looking almost peaceful. The nurse met him outside with the disinfectant bottle and told him to take the lift.

The smell of disinfectant from his spectacles helped wake him up. By the time he reached the ground floor he was almost awake. Mary was there waiting for him in a mask and the rest of it. 'We've got another case,' she said, handing him a bundle of SPGs. 'It's one of the detainees. It might be someone from that crowd of shoppers. I want you to try to identify her.'

He got into the garments as clumsily as the first time, nearly tearing the gown in his efforts to get the velcro strips apart. 'There were dozens of shoppers on the High,' he said, pulling the gloves on. 'And I was watching Badri. I doubt that I could identify anyone on that street.'

'I know,' Mary said. She led the way down the corridor and through the door to Casualties. It seemed like years since he'd been there.

Ahead, a cluster of people, all anonymous in paper, were wheeling a stretcher trolley in. The house officer, also papered, was taking information from a thin, frightened-looking woman in a wet mackintosh and matching rain hat.

'Her name is Beverly Breen,' the woman told him in a feint voice, '226 Plover Way, Surbiton. I knew something was wrong. She kept saying we needed to take the tube to Northampton.'

She was carrying an umbrella and a large handbag, and when the house officer asked for the patient's NHS number, she leaned the umbrella against the admissions desk, opened the handbag and looked through it.

'She was just brought in from the tube station complaining of headache and chills,' Mary said. 'She was waiting to be assigned lodging.'

She signalled the medics to stop the stretcher trolley and pulled the blanket back from the woman's neck and chest so he could get a better look at her, but he didn't need it.

The woman in the wet mac had found the card. She handed it to the officer, picked up the umbrella, the handbag and a sheaf of varicoloured papers, and came over to the stretcher trolley carrying them. The umbrella was a large one. It was covered with lavender violets.

'Badri collided with her on the way back to the net,' Dunworthy said.

'Are you absolutely certain?' Mary said.

He pointed at the woman's friend, who had sat down now and was filling in forms. 'I recognise the umbrella.'

'What time was that?' she said.

'I'm not positive. Half past one?'

'What type of contact was it? Did he touch her?'

'He ran straight into her,' he said, trying to recall the scene. 'He collided with the umbrella, and then he told her he was sorry, and she yelled at him for a bit. He picked up the umbrella and handed it to her.

'Did he cough or sneeze?'

'I can't remember.'

The woman was being wheeled into Casualties. Mary stood up. 'I want her put in Isolation,' she said, and started after them.

The woman's friend stood up, dropping one of the forms and clutching the others awkwardly to her chest. 'Isolation?' she said frightenedly. 'What's wrong with her?'

'Come with me, please,' Mary said to her and led her off somewhere to have her blood taken and her friend's umbrella spritzed with disinfectant before Dunworthy could ask her whether she wanted him to wait for her. He started to ask the registrar and then sat down tiredly in one of the chairs against the wall. There was an inspirational brochure on the chair next to him. Its tide was 'The Importance of a Good Night's Sleep'.

His neck hurt from his uncomfortable sleep on the campstool, and his eyes were smarting again. He supposed he should go back up to Badri's room, but he wasn't certain he had the energy to put on another set of SPGs. And he didn't think he could bear to wake Badri and ask him who else would be shortly wheeled into Casualties with a temp of 39.5.

At any rate Kivrin wouldn't be one of them. It was half past four. Badri had collided with the woman with the lavender umbrella at half past one. That meant an incubation of fifteen hours, and fifteen hours ago Kivrin had been fully protected.

Mary came back, her cap off and her mask dangling from her neck. Her hair was in disarray and she looked as bone-weary as Dunworthy felt.

'I'm discharging Mrs Gaddson,' she told the registrar. 'She's to be back here at seven for a blood test.' She came over to where Dunworthy was sitting. 'I'd forgotten all about her,' she said, smiling. 'She was rather upset. She threatened to sue me for unlawfully detaining her from William.'

'She should get along well with my bell ringers. They're threatening to go to court over involuntary breach of contract.'

Mary ran her hand through her disorderly hair. 'We got an ident from the World Influenza Centre on the influenza virus.'

She stood up as if she had had a sudden infusion of energy. 'I could do with a cup of tea,' she said. 'Come along.'

Dunworthy glanced at the registrar, who was watching them attentively, and hauled himself to his feet.

'I'll be in the surgical waiting-room,' Mary said to the registrar.

'Yes, Doctor,' the registrar said. 'I couldn't help overhearing your conversation . . .' she said hesitantly.

Mary stiffened.

'You told me you were discharging Mrs Gaddson, and then I heard you mention the name "William", and I was just wondering if Mrs Gaddson is by any chance William Gaddson's mother.'

'Yes,' Mary said, looking puzzled.

'You're a friend of his?' Dunworthy said, wondering if she would blush like the blonde student nurse.

She did. 'I've come to know him rather well this vac. He's stayed up to read Petrarch.'

'Among other things,' Dunworthy said and, while she was busy blushing, steered Mary past the 'NO ENTRANCE: ISOLA-TION AREA' sign and down the corridor.

'What in heaven's name was that all about?' she asked.

'Sickly William is even more self-sufficient than we had at first assumed,' he said, and opened the door to the waiting-room.

Mary flicked the light on and went over to the tea trolley. She shook the electric kettle and disappeared into the WC with it. He sat down. Someone had taken away the tray of blood-testing equipment and moved the end table back to its proper place, but Mary's shopping bag was still sitting in the middle of the floor. He leaned forward and moved it over next to the chairs.

Mary reappeared with the kettle. She bent and plugged it in. 'Did you have any luck discovering Badri's contacts?' she said.

'If you could call it that. He went to a Christmas dance in Headington last night. He took the tube both ways. How bad is it?'

Mary opened two tea packets and draped them over the cups. 'There's only powdered milk, I'm afraid. Do you know if he's had any contact recently with someone from the States?'

'No. Why?'

'Do you take sugar?'

'How bad is it?'

She poured powdered milk into the cups. 'The bad news is that Badri's very ill.' She spooned in sugar. 'He had his seasonals through the University, which requires broader-spectrum protection than the NHS. He should be completely protected against a five-point shift, and partially resistant to a ten-point shift. But he's exhibiting full influenza symptoms, which indicates a major mutation.'

The kettle was screaming. 'Which means an epidemic.'

'Yes.'

'A pandemic?'

'Possibly. If the WIC can't sequence the virus quickly, or the staff bolts. Or the quarantine doesn't hold.'

She unplugged the kettle and poured hot water into their cups. 'The good new is that the WIC thinks it's an influenza that originated in South Carolina.' She brought a cup over to Dunworthy. 'In which case it's already been sequenced and an analogue and vaccine manufactured, it responds well to anti-microbials and symptomatic treatment, and it's not fatal.'

'How long is its incubation period?'

'Twelve to forty-eight hours.' She stood against the tea trolley and took a sip of tea. 'The WIC is sending blood samples to the CDC in Atlanta for matching, and they're sending their recommended course of treatment.'

'When did Kivrin check into Infirmary on Monday for her antivirals?'

'Three o'clock,' Mary said. 'She was here until nine the next morning. I kept her overnight to ensure she got a good night's sleep.'

'Badri says he didn't see her yesterday,' Dunworthy said, 'but he could have had contact with her on Monday before she went into Infirmary.'

'She'd need to have been exposed before her antiviral inoculation, and the virus have had a chance to replicate unchecked for her to be in danger, James,' Mary said. 'Even if she did see Badri on Monday or Tuesday, she's in less danger of developing symptoms than you are.' She looked seriously at him over her teacup. 'You're still worried over the fix, aren't you?'

He half-shook his head. 'Badri says he checked the apprentice's coordinates and they were correct, and he'd already told Gilchrist the slippage was minimal,' he said, wishing Badri had answered him when he asked him about the slippage.

'What else is there that can have gone wrong?' Mary asked.

'I don't know. Nothing. Except that she's alone in the Middle Ages.'

Mary set her cup of tea down on the trolley. 'She may be safer there than here. We're going to have a good many ill patients. Influenza spreads like wildfire, and the quarantine will only make it worse. The medical staff are always the first exposed. If they come down with it, or the supply of antimicrobials gives out, this century could be the one that's a ten.'

She pushed her hand tiredly over her untidy hair. 'Sorry, it's the fatigue speaking. This isn't the Middle Ages, after all. It's not even the twentieth century. We have metabolisers and adjuvants, and if it's the South Carolina virus, we've an analogue and a vaccine. But I'm still glad Colin and Kivrin are safely out of this.'

'Safely in the Middle Ages,' Dunworthy said.

Mary smiled at him. 'With the cut-throats.'

The door banged open. A tallish blond boy with large feet and a rugby duffel came in, dripping water on the floor.

'Colin!' Mary said.

'So this is where you've got to,' Colin said. 'I've been looking everywhere for you.'

—❊—

Transcript from the Domesday Book
(000893–000898)

Mr Dunworthy, *ad adjuvandum me festina.**

—❊—

* *Translation*: Make haste to help me.

BOOK TWO

In the bleak midwinter
    Frosty wind made moan,
Earth stood hard as iron,
    Water like a stone;
Snow had fallen, snow on snow,
    Snow on snow,
In the bleak midwinter
    Long ago.

CHRISTINA ROSSETTI

CHAPTER TEN

The fire was out. Kivrin could still smell smoke in the room, but she knew it was from a fire burning in a hearth somewhere. It's no wonder, she thought, chimneys didn't become extant in England until the late fourteenth century, and this is only 1320. And as soon as she had formed the thought, awareness of the rest of it came: I am in 1320, and I've been ill. I've had a fever.

For a while she didn't think any further than that. It was peaceful just to lie there and rest. She felt worn out, as if she had come through some terrible ordeal that took all her strength. I thought they were trying to burn me at the stake, she thought. She remembered struggling against them and the flames leaping up, licking at her hands, burning her hair.

They had to cut off my hair, she thought and wondered if that were a memory or something she had dreamed. She was too tired to raise her hand to her hair, too tired even to try to remember. I have been very ill, she thought. They gave me the last rites. 'There is naught to fear,' he had said. 'You do but go home again.' *Requiescat in pace.* And slept.

When she woke again it was dark in the room, and a bell was ringing a long way off. She had the idea that it had been ringing for a long time, the way the lone bell had rung when she came through, but after a minute another one chimed in, and then one so close it seemed to be just outside the window, drowning out the others as they rang. Matins, Kivrin thought, and seemed to remember them ringing like that before, a ragged, out-of-tune chiming that matched the beating of her heart, but that was impossible.

She must have dreamed it. She had dreamed they were

burning her at the stake. She had dreamed they cut off her hair. She had dreamed the contemps spoke a language she didn't understand.

The nearest bell stopped, and the others went on for a while, as if glad of the opportunity to make themselves heard, and Kivrin remembered that, too. How long had she been here? It had been night, and now it was morning. It seemed like one night, but now she remembered the faces leaning over her. When the woman had brought her the cup and again when the priest had come in, and the cutthroat with him, she had been able to see them clearly, without the flicker of unsteady candlelight. And in between she remembered darkness and the smoky light of tallow lamps and the bells, ringing and stopping and ringing again.

She felt a sudden stab of panic. How long had she been lying here? What if she had been ill for weeks and had already missed the rendezvous? But that was impossible. People weren't delirious for weeks, even if they had typhoid fever, and she couldn't have typhoid fever. She had had her inoculations.

It was cold in the room, as if the fire had gone out in the night. She felt for the bed coverings, and hands came up out of the dark immediately and pulled something soft over her shoulders.

'Thank you,' Kivrin said, and slept.

The cold woke her again, and she had the feeling she had only slept a few moments, though there was a little light in the room now. It came from a narrow window recessed in the stone wall. The window's shutters had been opened, and that was where the cold was coming from, too.

A woman was standing on tiptoe on the stone seat under the window, fastening a cloth over the opening. She was wearing a black robe and a white wimple and coif, and for a moment Kivrin thought, I'm in a nunnery, and then remembered that women in the 1300s covered their hair when they were married. Only unmarried girls wore their hair loose and uncovered.

The woman didn't look old enough to be married, or to be a nun either. There had been a woman in the room while she was ill, but that woman had been much older. When Kivrin had clutched at her hands in her delirium, they had been rough and wrinkled, and the woman's voice had been harsh with age, though perhaps that had been part of the delirium, too.

The woman leaned into the light from the window. The white coif was yellowed and it was not a robe, but a kittle like Kivrin's, with a dark green surcote over it. It was badly dyed and looked like it had been made from a burlap sack, the weave so large Kivrin could see it easily even in the dim light. She must be a servant, then, but servants didn't wear linen wimples or carry bunches of keys like the one that hung from the woman's belt. She had to be a person of some importance, the housekeeper, perhaps.

And this was a place of importance. Probably not a castle, because the wall the bed lay up against wasn't stone – it was unfinished wood – but very likely a manor house of at least the first order of nobility, a minor baron, and possibly higher than that. The bed she was lying in was a real bed with a raised wooden frame and hangings and stiff linen sheets, not just a pallet, and the coverings were fur. The stone seat under the window had embroidered cushions on it.

The woman tied the cloth to little projections of stone on either side of the narrow window, stepped down from the window seat and leaned over to get something. Kivrin couldn't see what it was because the bed hangings obstructed her view. They were heavy, almost like rugs, and had been pulled back and tied with what looked like rope.

The woman straightened up again, holding a wooden bowl, and then, catching her skins up with her free hand, stepped on to the window seat and began brushing something thick on to the cloth. Oil, Kivrin thought. No, wax. Waxed linen used in place of glass in windows. Glass was supposed to have been common in fourteenth-century manor houses. The nobility were supposed to have carried glass windows along with the luggage and the furniture when they travelled from house to house.

I must get this on the corder, Kivrin thought, that some manor houses didn't have glass windows, and she raised her hands and pressed them together, but the effort of holding them up was too great and she let them fall back on to the coverings.

The woman glanced over towards the bed and then turned back to the window and went on painting the cloth with long, unconcerned strokes. I must be getting better, Kivrin thought. She was right by the bed the whole time I was ill. She wondered again how long that time had been. I will have to find out, she thought, and then I must find the drop.

It couldn't be very far. If this was the village she had intended to go to, the drop wasn't more than a mile away. She tried to remember how long the trip to the village had taken. It had seemed to take a long time. The cut-throat had put her on a white horse, and it had had bells on its harness. But he wasn't a cut-throat. He was a kind-looking young man with red hair.

She would have to ask the name of the village she had been brought to, and hopefully it would be Skendgate. But even if it wasn't, she would know from the name where she was in relation to the drop. And, of course, as soon as she was a little stronger, they could show her where it was.

What is the name of this village you have brought me to? She had not been able to think of the words last night but that was because of the fever, of course. She had no trouble now. Mr Latimer had spent months on her pronunciation. They would certainly be able to understand, '*In whatte londe am I?*' or even, '*Whatte be thisse holding?*' and even if there were some variation in local dialect, the interpreter would automatically correct it.

'*Whatte place hast thou brotte me?*' Kivrin said.

The woman turned, looking startled. She stepped down from the window seat, still holding the bowl in one hand and the brush in the other, only it wasn't a brush, Kivrin could see as she approached the bed. It was a squarish wooden spoon with a nearly flat bowl.

'*Gottebae plaise tthar tleve,*' the woman said, holding spoon and bowl together in front of her. '*Beth naught agast.*'

The interpreter was supposed to translate what was said immediately. Maybe Kivrin's pronunciation was all off, so far off that the woman thought she was speaking a foreign language and was trying to answer her in clumsy French or German.

'*Whatte place hast thou brotte me?*' she said slowly so the interpreter would have time to translate what she said.

'*Wick londebay yae comen lawdayke awtreen godelae deynorm andoar sic straunguwlondes. Spekefaw eek waenoot awfthy taloorbrede.*'

'*Lawyes sharess loostee?*' a voice said.

The woman turned around to look at a door Kivrin couldn't see, and another woman came in, much older, her face under the coif wrinkled and her hands the hands Kivrin remembered from her delirium, rough and old. She was wearing a silver chain and carrying a small leather chest. It looked like the casket Kivrin had brought through with her, but it was smaller and bound with iron instead of brass. She set the casket down on the window seat.

'*Auf specheryit darmayt?*'

She remembered the voice, too, harsh and almost angry-sounding, speaking to the woman by Kivrin's bed as if she were a servant. Well, perhaps she was, and this was the lady of the house, though her coif was no whiter, her dress no finer. But there weren't any keys at her belt, and now Kivrin remembered that it wasn't the housekeeper who carried the keys but the lady of the house.

The lady of the manor in yellowed linen and badly dyed burlap, which meant that Kivrin's dress was all wrong, as wrong as Latimer's pronunciations, as wrong as Dr Ahrens' assurances that she would not get any mediaeval diseases.

'I had my inoculations,' she murmured, and both women turned to look at her.

'*Ellavih swot wardesdoor feenden iss?*' the older woman asked sharply. Was she the younger woman's mother, or her mother-in-law, or her nurse? Kivrin had no idea. None of the words she'd said, not even a proper name or a form of address, separated itself out.

'*Maetinkerr woun dahest wexe hoordoumbe,*' the younger woman said, and the older one answered, '*Nor nayte bawcows derouthe.*'

Nothing. Shorter sentences were supposed to be easier to translate, but Kivrin couldn't even tell whether she said one word or several.

The younger woman's chin in the tight coif lifted angrily. '*Certessan, shreevadwomn wolde nadae seyvous,*' she said sharply.

Kivrin wondered if they were arguing over what to do with her. She pushed on the coverlet with her weak hands, as if she could push herself away from them, and the young woman set down her bowl and spoon and came immediately up beside the bed.

133

'*Spaegun yovor tongawn glais?*' she said, and it might be 'Good morning,' or 'Are you feeling better?' or 'We're burning you at dawn,' for all Kivrin knew. Perhaps her illness was keeping the interpreter from working. Perhaps when the fever went down, she would understand everything they said.

The old woman knelt beside the bed, holding a small silver box at the end of the chain between her folded hands, and began to pray. The young woman leaned forward to look at Kivrin's forehead and then reached around behind her head, doing something that pulled at Kivrin's hair, and she realised they must have bandaged the wound on her forehead. She touched her hand to the cloth and then put it on her neck, feeling for her tangled locks, but there was nothing there. Her hair ended in a ragged fringe just below her ears.

'*Vae motten tiyez thynt,*' the young woman said worriedly. '*Far thotyiwort wount sorr.*' She was giving Kivrin some kind of explanation, though Kivrin couldn't understand it, and actually she did understand it: she had been very ill, so ill she had thought her hair was on fire. She remembered someone – the old woman? – trying to grab at her hands and her flailing wildly at the flames. They had had no alternative.

And Kivrin had hated the unwieldy mass of hair and the endless time it took to brush it, had worried about how mediaeval women wore their hair, whether they braided it or not, and wondered how on earth she was going to get through two weeks without washing it. She should be glad they had cut it off, but all she could think of was Joan of Arc, who had had short hair, whom they had burned at the stake.

The young woman had drawn her hands back from the bandage and was watching Kivrin, looking frightened. Kivrin smiled at her, a little quaveringly, and she smiled back. She had a gap where two teeth were missing on the right side of her mouth, and the tooth next to the gap was brown, but when she smiled she looked no older than a first-year student.

She finished untying the bandage and laid it on the coverlet. It was the same yellowed linen as her coif, but torn into fraying strips and stained with brownish blood. There was more blood than

Kivrin would have thought there would be. Mr Gilchrist's wound must have started bleeding again.

The woman touched Kivrin's temple nervously, as if she wasn't sure what to do. '*Vexeyaw hongroot?*' she said, and put one hand behind Kivrin's neck and helped her raise her head.

Her head felt terribly light. That must be because of my hair, Kivrin thought.

The older woman handed the young one a wooden bowl, and she put it to Kivrin's lips. Kivrin sipped carefully at it, thinking confusedly that it was the same bowl that had held the wax. It wasn't, and it wasn't the drink they'd given her before. It was a thin, grainy gruel, less bitter than the drink last night, but with a greasy aftertaste.

'*Thasholde nayive gros vitaille towayte,*' the older woman said, her voice harsh with impatient criticism.

Definitely her mother-in-law, Kivrin thought.

'*Shimote lese hoor fource,*' the young woman answered back mildly.

The gruel tasted good. Kivrin tried to drink it all, but after only a few sips she felt worn out.

The young woman handed the bowl to the older one, who had come round to the side of the bed too, and eased Kivrin's head back down on to the pillow. She picked up the bloody bandage, touched Kivrin's temple again as if she were debating whether to put the bandage back on again, and then handed it to the other woman, who set it and the bowl down on the chest that must be at the foot of the bed.

'*Lo, liggethsteallouw,*' the young woman said, smiling her gap-toothed smile, and there was no mistaking her tone even though she couldn't make out the words at all. The woman had told her to go to sleep. She closed her eyes.

'*Durmidde shoalaushrekkeynow,*' the older woman said, and they left the room, shutting the heavy door behind them.

Kivrin repeated the words slowly to herself, trying to catch some familiar word. The interpreter was supposed to enhance her ability to separate out phonemes and recognise syntactical patterns, not just store Middle English vocabulary, but she might as well be listening to Serbo-Croatian.

And maybe I am, she thought Who knows where they've

brought me? I was delirious. Maybe the cut-throat put me on a boat and took me across the Channel. She knew that wasn't possible. She remembered most of the night's journey, even though it had a disjointed, dreamlike quality to it. I fell off the horse, she thought, and a redheaded man picked me up. And we came past a church.

She frowned, trying to remember more about the direction they had travelled. They had headed into the woods, away from the thicket, and then come to a road, and the road forked, and that was where she had fallen off. If she could find the fork in the road perhaps she could find the drop from there. The fork was only a little way from the church.

But if the drop was that close, she was in Skendgate and the women were speaking Middle English, but if they were speaking Middle English, why couldn't she understand them?

Maybe I hit my head when I fell off the horse, and it's done something to the interpreter, she thought, but she had not hit her head. She had let go and slid down until she was sitting on the road. It's the fever, she thought. It's somehow keeping the interpreter from recognising the words.

It recognised the Latin, she thought, and a little knot of fear began to form in her chest. It recognised the Latin, and I can't be ill. I had my inoculations. She remembered suddenly that her antiviral inoculation had itched and made a welt under her arm, but Dr Ahrens had checked it just before she came through. Dr Ahrens had said it was all right. And none of her other inoculations had itched except the plague inoculation. I can't have the plague, she thought. I don't have any of the symptoms.

Plague victims had huge lumps under their arms and on the insides of their thighs. They vomited blood, and the blood vessels under their skin ruptured and turned black. It wasn't the plague, but what was it and how had she contracted it? She had been inoculated against every major disease extant in 1320, and anyway, she hadn't been exposed to any disease. She had begun to have symptoms as soon as she came through, before she had even met anyone. Germs didn't just hover near a drop, waiting for someone to come through. They had to be spread by contact or sneezing or fleas. The plague had been spread by fleas.

It's not the plague, she told herself firmly. People who have the plague don't wonder if they have it. They're too busy dying.

It wasn't the plague. The fleas that had spread it lived on rats and humans, not out in the middle of a forest, and the Black Death hadn't reached England till 1348. It must be some mediaeval disease Dr Ahrens hadn't known about. There had been all sorts of strange diseases in the Middle Ages – the king's evil and St Vitus' dance and unnamed fevers. It must be one of them, and it had taken her enhanced immune system a while to figure out what it was and begin fighting it. But now it had, and her temperature was down and the interpreter would begin working. All she had to do was rest and wait and get better. Comforted by that thought she closed her eyes again and slept.

Someone was touching her. She opened her eyes. It was the mother-in-law. She was examining Kivrin's hands, turning them over and over again in hers, rubbing her chapped forefinger along the backs, scrutinising the nails. When she saw Kivrin's eyes were open, she dropped her hands, as if in disgust, and said, '*Sheavost ahvheigh parage attelest, baht hoore der wikkonasshae haswfolletwe?*'

Nothing. Kivrin had hoped that somehow, while she slept, the interpreter's enhancers would have sorted and deciphered everything she'd heard, and she would wake to find the interpreter working. But their words were still unintelligible. It sounded a little like French, with its dropped endings and delicate rising inflections, but Kivrin knew Norman French – Mr Dunworthy had made her learn it – and she couldn't make out any of the words.

'*Hastow naydepesse?*' the old woman said.

It sounded like a question, but all French sounded like a question.

The old woman took hold of Kivrin's arm with one rough hand and put her other arm around her, as if to help her up. I'm too ill to get up, Kivrin thought. Why would she make me get up? To be questioned? To be burned?

The younger woman came into the room, carrying a footed cup. She set it down on the window seat and came to take Kivrin's other arm. '*Hastontee natour yowrese?*' she asked, smiling her gap-toothed smile at Kivrin, and Kivrin thought, maybe they're taking me to the bathroom, and made an effort to sit up and put her legs over the side of the bed.

She was immediately dizzy. She sat, her bare legs dangling over the side of the high bed, waiting for it to pass. She was wearing her linen shift and nothing else. She wondered where her clothes were. At least they had let her keep her shift. People in the Middle Ages didn't usually wear anything to bed.

People in the Middle Ages didn't have indoor plumbing either, she thought, and hoped she wouldn't have to go outside to a privy. Castles sometimes had enclosed garderobes, or corners over a shaft that had to be cleaned out at the bottom, but this wasn't a castle.

The young woman put a thin, folded blanket around Kivrin's shoulders like a shawl, and they both helped her off the bed. The planked wooden floor was icy. She took a few steps and was dizzy all over again. I'll never make it all the way outside, she thought.

'*Wotan shay wootes nawdaor youse der jordane?*' the old woman said sharply, and Kivrin thought she recognised *jardin*, the French for garden, but why would they be discussing gardens?

'*Thanway maunhollp anhour,*' the young woman said, putting her arm round Kivrin and draping Kivrin's arm over her shoulders. The old woman gripped her other arm with both hands. She scarcely came to Kivrin's shoulder, and the young woman didn't look like she weighed more than ninety pounds, but between them they walked her to the end of the bed.

Kivrin got dizzier with every step. I'll never make it all the way outside, she thought, but they had stopped at the end of the bed. There was a chest there, a low wooden box with a bird or possibly an angel carved roughly into the top. On it lay a wooden basin full of water, the bloody bandage that had been round Kivrin's forehead, and a smaller, empty bowl. Kivrin, concentrating on not falling over, didn't realise what it was until the old woman said, '*Swoune nawmaydar oupondre yorresette,*' and pantomimed lifting her heavy skirts and sitting on it.

A chamber pot, Kivrin thought gratefully. Mr Dunworthy, chamber pots were extant in county village manor houses in 1320. She nodded to show she understood and let them ease her down on to it, though she was so dizzy she had to grab at the heavy bed hangings to keep from falling, and her chest hurt so badly when she tried to stand up again that she doubled over.

'*Maisry!*' the old woman shouted towards the door. '*Maisry, com un'dtvae holpoon!*' and the inflection indicated clearly that she was calling someone – Marjorie? Mary? – to come and help, but no one appeared, so perhaps she was wrong about that, too.

She straightened a little, testing the pain, and then tried to stand up, and the pain had lessened a little, but they still had nearly to carry her back to the bed, and she was exhausted by the time she was back under the bed coverings. She closed her eyes.

'*Slaeponpon donu paw daton,*' the young woman said, and she had to be saying 'Rest,' or 'Go to sleep,' but she still couldn't decipher it. The interpreter's broken, she thought, and the little knot of panic started to form again, worse than the pain in her chest.

It can't be broken, she told herself. It's not a machine. It's a chemical syntax and memory enhancer. It can't be broken. It could only work with words in its memory, though, and obviously Mr Latimer's Middle English was useless. *Whan that Aprille with his shoures sote.* Mr Latimer's pronunciations were so far off the interpreter couldn't recognise what it was hearing as the same words, but that didn't mean it was broken. It only meant it had to collect new data, and the few sentences it had heard so far weren't enough.

It recognised the Latin, she thought, and the panic stabbed at her again, but she resisted it. It had been able to recognise the Latin because the rite of extreme unction was a set piece. She had already known what words should be there. The words the women spoke weren't a set piece, but they were still decipherable. Proper names, forms of address, nouns and verbs and prepositional phrases would appear in set positions that repeated again and again. They would separate themselves out rapidly, and the interpreter would be able to use them as the key to the rest of the code. And what she needed to do now was collect data, listen to what was said without even trying to understand it, and let the interpreter work.

'*Thin keowre hoorwoun desmoortale?*' the young woman asked.

'*Got tallon wottes,*' the old woman said.

A bell began to ring, far away. Kivrin opened her eyes. Both women had turned to look at the window, even though they couldn't see through the linen.

'*Bere wichebay gansanon,*' the young woman said.

The old woman didn't answer. She was staring at the window, as if she could see past the stiffened linen, her hands clasped in front of her as if in prayer.

'*Aydreddit ister fayve riblaun,*' the young woman said, and in spite of her resolution, Kivrin tried to make it into 'It is time for vespers,' or 'There is the vespers bell,' but it wasn't vespers. The bell went on tolling, and no other bells joined in. She wondered if it was the bell she had heard before, ringing all alone in the late afternoon.

The old woman turned abruptly away from the window. '*Nay, Elwiss, itbahn diwolffin.*' She picked up the chamber pot from the wooden chest. '*Gawynha thesspyd—*'

There was a sudden scuffling outside the door, a sound of footsteps running up stairs, and a child's voice crying, '*Modder! Eysmertemay!*'

A little girl burst into the room, blonde plaits and cap strings flying, nearly colliding with the old woman and the chamber pot. The child's round face was red and smeared with tears.

'*Wol yadothoos forshame ahnyous!*' the old woman growled at her, lifting the treacherous bowl out of reach. '*Yowe maun naroonso inhus.*'

The little girl paid no attention to her. She ran straight at the young woman, sobbing, '*Rawzamun hattmay smerte, Modder!*'

Kivrin gasped. *Modder.* That had to be 'mother'.

The little girl held up her arms and her mother, oh, yes, definitely mother, picked her up. She fastened her arms around her mother's neck and began to howl.

'*Shh, ahnyous, shh,*' the mother said. That guttural's a G, Kivrin thought. A hacking German G. Shh, Agnes.

Still holding her, the mother sat down on the window seat. She wiped at the tears with the tail of her coif. '*Spekenaw dothass bifel, Agnes.*'

Yes, definitely Agnes. And *speken* was 'tell'. Tell me what happened.

'*Shayoss mayswerte!*' Agnes said, pointing at another child who had just come into the room. The second girl was considerably older, nine or ten at least. She had long brown hair that hung down her back and was held in place by a dark blue kerchief.

'*Itgan naso, ahnyous,*' she said. '*Tha pighte rennin gawn derstayres,*' and there was no mistaking that combination of affection and contempt. She didn't look like the blonde little girl, but Kivrin was willing to bet this dark-haired girl was the little one's older sister. '*Shay pighte renninge ahndist eyres, Modder.*'

'Mother' again, and *shay* was 'she' and *pighte* must be 'fell'. It sounded French, but the key to this was German. The pronunciations, the constructions, were German. Kivrin could almost feel it click into place.

'*Na comfitte hoor thusselwys,*' the older woman said. '*She hathnau woundes. Hoor teres been fornaught meis gain thy pitye.*'

'*Hoor may ganful bloody,*' the woman said, but Kivrin couldn't hear her. She was hearing instead the interpreter's translation, still clumsy and obviously more than a beat behind, but a translation:

'Don't pamper her, Eliwys. She is not injured. Her tears are but to get your attention.'

And the mother, whose name was Eliwys, 'Her knee is bleeding.'

'*Rossmunt, brangund oorwarsted frommecofre,*' she said, pointing at the foot of the bed, and the interpreter was right behind her. 'Rosemund, fetch me the cloth on the chest.' The ten-year-old moved immediately towards the chest at the foot of the bed.

The older girl was Rosemund, and the little one was Agnes, and the impossibly young mother in her wimple and coif was Eliwys.

Rosemund held out a frayed cloth that must surely be the one Eliwys had taken off Kivrin's forehead.

'Touch it not! Touch it not!' Agnes screamed, and Kivrin wouldn't have even needed the interpreter for that one. It was still far more than a beat behind.

'I would but tie a cloth to stop the bleeding,' Eliwys said, taking the rag from Rosemund. Agnes tried to push it away. 'The cloth will not—' There was a blank space as if the interpreter didn't know a word, and then, '—you, Agnes.' The word was obviously 'hurt' or 'harm', and Kivrin wondered if the interpreter had not had the word in its memory and why it couldn't have come up with an approximation from context.

'—*will* penaunce,' Agnes shouted, and the interpreter echoed, 'It will—' and then the blank again. The space must be so that she could hear the actual word and make her own guess at its meaning. It wasn't a bad idea, but the interpreter was so far behind the space that Kivrin couldn't hear the word she was intended to. If the interpreter did this every time it didn't recognise a word, she was in serious trouble.

'It *will* penaunce,' Agnes wailed, pushing her mother's hand away from her knee. 'It *will* pain,' the interpreter whispered, and Kivrin felt relieved that it had managed to come up with something, even though 'to pain' was scarcely a verb.

'How came you to fall?' Eliwys asked to distract Agnes.

'She was running up the stairs,' Rosemund said. 'She was running to give you the news that . . . had come.'

The interpreter left a space again, but Kivrin caught the word this time. Gawyn, which was probably a proper name, and the interpreter had apparently reached the same conclusion because by the time Agnes had shrieked, '*I* would have told Mother Gawyn had come,' the interpreter included it in the translation.

'*I* would have told,' Agnes said, really crying now, and buried her face against her mother, who promptly took advantage of the opportunity to tie the bandage around Agnes' knee.

'You can tell me now,' she said.

Agnes shook her buried head.

'You tie the bandage too loosely, daughter-in-law,' the older woman said. 'It will but fall away.'

The bandage looked tight enough to Kivrin, and obviously any attempt to bind the wound tighter would result in renewed screams. The old woman was still holding the chamber pot in both hands. Kivrin wondered why she didn't go empty it.

'Shh, shh,' Eliwys said, rocking the little girl gently and patting her back. 'I would fain have you tell me.'

'Pride goes before a fall,' the old woman said, seemingly determined to make Agnes cry again. 'You were to blame that you fell. You should not have run on the stairs.'

'Was Gawyn riding a white mare?' Eliwys asked.

A white mare. Kivrin wondered if Gawyn could be the man who had helped her on to his horse and brought her to the manor.

'Nay,' Agnes said in a tone that indicated her mother had made some sort of joke. 'He was riding his own black stallion, Gringolet. And he rode up to me and said, "Good Lady Agnes, I would speak with your mother."'

'Rosemund, your sister was hurt because of your carelessness,' the old woman said. She hadn't succeeded in upsetting Agnes, so she'd decided to go after some other victim. 'Why were you not tending her?'

'I was at my broidery,' Rosemund said, looking to her mother for support. 'Maisry was to keep watch over her.'

'Maisry went out to see Gawyn,' Agnes said, sitting up on her mother's lap.

'And dally with the stableboy,' the old woman said. She went to the door and shouted, 'Maisry!'

Maisry. That was the name the old woman had called out before, and now the interpreter wasn't even leaving spaces when it came to proper names. Kivrin didn't know who Maisry was, probably a servant but if the way things were going was any indication, Maisry was going to be in a lot of trouble. The old woman was determined to find a victim, and the missing Maisry seemed perfect.

'Maisry!' she shouted again, and the name echoed.

Rosemund took the opportunity to go and stand beside her mother. 'Gawyn bade us tell you he begged leave to come and speak with you.'

'Waits he below?' Eliwys asked.

'Nay. He went first to the church to speak of the lady with Father Rock.'

Pride goes before a fall. The interpreter was obviously getting overconfident. Father Rolfe, perhaps, or Father Peter. Obviously not Father Rock.

'Why went he to speak to Father Rock?' the old woman demanded coming back into the room.

Kivrin tried to hear the real word under the maddening whisper of the translation. Roche. The French word for 'rock'. Father Roche.

'Mayhap he has found somewhat of the lady,' Eliwys said, glancing at Kivrin. It was the first indication she, or anyone, had given that they remembered Kivrin was in the room. Kivrin quickly closed her eyes to make them think she was asleep so they would go on discussing her.

'Gawyn rode out this morning to seek the ruffians,' Eliwys said. Kivrin opened her eyes to slits, but she was no longer looking at her. 'Mayhap he has found them.' She bent and tied the dangling strings of Agnes' linen cap. 'Agnes, go to the church with Rosemund and tell Gawyn we would speak with him in the hall. The lady sleeps. We must not disturb her.'

Agnes darted for the door, shouting, '*I* would be the one to tell him, Rosemund.'

'Rosemund, let your sister tell,' Eliwys called after them. 'Agnes, do not run.'

The girls disappeared out the door and down the invisible stairs, obviously running.

'Rosemund is near grown,' the old woman said. 'It is not seemly for her to run after your husband's men. Ill will come of your daughters being untended. You would do wisely to send to Oxenford for a nurse.'

'No,' Eliwys said with a firmness Kivrin wouldn't have guessed at. 'Maisry can keep watch over them.'

'Maisry is not fit to watch sheep. We should not have come from Bath in such haste. Certes we could have waited till—' something.

The interpreter left a gap again, and Kivrin didn't recognise the phrase, but she had caught the important facts. They had come from Bath. They were near Oxford.

'Let Gawyn fetch a nurse. And a leech-woman to see to the lady.'

'We will send for no one,' Eliwys said.

'To—' another place name the interpreter couldn't manage. 'Lady Yvolde has repute with injuries. And she would gladly lend us one of her waiting women for a nurse.'

'No,' Eliwys said. 'We will tend her ourselves. Father Roche—'

'Father Roche,' she said contemptuously. 'He knows naught of medicine.'

But I understood everything he said, Kivrin thought. She remembered his quiet voice chanting the last rites, his gentle touch on her temples, her palms, the soles of her feet. He had told her not to be afraid and asked her her name. And held her hand.

'If the lady is of noble birth,' the older woman said, 'would you have it told you let an ignorant village priest tend her? Lady Yvolde—'

'We will send for no one,' Eliwys said, and for the first time Kivrin realised she was afraid. 'My husband bade us keep here till he come.'

'He had sooner have come with us.'

'You know he could not,' Eliwys said. 'He will come when he can. I must go to speak with Gawyn,' she said, walking past the old woman to the door. 'Gawyn told me he would search the place where first he found the lady to seek for signs of her attackers. Mayhap he has found somewhat that will tell us what she is.'

The place where first he found the lady. Gawyn was the man who had found her, the man with the red hair and the kind face who had helped her on to his horse and brought her here. That much at least she hadn't dreamed, though she must have dreamed the white horse. He had brought her here, and he knew where the drop was.

'Wait,' Kivrin said. She pushed herself up against the pillows. 'Wait. Please. I would speak with Gawyn.'

The women stopped. Eliwys came around beside the bed, looking alarmed.

'I would speak with the man called Gawyn,' Kivrin said carefully, waiting before each word until she had the translation. Eventually the process would be automatic, but for now she thought the word and then waited till the interpreter translated it and repeated it out loud. 'I must discover this place where he found me.'

Eliwys laid her hand on Kivrin's forehead, and Kivrin brushed it impatiently away.

'I would speak with Gawyn,' she said.

'She has no fever, Imeyne,' Eliwys said to the old woman, 'and

145

yet she tries to speak, though she knows we cannot understand her.'

'She speaks in a foreign tongue,' Imeyne said, making it sound criminal. 'Mayhap she is a French spy.'

'I'm not speaking French,' Kivrin said. 'I'm speaking Middle English.'

'Mayhap it is Latin,' Eliwys said. 'Father Roche said she spoke in Latin when he shrove her.'

'Father Roche can scarce say his Paternoster,' Lady Imeyne said. 'We should send to—' the unrecognisable name again. Kersey? Courcy?

'I would speak with Gawyn,' Kivrin said in Latin.

'Nay,' Eliwys said. 'We will await my husband.'

The old woman wheeled angrily, slopping the contents of the chamber pot on to her hand. She wiped it off on to her skirt and went out the door, slamming it shut behind her. Eliwys started after her.

Kivrin grabbed at her hands. 'Why don't you understand me?' she said. 'I understand you. I have to talk to Gawyn. He has to tell me where the drop is.'

Eliwys disengaged Kivrin's hand. 'There, you mustn't cry,' she said kindly. 'Try to sleep. You must rest, so you can go home.'

⊷⊶

Transcript from the Domesday Book
(000915–001284)

I'm in a lot of trouble, Mr Dunworthy. I don't know where I am and I can't speak the language. Something's gone wrong with the interpreter. I can understand some of what the contemps say, but they can't understand me at all. And that's not the worst of it.

I've caught some sort of disease. I don't know what it is. It's not the plague because I don't have any of the right symptoms and because I'm getting better. And I had a plague inoculation. I had all my inoculations and T-cell enhancement and everything, but one of them must not have worked or else this is some Middle Ages disease there aren't any inoculations for.

The symptoms are headache and fever and dizziness, and I get a pain in my chest when I try to move. I was delirious for a while, which is why I don't know where I am. A man named Gawyn brought me here on his horse, but I don't remember very much about the trip except that it was dark and it seemed to take hours. I'm hoping I was wrong and the fever made it seem longer, and I'm in Ms Montoya's village after all.

It could be Skendgate. I remember a church, and I think this is a manor house. I'm in a bedroom or a solar, and it's not just a loft because there are stairs, so that means the house of a minor baron at least. There's a window, and as soon as the dizziness subsides I'll climb up on the window seat and see if I can see the church. It has a bell – it rang for vespers just now. The one at Ms Montoya's village didn't have a bell tower, and that makes me afraid I'm not in the right place. I know we're fairly close to Oxford, because one of the contemps talked about fetching a doctor from there. It's also close to a village called Kersey – or Courcy – which is not one of the villages on the map of Ms Montoya's I memorised, but that could be the name of the landowner.

Because of being out of my head, I'm not sure of my temporal location either. I've been trying to remember, and I think I've only been ill for two days, but it might be more. And I can't ask them what day it is because they don't understand me, and I can't get out of bed without falling over, and they've cut my hair off, and I don't know what to do. What happened? Why won't the interpreter work? Why didn't the T-cell enhancement?

(Break)

There's a rat under my bed I can hear it scrabbling in the dark.

<hr>

CHAPTER ELEVEN

They couldn't understand her. Kivrin had tried to communicate with Eliwys, to *make* her understand, but she had merely smiled kindly, uncomprehendingly, and told Kivrin to rest.

'Please,' Kivrin had said as Eliwys started for the door. 'Don't leave. This is important. Gawyn is the only one who knows where the drop is.'

'Sleep,' Eliwys said. 'I will be back in a little.'

'You have to let me see him,' Kivrin said desperately, but Eliwys was already nearly to the door. 'I don't know where the drop is.'

There was a clattering on the stairs. Eliwys opened the door and said, 'Agnes, I bade you go tell—'

She stopped in midsentence and took a step back. She did not look frightened or even upset but her hand on the frame jerked a little, as if she would have slammed the door, and Kivrin's heart began to pound. This is it, she thought wildly. They've come to take me to the stake.

'Good morning, my lady,' a man's voice said. 'Your daughter Rosemund told me I would find you in hall, but I did not.'

He came into the room. Kivrin couldn't see his face. He was standing at the foot of the bed, hidden from her by the hangings. She tried to shift her head so she could see him, but the movement made her head spin violently. She lay back down.

'I thought I would find you with the wounded lady,' the man said. He was wearing a padded jerkin and leather hose. And a sword. She could hear it clank as he took a step forward. 'How does she?'

'She fares better today,' Eliwys said. 'My husband's mother has gone to brew her a decoction of woundwort for her injuries.'

148

She had taken her hand from the door, and his comment about 'your daughter Rosemund' surely meant that this was Gawyn, the man she had sent to look for Kivrin's attackers, but Eliwys had taken two more steps backward as he spoke, and her face looked guarded, wary. The thought of danger flickered through Kivrin's mind again, and she wondered suddenly if she might have not dreamed Mr Dunworthy's cut-throat after all, if that man, with his cruel face, might be Gawyn.

'Found you aught that might tell us of the lady's identity?' Eliwys said carefully.

'Nay,' he said. 'Her goods had all been stolen and the horses taken. I hoped the lady might tell me somewhat of her attackers, how many there were and from what direction they came upon her.'

'I fear she cannot tell you anything,' Eliwys said.

'Is she mute then?' he said and moved so she could see him.

He was not so tall as Kivrin remembered him, standing over her, and his hair looked less red and more blond in the daylight, but his face still looked as kind as when he had set her on his horse. His black horse, Gringolet.

After he had found her in the clearing. He was not the cut-throat – she had dreamed the cut-throat, conjured him out of her delirium and Mr Dunworthy's fears, along with the white horse and the Christmas carols – and she must be misunderstanding Eliwys' reactions the way she had misunderstood their getting her up to use the chamber pot.

'She is not mute, but speaks in some strange tongue I do not know,' Eliwys said. 'I fear her injuries have addled her wits.' She came round to the side of the bed and Gawyn followed her. 'Good lady. I have brought my husband's *privé*, Gawyn.'

'Good day, my lady,' Gawyn said, speaking slowly and over-distinctly, as if he thought Kivrin were deaf.

'It was he who found you in the woods,' Eliwys said.

Where in the woods? Kivrin thought desperately.

'I am pleased that your wounds are healing,' Gawyn said, emphasising every word. 'Can you tell me of the men who attacked you?'

I don't know if I can tell you anything, she thought, afraid to

149

speak for fear he wouldn't understand her either. He had to understand her. He knew where the drop was.

'How many men were there?' Gawyn said. 'Were they on horseback?'

Where did you find me? she thought, emphasising the words the way Gawyn had. She waited for the interpreter to work out the whole sentence, listening carefully to the intonations, checking them against the language lessons Mr Dunworthy had given her.

Gawyn and Eliwys were waiting, watching her intently. She took a deep breath. 'Where did you find me?'

They exchanged quick glances, his surprised, hers saying plainly, 'you *see*?'

'She spoke thus that night,' he said. 'I thought it was her injury that made her speak so.'

'And so I do,' Eliwys said. 'My husband's mother thinks she is of France.'

He shook his head. 'It is not French she speaks.' He turned back to Kivrin. 'Good lady,' he said, nearly shouting, 'came you from another land?'

Yes, Kivrin thought, another land, and the only way back is the drop, and only you know where it is.

'Where did you find me?' she said again.

'Her goods were all taken,' Gawyn said, 'but her wagon was of rich make, and she had many boxes.'

Eliwys nodded. 'I fear she is of high birth and her people seeking her.'

'In what part of the woods did you *find* me?' Kivrin said, her voice rising.

'We are upsetting her,' Eliwys said. She leaned over Kivrin and patted her hand. 'Shh. Take your rest.' She moved away from the bed, and Gawyn followed.

'Would you have me ride to Bath to Lord Guillaume?' Gawyn said, out of sight behind the hangings.

Eliwys stepped back the way she had when he first came in, as if she were afraid of him. But they had stood side by side at the bed, their hands nearly touching. They had spoken together like old friends. This wariness must be coming from something else.

'Would you have me bring your husband?' Gawyn said.

'Nay,' Eliwys said, looking down at her hands. 'My lord has enough to worry him, and he cannot leave until the trial is finished. And he bade you stay with us and guard us.'

'By your leave, then, I will return to the place where the lady was set upon and search further.'

'Aye,' Eliwys said, still not looking at him. 'In their haste, some token may have fallen to the ground nearby that will tell us of her.'

The place where the lady was set upon, Kivrin recited under her breath, trying to hear his words under the interpreter's translation and memorise them. The place where I was set upon.

'I will take my leave and ride out again,' Gawyn said.

Eliwys looked up at him. 'Now?' she said. 'It grows dark.'

'Show me the place where I was set upon,' Kivrin said.

'I do not fear the dark, Lady Eliwys,' he said, and strode out, the sword clanking.

'Take me with you,' Kivrin said, but it was no use. They were already gone and the interpreter was broken. She had deceived herself into thinking it was working. She had understood what they were saying because of the language lessons Mr Dunworthy had given her, not because of the interpreter, and perhaps she was only deceiving herself that she understood them.

Perhaps the conversation had not been about who she was at all, but about something else altogether – finding a missing sheep or putting her on trial.

The lady Eliwys had shut the door when they went out, and Kivrin couldn't hear anything. Even the tolling bell had stopped, and the light from the waxed linen was faintly blue. It grows dark.

Gawyn had said he was going to ride back to the drop. If the window overlooked the courtyard, she might at least be able to see which way he rode out. It is not far, he had said. If she could just see the direction he rode, she could find the drop herself.

She pushed herself up in the bed, but even that much exertion made the pain in her chest stab again. She put her feet over the side, but the action made her dizzy. She lay back against the pillow and closed her eyes.

Dizziness and fever and a pain in the chest. What were those symptoms of? Smallpox started out with fever and chills, and the pox didn't appear until the second or third day. She lifted her arm up to see if there were the beginnings of the pox. She had no idea how long she had been ill, but it couldn't be smallpox because the incubation period was ten to twenty-one days. Ten days ago she had been in hospital in Oxford, where the smallpox virus had been extinct for nearly a hundred years.

She had been in hospital, getting inoculated against all of them: smallpox, typhoid fever, cholera, plague. So how could it be any of them? And if it wasn't any of them, what was it? Saint Vitus' dance? She had told herself that before, that this was something she had not been vaccinated against but she had had her immune system augmented too, to fight off any infection.

There was a sound of running on stairs. 'Modder!' a voice that she already recognised as Agnes' shouted. 'Rosemund waited not!'

She didn't burst into the room with quite as much violence because the heavy door was shut and she had to push it open, but as soon as she had squeezed through she raced for the window seat, wailing.

'Modder! *I* would have told Gawyn!' she sobbed, and then stopped when she saw her mother wasn't in the room. The tears stopped too, Kivrin noticed.

Agnes stood by the window for a minute, as if she were debating whether to try this scene at a later time, and then ran back to the door. Halfway there, she spied Kivrin and stopped again.

'I know who you are,' she said, coming round to the side of the bed. She was scarcely tall enough to see over the bed. Her cap strings had come undone again. 'You are the lady Gawyn found in the wood.'

Kivrin was afraid that her answer, garbled as the interpreter obviously made it, would frighten the little girl. She pushed herself up a little against the pillows and nodded.

'What befell your hair?' Agnes asked. 'Did the robbers steal it?'

Kivrin shook her head, smiling at the odd idea.

'Maisry says the robbers stole your tongue,' Agnes said. She pointed at Kivrin's forehead. 'Hurt you your head?'

Kivrin nodded.

'I hurt my knee,' she said, and tried to pick it up with both hands so Kivrin could see the dirty bandage. The old woman was right. It was already slipping. She could see the wound under it. Kivrin had supposed it was just a skinned knee, but the wound looked fairly deep.

Agnes tottered, let go of the knee and leaned against the bed again. 'Will you die?'

I don't know, Kivrin thought, thinking of the pain in her chest. The mortality rate for smallpox had been 75 per cent in 1320, and her augmented immune system wasn't working.

'Brother Hubard died,' Agnes said wisely. 'And Gilbert. He fell from his horse. I saw him. His head was all red. Rosemund said Brother Hubard died of the blue sickness.'

Kivrin wondered what the blue sickness was – choking perhaps, or apoplexy – and if he was the chaplain that Eliwys' mother-in-law was so eager to replace. It was usual for noble households to travel with their own priests. Father Roche was apparently the local priest, probably uneducated and possibly even illiterate, though she had understood his Latin perfectly well. And he had been kind. He had held her hand and told her not to be afraid. There are nice people in the Middle Ages, Mr Dunworthy, she thought. Father Roche and Eliwys and Agnes.

'My father said he would bring me a magpie when he comes from Bath,' Agnes said. 'Adeliza has a tercel. She lets me hold him sometimes.' She held her bent arm up and out, the dimpled fist closed as if a falcon were perched on her imaginary gauntlet. 'I have a hound.'

'What is your hound's name?' Kivrin asked.

'I call him Blackie,' Agnes said, though Kivrin was certain that was only the interpreter's version. More likely she had said Black-amon or Blakkin. 'He is black. Have you a hound?'

Kivrin was too surprised to answer. She had spoken and made herself understood. Agnes hadn't even acted like her pronunciation was unusual. She had spoken without thinking about the interpreter or waiting for it to translate, and perhaps that was the secret.

'Nay, I have no hound,' she said finally, trying to duplicate what she'd done before.

'I will teach my magpie to talk. I will teach him to say, "Good morrow, Agnes."'

'Where is your hound?' Kivrin said, trying again. The words sounded different to her, lighter, with that murmuring French inflection she had heard in the women's speech.

'Do you wish to see Blackie? He is in the stable,' Agnes said. It sounded like a direct response, but the way Agnes talked it was difficult to tell. She might simply have been volunteering information. To be sure, Kivrin would have to ask her something completely off the subject and something with only one answer.

Agnes was stroking the soft fur of the bed covering and humming a toneless little tune.

'What is your name?' Kivrin asked, trying to let the interpreter control her words. It translated her modern sentence into something like, '*How are you cleped?*' which she was not sure was correct, but Agnes didn't hesitate.

'Agnes,' the little girl said promptly. 'My father says I may have a tercel when I am old enough to ride a mare. I have a pony.' She stopped stroking the fur, propped her elbows on the edge of the bed and rested her chin in her little hands. 'I know your name,' she said, sounding smugly pleased. 'It is Katherine.'

'What?' Kivrin said blankly. Katherine. How had they come up with Katherine? Her name was supposed to be Isabel. Was it possible that they thought they knew who she was?

'Rosemund said none knew your name,' she went on, looking smug, 'but I heard Father Roche tell Gawyn you were called Katherine. Rosemund said you could not speak, but yet you *can*.'

Kivrin had a sudden image of the priest bending over her, his face obscured by the flames that seemed constantly in front of her, saying in Latin, 'What is your name that you might be shriven?'

And she, trying to form the word though her mouth was so dry she could hardly speak, afraid she would die and they would never know what had happened to her.

'*Are* you called Katherine?' Agnes was demanding, and she could hear the little girl's voice clearly under the interpreter's translation. It sounded just like Kivrin.

'Aye,' Kivrin said, and felt like crying.

'Blackie has a—' Agnes said. The interpreter didn't catch the word. *Karette? Chavette?* 'It is red. Do you wish to see it?' and before

Kivrin could stop her, she went running out through the still partly opened door.

Kivrin waited, hoping she would come back and that a *karette* wasn't alive, wishing she had asked where she was and how long she'd been here, though Agnes was probably too young to know. She looked no more than three, though of course she would be much smaller than a modern three-year-old. Five, then, or possibly six. I should have asked her how old she was, Kivrin thought, and then remembered that she might not know that either. Joan of Arc hadn't known how old she was when the Inquisitors asked her at her trial.

At least she could ask questions, Kivrin thought. The interpreter was not broken after all. It must have been temporarily stymied by the strange pronunciations, or affected somehow by her fever, but it was all right now, and Gawyn knew where the drop was and could show it to her.

She sat up straighter among the pillows so she could see the door. The effort hurt her chest and made her dizzy, and her head ached. She anxiously felt her forehead and then her cheeks. They felt warm, but that could be because her hands were cold. It was icy in the room, and on her excursion to the chamber pot, she hadn't seen any sign of a brazier or even a warming pan.

Had warming pans been invented yet? They must have. Otherwise how would people have survived the Little Ice Age? It was so cold.

She was beginning to shiver. Her fever must be going back up. Were they supposed to come back? In History of Meds she had read about fevers breaking, and after that the patient was weak, but the fever didn't come back, did it? Of course it did. What about malaria? Shivering, headache, sweats, recurring fever. Of course they came back.

Well, it obviously wasn't malaria. Malaria had never been endemic to England, mosquitoes didn't live in Oxford in midwinter and never had, and the symptoms were wrong. She hadn't experienced any sweating, and the shivering she was having was due to fever.

Typhus produced headache and a high fever, and it was transmitted by body lice and rat fleas, both of which were endemic to England in the Middle Ages and probably endemic to the bed she was lying on, but the incubation period was too long, nearly two weeks.

Typhoid fever's incubation period was only a few days, and it caused headache, aching in the limbs and high fever, too. She didn't think it was a recurring fever, but she remembered it was normally highest at night, so that must mean it went down during the day and then up again in the evening.

Kivrin wondered what time it was. Eliwys had said, 'It grows dark,' and the light from the linen-covered window was faintly blue, but the days were short in December. It might only be midafternoon. She felt sleepy, but that was no sign either. She had slept off and on all day.

Drowsiness was a symptom of typhoid fever. She tried to remember the others from Dr Ahrens' 'short course' in mediaeval medicine. Nosebleeds, coated tongue, rose-coloured rash. The rash wasn't supposed to appear until the seventh or eighth day, but Kivrin pulled her shift up and looked at her stomach and chest. No rash, so it couldn't be typhoid. Or smallpox. With smallpox, the pox started appearing by the second or third day.

She wondered what had happened to Agnes. Perhaps someone had belatedly had the good sense to bar her from the sickroom, or perhaps the unreliable Maisry was actually watching her. Or, more likely, she had stopped to see her puppy in the stable and forgotten she was going to show her *chavotte* to Kivrin.

The plague started out with a headache and a fever. It can't be the plague, Kivrin thought. You don't have any of the symptoms. Buboes that grew to the size of oranges, a tongue that swelled till it filled the whole mouth, subcutaneous haemorrhages that turned the whole body black. You don't have the plague.

It must be some sort of flu. It was the only disease that came on so suddenly, and Dr Ahrens had been upset over Mr Gilchrist's moving the date up because the antivirals wouldn't take full effect until the twenty-fourth, and she'd only have partial immunity. It had to be the flu. What was the treatment for the flu? Antivirals, rest, fluids.

Well then, rest, she told herself, and closed her eyes.

She did not remember falling asleep, but she must have,

because the two women were in the room again, talking, and Kivrin had no memory of their having come in.

'What said Gawyn?' the old woman said. She was doing something with a bowl and a spoon, mashing the spoon against the side of it. The iron-bound casket sat open beside her, and she reached into it, pulled out a small cloth bag, sprinkled the contents into the bowl and stirred it again.

'He found naught among her belongings that might tell us the lady's origins. Her goods had all been stolen, the chests broken open and emptied of all that might identify her. But he said her wagon was of rich make. Certes, she is of good family.'

'And certes, her family searches for her,' the old woman said. She had set down the bowl and was tearing cloth with a loud ripping sound. 'We must send to Oxenford and tell them she lies safe with us.'

'No,' Eliwys said, and Kivrin could hear the resistance in her voice. 'Not to Oxenford.'

'What have you heard?'

'I have heard naught,' Eliwys said, 'but that my lord bade us keep here. He will be here within the week if all goes well.'

'If all had gone well he would have been here now.'

'The trial had scarce begun. Mayhap he is on his way home even now.'

'Or mayhap—' another one of those untranslatable names, Torquil? 'waits to be hanged and my son with him. He should not have meddled in such a matter.'

'He is a friend, and guiltless of the charges.'

'He is a fool, and my son more fool for testifying on his behalf. A friend would have bade him leave Bath.' She ground the spoon into the side of the bowl again. 'I have need of mustard for this,' she said and stepped to the door. 'Maisry!' she called, and went back to tearing the cloth. 'Found Gawyn aught of the lady's attendants?'

Eliwys sat down on the window seat. 'No, nor of their horses nor hers.'

A girl with a pocked face and greasy hair hanging over it came in. Surely this couldn't be Maisry, who dallied with stableboys instead of watching her charges? She bent her knee in a curtsy that was more of a stumble and said. '*Wotwardstu, Lawttymayseen?*'

Oh, no, Kivrin thought. What's wrong with the interpreter now?

'Fetch me the pot of mustard from the kitchen and tarry not,' the old woman said, and the girl started for the door. 'Where are Agnes and Rosemund? Why are they not with you?'

'*Shiyrouthamay*,' she said sullenly.

Eliwys stood up. 'Speak up,' she said sharply.

'They hide [something] from me.'

It wasn't the interpreter after all. It was simply the difference of the Norman English the nobles spoke and the still Saxon-sounding dialect of the peasants, neither of which sounded anything like the Middle English Mr Latimer had blithely taught her. It was a wonder the interpreter was picking up anything at all.

'I was seeking them when Lady Imeyne called, good lady,' Maisry said, and the interpreter got it all, though it was taking several seconds. It gave an imbecilic slowness to Maisry's speech, which might or might not be appropriate.

'Where did you look for them? In the stable?' Eliwys said, and brought her hands together on either side of Maisry's head like a pair of cymbals. Maisry howled and clapped a dirty hand to her left ear. Kivrin shrank back against the pillows.

'Go and fetch the mustard to Lady Imeyne and find you Agnes.'

Maisry nodded, not looking particularly frightened but still holding her ear. She stumbled another curtsy and went out no more quickly than she had come in. She seemed less upset by the sudden violence than Kivrin was, and Kivrin wondered if Lady Imeyne would get her mustard any time soon.

It was the swiftness and the calmness of the violence that had surprised her. Eliwys had not even seemed angry, and as soon as Maisry was gone she went back to the window seat, sat down and said quietly, 'The lady could not be moved though her family did come. She can bide with us until my husband returns. He will be here by Christmas surely.'

There was noise on the stairs. Apparently she had been wrong, Kivrin thought, and the ear boxing had done some good. Agnes rushed in, clutching something to her chest.

'Agnes!' Eliwys said. 'What do you here?'

'I brought my—' the interpreter still didn't have it. *Charette?* – 'to show the lady.'

'You are a wicked child to hide from Maisry and come hence to disturb the lady,' Imeyne said. 'She suffers greatly from her injuries.'

'But she told me she wished to see it.' She held it up. It was a toy two-wheeled cart painted red and gilt.

'God punishes those who bear false witness with everlasting torment,' Lady Imeyne said, grabbing the little girl roughly. 'The lady cannot speak. You know full well.'

'She spoke to me,' Agnes said sturdily.

Good for you, Kivrin thought. Everlasting torment. What horrible things to threaten a child with. But this was the Middle Ages, when priests talked constantly of the last days and the final judgment, of the pains of hell.

'She told me she wished to see my wagon,' Agnes said. 'She said she did not have a hound.'

'You are making up tales,' Eliwys said. 'The lady cannot speak,' and Kivrin thought, I have to stop this. They'll box her ears, too.

She pushed herself up on her elbows. The effort left her breathless. 'I spoke with Agnes,' she said, praying the interpreter would do what it was supposed to. If it chose to blink out again at this moment and ended up getting Agnes a beating, that would be the last straw. 'I bade her bring her cart to me.'

Both women turned and looked at her. Eliwys' eyes widened. The old woman looked astonished and then angry, as if she thought Kivrin had deceived them.

'I told you,' Agnes said, and marched over to the bed with the wagon.

Kivrin lay back against the pillow, exhausted. 'What is this place?' she asked.

It took Eliwys a moment to recover herself. 'You rest safely in the house of my lord and husband—' The interpreter had trouble with the name. It sounded like Guillaume D'Iverie or possibly Devereaux.

Eliwys was looking at her anxiously. 'My husband's *privé* found you in the woods and brought you hence. You had been set upon by robbers and grievously injured. Who attacked you?'

'I know not,' Kivrin said.

'I am called Eliwys, and this is the mother of my husband, the Lady Imeyne. What is your name?'

And now was the time to tell them the whole carefully researched story. She had told the priest her name was Katherine, but Lady Imeyne had already made it clear she put no stock in anything he said. She didn't even believe he could speak Latin. Kivrin could say he had misunderstood, that her name was Isabel de Beauvrier. She could tell them she had called out her mother's, her sister's name in her delirium. She could tell them she had been praying to St Catherine.

'Of what family are you?' Lady Imeyne asked.

It was a very good story. It would establish her identity and position in society and would ensure that they wouldn't try to send for her family. Yorkshire was too far away, and the road north was impassable.

'Whither were you bound?' Eliwys said.

Mediaeval had thoroughly researched the weather and the road conditions. It had rained every day for two weeks in December, and there had been a hard frost to freeze the mired roads till late January. But she had seen the road to Oxford. It had been dry and clear. And Mediaeval had thoroughly researched the colour of her dress and the prevalence of glass windows among the upper classes. They had thoroughly researched the language.

'I remember not,' Kivrin said.

'Naught?' Eliwys said, and turned to Lady Imeyne. 'She remembers naught.' They think I'm saying 'naught', Kivrin thought, that I don't remember anything. The inflection, the pronunciation didn't differentiate between the two words.

'It is her wound,' Eliwys said. 'It has shaken her memory.'

'No . . . nay . . .' Kivrin said. She was not supposed to feign amnesia. She was supposed to be Isabel de Beauvrier, from the East Riding. Just because the roads were dry here didn't mean they weren't impassable further north, and Eliwys would not even let Gawyn ride to Oxford to get news of her or to Bath to fetch her husband. She surely wouldn't send him to the East Riding.

'Can you not even remember your own name?' Lady Imeyne said impatiently, leaning so close that Kivrin could smell her breath. It was very foul, an odour of decay. She must have rotting teeth, too.

'What is your name?'

Mr Latimer had said Isabel was the most common woman's name in the 1300s. How common was Katherine? And Mediaeval didn't know the daughters' names. What if Yorkshire wasn't distant enough, after all, and Lady Imeyne knew the family? She would take it as further proof that she was a spy. She had better stay with the common name and tell them she was Isabel de Beauvrier.

The old woman would be only too happy to believe that the priest had got her name wrong. It would be further proof of his ignorance, of his incompetence, further reason to send to Bath for a new chaplain. But he had held Kivrin's hand, he had told her not to be afraid.

'My name is Katherine,' she said.

———&&&———

Transcript from the Domesday Book
(001300–002018)

I'm not the only one in trouble, Mr Dunworthy. I think the contemps who've taken me in are, too.

The lord of the manor, Lord Guillaume, isn't here. He's in Bath, testifying at the trial of a friend of his, which is apparently a dangerous thing to do. His mother, Lady Imeyne, called him a fool for getting mixed up in it, and Lady Eliwys, his wife, seems worried and nervous.

They've come here in a great hurry and without servants. Fourteenth-century noblewomen had at least one lady-in-waiting apiece, but neither Eliwys nor Imeyne has any, and they left the children's – Guillaume's two little girls are here – nurse behind. Lady Imeyne wanted to send for a new one, and a chaplain, but Lady Eliwys won't let her.

I think Lord Guillaume must be expecting trouble and has spirited his womenfolk away here to keep them safe. Or possibly the trouble's already happened – Agnes, the littler of the two girls, told me about the chaplain's death and someone named Gilbert whose 'head was all red', so perhaps there's already been bloodshed and the women have come here to escape it. One of Lord Guillaume's *privés* has come with them and he's fully armed.

There weren't any major uprisings against Edward II in Oxfordshire in 1320, although no one was very happy with the king and his favourite, Hugh Despenser, and there were plots and minor skirmishes everywhere else. Two of the barons, Lancaster and Mortimer, took sixty-three manors away from the Despensers that year – this year. Lord Guillaume – or his friend – may have got involved in one of those plots.

It could be something else entirely, of course, a land dispute or something. People in the 1300s spent almost as much time in court as the contemps in the last part of the twentieth century. But I don't think so. Lady Eliwys jumps at every sound and she's forbidden Lady Imeyne to tell the neighbours they're here.

I suppose in one way this is a good thing. If they aren't telling anyone they're here, they won't tell anyone about me or send messengers to try to find out who I am. On the other hand, there is the chance of armed men kicking in the door at any moment. Or of Gawyn, the only person who knows where the drop is, getting killed defending the manor.

(Break)

15 December 1320 (Old Style). The interpreter is working now, more or less, and the contemps seem to understand what I'm saying. I can understand them, though their Middle English bears no resemblance to what Mr Latimer taught me. It's full of inflections and has a much softer French sound. Mr Latimer wouldn't even recognise his '*When that Aprille with his shoures sote.*'

The interpreter translates what the contemps say with the syntax and some of the words intact, and at first I tried to phrase what I said the same way, saying 'Aye' and 'Nay' and 'I remember naught of whence I came,' but thinking about it's deadly – the interpreter takes for ever to come up with a translation and I stammer and struggle with the pronunciations. So I just speak modern English and hope what comes out of my mouth is close to being right, and that the interpreter isn't slaughtering the idioms and the inflections. Heaven only knows how I sound. Like a French spy probably.

The language isn't the only thing off. My dress is all wrong, of far too fine a weave, and the blue is too bright dyed with woad or not. I haven't seen any bright colours at all. I'm too tall, my teeth are too good and my hands are wrong, in spite of my muddy labours at the dig. They should not only have been dirtier, but I should have chilblains. Everyone's hands, even the children's, are chapped and bleeding. It is, after all, December.

December the fifteenth. I overheard part of an argument between Lady Imeyne and Lady Eliwys about getting a replacement chaplain, and Imeyne said, 'There is more than time enough to send. It is full ten days till Christ's mass.' So tell Mr Gilchrist I've ascertained my temporal location, at least. But I don't know how far from the drop I am. I've tried to remember Gawyn bringing me here, but that whole night is hopelessly muddled and part of what I remember didn't happen. I remember a white horse that had bells on its harness, and the bells were playing Christmas carols, like the carillon in Carfax Tower.

The fifteenth of December means it's Christmas Eve there, and you'll be giving your sherry party and then walking over to St Mary the Virgin's for the interchurch service. It is hard to comprehend that you are over seven hundred years away. I keep thinking that if I got out of bed (which I can't because I'm too dizzy – think my temp is back up) and opened the door I would find not a mediaeval hall but Brasenose's lab, and all of you waiting for me, Badri and Dr Ahrens and you, Mr Dunworthy, polishing your spectacles and saying I told you so. I wish you were.

CHAPTER TWELVE

Lady Imeyne did not believe Kivrin's story about having amnesia. When Agnes brought her hound, which turned out to be a tiny black puppy with huge feet, in to Kivrin, she said, 'This is my hound, Lady Kivrin.' She held it out to Kivrin, clutching its fat middle. 'You can pet him. Do you remember how?'

'Yes,' Kivrin said, taking the puppy out of Agnes' too-tight grasp and stroking its baby-soft fur. 'Aren't you supposed to be at your sewing?'

Agnes took the puppy back from her. 'Grandmother went to chide with the steward, and Maisry went out to the stable.' She twisted the puppy round to give it a kiss. 'So I came to speak to you. Grandmother is very angry. The steward and all his family were living in the hall when we came hence.' She gave the puppy another kiss. 'Grandmother says it is his wife who tempts him to sin.'

Grandmother. Agnes had not said anything like 'grandmother'. The word hadn't even existed until the eighteenth century, but the interpreter was taking huge, disconcerting leaps now, though it left Agnes' mispronunciation of Katherine intact and sometimes left blanks in places where the meaning should have been obvious from context. She hoped her subconscious knew what it was doing.

'Are you a *daltriss*, Lady Kivrin?' Agnes said.

Her subconscious obviously didn't know what it was doing. 'What?' she asked.

'A *daltriss*,' Agnes said. The puppy was trying desperately to squirm out of Agnes' grip. 'Grandmother says you are one. She says a wife fleeing to her lover would have good cause to remember naught.'

An adultress. Well, at least it was better than a French spy. Or perhaps Lady Imeyne thought she was both.

Agnes kissed the puppy again. 'Grandmother said a lady had no good cause to travel through the woods in winter.'

Lady Imeyne was right, Kivrin thought, and so was Mr Dunworthy. She still had not found out where the drop was, although she had asked to speak with Gawyn when Lady Eliwys came in the morning to bathe her temple.

'He has ridden out to search for the wicked men who robbed you,' Eliwys had said, putting an ointment on Kivrin's temple that smelled like garlic and stung horribly. 'Do you remember aught of them?'

Kivrin had shaken her head, hoping her faked amnesia wouldn't end in some poor peasant's being hanged. She could scarcely say, 'No, that isn't the man,' when she supposedly couldn't remember anything.

Perhaps she shouldn't have told them she couldn't remember anything. The probability that they would have known the de Beauvriers was very small, and her lack of an explanation had obviously made Imeyne even more suspicious of her.

Agnes was trying to put her cap on the puppy. 'There are wolves in the woods,' she said. 'Gawyn slew one with his axe.'

'Agnes, did Gawyn tell you of his finding me?' Kivrin asked.

'Aye. Blackie likes to wear my cap,' she said, tying the strings in a choking knot.

'He doesn't act like it,' Kivrin said. 'Where did Gawyn find me?'

'In the woods,' Agnes said. The puppy twisted out of the cap and nearly fell off the bed. She set it in the middle of the bed and lifted it by its front paws. 'Blackie can dance.'

'Here. Let me hold it,' Kivrin said, to rescue the poor thing. She cradled it in her arms. 'Where in the woods did Gawyn find me?'

Agnes stood on tiptoe, trying to see the puppy. 'Blackie sleeps,' she whispered.

The puppy was asleep, exhausted from Agnes' attentions.

Kivrin laid it beside her on the fur bed covering. 'Was the place he found me far from here?'

'Aye,' Agnes said, and Kivrin could tell she had no idea.

This was no use. Agnes obviously didn't know anything. She would have to talk to Gawyn. 'Has Gawyn returned?'

'Aye,' Agnes said, stroking the sleeping puppy. 'Would you speak with him?'

'Yes,' Kivrin said.

'*Are* you a *daltriss*?'

It was difficult to follow Agnes' conversational jumps. 'No,' she said, and then remembered she was not supposed to be able to remember anything. 'I don't remember anything about who I am.'

Agnes petted Blackie. 'Grandmother says only a *daltriss* would ask so boldly to speak with Gawyn.'

The door opened and Rosemund came in. 'They're looking for you everywhere, simplehead,' she said, her hands on her hips.

'I was speaking with Lady Kivrin,' Agnes said with an anxious glance at the coverlet where Blackie lay, nearly invisible against the sable fur. Apparently hounds were not allowed inside. Kivrin pulled the rough sheet up over it so Rosemund wouldn't see.

'Mother said the lady must rest so that her wounds will heal,' Rosemund said sternly. 'Come. I must tell Grandmother I found you.' She led the little girl out of the room.

Kivrin watched them leave, hoping fervently that Agnes wouldn't tell Lady Imeyne Kivrin had asked again to speak to Gawyn. She had thought she had a good excuse to talk to Gawyn, that they would understand that she was anxious to find out about her belongings and her attackers. But it was 'unseemly' for unmarried noblewomen in the 1300s to 'boldly ask' to speak to young men.

Eliwys could talk to him because she was the head of the house with her husband gone, and his employer, and Lady Imeyne was his lord's mother, but Kivrin should have waited until Gawyn spoke to her and then answered him 'with all modesty as fits a maid'. But I must talk to him, she thought. He's the only one who knows where the drop is.

Agnes came dashing back in and snatched up the sleeping

puppy. 'Grandmother was very angry. She thought I had fallen in the well,' Agnes said, and ran back out again.

And no doubt 'Grandmother' had boxed Maisry's ears because of it, Kivrin thought. Maisry had already been in trouble once today for losing Agnes, who had come to show Kivrin Lady Imeyne's silver chain, which she said was 'a rillieclary', a word that defeated the interpreter. Inside the little box, she told Kivrin, was a piece of the shroud of St Stephen. Maisry had had her pocked cheek slapped by Imeyne for letting Agnes take the reliquary and for not watching her, though not for letting the little girl in the sickroom.

None of them seemed concerned at all about the little girls getting close to Kivrin or to be aware that they might catch what she had. Neither Eliwys nor Imeyne took any precautions in caring for her.

The contemps hadn't understood the mechanics of disease transmission, of course – they believed it was a consequence of sin and epidemics were a punishment from God – but they had known about contagion. The motto of the Black Death had been 'Depart quickly, go far, tarry long', and there had been quarantines before that.

Not here, Kivrin thought, and what if the little girls come down with this? Or Father Roche?

He had been near her all through her fever, touching her, asking her name. She frowned, trying to remember that night. She had fallen off the horse, and then there was a fire. No, she had imagined that in her delirium. And the white horse. Gawyn's horse was black.

They had ridden through a wood and down a hill past a church, and the cut-throat had – it was no use. The night was a shapeless dream of frightening faces and bells and flames. Even the drop was hazy, unclear. There had been an oak tree and willows, and she had sat down against the wagon wheel because she felt so dizzy, and the cut-throat had . . . No, she had imagined the cut-throat. And the white horse. Perhaps she had imagined the church as well.

She would have to ask Gawyn where the drop was, but not in front of Lady Imeyne, who thought she was a *daltriss*. She had to get well, to get enough strength to get out of bed and go down to the hall, out to the stable, to find Gawyn to speak to him alone. She had to get better.

She was a little stronger, though she was still too weak to walk to the chamber pot unaided. The dizziness was gone, and the fever, but her shortness of breath persisted. They apparently thought she was improving, too. They had left her alone most of the morning, and Eliwys had only stayed long enough to smear on the foul-smelling ointment. And have me make improper advances towards Gawyn, Kivrin thought.

Kivrin tried not to worry about what Agnes had told her or why the antivirals hadn't worked or how far the drop was, and to concentrate on getting her strength back. No one came in all afternoon, and she practised sitting up and putting her feet over the side of the bed. When Maisry came with a rushlight to help her to the chamber pot, she was able to walk back to the bed by herself.

It grew colder in the night, and when Agnes came to see her in the morning, she was wearing a red cloak and hood of very thick wool and white fur mittens. 'Do you wish to see my silver buckle? Sir Bloet gave it me. I will bring it on the morrow. I cannot come today, for we go to cut the Yule log.'

'The Yule log?' Kivrin said, alarmed. The ceremonial log had traditionally cut on the twenty-fourth, and this was only supposed to be the seventeenth. Had she misunderstood Lady Imeyne?

'Aye,' Agnes said. 'At home we do not go till Christmas Eve, but it is like to storm and Grandmother would have us ride out to fetch it while it is yet fine weather.'

Like to storm, Kivrin thought. How would she recognise the drop if it snowed? The wagon and her boxes were still there, but if it snowed more than a few inches she would never recognise the road.

'Does everyone go to fetch the Yule log?' Kivrin asked.

'Nay. Father Roche called Mother to tend a sick cottar.'

That explained why Imeyne was playing the tyrant, bullying Maisry and the steward and accusing Kivrin of adultery. 'Does your grandmother go with you?'

'Aye,' she said. 'I will ride my pony.'

'Does Rosemund go?'

'Aye.'

'And the steward?'

'Aye,' she said impatiently. 'All the village goes.'

'Does Gawyn?'

'*Nay*,' she said, as if that were self-evident. 'I must go out to the stable and bid Blackie farewell,' She ran off.

Lady Imeyne was going, and the steward, and Lady Eliwys was somewhere nursing a peasant who was ill. And Gawyn, for some reason that was obvious to Agnes but not to her, wasn't. Perhaps he had gone with Eliwys. But if he hadn't, if he were staying here to guard the manor, she could talk to him alone.

Maisry was obviously going. When she brought Kivrin's breakfast she was wearing a rough brown poncho and had ragged strips of cloth wrapped round her legs. She helped Kivrin to the chamber pot carried it out and brought up a brazier full of hot coals, moving with more speed and initiative than Kivrin had seen before.

Kivrin waited an hour after Maisry left, until she was sure they were all gone, and then got out of bed and walked to the window seat and pulled the linen back. She could not see anything except branches and dark grey sky, but the air was even colder than that in the room. She climbed up on the window seat.

She was above the courtyard. It was empty, and the large wooden gate stood open. The stones of the courtyard and of the low thatched roofs around it looked wet. She stuck her hand out, afraid it had already begun to snow, but she couldn't feel any moisture. She climbed down, holding on to the ice-cold stones, and huddled by the brazier.

It gave off almost no heat. Kivrin hugged her arms to her chest, shivering in her thin shift. She wondered what they had done with her clothes. Clothes were hung on poles beside the bed in the Middle Ages, but this room had no poles, and no hooks either.

Her clothes were in the chest at the foot of the bed, neatly folded. She took them out, grateful that her boots were still there, and then sat on the closed lid of the chest for a long time, trying to catch her breath.

I have to speak to Gawyn this morning, she thought, willing her body to be strong enough. It's the only time everyone will be gone. And it's going to snow.

She dressed, sitting down as much as possible and leaning against the bedposts to pull her hose and boots on, and then went back over to the bed. I'll rest a little, she thought, just till I'm warmed through, and was immediately asleep.

The bell woke her, the one from the south-west she had heard when she came through. It had rung all yesterday and then stopped, and Eliwys had gone over to the window and stood there for a while, as if trying to see what had happened. The light from the window was dimmer, but it was only that the clouds were thicker, lower. Kivrin put on her cloak and opened the door. The stairs were steep, set into the stone side of the hall, and had no railing. Agnes was lucky she had only skinned her knee. She might have pitched headlong on to the floor below. Kivrin kept her hand on the wall and rested halfway, looking at the hall.

I'm really here, she thought. It really is 1320. The hearth in the middle of the room glowed a dull red with the banked coals, and there was a little light from the smoke hole above it and the high, narrow windows, but most of the hall was in shadow.

She stopped where she was, peering into the smoky gloom, trying to see if anyone was there. The high seat, with its carved back and arms, sat against the end wall with Lady Eliwys' slightly lower, slightly less ornate one next to it. There were tapestries on the wall behind them and a ladder at the far end of the wall to what must be a loft. Heavy wooden tables hung along the other walls above the wide benches, and a narrower bench sat next to the wall just below the stairs. The beggar's bench. And the wall it sat against was the screens.

Kivrin came down the rest of the stairs and tiptoed across to the screens, her feet crunching loudly on the dried rushes scattered on the floor. The screens were really a partition, an inside wall that shut off the draught from the door.

Sometimes the screens formed a separate room, with box beds in either end, but behind these there was only a narrow passage, with the missing hooks for hanging up cloaks. There were no cloaks there now. Good, Kivrin thought, they're all gone.

The door was open. On the floor next to it was a pair of shaggy boots, a wooden bucket and Agnes' cart. Kivrin stopped in the little anteroom to catch her already ragged breath, wishing she could sit down a moment, and then looked carefully out of the door and went outside.

There was no one in the enclosed courtyard. It was cobbled with flattish yellow stones, but the centre of it, where a water trough hollowed out of a tree stood, was deep in mud. There were trampled hoofprints and footprints all around it, and several puddles of brown water. A thin, mangy-looking chicken was drinking fearlessly from one of the pools. Chickens had only been raised for their eggs. Pigeons and doves had been the chief meat fowls in the 1300s.

And there was the dovecote by the gate, and the thatch-roofed building next to it must be the kitchen, and the other, smaller buildings the storehouses. The stable, with its wide doors, stood along the other side, and then a narrow passage, and then the big stone barn.

She tried the stable first. Agnes' puppy came bounding out to meet her on its clumsy feet, yipping happily, and she had hastily to push it back inside and shut the heavy wooden door. Gawyn obviously wasn't in there. He wasn't in the barn either, or in the kitchen or in the other buildings, the largest of which turned out to be the brewhouse. Agnes had said he wasn't going with the procession to cut the Yule log as if it were something obvious, and Kivrin had assumed he had to stay here to guard the manor, but now she wondered if he had gone with Eliwys to visit the cottar.

If he has, she thought, I'll have to go find the drop myself. She started towards the stable again, but halfway there she stopped. She would never be able to get up on a horse by herself, feeling as weak as she did, and if she did somehow manage it, she was too dizzy to stay on. And too dizzy to go looking for the drop. But I have to, she thought. They're all gone, and it's going to snow.

She looked towards the gate and then the passage between the barn and the stable, wondering which way to go. They had come down a hill, past a church. She remembered hearing the bell. She didn't remember the gate or the courtyard, but that was most likely the way they had come.

She walked across the cobbles, sending the chicken clucking frantically over to the shelter of the well, and looked out the gate at the road. It crossed a narrow stream with a long bridge and wound off to the south into the trees. But there wasn't any hill, and no church, no village, no indication that that was the way to the drop.

There had to be a church. She had heard the bell, lying in bed. She walked back into the courtyard and across to the muddy path. It led past a round wattle pen with two dirty pigs in it, and the privy, unmistakable in its smell, and Kivrin was afraid that the path was only the way to the outhouse, but it wound round behind the privy and opened out on to a green.

And there was the village. And the church, sitting at the far end of the green just the way Kivrin remembered it, and beyond it was the hill they had come down.

The green didn't look like a green. It was a ragged open space with huts on one side and the willow-edged stream on the other, but there was a cow grazing on what was left of the grass and a goat tethered to a big leafless oak. The huts straggled along the near side between piles of hay and muck heaps, getting smaller and more shapeless the further they were from the manor house, but even the one closest to the manor house, which should be the steward's, was nothing but a hovel. It was all smaller and dirtier and more tumbledown than the illustrations in the history vids. Only the church looked the way it was supposed to.

The bell tower stood separate from it, between the churchyard and the green. It had obviously been built later than the church with its Norman round-arched windows and greyed stone. The tower was tall and round, and its stone was yellower, almost golden.

A track, no wider than the road near the drop, led past the churchyard and the tower and up the hill into the woods.

That's the way we came, Kivrin thought, and started across the green, but as soon as she stepped out of the shelter of the barn, the wind hit her. It went through her cloak as if it were nothing, and seemed to stab into her chest. She pulled the cloak tight around her neck, held it with her flattened hand against her chest, and went on.

The bell in the south-west began again. She wondered what

it meant. Eliwys and Imeyne had talked about it, but that was before she could understand what they were saying, and when it began again yesterday, Eliwys hadn't even acted like she heard it. Perhaps it was something to do with Advent. The bells were supposed to ring at twilight on Christmas Eve and then for an hour before midnight, Kivrin knew. Perhaps they rang at other times during Advent as well.

The track was muddy and rutted. Kivrin's chest was beginning to hurt. She pressed her hand tighter against it and went on, trying to hurry. She could see movement out beyond the fields. They would be the peasants coming back with the Yule log, or getting in the animals. She couldn't make them out. It looked as if it were already snowing out there. She must hurry.

The wind whipped her cloak around her and swirled dead leaves past her. The cow moved off the green, its head down, into the shelter of the huts. Which were no shelter at all. They seemed hardly taller than Kivrin and as if they had been bundled together out of sticks and propped in place, and they didn't stop the wind at all.

The bell continued to ring, a slow, steady tolling, and Kivrin realised she had slowed her tread to match it. She mustn't do that. She must hurry. It might start snowing any minute. But hurrying made the pain stab so sharply she began to cough. She stopped, bent double with the coughing.

She was not going to make it. Don't be foolish, she told herself, you have to find the drop. You're ill. You have to get back home. Go as far as the church and you can rest inside for a minute.

She started on again, willing herself not to cough, but it was no use. She couldn't breathe. She couldn't make it to the church, let alone the drop. You have to make it she shouted to herself over the pain. You have to will yourself to make it.

She stopped again, bending over against the pain. She had been worried that a peasant would come out of one of the huts, but now she wished someone would so they could help her back to the manor. They wouldn't. They were all out in this freezing wind, bringing in the Yule log and gathering up the animals. She looked out towards the fields. The distant figures who had been out there were gone.

She was opposite the last hut. Beyond it was a scattering of ramshackle sheds she hoped no one lived in, and surely nobody did. They must be outbuildings – cowbyres and granaries – and beyond them, surely not that far away, the church. Perhaps if I take it slowly, she thought, and started towards the church again. Her whole chest jarred at every step. She stopped, swaying a little, thinking, I mustn't faint. No one knows where I am.

She turned and looked back at the manor house. She couldn't even get back to the hall. I have to sit down, she thought, but there was nowhere to sit in the muddy track. Lady Eliwys was tending the cottar, Lady Imeyne and the girls and the entire village were out cutting the Yule log. No one knows where I am.

The wind was picking up, coming now not in gusts but in a straight, determined push across the fields. I must try to get back to the house, Kivrin thought, but she couldn't do that either. Even standing was too much of an effort. If there were anywhere to sit she would sit down, but the space between the huts, right up to their fences, was all mud. She would have to go into the hut.

It had a rickety wattle fence round it, made by weaving green branches between stakes. The fence was scarcely knee-high and wouldn't have kept a cat out, let alone the sheep and cows it was intended against. Only the gate had supports even waist-high, and Kivrin leaned gratefully against one of them. 'Hello,' she shouted into the wind, 'is anyone there?'

The front door of the hut was only a few steps from the gate, and the hut couldn't be soundproof. It wasn't even windproof. She could see a hole in the wall where the daubed clay and chopped straw had cracked and fallen away from the matted branches underneath. They could surely hear her. She lifted the loop of leather that held the gate shut, went in and knocked on the low, planked door.

There was no answer, and Kivrin hadn't expected any. She shouted again, 'Is anyone home?' not even bothering to listen to how the interpreter translated it, and tried to lift the wooden bar that lay across it. It was too heavy. She tried to slide it out of the notches cut in the protruding frame, but she couldn't. The hut looked like it could blow away at any minute, and she couldn't get the door open. She would have to tell Mr Dunworthy mediaeval huts weren't as flimsy as they looked. She leaned against the door, holding her chest.

Something made a sound behind her and she turned, already saying, 'I'm sorry I intruded into your garden.' It was the cow, leaning casually over the fence and browsing among the brown leaves, hardly reaching at all.

She would have to go back to the manor. She used the gate for support, making sure she shut it behind her and looped the leather back over the stake, and then the cow's bony back. The cow followed with her a few steps, as if it thought Kivrin was leading it in to be milked, and then went back to the garden.

The door of one of the sheds that nobody could possibly live in opened, and a barefoot boy came out. He stopped, looking frightened.

Kivrin tried to straighten up. 'Please,' she said, breathing hard between the words, 'may I rest a while in your house?'

The boy stared dumbly at her, his mouth hanging open. He was hideously thin, his arms and legs no thicker than the twigs in the hut fences.

'Please, run and tell someone to come. Tell them I'm ill.'

He can no more run than I can, she thought as soon as she said it. The boy's feet were blue with cold. His mouth looked sore, and his cheeks and upper lip were smeared with dried blood from a nosebleed. He's got scurvy, Kivrin thought, he's worse off than I am, but she said again, 'Run to the manor and bid them come.'

The boy crossed himself with a chapped, bony hand. '*Bighaull emeurdroud ooghattund enblasthardey,*' he said, backing into the hut.

Oh, no, Kivrin thought despairingly. He can't understand me, and I don't have the strength to try to make him. 'Please help me,' she said, and the boy looked almost like he understood that. He took a step towards her and then darted suddenly away in the direction of the church.

'Wait!' Kivrin called.

He darted past the cow and round the fence and disappeared behind the hut Kivrin looked at the shed. It could scarcely even be called that. It looked more like a haystack – grass and pieces of thatch wadded into the spaces between the poles, but its door was a mat of sticks tied together with blackish rope, the kind of door you could blow down with one good breath, and the boy had left it open. She stepped over the raised doorstep and went into the hut.

It was dark inside and so smoky Kivrin couldn't see anything. It smelled terrible. Like a stable. Worse than a stable. Mingled with the barnyard smells were smoke and mildew and the nasty odour of rats. Kivrin had had to bend over almost double to get through the door. She straightened and hit her head on the sticks that served as crossbeams.

There was nowhere to sit in the hut, if that was really what it was. The floor was as covered with sacks and tools as if it was a shed after all, and there was no furniture except an uneven table whose rough legs splayed unevenly from the centre. But the table had a wooden bowl and a heel of bread on it, and in the centre of the hut, in the only cleared space, a little fire was burning in a shallow, dug-out hole.

It was apparently the source of all the smoke even though there was a hole in the ceiling above it for a draught. It was a little fire, only a few sticks, but the other holes in the unevenly stuffed walls and roof drew the smoke too, and the wind, coming in from everywhere, gusted it round the cramped hut. Kivrin started to cough, which was a terrible mistake. Her chest felt as if it would break apart with every spasm.

Gritting her teeth to keep from coughing, she eased herself down on a sack of onions, holding on to the spade propped against it and then the fragile-looking wall. She felt immediately better as soon as she was sitting down, even though it was so cold she could see her breath. I wonder how this place smells in the summer? she thought. She wrapped her cloak around her, folding the tails like a blanket across her knees.

There was a cold draught along the floor. She tucked the cloak around her feet and then picked up a bill hook lying next to the sack and poked at the meagre fire with it. The fire blazed up halfheartedly, illuminating the hut and making it look more than ever like a shed. A low lean-to had been built on at one side, probably for a stable because it was partitioned off from the rest of the hut by an even lower fence than the cottage had had. The fire wasn't bright enough for Kivrin to see into the lean-to corner, but a scuffling sound came from it.

A pig, maybe, although the peasants' pigs were supposed to have been slaughtered by now, or maybe a milchgoat. She poked at the fire again, trying to get a little more light on the corner.

The scuffling sound came from in front of the pathetic fence, from a large dome-shaped cage. It was elaborately out of place in the filthy corner with its smooth curved metal bands, its complicated door, its fancy handle. Inside the cage, its eyes glinting in the firelight Kivrin had stirred up, was a rat.

It sat on its haunches, its handlike paws holding the chunk of cheese that had tempted it into imprisonment, watching Kivrin. There were several other crumbled and probably mouldy bits of cheese on the floor of the cage. More food than in this entire hut, Kivrin thought, sitting very still on the lumpy sack of onions. One wouldn't think they had anything worth protecting from a rat.

She had seen a rat before, of course, in History of Psych and when they tested her for phobias during her first year, but not this kind. Nobody had seen this kind, in England at least, in fifty years. It was a very pretty rat actually, with silky black fur, not much bigger than History of Psych's white laboratory rats, not nearly as big as the brown rat she'd been tested with.

It looked much cleaner than the brown rat, too. It had looked like it belonged in the sewers and drains and tube tunnels it had no doubt come out of, with its matted dust-brown coat and long, obscenely naked tail. When she had first started studying the Middle Ages, she had been unable to understand how the contemps had tolerated the disgusting things in their barns, let alone their houses. The thought of the one in the wall by her bed had filled her with revulsion. But this rat was actually quite clean-looking, with its black eyes and shiny coat. Certainly cleaner than Maisry, and probably more intelligent. Harmless-looking.

As if to prove her point, the rat took another dainty nibble on the cheese.

'You're not harmless, though,' Kivrin said. 'You're the scourge of the Middle Ages.'

The rat dropped the chunk of cheese and took a step forward, its whiskers twitching. It took hold of two of the metal bars with its pinkish hands and looked appealingly through them.

'I can't let you out, you know,' Kivrin said, and its ears pricked up as if it understood her. 'You eat precious grain and contaminate food and carry fleas and in another twenty-eight years you and your chums will wipe out half of Europe. You're what Lady Imeyne should be worrying about instead of French spies and illiterate priests.' The rat looked at her. 'I'd like to let you out, but I can't. The Black Death was bad enough as it was. It killed half of Europe. If I let you out, your descendants might make it even worse.'

The rat let go of the bars and began running around the cage, crashing against the bars, circling in frantic, random movements.

'I'd let you out if I could,' Kivrin said. The fire had nearly gone out. Kivrin stirred it again, but it was all ashes. The door she had left open in the hope that the boy would bring someone back looking for her banged shut, plunging the hut into darkness.

They won't have any idea where to look for me, Kivrin thought, and knew they weren't even looking yet. They all thought she was in the upstairs room, asleep. Lady Imeyne wouldn't check on her until she brought her her supper. They wouldn't even start to look for her until after vespers, and by then it would be dark.

It was very quiet in the hut. The wind must have died down. She couldn't hear the rat. A twig on the fire snapped once, and sparks flew on to the dirt floor.

Nobody knows where I am, she thought, and put her hand up to her chest as if she had been stabbed. Nobody knows where I am. Not even Mr Dunworthy.

But surely that wasn't true. Lady Eliwys might have come back and gone up to put more ointment on, or Maisry might have been sent home by Imeyne or the boy might have darted off to fetch the men from the fields, and they would be here any minute, even though the door was shut. And even if they didn't realise she was gone until after vespers, they had torches and lanterns and the parents of the boy with scurvy would come back to cook supper and find her and would go and fetch someone from the manor. No matter what happens, she told herself, you're not completely alone, and that comforted her.

Because she was completely alone. She had tried to convince herself she wasn't, that some reading on the net's screens had told

Gilchrist and Montoya something had gone wrong, that Mr Dunworthy had made Badri check and recheck everything, that they knew what had happened somehow and were holding the drop open. But they weren't. They no more knew where she was than Agnes and Lady Eliwys did. They thought she was safely in Skendgate, studying the Middle Ages, with the drop clearly located and the corder already half-full of observations about quaint customs and rotation of crops. They wouldn't even realise she was gone until they opened the drop in two weeks.

'And by then it will be dark,' Kivrin said.

She sat still, watching the fire. It was nearly out and there weren't any more sticks anywhere that she could see. She wondered if the boy had been left at home to gather faggots and what they would do for a fire tonight.

She was all alone, and the fire was going out and nobody knew where she was except the rat that was going to kill half of Europe. She stood up, cracking her head again, pushed the door of the hut open and went outside.

There was still no one in sight in the fields. The wind had died down and she could hear the bell from the south-west tolling clearly. A few flakes of snow drifted out of the grey sky. The little rise the church was on was completely obscured by snow. Kivrin started towards the church.

Another bell began. It was more to the south and closer, but with the higher, more metallic sound that meant it was a smaller bell. It tolled steadily too, but a little behind the first bell so that it sounded like an echo.

'Kivrin! lady Kivrin!' Agnes called. 'Where have you been?' She ran up beside Kivrin, her round little face red with exertion or cold. Or excitement. 'We've been looking everywhere for you.' She darted back in the direction she had come from, shouting, 'I found her! I found her!'

'Nay, you did not!' Rosemund said. 'We all saw her.' She hurried forward ahead of Lady Imeyne and Maisry, who had her ragged poncho thrown over her shoulders. Her ears were bright red. She looked sullen, which probably meant she had been blamed for Kivrin's disappearance or thought she was going to be, or maybe she was just cold. Lady Imeyne looked furious.

'You did not know it was Kivrin,' Agnes shouted, running back to Kivrin's side. 'You said you were not certain it was Kivrin. I was the one who found her.'

Rosemund ignored her. She took hold of Kivrin's arm. 'What has happened? Why did you leave your bed?' she asked anxiously. 'Gawyn came to speak with you and found that you had gone.'

Gawyn came, Kivrin thought weakly. Gawyn, who could have told me exactly where the drop is, and I wasn't there.

'Aye, he came to tell you that he had found no trace of your attackers, and that—'

Lady Imeyne came up. 'Whither were you bound?' she said, and it sounded like an accusation.

'I could not find my way back,' Kivrin said, trying to think what to say to explain her wandering about the village.

'Went you to meet someone?' Lady Imeyne demanded, and it was definitely an accusation.

'How could she go to meet someone?' Rosemund asked. 'She knows no one here and remembers naught of before.'

'I went to look for the place where I was found,' Kivrin said, trying not to lean on Rosemund. 'I thought maybe the sight of my belongings might . . .'

'Help you to remember,' Rosemund said. 'But—'

'You need not have risked your health to do so,' Lady Imeyne said. 'Gawyn has fetched them here this day.'

'Everything?' Kivrin asked.

'Aye,' Rosemund said, 'the wagon and all your boxes.'

The second bell stopped, and the first bell kept on alone, steadily, slowly, and surely it was a funeral. It sounded like the death of hope itself. Gawyn had brought everything to the manor.

'It is not meet to hold Lady Katherine talking in this cold,' Rosemund said, sounding like her mother. 'She has been ill. We must needs get her inside ere she catches a chill.'

I have already caught a chill, Kivrin thought. Gawyn had brought everything to the manor, all traces of where the drop had been. Even the wagon.

'You are to blame for this, Maisry,' Lady Imeyne said, pushing Maisry forward to take Kivrin's arm. 'You should not have left her alone.'

Kivrin flinched away from the filthy Maisry.

'Can you walk?' Rosemund asked, already buckling under Kivrin's weight. 'Should we bring the mare?'

'No,' Kivrin said. She somehow couldn't bear the thought of that, brought back like a captured prisoner on the back of a jangling horse. 'No,' she repeated. 'I can walk.'

She had to lean heavily on Rosemund's arm and Maisry's filthy one, and it was slow going, but she made it. Past the huts and the steward's house and the interested pigs, and into the courtyard. The stump of a big ash tree lay on the cobbles in front of the barn, its twisted roots catching the flakes of snow.

'She will have caught her death with her behaviour,' Lady Imeyne said, gesturing to Maisry to open the heavy wooden door. 'She will no doubt have a relapse.'

It began to snow in earnest. Maisry opened the door. It had a latch like the little door on the rat's cage. I should have let it go, Kivrin thought, scourge or not. I should have let it go.

Lady Imeyne motioned to Maisry and she came back to take Kivrin's arm again. 'No,' she said, and shrugged off her hand and Rosemund's and walked alone and without help through the door and into the darkness inside.

∟∞∟

Transcript from the Domesday Book
(005982–013198)

18 December 1320 (Old Style). I think I have pneumonia. I tried to go find the drop, but I didn't make it and I've had some sort of relapse or something. There's a stabbing pain under my ribs every time I take a breath and when I cough, which is constantly, it feels like everything inside is breaking to pieces. I tried to sit up a while ago and was instantly bathed in sweat, and I think my temp is back up. Those are all symptoms Dr Ahrens told me indicate pneumonia.

Lady Eliwys isn't back yet. Lady Imeyne put a horrible-smelling poultice on my chest and then sent for the steward's wife. I thought she wanted to 'chide with' her for usurping the manor, but when the steward's wife came, carrying her six-month-old baby, Imeyne told her, 'The wound has fevered her lungs,' and the steward's wife looked at my temple and then went out and came back without the baby and with a bowl full of a bitter-tasting tea. It must have had willow bark or something in it because my temp came down, and my ribs don't hurt quite so much.

The steward's wife is thin and small, with a sharp face and ash-blonde hair. I think Lady Imeyne is probably right about her being the one to tempt the steward 'into sin'. She came in wearing a fur-trimmed kirtle with sleeves so long they nearly dragged on the floor, and her baby wrapped in a finely woven wool blanket, and she talks in an odd slurred accent that I think is an attempt to mimic Lady Imeyne's speech.

'The embryonic middle class,' as Mr Latimer would say, *nouveau riche* and waiting for its chance, which it will get in thirty years when the Black Death hits and a third of the nobility is wiped out.

'Is this the lady was found in the woods?' she asked Lady Imeyne when she came in, and there wasn't any 'seeming modesty' in her manner. She smiled at Imeyne as if they were old chums and came over to the bed.

'Aye,' Lady Imeyne said, managing to get impatience, disdain and distaste all in one syllable.

The steward's wife was oblivious. She came over to the bed and then stepped back, the first person to show any indication they thought I might be contagious. 'Has she the [something] fever?' The interpreter didn't catch the word and I couldn't get it either because of her peculiar accent. Flouronen? Florentine?

'She has a wound to the head,' Imeyne said sharply. 'It has fevered her lungs.'

The steward's wife nodded. 'Father Roche told us how he and Gawyn found her in the woods.'

Imeyne stiffened at the familiar use of Gawyn's name, and the steward's wife *did* catch that and hurried out to brew up the willow bark. She even ducked a bow to Lady Imeyne when she left the second time.

Rosemund came in to sit with me after Imeyne left – I think they've assigned her to keep me from trying to escape again – and I asked her if it was true that Father Roche had been with Gawyn when he found me.

'Nay,' she said. 'Gawyn met Father Roche on the road as he brought you here and left you to his care that he might seek your attackers, but he found naught of them, and he and Father Roche brought you here. You need not worry over it. Gawyn has brought your things to the manor.'

I don't remember Father Roche being there, except in the sickroom, but if it's true, and Gawyn didn't meet him too far from the drop, maybe he knows where it is.

(Break)

I have been thinking about what Lady Imeyne said. 'The wound to her head has fevered her lungs,' she said. I don't think anyone here realises I'm ill. They let the little girls in the sickroom all the time, and none of them seems the least afraid, except the steward's wife, and as soon as Lady Imeyne told her I had 'fevered lungs' she came up to the bed without any hesitation.

But she was obviously worried about the possibility of my illness' being contagious, and when I asked Rosemund why she hadn't gone with her mother to see the cottar, she said, as if it were self-evident, 'She forbade me to go. The cottar is ill.'

I don't think they know I have a disease. I didn't have any obvious marker symptoms, like pox or a rash, and I think they put my fever and delirium down to my injuries. Wounds often became infected, and there were frequent cases of blood poisoning. There would be no reason to keep the little girls away from an injured person.

And none of them have caught it. It's been five days and if it is a virus, the incubation period should only be twelve to forty-eight hours. Dr Ahrens told me the most contagious period is before there are any symptoms, so maybe I wasn't contagious by the time the little girls started coming in. Or maybe this is something they've all had already and they're immune. The steward's wife asked if I had had the Florentine? Flahntin? fever, and Mr Gilchrist's convinced there was an influenza epidemic in 1320. Maybe that's what I caught.

It's afternoon. Rosemund is sitting in the window seat, sewing a piece of linen with dark red wool, and Blackie's asleep beside me. I've been thinking about how you were right, Mr Dunworthy. I wasn't prepared at all, and everything's completely different from the way I thought it would be. But you were wrong about it's not being like a fairy-tale.

Everywhere I look I see things from fairy-tales: Agnes' red cape and hood, and the rat's cage, and bowls of porridge, and the village's huts of straw and sticks that a wolf could blow down without half trying.

The bell tower looks like the one Rapunzel was imprisoned in, and Rosemund, bending over her embroidery with her dark hair and white cap and red cheeks, looks for all the world like Snow White.

(Break)

I think my fever is back up. I can smell smoke in the room. Lady Imeyne is praying, kneeling beside the bed with her Book of Hours. Rosemund told me they have sent for the steward's wife again. Lady Imeyne despises her. I must be truly ill for Imeyne to have sent for her. I wonder if they will send for the priest. If they do, I must ask him if he knows where Gawyn found me. It's so hot in here. This part is not like a fairy-tale at all. They only send for the priest when someone is dying, but Probability says there was a 72 per cent chance of dying of pneumonia in the 1300s. I hope he comes soon, to tell me where the drop is and hold my hand.

CHAPTER THIRTEEN

Two more cases, both students, came in while Mary was interrogating Colin on how he had got through the perimeter.

'It was *easy*,' Colin had said indignantly. 'They're trying to keep people from getting out, not getting in,' and had been about to give the particulars when the registrar came in.

Mary had made Dunworthy accompany her to the Casualties Ward to see if he could identify them. 'And *you* stay here,' she had told Colin. 'You've caused quite enough trouble for one night.'

Dunworthy didn't recognise either of the new cases, but it didn't matter. They were conscious and lucid and were already giving the house officer the names of all their contacts when he and Mary got there. He took a good look at each of them and shook his head. 'They might have been part of that crowd on the High Street. I can't tell,' he said.

'It's all right,' she said. 'You can go home if you like.'

'I thought I'd wait and have my blood test,' he said.

'Oh, but that isn't till—' she said, looking at her digital. 'Good Lord, it's past six.'

'I'll just go up and check on Badri,' he said, 'and then I'll be in the waiting-room.'

Badri was asleep, the nurse said. 'I wouldn't wake him.'

'No, of course not,' Dunworthy said and went back down to the waiting-room.

Colin was sitting cross-legged in the middle of the floor, digging in his duffel. 'Where's Great-aunt Mary?' he asked. 'She's a bit flakked at my showing up, isn't she?'

'She thought you were safely back in London,' Dunworthy

said. 'Your mother told her your train had been stopped at Barton.'

'It was. They made everyone get off and get on another train going back to London.'

'And you got lost in the changeover?'

'*No*. I overheard these people talking about the quarantine, and how there was this terrible disease and everybody was going to die and everything—' He stopped to rummage further in his duffel. He took out and replaced a large number of items, vids and a pocket vidder and a pair of scuffed and dirty runners. He was obviously related to Mary. 'And I didn't want to be stuck with Eric and miss all the excitement.'

'Eric?'

'My mother's live-in.' He pulled out a large red gob-stopper, picked off a few bits of lint and popped it in his mouth. It made a mumplike lump in his cheek. 'He is absolutely the most necrotic person in the world,' he said around the gobstopper. 'He has this flat down in Kent and there is absolutely *nothing* to do.'

'So you got off the train at Barton? What did you do then? Walk to Oxford?'

He took the gobstopper out of his mouth. It was no longer red. It was a mottled bluish-green colour. Colin looked critically at all sides of it and put it back in his mouth. 'Of course not. Barton's a long way from Oxford I took a taxi.'

'Of course,' Dunworthy said.

'I told the driver I was reporting the quarantine for my school paper and I wanted to get vids of the blockade. I had my vidder with me, you see, so it seemed the logical thing.' He held up the pocket vidder to illustrate, and then stuffed it back in the duffel and began digging again.

'Did he believe you?'

'I think so. He did ask me which school I went to but I just said, very offended, "You should be able to tell," and he said St Edward's, and I said, "Of course." He must have believed me. He took me to the perimeter, didn't he?'

And I was worried about what Kivrin would do if no friendly traveller came along, Dunworthy thought. 'What did you do then, give the police the same story?'

Colin pulled out a green wool jumper, folded it into a bundle and laid it on top of the open duffel. 'No. When I thought about it, it was rather a lame story. I mean, what is there to take pictures of, after all? It's not like a fire, is it? So I just walked up to the guard as if I were going to ask him something about the quarantine and then just at the last I dodged sideways and ducked under the barrier.'

'Didn't they chase you?'

'Of course. But not for more than a few streets. They're trying to keep people from getting out not in. And then I walked about a while till I found a call box.'

Presumably it had been pouring with rain this entire time but Colin hadn't mentioned it, and a collapsible umbrella wasn't among the items he'd rooted out of his bag.

'The hard part was finding Great-aunt Mary,' he said. He lay down with his head on the duffel. 'I went to her flat but she wasn't there. I thought perhaps she was still at the tube station waiting for me, but it was shut down.' He sat up, rearranged the wool jumper and lay back down. 'And then I thought, she's a doctor. She'll be at the Infirmary.'

He sat up again, punched the duffel into a different shape, lay down and closed his eyes. Dunworthy leaned back in the uncomfortable chair, envying the young. Colin was probably nearly asleep already, not at all frightened or disturbed by his adventures. He had walked all over Oxford in the middle of the night, or perhaps he had taken further taxis or pulled a collapsible bicycle out of his duffel, all by himself in a freezing winter rain, and he wasn't even fazed by the adventure.

Kivrin was all right. If the village wasn't where it was supposed to be she would walk until she found it, or take a taxi, or lie down somewhere with her head on her folded-up cloak, and sleep the uncountable sleep of youth.

Mary came in. 'Both of them went to a dance in Headington last night,' she said, dropping her voice when she saw Colin.

'Badri was there, too,' Dunworthy whispered back.

'I know. One of them danced with him. They were there from nine to two, which puts it at from twenty-five to thirty hours and well within a forty-eight-hour incubation period, if Badri's the one who infected them.'

'You don't think he did?'

'I think it's more likely all three of them were infected by the same person, probably someone Badri saw early in the evening, and the others later.'

'A carrier?'

She shook her head. 'People don't usually carry myxo-viruses without contracting the disease themselves, but he or she could have had only a mild manifestation or have been ignoring the symptoms.'

Dunworthy thought of Badri collapsing against the console and wondered how it were possible to ignore one's symptoms.

'And if,' Mary went on, 'this person was in South Carolina four days ago—'

'You'll have your link with the American virus.'

'And you can stop worrying over Kivrin. She wasn't at the dance in Headington,' she said. 'Of course, the connection is more likely to be several links away.'

She frowned and Dunworthy thought, several links that haven't checked in to hospital or even rung up a doctor. Several links who have all ignored their symptoms.

Apparently Mary was thinking the same thing. 'These bell ringers of yours, when did they arrive in England?'

'I don't know. But they only arrived in Oxford this afternoon, after Badri was at the net.'

'Well, ask them anyway. When they landed, where they've been, whether any of them have been ill. One of them might have relations in Oxford and have come up early. You've no American undergraduates in college?'

'No. Montoya's an American.'

'I hadn't thought of that,' Mary said. 'How long has she been here?'

'All term. But she might have been in contact with someone visiting from America.'

'I'll ask her when she comes in for her bloodwork,' she said. 'I'd like you to question Badri about any Americans he knows, or students who've been to the States on exchange.'

'He's asleep.'

'And so should you be,' she said. 'I didn't mean now.' She patted his arm. 'There's no necessity of waiting till seven. I'll send someone in to take blood and BP so you can go home to bed.' She took Dunworthy's wrist and looked at the temp monitor. 'Any chills?'

'No.'

'Headache?'

'Yes.'

'That's because you're exhausted.' She dropped his wrist. 'I'll send someone straight away.'

She looked at Colin, stretched out on the floor. 'Colin will have to be tested as well, at least till we're certain it's droplet.'

Colin's mouth had fallen open, but the gobstopper was still firmly in place in his cheek. Dunworthy wondered if he were likely to choke. 'What about your nephew?' he said. 'Would you like me to take him back to Balliol with me?'

She looked immediately grateful. 'Would you? I hate to burden you with him, but I doubt I'll be home till we get this under control.' She sighed. 'Poor boy. I hope his Christmas won't be too spoilt.'

'I wouldn't worry too much about it,' Dunworthy said.

'Well, I'm very grateful,' Mary said, 'and I'll see to the tests immediately.'

She left. Colin sat up immediately.

'What sort of tests?' Colin asked. 'Does this mean I might get the virus?'

'I sincerely hope not,' Dunworthy said, thinking of Badri's flushed face, his laboured breathing.

'But I might,' Colin said.

'The chances are very slim,' Dunworthy said. 'I shouldn't worry about it.'

'I'm not worried.' He held out his arm. 'I think I'm getting a rash,' he said eagerly, pointing to a freckle.

'That isn't a symptom of the virus,' Dunworthy said. 'Collect your things. I'm taking you home with me after the tests.' He gathered up his muffler and overcoat from the chairs he'd draped them over.

'What are the symptoms, then?'

'Fever and difficulty breathing,' Dunworthy said Mary's shopping bag was on the floor by Latimer's chair. He decided they'd best take it with them.

The nurse came in, carrying her bloodwork tray.

'I feel hot,' Colin said. He clutched his throat dramatically. 'I can't breathe.'

The nurse took a startled step backwards, clinking her tray.

Dunworthy grabbed Colin's arm. 'Don't be alarmed,' he said to the nurse. 'It's only a case of gobstopper poisoning.'

Colin grinned and bared his arm fearlessly for the blood test, then stuffed the jumper into the duffel and pulled on his still-damp jacket while Dunworthy had his blood drawn.

The nurse said, 'Dr Ahrens said you needn't wait for the results,' and left.

Dunworthy put on his overcoat, picked up Mary's shopping bag and led Colin down the corridor and out through the Casualties Ward. He couldn't see Mary anywhere, but she had said they needn't wait and he was suddenly so tired he couldn't stand.

They went outside. It was just beginning to get light out and still raining. Dunworthy hesitated under the hospital porch, wondering if he should ring for a taxi, but he had no desire to have Gilchrist show up for his tests while they were waiting and have to hear his plans for sending Kivrin to the Black Death and the battle of Agincourt. He fished Mary's collapsible umbrella out of her bag and put it up.

'Thank goodness you're still here,' Montoya said, skidding up on a bicycle, spraying water. 'I need to find Basingame.'

So do we all, Dunworthy thought, wondering where she had been during all those telephone conversations.

She got off the bike, pushed it up the rack and keyed the lock. 'His secretary said no one knows where he is. Can you believe that?'

'Yes,' Dunworthy said. 'I've been trying most of today – yesterday – to reach him. He's on holiday somewhere in Scotland, no one knows exactly where. Fishing, according to his wife.'

'At this time of year?' she said. 'Who would go fishing in

Scotland in December? Surely his wife knows where he is or has a number where he can be reached or something?'

Dunworthy shook his head.

'This is ridiculous! I go to all the trouble to get the National Health Board to grant me access to my dig, and Basingame's on vacation!' She reached under her slick and brought out a sheaf of coloured papers. 'They agreed to give me a waiver if the Head of History would sign an affidavit saying the dig was a project necessary and essential to the welfare of the University. How could he just go off like this without telling anybody?' She slapped the papers against her leg and raindrops flew everywhere. 'I have to get this signed before the whole dig floats away. Where's Gilchrist?'

'He should be here shortly for his blood tests,' Dunworthy said. 'If you manage to find Basingame, tell him he needs to come back immediately. Tell him we've got a quarantine here, we don't know where an historian is, and the tech is too ill to tell us.'

'Fishing,' Montoya said disgustedly, heading for Casualties. 'If my dig is ruined, he's going to have a lot to answer for.'

'Come along,' Dunworthy said to Colin, anxious to be gone before anyone else showed up. He held the umbrella so it would cover Colin too, and then gave up. Colin walked rapidly ahead, managing to hit nearly every puddle, then dawdled behind to look at shop windows.

There was no one on the streets, though whether that was from the quarantine or the early hour, Dunworthy couldn't tell. Perhaps they'll all be asleep, he thought, and we can sneak in and go straight to bed.

'I thought there'd be more going on,' Colin said sounding disappointed. 'Sirens and all that.'

'And dead-carts going through the streets, calling "Bring out your dead"?' Dunworthy said. 'You should have gone with Kivrin. Quarantines in the Middle Ages were far more exciting than this one's likely to be, with only four cases and a vaccine on its way from the States.'

'Who is this Kivrin person?' Colin asked. 'Your daughter?'

'She's my pupil. She's just gone to 1320.'

'Time travel? Apocalyptic!'

They turned the corner of the Broad. 'The Middle Ages,' Colin said. 'That's Napoleon, isn't it? Trafalgar and all that?'

'It's the Hundred Years War,' Dunworthy said, and Colin looked blank. What are they teaching children in the schools these days? he thought. 'Knights and ladies and castles.'

'The Crusades?'

'The Crusades are a bit earlier.'

'That's where I'd want to go. The Crusades.'

They were at Balliol's gate. 'Quiet, now,' Dunworthy said. 'Everyone will be asleep.'

There was no one at the porter's gate, and no one in the front quadrangle. Lights were on in the hall, the bell ringers having breakfast probably, but there were no lights in the senior common room, and none in Salvin. If they could get up the stairs without seeing anyone and without Colin's suddenly announcing he was hungry, they might make it safely to his rooms.

'Shhh,' he said, turning back to caution Colin, who had stopped in the quad to take out his gobstopper and examine its colour, which was now a purplish-black. 'We don't want to wake everyone,' he said, his finger to his lips, turned round and collided with a couple in the doorway.

They were wearing rain slicks and embracing energetically, and the young man seemed oblivious to the collision, but the young woman pulled free and looked frightened. She had short red hair and was wearing a student nurse's uniform under her slick. The young man was William Gaddson.

'Your behaviour is inappropriate to both the time and the place,' Dunworthy said sternly. 'Public displays of affection are strictly forbidden in college. It is also ill-advised, since your mother may arrive at any moment.'

'My mother?' he said, looking as dismayed as Dunworthy had when he saw her coming down the corridor with her suitcase. 'Here? In Oxford? What's she doing here? I thought there was a quarantine on.'

'There is, but a mother's love knows no bounds. She is concerned about your health, as am I, considering the circumstances.' He frowned at William and the young woman, who giggled. 'I would suggest you escort your fellow-perpetrator home and then make preparations for your mother's arrival.'

'Preparations?' he said, looking truly stricken. 'You mean she's staying?'

'She has no alternative, I'm afraid. There is a quarantine on.

Lights came on suddenly inside the staircase and Finch emerged. 'Thank goodness you're here, Mr Dunworthy,' he said.

He had a sheaf of coloured papers too, which he waved at Dunworthy. 'National Health has just sent over *another* thirty detainees. I told them we hadn't any room but they wouldn't listen, and I don't know what to do. We simply do not have the necessary supplies for all those people.'

'Lavatory paper,' Dunworthy said.

'Yes!' Finch said, brandishing the papers. 'And food stores. We went through half the eggs and bacon this morning alone.'

'Eggs and bacon?' Colin said. 'Are there any left?'

Finch looked enquiringly at Colin and then at Dunworthy.

'He's Dr Ahrens' nephew,' he said, and before Finch could start off again, 'he'll stay in my rooms.'

'Well, good, because I simply *cannot* find space for another person.'

'We have both been up all night, Mr Finch, so—'

'Here's the list of supplies as of this morning.' He handed Dunworthy a dampish blue paper. 'As you can see—'

'Mr Finch, I appreciate your concern about the supplies, but surely this can wait until after—'

'This is a list of your telephone calls with the ones you need to return marked with asterisks. This is a list of your appointments. The vicar wishes you to be at St Mary's at a quarter past six tomorrow to rehearse the Christmas Eve service.'

'I will return all these calls, but *after* I—'

'Dr Ahrens telephoned twice. She wanted to know what you've found out about the bell ringers.'

Dunworthy gave up. 'Assign the new detainees to Warren and Basevi, three to a room. There are extra cots in the cellar of the hall.'

Finch opened his mouth to protest.

'They'll simply have to put up with the paint smell.'

He handed Colin Mary's shopping bag and the umbrella. 'That building over there with the lights on is the hall,' he said, pointing at the door. 'Go tell the scouts you want some breakfast and then get one of them to let you into my rooms.'

He turned to William, who was doing something with his hands under the student nurse's rain slick. 'Mr Gaddson, find your accomplice a taxi and then find the students who've been here during vac and ask them whether they've been to the States in the past week or had contact with anyone who has. Make a list. You haven't been to the States recently, have you?'

'No, sir,' he said, removing his hands from the nurse. 'I've been up the whole vac, reading Petrarch.'

'Ah, yes, Petrarch,' Dunworthy said. 'Ask the students what they know about Badri Chaudhuri's activities from Monday on and question the staff. I need to know where he was and who he was with. I want the same sort of report on Kivrin Engle. Do a thorough job, and refrain from further public displays of affection, and I'll arrange for your mother to be assigned a room as far from you as possible.'

'Thank you, sir,' William said. 'That would mean a great deal to me, sir.'

'Now, Mr Finch, if you'll tell me where I might find Ms Taylor?'

Finch handed him more sheets, with the room assignments on them, but Ms Taylor wasn't there. She was in the junior common room with her bell ringers and, apparently, the still-unassigned detainees.

One of them, an imposing woman in a fur coat, grabbed his arm as soon as he came in. 'Are you in charge of this place?' she demanded.

Clearly not, Dunworthy thought. 'Yes,' he said.

'Well, what are you going to do about getting us someplace to sleep? We've been up all night.'

'So have I, madam,' Dunworthy said, afraid this was Ms Taylor. She had looked thinner and less dangerous on the telephone, but visuals could be deceiving and the accent and the attitude were unmistakable. 'You wouldn't be Ms Taylor?'

'I'm Ms Taylor,' a woman in one of the wing chairs said. She stood up. She looked even thinner than she had on the telephone and apparently less angry. 'I spoke with you on the phone earlier,' she said, and the way she said it they might have had a pleasant chat about the intricacies of change ringing. 'This is Ms Piantini, our tenor,' she said, indicating the woman in the fur coat.

Ms Piantini looked like she could yank Great Tom straight off its moorings. She had obviously not had any viruses lately.

'If I could speak with you privately for a moment, Ms Taylor?' He led her out into the corridor. 'Were you able to cancel your concert in Ely?'

'Yes,' she said. 'And Norwich. They were very understanding.' She leaned forward anxiously. 'Is it true it's cholera?'

'Cholera?' Dunworthy said blankly.

'One of the women who had been down at the station said it was cholera, that someone had brought it from India and people were dropping like flies.'

It had apparently not been a good night's sleep but fear that had worked the change in her manner. If he told her there were only four cases she would very likely demand they be taken to Ely.

'The disease is apparently a myxovirus,' he said carefully. 'When did your group come to England?'

Her eyes widened. 'You think we're the ones who brought it? We haven't been to India.'

'There is a possibility it is the same myxovirus as one reported in South Carolina. Are any of your members from South Carolina?'

'No,' she said. 'We're all from Colorado except Ms Piantini. She's from Wyoming. And none of us has been sick.'

'How long have you been in England?'

'Three weeks. We've been visiting all the Traditional Council chapters and doing handbell concerts. We rang a Boston Treble Bob at St Katherine's and Post Office Caters with three of the Bury St Edmunds chapter ringers, but of course neither of those was a new peal. A Chicago Surprise Minor—'

'And you all arrived in Oxford yesterday morning?'

'Yes.'

'None of your group came early, to see the sights or visit friends?'

'No,' she said, sounding shocked. 'We're on tour, Mr Dunworthy, not on vacation.'

'And you said that none of you had been ill?'

She shook her head. 'We can't afford to get sick. There are only six of us.'

'Thank you for your help,' Dunworthy said and sent her back down to the common room.

He rang up Mary, who couldn't be found, left a message and started down Finch's asterisks. He rang up Andrews, Jesus College, Mr Basingame's secretary, and St Mary's without getting through. He rang off, waited a five-minute interval and tried again. During one of the intervals, Mary phoned.

'Why aren't you in bed yet?' she demanded. 'You look exhausted.'

'I've been interrogating the bell ringers,' he said. 'They've been here in England for three weeks. None of them came to Oxford before yesterday afternoon and none of them are ill. Do you want me to come back and question Badri?'

'It won't do any good, I'm afraid. He's not coherent.'

'I'm trying to get through to Jesus to see what they know of his comings and goings.'

'Good,' she said. 'Ask his landlady, too. And get some sleep. I don't want you getting this.' She paused. 'We've got six more cases.'

'Any from South Carolina?'

'No,' she said, 'and none who couldn't have had contact with Badri. So he's still the index case. Is Colin all right?'

'He's having breakfast,' he said. 'He's fine. Don't worry about him.'

He didn't get to bed until after one-thirty in the afternoon. It took him two hours to get through to all the starred names on Finch's list, and another hour to discover where Badri lived. His landlady wasn't at home and when Dunworthy got back, Finch insisted on going over the complete inventory of supplies.

Dunworthy finally got away from him by promising to telephone the NHS and demand additional lavatory paper. He let himself into his rooms.

Colin had curled up on the window seat, his head on his pack and a crocheted laprobe over him. It didn't reach as far as his feet. Dunworthy took a blanket from the foot of the bed and covered him up, and sat down in the Chesterfield opposite to take off his shoes.

He was almost too tired to do that, though he knew he would regret it if he went to bed in his clothes. That was the province of the young and nonarthritic. Colin would wake refreshed in spite of digging buttons and constricting sleeves. Kivrin could wrap up in her too-thin white cloak and rest her head on a tree stump none the worse for wear, but if he so much as omitted a pillow or left his shirt on, he would wake stiff and cramped. And if he sat here with his shoes in his hand, he would not get to bed at all.

He heaved himself out of the chair, still holding the shoes, switched the light off and went into the bedroom. He put on his pyjamas and turned back the bed. It looked impossibly inviting.

I shall be asleep before my head hits the pillow, he thought, taking off his spectacles. He got into bed and pulled the covers up. Before I've even switched off the light, he thought, and switched off the light.

There was scarcely any light from the window, only a dull grey showing through the tangle of darker grey vines. The rain beat faintly against the leathery leaves. I should have drawn the curtains, he thought but he was too tired to get up again.

At least Kivrin wouldn't have to contend with rain. It was the little Ice Age. It would be snow, if anything. The contemps had slept huddled together by the hearth until it had finally occurred to someone to invent the chimney and the fireplace, and that hadn't been extant in Oxfordshire villages till the mid-fifteenth century. But Kivrin wouldn't care. She would curl up like Colin and sleep the easy, the unappreciated sleep of the young.

He wondered if it had stopped raining. He couldn't hear the patter of it on the window. Perhaps it had slowed to a drizzle or was getting ready to rain again. It was so dark, and too early for the afternoon to be drawing in. He drew his hand out from under the covers and looked at the illuminated numbers on his digital. Only two o'clock. He wondered what time it was where Kivrin was. He needed to phone Andrews again when he woke up and have him read the fix so they would know exactly where and when she was.

Badri had told Gilchrist there was minimal slippage, that he'd double-checked the first-year apprentice's coordinates and they were correct, but he wanted to make certain. Gilchrist had taken no precautions and even with precautions, things could go wrong. Today had proved that.

Badri had had the full course of antivirals. Colin's mother had seen him safely on to the tube and given him extra money. The first time Dunworthy had gone to London he had almost not made it back, and they had taken endless precautions.

It had been a simple there-and-back-again to test the on-site net. Only thirty years. Dunworthy was to go through to Trafalgar Square, take the tube from Charing Cross to Paddington and the 10.48 train to Oxford where the main net would be open. They had allowed plenty of time, checked and rechecked the net, researched the ABC and the tube schedules, double-checked the dates on the money. And when he had got to Charing Cross the tube station was closed. The lights in the ticket kiosks had been off, and an iron gate had been pulled across the entrance, in front of the wooden turnstiles.

He pulled the blankets up over his shoulder. Any number of things could have gone wrong with the drop, things no one had even thought of. It had probably never occurred to Colin's mother that Colin's train would be stopped at Barton. It had not occurred to any of them that Badri would suddenly fall forward into the console.

Mary's right, he thought, you've a dreadful streak of Mrs Gaddsonitis. Kivrin overcame any number of obstacles to get to the Middle Ages. Even if something goes wrong, she can handle it. Colin hadn't let a little thing like a quarantine stop him. And Dunworthy had made it safely back from London.

He had banged on the shut gate and then run back up the stairs to read the signs again, thinking that perhaps he had come in the wrong way. He hadn't. He had looked for a clock. Perhaps there had been more slippage than the checks indicated, he'd thought, and the Underground was shut down for the night. But the clock above the entrance said nine-fifteen.

'Accident,' a disreputable-looking man in a filthy cap said. 'They've shut down till they can get it cleaned up.'

'But I must take the Bakerloo line,' he stammered, but the man shuffled off.

He stood there staring into the darkened station, unable to think what to do. He hadn't brought enough money for a taxi, and Paddington was all the way across London. He'd never make the 10.48.

'Whah ya gan, mite?' a young man with a black leather jacket and green hair like a cockscomb said. Dunworthy could scarcely understand him. Punk, he thought. The young man moved menacingly closer.

'Paddington,' he said, and it came out as little more than a squeak.

The punk reached in his jacket pocket for what Dunworthy was sure was his switchblade, but he pulled out a laminated tube pass and began reading the map on the back. 'Yuh cuhn get District or Sahcle from Embankment Gaw dahn Craven Street and tike a left.'

He had run the whole way, certain the punk's gang would leap out at him and steal his historically accurate money at any moment, and when he got to Embankment he had had no idea how to work the ticket machine.

A woman with two toddlers had helped him, punching in the destination and amount for him and showing him how to insert his ticket in the slot. He had made it to Paddington with time to spare.

'Aren't there any *nice* people in the Middle Ages?' Kivrin had asked him, and of course there were. Young men with switchblades and tube maps had existed in all ages. So had mothers and toddlers and Mrs Gaddsons and Latimers. And Gilchrists.

He rolled over on to his other side. 'She will be perfectly all right,' he said aloud, but softly, so as not to wake Colin. 'The Middle Ages are no match for my best pupil.' He pulled the blanket up over his shoulder and closed his eyes, thinking of the young man with the green cockscomb poring over the map. But the image that floated before him was of the iron gate, stretched between him and the turnstiles, and the darkened station beyond.

19 December 1320 (Old Style). I'm feeling better. I can go three or four careful breaths at a time without coughing, and I was actually hungry this morning, though not for the greasy porridge Maisry brought me. I would kill for a plate of bacon and eggs.

And a bath. I am absolutely filthy. Nothing's been washed since I got here except my forehead, and the last two days Lady Imeyne has glued poultices made of strips of linen covered with a disgusting-smelling paste to my chest Between that, the intermittent sweats that I'm still having, and the bed (which hasn't been changed since the 1200s), I positively reek, and my hair, short as it is, is crawling. I'm the cleanest person here.

Dr Ahrens was right in wanting to cauterise my nose. Everyone, even the little girls, smells terrible, and it's the dead of winter and freezing cold in here. I can't imagine what it must be like in August. They all have fleas. Lady Imeyne stops even in midprayer to scratch, and when Agnes pulled down her hose to show me her knee, there were red bites all up and down her leg.

Eliwys, Imeyne and Rosemund have comparatively clean faces, but they don't wash their hands, even after emptying the chamber pot, and the idea of washing the dishes or changing the flock in the mattresses has yet to be invented By rights, they should all have long since died of infection, but except for scurvy and a lot of bad teeth, everyone seems to be in good health. Even Agnes' knee is healing nicely. She comes to show me the scab every day. And her silver buckle, and her wooden knight, and poor overloved Blackie.

She is a treasure trove of information, most of it volunteered without my even asking. Rosemund is 'in her thirteenth year', which means she's twelve, and the room they've been tending me in is her bower. It's hard to imagine she's of marriageable age, and thus has a private 'maiden's bower', but girls were frequently married at thirteen and fourteen in the 1300s. Eliwys can scarcely have been older than that when she married. Agnes also told me she has three older brothers, all of whom stayed in Bath with their father.

The bell in the south-west is Swindone. Agnes can name all the bells by the sound of their ringing. The distant one that always rings first is the Osney bell, the forerunner of Great Tom. The double bells are at Courcy, where Sir Bloet lives, and the two closest are Witenie and Esthcote. That means I'm close to Skendgate in location, and this could very well be Skendgate. It has the ash trees, it's about the right size and the church is in the right place. Ms Montoya may simply not have found the bell tower yet. Unfortunately, the name of the village is the one thing Agnes hasn't known.

She did know where Gawyn was. She told me he was out hunting my attackers, 'And when he finds them, he will slay them with his sword. Like that,' she said, demonstrating with Blackie. I'm not certain the things she tells me can always be depended upon. She told me King Edward is in France, and that Father Roche saw the Devil, dressed all in black and riding on a black stallion.

This last is possible. (That Father Roche told her that, not that he saw the Devil.) The line between the spiritual world and the physical wasn't clearly drawn until the Renaissance, and the contemps routinely saw visions of angels, the Last Judgment, the Virgin Mary.

Lady Imeyne complains constantly about how ignorant and illiterate and incompetent Father Roche is. She is still trying to convince Eliwys to send Gawyn to Osney to fetch a monk. When I asked her if she would send for him so he could pray with me (I decided that request couldn't possibly be considered 'overbold'), she gave me a half-hour recital of how he had forgotten part of the Venite, had blown the candles out instead of pinching them so that 'much wax is wasted', and filled the servant's heads with superstitious prate (no doubt of the Devil and his horse).

Village-level priests in the 1300s were merely peasants who'd been taught the mass by rote and a smattering of Latin. Everyone smells about the same to me, but the nobility viewed their serfs as a different species altogether, and I'm sure it offends Imeyne's aristocratic soul to have to tell her confession to this 'villein'!

He's no doubt as superstitious and illiterate as she claims. But he's not incompetent. He held my hand when I was dying. He told me not to be afraid. And I wasn't.

(Break)

I'm feeling better by leaps and bounds. This afternoon I sat up for half an hour, and tonight I went downstairs for supper. Lady Eliwys brought me a brown wadmal kirtle and mustard-coloured surcote to wear, and a sort of kerchief to cover my chopped-off hair (not a wimple and coif, so Eliwys must still think I'm a maiden, in spite of all Imeyne's talk about '*daltrisses*'). I don't know if my clothes were inappropriate or simply too nice to be worn for everyday. Eliwys didn't say anything. She and Imeyne helped me dress. I wanted to ask if I could wash before I put my new clothes on, but I'm afraid of doing anything that will make Imeyne more suspicious.

She watched me fasten my points and tie my shoes as it was, and kept a sharp eye on me all through dinner. I sat between the girls and shared a trencher with them. The steward was relegated to the very end of the table, and Maisry was nowhere to be seen. According to Mr Latimer, the parish priest ate at the lord's table, but Lady Imeyne probably doesn't like Father Roche's table manners either.

We had meat, I think venison, and bread. The venison tasted of cinnamon, salt, and the lack of refrigeration, and the bread was stone-hard, but it was better than porridge, and I don't think I made any mistakes.

Though I'm certain I must be making mistakes all the time, and that's why Lady Imeyne is so suspicious of me. My clothes, my hands, probably my sentence structure, are slightly (or not so slightly) off, and it all combines to make me seem foreign, peculiar – suspicious.

Lady Eliwys is too worried over her husband's trial to notice my mistakes, and the girls are too young. But Lady Imeyne notices everything and is probably making a list like the one she has for Father Roche. Thank goodness I didn't tell her I was Isabel de Beauvrier. She'd have ridden to Yorkshire, winter or no, to catch me out.

Gawyn came in after dinner. Maisry, who'd finally slunk in with a scarlet ear and a wooden bowl of ale, had dragged the benches over to the hearth and put several logs of fat pine on the fire, and the women were sewing by its yellow light.

Gawyn stopped in front of the screens, obviously just in from a hard ride, and for a minute no one noticed him. Rosemund was brooding over her embroidery. Agnes was pushing her cart back and forth with the wooden knight in it, and Eliwys was talking earnestly to Imeyne about the cottar, who apparently isn't doing very well. The smoke from the fire was making my chest hurt, and I turned my head away from it, trying to keep from coughing, and saw him standing there, looking at Eliwys.

After a moment Agnes ran her cart into Imeyne's foot, and Imeyne told her she was the Devil's own child, and Gawyn came on into the hall. I lowered my eyes and prayed he would speak to me.

He did, bowing on one knee in front of where I sat on the bench. 'Good lady,' he said. 'I am glad to see you improved.'

I had no idea what, if anything, was appropriate to say. I ducked my head lower.

He remained on one knee, like a servitor. 'I was told you remember naught of your attackers, Lady Katherine. Is it so?'

'Yes,' I murmured.

'Nor of your servants, where they might have fled?'

I shook my head, eyes still downcast.

He turned towards Eliwys. 'I have news of the renegades,

Lady Eliwys. I have found their trail. There were many of them, and they had horses.'

I'd been afraid he was going to say he'd caught some poor wood-gathering peasant and hanged him.

'I beg your leave to pursue them and avenge the lady,' he said, looking at Eliwys.

Eliwys looked uneasy, wary, the way she had when he came before. 'My husband bade us keep to this place till he comes,' she said, 'and he bade you stay with us to guard us. Nay.'

'You have not supped,' Lady Imeyne said in a tone that closed the matter.

Gawyn stood up.

'I thank you for your kindness, sir,' I said rapidly. 'I know it was you who found me in the woods.' I took a breath, and coughed. 'I beg you, will you tell me of the place you found me, where it is?' I had tried to say too much too fast. I began to cough, gasped too deep a breath and doubled over with the pain.

By the time I got the coughing under control, Imeyne had set meat and cheese on the table for Gawyn and Eliwys had gone back to her sewing, so I still don't know anything.

No, that's not true. I know why Eliwys looked so wary when he came in and why he made up a tale about a band of renegades. And what that conversation about '*daltrisses*' was all about.

I watched him standing there in the doorway looking at Eliwys, and I didn't need an interpreter to read his face. He's obviously in love with his lord's wife.

————∞∞∞————

CHAPTER FOURTEEN

Dunworthy slept straight through till morning.

'Your secretary wanted to wake you up, but I wouldn't let him,' Colin said. 'He said to give you these.' He thrust a messy sheaf of papers at him.

'What time is it?' Dunworthy said, sitting up stiffly in bed.

'Half past eight,' Colin said. 'All the bell ringers and DTs are in hall eating breakfast. Porridge.' He made a gagging sound. 'It was absolutely necrotic. Your secretary chap says we need to ration the eggs and bacon because of the quarantine.'

'Half past eight in the morning?' Dunworthy asked, blinking nearsightedly at the window. It was as dark and dismal as when he'd fallen asleep. 'Good Lord, I was supposed to have gone back to hospital to question Badri.'

'I know,' Colin said. 'Great-aunt Mary said to let you sleep, that you couldn't question him anyway because they're running tests.'

'She rang up?' Dunworthy asked, groping blindly for his spectacles on the bedstand.

'I went over this morning. To have my blood tested. Great-aunt Mary said to tell you we only need to come once a day for our blood tests.'

He hooked his spectacles over his ears and looked at Colin. 'Did she say whether they'd identified the virus?'

'Hunh-unh,' Colin said around a lump in his cheek. Dunworthy wondered if the gobstopper had been in his mouth all night, and if so why it hadn't diminished in size. 'She sent you the contacts charts.' He handed the papers to him. 'The lady we saw at the Infirmary rang up, too. The one on the bicycle.'

'Montoya?'

'Yes. She wanted to know if you knew how to get in touch with Mr Basingame's wife. I told her you'd ring her back. When does the post come, do you know?'

'The post?' Dunworthy said, looking through the stack.

'My mother didn't have my presents bought in time to send them on the tube with me,' Colin said. 'She said she'd send them by post. You don't think the quarantine will delay it, do you?'

Some of the papers Colin had handed him were stuck together, no doubt because of Colin's periodic examinations of his gobstopper, and most of them seemed to be not the contact charts but assorted memoranda from Finch. One of the heating vents in Salvin was stuck shut. The National Health Service ordered all inhabitants of Oxford and environs to avoid contact with infected persons. Mrs Basingame was in Torquay for Christmas. They were running very low on lavatory paper.

'You don't do you? Think it will delay it?' Colin asked.

'Delay what?' Dunworthy said.

'The *post*!' Colin said disgustedly. 'The quarantine won't delay it, will it? What time is it supposed to come?'

'Ten,' Dunworthy said. He sorted all the memoranda into one pile and opened a large manila envelope. 'It's usually a bit late at Christmas because of all the parcels and Christmas cards.'

The stapled sheets in the envelope weren't the contact charts either. They were William Gaddson's report on Badri's and Kivrin's whereabouts, neatly typed and organised into the morning, afternoon and evening of each day. It looked far neater than any essay he'd ever handed in. Amazing what a salutary influence a mother could have.

'I don't see why it should be,' Colin said. 'I mean, it's not as if it's people, is it, so it can't be contagious? Where does it come, to the hall?'

'What?'

'The *post*.'

'Porter's lodge,' Dunworthy said, reading the report on Badri. He had gone back to the net on Tuesday afternoon after he was at Balliol. Finch had spoken to him at two o'clock, when he had asked where Mr Dunworthy was, and again at a little before three, when Badri had given him the note. At some time between two and three, John Yi, a third-year student, had seen him cross the quad to the laboratory, apparently looking for someone.

At three the porter at Brasenose had logged Badri in. He had worked in the net until half past seven and then gone back to his flat and dressed for the dance.

Dunworthy phoned Latimer. 'When were you at the net on Tuesday afternoon?'

He blinked bewilderedly at Dunworthy from the screen. 'Tuesday?' he said, looking around as if he had mislaid something. 'Was that yesterday?'

'The day before the drop,' Dunworthy said. 'You went to the Bodleian in the afternoon.'

He nodded. 'She wanted to know how to say, "Help me, for I have been set upon by thieves."'

Dunworthy assumed by 'she' he meant Kivrin. 'Did Kivrin meet you at the Bodleian or at Brasenose?'

He put his hand to his chin, pondering. 'We had to work until late in the evening deciding on the form of the pronouns,' he said. 'The decay of pronominal inflections was advanced in the 1300s but not complete.'

'Did Kivrin come to the net to meet you?'

'The net?' Latimer said doubtfully.

'To the laboratory at Brasenose,' Dunworthy snapped.

'Brasenose? The Christmas Eve service isn't at Brasenose, is it?'

'The Christmas Eve service?'

'The vicar said he wished me to read the benediction,' Latimer said. 'Is it being held at Brasenose?'

'No. You met with Kivrin on Tuesday afternoon to work on her speech. Where did you meet her?'

'The word "thieves" was very difficult to translate. It derives from the Old English *theof*, but the—'

This was useless. 'The Christmas Eve service is at St Mary the Virgin's at seven,' he said and rang off.

He phoned the porter at Brasenose, who was *still* decorating his tree, and made him look up Kivrin in his log book. She hadn't been there on Tuesday afternoon.

He fed the contact charts into the console and entered the

additions from William's report. Kivrin hadn't seen Badri on Tuesday. Tuesday morning she had been in Infirmary and then with Dunworthy. Tuesday afternoon she'd been with Latimer and Badri would have been gone to the dance in Headington before they left the Bodleian. Monday from three on she was in Infirmary, but there was still a gap between twelve and half past two on Monday when she might have seen Badri.

He scanned the contact sheets they had filled in again. Montoya's was only a few lines long. She had filled in her contacts for Wednesday morning, but none for Monday and Tuesday, and she hadn't listed any information on Badri. He wondered why, and then remembered she had come in after Mary gave the instructions for filling in the forms.

Perhaps Montoya had seen Badri before Wednesday morning, or knew where he'd spent the gap between noon and half past two on Monday.

'When Ms Montoya phoned, did she tell you her telephone number?' he asked Colin. There was no answer. He looked up. 'Colin?'

He wasn't in the room, nor in the sitting-room, though his duffel was, its contents spread all over the carpet.

Dunworthy looked up Montoya's number at Brasenose and rang it up, not expecting any answer. If she was still looking for Basingame, that meant she hadn't got permission to go out to the dig and was doubtless at the NHS or the National Trust, badgering them to have it declared 'of irreplaceable value'.

He dressed and went across to the hall, looking for Colin. It was still raining, the sky the same sodden grey as the paving stones and the bark on the beech trees. He hoped that the bell ringers and detainees had breakfasted early and gone back to their assigned rooms, but it was a fond hope. He could hear the high hubbub of female voices before he was halfway across the quad.

'Thank goodness you're here, sir,' Finch said, meeting him at the door. 'The NHS just phoned. They want us to take twenty more detainees.'

'Tell them we can't,' Dunworthy said, looking through the crowd. 'We're under orders to avoid contact with infected persons. Have you seen Dr Ahrens' nephew?'

'He was just here,' Finch said, peering over the heads of the women, but Dunworthy had already spotted him. He was standing at the end of the table where the bell ringers were sitting, buttering several pieces of toast.

Dunworthy made his way to him. 'When Ms Montoya telephoned, did she tell you where she might be reached?'

'The one with the bicycle?' Colin said, smearing marmalade on the buttered toast.

'Yes.'

'No, she didn't.'

'Will you have breakfast, sir?' Finch said. 'I'm afraid there aren't any bacon and eggs, and we're getting very low on marmalade' – he glared at Colin – 'but there's porridge and—'

'Just tea,' Dunworthy said. 'She didn't mention where she was phoning from?'

'Do sit down,' Ms Taylor said. 'I've been wanting to speak to you about our Chicago Surprise.'

'What exactly did Ms Montoya say?' Dunworthy said to Colin.

'That nobody cared that her dig was being ruined and an invaluable link with the past was being lost, and what sort of person went fishing in the middle of winter anyway,' Colin said, scraping marmalade off the sides of the bowl.

'We're nearly out of tea,' Finch said, pouring Dunworthy a very pale cup.

Dunworthy sat down. 'Would you like some cocoa, Colin? Or a glass of milk?' Dunworthy asked.

'We're nearly out of milk,' Finch said.

'I don't need anything, thanks,' Colin said, slapping the slices of toast marmalade-sides together. 'I'm just going to take these with me out to the gate so I can wait for the post.'

'The vicar telephoned,' Finch said. 'He said to tell you you needn't be there to go over the order of worship until half past six.'

'Are they still holding the Christmas Eve service?' Dunworthy said. 'I shouldn't think anyone would come under the circumstances.'

'He said the Interchurch Committee had voted to hold it regardless,' Finch said, pouring a quarter-teaspoon of milk in the pallid tea and handing it to him. 'He said they felt carrying on as usual will help keep up morale.'

'We're going to perform several pieces on the handbells,' Ms Taylor said. 'It's hardly a substitute for a peal, of course, but it's something. The priest from Holy Re-Formed is going to read from the Mass in Time of Pestilence.'

'Ah,' Dunworthy said. 'That should help in keeping up morale.'

'Do I have to go?' Colin said.

'He has no business going out in this weather,' Mrs Gaddson said, appearing like a harpy with a large bowl of grey porridge. She set it in front of Colin. 'And no business being exposed to germs in a draughty church. He can stay here with me during the church service.' She pushed a chair up behind him. 'Sit down and eat your porridge.'

Colin looked beseechingly at Dunworthy.

'Colin, I left Ms Montoya's telephone number in my rooms,' Dunworthy said. 'Would you fetch it for me?'

'Yes!' Colin said, and was out of his chair like a shot.

'When that child comes down with the Indian flu,' Mrs Gaddson said, 'I hope you will remember that you were the one who encouraged him in his poor eating habits. It is clear to me what led to this epidemic. Poor nutrition and a complete lack of discipline. It's disgraceful, the way this college is run. I asked to be put in with my son William, but instead I've been assigned a room in another building altogether, and—'

'I'm afraid you'll have to take that up with Finch,' Dunworthy said. He stood up and wrapped Colin's marmaladed toast in a napkin. 'I'm needed at the Infirmary,' he said and escaped before Mrs Gaddson could start off again.

He went back to his rooms and rang up Andrews. The line was engaged. He rang up the dig, on the off-chance that Montoya had obtained her quarantine waiver, but there was no answer. He rang up Andrews again. Amazingly enough, the line was free. It rang three times and then switched to a message service.

'This is Mr Dunworthy,' he said. He hesitated and then gave the number of his rooms. 'I need to speak with you immediately. It's important.'

He rang off, pocketed the disk, picked up his umbrella and Colin's toast and walked out through the quad.

Colin was huddling under the shelter of the gate, looking anxiously down the street towards Carfax.

'I'm going to the Infirmary to see my tech and your great-aunt,' Dunworthy said, handing him the napkin-wrapped toast. 'Would you like to go with me?'

'No, thanks,' Colin said. 'I don't want to miss the post.'

'Well, for goodness' sake, go and fetch your jacket so Mrs Gaddson doesn't come out and begin haranguing you.'

'The Gallstone's already been,' Colin said. 'She tried to make me put on a muffler. A muffler!' He gave another anxious look down the street. 'I ignored her.'

'I hadn't thought of that,' Dunworthy said. 'I should be home in time for lunch. If you need anything, ask Finch.'

'Umm,' Colin said, obviously not listening. Dunworthy wondered what his mother was sending that merited such devotion. Obviously not a muffler.

He pulled his own muffler up round his neck and set off for Infirmary through the rain. There were only a few people in the streets and they kept out of each other's way, one woman stepping off the pavement altogether to avoid meeting Dunworthy.

Without the carillon banging away at 'It Came Upon the Midnight Clear', one would have had no idea at all that it was Christmas Eve. No one carried gifts or holly, no one carried parcels at all. It was as if the quarantine had knocked the memory of Christmas out of their heads completely.

Well, and hadn't it? He hadn't given a thought to shopping for gifts or a tree. He thought of Colin huddled at Balliol's gate and hoped his mother at least hadn't forgotten to send his gifts. On the way home he'd stop and get Colin a small present, a toy or a vid or something, something besides a muffler.

At the Infirmary, he was hustled immediately into Isolation and taken off to question the new cases. 'It's essential we establish an American connection,' Mary said. 'There's been a snag at the WIC. There's no one on duty who can run a sequencing because of the holidays. They're supposed to be at full readiness at all times, of course, but apparently it's after Christmas that they usually get problems – food poisonings and overindulgence masquerading as viruses – so they give time off before. At any rate, the CDC in Atlanta agreed to send the vaccine prototype to the WIC without a positive S-ident, but they can't begin manufacturing without a definite connection.'

She led him down a cordoned-off corridor. 'The cases are all following the profile of the South Carolina virus – high fever, body aches, secondary pulmonary complication, but unfortunately that's not proof.' She stopped outside a ward. 'You didn't find any American connections for Badri, did you?'

'No, but there are still a good many gaps. Do you want me to question him, as well?'

She hesitated.

'He's worse,' Dunworthy said.

'He's developed pneumonia. I don't know if he'll be able to tell you anything. His fever is still very high, which follows the profile. We have him on the antimicrobials and adjuvants which the South Carolina virus responded to.' She opened the door to the ward. 'The chart lists all the cases which have come in. Ask the nurse on duty which beds they're in.' She typed something into the console by the first bed. It lit up a chart as branching and intertwined as the big beech in the quad. 'You don't mind having Colin with you for another night, do you?'

'I don't mind in the slightest.'

'Oh, good. I doubt very much I'll be able to get home before tomorrow, and I do worry about him staying alone in the flat. I'm apparently the only one who does, however,' she said angrily. 'I finally got through to Deirdre down in Kent, and she wasn't even concerned. "Oh, is there a quarantine on?" she said. "I've been so rushed I haven't had time to catch the news," and then she proceeded to tell me all about her and her live-in's plans, with the clear implication that she'd have had no time at all for Colin and was glad she was rid of him. There are times when I'm convinced she's not my niece.'

'Did she send Colin's Christmas presents, do you know? He said she planned to send them by post.'

'I'm certain she's been far too *rushed* to remember to buy them, let alone send them. The last time Colin was with me for

Christmas, his gifts didn't arrive till Epiphany. Oh, which reminds me, do you know what's become of my shopping bag? It had my gifts for Colin in it.'

'I've got it at Balliol,' he said.

'Oh, good. I didn't finish my shopping, but if you'd wrap up the muffler and the other things, he'll have something under the tree, won't he?' She stood up. 'If you find any possible connection, come tell me immediately. As you can see, we've already traced several of the secondaries to Badri, but those may only be cross-connections, and the real connection could be someone else.'

She left, and he sat down beside the bed of the woman of the lavender umbrella.

'Ms Breen?' he said. 'I'm afraid I must ask you some questions.'

Her face was very red, and her breathing sounded like Badri's, but she answered his questions promptly and clearly. No, she hadn't been to America in the past month. No, she didn't know any Americans or anyone who'd been to America. But she had taken the tube up from London to shop for the day. 'At Blackwell's, you know,' and she had been all over Oxford shopping and then at the tube station, and there were at least five hundred people she had had contact with who might be the connection Mary was looking for.

It took him till past two to finish questioning the primaries and adding the contacts to the chart, none of which were the American connection though he had found out that two more of them had been to the dance in Headington.

He went up to Isolation, though he didn't have much hope of Badri's being able to answer his questions, but Badri seemed improved. He was sleeping when Dunworthy came in, but when Dunworthy touched his hand his eyes opened and focused on him.

'Mr Dunworthy,' he said. His voice was weak and hoarse. 'What are you doing here?'

Dunworthy sat down. 'How are you feeling?'

'It's odd, the things one dreams. I thought . . . I had such a headache . . .'

'I need to ask you some questions, Badri. Do you remember who you saw at the dance you went to in Headington?'

'There were so many people,' he said, and swallowed as if his throat hurt. 'I didn't know most of them.'

'Do you remember who you danced with?'

'Elizabeth—' he said, and it came out a croak. 'Sisu somebody, I don't know her last name,' he whispered. 'And Elizabeth Yakamoto.'

The grim-looking ward sister came in. 'Time for your X-ray,' she said without looking at Badri. 'You'll have to leave, Mr Dunworthy.'

'Could I have just a few more minutes? It's important,' he asked, but she was already tapping keys on the console.

He leaned over the bed. 'Badri, when you got the fix, how much slippage was there?'

'Mr Dunworthy,' the sister said insistently.

Dunworthy ignored her. 'Was there more slippage than you expected?'

'No,' Badri said huskily. He put his hand to his throat.

'How much slippage was there?'

'Four hours,' Badri whispered, and Dunworthy let himself be ushered out.

Four hours. Kivrin had gone through at half past twelve. That would have put her there at half past four, nearly sunset but still enough light left to see where she was, enough time to have walked to Skendgate, if necessary.

He went to find Mary and give her the two names of the girls Badri had danced with. Mary checked them against the list of new admissions. Neither of them were on it, and Mary told him he could go home and took his temp and bloods so he wouldn't have to come back. He was about to start home when they brought Sisu Fairchild in. He didn't make it home till nearly teatime.

Colin wasn't at the gate nor in hall, where Finch was nearly out of sugar and butter. 'Where's Dr Ahrens' nephew?' Dunworthy asked him.

'He waited by the gate all morning,' Finch said, anxiously counting over sugar cubes. 'The post didn't come till past one, and then he went over to his great-aunt's flat to see if the parcels had been sent there. I gather they hadn't. He came back looking very glum, and then about half an hour ago, he said suddenly,

"I've just thought of something," and shot out. Perhaps he'd thought of some other place the parcels might have been sent to.'

But weren't Dunworthy thought. 'What time do the shops close today?' he asked Finch.

'Christmas Eve? Oh, they're already closed, sir. They always close early on Christmas Eve, and some of them closed at noon due to the lack of trade. I've a number of messages, sir—'

'They'll have to wait,' Dunworthy said, snatched up his umbrella and went out again. Finch was right. The shops were all closed. He went down to Blackwell's, thinking they had surely stayed open, but they were shut up tight. They had already taken advantage of the selling points of the situation, though. In the window, arranged amid the snow-covered houses of the toy Victorian village, were self-help medical books, drug compendia and a brightly coloured paperback entitled *Laughing Your Way to Perfect Health*.

He finally found an open post office off the High, but it had only cigarettes, cheap sweets, and a rack of greeting cards, nothing in the way of suitable gifts for twelve-year-old boys. He went out without buying anything and then went back and purchased a pound's worth of toffee, a gobstopper the size of a small asteroid and several packets of a sweet that, looked like soap tablets. It wasn't much, but Mary had said she'd bought some other things.

The other things turned out to be a pair of grey woollen socks, even grimmer than the muffler, and a vocabulary improvement vid. There were crackers, at least, and sheets of wrapping paper, but a pair of socks and some toffee hardly made a Christmas. He looked round the study, trying to think what he had that might do.

Colin had said, 'Apocalyptic!' when Dunworthy had told him Kivrin was in the Middle Ages. He pulled down *The Age of Chivalry*. It only had illustrations, no holos, but it was the best he could do on short notice. He wrapped it and the rest of the presents hastily, changed his clothes and hurried over to St Mary the Virgin's in a downpour, ducking across the deserted courtyard of the Bodleian and trying to avoid the spilling gutters.

No one in their right mind would come out in this. Last year the weather had been dry and the church was still only half-full. Kivrin had gone with him. She had stayed up for the vac to study, and he had found her in the Bodleian and insisted on her coming to his sherry party and then to church.

'I shouldn't be doing this,' she'd said on the way to the church. 'I should be doing research.'

'You can do it at St Mary the Virgin's. Built in 1139 and all just as it was in the Middle Ages, including the heating system.'

'The interchurch service is authentic, too, I suppose,' she'd said.

'I have no doubt that in spirit it is as well meant and as fraught with foolishness as any mediaeval mass,' he had said.

He hurried down the narrow path next to Brasenose and opened the door of St Mary's to a blast of hot air. His spectacles steamed up. He stopped in the narthex and wiped them on the tail of his muffler, but they clouded up again immediately.

'The vicar's looking for you,' Colin said. He was wearing a jacket and shirt, and his hair was combed. He handed Dunworthy an order of service from a large stack he was holding.

'I thought you were going to stay at home,' Dunworthy said.

'With Mrs Gaddson? What a necrotic idea! Even church is better than that, so I told Ms Taylor I'd help carry the bells over.'

'And the vicar put you to work,' Dunworthy said, still trying to get his spectacles clear. 'Have you had any business?'

'Are you joking? The church is crammed.'

Dunworthy peered into the nave. The pews were already full, and folding chairs were being set up at the back.

'Oh, good, you're here,' the vicar said, bustling over with an armful of hymnals. 'Sorry about the heat. It's the furnace. The National Trust won't let us put in a new fused-air, but it's nearly impossible to get parts for a fossil-fuel. At the moment it's the thermostat that's gone wrong. The heat's either on or off.' He fished two slips of paper out of his cassock pocket and looked at them. 'You haven't seen Mr Latimer yet, have you? He's supposed to read the benediction.'

'No,' Dunworthy said. 'I reminded him of the time.'

'Yes, well, last year he muddled things and arrived an hour early.' He handed Dunworthy one of the slips of paper. 'Here's your Scripture. It's from the King James this year. The Church of the Millennium insisted on it, but at least it's not the People's

Common like last year. The King James may be archaic, but at least it's not criminal.'

The outside door opened and a knot of people, all taking down umbrellas and shaking out hats, came in, were order-of-serviced by Colin and went into the nave.

'I knew we should have used Christ Church,' the vicar said.

'What are they all doing here?' Dunworthy said. 'Don't they realise we're in the midst of an epidemic?'

'It's always this way,' the vicar said. 'I remember the beginning of the Pandemic. Largest collections ever taken. Later on you won't be able to get them out of their houses, but just now they want to huddle together for comfort.'

'And it's exciting,' the priest from Holy Re-Formed said. He was wearing a black turtleneck, bags, and a red and green plaid alb. 'One sees the same sort of thing during wartime. They come for the drama of the thing.'

'And spread the infection twice as fast, I should think,' Dunworthy said. 'Hasn't anyone told them the virus is contagious?'

'I intend to,' the vicar said. 'Your Scripture comes directly after the bell ringers. It's been changed. Church of the Millennium again. Luke 2:1–19.' He went off to distribute hymnals.

'Where is your pupil, Kivrin Engle?' the priest asked. 'I missed her at the Latin mass this afternoon.'

'She's in 1320, hopefully in the village of Skendgate, hopefully in out of the rain.'

'Oh, good,' the priest said. 'She so wanted to go. And how lucky she's missing all this.'

'Yes,' Dunworthy said. 'I suppose I should read through the Scripture at least once.'

He went into the nave. It was even hotter in there, and it smelled strongly of damp wool and damp stone. Laser candles flickered wanly in the windows and on the altar. The bell ringers were setting up two large tables in front of the altar and covering them with heavy red wool covers. Dunworthy stepped up to the lectern and opened the Bible to Luke.

'And it came to pass in those days, that there went out a decree from Caesar Augustus, that all the world should be taxed,' he read.

The King James *is* archaic, he thought. And where Kivrin is, it hasn't been written yet.

He went back out to Colin. People continued to stream in. The priest from Holy Re-Formed and the Muslim imam went across to Oriel for more chairs, and the vicar fiddled with the thermostat on the furnace.

'I saved us two seats in the second row,' Colin said. 'Do you know what Mrs Gaddson did at tea? She threw my gobstopper away. She said it was covered with germs. I'm glad my mother's not like that.' He straightened his stack of folded orders of service, which had shrunk considerably. 'I think what happened is her presents couldn't get through because of the quarantine, you know. I mean, they probably had to send provisions and things first.' He straightened the already straight pile again.

'Very likely,' Dunworthy said. 'When would you like to open your other gifts? Tonight or in the morning?'

Colin tried to look nonchalant. 'Christmas morning, please.' He gave an order of service and a dazzling smile to a lady in a yellow slicker.

'Well,' she snapped, snatching it out of his hand, 'I'm glad to see *someone*'s still got the Christmas spirit, even though there's a deadly epidemic on.'

Dunworthy went in and sat down. The vicar's attentions to the furnace didn't seem to have done any good. He took off his muffler and overcoat and draped them on the chair beside him.

It had been freezing last year. 'Extremely authentic,' Kivrin had whispered to him, 'and so was the Scripture. "Around then the politicos dumped a tax hike on the ratepayers,"' she'd said, quoting from the People's Common. She'd grinned at him. 'The Bible in the Middle Ages was in a language they didn't understand either.'

Colin came in and sat down on Dunworthy's coat and muffler. The priest from Holy Re-Formed stood up and wedged himself between the bell ringers' tables and the front of the altar. 'Let us pray,' he said.

There was a plump of kneeling pads on the stone floor, and everyone knelt.

' "O God, who have sent this affliction among us, say to Thy destroying angel, hold Thy hand and let not the land be made desolate, and destroy not every living soul." '

So much for morale, Dunworthy thought.

' "As in those days when the Lord sent a pestilence on Israel, and there died of the people from Dan to Bersabee seventy thousand men, so now we are in the midst of affliction and we beseech Thee to take away the scourge of Thy wrath from the faithful." '

The pipes of the ancient furnace began clanging, but it didn't seem to deter the priest. He went on for a good five minutes, mentioning a number of instances in which God had smitten the unrighteous and 'brought plagues among them' and then asked everyone to stand and sing, 'God Rest Ye Merry, Gentlemen, Let Nothing You Dismay.'

Montoya ducked in and sat down next to Colin. 'I have spent *all* day at the NHS,' she whispered, 'trying to get them to give me a dispensation. They seem to think I intend to run around spreading the virus. I *told* them I'd go straight to the dig, that there's no one out there to infect but do you think they'd listen?'

She turned to Colin. 'If I do get the dispensation, I'm going to need volunteers to help me. How would you like to dig up bodies?'

'He can't,' Dunworthy said hastily. 'His great-aunt won't let him.' He leaned across Colin and whispered, 'We're trying to determine Badri Chaudhuri's whereabouts on Monday afternoon from noon till half past two. Did you see him?'

'Shh,' the woman who had snapped at Colin said.

Montoya shook her head. 'I was with Kivrin, going over the map and the layout of Skendgate,' she whispered back.

'Where? At the dig?'

'No, at Brasenose.'

'And Badri wasn't there?' he asked, but there was no reason for Badri to have been at Brasenose. He hadn't asked Badri to run the drop until he met with him at half past two.

'No,' Montoya whispered.

'Shh!' the woman hissed.

'How long did you meet with Kivrin?'

'From ten till she had to go check into Infirmary, three, I think,' Montoya whispered.

'*Shh!*'

'I've got to go read a "Prayer to the Great Spirit",' Montoya whispered, standing up and starting along the row of chairs.

She read her American Indian chant, after which the bell ringers, wearing white gloves and determined expressions, played 'O Christ Who Interfaces with the World', which sounded a good deal like the banging of the pipes.

'They're absolutely necrotic, aren't they?' Colin whispered behind his order of service.

'It's late-twentieth-century atonal,' Dunworthy whispered back. 'It's supposed to sound dreadful.'

When the bell ringers appeared to be finished, Dunworthy mounted the lectern and read the Scripture. ' "And it came to pass in those days, that there went out a decree from Caesar Augustus, that all the world should be taxed . . ." '

Montoya stood up and edged her way past Colin to the side aisle and ducked out the door. He had wanted to ask her if she'd seen Badri at all on Monday or Tuesday or knew of any Americans he might have had contact with.

He could ask her tomorrow when they went for their bloodwork. He had found out the most important thing – that Kivrin hadn't seen Badri on Monday afternoon. Montoya had said she was with her from ten till three when she left for Infirmary. By that time Badri was already at Balliol meeting with him, and he hadn't come up from London until twelve, so Badri couldn't possibly have exposed her.

' "And the angel said unto them, Fear not: for, behold, I bring you good tidings of great joy, which shall be to all people . . ." '

No one seemed to be paying any attention. The woman who had snapped at Colin was wrestling her way out of her coat, and everyone else had already shed theirs and were fanning themselves with their orders of service.

He thought of Kivrin, at the service last year, kneeling on the stone floor, gazing raptly, intently at him while he read. She had not been listening either. She had been imagining Christmas Eve in 1320, when the Scripture was in Latin and candles flickered in the windows.

I wonder if it's the way she imagined it, he thought, and then remembered it wasn't Christmas Eve there. Where she was it was still two weeks away. If she was really there. If she was all right.

' ". . . but Mary kept all these things, and pondered them in her heart," ' Dunworthy finished and went back to his seat.

The imam announced the times of the Christmas Day services at all the churches, and read the NHS bulletin on avoiding contact with infected persons. The vicar began his sermon.

'There are *those*,' he said, looking hard at the priest from Holy Re-Formed, 'who think that diseases are a punishment from God, and yet Christ spent his life healing the sick, and were he here, I have no doubt he would cure those afflicted with this virus, just as he cured the Samaritan leper,' and launched into a ten-minute lecture on how to protect oneself from influenza. He listed the symptoms and explained droplet transmission.

'Drink fluids and rest,' he said, extending his hands out over the pulpit as if it were a benediction, 'and at the first sign of any of these symptoms, telephone your doctor.'

The bell ringers pulled on their white gloves again and accompanied the organ in 'Angels from the Realms of Glory', which actually sounded recognisable.

The minister from the Converted Unitarian Church mounted the pulpit. 'On this very night over two thousand years ago, God sent His Son, His precious child, into our world. Can you imagine what kind of incredible love it must have taken to do that? On that night Jesus left his heavenly home and went into a world full of dangers and diseases,' the minister said. 'He went as an ignorant and helpless babe, knowing nothing of the evil, of the treachery he would encounter. How could God have sent His only Son, His precious child, into such danger? The answer is love. Love.'

'Or incompetence,' Dunworthy muttered.

Colin looked up from his examination of his gobstopper and stared at him.

And after He'd let him go, He worried about Him every minute, Dunworthy thought. I wonder if He tried to stop it.

'It was love that sent Christ into the world, and love that made Christ willing, nay, eager to come.'

She's all right, he thought. The coordinates were correct. There was only four hours' slippage. She wasn't exposed to the flu. She's safely in Skendgate, with the rendezvous date determined and her corder already half-full of observations, healthy and excited and blissfully unaware of all this.

'He was sent into the world to help us in our trials and tribulations,' the minister said.

The vicar was signalling to Dunworthy. He leaned across Colin. 'I've just had word that Mr Latimer's ill,' the vicar whispered. He handed Dunworthy a folded sheet of paper. 'Will you read the benediction?'

'. . . a messenger from God, an emissary of love,' the minister said, and sat down.

Dunworthy went to the lectern. 'Will you please rise for the benediction?' he said, opening the sheet of paper and looking at it. 'Oh, Lord, stay Thy wrathful hand,' it began.

Dunworthy crumpled it up. 'Merciful Father,' he said, 'protect those absent from us, and bring them safely home.'

Transcript from the Domesday Book
(035850–037745)

20 December 1320. I'm nearly completely well. My enhanced T-cells or the antivirals or something must have finally kicked in. I can breathe in without it hurting, my cough's gone and I feel as though I could walk all the way to the drop, if I knew where it was.

The cut on my forehead is healed, too. Lady Eliwys looked at it this morning and then went and got Imeyne and had her examine it. 'It is a miracle,' Eliwys said delightedly, but Imeyne only looked suspicious. Next she'll decide I'm a witch.

It has become immediately apparent that now that I'm not an invalid, I'm a problem. Besides Imeyne thinking I'm spying or stealing the spoons, there's the difficulty of who I am – what my status is and how I should be treated – and Eliwys doesn't have the time or the energy to deal with it.

She has enough problems. Lord Guillaume still isn't here, his *privé* is in love with her and Christmas is coming. She's recruited half the village as servants and cooks, and they are out of a number of essential supplies that Imeyne insists they send to Oxford or Courcy for. Agnes adds to the problem by being underfoot and constantly running away from Maisry.

'You must send to Sir Bloet for a waiting woman,' Imeyne said when they found her playing in the barn loft. 'And for sugar. We have none for the subtlety nor the sweetmeats.'

Eliwys looked exasperated. 'My husband bade us—'

'I will watch Agnes,' I said, hoping the interpreter had translated 'waiting women' properly and that the history vids had been right, and the position of children's nurse was sometimes filled by women of noble birth. Apparently it was. Eliwys looked immediately grateful, and Imeyne didn't glare any more than usual. So I'm in charge of Agnes. And apparently Rosemund, who asked for help with her embroidery this morning.

The advantages of being their nurse is that I can ask them all about their father and the village, and I can go out to the stable and the church and find the priest and Gawyn. The disadvantage is that a good deal is being kept from the girls. Once already Eliwys stopped talking to Imeyne when Agnes and I came into the hall, and when I asked Rosemund why they had come here to stay, she said, 'My father deems the air is healthier at Ashencote.'

This is the first time anyone has mentioned the name of the village. There isn't any Ashencote on the map or in the *Domesday Book.* I suppose there's a chance it could be another 'lost village'. With a population of forty, it could easily have died out in the Black Death or been absorbed by one of the nearby towns, but I still think it's Skendgate.

I asked the girls if they knew of a village named Skendgate, and Rosemund said she'd never heard of it, which doesn't prove anything, since they're not from around here, but Agnes apparently asked Maisry, and she'd never heard of it either. The first written reference to the 'gate' (which was actually a weir) wasn't till 1360, and many of the Anglo-Saxon place names were replaced by Normanised ones or named after their new owners. Which bodes ill for Guillaume D'Iverie, and for the trial he still has not returned from. Unless this is another village altogether. Which bodes ill for me.

(Break)

Gawyn's feelings of courtly love for Eliwys are apparently not disturbed by dalliances with the servants. I asked Agnes to take me out to the stable to see her pony on the chance that Gawyn would be there. He was, in one of the boxes with Maisry, making less-than-courtly grunting noises. Maisry looked no more terrified than usual, and her hands were holding her skirts in a wad above her waist instead of clutching her ears, so it apparently wasn't rape. It wasn't *l'amour courtois* either.

I had hastily to distract Agnes and get her out of the stable, so I told her I wanted to go across the green to see the bell tower. We went inside and looked at the heavy rope.

'Father Roche rings the bell when someone dies,' Agnes said. 'If he does not, the Devil will come and take their soul, and they cannot go to heaven,' which, I suppose, is more of the superstitious prate that irritates Lady Imeyne.

Agnes wanted to ring the bell, but I talked her into going into the church to find Father Roche instead.

Father Roche wasn't there. Agnes told me that he was probably still with the cottar, 'who dies not though he has been shriven,' or was somewhere praying. 'Father Roche is wont to pray in the woods,' she said, peering through the rood screen to the altar.

The church is Norman, with a central aisle and sandstone pillars, and a flagged stone floor. The stained-glass windows are very narrow and small and of dark colours. They let in almost no light. Halfway up the nave is a single tomb, which may be the one I worked on out at the dig. It has an effigy of a knight on the top, his arms in gauntlets crossed over his breast, and his sword at his side. The carving on the side says, '*Requiescat cum Sanctis tuis in aeternum*'. May he rest with Thy saints for ever. The tomb at the dig had an inscription beginning '*Requiescat*', but that was all that had been excavated when I was there.

Agnes told me the tomb is her grandfather's, who died of a fever 'a long time ago', but it looks nearly new and therefore very different from the dig's tomb. It has a number of decorations the dig's tomb didn't have, but they might simply have broken or worn off.

Except for the tomb and a rough statue, the nave is completely empty. The contemps stood during church so there aren't any pews, and the practice of filling the nave with monuments and memorials didn't take hold until the 1500s.

A carved wooden rood screen, twelfth century, separates the nave from the shadowy recesses of the chancel and the altar. Above it, on either side of the crucifix, are two crude paintings of the Last Judgment. One is of the faithful entering heaven and the other of sinners being consigned to hell, but they seem nearly alike. Both are painted in garish reds and blues, and their expressions look equally dismayed.

The altar's plain, covered with a white linen cloth, with two silver candelabra on either side of it. The badly carved statue is not, as I'd assumed, the Virgin, but St Catherine of Alexandria. It has the foreshortened body and large head of pre-Renaissance sculpture, and an odd, squarish coif that stops just below her ears. She stands with one arm around a doll-sized child and the other holding a wheel. A short yellowish candle and two oil cressets were sitting on the floor in front of it.

'Lady Kivrin, Father Roche says you are a saint,' Agnes said when we went back outside.

It was easy to see where the confusion had come in this time, and I wondered if she'd done the same thing with the bell and the Devil on the black horse.

'I am named for St Catherine of Alexandria,' I said, 'as you are named for St Agnes, but we ourselves are not saints.'

She shook her head. 'He says in the last days God will send his saints to sinful man. He says when you pray, you speak in God's own tongue.'

225

I've tried to be careful about talking into the corder, to record my observations only when there's no one in the room, but I don't know about when I was ill. I remember that I kept asking him to help me, and you to come and get me. And if Father Roche heard me speaking modern English, he could very well believe I was speaking in tongues. At least he thinks I'm a saint, and not a witch, but Lady Imeyne was in the sickroom, too. I will have to be more careful.

(Break)

I went out to the stable again (after making sure Maisry was in the kitchen), but Gawyn wasn't there, and neither was Gringolet. My boxes and the dismanded remains of the wagon were, though Gawyn must have made a dozen trips to bring everything here. I looked through it all, and I can't find the casket. I'm hoping he missed it, and it's still by the road where I left it. If it is, it's probably completely buried in snow, but the sun is out today, and it's beginning to melt a little.

<hr>

CHAPTER FIFTEEN

Kivrin's recovery from pneumonia came so suddenly she was convinced that something had happened finally to activate her immune system. The pain in her chest abruptly went away and the cut on her forehead disappeared as if by magic.

Imeyne examined it suspiciously, as if she suspected Kivrin of faking her injury, and Kivrin was infinitely glad the wound had been real. 'You must thank God that He has healed you on this Sabbath day,' Imeyne said disapprovingly, and knelt beside the bed.

She had been to mass and was wearing her silver reliquary. She folded it between her palms – 'like the corder,' Kivrin thought – and recited the Paternoster, then pulled herself to her feet.

'I wish I could have gone with you to the mass,' Kivrin said.

Imeyne sniffed. 'I deemed you were too ill,' she said with an insinuating emphasis on the word 'ill', 'and it was but a poor mass.'

She launched into a recital of Father Roche's sins: he had read the gospel before the Kyrie, his alb was stained with candlewax, he had forgotten part of the Confiteor Deo. Listing his sins seemed to put her in a better mood and when she finished she patted Kivrin's hand and said, 'You are not yet fully healed. Stay you in bed yet another day.'

Kivrin did, using the time to record her observations on to the corder, describing the manor and the village and everyone she'd met so far. The steward came with another bowl of his wife's bitter tea, a dark, burly man who looked uncomfortable in his Sunday-best jerkin and a too-elaborate silver belt, and a boy about Rose-mund's age came in to tell Eliwys that her mare's forefoot was

227

'amiss'. But the priest didn't come again. 'He has gone to shrive the cottar,' Agnes told her.

Agnes was continuing to be an excellent informant, answering all of Kivrin's questions readily, whether she knew the answers or not, and volunteering all sorts of information about the village and its occupants. Rosemund was quieter and very much concerned with appearing grown-up. 'Agnes, it is childish to speak so. You must learn to keep a watch on your tongue,' she said repeatedly, a comment that happily had no effect whatsoever on Agnes. Rosemund did talk about her brothers and her father who 'has promised he will come to us for Christmas without fail'. She obviously worshipped him and missed him. 'I wish I had been a boy,' she said when Agnes was showing Kivrin the silver penny Sir Bloet had given her. 'Then I had stayed with Father in Bath.'

Between the two girls, and snatches of Eliwys' and Imeyne's conversations, plus her own observations, she was able to piece together a good deal about the village. It was smaller than Probability had predicted Skendgate would be, small even for a mediaeval village. Kivrin guessed it contained no more than forty people, including Lord Guillaume's family and the steward's. He had five children in addition to the baby.

There were two shepherds and several farmers, but it was 'the poorest of all Guillaume's holdings', Imeyne said, complaining again about them having to spend Christmas there. The steward's wife was the resident social climber, and Maisry's family the local ne'er-do-wells. Kivrin recorded everything, statistics and gossip, folding her hands in prayer whenever she had the chance.

The snow that had started when they brought her back to the manor continued all that night and into the next afternoon, snowing nearly a foot. The first day Kivrin was up, it rained, and Kivrin hoped the rain would melt the snow, but it merely hardened the crust to ice.

She was afraid she'd have no hope at all of recognising the drop without the wagon and boxes there. She would have to get Gawyn to show it to her, but that was easier said than done. He only came into the hall to eat or to ask Eliwys something, and Imeyne was always there, watching, when he was, so she didn't dare approach him.

Kivrin began taking the girls on little excursions – around the courtyard, out into the village – in the hope that she might run into him, but he was not in the barn or the stable. Gringolet was not there either. Kivrin wondered if he had gone after her attackers in spite of Eliwys' orders, but Rosemund said he was out hunting. 'He slays deer for the Christmas feast,' Agnes said.

No one seemed to care where she took the little girls or how long they were gone. Lady Eliwys nodded distractedly when Kivrin asked if she might take the little girls to the stable, and Lady Imeyne didn't even tell Agnes to fasten her cloak or wear her mittens. It was as if they had given the children over into Kivrin's care and then forgotten them.

They were very busy with preparations for Christmas. Eliwys had recruited every girl and old woman in the village and set them to baking and cooking. The two pigs were slaughtered and over half the doves killed and plucked. The courtyard was full of feathers and the smell of baking bread.

In the 1300s Christmas had been a two-week celebration with feasting and games and dancing, but Kivrin was surprised that Eliwys was doing all this under the circumstances. She must be convinced Lord Guillaume would really come for Christmas, as he'd promised.

Imeyne supervised the cleaning of the hall, complaining constantly about the poor conditions and the lack of decent help. This morning she had brought in the steward and another man to take down the heavy tables from the walls and set them on two trestles. She was supervising Maisry and a woman with the patchy white scars of scrofula on her neck while they scrubbed the table with sand and heavy brushes.

'There is no lavender,' she said to Eliwys. 'And not enough new rushes for the floor.'

'We shall have to make do with what we have, then,' Eliwys said.

'We have no sugar for the subtlety, either, and no cinnamon. At Courcy they are amply provided. He would welcome us.'

Kivrin was putting on Agnes' boots, getting ready to take her out to see her pony in the stable again. She looked up, alarmed.

'It is but a half-day's journey,' Imeyne said. 'Lady Yvolde's chaplain will likely say the mass, and—'

Kivrin didn't hear the rest of it because Agnes said, 'My pony is called Saracen.'

'Um,' Kivrin murmured, trying to hear the conversation. Christmas was a time when the nobility often went visiting. She should have thought of that before. They took their entire households and stayed for weeks, at least until Epiphany. If they went to Courcy, they might stay until long after the rendezvous.

'Father named him Saracen for that he has a heathen heart,' Agnes said.

'Sir Bloet will take it ill when he finds we have sat so near through Yule without a visit,' Lady Imeyne said. 'He will think the betrothal has gone amiss.'

'We cannot go to Courcy for Yule,' Rosemund said. She had been sitting on the bench across from Kivrin and Agnes, sewing, but now she stood up. 'My father promised without fail that he would come by Christmas. He will be ill-pleased to come and find us gone.'

Imeyne turned and glared at Rosemund. 'He will be ill-pleased to find his daughters grown so wild they speak when they will and meddle in matters that do not concern them.' She turned back to Eliwys, who was looking worried. 'My son would surely have the wit to seek us at Courcy.'

'My husband bade us stay here and wait till he comes,' Eliwys said. 'He will be pleased that we have done his bidding.' She went over to the hearth and picked up Rosemund's sewing, clearly putting an end to the conversation.

But not for long, Kivrin thought, watching Imeyne. The old woman pursed her lips angrily and pointed at a spot on the table. The woman with the scrofula scars immediately moved to scrub it.

Imeyne wouldn't let it rest. She would bring it up again, putting forth argument after argument why they should go to Sir Bloet, who had sugar and rushes and cinnamon. And an educated chaplain to say the Christmas masses. Lady Imeyne was determined not to hear mass from Father Roche. And Eliwys was more and more worried all the time. She might suddenly decide to go to Courcy for help, or even back to Bath. Kivrin had to find the drop.

She tied the dangling strings of Agnes' cap and pulled the hood of her cloak up over her head.

'I rode Saracen every day in Bath,' Agnes said. 'I would we could go riding here. I would take my hound.'

'Dogs do not ride horses,' Rosemund said. 'They run alongside.'

Agnes stuck her lip out stubbornly. 'Blackie is too little to run.'

'Why can you not go riding here?' Kivrin said to head off a fight.

'There is none to accompany us,' Rosemund said. 'In Bath our nurse and one of Father's *privés* rode with us.'

One of Father's *privés*. Gawyn could accompany them, and she could not only ask him where the drop was but also have him show it to her. Gawyn was here. She had seen him in the courtyard this morning, which was why she had suggested the trip to the stable, but having him ride with them was better.

Imeyne came over to where Eliwys was sitting. 'If we are to stay here, we must have game for the Christmas pie.'

Lady Eliwys set aside her sewing and stood up. 'I will bid the steward and his eldest son go hunting,' she said quietly.

'Then will there be no one to fetch the ivy and the holly.'

'Father Roche goes out to gather it this day,' Lady Eliwys said.

'He gathers it for the church,' Lady Imeyne said. 'Will you have none in the hall, then?'

'We'll fetch it,' Kivrin said.

Eliwys and Imeyne both turned to look at her. Mistake, Kivrin thought. She had been so intent on finding a way to speak to Gawyn she had forgotten everything else, and now she had spoken without being spoken to and 'meddled in matters' that obviously didn't concern her. Lady Imeyne would be more convinced than ever that they should go to Courcy and get a proper nurse for the girls.

'I'm sorry if I spoke out of turn, good lady,' she said, ducking her head. 'I know there is much to do and there are few to do it. Agnes and Rosemund and I might easily ride into the woods to fetch the holly.'

'Aye,' Agnes said eagerly. 'I could ride Saracen.'

Eliwys started to speak, but Imeyne interrupted her. 'Have you no fear of the woods then, though you are only lately healed of your injuries?'

Mistake upon mistake. She was supposed to have been attacked and left for dead, and here she was volunteering to take two little girls into the same woods.

'I didn't mean that we should go alone,' Kivrin said, hoping she wasn't making it worse. 'Agnes told me that she rode out with one of your husband's men to guard her.'

'Aye,' Agnes piped up. 'Gawyn can ride with us, and my hound Blackie.'

'Gawyn is not here,' Imeyne said, and then turned quickly back to the women scrubbing the table in the silence that followed.

'Where has he gone?' Eliwys said, quietly enough, but her cheeks had flushed bright red.

Imeyne took Maisry's rag away from her and began scrubbing at a spot on the table. 'He has undertaken an errand for me.'

'You have sent him to Courcy,' Eliwys said, and it was a statement, not a question.

Imeyne turned back to face her. 'It is not meet for us to be so close to Courcy and yet send no greeting. He will say we have cast him off, and we can ill afford in these times to anger such a man as powerful as—'

'My husband bade us tell no one we were here,' Eliwys cut in.

'My *son* did not bid us to slight Sir Bloet and lose him his goodwill, now when it may be sorely needed.'

'What did you bid him say to Sir Bloet?'

'I bade him deliver kind greetings,' Imeyne said, twisting the rag in her hands. 'I bade him say we would be glad to receive them for Christmas.' She lifted her chin defiantly. 'We could do aught else, with our two families to be joined so soon in marriage. They will bring provisions for the Christmas feast, and servants—'

'And Lady Yvolde's chaplain to say the mass?' Eliwys asked coldly.

'Do they come here?' Rosemund asked. She had stood up again, and her sewing had slid off her knees and on to the floor.

Eliwys and Imeyne looked at her blankly, as if they had forgotten there was anyone else in the hall, and then Eliwys turned on Kivrin. 'Lady Katherine,' she snapped, 'were you not taking the children to gather greens for the hall?'

'We cannot go without Gawyn,' Agnes said.

'Father Roche can ride with you,' Eliwys said.

'Yes, good lady,' Kivrin said. She took Agnes' hand to lead her from the room.

'Do they come here?' Rosemund asked again, and her cheeks were nearly as red as her mother's.

'I know not,' Eliwys said. 'Go with your sister and Lady Katherine.'

'I am to ride Saracen,' Agnes said, and tore free of Kivrin's hand and ran out of the hall.

Rosemund looked as if she were going to say something and then went to get her cloak from the passage behind the screens.

'Maisry,' Eliwys said. 'The table looks well enough. Go and fetch the saltcellar and the silver platter from the chest in the loft.'

The woman with the scrofula scars scurried out of the room and even Maisry didn't dawdle going up the ladder. Kivrin pulled her cloak on and tied it hastily, afraid Lady Imeyne would say something else about her being attacked, but neither of the women said anything. They stood, Imeyne still twisting the rag between her hands, obviously waiting for Kivrin and Rosemund to be gone.

'Does—' Rosemund said, and then ran off after Agnes.

Kivrin hurried after them. Gawyn was gone, but she had permission to go into the woods and transportation. And the priest to go with them. Rosemund had said Gawyn had met him on the road when he was bringing her to the manor. Perhaps Gawyn had taken him to the clearing.

She practically ran across the courtyard to the stable, afraid that at the last minute Eliwys would call across the courtyard to her that she had changed her mind, Kivrin was not well enough and the woods were too dangerous.

The girls had apparently had the same idea. Agnes was already on her pony and Rosemund was cinching the girth on her mare's saddle. The pony wasn't a pony at all; it was a sturdy sorrel scarcely smaller than Rosemund's mare and Agnes looked impossibly high up on the high-backed saddle. The boy who had told Eliwys about the mare's foot was holding the reins.

'Do not stand gawking, Cob!' Rosemund snapped at him. 'Saddle the roan for Lady Katherine!'

He obediently let go of the reins. Agnes leaned far forward to grab them.

'*Not* Mother's mare!' Rosemund said. 'The *roncin!*'

'We will ride to the church, Saracen,' Agnes said, 'and tell Father Roche we would go with him, and then we will go riding. Saracen loves to go riding.' She leaned much too far forward to pat the pony's cropped mane, and Kivrin had to keep herself from grabbing for her.

She was obviously perfectly able to ride – neither Rosemund nor the boy saddling Kivrin's horse gave her a glance – but she looked so tiny perched up there in the saddle with her soft-soled boot in the jerked-up stirrup, and she was no more capable of riding carefully than she was of walking slowly.

Cob saddled the roan, led it out and then stood there, waiting.

'Cob!' Rosemund said rudely. He bent down and made a step out of his linked hands. Rosemund stepped up on it and swung into the saddle. 'Do not stand there like a witless fool. Help Lady Katherine.'

He hurried awkwardly over to give Kivrin a hand up. She hesitated, wondering what was wrong with Rosemund. She had obviously been upset by the news that Gawyn had gone to Sir Bloet's. Rosemund hadn't seemed to know anything about her fathers trial, but perhaps she was aware of more than Kivrin, or her mother and grandmother, thought.

'A man as powerful as Sir Bloet,' Imeyne had said, and 'his goodwill may be sorely needed.' Perhaps Imeyne's invitation was not as self-serving as it seemed. Perhaps it meant Lord Guillaume was in even more trouble than Eliwys imagined, and Rosemund, sitting quietly at her sewing, had figured that out.

'Cob!' Rosemund snapped, though he was clearly waiting for Kivrin to mount. 'Your dawdling will make us miss Father Roche!'

Kivrin smiled reassuringly at Cob, and put her hands on the boy's shoulder. One of the first things Mr Dunworthy had insisted on was riding lessons, and she had managed fairly well. The sidesaddle hadn't been introduced until the 1390s, which was a blessing, and mediaeval saddles had a high saddlebow and cantle. This saddle was even higher in the back than the one she'd learned on.

But I'll probably be the one to fall off, not Agnes, she thought, looking at Agnes perched confidently on her pony. She wasn't even holding on but was twisted around messing with something in the saddlebag behind her.

'Let us be gone!' Rosemund said impatiently.

'Sir Bloet says he will bring me a silver bridle-chain for Saracen,' she said, still fussing with the saddlebag.

'Agnes! Stop dawdling and *come*,' Rosemund said.

'Sir Bloet says he will bring it when he comes at Easter.'

'Agnes!' Rosemund said. 'Come! It is like to rain.'

'Nay, it will not,' Agnes said unconcernedly. 'Sir Bloet—'

Rosemund turned furiously on her sister. 'Oh, and can you now soothe the weather? You are naught but a babe! A mewling babe!'

'Rosemund!' Kivrin said. 'Don't speak that way to your sister.' She stepped up to Rosemund's mare and took hold of the loosely looped reins. 'What's the matter, Rosemund? Is something troubling you?'

Rosemund pulled the reins sharply taut. 'Only that we dawdle here while the *babe* prattles!'

Kivrin let go of the reins, frowning, and let Cob make a step of his laced fingers for her foot so she could mount. She had never seen Rosemund act like this.

They rode out of the courtyard past the now-empty pigpens and out on to the green. It was a leaden day, with a low blanketing layer of heavy clouds and no wind at all. Rosemund was right about it being 'like to rain'. There was a damp, misty feeling to the cold air. She kicked her horse into a faster walk.

The village was obviously getting ready for Christmas. Smoke was coming from every hut, and two men were at the far end of the green, chopping wood and throwing it on to an already huge pile. A large, blackened chunk of meat – the goat? – was roasting over a spit beside the steward's house. The steward's wife was in front, milking the bony cow Kivrin had leaned against the day she tried to find the drop. She and Mr Dunworthy had had a fight over whether she needed to learn to milk. She had told him no cows were milked in winter in the 1300s, that the contempts let them go dry and used goat's milk for cheese. She had also told him goats were not meat animals.

'Agnes!' Rosemund said furiously.

Kivrin looked up. Agnes had come to a stop and was twisted backwards in her saddle again. She obediently moved forward again, but Rosemund said, 'I will wait for you no longer, ninny!' and kicked her horse into a trot, scattering the chickens and practically running down a barefoot little girl with an armload of faggots.

'Rosemund!' Kivrin called, but she was already out of earshot, and Kivrin didn't want to leave Agnes' side to go after her.

'Is your sister angry over fetching the holly?' Kivrin asked Agnes, knowing that wasn't it, but hoping Agnes would volunteer something else.

'She is ever cross-grained,' Agnes said. 'Grandmother will be wroth that she rides so childishly.' She trotted her pony decorously across the green, a model of maturity, nodding her head to the villagers.

The little girl Rosemund had almost run down stopped and stared at them, her mouth open. The steward's wife looked up as they passed and smiled, and then went on milking, but the men who were cutting wood took off their caps and bowed.

They rode past the hut where Kivrin had taken shelter the day she tried to find the drop. The hut she had sat in while Gawyn was bringing her things back to the manor.

'Agnes,' Kivrin said, 'did Father Roche go with you when you went after the Yule log?'

'Aye,' Agnes said. 'He had to bless it.'

'Oh,' Kivrin said, disappointed. She had hoped perhaps he had gone with Gawyn to fetch her things and knew where the drop was. 'Did anyone help Gawyn bring my things to the manor?'

'Nay,' Agnes said, and Kivrin couldn't tell whether she really knew or not. 'Gawyn is very strong. He killed four wolves with his sword.'

That sounded unlikely, but so did his rescuing a maiden in the woods. And it was obvious he would do anything if he thought it would win him Eliwys' love, even to dragging the wagon home single-handed.

'Father Roche is strong,' Agnes said.

'Father Roche has *gone*,' Rosemund said, already off her horse. She had tied it to the lychgate and was standing in the churchyard, her hands on her hips.

'Have you looked in the church?' Kivrin asked.

'Nay,' Rosemund said sullenly. 'But look how cold it grows. Father Roche would have more wit than to wait here till it snows.'

'We will look in the church,' Kivrin said, dismounting and holding her arms to Agnes. 'Come on, Agnes.'

'Nay,' Agnes said, sounding almost as stubborn as her sister, 'I would wait here with Saracen.' She patted the pony's mane.

'Saracen will be fine,' Kivrin said. She reached for the little girl and lifted her down. 'Come on, we'll look in the church first.' She took her hand and opened the lychgate to the churchyard.

Agnes didn't protest, but she kept glancing anxiously over her shoulder at the horses. 'Saracen likes not to be left alone.'

Rosemund stopped in the middle of the churchyard and turned round, her hands on her hips. 'What are you hiding, you wicked girl? Did you steal apples and put them in your saddlebags?'

'No!' Agnes said, alarmed, but Rosemund was already striding towards the pony. 'Stay from there! It is not your pony!' Agnes shouted. 'It is mine!'

Well, we won't have to go and find the priest, Kivrin thought If he's here, he'll come out to see what all the noise is.

Rosemund was unbuckling the straps to the saddlebag. 'Look!' she said, and held up Agnes' puppy by the scruff of its neck.

'Oh, Agnes,' Kivrin said.

'You are a wicked girl,' Rosemund said. 'I should take it to the river and drown it.' She turned in that direction.

'Nay!' Agnes wailed and ran to the lychgate. Rosemund immediately held the puppy up out of Agnes' reach.

This has gone absolutely far enough, Kivrin thought. She stepped forward and took the puppy away from Rosemund. 'Agnes, stop howling. Your sister won't hurt your puppy.'

The puppy scrabbled against Kivrin's shoulder, trying to lick her cheek. 'Agnes, hounds can't ride horses. Blackie wouldn't be able to breathe in your saddlebag.'

'I could carry him,' Agnes said, but not very hopefully. 'He wanted to ride my pony.'

'He had a nice ride to the church,' Kivrin said firmly. 'And he will have a nice ride back to the stable.' He was trying to bite her ear. She gave him to Rosemund, who took hold of the back of his neck. 'It's just a baby, Agnes. It must go back to its mother now and sleep.'

'You are the babe, Agnes!' Rosemund said, so furiously Kivrin was not sure she trusted her to take the puppy back. 'To put a hound upon a horse! And now we must waste yet more time taking it back! I shall be glad when I am grown and no longer have to do with babes!'

She mounted, still holding the puppy up by his neck, but once she was in her saddle, she wrapped him almost tenderly in the corner of her cloak and cupped him against her chest. She took the reins with her free hand and turned the horse. 'Father Roche has *surely* gone by now!' she said angrily and galloped off.

Kivrin was afraid she was probably right. The racket they had made had almost been enough to wake the dead under the wooden tombstones, but no one had appeared from the church. He had no doubt left before they arrived and now was long gone, but Kivrin took Agnes' hand and led her into the church.

'Rosemund is a wicked girl,' Agnes said.

Kivrin felt inclined to agree with her, but she could hardly say that, and she didn't feel much like defending Rosemund, so she didn't say anything.

'Nor am I a babe,' Agnes said, looking up at Kivrin for confirmation, but there was nothing to say to that either. Kivrin pushed the heavy door open and stood looking into the church.

There was no one there. It was dim almost to blackness in the nave, the grey day outside sending no light at all through the narrow stained-glass windows, but the half-open door gave enough light to see it was empty.

'Mayhap he is in the chancel,' Agnes said. She squeezed past Kivrin into the dark nave, knelt, crossed herself and then looked impatiently back over her shoulder at Kivrin.

There was no one in the chancel either. She could see from there that there were no candles lit on the altar, but Agnes wasn't going to be satisfied till they had searched the whole church. Kivrin knelt and made her obeisance beside her, and they walked up to the rood screen through the near darkness. The candles in front of the statue of St Catherine had been extinguished. She could smell the sharp scent of tallow and smoke. She wondered if Father Roche had snuffed them out before he left. Fire would have been a huge problem, even in a stone church, and there were no votive dishes for the candles to burn down safely in.

Agnes went right up to the rood screen, pressed her face against the cutout wood and called, 'Father Roche!' She turned around immediately and announced, 'He isn't here, Lady Kivrin. Mayhap he is in his house,' she said, and ran out of the priest's door.

Kivrin was sure Agnes was not supposed to do that, but there was nothing to do but follow her across the churchyard to the nearest house.

It had to belong to the priest because Agnes was already standing outside the door yelling 'Father Roche!' and of course the priest's house was next to the church, but Kivrin was still surprised.

The house was as ramshackle as the hut she had rested in and not much larger. The priest was supposed to get a tithe of everyone's crops and livestock, but there were no animals in the narrow yard except for a few scraggly chickens, and less than an armload of wood stacked in front.

Agnes had started banging on the door, which looked as insubstantial as the hut's, and Kivrin was afraid she'd knock it open and walk straight in, but before she could get to her, Agnes turned and said, 'Mayhap he is in the bell tower.'

'No, I don't think so,' Kivrin said, taking Agnes' hand so she didn't go tearing off through the churchyard again. They started walking back toward the lychgate. 'Father Roche does not ring the bell again till vespers.'

'He might,' Agnes said, cocking her head as if listening for it.

Kivrin listened, too, but there was no sound, and she realised suddenly that the bell in the south-west had stopped. It had rung almost nonstop while she had the pneumonia, and she had heard it when she went out to the stable the second time, looking for Gawyn, but she didn't remember whether it had rung since then or not.

'Heard you that, Lady Kivrin?' Agnes said. She pulled her hand out of Kivrin's grasp and ran off, not towards the bell tower, but round the end of the church to the north side. 'See you?' she crowed, pointing at what she'd found. 'He has not gone.'

It was the priest's white donkey, placidly pulling at the weeds sticking up through the snow. It had a rope bridle on and several burlap bags over its back, obviously empty, obviously intended for the holly and ivy.

'He *is* in the bell tower, I trow,' Agnes said, and darted back the way she'd come.

Kivrin followed her round the church and into the churchyard, watching Agnes disappear into the tower. She waited, wondering where else they should look. Perhaps he was tending someone ill in one of the huts.

She caught a flicker of movement through the church window. A light. Perhaps while they were looking at the donkey he had come back. She pushed the priests door open and looked inside. A candle had been lit in front of St Catherine's statue. She could see its faint glow at the statue's feet.

'Father Roche?' she called softly. There was no answer. She stepped inside, letting the door shut behind her, and went over to the statue.

The candle was set between the statue's blocklike feet. St Catherine's rough face and hair were in shadow, looming protectively over the small adult figure who was supposed to be a little girl. She knelt and picked up the candle. It had just been lit. It hadn't even had time to melt the tallow in the well around the wick.

Kivrin looked down the nave. She couldn't see anything, holding the candle. It lit the floor and St Catherine's boxlike wimple and put the rest of the nave in total darkness.

She took a few steps down the nave, still holding the candle. 'Father Roche?'

It was utterly silent in the church, the way it had been in the woods that day when she came through. Too silent, as if someone was there, standing beside the tomb or behind one of the pillars, waiting.

'Father Roche?' she called clearly. 'Are you there?'

There was no answer, only that hushed, waiting silence. There wasn't anyone in the woods, she told herself, and took a few more steps forward into the gloom. There was no one beside the tomb. Imeyne's husband lay with his hands folded across his breast and his sword at his side, peaceful and silent. There was no one by the door either. She could see it now, in spite of the candle's blinding light. There was no one there.

She could feel her heart pounding the way it had in the forest, so loud it could be covering up the sound of footsteps, of breathing, of someone standing there waiting. She whirled around, the candle tracing a fiery trail in the air as she turned.

He was right behind her. The candle nearly went out. It bent, flickering, and then steadied, lighting his cut-throat's face from below the way it had with the lantern.

'What do you want?' Kivrin said, so breathlessly almost no sound came out. 'How did you get in here?'

The cut-throat didn't answer her. He simply stared at her the way he had in the clearing. I didn't dream him, she thought frightenedly. He was there. He had intended – what? to rob her? to rape her? – and Gawyn had frightened him off.

She took a step backwards. 'I said, what do you want? Who are you?'

She was speaking English. She could hear it echoing hollowly in the cold stone space. Oh, no, she thought don't let the interpreter break down now.

'What are you doing here?' she said, forcing herself to speak more slowly and heard her own voice saying, '*Whette wolde thou withe me?*'

He put his hand out towards her, a huge hand, dirty and reddened, a cut-throat's hand, as if he would touch her cropped hair.

'Go away,' she said. She stepped backwards again and came up against the tomb. The candle went out. 'I don't know who you are or what you want, but you'd better go away.' It was English again, but what difference did it make, he wanted to rob her, to kill her, and where was the priest? 'Father Roche!' she cried desperately. 'Father Roche!'

There was a sound at the door, a bang and then the scrape of wood on stone, and Agnes pushed the door open. 'There you are,' she said happily. 'I have looked everywhere for you.'

The cut-throat glanced at the door.

'Agnes!' Kivrin shouted. 'Run!'

The little girl froze, her hand still on the heavy door.

'Get away from here!' Kivrin shouted, and realised with horror that it was still English. What was the word for 'run'?

The cut-throat took another step towards Kivrin. She shrank back against the tomb.

'*Renne!* Flee, Agnes!' she cried, and then the door crashed shut and Kivrin was running across the stone floor and out the door after her, dropping the candle as she ran.

Agnes was almost to the lychgate, but she stopped as soon as Kivrin was out the door and ran back to her.

'No!' Kivrin shouted, waving her on. 'Run!'

'Is it a wolf?' Agnes asked, wide-eyed.

There was no time to explain or try to coax her to run. The men who had been cutting wood had disappeared. She scooped Agnes up in her arms and ran towards the horses. 'There was a wicked man in the church!' she said, setting Agnes on her pony.

'A wicked man?' Agnes asked, ignoring the reins Kivrin was thrusting at her. 'Was it one of those who set upon you in the woods?'

'Yes,' Kivrin said, untying the reins. 'You must ride as fast as you can to the manor house. Don't stop for anything.'

'I didn't see him,' Agnes said.

She probably hadn't. Coming in from outside, she wouldn't have been able to see anything in the church's gloom.

'Was he the man who stole your goods and gear and cracked your skull?'

'Yes,' Kivrin said. She reached for the reins and started to untie them.

'Was the wicked man hiding in the tomb?'

'What?' Kivrin said. She couldn't get the stiff leather untied. She glanced anxiously back at the church door.

'I saw you and Father Roche by the tomb. Was the wicked man hiding in Grandfather's grave?'

CHAPTER SIXTEEN

Father Roche.

The stiff reins came suddenly loose in Kivrin's hands. 'Father Roche?'

'I went in the bell tower, but he was not there. He was in the church,' Agnes said. 'Why was the wicked man hiding in Grandfather's tomb, Lady Kivrin?'

Father Roche. But it couldn't be. Father Roche had given her the last rites. He had anointed her temples and the palms of her hands.

'Will the wicked man hurt Father Roche?' Agnes asked.

He couldn't be Father Roche. Father Roche had held her hand. He had told her not to be afraid. She tried to call up the face of the priest. He had leaned over her and asked her her name, but she hadn't been able to see his face because of all the smoke.

And while he was giving her the last rites, she had seen the cut-throat, she had been afraid because they had let him in the room, she had tried to get away from him. But it hadn't been a cut-throat at all. It had been Father Roche.

'Is the wicked man coming?' Agnes said, looking anxiously at the church door.

It all made sense. The cut-throat leaning over her in the clearing, putting her on the horse. She had thought it was a vision from her delirium, but it wasn't. It had been Father Roche, come to help Gawyn bring her to the manor.

'The wicked man isn't coming,' Kivrin said. 'There isn't any wicked man.'

'Hides he still in the church?'

'No. I was wrong. There isn't any wicked man.'

Agnes looked unconvinced. 'You cried out,' she said.

Kivrin could hear her telling her grandmother, 'Lady Katherine and Father Roche were in the church together and she cried out.' Lady Imeyne would be delighted to have this to add to her litany of Father Roche's sins. And to Kivrin's list of suspicious behaviour.

'I know I cried out,' Kivrin said. 'It was dark in the church. Father Roche came upon me suddenly and I was frightened.'

'But it was Father Roche,' Agnes said as if she could not imagine anyone being frightened by him.

'When you and Rosemund play at hiding and she jumps suddenly at you from behind a tree, you cry out,' Kivrin said desperately.

'One time Rosemund hid in the loft when I was looking at my hound, and she jumped down. I was so affrighted I cried out. Like this,' Agnes said, and let out a bloodcurdling shriek. 'And another time it was dark in the hall and Gawyn jumped out from behind the screens and he said "Fie!" and I cried out and—'

'That's right,' Kivrin said, 'it was dark in the church.'

'Did Father Roche jump out at you and say "Fie"?'

Yes, Kivrin thought. He leaned over me, and I thought he was a cut-throat. 'No,' she said. 'He didn't do anything.'

'Go we still with Father Roche for the holly?'

If I haven't frightened him away, Kivrin thought. If he hasn't left while we've stood here talking.

She lifted Agnes down. 'Come on. We must go find him.'

She didn't know what she'd do if he'd already gone. She couldn't take Agnes back to the manor to tell Lady Imeyne how she had screamed. And she couldn't go back without explaining to Father Roche. Explaining what? That she'd thought he was a robber, a rapist? That she'd thought he was a nightmare from her delirium?

'Must we go into the church again?' Agnes asked reluctantly.

'It's all right. There's no one there except Father Roche.'

In spite of Kivrin's assurances, Agnes was unwilling to go back in the church. She hid her head in Kivrin's skirts when Kivrin opened the door, and clung to her leg.

'It's all right,' Kivrin said, peering into the nave. He was no longer by the tomb. The door shut behind her, and she stood there with Agnes pressed against her, waiting for her eyes to adjust to the darkness. 'There's nothing to be afraid of.'

He's not a cut-throat, she told herself. There's nothing to be afraid of. He gave you the last rites. He held your hand. But her heart was pounding.

'Is the wicked man there?' Agnes whispered, her head jammed against Kivrin's knee.

'There isn't any wicked man,' she said, and then saw him. He was standing in front of St Catherine's statue. He was holding the candle Kivrin had dropped, and he bent and set it in front of the statue, and then straightened again.

She had thought perhaps it had been some trick of the darkness and the candle's flame, lighting his face from below, and he wasn't the cut-throat after all, but he was. He had worn a hood over his head that night, so she couldn't see his tonsure, but he was bending over the statue the way he had bent over her. Her heart began to pound again.

'Where is Father Roche?' Agnes said, raising her head. 'There he is,' she said, and ran towards him.

'No—' Kivrin said, and started after her. 'Don't—'

'Father Roche!' Agnes shouted. 'Father Roche! We have been seeking you!' She had obviously forgotten all about the wicked man. 'We looked in the church and we looked in the house, but you were not there!'

She was running full tilt at him. He turned and bent down and scooped Agnes up into his arms all in one motion.

'I sought you in the bell tower, but you were not there,' Agnes said without the slightest trace of fear. 'Rosemund said you had gone.'

Kivrin stopped even with the last pillar, trying to get her heart to slow down.

'Were you hiding?' Agnes asked. She put one arm trustingly around his neck. 'Once Rosemund hid in the barn and jumped down on me. I cried out in a loud voice.'

'Why did you seek me, Agnes?' he said. 'Is someone ill?'

He pronounced Agnes '*Agnus*', and he had nearly the same accent as the boy with the scurvy. The interpreter took a catch step before it translated what he'd said, and Kivrin felt a fleeting surprise that she couldn't understand him. She had understood everything he said in the sickroom.

He must have been speaking Latin to me, she thought, because there was no mistaking his voice. It was the voice that had said the last rites, the voice that had told her not to be afraid. And she wasn't afraid. At the sound of his voice, her heart had stopped pounding.

'Nay, none are ill,' Agnes said. 'We would go with you to gather ivy and holly for the hall. Lady Kivrin and Rosemund and Saracen and I.'

At the words 'Lady Kivrin', Roche turned and saw her standing there by the pillar. He set Agnes down.

Kivrin put out her hand to the pillar for support. 'I beg your pardon, Holy Father,' she said. 'I'm so sorry I screamed and ran from you. It was dark, and I didn't recognise you—'

The interpreter, still a half-beat behind, translated that as 'I knew you not.'.

'She knows naught,' Agnes interrupted. 'The wicked man struck her on the head, and she remembers naught save for her name.'

'I had heard this,' he said, still looking at Kivrin. 'Is it true you have no memory of why you have come among us?'

She felt the same longing to tell him the truth that she had felt when he'd asked her her name. I'm an historian, she wanted to say. I came here to observe you, and I fell ill, and I don't know where the drop is.

'She remembered naught of who she is,' Agnes said. 'She did not yet remember how to speak. I had to teach her.'

'You remember naught of who you are?' he asked.

'No.'

'And naught of your coming here?' he said.

She could answer that truthfully at least. 'No,' she said. 'Except that you and Gawyn brought me to the manor.'

Agnes was obviously tired of the conversation. 'Might we go with you now to gather holly?'

He didn't act as if he'd heard her. He extended his hand as if he were going to bless Kivrin, but he touched her temple instead and she realised that was what he had intended to do before, beside the tomb. 'You have no wound,' he said.

'It's healed,' she said.

'We wish to go now,' Agnes said, tugging on Roche's arm. He raised his hand, as if to touch her temple again, and then withdrew it. 'You must not fear,' he said. 'God has sent you among us for some good purpose.'

No, he hasn't, Kivrin thought. He hasn't sent me here at all. Mediaeval sent me. But she felt comforted.

'Thank you,' she said.

'I would go *now*!' Agnes said, tugging on Kivrin's arm. 'Go fetch your donkey,' she told Father Roche, 'and we will fetch Rosemund.'

Agnes started down the nave, and Kivrin had no choice but to go with her to keep her from running. The door banged open just before they reached it and Rosemund looked in, blinking.

'It is raining. Found you Father Roche?' she demanded.

'Took you Blackie to the stable?' Agnes asked.

'Aye. You were too late, then, and Father Roche had gone?'

'Nay. He is here, and we are to go with him. He was in the church and Lady Kivrin—'

'He has gone to fetch his donkey,' Kivrin said to keep Agnes from launching into the story of what had happened.

'I was affrighted that time when you jumped from the loft, Rosemund,' Agnes said, but Rosemund had already stamped off to her horse.

It wasn't raining, but there was a fine mist in the air. Kivrin helped Agnes into her saddle and mounted the roan, using the lychgate as a step. Father Roche led the donkey out to them, and they started off on the track past the church and up through the little band of trees behind it, along a little space of snow-covered meadow and on into the woods.

'There are wolves in these woods,' Agnes said. 'Gawyn killed one.'

Kivrin scarcely heard her. She was watching Father Roche walking beside his donkey, trying to remember the night he had brought her to the manor. Rosemund had said Gawyn had met him on the road and he had helped Gawyn bring her the rest of the way to the manor, but that couldn't be right.

He had leaned over her as she sat against the wagon wheel. She could see his face in the flickering light from the fire. He had said something to her she didn't understand, and she had said, 'Tell Mr Dunworthy to come and get me.'

'Rosemund does not ride in seemly fashion for a maid,' Agnes said primly.

She had ridden out ahead of the donkey and was nearly out of sight where the road curved, waiting impatiently for them to catch up.

'Rosemund!' Kivrin called, and Rosemund galloped back, nearly colliding with the donkey and then pulling her mare's reins up short.

'Can we go no faster than this?' she demanded, wheeled around, and rode ahead again. 'We will never finish ere it rains.'

They were riding in thick woods now, the road scarcely wider than a bridle path. Kivrin looked at the trees trying to remember having seen them. They passed a thicket of willows, but it was set too far back from the road, and a trickle of ice-bordered water ran next to it.

There was a huge sycamore on the other side of the path. It stood in a little open space, draped with mistletoe. Beyond it was a line of wild service trees, so evenly spaced they might have been planted. She didn't remember ever having seen any of this before.

They had brought her along this road, and she'd hoped that something might trigger her memory, but nothing looked familiar at all. It had been too dark and she had been too ill.

All she really remembered was the drop, though it had the same hazy, unreal quality as the trip to the manor. There had been a clearing and an oak and a thicket of willows. And Father Roche's face bending over her as she sat against the wagon wheel.

He must have been with Gawyn when he found her, or else Gawyn had brought him back to the drop. She could see his face clearly in the light from the fire. And then she'd fallen off the horse at the fork.

They hadn't come to any fork yet. She hadn't even seen any paths, though she knew they had to be there, cutting from village to village and leading to the fields and the hut of the sick cottar Eliwys had gone to see.

They climbed a low hill, and at the top of it Father Roche looked back to see if they were following. He knows where the drop is, Kivrin thought. She had hoped he had some idea where it was, that Gawyn had described it to him or told him which road it lay along, but he hadn't had to. Father Roche already knew where the drop was. He had been there.

Agnes and Kivrin came to the top of the hill, but all she could see was trees, and below them more trees. They had to be in Wychwood Forest, but if they were, there were over a hundred square kilometres in which the drop could be hidden. She would never have found it on her own. She could scarcely see ten metres into the undergrowth.

She was amazed at the thickness of the woods as they came down the hill into the heart of them. There were clearly no paths between the trees here. There was scarcely any space at all, and what there was, was filled with fallen branches and tangled thickets and snow.

She had been wrong about not recognising anything – she knew these woods after all. It was the forest Snow White had got lost in, and Hansel and Gretel, and all those princes. There were wolves in it, and bears, and perhaps even witches' cottages, and that was where all those stories had come from, wasn't it, the Middle Ages? And no wonder. Anyone could get lost in here.

Roche stopped and stood beside his donkey while Rosemund cantered back to him and they caught up, and Kivrin wondered wryly if he had lost his way. But as soon as they came up to him, he plunged off through a thicket and on to an even narrower path that wasn't visible from the road.

Rosemund couldn't pass Father Roche and his donkey without shoving them aside, but she followed nearly treading on the donkey's hind hooves, and Kivrin wondered again what was bothering her. 'Sir Bloet has many powerful friends,' Lady Imeyne had said. She had called him an ally, but Kivrin wondered if he really was, or if Rosemund's father had told her something about him that made her so distressed at the prospect of his coming to Ashencote.

They went a short way along the path, past a thicket of willows that looked like the one by the drop, and then turned off the path, squeezing through a stand of firs and emerging next to a holly tree.

Kivrin had been expecting holly bushes like the ones in Brasenose's quad, but this was a tree. It towered over them, spreading out above the confines of the spruces, its red berries bright among the masses of glossy leaves.

Father Roche began taking the sacks from the back of the donkey, Agnes attempting to help him. Rosemund pulled a short, fat-bladed knife out of her girdle and began hacking at the sharp-leaved lower branches.

Kivrin waded through the snow to the other side of the tree. She had caught a glimpse of white she thought might be the stand of birches, but it was only a branch, half-fallen between two trees and covered with snow.

Agnes appeared, with Roche behind her carrying a wicked-looking dagger. Kivrin had thought that knowing who he was would work some transformation, but he still looked like a cut-throat, standing there looming over Agnes.

He handed Agnes one of the coarse bags. 'You must hold the bag open like this,' he said, bending down to show her how the top of the bag should be folded back, 'and I will put the branches into it.' He began chopping at the branches, oblivious to the spiky leaves. Kivrin took the branches from him and put them in the bag carefully, so the stiff leaves wouldn't break.

'Father Roche,' she said, 'I wanted to thank you for helping me when I was ill and for bringing me to the manor when I—'

'When that you were fallen,' he said, hacking at a stubborn branch.

She had intended to say, 'when I was set upon by thieves', and his response surprised her. She remembered falling off the horse and wondered if that was when he had come along. But if it was, they had already come a long way from the drop, and he wouldn't know where it was. And she remembered him *there*, at the drop.

There was no point in speculating. 'Do you know the place where Gawyn found me?' she asked, and held her breath.

'Aye,' he said, sawing at a thick branch.

She felt suddenly sick with relief. He knew where the drop was. 'Is it far from here?'

'Nay,' he said. He wrenched the branch off.

'Would you take me there?' Kivrin asked.

'Why would you go there?' Agnes asked, spreading her arms out wide to keep the bag open. 'What if the wicked men be still there?'

Roche was looking at her as if he were wondering the same thing.

'I thought that if I saw the place, I might remember who I am and where I came from,' she said.

He handed her the branch, holding it so she could take it without being stabbed. 'I will take you there,' he said.

'Thank you,' Kivrin said. Thank you. She slid the branch in next to the others, and Roche tied the top shut and hoisted the bag over his shoulder.

Rosemund appeared, dragging her bag in the snow behind her. 'Are you not finished yet?' she said.

Roche took her bag too, and tied them on the donkey's back. Kivrin lifted Agnes on to her pony and helped Rosemund mount, and Father Roche knelt and linked his big hands so Kivrin could step up into the stirrup.

He had helped her back on the white horse when she fell off. When that she was fallen. She remembered his big hands steadying her. But they had come a long way from the drop by then, and why would Gawyn have taken Roche all the way back to the drop? She did not remember going back, but it was all so dim and confused. In her delirium it must have seemed further than it was.

Roche led the donkey back through the firs and on to the path, going back the way they had come. Rosemund let him get ahead and then said, in a voice just like Imeyne's, 'Where goes he now? The ivy lies not this way.'

'We go to see the place where Lady Katherine was set upon,' Agnes said.

Rosemund looked at Kivrin suspiciously. 'Why would you go thence?' she asked. 'Your goods and gear have already been fetched to the manor.'

'She wots that if she sees the place she will remember

somewhat,' Agnes said. 'Lady Kivrin, if you remember you who you are, must you return home?'

'Certes, she will,' Rosemund said. 'She must needs return to her family. She cannot stay with us for ever.' She was only doing this to provoke Agnes, and it worked.

'She *can*!' Agnes said. 'She will be our nurse.'

'Why would she wish to stay with such a mewling babe?' Rosemund said, kicking her horse into a trot.

'I am no babe!' Agnes called after her. 'You are the babe!' She rode back to Kivrin. 'I do not wish you to leave me!'

·'I won't leave you,' she said. 'Come, Father Roche is waiting.'

He was at the road, and as soon as they rode up he started on. Rosemund was already far ahead, dashing along the snow-filled path, sending up sprays of snow.

They crossed a little stream and came to a fork, the part they were on curving away to the right, the other continuing nearly straight for a hundred metres or so and then taking a sharp turn to the left. Rosemund sat at the fork, letting her horse stamp and toss its head to express her impatience.

I fell off the white horse at a fork in the road, Kivrin thought, trying to remember the trees, the road, the little stream, anything. There were dozens of forks along the paths that crisscrossed Wychwood Forest and no reason to think this was the one, but it apparently was. Father Roche turned right at the fork and went a few metres and then plunged into the woods, leading the donkey.

There were no willows where he left the road, and no hill. He must be going back the way Gawyn had brought her. She remembered them going a long way through the woods before they came to the fork.

They followed him into the trees, Rosemund in the rear, and almost immediately had to dismount and lead their horses. Roche wasn't following any path that Kivrin could see. He picked his way through the snow, ducking under low branches that showered snow down on his neck, and skirting around a spiny clump of blackthorn.

Kivrin tried to memorise the scenery so she could find her way back here, but it all had a defeating sameness. As long as there was snow she could follow their footprints and hoofprints. She would have to come back alone before it melted and mark the trail with notches or scraps of cloth or something. Or breadcrumbs, like Hansel or Gretel.

It was easy to see how they, and Snow White, and the princes, had got lost in the woods. They had only gone a few hundred metres and already, looking back, Kivrin wasn't sure which direction the road lay, even with the footprints. Hansel and Gretel could have wandered for months and never found their way back home, or found the witch's cottage either.

Father Roche's donkey stopped.

'What is it?' Kivrin asked.

Father Roche led the donkey off to the side and tied it to an alder tree. 'This is the place.'

It wasn't the drop. It was scarcely even a clearing, only a space where an oak tree had spread out its branches and kept the other trees from growing. It made almost a tent, and under it the ground was only powdered with snow.

'Can we build a fire?' Agnes asked, walking under the branches to the remains of a campfire. A fallen log had been dragged over to it. Agnes sat down on it. 'I am cold,' she said, poking at the blackened stones with her foot.

It hadn't burned very long. The sticks were barely charred. Someone had kicked dirt on it to put it out. Father Roche had squatted in front of her, the light from the fire flickering on his face.

'Well?' Rosemund said impatiently. 'Do you remember aught?'

She had been here. She remembered the fire. She had thought they were lighting it for the stake. But that couldn't be right. Roche had been at the drop. She remembered him leaning over her as she sat against the wagon wheel.

'Are you sure this is the place where Gawyn found me?'

'Aye,' he said, frowning.

'If the wicked man comes, I will fight him with my dirk,' Agnes said, pulling one of the half-charred sticks out of the fire and brandishing it in the air. The blackened end broke off. Agnes squatted next to the fire and pulled out another stick and then sat down on the ground, her back against the log, and struck the two sticks together. Pieces of charred wood flew off them.

Kivrin looked at Agnes. She had sat against the log while they made the fire, and Gawyn had leaned over her, his hair red in the fire's light, and said something to her that she couldn't understand. And then he had put the fire out, kicking it apart with his boots, and the smoke had come up and blinded her.

'Have you remembered you?' Agnes said, tossing the sticks back among the stones.

Roche was still frowning at her. 'Are you ill, Lady Katherine?' he asked.

'No,' she said, trying to smile. 'It was just . . . I'd hoped that if I saw the place where I was attacked, I might remember.'

He looked at her solemnly a moment, the way he had in the church, and then turned and went over to his donkey. 'Come,' he said.

'Have you remembered?' Agnes insisted, clapping her fur mittens together. They were covered with soot.

'Agnes!' Rosemund said. 'Look you how you have dirtied your mittens.' She pulled Agnes roughly to her feet. 'And you have ruined your cloak, sitting in the cold snow. You wicked girl!'

Kivrin pulled the two girls apart. 'Rosemund, untie Agnes' pony,' she said. 'It is time to go gather the ivy.' She brushed the snow off Agnes' cloak and wiped ineffectually at the white fur.

Father Roche was standing by his donkey, waiting for them, still with that odd, sober expression.

'We'll clean your mittens when we get home,' she said hastily. 'Come, we must go with Father Roche.'

Kivrin took the mare's reins and followed the girls and Father Roche back the way they had come for a few metres and then in another direction that brought them almost immediately out on to a road. She couldn't see the fork, and she wondered if they were further along the road or on a different road altogether. It all looked the same – willows and little clearings and oak trees.

It was clear what had happened. Gawyn had tried to take her to the manor, but she had been too ill. She had fallen off his horse and he had taken her into the woods and built a campfire and left her there, propped against the fallen log, while he went for help.

Or he had intended to build a fire and stay there with her until morning, and Father Roche had seen the campfire and come to

254

help, and between them they had taken her to the manor. Father Roche had no idea where the drop was. He had assumed Gawyn had found her there, under the oak tree.

The image of him leaning over her as she sat against the wagon wheel was part of her delirium. She had dreamed it as she lay in the sickroom, the way she had dreamed the bells and the stake and the white horse.

'Where does he go now?' Rosemund asked peevishly, and Kivrin felt like slapping her. 'There is ivy nearer to home. And now it begins to rain.'

She was right. The mist was turning into a drizzle.

'We could have been finished and home ere now if the babe Agnes had not brought her puppy!' She galloped off ahead again, and Kivrin didn't even try to stop her.

'Rosemund is a churl,' Agnes said.

'Yes,' Kivrin said. 'She is. Do you know what's the matter with her?'

'It is because of Sir Bloet,' Agnes said. 'She is to wed him.'

'What?' Kivrin said. Imeyne had said something about a wedding, but she'd assumed one of Sir Bloet's daughters was to marry one of Lord Guillaume's sons. 'How can Sir Bloet marry Rosemund? Isn't he already married to Lady Yvolde?'

'Nay,' Agnes said, looking surprised. 'Lady Yvolde is Sir Bloet's sister.'

'But Rosemund isn't old enough,' she said, and knew she was. Girls in the 1300s had frequently been betrothed before they were of age, sometimes even at birth. Marriage in the Middle Ages had been a business arrangement, a way to join lands and enhance social standing, and Rosemund had no doubt been groomed from Agnes' age to be married to someone like Sir Bloet. But every mediaeval story of virginal girls married to toothless, dissipated old men came to her in a rush.

'Does Rosemund like Sir Bloet?' Kivrin asked. Of course she didn't like him. She had been hateful, ill-tempered, nearly hysterical ever since she heard he was coming.

'*I* like him,' Agnes said. 'He is to give me a silver bridlechain when they wed.'

Kivrin looked ahead at Rosemund, waiting far down the road.

Sir Bloet might not be old and dissipated at all. She was assuming that the way she had assumed Lady Yvolde was his wife. He might be young, and Rosemund's bad temper might only be nervousness. Or she might change her mind about him before the wedding. Girls weren't usually married till they were fourteen or fifteen, certainly not before they started exhibiting signs of maturation.

'When are they to be married?' Kivrin asked Agnes.

'At Eastertide,' Agnes said.

They had come to another fork. This one was much narrower, the two roads running nearly parallel for a hundred metres before the one Rosemund had taken started up a low hill.

Twelve years old and to be married in three months. No wonder Lady Eliwys hadn't wanted Sir Bloet to know they were here. Perhaps she didn't approve of Rosemund marrying so young, and the betrothal had only been arranged to get her husband out of the trouble he was in.

Rosemund rode to the top of the hill and galloped back to Father Roche. 'Where do you lead us?' she demanded. 'We come soon to open ground.'

'We are nearly there,' Father Roche said mildly.

She wheeled her mare round and galloped out of sight over the hill, reappeared, galloped back nearly to Kivrin and Agnes, turned the mare sharply, and rode ahead again. Like the rat in the trap, Kivrin thought, frantically looking for a way out.

The drizzle was turning into a sleety rain. Father Roche pulled his hood up over his tonsured head and led the donkey up the low hill. It plodded steadily up the incline to the top, and then stopped Father Roche jerked on the reins, and the donkey pulled back against them.

Kivrin and Agnes caught up to him. 'What's wrong?' Kivrin asked.

'Come, Balaam,' Father Roche said, and took hold of the reins with both his huge hands, but the donkey didn't budge. It strained against the priest, digging in its rear hooves and leaning back so it was nearly sitting.

'Mayhap he likes not the rain,' Agnes said.

'Can we help?' Kivrin asked.

'Nay,' he said, waving them past him. 'Ride ahead. It will go better with him if the horses are not here.'

He wrapped the reins round his hand and went round behind as if he intended to push. Kivrin rode over the crest with Agnes, looking back to make sure the donkey didn't suddenly kick him in the head. They started down the other side.

The forest below them was veiled in rain. It was already melting the snow from the road, and the bottom of the hill was a muddy bog. There were thick bushes on either side, covered with snow. Rosemund sat at the top of the next hill. It had trees only halfway up its sides, and above them there was an expanse of snow. And beyond that, Kivrin thought, is an open plain and a view of the road, and Oxford.

'Where are you going, Kivrin? Wait!' Agnes cried, but Kivrin was already down the hill and off her roan shaking the snow-covered bushes, trying to see if they were willows. They were, and beyond them she could see the crown of a big oak. She threw the roan's reins over the reddish willow branches, and pushed into the thicket. The snow had frozen the willow branches together. She struck at them, and snow showered down on her. A flurry of birds launched itself into the air, screeching. She fought her way through the snowy branches and pushed through to the clearing that had to be there. It was.

And there was the oak, and beyond it, away from the road, the stand of white-trunked birches that had looked like thinner woods. It had to be the drop.

But it didn't look right. The clearing had been smaller, hadn't it? And the oak had had more leaves on it, more nests. There was a blackthorn bush to one side of the clearing, its purple-black buds poking out from the vicious thorns. She didn't remember it being there. She would surely have remembered that, wouldn't she?

It's the snow, she thought, it's making the clearing look larger. It was nearly half a metre deep here, and smooth, untouched. It didn't look as if anyone had ever been here.

'Is this the place where Father Roche would have us gather ivy?' Rosemund said, pushing through the thicket. She looked round the clearing, her hands on her hips. 'There is no ivy here.'

There had been ivy, hadn't there, wound around the base of

the oak, and mushrooms? It's the snow, she thought. The snow has covered up all the distinguishing landmarks. And the tracks, where Gawyn had dragged away the wagon and the boxes.

The casket – Gawyn had not brought the casket back to the manor. He hadn't seen it because she'd hidden it in the weeds by the road.

She pushed past Rosemund through the willows, not even trying to avoid the showering snow. The casket would be buried in snow, too, but it wasn't as deep by the road, and the casket was nearly forty centimetres tall.

'Lady Katherine!' Rosemund shouted, right behind her. 'Where would you *now*?'

'Kivrin!' Agnes said, a pathetic echo. She had tried to climb down off her pony in the middle of the road, but she had got her foot caught in the stirrup. 'Lady Kivrin, come you here!'

Kivrin looked at her blindly for a moment, and then glanced up the hill.

Father Roche was still at the top, struggling with the donkey. She had to find the casket before he came. 'Stay on your pony, Agnes,' she said and began scrabbling at the snow under the willows.

'What do you seek?' Rosemund said. 'There is no ivy here!'

'Lady Kivrin, you come now!' Agnes said.

Perhaps the snow had bent the willows over, and the casket was further in underneath them. She bent over, clinging to the thin, brittle branches, and tried to sweep the snow aside. But the trunk wasn't there. She had seen that as soon as she started. The willows had protected the weeds and the ground underneath them. There were only a few centimetres of snow. But if this is the place, it must be here, Kivrin thought numbly. If this is the place.

'Lady Kivrin!' Agnes shouted, and Kivrin glanced back at her. She had managed to get down off her pony and was running towards Kivrin.

'Don't run,' Kivrin started to say, but she didn't get it half out before Agnes caught her foot on one of the ruts and went down.

It knocked the breath out of her, and Kivrin and Rosemund were both to her before she even started to cry. Kivrin scooped her into her arms and pushed her hand against Agnes' middle to straighten her and make her take a breath.

Agnes gasped, and then drew in a long breath and began to shriek.

'Go and fetch Father Roche,' Kivrin said to Rosemund. 'He's at the top of the hill. His donkey baulked.'

'He is already coming,' Rosemund said. Kivrin turned her head. He was running clumsily down the hill, without the donkey, and Kivrin almost called out 'Don't run!' to him, too, but he could not have heard her over Agnes' screaming.

'Shh,' Kivrin said. 'You're all right. You just had the wind knocked out of you.'

Father Roche caught up to them, and Agnes immediately flung herself across into his arms. He hugged her against him. 'Hush, *Agnus*,' he murmured in his wonderful comforting voice. 'Hush.' Her screams quieted to sobs.

'Where did you hurt yourself?' Kivrin asked, brushing the snow from Agnes' cloak. 'Did you scrape your hands?'

Father Roche turned her round in his arms so Kivrin could take her white fur mittens off her. Her hands were bright red, but they weren't scraped. 'Where did you hurt yourself?'

'She is not hurt,' Rosemund said. 'She cries because she is a babe!'

'I am *not* a babe!' Agnes said with such force she nearly flung herself out of Father Roche's arms. 'I struck my knee on the ground.'

'Which one?' Kivrin asked. 'The one you hurt before?'

'Yes! Do not look!' she said as Kivrin reached for her leg.

'All right, I won't,' Kivrin said. The knee had been scabbing over. She had probably knocked the scab loose. Unless it was bleeding badly enough to soak through her leather hose, there was no point in making her colder by undressing her here in the snow. 'But you must let me look at it at home.'

'Can we go thence now?' Agnes asked.

Kivrin looked helplessly across at the thicket. This had to be the place. The willows, the clearing, the treeless crest. It had to be the place. Perhaps she had put the casket further back in the thicket than she thought, and the snow—

'I would go home *now*!' Agnes said, and began to sob. 'I am *cold*!'

'All right.' Kivrin nodded. Agnes' mittens were too wet to put back on her. Kivrin took off her borrowed gloves and gave them to her. They went all the way up Agnes' arms, which delighted her, and Kivrin began to think she had forgotten about her knee, but when Father Roche tried to put her on her pony, she sobbed, 'I would ride with you.'

Kivrin nodded again and got on her roan. Father Roche handed Agnes up to her and led Agnes' pony up the hill. The donkey was standing at the top, by the side of the road, eating the weeds that poked up through the thin snow.

Kivrin looked back at the thicket through the rain, trying to see the clearing. It's surely the drop, she told herself, but she wasn't sure. Even the hill looked somehow wrong from here.

Father Roche took hold of the donkey's reins, and the donkey immediately stiffened and dug in its hooves, but as soon as Father Roche turned its head and started down the far side of the hill with Agnes' pony, it came willingly.

The rain was melting the snow, and Rosemund's mare slipped a little as she galloped it on the straight stretch back to the fork. She slowed it to a trot.

At the next fork, Roche took the left-hand way. There were willows all along it, and oak trees, and muddy ruts at the bottom of every hill.

'Do we go home now, Kivrin?' Agnes said, shivering against her.

'Yes,' Kivrin said. She pulled the tail of her cloak forward over Agnes. 'Does your knee still hurt?'

'Nay. We did not gather any ivy.' She sat up straight and twisted round to look at Kivrin. 'Did you remember you when you saw the place?'

'No,' Kivrin said.

'Good,' Agnes said, settling back against her. 'Now you must stay with us for ever.'

CHAPTER SEVENTEEN

Andrews did not telephone Dunworthy until late afternoon on Christmas Day. Colin had, of course, insisted on getting up at an ungodly hour to open his small pile of gifts.

'Are you going to stay in bed all day?' he'd demanded while Dunworthy groped for his spectacles. 'It's nearly eight o'clock.'

It was in fact a quarter past six, pitch-black outside, too dark even to see if it was still raining. Colin had had a good deal more sleep than he had. After the interchurch service, Dunworthy had sent Colin back to Balliol and gone to Infirmary to find out about Latimer.

'He has a fever, but no lung involvement thus far,' Mary had told him. 'He came in at five, said he'd started feeling headachy and confused around one. Forty-eight hours on the button. There's obviously no need to question him to find out who he contracted it from. How are *you* feeling?'

She had made him stay for blood tests, and then a new case had come in and he'd waited to see if he could identify him. It was nearly one before he'd gone to bed.

Colin handed Dunworthy a cracker and insisted he snap it, put on the yellow tissue paper crown, and read his motto aloud. It said, 'When are Santa's reindeer most likely to come inside? When the door is open.'

Colin was already wearing his red crown. He sat on the floor and opened his gifts. The soap tablets were a huge success. 'See,' Colin said, sticking out his tongue, 'they turn it different colours.' They did, also his teeth and the edges of his lips.

He seemed pleased with the book, though it was obvious he

wished there were holos. He flipped through the pages, looking at the illustrations.

'Look at this,' he said, thrusting the volume at Dunworthy, who was still trying to wake up.

It was a knight's tomb, with the standard carved effigy in full armour on top, his face and posture the image of eternal rest, but on the side, in an inset frieze like a window into the tomb, the dead knight's corpse struggled up in his coffin, his tattered flesh falling away from him like grave wrappings, his skeleton's hands curved into frantic claws, his face a skull's empty-socketed horror. Worms crawled in and out between his legs, over and under his sword. 'Oxfordshire, c 1350', the caption read. 'An example of the macabre tomb decoration prevalent following the bubonic plague.'

'Isn't it apocalyptic?' Colin said delightedly.

He was even polite about the muffler. 'I suppose it's the thought that counts, isn't it?' he said, holding it up by one end, and then after a minute, 'Perhaps I can wear it when I visit the sick. They won't care what it looks like.'

'Visit what sick?' Dunworthy asked.

Colin got up off the floor and went over to his duffel and began rummaging through it. 'The vicar asked me last night if I'd run errands for him, check on people and take them medicine and things.'

He fished a paper bag out of the duffel. 'This is your present,' he said, handing it to Dunworthy. 'It's not wrapped,' he added unnecessarily. 'Finch said we ought to save paper for the epidemic.'

Dunworthy opened the bag and pulled out a flattish red book.

'It's an appointment calendar,' Colin said. 'It's so you can mark off the days till your girl gets back.' He opened it to the first page. 'See, I made sure to get one that had December.'

'Thank you,' Dunworthy said, opening it. Christmas. The Slaughter of the Innocents. New Year's. Epiphany. 'That was very thoughtful.'

'I wanted to get you this model of Carfax Tower that plays "I Heard the Bells on Christmas Day",' Colin said, 'but it cost twenty pounds!'

The telephone rang, and Colin and Dunworthy both dived for it. 'I'll bet it's my mother,' Colin said.

It was Mary, calling from the Infirmary. 'How are you feeling?'

'Half-asleep,' Dunworthy said.

Colin grinned at him.

'How's Latimer?' Dunworthy asked.

'Good,' Mary said. She was still wearing her lab coat, but she'd combed her hair and she looked cheerful. 'He seems to have a very mild case. We've established a connection with the South Carolina virus.'

'Latimer was in South Carolina?'

'No. One of the students I had you question last night . . . good Lord, I mean two night ago. I'm losing all track of time. One of the ones who'd been at the dance in Headington. He lied at first because he'd skipped off from his college to see a young woman and left a friend to cover for him.'

'Skipped off to South Carolina?'

'No, London. But the young woman was from the States. She'd flown in from Texas and changed planes in Charleston, South Carolina. The CDC's working to find out what cases were in the airport. Let me speak to Colin. I want to wish him a happy Christmas.'

Dunworthy put him on, and he launched into a recital of his gifts, down to and including the motto in his cracker. 'Mr Dunworthy gave me a book about the Middle Ages.' He held it up to the screen. 'Did you know they cut off people's heads for stealing and stuck them up on London Bridge?'

'Thank her for the muffler, and don't tell her you're running errands for the vicar,' Dunworthy whispered, but Colin was already holding the receiver out to him. 'She wants to speak to you again.'

'It's clear you're taking good care of him,' Mary said. 'I'm very grateful. I haven't been home yet, and I should have hated him to be alone on Christmas. I don't suppose the promised gifts from his mother have arrived?'

'No,' Dunworthy said cautiously, looking at Colin, who was looking at the pictures in the Middle Ages book.

'Nor telephoned,' she said disgustedly. 'The woman hasn't a

drop of maternal blood in her body. For all she knows, Colin might be lying in hospital with a temp of forty degrees, mightn't he?'

'How is Badri?' Dunworthy asked.

'The fever was down a bit this morning, but there's still a good deal of lung involvement. We're putting him on synthamycin. The South Carolina cases have responded very well to it.' She promised to try to come over for Christmas dinner and then rang off.

Colin looked up from his book. 'Did you know in the Middle Ages they burned people at the stake?'

Mary didn't come nor telephone, and neither did Andrews. Dunworthy sent Colin over to hall for breakfast and tried phoning the tech, but all the lines were engaged, 'due to the holiday crush,' the computer voice said, obviously not reprogrammed since the beginning of the quarantine. It advised him to delay all nonessential calls until the next day. He tried twice more, with the same result.

Finch came over, bearing a tray. 'Are you all right, sir?' he said anxiously. 'You're not feeling ill?'

'I'm not feeling ill. I'm waiting for a trunk call to come through.'

'Oh, thank goodness, sir. When you didn't come over for breakfast I feared the worst.' He took the rain-spotted cover off the tray. 'I'm afraid it's a poor sort of Christmas breakfast, but we're nearly out of eggs. I don't know what sort of Christmas dinner it will be. There isn't a goose left inside the perimeter.'

It actually seemed to be quite a respectable breakfast, a boiled egg, kippers, muffins with jam.

'I tried for a Christmas pudding, sir, but we're nearly out of brandy,' Finch said, pulling a plastic envelope out from under the tray and handing it to Dunworthy.

He opened it. On top was an NHS directive headed: 'Early Symptoms of Influenza. 1.) Disorientation. 2.) Headache. 3.) Muscle Aches. Avoid contracting it. Wear your NHS regulation face mask at all times.'

'Face mask?' Dunworthy asked.

'The NHS delivered them this morning,' Finch said. 'I don't

know how we're going to manage the washing up. We're nearly out of soap.'

There were four other directives, all similar in tone, and a note from William Gaddson with a printout of Badri's credit account for Monday the twentieth of December attached. Badri had apparently spent that missing time from noon to half past two Christmas shopping. He had purchased four books, paperback, at Blackwell's, a muffler, red, and a digital carillon, miniature, at Debenham's. Wonderful. That meant dozens and dozens more contacts.

Colin came in carrying a napkinful of muffins. He was still wearing his paper crown, which was a good deal the worse for the rain.

'It would reassure everyone, sir,' Finch said, 'if after your call comes through you'd come over to hall. Mrs Gaddson particularly is convinced you've come down with the virus. She said you'd contracted it through poor ventilation in the dormitories.'

'I'll put in an appearance,' Dunworthy promised.

Finch went to the door and then turned back. 'About Mrs Gaddson, sir. She's behaving dreadfully, criticising the college and demanding that she be moved in with her son. She's completely undermining morale.'

'I'll say,' Colin said, dumping the muffins on the table. 'The Gallstone told me hot bread was bad for my immune system.'

'Isn't there some sort of volunteer work she could do at Infirmary or something?' Finch asked. 'To keep her out of college?'

'We can hardly inflict her on poor helpless flu victims. It might kill them. What about asking the vicar? He was looking for volunteers to run errands.'

'The vicar?' Colin said. 'Have a heart, Mr Dunworthy. *I'm* working for the vicar.'

'The priest from Holy Re-Formed then,' Dunworthy said. 'He's fond of reciting the Mass in Time of Pestilence for morale. They should get along swimmingly.'

'I'll phone him straight away,' Finch said, and left.

Dunworthy ate his breakfast, except for the muffin, which Colin appropriated, and then took the empty tray over to hall, leaving orders for Colin to come get him *immediately* if the tech rang up. It was still raining, the trees black and dripping and the Christmas tree lights spotted with rain.

Everyone was still at table except for the bell ringers, who stood off to one side in their white gloves, their handbells on the table in front of them. Finch was demonstrating the wearing of the NHS regulation masks, pulling off the tapes at either side and pressing them to his cheeks.

'You don't look well at all, Mr Dunworthy,' Mrs Gaddson said. 'And no wonder. The conditions in this college are appalling. It is a wonder to me that there has not been an epidemic before this. Poor ventilation and an extremely uncooperative staff. Your Mr Finch was quite rude to me when I spoke to him about moving into my son's rooms. He told me *I* had chosen to be in Oxford during a quarantine, and that I had to take whatever accommodation I was given.'

Colin came skidding in. 'There's someone on the telephone for you,' he said.

Dunworthy started past her, but she placed herself solidly in his way. 'I told Mr Finch that *he* might be content to stay at home when his son was in danger, but that I was not.'

'I'm afraid I'm wanted on the telephone,' Dunworthy said.

'I told him no real mother could fail to go when her child was alone and ill in a faraway place.'

'Mr *Dun*worthy,' Colin said. 'Come along!'

'Of course you clearly have no idea what I'm talking about. Look at this child!' She grabbed Colin by the arm. 'Running about in the pouring rain with no coat on!'

Dunworthy took advantage of her shift in position to get past her.

'You obviously care nothing about your boy's catching the Indian flu,' she said. Colin wrenched free. 'Letting him gorge himself on muffins and go about soaked to the skin.'

Dunworthy sprinted across the quad Colin at his heels.

'I shall not be surprised if this virus turns out to have originated here in Balliol,' Mrs Gaddson shouted after them. 'Sheer negligence, that's what it is. Sheer negligence!'

Dunworthy burst into the room and snatched up the phone.

There was no picture. 'Andrews,' he shouted. 'Are you there? I can't see you.'

'The telephone system's overbooked,' Montoya said. 'They've cut the visual. It's Lupe Montoya. Is Mr Basingame salmon or trout?'

'What?' Dunworthy said, frowning at the blank screen.

'I've been calling fishing guides in Scotland all morning. *When* I could get through. They say where he's gone depends on whether he's salmon or trout. What about friends? Is there someone in the University he goes fishing with who might know?'

'I don't know,' Dunworthy said. 'Ms Montoya, I'm afraid I'm waiting for a most important—'

'I've tried everything else – hotels, inns, boat rentals, even his barber. I tracked his wife down in Torquay, and she said he didn't tell her where he was going. I hope that doesn't mean he's off somewhere with a woman and not really in Scotland at all.'

'I hardly think Mr Basingame—'

'Yes, well, then, why doesn't anyone know where he is? And why hasn't he called in now that the epidemic's all over the papers and the vids?'

'Ms Montoya, I—'

'I suppose I'll have to call both the salmon *and* trout guides. I'll let you know if I find him.'

She rang off finally, and Dunworthy put the receiver down and stared at it, certain Andrews had tried to ring while he was on the line with Montoya.

'Didn't you say there were a lot of epidemics in the Middle Ages?' Colin asked. He was sitting in the window seat with the Middle Ages book on his knees, eating muffins.

'Yes.'

'Well, I can't find them in this book. How do you spell it?'

'Try Black Death,' Dunworthy said.

Dunworthy waited an anxious quarter of an hour and then tried to ring Andrews again. The lines were still jammed.

'Did you know the Black Death was in Oxford?' Colin said. He had polished off the muffins and was back to the soap tablets. 'At Christmas. Just like us!'

'Influenza scarcely compares with the plague,' he said,

watching the telephone as if he could will it to ring. 'The Black Death killed one third to one half of Europe.'

'I know,' Colin said. 'And the plague was a lot more interesting. It was spread by rats, and you got these enormous bobos—'

'Buboes.'

'Buboes under your arms, and they turned black and swelled up till they were enormous and then you died! The flu doesn't have anything like that,' he said, sounding disappointed.

'No.'

'And the flu's only one disease. There were three sorts of plague. Bubonic, that's the one with the buboes, pneumonic,' he said, pronouncing the p. 'It went in your lungs and you coughed up blood and sep-tah-keem-ic—'

'Septicaemic.'

'Septicaemic, which went into your bloodstream and killed you in three hours and your body turned black all over! Isn't that apocalyptic?'

'Yes,' Dunworthy said.

The telephone rang just after eleven o'clock and Dunworthy snatched it up again, but it was Mary, saying she wouldn't be able to manage dinner. 'We've had five new cases this morning.'

'We'll come to Infirmary as soon as my trunk call has come through,' Dunworthy promised. 'I'm waiting for one of my techs to phone. I'm going to have him come and read the fix.'

Mary looked wary. 'Have you cleared this with Gilchrist?'

'Gilchrist! He's busy planning to send Kivrin to the Black Death!'

'Nevertheless, I don't think you should do this without telling him. He *is* Acting Head, and there's no point in antagonising him. If something *has* gone wrong, and Andrews needs to abort the drop, you'll need his cooperation.' She smiled at Dunworthy. 'We'll discuss it when you come. And when you're here, I want you to have an inoculation.'

'I thought you were waiting for the analogue.'

'I was, but I'm not satisfied with the way the primary cases are responding to Atlanta's recommended course of treatment. A few of them are showing a slight improvement, but Badri is worse, if anything. I want all high-risk people to have T-cell enhancement.'

268

Andrews still hadn't phoned by noon. Dunworthy sent Colin over to Infirmary to be inoculated. He came back looking pained.

'As bad as all that?' Dunworthy asked.

'Worse,' Colin said, flinging himself down on the window seat. 'Mrs Gaddson caught me coming in. I was rubbing my arm, and she demanded to know where I'd been and why I was getting inoculated instead of William.' He looked reproachfully at Dunworthy. 'Well, it hurts! She said if anyone was high-risk it was poor Willy and it was absolute necrophilia for me to be jabbed instead of him.'

'Nepotism.'

'Nepotism. I hope the priest finds her an absolutely cadaverous job.'

'How was your Great-aunt Mary?'

'I didn't see her. They were awfully busy, beds in the corridor and everything.'

Colin and Dunworthy took turns going over to hall for Christmas dinner. Colin was back in something less than fifteen minutes. 'The bell ringers started to play,' he said. 'Mr Finch said to tell you we're out of sugar and butter and nearly out of cream.' He pulled a jam tart out of his jacket pocket. 'Why is it they never run out of Brussels sprouts?'

Dunworthy gave him orders to come and tell him at once if Andrews phoned and to take down any other messages, and went over. The bell ringers were in full cry, jangling away at a Mozart canon.

Finch handed Dunworthy a plate that seemed to be mostly Brussels sprouts. 'We're nearly out of turkey, I'm afraid, sir,' he said. 'I'm glad you've come. It's almost time for the royal Christmas message.'

The bell ringers finished the Mozart to enthusiastic applause, and Ms Taylor came over, still wearing her white gloves. 'There you are, Mr Dunworthy,' she said. 'I missed you at breakfast, and Mr Finch said you were the one to talk to. We need a practice room.'

He was tempted to say, 'I'd no idea you practised.' He ate a Brussels sprout.

'A practice room?'

'Yes. So we can practise our Chicago Surprise Minor. I've arranged with the dean of Christ Church to ring our peal here on New Year's Day, but we have to have somewhere to practise. I told Mr Finch the big room in Beard would be perfect—'

'The senior common room.'

'But Mr Finch said it was being used as store-room for supplies.'

What supplies? he thought. According to Finch, they were either out or nearly out of everything save Brussels sprouts.

'And he said the lecture rooms were being kept to use as an infirmary. We have to have a quiet place where we can focus. The Chicago Surprise Minor is very complicated. The in-and out-of-course changes and the lead end alterations require complete concentration. And of course there's the extra dodging.'

'Of course,' Dunworthy said.

'The room doesn't have to be large, but it does need to be secluded. We've been practising here in the dining-room, but there are people in and out all the time and the tenor keeps losing her place.'

'I'm sure we can find something.'

'Of course with seven bells, we should be doing Triples, but the North American Council rang Philadelphia Triples here last year, and did a very sloppy job of it, too, as I understand. The tenor a full count behind and absolutely terrible stroking. Which is an-other reason we've got to have a good practice room. Stroking is so important.'

'Of course,' Dunworthy said.

Mrs Gaddson appeared in the far doorway, looking fierce and maternal. 'I'm afraid I have an important trunk call coming in,' he said, standing up so that Ms Taylor was between him and Mrs Gaddson.

'Trunk call?' Ms Taylor said, shaking her head. 'You English! I don't understand what you're saying half the time.'

Dunworthy escaped out of the buttery door, promising to find a practice room so that they could perfect their snapping leads, and went back up to his rooms. Andrews hadn't phoned. There was one message, from Montoya. 'She said to tell you "never mind",' Colin said.

'That's all? She didn't say anything else?'

'No. She said, "Tell Mr Dunworthy never mind." '

He wondered if she had by some miracle located Basingame and obtained his signature or if she had merely found out whether he was 'salmon' or 'trout'. He debated ringing her back, but he was afraid the lines would choose that moment to unjam and Andrews would phone.

He didn't, or they didn't, until nearly four. 'I'm terribly sorry I didn't ring you sooner,' Andrews said.

There was still no picture, but Dunworthy could hear music and talk in the background. 'I was away till last night, and I've had a good deal of trouble getting through to you,' Andrews said. 'The lines have been engaged, the holiday crush, you know. I've been trying every—'

'I need you to come up to Oxford,' Dunworthy cut in. 'I need you to read a fix.'

'Of course, sir,' Andrews said promptly. 'When?'

'As soon as possible. This evening?'

'Oh,' he said, less promptly. 'Would tomorrow do? My live-in won't get in till late tonight, so we'd planned on having our Christmas tomorrow, but I could get a train up in the afternoon or evening. Will that do, or is there a limit on taking the fix?'

'The fix is already taken, but the tech's come down with a virus and I need someone to read it,' Dunworthy said. There was a sudden burst of laughter from Andrews' end. Dunworthy raised his voice. 'What time do you think you can be here?'

'I'm not certain. Can I ring you back tomorrow and tell you when I'll be coming in on the tube?'

'Yes, but you can only take the tube as far as Barton. You'll need to take a taxi from there to the perimeter. I'll arrange for you to be let through. All right, Andrews?'

He didn't answer, though Dunworthy could still hear the music. 'Andrews?' Dunworthy said. 'Are you still there?' It was maddening not to be able to see.

'Yes, sir,' Andrews said, but warily. 'What was it you said you wanted me to do?'

'Read a fix. It's already been taken, but the tech—'

'No, the other bit. About taking the train to Barton.'

'Take the train to Barton,' Dunworthy said loudly and carefully. 'That's as far as it goes. From there, you'll have to get a taxi to the quarantine perimeter.'

'Quarantine?'

'Yes,' Dunworthy said, irritated. 'I'll arrange for you to be allowed into the quarantine area.'

'What sort of quarantine?'

'A virus,' he said. 'You haven't heard about it?'

'No, sir. I was running an on-site in Florence. I only arrived back this afternoon. Is it serious?' He did not sound frightened, only interested.

'Eighty-one cases so far,' Dunworthy said.

'Eighty-two,' Colin said from the window seat.

'But they've identified it, and the vaccine's on the way. There haven't been any fatalities.'

'But a lot of unhappy people who wanted to be home for Christmas, I'll wager,' he said. 'I'll call you in the morning, then, as soon as I know what time I'll arrive.'

'Yes,' Dunworthy shouted to make sure Andrews could hear over the background noise. 'I'll be here.'

'Right,' Andrews said. There was another burst of laughter and then silence as he rang off.

'Is he coming?' Colin asked.

'Yes. Tomorrow.' He punched in Gilchrist's number.

Gilchrist appeared, sitting at his desk and looking belligerent. 'Mr Dunworthy, if this is about pulling Ms Engle out—'

I would if I could Dunworthy thought, and wondered if Gilchrist truly didn't realise Kivrin had already left the drop site and wouldn't be there if they did open the net.

'No,' he said. 'I've located a tech who can come and read the fix.'

'Mr Dunworthy, may I remind you—'

'I am fully aware that you are in charge of this drop,' Dunworthy said, trying to keep his temper. 'I was merely trying to help. Knowing the difficulty of finding techs over vac, I telephoned one in Reading. He can be here tomorrow.'

Gilchrist pursed his lips disapprovingly. 'None of this would be necessary if your tech hadn't fallen ill, but as he has, I suppose this will have to do. Have him report to me as soon as he arrives.'

Dunworthy managed to say goodbye civilly, but as soon as the screen went blank he slammed the receiver down, yanked it up again and began stabbing numbers. He would find Basingame if it took all afternoon.

But the computer came on and informed him all lines were engaged again. He laid the receiver down and stared at the blank screen.

'Are you waiting for another call?' Colin asked.

'No.'

'Then can we walk over to Infirmary? I've a present for Great-aunt Mary.'

And I can see about getting Andrews into the quarantine area, he thought. 'Excellent idea. You can wear your new muffler.'

Colin stuffed it in his jacket pocket. 'I'll put it on when we get there,' he said, grinning. 'I don't want anyone to see me on the way.'

There was no one to see them. The streets were completely deserted not even any bicycles or taxis. Dunworthy thought of the vicar's remark that when the epidemic took hold people would hole up in their houses. Either that or they had been driven inside by the sound of the Carfax carillon, which was not only still banging away at 'The Carol of the Bells' but seemed louder, echoing through the empty streets. Or they were napping after too much Christmas dinner. Or they knew enough to keep in out of the rain.

They saw no one at all until they got to Infirmary. A woman in a Burberry stood in front of the Casualties Ward holding a picket sign that said 'Ban Foreign Diseases'. A man wearing a regulation face mask opened the door for them and handed Dunworthy a very damp flyer.

Dunworthy asked at the admission desk for Mary and then read the flyer. In boldface type it said 'FIGHT INFLUENZA. VOTE TO SECEDE FROM THE EC.' Underneath was a paragraph: 'Why will you be separated from your loved ones this Christmas? Why are you forced to stay in Oxford? Why are you in danger of getting ill and *dying*? Because the EC allows infected foreigners to enter England, and England doesn't have a thing to say about it. An Indian immigrant carrying a deadly virus—'

Dunworthy didn't read the rest. He turned it over. It read, 'A Vote for Secession is a Vote for Health. Committee for an Independent Great Britain.'

Mary came in, and Colin grabbed his muffler out of his pocket and wrapped it hastily round his neck. 'Happy Christmas,' he said. 'Thank you for the muffler. Shall I open your cracker for you?'

'Yes, please,' Mary said. She looked tired. She was wearing the same lab coat she had had on two days ago. Someone had pinned a cluster of holly to the lapel.

Colin snapped the cracker.

'Put your hat on,' he said, unfolding a blue paper crown.

'Have you managed to get any rest at all?' Dunworthy asked.

'A bit,' she said, putting the crown on over her untidy grey hair. 'We've had thirty new cases since noon, and I've spent most of the day trying to get the sequencing from the WIC, but the lines are jammed.'

'I know,' Dunworthy said. 'Can I see Badri?'

'Only for a minute or two.' She frowned. 'He's not responding at all to the synthamycin, and neither are the two students from the dance in Headington. Beverly Breen is a bit improved.' She frowned. 'It worries me. Have you had your enhancement?'

'Not yet. Colin's had his.'

'And it hurt like blood,' Colin said, unfolding the slip of paper inside the cracker. 'Shall I read your motto for you?'

She nodded.

'I need to bring a tech into the quarantine area tomorrow to read Kivrin's fix,' Dunworthy said. 'What must I do to arrange it?'

'Nothing so far as I know. They're trying to keep people in, not out.'

The registrar took Mary aside, and spoke softly and urgently to her.

'I must go,' she said. 'I don't want you to leave till you've had your enchancement. Come back down here when you've seen Badri. Colin, you wait here for Mr Dunworthy.'

Dunworthy went up to Isolation. There was no one at the desk so he wrestled his way into a set of SPGs, remembering to put the gloves on last, and went inside.

The pretty nurse who had been so interested in William was taking Badri's pulse, her eyes on the screens. Dunworthy stopped at the foot of the bed.

Mary had said Badri wasn't responding, but Dunworthy was still shocked by the sight of him. His face was dark with fever again, and his eyes looked bruised, as if someone had hit him. His right arm was hooked to an elaborate cannula. It was bruised a purple-blue on the inside of the elbow. The other arm was worse, black all along the forearm.

'Badri?' he said, and the nurse shook her head.

'You can only stay a moment,' she said.

Dunworthy nodded.

She laid Badri's unresisting hand down at his side, typed something on the console and went out.

Dunworthy sat down beside the bed and looked up at the screens. They looked the same, still indecipherable, the graphs and jags and generating numbers telling him nothing. He looked at Badri, who lay there looking battered, beaten. He patted his hand gently and stood up to go.

'It was the rats,' Badri murmured.

'Badri?' Dunworthy said gently. 'It's Mr Dunworthy.'

'Mr Dunworthy . . .' Badri said, but he didn't open his eyes. 'I'm dying, aren't I?'

He felt a twinge of fear. 'No, of course not,' he said heartily. 'Where did you get that idea?'

'It's always fatal,' Badri said.

'What is?'

Badri didn't answer. Dunworthy sat with him until the nurse came in, but he didn't say anything else.

'Mr Dunworthy?' she said. 'He needs to rest.'

'I know.' He walked to the door and then looked back at Badri, lying in the bed. He opened the door.

'It killed them all,' Badri said. 'Half of Europe.'

Colin was standing at the registrar's desk when he came back down, telling her about his Christmas gifts. 'My mother's gifts didn't arrive because of the quarantine. The postman wouldn't let them through.'

Dunworthy told the registrar about the T-cell enhancement and she nodded and said, 'It will just be a moment.'

They sat down to wait. It killed them all, Dunworthy thought. Half of Europe.

'I didn't get to read her her motto,' Colin said. 'Would you like to hear it?' He didn't wait for an answer. 'Where was Father Christmas when the lights went out?' He waited expectantly.

Dunworthy shook his head.

'In the dark.'

He took his gobstopper out of his pocket, unwrapped it and stuck it in his mouth. 'You're worried about your girl, aren't you?'

'Yes.'

He folded up the gobstopper wrapper into a tiny packet. 'What I don't understand is, why can't you go get her?'

'She isn't there. We must wait for the rendezvous.'

'No, I mean why can't you go back to the same time you sent her through and get her while she was still there? Before anything happened? I mean you can go to any time you want, can't you?'

'No,' he said. 'You can *send* an historian to any time, but once she's there, the net can only operate in real time. Did you study the paradoxes at school?'

'Yes,' Colin said, but he sounded uncertain. 'They're like time-travel rules?'

'The space-time continuum doesn't allow paradoxes,' Dunworthy said. 'It would be a paradox if Kivrin made something happen that hadn't happened, or if she caused an anachronism.'

Colin was still looking uncertain.

'One of the paradoxes is that no one can be in two places at the same time. She's already been in the past for four days. There's nothing we can do to change that. It's already happened.'

'Then how does she get back?'

'When she went through, the tech took what's called a fix. It tells the tech exactly where she is, and it acts as a . . . um . . .' he groped for an understandable word. 'A tether. It ties the two times together so the net can be reopened at a certain time, and she can be picked up.'

'Like, "I'll meet you at the church at half past six"?'

'Exactly. It's called a rendezvous. Kivrin's is in two weeks. The twenty-eighth of December. On that day the tech will open the net and Kivrin will come back through.'

'I thought you said it was the same time there. How can the twenty-eighth be two weeks from now?'

'They used a different calendar in the Middle Ages. It's December the seventeenth there. Our rendezvous date is the sixth of January.' If she's there. If I can find a tech to open the net.

Colin pulled out his gobstopper and looked at it thoughtfully. It was a mottled bluish-white and looked rather like a map of the moon. He stuck it back in his mouth.

'So, if I went to 1320 on the twenty-sixth of December, I could have Christmas twice.'

'Yes, I suppose so.'

'Apocalyptic,' he said. He unfolded the gobstopper wrapper and folded it into an even tinier packet. 'I think they've forgotten about you, don't you?'

'It's beginning to look that way,' Dunworthy said. The next time a house officer came through, Dunworthy stopped him and told him he was waiting for T-cell enchancement.

'Oh?' he said, looking surprised. 'I'll try to find out about it.' He disappeared into Casualties.

They waited some more. 'It was the rats,' Badri had said. And that first night he had asked Dunworthy, 'What year is it?' But he had said there was minimal slippage. He had said the apprentice's calculations were correct.

Colin took his gobstopper out and examined it several times for change in colour. 'If something terrible happened, couldn't you break the rules?' he said, squinting at it. 'If she got her arm cut off or she died or a bomb blew her up or something?'

'They're not rules, Colin. They're scientific laws. We couldn't break them if we tried. If we attempted to reverse events that had already happened, the net wouldn't open.'

Colin spat his gobstopper into the wrapper and folded the wrinkled paper carefully around it. 'I'm sure your girl's all right,' he said.

He jammed the wrapped gobstopper in his jacket pocket and

pulled out a lumpy parcel. 'I forget to give Great-aunt Mary her Christmas present,' he said.

He jumped up and started into Casualties before Dunworthy could caution him to wait, got opposite the door and came tearing back.

'Blood! The Gallstone's here!' he said. 'She's coming this way.'

Dunworthy stood up. 'That's all that's needed.'

'This way,' Colin said. 'I came in the back door the night I got here.' He sprinted off in the other direction. 'Come on!'

Dunworthy could not manage a sprint, but he walked quickly down the labyrinth of corridors Colin indicated and out of a service entrance into a side street. A man in a sandwich board was standing outside the door in the rain. The sandwich board said, 'The doom we feared is upon us,' which seemed oddly fitting.

'I'll make certain she didn't see us,' Colin said, and dashed round to the front.

The man handed Dunworthy a flyer. 'THE END OF TIME IS NEAR!' it said in fiery capital letters. ' "Fear God, for the hour of His judgment is come." Revelation 14:7.'

Colin waved to Dunworthy from the corner. 'It's all right,' Colin said, slightly out of breath. 'She's inside shouting at the registrar.'

Dunworthy handed the flyer back to the man and followed Colin. He led the way along the side street to Woodstock Road. Dunworthy looked anxiously towards the door of Casualties but he couldn't see anyone, not even the anti-EC picketers.

Colin sprinted another block and then slowed to a walk. He pulled the packet of soap tablets out of his pocket and offered Dunworthy one.

He declined.

Colin popped a pink one in his mouth and said, none too clearly, 'This is the best Christmas I've ever had.'

Dunworthy pondered that sentiment for several blocks. The carillon was massacring 'In the Bleak Midwinter', which also seemed fitting, and the streets were still deserted, but as they turned down the Broad a familiar figure hurried towards them, hunched against the rain.

'It's Mr Finch,' Colin said.

'Good Lord,' Dunworthy said. 'What do you suppose we've run out of now?'

'I hope it's Brussels sprouts.'

Finch had looked up at the sound of their voices. 'There you are, Mr Dunworthy. Thank goodness. I've been looking for you everywhere.'

'What is it?' Dunworthy said. 'I told Ms Taylor I'd see about a practice room.'

'It isn't that, sir. It's the detainees. Two of them are down with the virus.'

⥈

Transcript from the Domesday Book
(032631–034122)

21 December 1320 (Old Style). Father Roche doesn't know where the drop is. I made him take me to the place where Gawyn met him, but even standing in the clearing didn't jog my memory. It's obvious Gawyn didn't come across him until he was a long way from the drop, and by that time I was completely delirious.

And I realised today I'll never be able to find the drop on my own. The woods are too big, and they're full of clearings and oak trees and willow thickets that all look alike now that it's snowed I should have marked the drop with something besides the casket.

Gawyn will have to show me where the drop is and he's not back yet. Rosemund told me it's only a half-day's ride to Courcy, but that he will probably spend the night there because of the rain.

It's been raining hard since we got back, and I suppose I should be happy since it may melt the snow, but it makes it impossible for me to go out and look for the drop, and it's freezing in the manor house. Everyone's wearing their cloaks and huddling next to the fire.

What *do* the villagers do? Their huts can't even keep the wind out, and the one I was in had no sign of a blanket.

They must be literally freezing, and Rosemund said the steward said it was going to rain till Christmas Eve.

Rosemund apologised for her ill-tempered behaviour in the woods and told me, 'I was wroth with my sister.'

Agnes had nothing to do with it – what upset her was obviously the news that her fiancé had been invited for Christmas, and when I had a chance with Rosemund alone, I asked her if she was worried over her marriage.

'My father has arranged it,' she said, threading her needle. 'We were betrothed at Martinmas. We are to be wed at Easter.'

'And it is with your consent?' I asked.

'It is a good match,' she said. 'Sir Bloet is highly placed, and he has holdings that adjoin my father's.'

'Do you like him?'

She stabbed the needle into the linen in the wooden frame. 'My father would never let me come to harm,' she said, and pulled the long thread through.

She didn't volunteer anything else, and all I could get out of Agnes was that Sir Bloet was nice and had brought her a silver penny, no doubt as part of the betrothal gifts.

Agnes was too concerned about her knee to tell me anything else. She stopped complaining about it halfway home, and then limped exaggeratedly when she got down off the roan. I thought she was just trying to get attention, but when I looked at it, the scab had come off completely. The area around it is red and swollen.

I washed it off, wrapped it in as clean a cloth as I could find (I'm afraid it may have been one of Imeyne's coifs – I found it in the chest at the foot of the bed), and made her sit quietly by the fire and play with her knight, but I'm worried. If it gets infected, it could be serious. There weren't any antimicrobials in the 1300s.

Eliwys is worried, too. She clearly expected Gawyn back tonight, and has been going to stand by the screens all day, looking out of the door. I have not been able to figure out how she feels about Gawyn. Sometimes, like today, I think she loves him, and is afraid of what that means for both of them. Adultery was a mortal sin in the eyes of the Church, and often a dangerous one. But most of the time I am convinced that his *amour* is completely unrequited, that she is so worried about her husband that she doesn't know Gawyn exists.

The pure, unattainable lady was the ideal of courtly romances, but it's clear he doesn't know whether or not she loves him either. His rescuing me in the wood and his story of the renegades was only an attempt to impress her (which would have been much more impressive if there *had* been twenty renegades, all armed with swords and maces and battle axes). He would obviously do anything to win her, and Lady Imeyne knows it. Which is why, I think, he's been sent off to Courcy.

⸺⸙⸺

CHAPTER EIGHTEEN

By the time they got back to Balliol, two more of the detainees were down with the virus. Dunworthy sent Colin to bed and helped Finch get the detainees to bed and phone the Infirmary.

'All our ambulances are out,' the registrar told him. 'We'll send one as soon as possible.'

As soon as possible was midnight. He didn't get back and to bed till past one.

Colin was asleep on the cot Finch had set up for him, *The Age of Chivalry* next to his head. Dunworthy debated pulling the book away but he didn't want to risk waking him. He went in to bed.

Kivrin could not be in the plague. Badri had said there was four hours' slippage, and the plague had not hit England until 1348. Kivrin had been sent to 1320.

He turned over and closed his eyes determinedly. She could not be in the plague. Badri was delirious. He had said all sorts of things, talked about lids and breaking china as well as rats. None of it made any sense. It was the fever speaking. He had told Dunworthy to back up. He had given him imaginary notes. None of it meant anything.

'It was the rats,' Badri had said. The contemps hadn't known it was spread by fleas on the rats. They had had no idea what caused it. They had accused everyone – Jews and witches and the insane. They had murdered halfwits and hanged old women. They had burned strangers at the stake.

He got out of bed and padded into the sitting-room. He tiptoed around Colin's cot and slid *The Age of Chivalry* out from under Colin's head. Colin stirred but didn't wake.

Dunworthy sat on the window seat and looked up the Black

Death. It had started in China in 1333, and moved west on trading ships to Messina in Sicily and from there to Pisa. It had spread through Italy and France – eighty thousand dead in Siena, a hundred thousand in Florence, three hundred thousand in Rome – before it crossed the Channel. It had reached England in 1348, 'a little before the Feast of St John the Baptist,' the twenty-fourth of June.

That meant a slippage of twenty-eight years. Badri had been worried about too much slippage, but he had been talking of weeks, not years.

He reached over the cot to the bookcase and took down Fitzwiller's *Pandemics*.

'What are you doing?' Colin asked sleepily.

'Reading about the Black Death,' he whispered. 'Go back to sleep.'

'They didn't call it that,' Colin mumbled round his gob-stopper. He rolled over, wrapping himself in his blankets. 'They called it the blue sickness.'

Dunworthy took both books back to bed with him. Fitzwiller gave the date of the plague's arrival in England as St Peter's Day, the twenty-ninth of June, 1348. It had reached Oxford in December, London in October of 1349, and then moved north and back across the Channel to the Low Countries and Norway. It had gone everywhere except Bohemia, and Poland, which had a quarantine, and oddly, parts of Scotland.

Where it had gone, it had swept through the countryside like the Angel of Death, devastating entire villages, leaving no one alive to administer the last rites or bury the putrefying bodies. In one monastery, all but one of the monks had died.

The single survivor, John Clyn, had left a record: 'And lest things which should be remembered perish with time and vanish from the memory of those who are to come after us,' he had written, 'I, seeing so many evils and the whole world, as it were, placed within the grasp of the Evil One, being myself as if among the dead, I, waiting for death, have put into writing all the things that I have witnessed.'

He had written it all down, a true historian, and then had apparently died himself, all alone. His writing on the manuscript trailed off, and below it, in another hand, someone had written, 'Here, it seems, the author died.'

Someone knocked on the door. It was Finch in his bathrobe, looking bleary-eyed and distraught. 'Another one of the detainees, sir,' he said.

Dunworthy put his finger to his lips and stepped outside the door with him. 'Have you telephoned Infirmary?'

'Yes, sir, and they said it would be several hours before they can dispatch an ambulance. They said to isolate her and give her dimantadine and orange juice.'

'Which I suppose we're nearly out of,' Dunworthy said irritably.

'Yes, sir, but that's not the problem. She won't cooperate.'

Dunworthy made Finch wait outside the door while he dressed and found his face mask, and they went across to Salvin. A huddle of detainees were standing by the door, dressed in an odd assortment of underthings, coats, and blankets. Only a few of them were wearing their face masks. By the day after tomorrow they'll all be down with it, Dunworthy thought.

'Thank goodness you're here,' one of the detainees said fervently. 'We can't do a thing with her.'

Finch led him over to the detainee, who was sitting upright in bed. She was an elderly woman with sparse white hair, and she had the same fever-bright eyes, the same frenetic alertness Badri had had that first night.

'Go away!' she said when she saw Finch and made a slapping motion at him. She turned her burning eyes on Dunworthy. 'Daddy!' she cried, and then stuck her lower lip out in a pout. 'I was very naughty,' she said in a childish voice. 'I ate all the birthday cake, and now I have a stomach ache.'

'Do you see what I mean, sir?' Finch put in.

'Are the Indians coming, Daddy?' she asked. 'I don't like Indians. They have bows and arrows.'

It took them until morning to get her on to a cot in one of the lecture rooms. Dunworthy eventually had to resort to saying, 'Your daddy wants his good girl to lie down now,' and just after they had her quieted down, the ambulance came. 'Daddy!' she wailed when they shut the doors. 'Don't leave me here all alone!'

'Oh, dear,' Finch said when the ambulance drove off. 'It's past breakfast time. I do hope they haven't eaten all the bacon.'

He went off to ration supplies, and Dunworthy went back to his rooms to wait for Andrews' call. Colin was halfway down the staircase, eating a piece of toast and pulling on his jacket. 'The vicar wants me to help collect clothes for the detainees,' he said with his mouth full of toast. 'Great-aunt Mary telephoned. You're to ring her back.'

'But not Andrews?'

'No.'

'Has the visual been restored?'

'No.'

'Wear your regulation face mask,' Dunworthy called after him, 'and your muffler!'

He rang up Mary and waited impatiently for nearly five minutes until she came to the telephone.

'James?' Mary's voice said. 'It's Badri. He's asking for you.'

'He's better, then?'

'No. His fever's still very high, and he's become quite agitated, keeps calling your name, insists he has something to tell you. He's working himself into a very bad state. If you could come and speak with him, it might calm him down.'

'Has he said anything about the plague?' he asked.

'The *plague*?' she said, looking annoyed. 'Don't tell me *you've* been infected by these ridiculous rumours that are flying about, James – that it's cholera, that it's breakbone fever, that it's a recurrence of the Pandemic—'

'No,' Dunworthy said. 'It's Badri. Last night he said, "It killed half of Europe," and, "It was the rats." '

'He's delirious, James. It's the fever. It doesn't mean anything.'

She's right, he told himself. The detainee ranted on about Indians with bows and arrows, and you didn't begin looking for Sioux warriors. She had conjured up too much birthday cake as an explanation for her being ill, and Badri had conjured up the plague. It didn't mean anything.

Nevertheless, he said he would be there immediately and went to find Finch. Andrews hadn't specified what time he would call, but Dunworthy couldn't risk leaving the phone unattended. He wished he'd made Colin stay while he spoke to Mary.

Finch would very likely be in hall, guarding the bacon with his life. He took the receiver off the hook so the phone would sound engaged and went across the quad to the hall.

Ms Taylor met him at the door. 'I was just coming to look for you,' she said. 'I heard some of the detainees came down with the virus last night.'

'Yes,' he said, scanning the hall for Finch.

'Oh, dear. So I suppose we've all been exposed.'

He couldn't see Finch anywhere.

'How long is the incubation period?' Ms Taylor asked.

'Twelve to forty-eight hours,' he said. He craned his neck, trying to see over the heads of the detainees.

'That's awful,' Ms Taylor said. 'What if one of us comes down with it in the middle of the peal? We're Traditional, you know, not Council. The rules are very explicit.'

He wondered why Traditional, whatever that might be, had deemed it necessary to have rules concerning change ringers infected with influenza.

'Rule Three,' Ms Taylor said. ' "Every man must stick to his bell without interruption." It isn't as if we can put somebody else in halfway through if one of us suddenly keels over. And it would ruin the rhythm.'

He had a sudden image of one of the bell ringers in her white gloves collapsing and being kicked out of the way so as not to disrupt the rhythm.

'Aren't there any warning symptoms?' Ms Taylor asked.

'No,' he said.

'That paper the NHS sent round said disorientation, fever and headache, but that isn't any good. The bells always give us headaches.'

I can imagine, he thought, looking for William Gaddson or one of the other undergraduates he could get to listen for the phone.

'If we were Council, of course, it wouldn't matter. They let people substitute right and left. During a peal of Tittum Bob Maxims at York, they had nineteen ringers. Nineteen! I don't see how they can even call it a peal.'

None of his undergraduates appeared to be in hall, Finch had no doubt barricaded himself in the buttery, and Colin was long gone. 'Are you still in need of a practice room?' he asked Ms Taylor.

'Yes, unless one of us comes down with this thing. Of course, we could do Stedmans, but that would hardly be the same thing, would it?'

'I'll let you use my sitting-room if you will answer the telephone and take down any messages for me. I am expecting an important trunk – long-distance – call so it's essential that someone be in the room at all times.'

He led her back to his rooms.

'Oh, it's not very big, is it?' she said. 'I'm not sure there's room to work on our raising. Can we move the furniture around?'

'You may do anything you like, so long as you answer the telephone and take down any messages. I'm expecting a call from Mr Andrews. Tell him he doesn't need clearance to enter the quarantine area. Tell him to go straight to Brasenose and I'll meet him there.'

'Well, all right, I guess,' she said as if she were doing him a favour. 'At least it's better than that draughty cafeteria.'

He left her rearranging furniture, not at all convinced that it was a good idea to entrust her with this, and hurried off to see Badri. He had something to tell him. *It killed them all. Half of Europe.*

The rain had subsided to little more than a fine mist, and the anti-EC picketers were gathered in force in front of the Infirmary. They had been joined by a number of boys Colin's age wearing black face plasters and shouting. 'Let my people go!'

One of them grabbed Dunworthy's arm. 'The government's got no right to keep you here against your will,' he said, thrusting his striped face up to Dunworthy's face mask.

'Don't be a fool,' Dunworthy said. 'Do you want to start another pandemic?'

The boy let go his arm, looking confused, and Dunworthy escaped inside.

Casualties was full of patients on stretcher trolleys, and there was one standing next to the elevator. An imposing-looking nurse in voluminous SPGs was standing next to it, reading something to the patient from a polythene-wrapped book.

' "Whoever perished, being innocent?" ' she said, and he realised with dismay that it wasn't a nurse. It was Mrs Gaddson.

' "Or where were the righteous cut off?" ' she recited.

She stopped and thumbed through the thin pages of the Bible, looking for another cheering passage, and he ducked down the side corridor and into a stairwell, eternally grateful to the NHS for issuing face masks.

' "The Lord shall smite thee with a consumption," ' she intoned, her voice resounding through the corridor as he fled, ' "and with a fever, and with an inflammation." '

And He shall smite thee with Mrs Gaddson, he thought, and she shall read you Scriptures to keep your morale up.

He went up the stairs to Isolation, which had now apparently taken over most of the first floor.

'*Here* you are,' the nurse said. It was the pretty blonde student nurse again. He wondered if he should warn her about Mrs Gaddson.

'I'd nearly given you up,' she said. 'He's been calling for you all morning.' She handed him a set of SPGs, and he put them on and followed her in.

'He was frantic for you half an hour ago,' she whispered, 'kept insisting he had something to tell you. He's a bit better now.'

He looked, in fact, considerably better. He had lost the dark, frightening flush, and though he was still a bit pale under his brown skin, he looked almost like his old self. He was half-sitting against several pillows, his knees up and his hands lying lightly on them, the fingers curved. His eyes were closed.

'Badri,' the nurse said, putting her imperm-gloved hand on his shoulder and bending close to him. 'Mr Dunworthy's here.'

He opened his eyes. 'Mr Dunworthy?'

'Yes.' She nodded across the bed, indicating him. 'I told you he'd come.'

Badri sat up straighter against the pillows, but he didn't look at Dunworthy. He looked intently ahead.

'I'm here, Badri,' Dunworthy said, moving forward so he was in his line of vision. 'What was it you wanted to tell me?'

Badri continued to look straight ahead and his hands began moving restlessly on his knees. Dunworthy glanced at the nurse.

'He's been doing that,' she said. 'I think he's typing.' She looked at the screens and went out.

He was typing. His wrists rested on his knees, and his fingers tapped the blanket in a complex sequence. His eyes stared at something in front of him – a screen? – and after a moment he frowned. 'That can't be right,' he said and began typing rapidly.

'What is it, Badri?' Dunworthy said. 'What's wrong?'

'There must be an error,' Badri said. He leaned slightly sideways and said, 'Give me a line-by-line on the TAA.'

He was speaking into the console's ear, Dunworthy realised. He's reading the fix, he thought. 'What can't be right, Badri?'

'The slippage,' Badri said, his eyes fixed on the imaginary screen. 'Readout check,' he said into the ear. 'That *can't* be right.'

'What's wrong with the slippage?' Dunworthy asked. 'Was there more slippage than you expected?'

Badri didn't answer. He typed for a moment, paused, watching the screen, and began typing frantically.

'How much slippage was there, Badri?' Dunworthy said.

He typed for a full minute and then stepped and looked up at Dunworthy. 'So worried,' he said thoughtfully.

'Worried about what Badri?' Dunworthy said.

Badri suddenly flung the blanket back and grabbed for the bed rails. 'I have to find Mr Dunworthy,' he said. He yanked at his cannula, pulling at the tape.

The screens behind him went wild, spiking crazily and beeping. Somewhere outside an alarm went off.

'You mustn't do that,' Dunworthy said, reaching across the bed to stop him.

'He's at the pub,' Badri said, ripping at the tape.

The screens went abruptly flatline. 'Disconnect,' a computer voice said. 'Disconnect.'

The nurse banged in. 'Oh, dear, that's twice he's done that,' she said. 'Mr Chaudhuri, you mustn't do that. You'll pull your cannula out.'

'Go and get Mr Dunworthy. Now,' he said. 'There's something

wrong,' but he lay back and let her cover him up. 'Why doesn't he come?'

Dunworthy waited while the nurse retaped the cannula and reset the screens, watching Badri. He looked worn out and apathetic, almost bored. A new bruise was already forming above the cannula.

The nurse left with, 'I think I'd best call down for a sedative.'

As soon as she was gone, Dunworthy said, 'Badri, it's Mr Dunworthy. You wanted to tell me something. Look at me, Badri. What is it? What's wrong?'

Badri looked at him but without interest.

'Was there too much slippage, Badri? Is Kivrin in the plague?'

'I don't have time,' Badri said. 'I was out there Saturday and Sunday.' He began typing again, his fingers moving ceaselessly on the blanket. 'That can't be right.'

The nurse came back with a drip bottle. 'Oh, good,' he said, and his expression relaxed and softened, as if a great weight had been lifted. 'I don't know what happened I had such a terrific headache.'

He closed his eyes before she had even hooked the drip to the cannula and began to snore softly.

The nurse led him out. 'If he wakes and calls for you again, where can you be reached?' she asked.

He gave her the number. 'What exactly did he say?' he asked, stripping off his gown. 'Before I arrived?'

'He kept calling your name and saying he had to find you, that he had to tell you something important.'

'Did he say anything about rats?' he said.

'No. Once he said he had to find Karen – or Katherine—'

'Kivrin.'

She nodded. 'Yes. He said, "I must find Kivrin. Is the laboratory open?" And then he said something about a lamb, but nothing about rats, I don't think. A good deal of the time I can't make it out.'

He threw the imperm gloves into the bag. 'I want you to write down everything he says. Not the unintelligible parts,' he added before she could object. 'But everything else. I'll be back this afternoon.'

'I'll try,' she said. 'It's mostly nonsense.'

He went downstairs. It was mostly nonsense, feverish ramblings that meant nothing, but he went outside to get a taxi. He wanted to get back to Balliol quickly, to speak to Andrews, to get him up here to read the fix.

'That can't be right,' Badri had said, and it had to be the slippage. Could he have somehow misread the figure, thought it was only four hours and then discovered, what? That it was four years? Or twenty-eight?

'You'll get there faster walking,' someone said. It was the boy with the black face plasters. 'If you're waiting for a taxi, you'll stand there for ever. They've all been commandeered by the bloody government.'

He gestured towards one just pulling up to the door of Casualties. It had an NHS placard in the side window.

Dunworthy thanked the boy and started back to Balliol. It was raining again and he waited rapidly, hoping that Andrews had already telephoned, that he was already on his way. 'Go and get Mr Dunworthy immediately,' Badri had said. 'Now. There's something wrong,' and he was obviously reliving his actions after he had got the fix, when he had run through the rain to the Lamb and Cross to fetch him. 'That can't be right,' he had said.

He half-ran across the quad and up to his rooms. He was worried Ms Taylor wouldn't have been able to hear the telephone's bell over her bell ringers' clanging, but when he opened the door, he found them standing in a circle in the middle of his sitting-room in their face masks, their arms raised and hands folded as if in supplication, bringing their hands down in front of them and bending their knees one after the other in solemn silence.

'Mr Basingame's scout called,' Ms Taylor said, rising and stooping. 'He said he thought Mr Basingame was somewhere in the Highlands. And Mr Andrews said you were to call him back. He just called.'

Dunworthy put the trunk call through, feeling immensely relieved. While he waited for Andrews to answer, he watched the curious dance and tried to determine the pattern. Ms Taylor seemed to bob on a semi regular basis, but the others did their odd curtsies in no order he could detect. The largest one, Ms Piantini, was counting to herself, frowning in concentration.

'I've obtained clearance for you to enter the quarantine area. When are you coming up?' he said as soon as the tech answered.

'That's the thing, sir,' Andrews said. There was a visual, but it was too fuzzy to read his expression. 'I don't think I'd better. I've been watching all about the quarantine on the vids, sir. They say this Indian flu is extremely dangerous.'

'You needn't come in contact with any of the cases,' Dunworthy said. 'I can arrange for you to go straight to Brasenose's laboratory. You'll be perfectly safe. This is extremely important.'

'Yes, sir, but the vidders say it might have been caused by the University's heating system.'

'The heating system?' Dunworthy said. 'The University has no heating system, and the individual ones of the colleges are over a hundred years old and incapable of heating, let alone infecting.' The bell ringers turned as one to look at him, but they did not break rhythm. 'It has absolutely nothing to do with the heating system. Or India, or the wrath of God. It began in South Carolina. The vaccine is already on the way. It's perfectly safe.'

Andrews looked stubborn. 'Nevertheless, sir, I don't think it would be wise for me to come.'

The bell ringers abruptly stopped. 'Sorry,' Ms Piantini said, and they started again.

'This fix must be read. We have an historian in 1320, and we don't know how much slippage there has been. I'll see to it that you're paid for hazardous duty,' Dunworthy said, and then realised that was exactly the wrong approach. 'I can arrange for you to be isolated or wear SPGs or—'

'I could read the fix from here,' Andrews said. 'I've a friend who'll set up the access connections. She's a student at Shrewsbury.' He paused. 'It's the best I can do. Sorry.'

'Sorry,' Ms Piantini said again.

'No, no, you ring in second's place,' Ms Taylor said. 'You dodge two-three up and down and three-four down and then lead a whole pull. And keep your eyes on the other ringers, not on the floor. One-two-and-off!' They started their minuet again.

'I simply can't take the risk,' Andrews said.

It was clear he couldn't be persuaded. 'What is the name of your friend at Shrewsbury?' Dunworthy asked.

'Polly Wilson,' Andrews said, sounding relieved. He gave Dunworthy her number. 'Tell her you need a remote read, IA enquiry and bridge transmit. I'll stay by this number.' He moved to ring off.

'Wait!' Dunworthy said. The bell ringers glanced disapprovingly at him. 'What would the maximal slippage be on a drop to 1320?'

'I've no idea,' Andrews said promptly. 'Slippage is difficult to predict. There are so many factors.'

'An estimate,' Dunworthy said. 'Could it be twenty-eight years?'

'Twenty-eight *years*?' Andrews said, and the amazed tone sent a gust of relief through Dunworthy. 'Oh, I wouldn't think so. There's a general tendency towards greater slippage the further back you go, but the increase isn't exponential. The parameter checks will tell you.'

'Mediaeval didn't do any.'

'They sent an historian back without parameter checks?' Andrews sounded shocked.

'Without parameter checks, without unmanneds, without recon tests,' Dunworthy said. 'Which is why it's essential I get this fix read. I want you to do something for me.'

Andrews stiffened.

'You don't have to come here to do it,' he said rapidly. 'Jesus has an on-site set-up in London. I want you to go over there and run parameter checks on a drop to noon, 13 December 1320.'

'What are the locational coordinates?'

'I don't know. I'll get them when I go to Brasenose. I want you to telephone me here as soon as you've determined maximal slippage. Can you do that?'

'Yes,' he said, but he was looking doubtful again.

'Good I'll telephone Polly Wilson. Remote read, IA enquiry, bridge transmit. I'll ring you back as soon as she's got it set up at Brasenose,' Dunworthy said, and rang off before Andrews could renege.

He held on to the receiver, watching the bell ringers. The order changed each time, but Ms Piantini apparently did not lose count again.

He telephoned Polly Wilson and gave her the specifications Andrews had dictated, wondering if she had been watching the vidders too, and would be afraid of Brasenose's heating system, but she said promptly, 'I'll need to find a gateway. I'll meet you there in three-quarters of an hour.'

He left the bell ringers still bobbing and went over to Brasenose. The rain had slowed to a fine mist and there were more people on the streets, though many of the shops were closed. Whoever was in charge of the Carfax carillon had either come down with the flu or forgotten about it because of the quarantine. It was still playing 'Bring a Torch, Jeanette Isabella', or possibly 'O Tannenbaum'.

There were three picketers outside an Indian grocer's and a half dozen more outside Brasenose with a large banner they were holding between them that read 'TIME TRAVEL IS A HEALTH THREAT'. He recognised the young woman on the end as one of the medics from the ambulance.

Heating systems and the EC and time travel. During the Pandemic it had been the American germ warfare programme and air conditioning. Back in the Middle Ages they had blamed Satan and the appearance of comets for their epidemics. Doubtless when the fact that the virus had originated in South Carolina was revealed, the Confederacy, or Southern fried chicken, would be blamed.

He went in the gate to the porter's desk. The Christmas tree was sitting on one end of it, the angel perched atop it. 'I have a student from Shrewsbury meeting me to set up some communications equipment,' he told the porter. 'We'll need to be let into the laboratory.'

'The laboratory is restricted, sir,' the porter said.

'Restricted?'

'Yes, sir. It's been locked and no one's allowed in.'

'Why? What's happened?'

'It's because of the epidemic, sir.'

'The epidemic?'

'Yes, sir. Perhaps you'd better speak with Mr Gilchrist, sir.'

'Perhaps I had. Tell him I'm here, and I need to be let into the laboratory.'

'I'm afraid he's not here just now.'

'Where is he?'

'At the Infirmary, I believe. He—'

Dunworthy didn't wait to hear the rest. Halfway to the Infirmary it occurred to him that Polly Wilson would be left waiting with no idea where he'd gone, and as he came up to the hospital it came to him that Gilchrist might be there because he'd come down with the virus.

Good, he thought, it's what he deserves, but Gilchrist was in the little waiting-room, hale and hearty, wearing an NHS face mask, rolling up his sleeve in preparation for the inoculation a nurse was holding.

'Your porter told me the laboratory's restricted,' he said, stepping between them. 'I need to get into it. I've found a tech to do a remote fix. We need to set up transmission equipment.'

'I'm afraid that's impossible,' Gilchrist said. 'The laboratory is under quarantine until the source of the virus is determined.'

'The source of the virus?' he said incredulously. 'The virus originated in South Carolina.'

'We will not be certain of that until we've obtained positive identification. Until then, I felt it was best to minimise all possible risks to the University by restricting access to the laboratory. Now, if you will excuse me, I'm here to receive my immune system enhancement.' He started past Dunworthy towards the nurse.

Dunworthy put out his arm to stop him. '*What* risks?'

'There has been considerable public concern that the virus was transmitted through the net.'

'Public concern? Do you mean those three halfwits with the banner outside your gate?' he shouted.

'This is a hospital, Mr Dunworthy,' the nurse said. 'Please keep your voice down.'

He ignored her. 'There has been "considerable public concern", as you call it, that the virus was caused by liberal immigration laws,' he said. 'Do you intend to secede from the EC as well?'

Gilchrist's chin went up, and the pinched lines appeared by his nose, visible even through the mask. 'As Acting Head of the History Faculty, it is my responsibility to act in the University's interest. Our position in the community, as I'm certain you're aware, depends on maintaining the goodwill of the townspeople. I felt it important to calm the public's fears by closing the laboratory until the sequencing arrives. If it indicates that the virus is from South Carolina, then of course the laboratory will be reopened immediately.'

'And in the meantime, what about *Kivrin*?'

'If you cannot keep your voice down,' the nurse said, 'I shall be forced to report you to Dr Ahrens.'

'Excellent. Go and fetch her,' Dunworthy told her. 'I want her to tell Mr Gilchrist how ridiculous he's being. This virus cannot possibly have come through the net.'

The nurse stamped out.

'If your protesters are too ignorant to understand the laws of physics,' Dunworthy said, 'surely they can understand the simple fact that this was a *drop*. The net was only open *to* 1320, not *from* it. Nothing came through from the past.'

'If that is the case, then Ms Engle is not in any danger, and it will do no harm to wait for the sequencing.'

'Not in any danger? You don't even know where she is!'

'Your tech obtained the fix, and indicated the drop was successful and that there was minimal slippage,' Gilchrist said. He rolled down his sleeve and carefully buttoned the cuff. 'I'm satisfied Ms Engle is where she's supposed to be.'

'Well, I'm not. And I won't be until I know Kivrin made it through safely.'

'I see I must remind you again that Ms Engle is my responsibility, not yours, Mr Dunworthy.' He donned his coat. 'I must do as I think best.'

'And you think it best to set up a quarantine around the laboratory to placate a handful of crackpots,' he said bitterly. 'There is also "considerable public concern" that the virus is a judgment from God. What do you intend to do to maintain the goodwill of those townspeople? Resume burning martyrs at the stake?'

'I resent that remark. And I resent your constant interference in matters which do not concern you. You have been determined from the first to undermine Mediaeval, to keep it from gaining access to time travel, and now you are determined to undermine my authority. May I remind you that I am Acting Head of History in Mr Basingame's absence, and as such—'

'What you are is an ignorant, self-important fool who should never have been trusted with Mediaeval, let alone Kivrin's safety!'

'I see no reason to continue this discussion,' Gilchrist said. 'The laboratory is under quarantine. It will remain so until we obtain the sequencing.' He walked out.

Dunworthy started after him and nearly collided with Mary. She was wearing SPGs and reading a chart.

'You will not believe what Gilchrist's done now,' he said. 'A group of picketers convinced him the virus came through the net, and he's barricaded the laboratory.'

She didn't say anything or even look up from the chart.

'Badri said this morning that the slippage figures can't be right. He said over and over, 'There's something wrong.''

She looked up at him distractedly and back at the chart.

'I have a tech ready to read Kivrin's fix remotely, but Gilchrist's locked the doors,' he said. 'You must talk to him, tell him the virus has been firmly established as originating in South Carolina.'

'It hasn't.'

'What do you mean, it hasn't? Did the sequencing arrive?'

She shook her head. 'The WIC located their tech, but she's still running it. But her preliminary read indicates it's not the South Carolina virus.' She looked up at him. 'And I know it's not.' She looked back at the chart. 'The South Carolina virus had a zero mortality rate.'

'What do you mean? Has something happened to Badri?'

'No,' she said, shutting the chart and holding it to her chest. 'Beverly Breen.'

He must have looked blank. He had thought she was going to say Latimer.

'The woman with the lavender umbrella,' she said, and sounded angry. 'She died just now.'

22 December 1320 (Old Style). Agnes' knee is worse. It's red and painful (an understatement – she screams when I try to touch it) and she can scarcely walk. I don't know what to do – if I tell Lady Imeyne, she'll put one of her poultices on it and make it worse, and Eliwys is distracted and obviously worried.

Gawyn still isn't back. He should have been home by noon yesterday, and when he hadn't shown up by vespers, Eliwys accused Imeyne of sending him to Oxford.

'I have sent him to Courcy, as I told you,' Imeyne said defensively. 'No doubt the rain keeps him.'

'Only to Courcy?' Eliwys said angrily. 'Or have you sent him otherwhere for a new chaplain?'

Imeyne drew herself up. 'Father Roche is not fit to say the Christmas masses if Sir Bloet and his company come,' she said. 'Would you be shamed before Rosemund's fiancé?'

Eliwys went absolutely white. 'Where have you sent him?'

'I have sent him with a message to the bishop, saying that we are in sore need of a chaplain,' she said.

'To Bath?' Eliwys said, and raised her hand as if she would strike her.

'Nay. Only to Cirencestre. The archdeacon was to lie at the abbey for Yule. I bade Gawyn give him the message. One of his churchmen will bear it thence. Though, certes, things go not so ill in Bath that Gawyn could not go thence himself without harm, else my son would have quitted it.'

'Your *son* will be ill-pleased to find we have disobeyed him. He bade us, and Gawyn, keep to the manor till he come.'

She still sounded furious, and as she lowered her hand, she clenched it into a fist, as if she would have liked to box Imeyne's ears the way she does Maisry's. But the colour had come back in her cheeks as soon as Imeyne said, 'Cirencestre,' and I think she was at least a little relieved.

'Certes, things go not so ill in Bath that Gawyn could not go thence without harm,' Imeyne said, but it's obvious Eliwys doesn't think he can. Is she afraid he'd ride into a trap or that he might lead Lord Guillaume's enemies here? And are things going so 'ill' that Guillaume can't quit Bath?

Perhaps all three. Eliwys has been to the door to look out into the rain at least a dozen times this morning, and she's in as bad a temper as Rosemund was in the woods. Just now she asked Imeyne if she was certain the archdeacon was at Cirencestre. She's obviously worried that if he wasn't, Gawyn will have taken the message into Bath himself.

Her fear has infected everyone. Lady Imeyne has slunk off into a corner with her reliquary to pray, Agnes whines and Rosemund sits with her embroidery in her lap, staring blindly at it.

(Break)

I took Agnes to Father Roche this afternoon. Her knee was much worse. She couldn't walk at all, and there was what looked like the beginning of a red streak above it. I couldn't tell for certain – the entire knee is red and swollen – but I was afraid to wait.

There was no cure for blood poisoning in 1320, and it's my fault her knee is infected. If I hadn't insisted on going to look for the drop, she wouldn't have fallen. I know the paradoxes aren't supposed to let my presence here have any effect on what happens to the contemps, but I couldn't take that chance. I wasn't supposed to be able to catch anything, either.

So when Imeyne went up to the loft, I carried Agnes over to the church to ask him to treat her. It was pouring by the time we got there, but Agnes wasn't whining over getting wet, and that frightened me more than the red streak.

The church was dark and smelled musty. I could hear Father Roche's voice from the front of the church, and it sounded like he was talking to someone. 'Lord Guillaume has still not arrived from Bath. I fear for his safety,' he said.

I thought perhaps Gawyn had come back, and I wanted

to hear what they said about the trial, so I didn't go forward. I stood there with Agnes in my arms and listened.

'It has rained these two days,' Roche said, 'and there is a bitter wind from the west. We have had to bring the sheep in from the fields.'

After a minute of peering into the dark nave, straining to see, I finally made him out. He was on his knees in front of the rood screen, his big hands folded together in prayer.

'The steward's babe has a colic on the stomach and cannot keep his milk down. Tabord the Cottar fares ill.'

He wasn't praying in Latin, and there was none of the priest at Holy Re-Formed's singsong chanting or the vicar's oratory in his voice. He sounded businesslike and matter-of-fact, the way I sound now, talking to you.

God was supposed to be very real to the contemps in the 1300s, more vivid than the physical world they inhabited. 'You do but go home again,' Father Roche told me when I was dying, and that's what the contemps are supposed to have believed – that the life of the body is illusory and unimportant, and the real life is that of the eternal soul, as if they were only visiting life the way I am visiting this century, but I haven't seen much evidence of it. Eliwys dutifully murmurs her *aves* at vespers and matins and then rises and brushes off her kirtle as if her prayers had nothing to do with her worries over her husband or the girls or Gawyn. And Imeyne, for all her reliquary and her Book of Hours, is concerned only about her social standing. I'd seen no evidence that God was real at all to them till I stood there in the damp church, listening to Father Roche.

I wonder if he sees God and heaven as clearly as I can see you and Oxford, the rain falling in the quad and your spectacles steaming up so you have to take them off and polish them on your muffler. I wonder if they seem as close as you do, and as difficult to get to.

'Preserve our souls from evil and bring us safely into heaven,' Roche said, and as if that were a cue, Agnes sat up in my arms and said, 'I want Father Roche.'

Father Roche stood up and started towards us. 'What is it? Who is there?'

'It is Lady Katherine,' I said. 'I have brought Agnes. Her knee is—' What? Infected? 'I would have you look at her knee.'

He tried to look at it, but it was too dark in the church so he carried her over to his house. It was scarcely lighter there. His house is not much larger than the hut I took shelter in, and no higher. He had to stoop the whole time we were there to keep from bumping his head against the rafters.

He opened the shutter on the only window, which let the rain blow in, and then lit a rushlight and set Agnes on a crude wooden table. He untied the bandage, and she flinched away from him.

'Sit you still, *Agnus*,' he told her, 'and I will tell you how Christ came to earth from far heaven.'

'On Christmas Day,' Agnes said.

Roche felt around the wound poking at the swollen parts, talking steadily ' "And the shepherds stood afraid, for they knew not what this glittering light was. And sounds they heard as of bells rung in heaven. But they beheld it was God's angel come down to them." '

Agnes had screamed and pushed my hands away when I tried to touch her knee, but she let Roche prod the red area with his huge fingers. There was definitely the beginning of a red streak. Roche touched it gently and brought the rushlight closer.

' "And there came from a far land," ' he said, squinting at it, ' "three kings bearing gifts." ' He touched the red streak again, gingerly, and then folded his hands together, as if he were going to pray, and I thought, Don't pray. *Do* something.

He lowered his hands and looked across at me. 'I fear the wound is poisoned,' he said. 'I will make an infusion of hyssop to draw the venom out.' He went over to the hearth, stirred up a few lukewarm-looking coals, and poured water into an iron pot from a bucket.

The bucket was dirty, the pot was dirty, the hands he'd

felt Agnes' wound with were dirty and, standing there, watching him set the pot on the fire and dig into a dirty bag, I was sorry I'd come. He wasn't any better than Imeyne. An infusion of leaves and seeds wouldn't cure blood poisoning any more than one of Imeyne's poultices, and his prayers wouldn't help either, even if he did talk to God as if He were really there.

I almost said, 'Is that all you can do?' and then realised I was expecting the impossible. The cure for infection was penicillin, T-cell enhancement, antiseptics, none of which he had in his burlap bag.

I remember Mr Gilchrist talking about mediaeval doctors in one of his lectures. He talked about what fools they were for bleeding people and treating them with arsenic and goat's urine during the Black Death. But what did he expect them to do? They didn't have analogues or anti-microbials. They didn't even know what caused it. Standing there, crumbling dried petals and leaves between his dirty fingers, Father Roche was doing the best he could.

'Do you have wine?' I asked him. 'Old wine?'

There's scarcely any alcohol in the small ale and not much more in their wine, but the longer it's stood, the higher the alcoholic content, and alcohol is an antiseptic.

'I have remembered me that old wine poured into a wound may sometimes stop infections,' I said.

He didn't ask me what 'infection' was or how I was able to remember that when I supposedly can't remember any-thing else. He went immediately across to the church and got an earthenware bottle full of strong-smelling wine, and I poured it on to the bandage and washed the wound with it.

I brought the bottle home with me. I've hidden it under the bed in Rosemund's bower (in case it's part of the sacra-mental wine – that would be all Imeyne would need, she'd have Roche burned for a heretic) so I can keep cleaning it. Before she went to bed, I poured some straight on.

<hr />

CHAPTER NINETEEN

It rained till Christmas Eve, a hard, wintry rain that came through the smoke vent in the roof and made the fire hiss and smoke.

Kivrin poured wine on Agnes' knee at every chance she got, and by the afternoon of the twenty-third it looked a little better. It was still swollen but the red streak was gone. Kivrin ran across to the church, holding her cloak over her head, to tell Father Roche, but he wasn't there.

Neither Imeyne nor Eliwys had noticed Agnes' knee was hurt. They were trying frantically to get ready for Sir Bloet's family, if they were coming, cleaning the loft room so the women could sleep there, strewing dried rose petals over the rushes in the hall, baking an amazing assortment of manchets, puddings and pies, including a grotesque one in the shape of the Christ child in the manger, with braided pastry for swaddling clothes.

In the afternoon Father Roche came to the manor, drenched and shivering. He had gone out in the freezing rain to fetch ivy for the hall. Imeyne wasn't there – she was in the kitchen cooking the Christ child – and Kivrin made Roche come in and dry his clothes by the fire.

She called for Maisry, and when she didn't come went out across the courtyard to the kitchen and fetched him a cup of hot ale. When she returned with it, Maisry was on the bench beside Roche, holding her tangled, filthy hair back with her hand, and Roche was putting goose grease on her ear. As soon as she saw Kivrin she clapped her hand to her ear, probably undoing all the good of Roche's treatment, and scuttled out.

'Agnes' knee is better,' Kivrin told him. 'The swelling has gone down, and a new scab is forming.'

He didn't seem surprised, and she wondered if she'd been mistaken, if it hadn't been blood poisoning at all.

During the night the rain turned to snow. 'They will not come,' Lady Eliwys said the next morning, sounding relieved.

Kivrin had to agree with her. It had snowed nearly thirty centimetres in the night, and it was still coming down steadily. Even Imeyne seemed resigned to their not coming, though she kept on with the preparations, bringing down pewter trenchers from the loft and shouting for Maisry.

Around noon the snow stopped abruptly, and by two it had begun to clear, and Eliwys ordered everyone into their good clothes. Kivrin dressed the girls, surprised at the fanciness of their silk shifts. Agnes had a dark red velvet kirtle to wear over hers and her silver buckle, and Rosemund's leaf-green kirtle had long split sleeves and a low bodice that showed the embroidery on her yellow shift. Nothing had been said to Kivrin about what she should wear, but after she had taken the girls' hair out of braids and brushed it over their shoulders, Agnes said, 'You must put on your blue,' and got her dress out of the chest at the foot of the bed. It looked less out of place among the girl's finery, but the weave was still too fine, the colour too blue.

She didn't know what she should do about her hair. Unmarried girls wore their hair unbound on festive occasions, held back by a fillet or a ribbon, but her hair was too short for that, and only married women covered their hair. She couldn't just leave it uncovered – the chopped-off hair looked terrible.

Apparently Eliwys agreed. When Kivrin brought the girls back downstairs, she bit her lip and sent Maisry up to the loft room to fetch a thin, nearly transparent veil that she fastened with Kivrin's fillet halfway back on her head so that her front hair showed, but the ragged cut ends were hidden.

Eliwys' nervousness seemed to have returned with the improving weather. She started when Maisry came in from outside and then cuffed her for getting mud on the floor. She suddenly thought of a dozen things that weren't ready and found fault with everyone. When Lady Imeyne said for the dozenth time, 'If we had gone to Courcy . . .' Eliwys nearly snapped her head off.

Kivrin had thought it was a bad idea to dress Agnes before the last possible minute, and by midafternoon the little girl's embroidered sleeves were grubby and she had spilled flour all down one side of the velvet skirt.

By late afternoon Gawyn had still not returned, everyone's nerves were at the snapping point, and Maisry's ears were bright red. When Lady Imeyne told Kivrin to take six beeswax candles to Father Roche, she was delighted with the chance to get the girls out of the house.

'Tell him they must last through both the masses,' Imeyne said irritably, 'and poor masses will they be for our Lord's birth. We should have gone to Courcy.'

Kivrin got Agnes into her cloak and called Rosemund, and they walked across to the church. Roche wasn't there. A large yellowish candle with bands marked on it sat in the middle of the altar, unlit. He would light it at sunset and use it to keep track of the hours till midnight. On his knees in the icy church.

He wasn't in his house either. Kivrin left the candles on the table. On the way back across the green, they saw Roche's donkey by the lychgate licking the snow.

'We forgot to feed the animals,' Agnes said.

'Feed the animals?' Kivrin asked warily, thinking of their clothes.

'It is Christmas Eve,' Agnes said. 'Fed you not the animals at home?'

'She remembers not,' Rosemund said. 'On Christmas Eve we feed the animals in honour of our Lord that he was born in a stable.'

'Do you remember naught of Christmas then?' Agnes asked.

'A little,' Kivrin said, thinking of Oxford on Christinas Eve, of the shops in Carfax decorated with plastene evergreens and laser lights and jammed with last-minute shoppers, the High full of bicycles, and Magdalen Tower showing dimly through the snow.

'First they ring the bells and then you get to eat and then mass and then the Yule log,' Agnes said.

'You have turned it all about,' Rosemund said. 'First we light the Yule log and then we go to mass.'

'*First* the bells,' Agnes said, glaring at Rosemund, 'and then mass.'

They went to the barn for a sack of oats and some hay and took them across to the stable to feed the horses. Gringolet wasn't among them, which meant Gawyn still wasn't back. She must speak with him as soon as he returned. The rendezvous was less than a week away, and she still had no idea where the drop was. And with Lord Guillaume coming, everything might change.

Eliwys had only put off doing anything with her till her husband came, and she had told the girls again this morning she expected him today. He might decide to take Kivrin to Oxford, or London, to look for her family, or Sir Bloet might offer to take her back with them to Courcy. She had to talk to him soon. But with guests here it would be much easier to catch him alone, and in all the bustle and busyness of Christmas, she might even get him to show her the place.

Kivrin dawdled as long as she could with the horses, hoping Gawyn might come back, but Agnes got bored and wanted to go feed corn to the chickens. Kivrin suggested they go feed the steward's cow.

'It is not our cow,' Rosemund snapped.

'She helped me on that day when I was ill,' she said, thinking of how she had leaned against the cow's bony back the day she tried to find the drop. 'I would thank her for her kindness.'

They went past the pen where the pigs had lately been, and Agnes said, 'Poor piglings. I would have fed them an apple.'

'The sky to the north darkens again,' Rosemund said. 'I think they will not come.'

'Ay, but they will,' Agnes said. 'Sir Bloet has promised me a trinket.'

The steward's cow was in almost the same place Kivrin had found it, behind the second to the last hut, eating what was left of the same blackening pea vines.

'Good Christmas, Lady Cow,' Agnes said, holding a handful of hay a good metre from the cow's mouth.

'They speak only at midnight,' Rosemund said.

'I would come see them at midnight, Lady Kivrin,' Agnes said. The cow strained forward. Agnes edged back.

'You cannot, simplehead,' Rosemund said. 'You will be at mass.'

The cow extended her neck and took a large-hoofed step forward. Agnes retreated. Kivrin gave the cow a handful of hay.

Agnes watched enviously. 'If all are at mass, how do they know the animals speak?' she asked.

Good point, Kivrin thought.

'Father Roche says it is so,' Rosemund said.

Agnes came out from behind Kivrin's skirts and picked up another handful of hay. 'What do they say?' She pointed it in the cow's general direction.

'They say you know not how to feed them,' Rosemund said.

'They do *not*,' Agnes said, thrusting her hand forward. The cow lunged for the hay, mouth open, teeth bared. Agnes threw the handful of hay at it and ran behind Kivrin's back. 'They praise our blessed Lord. Father Roche said it.'

There was a sound of horses. Agnes ran between the huts. 'They are come!' she shouted, running back. 'Sir Bloet is here. I saw them. They ride now through the gate.'

Kivrin hastily scattered the rest of the hay in front of the cow. Rosemund took a handful of oats out of the bag and fed them to the cow, letting it nuzzle the grain out of her open hand.

'Come, Rosemund!' Agnes said. 'Sir Bloet is here!'

Rosemund rubbed what was left of the oats off her hand. 'I would feed Father Roche's donkey,' she said, and started towards the church, not even glancing in the direction of the manor.

'But they've *come*, Rosemund,' Agnes shouted, running after her. 'Do you not want to see what they have brought?'

Obviously not. Rosemund had reached the donkey, which had found a tuft of foxtail grass sticking out of the snow next to the lychgate. She bent and stuck a handful of oats under its muzzle, to its complete uninterest, and then stood there with her hand on its back, her long dark hair hiding her face.

'Rosemund!' Agnes said, her face red with frustration. 'Did you not hear me? They have *come*!'

The donkey nudged the oats out of the way and clamped its yellow teeth around a large head of the grass. Rosemund continued to offer it the oats.

'Rosemund,' Kivrin said, 'I will feed the donkey. You must go to greet your guests.'

'Sir Bloet said he would bring me a trinket,' Agnes said.

Rosemund opened her hands and let the oats fall. 'If you like him so well, why do you not ask Father to let you marry him?' she said, and started for the manor.

'I am too little,' Agnes said.

So is Rosemund, Kivrin thought, grabbing Agnes' hand and starting after her. Rosemund walked rapidly ahead, her chin in the air, not bothering to lift her dragging skirts, ignoring Agnes' repeated pleas to 'Wait, Rosemund.'

The party had already passed into the courtyard, and Rosemund was already to the sty. Kivrin picked up the pace, pulling Agnes along at a run, and they all arrived in the courtyard at the same time. Kivrin stopped, surprised.

She had expected a formal meeting, the family at the door with stiff speeches and polite smiles, but this was like the first day of term – everyone carrying in boxes and bags, greeting each other with exclamations and embraces, talking at the same time, laughing. Rosemund hadn't even been missed. A large woman wearing an enormous starched coif grabbed Agnes up and kissed her, and three young girls clustered around Rosemund, squealing.

Servants, obviously in their holiday best too, carried covered baskets and an enormous goose into the kitchen, and led the horses into the stable. Gawyn, still on Gringolet, was leaning down to speak to Imeyne. Kivrin heard him say, 'Nay, the bishop is at Wiveliscombe,' but Imeyne didn't look unhappy, so he must have got the message to the archdeacon.

She turned to help a young woman in a vivid blue cloak even brighter than Kivrin's kirtle down from her horse, and led her over to Eliwys, smiling. Eliwys was smiling, too.

Kivrin tried to make out which was Sir Bloet, but there were at least a half-dozen mounted men, all with silver-chased bridles and fur-trimmed cloaks. None of them looked decrepit, thank goodness, and one or two were quite presentable-looking. She turned to ask Agnes which one he was, but she was still in the grip of the starched coif, who kept patting her head and saying, 'You have grown so I scarce knew you.' Kivrin stifled a smile. Some things truly never changed.

Several of the newcomers had red hair, including a woman

nearly as old as Imeyne, who nevertheless wore her faded pink hair down her back like a young girl. She had a pinched, unhappy-looking mouth and was obviously dissatisfied with the way the servants were unloading things. She snatched one over-loaded basket out of the hands of a servant who was struggling with it and thrust it at a fat man in a green velvet kirtle.

He had red hair, too, and so did the nicest looking of the younger men. He was in his late twenties, but he had a round, open, freckled face and a pleasant expression at least.

'Sir Bloet!' Agnes cried, and flung herself past Kivrin and against the knees of the fat man.

Oh, no, Kivrin thought. She had assumed the fat man was married to the pink-tressed shrew or the woman in the starched coif. He was at least fifty, and nearly twenty stone, and when he smiled at Agnes his large teeth were brown with decay.

'Have you no trinket for me?' Agnes was demanding, tugging on the hem of his kirtle.

'Ay,' he said, looking forward where Rosemund still stood talking to the other girls, 'for you and for your sister.'

'I will fetch her,' Agnes said, and darted across to Rosemund before Kivrin could stop her. Bloet lumbered after her. The girls giggled and parted as he approached, and Rosemund shot a murderous look at Agnes and then smiled and extended her hand to him. 'Good day and welcome, sir,' she said.

Her chin was up about as far as it would go, and there were two spots of feverish red in her pale cheeks, but Bloet apparently took these for shyness and excitement. He took her little fingers in his own fat ones and said, 'Surely you will not greet your husband with such formality come spring.'

The spots got redder. 'It is still winter, sir.'

'It will be spring soon enough,' he said and laughed, showing his brown teeth.

'Where is my trinket?' Agnes demanded.

'Agnes, be not so greedy,' Eliwys said, coming to stand between her daughters. 'It is a poor welcome to demand gifts of a guest.' She smiled at him, and if she dreaded this marriage, she showed no sign of it. She looked more relaxed than Kivrin had yet seen her.

'I promised my sister-in-law a trinket,' he said, reaching into his too-tight belt and bringing out a little cloth bag, 'and my betrothed a bride-gift.' He fumbled in the little bag and brought out a brooch set with stones. 'A lovenot for my bride,' he said, unfastening the clasp. 'You must think of me when you wear it.'

He moved forward, puffing, to pin it to her cloak. I hope he has a stroke, Kivrin thought. Rosemund stood stock-still, her cheeks sharply red, while his fat hands fumbled at her neck.

'Rubies,' Eliwys said delightedly. 'Do you not thank your betrothed for his goodly gift, Rosemund?'

'I thank thee for the brooch,' Rosemund said tonelessly.

'Where is *my* trinket?' Agnes said, dancing on one foot, then the other while he reached in the little bag again and brought out something clenched in his fist. He stooped down to Agnes' level, breathing hard, and opened his hand.

'It is a bell!' Agnes said delightedly, holding it up and shaking it. It was brass and round, like a horse's sleigh bell, and had a metal loop at the top.

Agnes insisted on Kivrin taking her up to the bower to fetch a ribbon to thread through it so she could wear it around her wrist for a bracelet. 'My father brought me this ribbon from the fair,' Agnes said, pulling it out of the chest Kivrin's clothes had been kept in. It was patchily dyed and so stiff Kivrin had trouble threading it through the hole. Even the cheapest ribbons at Woolworth's or the paper ribbons used for wrapping Christmas presents were better than this obviously treasured one.

Kivrin tied it to Agnes' wrist, and they went back downstairs. The bustle and unloading had moved inside, servants carrying chests and bedding and what looked like early versions of the carpet bag into the hall. She needn't have worried about Sir Bloet *et al* carrying her off. It looked like they were here for the winter at the least.

She needn't have worried about them discussing her fate either. None of them had so much as cast a glance at her, even when Agnes insisted on going over to her mother and showing off her bracelet. Eliwys was deep in conversation with Bloet, Gawyn and the nice-looking man, who must be a son or a nephew, and Eliwys was twisting her hands again. The news from Bath must be bad.

Lady Imeyne was at the end of the hall, talking to the stout woman and a pale-looking man in a cleric's robe, and it was clear from the expression on her face that she was complaining about Father Roche.

Kivrin took advantage of the noisy confusion to pull Rosemund away from the other girls and ask her who everyone was. The pale man was Sir Bloet's chaplain, which she had more or less figured out. The lady in the bright blue cloak was his foster daughter. The stout woman with the starched coif was Sir Bloet's brother's wife, come up from Dorset to stay with him. The two redheaded young men and the giggling girls were all hers. Sir Bloet didn't have any children.

Which of course was why he was marrying one, with, apparently, everyone's approval. The carrying on of the line was the all-important concern in 1320. The younger the woman, the better her chance of producing enough heirs that one at least would survive to adulthood, even if its mother didn't.

The shrew with the faded red hair was, horror of horrors, Lady Yvolde, his unmarried sister. She lived at Courcy with him and, Kivrin saw, watching her shouting at poor Maisry for dropping a basket, had a bunch of keys at her belt. That meant she ran the household, or would until Easter. Poor Rosemund wouldn't stand a chance.

'Who are all the others?' Kivrin asked, hoping there might be at least one ally for Rosemund among them.

'Servants,' Rosemund said, as if it were obvious, and ran back to the girls.

There were at least twenty of them, not counting the grooms who were putting the horses up, and nobody, not even the nervous Eliwys, seemed surprised by their number. She had read that noble households had dozens of servants, but had thought those figures must be off. Eliwys and Imeyne had scarcely any servants at all, had had to put practically the whole village to work to get ready for Yule, and although she had put part of it down to their being in trouble, she had also thought the numbers of attendants for the rural manors must have been exaggerated. They obviously weren't.

The servants swarmed over the hall, serving supper. Kivrin had not known whether they would eat an evening meal at all, since Christmas Eve was a fast day, but as soon as the pale chaplain finished reading vespers, obviously on Lady Imeyne's orders, the herd of servants trooped in with a meal of bread, watered wine and dried cod that had been soaked in lyewater and then roasted.

Agnes was so excited she didn't eat a bite, and after supper had been cleared away she refused to come and sit quietly by the hearth, but ran round the hall, ringing her bell and pestering the dogs.

Sir Bloet's servants and the steward brought in the Yule log and dumped it on the hearth, scattering sparks everywhere. The women stepped back, laughing, and the children screamed with delight. Rosemund as eldest child of the house, lit the log with a faggot saved from the Yule log the year before, touching it gingerly to the tip of one of the crooked roots. There was laughter and applause when it caught, and Agnes waved her arm wildly to make her bell ring.

Rosemund had said earlier that the children were allowed to stay up for the mass at midnight, but Kivrin had hoped she could at least coax Agnes to lie down on the bench beside her and take a nap. Instead, as the evening progressed, Agnes got wilder and wilder, shrieking and ringing her bell till Kivrin had to take it away from her.

The women sat down by the hearth, talking quietly. The men stood in little groups, their arms folded across their chests, and several times they all went outside, except for the chaplain, and came back in stamping the snow off their feet and laughing. It was obvious from their red faces and Imeyne's look of disapproval that they had been out in the brew house with a keg of ale, breaking their fast.

When they came in the third time, Bloet sat down across the hearth and stretched out his legs to the fire, watching the girls. The three gigglers and Rosemund were playing blind man's bluff. When Rosemund blindfolded came close to the benches, Bloet reached out and pulled her on to his lap. Everyone laughed.

Imeyne spent the long evening sitting by the chaplain, reciting her grievances against Father Roche to him. He was ignorant, he was clumsy, he had said the Confiteor before Adjutorum during the mass last Sunday. And he was out there in that ice-cold church on his knees, Kivrin thought, while the chaplain warmed his hands at the fire and shook his head disapprovingly.

The flare died down to glowing embers. Rosemund slid off Bloet's lap and ran back to the game. Gawyn told the story of how he had killed six wolves, watching Eliwys the whole time. The chaplain told a story about a dying woman who had made false confession. When the chaplain had touched her forehead with the holy oil, her skin had smoked and turned black before his eyes.

Halfway through the chaplain's story, Gawyn stood up, rubbed his hands over the fire and went over to the beggar's bench. He sat down and pulled off his boot.

After a minute Eliwys stood up and went over to him. Kivrin couldn't hear what she said to him but he stood up, the boot still in his hand.

'The trial is once more delayed,' Kivrin heard Gawyn say. 'The judge who was to hear it is taken ill.'

She couldn't hear Eliwys' answer, but Gawyn nodded and said, 'It is good news. The new judge is from Swindone and less kindly disposed to King Edward,' but neither of them looked like it was good news. Eliwys was nearly as white as she had been when Imeyne told her she'd sent Gawyn to Courcy.

She twisted her heavy ring. Gawyn sat down again, brushed the rushes from the bottom of his hose and pulled the boot on, and then looked up again and said something. Eliwys turned her head aside and Kivrin couldn't see her expression for the shadows, but she could see Gawyn's.

And so could anyone else in the hall, Kivrin thought, and looked hastily around to see if the couple had been observed. Imeyne was deep in complaint with the chaplain but Sir Bloet's sister was watching, her mouth tight with disapproval, and so, on the opposite side of the fire, were Bloet and the other men.

Kivrin had hoped she might have a chance to speak with Gawyn tonight, but she obviously could not among all these watchful people. A bell rang, and Eliwys started and looked towards the door.

'It is the Devil's knell,' the chaplain said quietly, and even the children stopped their games to listen.

In some villages the contemps had rung the bell once for each year since the birth of Christ. In most it had only been tolled for the hour before midnight, and Kivrin doubted whether Roche, or even the chaplain, could count high enough to toll the years, but she began keeping count anyway.

Three servants came in, bearing logs and kindling, and replenished the fire. It flared up brightly, throwing huge, distorted shadows on the walls. Agnes jumped up and pointed, and one of Sir Bloet's nephews made a rabbit with his hands.

Mr Latimer had told her that the contemps had read the future in the Yule log's shadows. She wondered what the future held for them, Lord Guillaume in trouble and all of them in danger.

The king had forfeited the lands and property of convicted criminals. They might be forced to live in France or to accept charity from Sir Bloet and endure snubs from the steward's wife.

Or Lord Guillaume might come home tonight with good news and a falcon for Agnes, and they would all live happily ever after. Except Eliwys. And Rosemund. What would happen to her?

It's already happened, Kivrin thought wonderingly. The verdict is already in and Lord Guillaume's come home and found out about Gawyn and Eliwys. Rosemund's already been handed over to Sir Bloet. And Agnes has grown up and married and died in childbirth, or of blood poisoning, or cholera, or pneumonia.

They've all died, she thought, and couldn't make herself believe it. They've all been dead over seven hundred years.

'Look!' Agnes shrieked. 'Rosemund has no head!' She pointed to the distorted shadows the fire cast on the walls as it flared up. Rosemund's, oddly elongated, ended at the shoulders.

One of the redheaded boys ran over to Agnes. 'I have no head either!' he said, jumping on tiptoe to change the shadow's shape.

'You have no head, Rosemund,' Agnes shouted happily. 'You will die ere the year is out.'

'Say not such things,' Eliwys said, starting towards her. Everyone looked up.

'Kivrin has a head,' Agnes said. 'I have a head but poor Rosemund has none.'

Eliwys caught hold of Agnes by both arms. 'Those are but foolish games,' she said. 'Say not such things.'

'The shadow—' Agnes said, looking like she was going to cry.

'Sit you down by Lady Katherine and be still,' Eliwys said. She brought her over to Kivrin and almost pushed her on to the bench. 'You are grown too wild.'

Agnes huddled next to Kivrin, trying to decide whether to cry or not. Kivrin had lost count, but she picked up where she had left off. Forty-six, forty-seven.

'I want my bell,' Agnes said, climbing off the bench.

'Nay, we must sit quietly,' Kivrin said. She took Agnes on to her lap.

'Tell me of Christmas.'

'I can't, Agnes. I can't remember.'

'Do you remember *naught* that you can tell me?'

I remember it all, Kivrin thought. The shops are full of ribbons, satin and mylar and velvet, red and gold and blue, brighter even than my woad-dyed cloak, and there's light everywhere and music. Great Tom and Magdalen's bells and Christmas carols.

She thought of the Carfax carillon, trying to play 'It Came Upon the Midnight Clear', and the tired old piped carols in the shops along the High. Those carols haven't even been written yet, Kivrin thought, and felt a sudden wash of homesickness.

'I would ring my bell,' Agnes said, struggling to get off Kivrin's lap. 'Give it to me.' She held out her wrist.

'I will tie it on if you will lie down a little on the bench beside me,' Kivrin said.

She started to pucker up into a pout again. 'Must I sleep?'

'No. I will tell you a story,' Kivrin said, untying the bell from her own wrist, where she had put it for safekeeping. 'Once—' she said and then stopped, wondering if 'once upon a time' dated as far back as 1320 and what sort of stories the contemps told their children. Stories about wolves and about witches whose skin turned black when they were given extreme unction.

'There once was a maiden,' she said, tying the bell on Agnes' chubby wrist. The red ribbon had already begun to fray at the edges. It wouldn't tolerate many more knottings and unknottings. She bent over it. 'A maiden who lived—'

'Is this the maiden?' a woman's voice said.

Kivrin looked up. It was Bloet's sister Yvolde, with Imeyne

behind her. She stared at Kivrin, her mouth pinched with disapproval, and then shook her head.

'Nay, this is not Uluric's daughter,' she said. 'That maid was short and dark.'

'Nor de Ferrers' ward?' Imeyne said.

'She is dead,' Yvolde said. 'Do you remember naught of who you are?' she asked Kivrin.

'Nay, good lady,' Kivrin said, remembering too late that she was supposed to keep her eyes modestly on the floor.

'She was struck upon the head,' Agnes volunteered.

'Yet you remember your name and how to speak. Are you of good family?'

'I do not remember my family, good lady,' Kivrin said, trying to keep her voice meek.

Yvolde sniffed. 'She sounds of the west. Have you sent to Bath for news?'

'Nay,' Imeyne said. 'My son's wife would wait on his arrival. You have heard naught from Oxenford?'

'Nay, but there is much illness there,' Yvolde said.

Rosemund came up. 'Know you Lady Katherine's family, Lady Yvolde?' she asked.

Yvolde turned her pinched look on her. 'Nay. Where is the brooch my brother gave you?'

'I . . . 'tis on my cloak,' Rosemund stammered.

'Do you not honour his gifts enough to wear them?'

'Go and fetch it,' Lady Imeyne said. 'I would see this brooch.'

Rosemund's chin went up, but she went over to the outer wall where the cloaks hung.

'She shows as little eagerness for my brother's gifts as for his presence,' Yvolde said. 'She spoke not once to him at supper.'

Rosemund came back, carrying her green cloak with the brooch pinned to it. She showed it wordlessly to Imeyne. 'I would see it,' Agnes said, and Rosemund bent down to show her.

The brooch had red stones set on a round gold ring, and the pin in the centre. It had no hinge, but had to be pulled up and stuck through the garment. Letters ran around the outside of the ring: '*Io suiicien lui dami amo.*'

'What does it say?' Agnes said, pointing to the letters ringing the gold circle.

'I know not,' Rosemund said in a tone that clearly meant 'And I don't care.'

Yvolde's jaw tightened, and Kivrin said hastily, 'It says, "You are here in place of the friend I love," Agnes,' and then realised sickly what she had done. She looked up at Imeyne, but Imeyne didn't seem to have noticed anything.

'Such words should be on your breast instead of hanging on a peg,' Imeyne said. She took the brooch and pinned it to the front of Rosemund's kirtle.

'And you should be at my brother's side as befits his betrothed,' Yvolde said, 'instead of playing childish games.' She extended her hand in the direction of the hearth where Bloet was sitting, nearly asleep and obviously the worse for all the trips outside, and Rosemund looked beseechingly at Kivrin.

'Go and thank Sir Bloet for such a generous gift,' Imeyne said coldly.

Rosemund handed Kivrin her cloak and started towards the hearth.

'Come, Agnes,' Kivrin said. 'You must rest.'

'I would listen to the Devil's knell,' Agnes said.

'Lady Katherine,' Yvolde said, and there was an odd emphasis on the word 'Lady,' 'you told us you remembered naught. Yet you read Lady Rosemund's brooch with ease. Can you read, then?'

I can read, Kivrin thought, but fewer than a third of the contemps could, and even fewer of women.

She glanced at Imeyne, who was looking at her the way she had the first morning she was here, fingering her clothes and examining her hands.

'No,' Kivrin said, looking Yvolde directly in the eye, 'I fear I cannot read even the Paternoster. Your brother told us what the words meant when he gave the brooch to Rosemund.'

'Nay, he did not,' Agnes said.

'You were looking at your bell,' Kivrin said, thinking, Lady Yvolde will never believe that, she'll ask him and he'll say he never spoke to me.

But Yvolde seemed satisfied. 'I did not think such a one as she

317

would be able to read,' she said to Imeyne. She gave her her hand, and they walked over to Sir Bloet.

Kivrin sank down on the bench.

'I would have my bell,' Agnes said.

'I will not tie it on unless you lie down.'

Agnes crawled into her lap. 'You must tell me the story first. Once there was a maiden.'

'Once there was a maiden,' Kivrin said. She looked at Imeyne and Yvolde. They had sat down next to Sir Bloet and were talking to Rosemund. She said something, her chin up and her cheeks very red. Sir Bloet laughed, and his hand closed over the brooch and then slid down over Rosemund's breast.

'*Once there was a maiden*—' Agnes said insistently.

'—who lived at the edge of a great forest,' Kivrin said. ' "Do not go into the forest alone," her father said—'

'But she would not heed him,' Agnes said, yawning.

'No, she wouldn't heed him. Her father loved her and cared only for her safety, but she wouldn't listen to him.'

'What was in the woods?' Agnes asked, nestling against Kivrin.

Kivrin pulled Rosemund's cloak up over her. Cut-throats and thieves, she thought. And lecherous old men and their shrewish sisters. And illicit lovers. And husbands. And judges. 'All sorts of dangerous things.'

'Wolves,' Agnes said sleepily.

'Yes, wolves.' She looked at Imeyne and Yvolde. They had moved away from Sir Bloet and were watching her, whispering.

'What happened to her?' Agnes said sleepily, her eyes already closing.

Kivrin cradled her close. 'I don't know,' she murmured. 'I don't know.'

CHAPTER TWENTY

Agnes could not have been asleep more than five minutes before the bell stopped and then began to ring again, more quickly, calling them to mass!

'Father Roche begins too soon. It is not midnight yet,' Lady Imeyne said, and it wasn't even out of her mouth before the other bells started: Wychlade and Bureford and, far away to the east, too far to be more than a breath of an echo, the bells of Oxford.

There are the Osney bells, and there's Carfax, Kivrin thought, and wondered if they were ringing at home tonight, too.

Sir Bloet heaved himself to his feet and then helped his sister up. One of their servants hurried in with their cloaks and a squirrel-fur-lined mantle. The chattering girls pulled their cloaks from the pile and fastened them, still chattering. Lady Imeyne shook Maisry, who'd fallen asleep on the beggars bench, and told her to fetch her Book of Hours, and Maisry shuffled off to the loft ladder, yawning. Rosemund came over and reached with exaggerated carefulness for her cloak, which had slid off Agnes' shoulders.

Agnes was dead to the world. Kivrin hesitated, hating to have to wake her up, but fairly sure even exhausted five-year-olds weren't excepted from this mass. 'Agnes,' she said softly.

'You must needs carry her to the church,' Rosemund said, struggling with Sir Bloet's gold brooch. The steward's youngest boy came and stood in front of Kivrin with her white cloak, dragging it on the rushes.

'Agnes,' Kivrin said again, and jostled her a little, amazed that the church bell hadn't waked her. It sounded louder and closer

319

than it ever did for matins or vespers, its overtones nearly drowning out the other bells.

Agnes' eyes flew open. 'You did not wake me,' she said sleepily to Rosemund, and then more loudly as she came awake, 'You promised to wake me.'

'Get into your cloak,' Kivrin said. 'We must go to church.'

'Kivrin, I would wear my bell.'

'You're wearing it,' Kivrin said, trying to fasten Agnes' red cape without stabbing her in the neck with the pin of the clasp.

'Nay, I have it not,' Agnes said, searching her arm. 'I would wear my *bell*!'

'Here it is,' Rosemund said, picking it up off the floor. 'It must have fallen from your wrist. But it is not meet to wear it now. This bell calls us to mass. The Christmas bells come after.'

'I shall not ring it,' Agnes said. 'I would only wear it.'

Kivrin didn't believe that for a minute, but everyone else was ready. One of Sir Bloet's men was lighting the horn lanterns with a brand from the fire and handing them to the servants. She hastily tied the bell to Agnes' wrist and took the girls by the hand.

Lady Eliwys laid her hand on Sir Bloet's upheld one. Lady Imeyne signalled to Kivrin to follow with the little girls, and the others fell in behind them solemnly, as if it were a procession, Lady Imeyne with Sir Bloet's sister, and then the rest of Sir Bloet's entourage. Lady Eliwys and Sir Bloet led the way out into the courtyard, through the gate and on to the green.

It had stopped snowing and the stars had come out. The village lay silent under its covering of white. Frozen in time, Kivrin thought. The dilapidated buildings looked different, the staggering fences and filthy daubed huts softened and graced by the snow. The lanterns caught the crystalline facets of the snowflakes and made them sparkle, but it was the stars that took Kivrin's breath away, hundreds of stars, thousands of stars, and all of them sparkling like jewels in the icy air. 'It shines,' Agnes said, and Kivrin didn't know whether she was talking about the snow or the sky.

The bell tolled evenly, calmly, its sound different again out in the frosty air – not louder, but fuller and somehow clearer. Kivrin could hear all the other bells now and recognise them, Esthcote and Witenie and Chertelintone, even though they sounded different, too. She listened for the Swindone bell, which had rung all this time, but she couldn't hear it. She couldn't hear the Oxford bells either. She wondered if she had only imagined them.

'You are ringing your bell, Agnes,' Rosemund said.

'I am not,' Agnes said. 'I am only walking.'

'Look at the church,' Kivrin said. 'Isn't it beautiful?'

It flamed like a beacon at the other end of the green, lit from inside and out, the stained-glass windows throwing wavering ruby and sapphire lights on the snow. There were lights all around it, too, filling the churchyard all the way to the bell tower. Torches. She could smell their tarry smoke. More torches made their way in from the white fields, winding down from the hill behind the church.

She thought suddenly of Oxford on Christmas Eve, the shops lit for last-minute shopping and the windows of Brasenose shining yellow on to the quad. And the Christmas tree at Balliol lit with multicoloured strings of laser lights.

'I would that we had come to you for Yule,' Lady Imeyne said to Lady Yvolde. 'Then we had had a proper priest to say the masses. This place's priest can but barely say the Paternoster.'

This place's priest just spent hours kneeling in an ice-cold church, Kivrin thought, hours kneeling in hose that have holes in the knees, and now this place's priest is ringing a heavy bell that has had to be tolled for an hour and will shortly go through an elaborate ceremony that he has had to memorise because he cannot read.

'It will be a poor sermon and a poor mass, I fear,' Lady Imeyne said.

'Alas, there are many who do not love God in these days,' Lady Yvolde said, 'but we must pray to God that He will set the world right and bring men again to virtue.'

Kivrin doubted if that answer was what Lady Imeyne wanted to hear.

'I have sent to the Bishop of Bath to send us a chaplain,' Imeyne said, 'but he has not yet come.'

'My brother says there is much trouble in Bath,' Yvolde said.

They were almost to the churchyard. Kivrin could make out

faces now, lit by the smoky torches and by little oil cressets some of
the women were carrying. Their faces, reddened and lit from
below, looked faintly sinister. Mr Dunworthy would think they
were an angry mob, Kivrin thought, gathered to burn some poor
martyr at the stake. It's the light, she thought. Everyone looks like
a cut-throat by torchlight. No wonder they invented electricity.

They came into the churchyard. Kivrin recognised some of the
people near the church doors: the boy with the scurvy who had
run from her, two of the young girls who'd helped with the
Christmas baking, Cob. The steward's wife was wearing a cloak
with an ermine collar and carrying a metal lantern with four tiny
panes of real glass. She was talking animatedly to the woman with
the scrofula scars who had helped put up the holly. They were all
talking and moving around to keep warm, and one man with a
black beard was laughing so hard his torch swept dangerously
close to the steward's wife's wimple.

Church officials had eventually had to do away with the midnight mass because of all the drinking and carousing, Kivrin
remembered, and some of these parishioners definitely looked
like they had spent the evening breaking fasts. The steward was
talking animatedly to a rough-looking man Rosemund pointed
out as Maisry's father. Both their faces were bright red from the
cold or the torchlight or the liqueur or all three, but they seemed
gay rather than dangerous. The steward kept punctuating what he
was saying with hard, thunking claps on Maisry's father's shoulder, and every time he did it the father laughed, a happy helpless
giggle that made Kivrin think he was much brighter than she had
supposed.

The steward's wife grabbed for her husband's sleeve, and he
shook her off, but as soon as Lady Eliwys and Sir Bloet came
through the lychgate, he and Maisry's father fell back promptly to
make a clear path into the church. So did all the others, falling
silent as the entourage passed through the churchyard and in the
heavy doors, and then beginning to talk again, but more quietly,
as they came into the church behind them.

Sir Bloet unbuckled his sword and handed it to a servant, and
he and Lady Eliwys knelt and genuflected as soon as they were in

the door. They walked almost to the rood screen together and knelt again.

Kivrin and the little girls followed. When Agnes crossed herself, her bell jangled hollowly in the church. I'll have to take it off her, Kivrin thought, and wondered if she should step out of the procession now and take Agnes off to the side by Lady Imeyne's husband's tomb and undo it, but Lady Imeyne was waiting impatiently at the door with Sir Bloet's sister.

She led the girls to the front. Sir Bloet had already lumbered to his feet again. Eliwys stayed on her knees a little longer, and then stood, and Sir Bloet escorted her to the north side of the church, bowed slightly and walked over to take his place on the men's side.

Kivrin knelt with the little girls, praying Agnes wouldn't make too much noise when she crossed herself again. She didn't, but when Agnes got to her feet she snagged her foot in the hem of her robe and caught herself with a clanging almost as loud as the bell still tolling outside. Lady Imeyne was, of course, right behind them. She glared at Kivrin.

Kivrin took the girls to stand beside Eliwys. Lady Imeyne knelt, but Lady Yvolde made only an obeisance. As soon as Imeyne rose, a servant hurried forward with a dark-velvet-covered prie-dieu and laid it on the floor next to Rosemund for Lady Yvolde to kneel on. Another servant had laid one in front of Sir Bloet on the men's side and was helping him get down on his knees on it. He puffed and clung to the servant's arm as he lowered his bulk, and his face got very red.

Kivrin looked at Lady Yvolde's prie-dieu longingly, thinking of the plastic kneeling pads that hung on the backs of the chairs in St Mary's. She had never realised until now what a blessing they were, what a blessing the hard wooden chairs were either until they stood again and she thought about how they would have to remain standing through the whole service.

The floor was cold. The church was cold, in spite of all the lights. They were mostly cressets, set along the walls and in front of the holly-banked statue of St Catherine, though there was a tall, thin, yellowish candle set in the greenery of each of the windows, but the effect was probably not what Father Roche had intended.

The bright flames only made the coloured panes of glass darker, almost black.

More of the yellowish candles were in the silver candelabra on either side of the altar, and holly was heaped in front of them and along the top of the rood screen, and Father Roche had set Lady Imeyne's beeswax candles in among the sharp, shiny leaves. He'd done a job of decorating the church that should please even Lady Imeyne, Kivrin thought, and glanced at her.

She was holding her reliquary between her folded hands, but her eyes were open, and she was staring at the top of the rood screen. Her mouth was tight with disapproval, and Kivrin supposed she hadn't wanted the candles there, but it was the perfect place for them. They illuminated the crucifix and the Last Judgment and lit nearly the whole nave.

They made the whole church seem different, homier, more familiar, like St Mary's on Christmas Eve. Dunworthy had taken her to the interchurch service last Christmas. She had planned to go to midnight mass at the Holy Re-Formed to hear it said in Latin, but there hadn't been a midnight mass. The priest had been asked to read the gospel for the interchurch service, so he had moved the mass to four in the afternoon.

Agnes was fiddling with her bell again, lady Imeyne turned and glared at her across her piously folded hands, and Rosemund leaned across Kivrin and shhhed her.

'You mustn't ring your bell until the mass is over,' Kivrin whispered, bending close to Agnes so no one else could hear her.

'I rang it *not*,' Agnes whispered back in a voice that could be heard all over the church. 'The ribbon binds too tight. See you?'

Kivrin couldn't see any such thing. In fact if she had taken the time to tie it tighter it wouldn't be ringing at every movement, but there was no way she was going to argue with an overtired child when the mass was going to begin any minute. She reached for the knot.

Agnes must have been trying to pull the bell off over her wrist. The already-fraying ribbon had tightened into a solid little knot. Kivrin picked at its edges with her fingernails, keeping an eye on the people behind her. The service would start with a procession;

Father Roche and his acolytes, if he had any, would come down the aisle bearing the holy water and chanting the Asperges.

Kivrin pulled on the ribbon and both sides of the knot, tightening it beyond any hope of ever getting it off without cutting it, but getting a little more slack. It still wasn't enough to get the ribbon off. She glanced back at the church door. The bell had stopped, but there was still no sign of Father Roche and no aisle for him to come up either. The townsfolk had crowded in, filling the whole rear of the church. Someone had lifted a child up on to Imeyne's husband's tomb and was holding him there so he could see, but there wasn't anything to see yet.

She went back to working on the bell. She got two fingers under the ribbon and pulled up on it, trying to stretch it.

'Tear it *not!*' Agnes said in that carrying stage whisper of hers. Kivrin took hold of the bell and hastily pulled it round so it lay in Agnes' palm.

'Hold it like this,' she whispered, cupping Agnes' fingers over it. 'Tightly.'

Agnes obligingly clenched her little fist. Kivrin folded Agnes' other hand over the top of the fist in a so-so facsimile of a praying attitude and said softly, 'Hold tight to the bell, and it will not ring.'

Agnes promptly pressed her hands to her forehead in an attitude of angelic piety.

'Good girl,' Kivrin said, and put her arm round her. She glanced back at the church doors. They were still closed She breathed a sigh of relief and turned back to face the altar.

Father Roche was standing there. He was dressed in an embroidered white stole and a yellowed white alb with a hem more frayed than Agnes' ribbon, and was holding a book. He had obviously been waiting for her, had obviously stood there watching her the whole time she tended to Agnes, but there was no reproof in his face or even impatience. His face held some other expression entirely, and she was reminded suddenly of Mr Dunworthy, standing and watching her through the thin-glass partition.

Lady Imeyne cleared her throat, a sound that was almost a growl, and he seemed to come to himself. He handed the book to Cob, who was wearing a grimy cassock and a pair of too-large leather shoes, and knelt in front of the altar. Then he took the book back and began saying the lections.

Kivrin said them to herself along with him, thinking the Latin and hearing the echo of the interpreter's translation.

'"Whom saw ye, O Shepherds?"' Father Roche recited in Latin, beginning the responsory. '"Speak tell us who hath appeared on the earth."'

He stopped frowning at Kivrin.

He's forgotten it, she thought. She glanced anxiously at Imeyne, hoping she wouldn't realise there was more to come, but Imeyne had raised her head and was scowling at him, her jaw in the silk wimple clenched.

Roche was still frowning at Kivrin. '"Speak, what saw ye?"' he said, and Kivrin gave a sigh of relief. '"Tell us who hath appeared."'

That wasn't right. She mouthed the next line, willing him to understand it. '"We saw the newborn Child."'

He gave no indication that he had seen what she said, though he was looking straight at her. 'I saw . . .' he said, and stopped again.

'"We saw the newborn Child,"' Kivrin whispered, and could feel Lady Imeyne turning to look at her.

'"And angels singing praise unto the Lord,"' Roche said, and that wasn't right either, but Lady Imeyne turned back to the front to fasten her disapproving gaze on Roche.

The bishop would no doubt hear about this, and about the candles and the fraying hem, and who knew what other errors and infractions he had committed.

'"Speak, what saw ye?"' Kivrin mouthed, and he seemed suddenly to come to himself.

'"Speak, what saw ye?"' he said clearly. '"And tell us of the birth of Christ. We saw the newborn Child and angels singing praise unto the Lord."'

He began the Confiteor Deo, and Kivrin whispered it along with him, but he got through it without any mistakes, and Kivrin began to relax a little, though she watched him closely as he moved to the altar for the Ordmus Te.

He was wearing a black cassock under the alb, and both of

them looked like they had once been richly made. They were much too short for Roche. She could see a good ten centimetres of his worn brown hose below the cassock's hem when he bent over the altar. The alb and cassock had probably belonged to the priest before him, or were cast-offs of Imeyne's chaplain.

The priest of Holy Re-Formed had worn a polyester alb over a brown jumper and jeans. He had assured Kivrin that the mass was completely authentic, in spite of its being held in midafternoon. The antiphon dated from the eighth century, he had told her, and the gruesomely detailed stations of the cross were exact copies of Turin's. But the church had been a converted stationer's shop, they had used a folding table for an altar, and the Carfax carillon outside had been busily destroying 'It Came Upon the Midnight. Clear'.

'*Kyrie eléson*,' Cob said, his hands folded in prayer.

'*Kyrie eléson*,' Father Roche said.

'*Christe eléson*,' Cob said.

'*Christe eléson*,' Agnes said brightly.

Kivrin hushed her, her finger to her lips. Lord have mercy. Christ have mercy. Lord have mercy.

They had used the Kyrie at the interchurch service, probably because of some deal Holy Re-Formed's priest had struck with the vicar in return for moving the time of the mass, and the minister of the Church of the Millennium had refused to recite it and had looked coldly disapproving throughout Like Lady Imeyne.

Father Roche seemed all right now. He said the Gloria and the gradual without faltering and began the gospel. '*Inituim sancti Evangelii secundum Luke*', he said, and began to read haltingly in Latin. ' "Now it came to pass in those days that a decree went forth from Caesar Augustus that a census of the whole world be taken." '

The vicar had read the same verses at St Mary's. He had read it from the People's Common Bible, which had been insisted on by the Church of the Millennium, and it had begun, 'Around then the politicos dumped a tax hike on the ratepayers,' but it was the same gospel Father Roche was laboriously reciting.

' "And suddenly there was with the angel a multitude of the heavenly host praising God and saying, Glory to God in the highest and on earth peace among men of goodwill." ' Father Roche kissed the gospel. '*Per evangélica dicta deléantur nostra delicta.*'

The sermon should come next, if there was one. In most village churches the priest only preached at the major masses, and even then it was usually no more than a catechism lesson, the listing of the seven deadly sins or the seven Acts of Mercy. The high mass on Christmas morning was probably when the sermon would be.

But Father Roche stepped out in front of the central aisle, which had nearly closed up again as the villagers leaned against the pillars and each other, trying to find a more comfortable position, and began to speak.

'In the days when Christ came to earth from heaven, God sent signs that men might know his coming, and in the last days also will there be signs. There will be famines and pestilence, and Satan will ride abroad in the land.'

Oh, no, Kivrin thought, don't talk about seeing the Devil riding a black horse.

She glanced at Imeyne. The old woman looked furious, but it wouldn't matter what he'd said, Kivrin thought. She'd been determined to find mistakes and lapses she could tell the bishop about. Lady Yvolde looked mildly irritated and everyone else had the look of tired patience people always got when listening to a sermon, no matter what the century. Kivrin had seen the same look in St Mary's last Christmas.

The sermon at St Mary's had been on rubbish disposal, and the dean of Christ Church had begun it by saying, 'Christianity began in a stable. Will it end in a sewer?'

But it hadn't mattered. It had been midnight, and St Mary's had had a stone floor and a real altar, and when she'd closed her eyes, she'd been able to shut out the carpeted nave and the umbrellas and the laser candles. She had pushed the plastic kneeling pad out of her way and knelt on the stone floor and imagined what it would be like in the Middle Ages.

Mr Dunworthy had told her it wouldn't be like anything she had imagined, and he was right, of course. But not about this mass. She had imagined it just like this, the stone floor, and the murmured Kyrie, the smells of incense and tallow and cold.

'The Lord will come with fire and pestilence, and all will perish,' Roche said, 'but even in the last days, God's mercy will not forsake us. He will send us help and comfort and bring us safely unto heaven.'

Safely unto heaven. She thought of Mr Dunworthy. 'Don't go,' he had said. 'It won't be anything like you imagine.' And he was right. He was always right.

But even he, with all his imagining of smallpox and cutthroats and witchburnings, would never have imagined this: that she was lost. That she didn't know where the drop was and the rendezvous was less than a week away. She looked across the aisle at Gawyn, who was watching Eliwys. She had to talk to him after the mass.

Father Roche moved to the altar to begin the mass proper. Agnes leaned against Kivrin, and Kivrin put her arm round her. Poor thing, she must be exhausted. Up since before dawn and all that wild running around. She wondered how long the mass would take.

The service at St Mary's had taken an hour and a quarter, and halfway through the offertory Dr Ahrens' bleeper had gone off. 'It's a baby,' she'd whispered to Kivrin and Dunworthy as she hurried out, 'how appropriate.'

I wonder if they're in church now, she thought and then remembered it wasn't Christmas there. They had had Christmas three days after she arrived, while she was still ill. It would be what? The second of January, Christmas Vac nearly over and all the decorations taken down.

It was starting to get hot in the church, and the candles seemed to be taking all the air. She could hear shiftings and shufflings behind her as Father Roche went through the ritualised steps of the mass, and Agnes sank further and further against her. She was glad when they reached the Sanctus and she could kneel.

She tried to imagine Oxford on the second of January, the shops advertising New Year's sales and the Carfax carillon silent. Dr Ahrens would be at the Infirmary dealing with post-holiday stomach upsets and Mr Dunworthy would be getting ready for Hilary term. No, he's not, she thought, and saw him standing behind the thin-glass. He's worrying about me.

Father Roche raised the chalice, knelt, kissed the altar. There was more shuffling, and a whispering on the men's side of the church. She looked across. Gawyn was sitting back on his heels, looking bored. Sir Bloet was asleep.

So was Agnes. She had collapsed so completely against Kivrin there would be no way she could stand for the Paternoster. She didn't even try. When everyone else stood for it, Kivrin took the opportunity to gather Agnes in more closely and shift her head to a better position. Kivrin's knee hurt. She must have knelt in the depression between two stones. She shifted it, raising it slightly and cramming a fold of her cloak under it.

Father Roche put a piece of bread in the chalice and said the Haec Commixtio, and everyone knelt for the Agnus dei. '*Agnus dei, qui tollis peccata mundi: miserere nobis,*' he chanted. ' "Lamb of God, who takest away the sins of the world, have mercy upon us." '

Agnus dei. Lamb of God. Kivrin smiled down at Agnes. She was sound asleep, her body a dead weight against Kivrin's side and her mouth slackly open, but her fist was still clenched tightly over the little bell. My lamb, Kivrin thought.

Kneeling on St Mary's stone floor she had envisioned the – candles and the cold, but not Lady Imeyne, waiting for Roche to make a mistake in the mass, not Eliwys or Gawyn or Rosemund. Not Father Roche, with his cut-throat's face and worn-out hose.

She could never in a hundred years, in seven hundred and thirty-four years, have imagined Agnes, with her puppy and her naughty tantrums, and her infected knee. I'm glad I came, she thought. In spite of everything.

Father Roche made the sign of the cross with the chalice and drank it. '*Dominus vobiscum,*' he said and there was a general commotion behind Kivrin. The main part of the show was over, and people were leaving now, to avoid the crush. Apparently there was no deference to the lord's family when it came to leaving. Or even in waiting till they were outside to begin talking. She could scarcely hear the dismissal.

'*Ite, Missa est,*' Father Roche said over the din, and Lady Imeyne was in the aisle before he could even lower his raised hand looking like she intended to leave for Bath and the bishop immediately.

'Saw you the tallow candles by the altar?' she said to Lady Yvolde. 'I *bade* him use the beeswax candles that I gave him.'

Lady Yvolde shook her head and looked darkly at Father Roche, and the two of them swept out with Rosemund right at their heels.

Rosemund obviously had no intention of walking back to the manor with Sir Bloet if she could help it, and this should do it. The villagers had closed in behind the three women, talking and laughing. By the time Sir Bloet huffed and puffed his way to his feet, they would be all the way to the manor.

Kivrin was having trouble getting up herself. Her foot had gone to sleep and Agnes was dead to the world. 'Agnes,' she said. 'Wake up. It's time to go home.'

Sir Bloet had got to his feet, his face nearly purple with the effort, and had come across to offer Eliwys his arm. 'Your daughter has fallen asleep,' he said.

'Aye,' Eliwys said, glancing at Agnes.

She took his arm and they started out.

'Your husband has not come as he promised.'

'Nay,' Kivrin heard Eliwys say. Her grip tightened on his arm.

Outside, the bells began to ring all at once, and out of time, a wild, irregular chiming. It sounded wonderful. 'Agnes,' Kivrin said, shaking her, 'it's time to ring your bell.'

She didn't even stir. Kivrin tried to get the sleeping child on to her shoulder. Her arms flopped limply over Kivrin's shoulders, and the bell jangled.

'You waited all night to ring your bell,' Kivrin said, getting to one knee. 'Wake up, lamb.'

She looked around for someone to help her. There was scarcely anyone left in the church. Cob was making the rounds of the windows, pinching the candle flames out between his chapped fingers. Gawyn and Sir Bloet's nephews were at the back of the nave, buckling on their swords. Father Roche was nowhere to be seen. She wondered if he was the one ringing the bell with such joyous enthusiasm.

Her numb foot was beginning to tingle. She flexed it in the thin shoe and then put her weight on it. It felt terrible, but she could stand on it. She hoisted Agnes further over her shoulder and tried to stand up. Her foot caught in the hem of her skirt and she pitched forward.

Gawyn caught her. 'Good lady Katherine, my lady Eliwys bade me come to help you,' he said, steadying her. He lifted Agnes easily out of her arms and on to his shoulder, and strode out of the church, Kivrin hobbling beside him.

'Thank you,' Kivrin said when they were out of the jammed churchyard. 'My arms felt like they were going to fall off.'

'She is a stout lass,' he said.

Agnes' bell slid off her wrist and fell on to the snow, clattering with the other bells as it fell. Kivrin stooped and picked it up. The knot was almost too small to be seen, and the short ends of ribbon beyond it were frayed into thin threads, but the moment she took hold of it, the knot came undone. She tied it on Agnes' dangling wrist with a little bow.

'I am glad to assist a lady in distress,' Gawyn said, but she didn't hear him.

They were all alone on the green. The rest of the family was nearly to the manor gate. She could see the steward holding the lantern over Lady Imeyne and Lady Yvolde as they started into the passage. There were a lot of people still in the churchyard, and someone had built a bonfire next to the road and people were standing around it, warming their hands and passing a wooden bowl of something, but here, halfway across the green, they were all alone. The opportunity she had thought would never come was here.

'I wanted to thank you for trying to find my attackers, and for rescuing me in the woods and bringing me here,' she said. 'When you found me, how far from here was the place? Could you take me to it?'

He stopped and looked at her. 'Did they not tell you?' he said. 'All of your goods and gear that were found I brought to the manor. The thieves had taken your belongings, and though I rode after them, I fear I found naught.' He started walking again.

'I know you brought my boxes here. Thank you. But that wasn't why I wanted to see the place you found me,' Kivrin said rapidly, afraid they would catch up with the others before she finished asking him.

Lady Imeyne had stopped and was looking back their way. She had to get it asked before Imeyne sent the steward back to see what was keeping them.

'I lost my memory when I was injured in the attack,' she said. 'I thought if I could see the place where you found me, I might remember something.'

He had stopped again and was looking at the road above the church. There were lights there, bobbing unsteadily and coming rapidly nearer. Latecomers to church?

'You're the only one who knows where the place is,' Kivrin said, 'or I wouldn't bother you, but if you could just tell me where it is, I could—'

'There is nothing there,' he said vaguely, still looking at the lights. 'I brought your wagon and your boxes to the manor.'

'I *know*,' Kivrin said, 'and I thank you, but—'

'They are in the barn,' he said. He turned at the sound of horses. The bobbing lights were lanterns carried by men on horseback. They galloped past the church and through the village, at least a half dozen of them, and pulled up short where Lady Eliwys and the others were standing.

It's her husband, Kivrin thought, but before she could finish her thought, Gawyn had thrust Agnes into her arms and taken off towards them, pulling his sword as he ran.

Oh, no, Kivrin thought, and began to run too, clumsy under Agnes' weight. It wasn't her husband. It was the men who were after them, the reason they were hiding, the reason Eliwys had been so angry at Imeyne for telling Sir Bloet they were here.

The men with the torches had got down off their horses. Eliwys walked forward to one of the three men still on horseback and then fell to her knees as if she had been struck.

No, oh no, Kivrin thought, out of breath. Agnes' bell jangled wildly as she ran.

Gawyn ran up to them, his sword flashing in the lantern light, and then he was on his knees too. Eliwys stood up and stepped forward to the men on horseback, her aim out in a gesture of welcome.

Kivrin stopped, out of breath. Sir Bloet came forward, knelt, stood up. The men on horseback flung back their hoods. They were wearing hats of some kind, or crowns. Gawyn, still on his knees, sheathed his sword. One of the men on horseback raised his hand, and something glittered.

'What is it?' Agnes said sleepily.

'I don't know,' Kivrin said.

Agnes twisted round in Kivrin's arms so she could see. 'It is the three kings,' she said wonderingly.

Transcript from the Domesday Book
(064996–065537)

Christmas Eve 1320 (Old Style). An envoy from the bishop has arrived along with two other churchmen. They rode in just after midnight mass. Lady Imeyne is delighted. She's convinced they've come in response to her message demanding a new chaplain, but I'm not convinced of that. They've come without any servants, and there's an air of nervousness about them, as if they were on some secret, hurried mission.

It has to concern Lord Guillaume, though the Assizes are a secular court, not an ecclesiastical one. Perhaps the bishop is a friend of Lord Guillaume's or of King Edward II's, and they've come to strike some sort of deal with Eliwys for his freedom.

Whatever their reason for being here, they're here in style. Agnes thought they were the three Magi when she first saw them, and they do look like royalty. The bishop's envoy has a thin, aristocratic face, and they are all dressed like kings. One of them has a purple velvet cloak with the design of a white cross sewn in silk on the back of it.

Lady Imeyne immediately latched on to him with her sad story of how ignorant, clumsy, generally impossible Father Roche is. 'He deserves not a parish,' she said. Unfortunately (and luckily for Father Roche) he was not the envoy, but only his clerk. The envoy was the one in the red, also very impressive, with gold embroidery and a sable hem.

The third is a Cistercian monk – least, he wears the white

habit of one, though it's made of even finer wool than my cloak and has a silk cord for a sash, and he wears a ring fit for a king on each of his fat fingers, but he doesn't act like a monk. He and the envoy both demanded wine before they'd even dismounted, and it's obvious the clerk had already drunk a good deal before he got here. He slipped just now getting off his horse and had to be supported into the hall by the fat monk.

(Break)

I was apparently wrong about the reason for their coming here. Eliwys and Sir Bloet went off in a corner with the bishop's envoy as soon as they got in the house, but they only talked to him for a few minutes, and I just heard her tell Imeyne, 'They have heard naught of Guillaume.'

Imeyne didn't seem surprised or even particularly concerned at this news. It's clear she thinks they're here to bring her a new chaplain and she is falling all over them, insisting that the Christmas feast be brought in immediately and that the bishop's envoy sit in the high seat. They seem more interested in drinking than in eating. Imeyne fetched them cups of wine herself, and they've already gone through them and called for more. The clerk caught hold of Maisry's skirt as she brought the pitcher, pulled her in hand over hand, and stuck his hand down her shift. She, of course, clapped her hands over her ears.

The one good thing about them being here is that they add tremendously to the general confusion. I only had a moment to talk to Gawyn, but sometime in the next day or so I'll surely be able to speak to him without anyone noticing – especially since Imeyne's attention is riveted on the envoy, who just grabbed the pitcher from Maisry and poured his wine himself – and get him to show me where the drop is. There's plenty of time. I have nearly a week.

CHAPTER TWENTY-ONE

Two more people died on the twenty-eighth, both of them primaries who had been at the dance in Headington, and Latimer had a stroke.

'He developed myocarditis, which caused a thrombo-embolism,' Mary had said when she phoned. 'At this point he's completely unresponsive.'

Over half of Dunworthy's detainees were down with the flu, and there was only room in Infirmary for the most severe cases. Dunworthy and Finch, and a detainee William had found who'd had a year of nurse's training, gave temps and dispensed orange juice round the clock. Dunworthy made up cots and gave medications.

And worried. When he had told Mary about Badri's saying 'That can't be right,' of his saying 'It was the rats,' she had said, 'It's the fever, James. It has no connection with reality. I've one patient who keeps talking about the queen's elephants,' but he could not get the idea of Kivrin's being in 1348 out of his mind.

'What year is it?' Badri had said that first night, and 'That can't be right.'

Dunworthy had telephoned Andrews after his argument with Gilchrist and told him he couldn't get access to Brasenose's net.

'It doesn't matter,' Andrews had said. 'The locational coordinates aren't as critical as the temporals. I'll get an L-and-L on the dig from Jesus. I've already talked to them about doing the parameter checks, and they said it's all right.'

The visuals had been off again, but he had sounded nervous, as if he was afraid Dunworthy would broach the subject again of his coming to Oxford. 'I've done some research on slippage,' he said.

'There are no theoretical limits, but in practice the minimal slippage is always greater than zero, even in uninhabited areas. Maximal slippage has never gone above five years, and those were all unmanneds. The greatest slippage on a manned drop was a seventeenth-century remote – two hundred and twenty-six days.'

'Is there anything else it could be?' Dunworthy had asked. 'Anything besides the slippage that could go wrong?'

'If the coordinates are correct, nothing,' Andrews had said and promised to report as soon as he'd done the parameter checks.

Five years was 1325. The plague had not even begun in China then, and Badri had told Gilchrist there was minimal slippage. And it couldn't be the coordinates. Badri had checked them before he fell ill. But the fear continued to nag at him, and he spent the few free moments he could snatch telephoning techs, trying to find someone willing to come read the fix when the sequencing arrived and Gilchrist opened the laboratory again. It was supposed to have arrived yesterday, but when Mary phoned she had still been waiting for it.

She phoned again in the late afternoon. 'Can you set up a ward?' she asked. The visuals were back on. Her SPGs looked like she'd slept in them, and her mask dangled from her neck by one tie.

'I've already set up a ward,' he said. 'It's full of detainees. We've got thirty-one cases as of this afternoon.'

'Do you have space to set up another one? I don't need it yet,' she said tiredly, 'but at this rate I will. We're nearly at capacity here, and several of the staff are either down with it or are refusing to come in.'

'And the sequencing hasn't come yet?' he asked.

'No. The WIC just phoned. They got a faulty result the first time through and had to run it again. It's supposed to be here tomorrow. Now they think it's a Uruguayan virus.' She smiled wanly. 'Badri hasn't been in contact with anyone from Uruguay, has he? How soon can you have the beds ready?'

'By this evening,' Dunworthy said, but Finch informed him they were nearly out of folding cots, and he had to go to the NHS and argue them out of a dozen. They didn't get the ward set up, in two of the Fellows' teaching rooms, until morning.

Finch, helping assemble the cots and make beds, announced that they were nearly out of clean linens, face masks and lavatory paper. 'We haven't enough for the detainees,' he said, tucking in a sheet, 'let alone all these patients. And we have no bandages at all.'

'It's not a war,' Dunworthy said. 'I doubt if there will be any wounded. Did you find out if any of the other colleges has a tech here in Oxford?'

'Yes, sir, I telephoned all of them, but none of them did.' He tucked a pillow beneath his chin. 'I've posted notices asking that everyone conserve lavatory paper, but it's done no good at all. The Americans are particularly wasteful.' He tugged the pillow slip up over the pillow. 'I do feel rather sorry for them, though. Helen came down with it last night, you know, and they haven't any alternates.'

'Helen?'

'Ms Piantini. The tenor. She has a fever of 39.7. The Americans won't be able to do their Chicago Surprise.'

Which is probably a blessing, Dunworthy thought. 'Ask them if they'll continue to keep watch on my telephone, even though they're no longer practising,' he said. 'I'm expecting several important calls. Did Andrews ring back?'

'No, sir, not yet. And the visual is off.' He plumped the pillow. 'It is too bad about the peal. They can do Stedmans, of course, but that's old hat. It does seem a pity there's no alternative solution.'

'Did you get the list of techs?'

'Yes, sir,' Finch said, struggling with a reluctant cot. He motioned with his head. 'It's there by the chalkboard.'

Dunworthy picked up the sheets of paper and looked at the one on top. It was filled with columns of numbers, all of them with the digits one to six, in varying order.

'That's not it,' Finch said, snatching the papers away. 'Those are the changes for the Chicago Surprise.' He handed Dunworthy a single sheet. 'Here it is. I've listed the techs by college with addresses and telephone numbers.'

Colin came in, wearing his wet jacket and carrying a roll of tape and a plastene-covered bundle. 'The vicar said I'm to put these up in all the wards,' he said, taking out a placard that read

'Feeling Disorientated? Muddled? Mental Confusion Can Be a Warning Sign of the Flu'.

He tore off a strip of tape and stuck the placard to the chalk-board. 'I was just posting these at the Infirmary, and what do you think the Gallstone was doing?' he said, taking another placard out of the bundle. It read 'Wear Your Face Mask'. He taped it to the wall above the cot Finch was making up. 'Reading the Bible to the patients.' He pocketed the tape. 'I hope *I* don't catch it.' He tucked the rest of the placards under his arm and started out.

'Wear your face mask,' Dunworthy said.

Colin grinned. 'That's what the Gallstone said. *And* she said, the Lord would smite anyone who heeded not the words of the righteous.' He pulled the grey plaid muffler out of his pocket. 'I wear this instead of a face mask,' he said, tying it over his mouth and nose highwayman fashion.

'Cloth cannot keep out microscopic viruses,' Dunworthy said.

'I know. It's the colour. It frightens them away.' He darted out.

Dunworthy rang Mary to tell her the ward was ready but couldn't get through, so he went over to Infirmary. The rain had let up a little and people, mostly wearing masks, were out again, coming back from the grocer's and queuing in front of the chemist's. But the streets seemed hushed, unnaturally silent.

Someone's turned the carillon off, Dunworthy thought. He almost regretted it.

Mary was in her office, staring at a screen. 'The sequencing's arrived,' she said before he could tell her about the ward.

'Have you told Gilchrist?' he said eagerly.

'No,' she said. 'It's not the Uruguay virus. Or the South Carolina.'

'What is it?'

'It's an H9N2. Both the South Carolina and the Uruguay were H3s.'

'Then where did it come from?'

'The WIC doesn't know. It's not a known virus. It's previously unsequenced.' She handed him a printout. 'It has a seven point mutation, which explains why it's killing people.'

He looked at the printout. It was covered with columns of

numbers, like Finch's list of changes, and as unintelligible. 'It has to come from somewhere.'

'Not necessarily. Approximately every ten years there's a major antigenic shift with epidemic potential, so it may have originated with Badri.' She took the printout back from him. 'Does he live around livestock, do you know?'

'Livestock?' he said. 'He lives in a flat in Headington.'

'Mutant strains are sometimes produced by the intersection of an avian virus with a human strain. The WIC wants us to check possible avian contacts and exposure to radiation. Viral mutations have sometimes been caused by X-rays.' She studied the printout as though it made sense. 'It's an unusual mutation. There's no recombination of the hemagluttinin genes, only an extremely large point mutation.'

No wonder she had not told Gilchrist. He had said he would open the laboratory when the sequencing arrived but this news would only convince him he should keep it closed.

'Is there a cure?'

'There will be as soon as an analogue can be manufactured. And a vaccine. They've already begun work on the prototype.'

'How long?'

'Three to five days to produce a prototype, then at least another five to manufacture, if they don't run into any difficulty with duplicating the proteins. We should be able to begin inoculating by the tenth.'

The tenth. And that was when they could *begin* giving immunisations. How long would it take to immunise the quarantine area? A week? Two? Before Gilchrist and the idiot protesters considered it safe to open the laboratory?

'That's too long,' Dunworthy said.

'I know,' Mary said, and sighed. 'God knows how many cases we'll have by then. There have been twenty new ones already this morning.'

'Do you think it's a mutant strain?' Dunworthy asked.

She thought about it. 'No. I think it's much more likely that Badri caught it from someone at that dance in Headington. There may have been New Hindus there, or Earthers, or someone else who doesn't believe in antivirals or modern medicine. The

340

Canadian goose flu of 2010, if you'll remember, was traced back to a Christian Science commune. There's a source. We'll find it.'

'And what about Kivrin in the meantime? What if you don't find the source by the rendezvous? Kivrin's supposed to come back on the sixth of January. Will you have it sourced by then?'

'I don't know,' she said wearily. 'She may not want to come back to a century that's rapidly becoming a ten. She may want to stay in 1320.'

If she's in 1320, he thought, and went up to see Badri. He had not mentioned rats since Christmas night. He was back to the afternoon at Bailiol when he had come looking for Dunworthy. 'Laboratory?' he murmured when he saw Dunworthy. He tried feebly to hand him a note and then seemed to sink into sleep, exhausted by the effort.

Dunworthy stayed only a few minutes and then went to see Gilchrist.

It was raining hard again by the time he reached Brasenose. The gaggle of picketers were huddling underneath their banner, shivering.

The porter was standing at the lodge desk, taking the decorations off the little Christmas tree. He glanced up at Dunworthy and looked suddenly alarmed. Dunworthy walked past him and through the gate.

'You can't go in there, Mr Dunworthy,' the porter called after him. 'The college is restricted.'

Dunworthy walked into the quad. Gilchrist's rooms were in the building behind the laboratory. He hurried towards them, expecting the porter to catch up to him and try to stop him.

The laboratory had a large yellow sign on it that read 'No Admittance Without Authorisation', and an electronic alarm attached to the door frame.

'Mr Dunworthy,' Gilchrist said, striding towards him through the rain. The porter must have phoned him. 'The laboratory is off-limits.'

'I came to see you,' Dunworthy said.

The porter came up, trailing a tinsel garland. 'Shall I phone for the University police?' he asked.

'That won't be necessary. Come up to my rooms,' he said to Dunworthy. 'I have something I want you to see.'

He led Dunworthy into his office, sat down at his cluttered desk and put on an elaborate mask with some sort of filters.

'I've just spoken to the WIC,' he said. His voice sounded hollow, as if it were coming from a great distance. 'The virus is a previously unsequenced virus whose source is unknown.'

'It's been sequenced now,' Dunworthy said, 'and the analogue and vaccine are due to arrive in a few days. Dr Ahrens has arranged for Brasenose to be given immunisation priority, and I'm attempting to locate a tech who can read the fix as soon as immunisation has been completed.'

'I'm afraid that's impossible,' Gilchrist said hollowly. 'I've been conducting research into the incidence of influenza in the 1300s. There are clear indications that a series of influenza epidemics in the first half of the fourteenth century severely weakened the populace, thereby lowering their resistance to the Black Death.'

He picked up an ancient-looking book. 'I have found six separate references to outbreaks between October 1318 and February 1321.' He held up a book and began to read. ' "After the harvest there came upon all of Dorset a fever so fierce as to leave many dead. This fever began with an aching in the head and confusion in all the parts. The doctors bled them, but many died in despite." '

A fever. In an age of fevers – typhoid and cholera and measles, all of them producing 'aching of the head and confusion in all the parts.'

'1319. The Bath Assizes for the previous year were cancelled,' Gilchrist said, holding up another book. ' "A malady of the chest that fell upon the court so that none, nor judge nor jury, were left to hear the cases," ' Gilchrist said. He looked at Dunworthy over the mask. 'You stated that the public's fears over the net were hysterical and unfounded. It would seem, however, that they are based in solid historical fact.'

Solid historical fact. References to fevers and maladies of the chest that could be anything, blood poisoning or typhus or any of a hundred nameless infections. All of which was beside the point.

'The virus cannot have come through the net,' he said. 'Drops have been made to the Pandemic, to World War I battles in which mustard gas was used, to Tel Aviv. Twentieth Century sent detection equipment to the site of St Paul's two days after the pinpoint was dropped. Nothing comes through.'

'So you say.' He held up a printout. 'Probability indicates a .003 per cent possibility of a microorganism being transmitted through the net and a 22.1 per cent chance of a viable myxovirus being within the critical area when the net was opened.'

'Where in God's name do you get these figures?' Dunworthy said. 'Pull them out of a hat? According to Probability,' he said, putting a nasty emphasis on the word, 'there was only a .04 per cent chance of anyone's being present when Kivrin went through, a possibility you considered statistically insignificant.'

'Viruses are exceptionally sturdy organisms,' Gilchrist said. 'They have been known to lie dormant for long periods of time, exposed to extremes of temperature and humidity, and still be viable. Under certain conditions they form crystals which retain their structure indefinitely. When put back into solution they become infective again. Viable tobacco mosaic crystals have been found dating from the sixteenth century. There is clearly a significant risk of the virus' penetrating the net if opened, and under the circumstances I cannot possibly allow the net to be opened.'

'The virus *cannot* have come through the net,' Dunworthy said.

'Then why are you so anxious to have the fix read?'

'*Because*—' Dunworthy said, and stopped to get control of himself. 'Because reading the fix will tell us whether the drop went as planned or whether something went wrong.'

'Oh, you'll admit there's a possibility of error then?' Gilchrist said. 'Then why not an error that would allow a virus through the net? As long as that possibility exists, the laboratory will remain locked. I'm certain Mr Basingame will approve of the course of action I've taken.'

Basingame, Dunworthy thought, that's what this is all about. It has nothing to do with the virus or the protesters or 'maladies of the chest' in 1318. This is all to justify himself to Basingame.

Gilchrist was Acting Head in Basingame's absence, and he had rushed through the reranking, rushed through a drop, intending

343

no doubt to present Basingame with a brilliant *fait accompli*. But he hadn't got it. Instead, he'd got an epidemic and a lost historian and people picketing the college, and now all he cared about was vindicating his actions, saving himself even though it meant sacrificing Kivrin.

'What about Kivrin? Does Kivrin approve of your course of action?' he said.

'Ms Engle was fully aware of the risks when she volunteered to go to 1320,' Gilchrist said.

'Was she aware you intended to abandon her?'

'This conversation is over, Mr Dunworthy.' Gilchrist stood up. 'I will open the laboratory when the virus has been sourced, and it has been proven to my satisfaction that there is no chance it came through the net.'

He showed Dunworthy to the door. The porter was waiting outside.

'I have no intention of allowing you to abandon Kivrin,' Dunworthy said.

Gilchrist crimped his lips under the mask. 'And I have no intention of allowing you to endanger the health of this community.' He turned to the porter. 'Escort Mr Dunworthy to the gate. If he attempts to enter Brasenose again, telephone the police.' He slammed the door.

The porter walked Dunworthy across the quad, watching him warily as if he thought he might turn suddenly dangerous.

I might, Dunworthy thought. 'I want to use your telephone,' he said when they reached the gate. 'University business.'

The porter looked nervous, but he set a telephone on the counter and watched while Dunworthy punched Balliol's number. When Finch answered, he said, 'We've got to locate Basingame. It's an emergency. Phone the Scottish Fishing Licence Bureau and compile a list of hotels and inns. And get me Polly Wilson's number.'

He wrote down the number, rang off and started to punch it in and then thought better of it and telephoned Mary.

'I want to help source the virus,' he said.

'Gilchrist wouldn't open the net,' she said.

'No,' he said. 'What can I do to help with the sourcing?'

'What you were doing before with the primaries. Trace the contacts, look for the things I told you about, exposure to radiation, proximity to birds or livestock, religions that forbid antivirals. You'll need the contacts charts.'

'I'll send Colin for them,' he said.

'I'll have someone get them ready. You'd better check Badri's contacts back four to six days, as well, in case the virus did originate with him. The time of incubation from a reservoir can be longer than a person-to-person incubation period.'

'I'll put William on it,' he said. He pushed the phone back at the porter, who immediately came round the counter and walked him out to the pavement. Dunworthy was surprised he didn't follow him all the way to Balliol.

As soon as he got there, he phoned Polly Wilson. 'Is there some way you can get into the net's console without having access to the laboratory?' he asked her. 'Can you go in directly through the University's computer?'

'I don't know,' she said. 'The University's computer is moated. I might be able to rig a battering ram, or worm in from Balliol's console. I'll have to see what the safeties are. Do you have a tech to read it if I can get it set up?'

'I'm getting one,' he said. He rang off.

Colin came in, dripping wet, to get another roll of tape. 'Did you know the sequencing came, and the virus is a *mutant*?'

'Yes,' Dunworthy said. 'I want you to go to Infirmary and get the contacts charts from your great-aunt.'

Colin set down his load of placards. The one on top read 'Do Not Have a Relapse'.

'They're saying it's some sort of biological weapon,' Colin said. 'They're saying it escaped from a laboratory.'

Not Gilchrist's, he thought bitterly. 'Do you know where William Gaddson is?'

'No.' Colin made a face. 'He's probably on the staircase *kissing* someone.'

He was in the buttery, embracing one of the detainees. Dunworthy told him to find out Badri's whereabouts from Thursday to Sunday morning and to obtain a copy of Basingame's credit records for December, and went back to his rooms to telephone techs.

One of them was running a net for Nineteenth Century in Moscow, and two of them had gone skiing. The others weren't at home, or perhaps, alerted by Andrews, they weren't answering.

Colin brought the contacts charts. They were a disaster. No attempt had been made to correlate any of the information except possible American connections, and there were too many contacts. Half of the primaries had been at the dance in Headington, two-thirds of them had gone Christmas shopping, all but two of them had ridden the tube. It was like looking for a needle in a haystack.

He spent half the night checking religious affiliations and running cross-matches. Forty-two of them were Church of England, nine Holy Re-Formed, seventeen unaffiliated. Eight were students at Shrewsbury College, eleven had stood in line at Debenham's to see Father Christmas, nine had worked on Montoya's dig, thirty had shopped at Blackwell's.

Twenty-one of them had cross-contacts with at least two secondaries, and Debenham's Father Christmas had had contact with thirty-two (all but eleven at a pub after his shift), but none of them could be traced to all the primaries except Badri.

Mary brought the overflow cases in the morning. She was wearing SPGs, but no mask. 'Are the beds ready?' she said.

'Yes. We've got two wards of ten beds each.'

'Good. I'll need all of them.'

They helped the patients into the makeshift ward and into bed and left them in the care of William's nurse trainee. 'The stretcher cases will be over as soon as we have an ambulance free,' Mary said, walking back across the quad with Dunworthy.

The rain had stopped completely and the sky was lighter, as if it might clear.

'When will the analogue arrive?' he asked.

'It'll be two days at the least,' she said.

They reached the gate. She leaned against the stone passageway. 'When all this is over, I'm going to go through the net,' she said. 'To some century where there aren't any epidemics, where there isn't any waiting or worrying or helpless standing by.'

She pushed her hand back over her grey hair. 'Some century that isn't a ten.' She smiled. 'Only there isn't one, is there?'

He shook his head.

'Did I ever tell you about the Valley of the Kings?' she said.

'You said you saw it during the Pandemic.'

She nodded. 'Cairo was quarantined, so we had to fly out of Addis Ababa, and on the way down I bribed the taxi driver to take us to the Valley of the Kings so I could see Tutankhamen's tomb,' she said. 'It was a foolhardy thing to do. The Pandemic had already reached Luxor, and we just missed being caught in the quarantine. We were shot at twice.' She shook her head. 'We might have been killed. My sister refused to get out of the car, but I went down the stairs and up to the door of the tomb, and I thought, this is what it was like when Carter found it.'

She looked at Dunworthy and through him, remembering it. 'When they found the door to the tomb, it was locked, and they were supposed to wait for the proper authorities to open it. Carter drilled a hole in the door, and held a candle up and looked through.' Her voice was hushed. 'Carnarvon said, "Can you see anything?" and Carter said, "Yes. Wonderful things."'

She closed her eyes. 'I've never forgotten that, standing there at that closed door. I can see it clearly even now.' She opened her eyes. 'Perhaps that's where I'll go when this is over. To the opening of King Tut's tomb.'

She leaned out of the gate. 'Oh, dear, it's started raining again. I must get back. I'll send the stretcher cases as soon as there's an ambulance.' She looked sharply at him. 'Why aren't you wearing your mask?'

'It causes my spectacles to steam up. Why aren't you wearing yours?'

'We're running out of them. You've had your T-cell enhancement, haven't you?'

He shook his head. 'I haven't had any time.'

'Make time,' she said. 'And wear your mask. You'll be of no help to Kivrin if you fall ill.'

I'm of no help to Kivrin now, he thought, walking back across to his rooms. I can't get into the laboratory, I can't get a tech to come to Oxford, I can't find Basingame. He tried to think who else he should contact. He'd checked every booking agent and fishing guide and boat rental in Scotland. There was no trace of the man. Perhaps Montoya was right and he wasn't in Scotland at all, but off in the tropics somewhere with a woman.

Montoya. He'd forgotten completely about her. He hadn't seen her since the Christmas Eve service. She'd been looking for Basingame then so he could sign the authorisation for her to go out to the dig, and then she had rung up on Christmas Day to ask whether Basingame was trout or salmon. And rung back with the message, 'Never mind.' Which might mean she had found out not only whether he was salmon or trout but the man himself.

He climbed the staircase to his rooms. If Montoya had located Basingame and got her authorisation, she would have gone straight out to the dig. She would not have waited to tell anyone. He was not even certain she knew he was looking for Basingame, too.

Basingame would surely have come back as soon as Montoya told him about the quarantine unless he had been stopped by bad weather or impassable roads. Or Montoya might not have told him about the quarantine. Obsessed as she was with the dig, she might merely have told him she needed his signature.

Ms Taylor, her four healthy bell ringers, and Finch were in his rooms, standing in a circle and bending their knees. Finch was holding a paper in one hand and counting under his breath. 'I was just going over to the ward to assign nurses,' he said sheepishly. 'Here's William's report.' He handed it to Dunworthy and scurried out.

Ms Taylor and her foursome gathered up their handbell cases. 'A Ms Wilson called,' Ms Taylor said. 'She said to tell you a battering ram won't work, and you'll have to go in through Brasenose's console.'

'Thank you,' Dunworthy said.

She went out, her four bell ringers in a line behind her.

He rang the dig. No answer. He rang Montoya's flat, her office at Brasenose, the dig again. There was no answer at any of them. He phoned her flat again and let it ring while he looked at William's report Badri had spent all day Saturday and Sunday morning working at the dig. William must have been in contact with Montoya to find that out.

He wondered suddenly about the dig itself. It was out in the country from Witney, on a National Trust farm. Perhaps it had ducks, or chickens, or pigs, or all three. And Badri had spent an entire day and a half working there, digging in the mud, a perfect chance to come in contact with a reservoir.

Colin came in, soaked to the skin. 'They ran out of placards,' he said, rummaging through his duffel. 'London's sending some more tomorrow.' He unearthed his gobstopper and popped it, lint and all, into his mouth. 'Do you know who's standing on your staircase?' he asked. He flung himself on to the window seat and opened his Middle Ages book. 'William and some girl. Kissing and talking all lovey-dovey. I could scarcely get past.'

Dunworthy opened the door. William disengaged himself reluctantly from a small brunette in a Burberry and came in.

'Do you know where Ms Montoya is?' Dunworthy asked.

'No. The NHS said she's out at the dig, but she's not answering the phone. She's probably out in the churchyard or somewhere on the farm and can't hear it. I thought of using a screamer, but then I remembered this girl who's reading archaeohistory and . . .' He nodded towards the small brunette. 'She told me she saw the assignment sheets out at the dig, and Badri was signed up for Saturday and Sunday.'

'A screamer? What's that?'

'You hook it to the line and it magnifies the ring on the other end. If the person's out in the garden or in the shower or something.'

'Can you put one on this phone?'

'They're a bit too complicated for me. I know a student who might be able to rig it, though. I've got her number in my rooms.' He left, holding hands with the brunette.

'You know, if Ms Montoya is at the dig, I could get you through the perimeter,' Colin said. He took his gobstopper out and examined it. 'It'd be easy. There are lots of places that aren't watched. The guards don't like to stand out in the rain.'

'I have no intention of breaking quarantine,' he said. 'We are trying to stop this epidemic, not spread it.'

'That's how the plague was spread during the Black Death,' Colin said, taking the gobstopper out and examining it. It was a sickly yellow. 'They kept trying to run away from it, but they just took it along with them.'

William stuck his head in the door. 'She says it'd take two days to set it up, but she's got one on her phone if you want to use that.'

Colin grabbed for his jacket. 'Can I go?'

'No,' Dunworthy said. 'And get out of those wet clothes. I don't want you catching the flu.' He went down the stairs with William.

'She's an undergraduate at Shrewsbury,' William said, heading off through the rain.

Colin caught up with them halfway across the quad. 'I can't catch it. I had my enhancement,' he said. 'They didn't have quarantines in the Black Death so it went everywhere.' He pulled his muffler out of his jacket pocket. 'Bodey Road's a good place to sneak through the perimeter. There's a pub on the corner by the blockade, and the guard nips in now and again for something to keep warm.'

'Fasten your jacket,' Dunworthy said.

The girl turned out to be Polly Wilson. She told Dunworthy she had been working on an optical traitor that could break into the console, but hadn't managed it yet. Dunworthy phoned the dig, but there was no answer.

'Let it ring,' Polly said. 'She may have a long trek to get to it. The screamer's got a range of half a kilometre.'

He let it ring for ten minutes, put the receiver down, waited five minutes, tried again and let it ring a quarter of an hour before admitting defeat. Polly was looking longingly at William, and Colin was shivering in his wet jacket. Dunworthy took him home and put him to bed.

'Or I could sneak through the perimeter and tell her to phone you,' Colin said, putting his gobstopper back in the duffel. 'If you're worried about being too old to go. I'm very good at getting through perimeters.'

Dunworthy waited till William returned the next morning and then went back to Shrewsbury and tried again, but to no avail. 'I'll set it to ring at half-hour intervals,' Polly said, walking him to the gate. 'You wouldn't know if William has any other girlfriends, would you?'

'No,' Dunworthy said.

The sound of bells clanged out suddenly from the direction of Christ Church, pealing loudly through the rain. 'Has someone switched that horrid carillon on again?' Polly asked, leaning out to listen.

'No,' he said. 'It's the Americans.' He cocked his head in the direction of the sound, trying to determine whether Ms Taylor had settled for Stedmans, but he could hear six bells, the ancient bells of Osney: Douce and Gabriel and Marie, one after the other, Clement and Hautclerc and Taylor. 'And Finch.'

They sounded remarkably good, not at all like the digital carillon, not at all like 'O Christ Who Interfaces with the World'. They rang out clearly and brightly, and Dunworthy could almost see the bell ringers in their circle in the belfry, bending their knees and raising their arms, Finch referring to his list of numbers.

'Every man must stick to his bell without interruption,' Ms Taylor had said. He had had nothing but interruptions, but he felt oddly cheered nonetheless. Ms Taylor had not been able to get her bell ringers to Norwich for Christmas Eve, but she had stuck to her bells, and they rang out deafeningly, deliriously overhead, like a celebration, a victory. Like Christmas morning. He would find Montoya. And Basingame. Or a tech who wasn't afraid of the quarantine. He would find Kivrin.

The telephone was ringing when he got back to Balliol. He galloped up the stairs, hoping it was Polly. It was Montoya.

'Dunworthy?' she said. 'Hi. It's Lupe Montoya. What's going on?'

'Where are you?' he demanded.

'At the dig,' she said, but that was already apparent. She was standing in front of the ruined nave of the church in the half-excavated mediaeval churchyard. He could see why she had been so anxious to get back to her dig. There was as much as a foot of water in places. She had draped a motley assortment of tarps and plastene sheets over the excavation, but rain was dripping in at a dozen places, and where the sagging coverings met, spilling down the edges in veritable waterfalls. Everything, the gravestones, the

351

battery lights she had clipped to the tarps, the shovels stacked against the wall, was covered in mud.

Montoya was covered in mud, too. She was wearing her terrorist jacket and thigh-high fisherman's waders like Basingame, wherever he was, might be wearing, and they were wet and filthy. The hand she was holding the telephone with was caked with dried mud.

'I've been ringing you for days,' Dunworthy said.

'I can't hear the phone over the pump.' She gestured towards something outside the picture, presumably the pump, though he couldn't hear anything save for the thump of rain on the tarps. 'It's just broken a belt and I don't have another one. I heard the bells. Do they mean the quarantine's over?'

'Hardly,' he said. 'We're in the midst of a full-scale epidemic. Seven hundred and eighty cases and sixteen deaths. Haven't you seen the papers?'

'I haven't seen anything or anybody since I got here. I've spent the last six days trying to keep this damned dig above water, but I can't do it all by myself. And without a pump.' She pushed her heavy black hair back from her face with a dirty hand. 'What were they ringing the bells for then, if the quarantine's not over?'

'A peal of Chicago Surprise Minor.'

She looked irritated. 'If the quarantine's as bad as all that, why aren't they doing something useful?'

They are, he thought. They made you telephone.

'I could certainly put them to work out here.' She pushed her hair back again. She looked nearly as tired as Mary. 'I was really hoping the quarantine had been lifted so I could get some people out here to help. How long do you think it will be?'

Too long, he thought, watching the rain cascade in between the tarps. You'll never get the help you need in time.

'I need some information about Basingame and Badri Chaudhuri,' he said. 'We're attempting to source the virus and we need to know who Badri had contact with. Badri worked at the dig on the eighteenth and the morning of the nineteenth. Who else was there when he was?'

'I was.'

'Who else?'

352

'No one. I've had a terrible time getting help all December. Every one of my archaeohistory students took off the day vac started. I've had to scrounge volunteers wherever I could.'

'You're certain you were the only two there?'

'Yes. I remember because we opened the knight's tomb on Saturday and we had so much trouble lifting the lid. Gillian Ledbetter was signed up to work Saturday, but she called at the last minute and said she had a date.'

With William, Dunworthy thought. 'Was anyone there with Badri on Sunday?'

'He was only here in the morning, and there was no one here then. He had to leave to go to London. Look, I've got to go. If I'm not going to get any help soon, I've got to get back to work.' She started to take the receiver away from her ear.

'Wait!' Dunworthy shouted. 'Don't hang up.'

She put the receiver back to her ear, looking impatient.

'I need to ask you some more questions. It's very important. The sooner we source this virus, the sooner the quarantine will be lifted and you can get assistance at the dig.'

She looked unconvinced, but she punched up a code, laid the receiver in its cradle and said, 'You don't mind if I work while we talk?'

'No,' Dunworthy said, relieved. 'Please do.'

She moved abruptly out-of-picture, returned and punched up something else. 'Sorry. It won't reach,' she said, and the screen went fuzzy while she, presumably, moved the phone to her new worksite. When the picture reappeared, Montoya was crouched in a mudhole by a stone tomb. Dunworthy supposed it was the one whose lid she and Badri had nearly dropped.

The lid which bore the effigy of a knight in full armour, his arms crossed over his mailed chest so that his hands in their heavy cuirasses lay on his shoulders and his sword at his feet, stood propped at a precarious angle against the side, obscuring the elaborate carved letters. '*Requiesc*—' was all he could see. *Requiescat in pace*. 'Rest in peace', a blessing the knight had obviously not been granted. His sleeping face under the carved helmet looked disapproving.

Montoya had draped a thin sheet of plastene over the open top.

It was beaded with water. Dunworthy wondered if the other side of the tomb bore a morbid carving of the horror that lay within, like the ones in Colin's illustration, and if it were as ghastly as the reality. Water spilled steadily into the head of the tomb, dragging the plastic down.

Montoya straightened bringing up with her a flat box filled with mud. 'Well?' she said, laying it across the corner of the tomb. 'You said you had some more questions?'

'Yes,' he said. 'You said there wasn't anyone else at the dig when Badri was there.'

'There wasn't,' she said, wiping sweat off her forehead. 'Whew, it's muggy in here.' She took off her terrorist jacket and draped it over the tomb lid.

'What about locals? People not connected with the dig?'

'If there'd been anyone here, I'd have recruited them.' She began sorting through the mud in the box, unearthing several brown stones. 'The lid weighed a ton, and we'd no sooner gotten it off than it started raining. I would've recruited anybody who happened by, but the dig's too far out for anyone to happen by.'

'What about the National Trust staff?'

She held the stones under the water to clean them. 'They're only here during the summer.'

He had hoped someone at the dig would turn out to be the source, that Badri had come in contact with a local, a National Trust staffer or a wandering duck hunter. But myxoviruses didn't have carriers. The mysterious local would have had to have the disease himself, and Mary had been in touch with every hospital and doctor's surgery in England. There hadn't been any cases outside the perimeter.

Montoya held the stones up one by one to the battery light clipped to one of the supporting posts, turning them in the light, looking at their still-muddy edges.

'What about birds?'

'Birds?' she said, and he realised it must sound as though he were suggesting she recruit passing sparrows to help raise the lid of the tomb.

'The virus may have been spread by birds. Ducks, geese,

354

chickens,' he said, even though he wasn't certain chickens were reservoirs. 'Are there any at the dig?'

'Chickens?' she said, holding one of the stones half-raised to the light.

'Viruses are sometimes caused by the intersection of animal and human viruses,' he explained. 'Fowl are the most common reservoirs, but fish are sometimes responsible. Or pigs. Are there any pigs there at the dig?'

She was still looking at him as though she thought he was daft. 'The dig's on a National Trust farm, isn't it?'

'Yes, but the actual farm's three kilometres away. We're in the middle of a barley field. There aren't any pigs around, or birds, or fish.' She went back to examining the stones.

No birds. No pigs. No locals. The source of the virus wasn't here at the dig either. Possibly it wasn't anywhere, and Badri's influenza had mutated spontaneously, as Mary had said happened occasionally, appearing out of thin air and descending on Oxford the way the plague had descended on the unwitting residents of this churchyard.

Montoya was holding the stones up to the light again, chipping with her fingernails at an occasional clot of mud and then rubbing at the surface, and he realised suddenly that what she was examining were bones. Vertebrae, perhaps, or the knight's toes. *Requiescat in pace.*

She found the one she had apparently been looking for, an uneven bone the size of a walnut, with a curved side. She dumped the rest back into the tray, rummaged in the pocket of her shirt for a short-handled toothbrush and began scrubbing at the concave edges, frowning.

Gilchrist would never accept spontaneous mutation as a source. He was too in love with the theory that some fourteenth-century virus had come through the net. And too in love with his authority as Acting Head of the History Faculty to give in, even if Dunworthy had found dudes swimming in the churchyard puddles.

'I need to get in touch with Mr Basingame,' he said. 'Where is he?'

'Basingame?' she said, still frowning at the bone. 'I don't have any idea.'

'But – I thought you'd found him. When you phoned Christmas Day you said you had to find him to authorise your NHS dispensation.'

'I know. I spent two full days calling every trout and salmon guide in Scotland before I decided I couldn't wait any longer. If you ask me, he's nowhere near Scotland.' She pulled a pocketknife out of her jeans and began scraping at the rough edge of the bone. 'Speaking of the NHS, would you do something for me? I keep calling their number but it's always busy. Would you run over there and tell them I've got to have some more help? Tell them the dig's of irreplaceable historical value, and it's going to be irretrievably lost if they don't send me at least five people. And a pump.' The knife snagged. She frowned and chipped some more.

'How did you get Basingame's authorisation if you didn't know where he was? I thought you'd said the form required his signature.'

'It did,' she said. An edge of bone flew suddenly off and landed on the plastene shroud. She examined the bone and dropped it back in the box, no longer frowning. 'I forged it.'

She crouched by the tomb again, digging for more bones. She looked as absorbed as Colin examining his gobstopper. He wondered if she even remembered that Kivrin was in the past, or if she had forgotten her as she seemed to have forgotten the epidemic.

He rang off, wondering if Montoya would even notice, and walked back to Infirmary to tell Mary what he had found out and to begin questioning the secondaries again, looking for the source. It was raining very hard, spilling off the downspouts and washing away things of irreplaceable historical value.

The bell ringers and Finch were still at it, ringing the changes one after another in their determined order, bending their knees and looking like Montoya, sticking to their bells. The sound pealed out loudly, leadenly, through the rain, like an alarum, like a cry for help.

Christmas Eve 1320 (Old Style). I don't have as much time as I thought. When I came in from the kitchen just now, Rosemund told me Lady Imeyne wanted me. Imeyne was deep in earnest conversation with the bishop's envoy, and I supposed from her expression that she was cataloguing Father Roche's sins, but as Rosemund and I came up she pointed to me and said, 'This is the woman I spake of.'

Woman, not maid, and her tone was critical, almost accusing. I wondered if she'd told the bishop her theory that I was a French spy.

'She says she remembers naught,' Lady Imeyne said, 'yet she can speak and read.' She turned to Rosemund. 'Where is your brooch?'

'It is on my cloak,' Rosemund said. 'I laid it in the loft.'

'Go and fetch it.'

Rosemund went, reluctantly. As soon as she was gone Imeyne said, 'Sir Bloet brought a loveknot brooch to my granddaughter with words on it in the Roman tongue.' She looked at me triumphantly. 'She told their meaning, and at the church this night she spoke the words of the mass ere the priest had said them.'

'Who taught you your letters?' the bishop's envoy asked, his voice blurred from the wine.

I thought of saying Sir Bloet had told me what the words meant, but I was afraid he'd already denied it. 'I know not,' I said. 'I have no memory of my life since I was waylaid in the woods, for I was struck upon the head.'

'When first she woke she spoke in a tongue none could understand,' Imeyne said, as if that were further proof, but I had no idea what she was trying to convict me of or how the bishop's envoy was involved.

'Holy Father, go you to Oxenford when you leave us?' she asked him.

357

'Aye,' he said, sounding wary. 'We can stay but a few days here.'

'I would have you take her with you to the good sisters at Godstow.'

'We go not to Godstow,' he said, which was clearly an excuse. The nunnery wasn't even five miles from Oxford. 'But I will enquire of the bishop for news of the woman on my return and send word to you.'

'I wot she is a nun for that she speaks in Latin and knows the passages of the mass,' Imeyne said. 'I would have you take her to their convent that they may ask among the nunneries who she may be.'

The bishop's envoy looked even more nervous, but he agreed. So I have till whenever they leave. A few days, the bishop's envoy said, and with luck that means they won't leave till after the Slaughter of the Innocents. But I plan to put Agnes to bed and talk to Gawyn as soon as possible.

CHAPTER TWENTY-TWO

Kivrin didn't get Agnes to bed till nearly dawn. The arrival of the 'three kings', as she continued to call them, had woken her completely and she refused to consider lying down for fear she might miss something, even though she was obviously exhausted.

She tagged after Kivrin as she tried to help Eliwys bring in the food for the feast, whining that she was hungry and then, when the tables were finally set and the feast began, refused to eat anything.

Kivrin had no time to argue with her. There was course after course to be brought across the courtyard from the kitchen, trenchers of venison and roast pork and an enormous pie Kivrin half-expected blackbirds to fly out of when the crust was cut. According to the priest at Holy Re-Formed, fasting was observed between the midnight mass and the high mass on Christmas morning, but everyone, including the bishop's envoy, ate heartily of the roast pheasant and goose and stewed rabbit in saffron gravy. And drank. The 'three kings' called constantly for more wine.

They had already had more than enough. The monk was leering at Maisry, and the clerk, drunk when he arrived, was nearly under the table. The bishop's envoy was drinking more than either of them, beckoning constantly to Rosemund to bring him the wassail bowl, his gestures growing broader and less clear with every drink.

Good, Kivrin thought. Perhaps he'll get so drunk he'll forget he promised Lady Imeyne he'd take me to the nunnery at Godstow. She took the bowl round to Gawyn, hoping to have an opportunity to ask him where the drop was, but he was laughing with some of Sir Bloet's men and they called to her for ale and more meat. By the time she got back to Agnes the little girl was sound asleep, her head nearly in her manchet. Kivrin picked her up carefully and carried her upstairs to Rosemund's bower.

Above them, the door opened. 'Lady Katherine,' Eliwys said, her arms full of bedding. 'I am grateful you are here. I have need of your help.'

Agnes stirred.

'Bring the linen sheets from the loft,' Eliwys said. 'The church-men will sleep in this bed, and Sir Bloet's sister and her women in the loft.'

'Where am I to sleep?' Agnes asked wriggling out of Kivrin's arms.

'We will sleep in the barn,' Eliwys said. 'But you must wait till we have made up the beds, Agnes. Go and play.'

Agnes didn't have to be encouraged. She hopped off down the stairs, waving her arm to make her bell ring.

Eliwys handed Kivrin the bedding. 'Take these to the loft and bring the miniver coverlid from my husband's carven chest.'

'How many days do you think the bishop's envoy and his men will stay?' Kivrin asked.

'I know not,' Eliwys said, looking worried. 'I pray not more than a fortnight or we shall not have meat enough. See you do not forget the good bolsters.'

A fortnight was more than enough, well past the rendezvous, and they certainly didn't look like they were going anywhere. When Kivrin climbed down from the loft with the sheets, the bishop's envoy was asleep in the high seat, snoring loudly, and the clerk had his feet on the table. The monk had one of Sir Bloet's waiting women backed into a corner and was playing with her kerchief. Gawyn was nowhere to be seen.

Kivrin took the sheets and coverlid to Eliwys, then offered to take bedding out to the barn. 'Agnes is very tired,' she said. 'I would put her to bed soon.'

Eliwys nodded absently, pounding at one of the heavy bolsters, and Kivrin ran downstairs and out into the courtyard. Gawyn was not in the stable nor the brewhouse. She lingered near the privy until two of the redheaded young men emerged, looking at her curiously, and then went on to the barn. Perhaps Gawyn had gone off with Maisry again, or joined the villagers' celebration on the green. She could hear the sound of laughter as she spread straw on the bare wooden floor of the loft.

She laid the furs and quilts on the straw and went down and out through the passageway to see if she could see him. The contemps had built a bonfire in front of the churchyard and were standing around it, warming their hands and drinking out of large horns. She could see the reddened faces of Maisry's father and the reeve in the firelight, but not Gawyn's.

He was not in the courtyard either. Rosemund was standing by the gate, wrapped in her cloak.

'What are you doing out here in the cold?' Kivrin asked.

'I am awaiting my father,' Rosemund said. 'Gawyn told me he expects him before day.'

'Have you seen Gawyn?'

'Aye. He is in the stable.'

Kivrin looked anxiously towards the stable. 'It's too cold to wait out here. You must go in the house, and I'll tell Gawyn to tell you when your father comes.'

'Nay, I will wait here,' Rosemund said. 'He promised he would come to us for Christmas.' Her voice quavered a little.

Kivrin held her lantern up. Rosemund wasn't crying, but her cheeks were red. Kivrin wondered what Sir Bloet had done now that had Rosemund hiding from him. Or perhaps it was the monk who had frightened her, or the drunken clerk.

Kivrin took her arm. 'You can wait as well in the kitchen, and it is warm there,' she said.

Rosemund nodded. 'My father promised he would come without fail.'

And do what? Kivrin wondered. Throw out the churchmen? Call off Rosemund's engagement to Sir Bloet? 'My father would never allow me to come to harm,' she had told Kivrin, but he was scarcely in a position to cancel the betrothal when the marriage settlement had already been signed, to alienate Sir Bloet, who had 'many powerful friends'.

Kivrin took Rosemund into the kitchen and told Maisry to heat a cup of wine for her. 'I'll go and tell Gawyn to come and get you as soon as your father comes,' she said, and went across to the stable, but Gawyn wasn't there, or in the brewhouse.

She went into the house, wondering if Imeyne had sent him on yet another of her errands. But Imeyne was sitting beside the obviously unwillingly wakened envoy, talking determinedly to him, and Gawyn was by the fire, surrounded by Sir Bloet's men, including the two who had come out of the privy. Sir Bloet sat on the near side of the hearth with his sister-in-law and Eliwys.

Kivrin sank down on the beggar's bench by the screens. There was no way to get near him, let alone ask him about the drop.

'Give him to me!' Agnes wailed. She and the rest of the children were over by the stairs to the bower, and the little boys were passing Blackie among them, petting him and playing with his ears. Agnes must have gone out to the stable to fetch the puppy while Kivrin was out in the barn.

'He's *my* hound!' Agnes said, grabbing at Blackie. The little boy wrenched the puppy away. 'Give him to me!'

Kivrin stood up.

'As I was riding through the woods, I came upon a maiden,' Gawyn said loudly. 'She had been set upon by thieves and was sore wounded, her head cut open and bleeding grievously.'

Kivrin hesitated, glancing towards Agnes, who was pounding on the little boy's arm, and then sat down again.

' "Fair maid," I said. "Who has done this fell thing?" ' Gawyn said, 'but she could not speak for her injuries.'

Agnes had the puppy back and was clutching it to her. Kivrin should go rescue the poor thing but she stayed where she was, moving a little so she could see past the sister-in-law's coif. Tell them where you found me, she willed Gawyn. Tell them where in the woods.

' "I am your liegeman and will find these evil knaves," I said, "but I fear to leave you in such sad plight," ' he said, looking towards Eliwys, 'but she had recovered herself and she begged me to go and find those who had harmed her.'

Eliwys stood up and walked to the door. She stood there for a moment, looking anxious, and then came and sat back down.

'No!' Agnes shrieked. One of Sir Bloet's redheaded nephews had Blackie now and was holding him above his head in one hand. If Kivrin didn't rescue it soon, they'd squeeze the poor dog to death, and there was no point in listening to any more of the Rescue of the Maiden in the Wood, which was obviously intended not to tell what had happened but to impress Eliwys. She walked over to the children.

'The robbers had not been long gone,' Gawyn said, 'and I found their trail with ease and followed it, spurring my steed after them.'

Sir Bloet's nephew was dangling Blackie by his front legs, and the puppy was whimpering pathetically.

'Kivrin!' Agnes cried, catching sight of her, and flung herself at Kivrin's legs. Sir Bloet's nephew immediately handed Kivrin the puppy and backed away, and the rest of the children scattered.

'You rescued Blackie!' Agnes said, reaching for him.

Kivrin shook her head. 'It is time to go to bed,' she said.

'I'm *not* tired!' Agnes said in a whine that was scarcely convincing. She rubbed her eyes.

'Blackie is tired,' Kivrin said, squatting down beside Agnes, 'and he won't go to bed unless you will lie down with him.'

That argument seemed to interest her and before she could find a flaw in it, Kivrin handed Blackie back to her, placing him in her arms like a baby, and scooped them both up. 'Blackie would have you tell him a story,' Kivrin said, starting for the door.

'Soon I found myself in a place that I knew not,' Gawyn said, 'a dark forest.'

Kivrin carried her charges outside and across the courtyard. 'Blackie likes stories about cats,' Agnes said, rocking the puppy gently in her arms.

'You must tell him a story about a cat then,' Kivrin said. She took the puppy while Agnes climbed up the ladder to the loft. He was already asleep, worn out from all the handling. Kivrin laid him in the straw next to the pallet.

'A wicked cat,' Agnes said, grabbing him up again. 'I am not going to sleep. I am only lying down with Blackie, so I need not take off my clothes.'

'No, you need not,' Kivrin said, covering Agnes and Blackie with a heavy fur. It was too cold in the barn for undressing.

'Blackie would fain wear my bell,' she said, trying to put the ribbon over his head.

'No, he wouldn't,' Kivrin said. She confiscated the bell and spread another fur over them. Kivrin crawled in next to the little girl. Agnes pushed her small body against Kivrin.

'Once there was a wicked cat,' Agnes said, yawning. 'Her father told her not to go into the forest, but she heeded him not.' She fought valiantly against falling asleep, rubbing her eyes and making up adventures for the wicked cat, but the darkness and the warmth of the heavy fur finally overcame her.

Kivrin continued to lie there, waiting till Agnes' breathing became light and steady, and then gently extricated Blackie from Agnes' grip and laid him in the straw.

Agnes frowned in her sleep and reached for him, and Kivrin wrapped her arms around her. She should get up and go look for Gawyn. The rendezvous was in less than a week.

Agnes stirred and snuggled closer, her hair against Kivrin's cheek.

And how will I leave you? Kivrin thought. And Rosemund? And Father Roche? And fell asleep.

When she woke, it was nearly light and Rosemund had crawled in beside Agnes. Kivrin left them sleeping, and crept down from the loft and across the grey courtyard, afraid she had missed the bell for mass, but Gawyn was still holding forth by the fire, and the bishop's envoy was still sitting in the high seat, listening to Lady Imeyne.

The monk was sitting in the corner with his arm around Maisry, but the clerk was nowhere to be seen. He must have passed out and been put to bed.

The children must also have been put to bed, and some of the women had apparently gone up to the loft to rest. Kivrin didn't see Sir Bloet's sister or the sister-in-law from Dorset.

' "Halt, knave!" I cried,' Gawyn said. ' "For I would fight you in fair combat." ' Kivrin wondered if this was still the Rescue or one of Sir Lancelot's adventures. It was impossible to tell, and if the purpose of it was to impress Eliwys, it was to no avail. She wasn't in the hall. What was left of Gawyn's audience didn't seem impressed either. Two of them were playing a desultory game of dice on the bench between them and Sir Bloet was asleep, his chin on his massive chest.

Kivrin obviously hadn't missed any opportunities to speak to Gawyn by falling asleep, and from the look of things there wouldn't be any for some time. She might as well have stayed in the loft with Agnes. She was going to have to make an opportunity – waylay Gawyn on his way to the privy or catch up with him on the way to mass and whisper, 'Meet me afterwards in the stable.'

The churchmen didn't look like they'd leave unless the wine gave out, but it was risky to cut it too close. The men might take a notion to go hunting tomorrow, or the weather might change, and whether the bishop's envoy and his flunkies left or not it was still only five days to the rendezvous. No, four. It was already Christmas.

'He aimed a savage blow,' Gawyn said, standing up to illustrate, 'and had it driven down as earnestly as he fainted, my head would have been cloven in twain.'

'Lady Katherine,' Imeyne said. She had stood up and was beckoning to Kivrin. The bishop's envoy was looking interestedly at her and her heart began to pound, wondering what mischief they had cooked up between them now, but before Kivrin could cross the hall, Imeyne left him and came across to her, carrying a linen-wrapped bundle.

'I would have you carry these to Father Roche for the mass,' she said, folding the linen back so Kivrin could see the wax candles inside. 'Bid him put these on the *altar* and say to him to pinch not the flames from the candles, for it breaks the wick. Bid him prepare the church that the bishop's envoy may say the Christmas mass. I would have the church look like a place of the Lord, not a pig's sty. And bid him put on a clean robe.'

So you get your proper mass after all, Kivrin thought, hurrying across the courtyard and along the passageway. And you've got rid of me. All you need now is to get rid of Roche, persuade the bishop's envoy to demote him or take him to Bicester Abbey.

There was no one on the green. The dying bonfire flickered palely in the grey light, and the snow that had melted round it was refreezing in icy puddles. The villagers must have gone to bed and she wondered if Father Roche had too, but there was no smoke from his house and no answer to her knock on the door. She went along the path and in the side door of the church. It was still dark inside, and colder than it had been at midnight.

'Father Roche,' Kivrin called softly, groping her way to the statue of St Catherine.

He didn't answer, but she could hear the murmur of his voice. He was behind the rood screen, kneeling in front of the altar.

'Guide those who have travelled far this night safely home and protect them from danger and illness along the way,' he said, and his soft voice reminded her of the night in the sickroom when she had been so ill, steady and comforting through the flames. And of Mr Dunworthy. She didn't call to him again, but stayed where she was, leaning against the icy statue and listening to his voice in the darkness.

'Sir Bloet and his family came from Courcy to the mass, and all their servants,' he said, 'and Theodulf Freeman from Henefelde. The snow stopped yestereve, and the skies showed clear for the night of Christ's holy birth,' he went on in that matter-of-fact voice that sounded just like she did, praying into the corder. The attendance tally for the mass and the weather report.

Light was beginning to come in through the windows now, and she could see him through the filigreed rood screen, his robe threadbare and dirty around the hem, his face coarse and cruel-looking in comparison with the aristocratic envoy, the thin-faced clerk.

'This blessed night as the mass ended a messenger from the bishop came and with him two priests, all three of great learning and goodness,' Roche prayed.

Don't be fooled by the gold and and fancy clothes, Kivrin thought. You're worth ten of them. 'The bishop's envoy will say the Christmas mass,' Imeyne had said and didn't seem to be troubled at all by the fact that he hadn't fasted or bothered to come to the church to prepare for the mass himself. You're worth fifty of them, Kivrin thought. A hundred.

'There is word from Oxenford of illness. Tord the Cottar fares better, though I bade him not come so far to the mass. Uctreda was too weak to come to the mass. I took her soup, but she ate it not. Walthef fell vomiting after the dancing from too much ale.

Gytha burned her hand upon the bonfire in plucking a brand from it. I shall not fear, though the last days come, the days of wrath and the final judgment, for You have sent much help.'

Much help. He wouldn't have any help if she stood here listening much longer. The sun was up now and in the rose and gold light from the windows she could see the drippings down the sides of the candlesticks, the tarnish on their bases, a big blot of wax on the altar cloth. The day of wrath and the final judgment would be the right words for what would happen if the church looked like this when Imeyne marched in to mass.

'Father Roche,' she said.

Roche turned immediately and then tried to stand up, his legs obviously stiff with the cold. He looked startled even frightened, and Kivrin said quickly, 'It's Katherine,' and moved forward into the light of one of the windows so he could see her.

He crossed himself, still looking frightened and she wondered if he had been half dozing at his prayers and was still not awake.

'Lady Imeyne sent me with candles,' she said, coming round the rood screen to him. 'She bade me tell you to set them in the silver candlesticks on either side of the altar. She bade me tell you—' She stopped, ashamed to be delivering Imeyne's edicts. 'I have come to help you prepare the church for mass. What would you have me do? Shall I polish the candlesticks?' She held out the candles to him.

He didn't take the candles or say anything, and she frowned wondering if in her eagerness to protect him from Imeyne's wrath she had broken some rule. Women were not allowed to touch the elements or the vessels of the mass. Perhaps they weren't allowed to handle the candlesticks either.

'Am I not allowed to help?' she asked. 'Should I not have come into the chancel?'

Roche seemed suddenly to come to himself. 'There is nowhere God's servants may not go,' he said. He took the candles from her and laid them on the altar. 'But such a one as you should not do such humble work.'

'It is God's work,' she said briskly. She took the half-burned candles out of the heavy branched candlestick. Wax had dripped down the sides. 'We'll need some sand,' she said, 'and a knife to scrape the wax off.'

He went to get them immediately, and while he was gone she hastily took the candles down from the rood screen and replaced them with tallow ones.

He came in with the sand, a fistful of filthy rags and a poor excuse for a knife. But it cut through wax and Kivrin started in on the altar cloth, scraping at the spot of wax, worried that they might not have much time. The bishop's envoy hadn't looked in any hurry to heave himself out of the high seat and prepare for the mass, but who knew how long he could hold out against Imeyne.

I don't have any time either, she thought, starting on the candlesticks. She had told herself there was plenty of time, but she had spent the entire night actively pursuing Gawyn and hadn't even got close to him. And tomorrow he might decide to go hunting or Rescuing Fair Maidens, or the bishop's envoy and his flunkies might drink up all the wine and set off in search of more, dragging her with them.

'There is nowhere God's servants may not go,' Roche had said. Except to the drop, she thought. Except home.

She scrubbed viciously with the wet sand at some wax embedded in the rim of the candlestick, and a piece flew off and hit the candle Roche was scraping. 'I'm sorry,' she said, 'Lady Imeyne—' and then stopped.

There was no point in telling him she was being sent away. If he tried to intercede for her with Lady Imeyne it would only make it worse, and she didn't want him shipped off to Osney for trying to help her.

He was waiting for her to finish her sentence. 'Lady Imeyne bade me tell you the bishop's envoy will say the Christmas mass,' she said.

'It will be a blessing to hear such holiness on the birthday of Christ Jesus,' he said, setting down the polished chalice.

The birthday of Christ Jesus. She tried to envision St Mary the Virgin's as it would look this morning, the music and the warmth, the laser candles glittering in the stainless-steel candlesticks, but it was like something she had only imagined, dim and unreal.

She stood the candlesticks on either side of the altar. They shone dully in the multicoloured light of the windows. She set three of Imeyne's candles in them and moved the left one a little closer to the altar so they were even.

There was nothing she could do about Roche's robe, which Imeyne knew full well was the only one he had. He had got wet sand on his sleeve, and she wiped it off with her hand.

'I must go wake Agnes and Rosemund for the mass,' she said, brushing at the front of his robe, and then went on almost without meaning to, 'Lady Imeyne has asked the bishop's envoy to take me with them to the nunnery at Godstow.'

'God has sent you to this place to help us,' he said. 'He will not let you be taken from it.'

I wish I could believe you, Kivrin thought, going back across the green. There was still no sign of life, though smoke was coming from a couple of the roofs, and the cow had been turned out. It was nibbling the grass near the bonfire where the snow had melted. Perhaps they're all asleep, and I can wake Gawyn and ask him where the drop is, she thought, and saw Rosemund and Agnes coming towards her. They looked considerably the worse for wear. Rosemund's leaf-green velvet dress was covered with wisps of straw and hay dust, and Agnes had it in her hair. She broke free of Rosemund as soon as she saw Kivrin and ran up to her.

'You're supposed to be asleep,' Kivrin said, brushing straw from her red kirtle.

'Some men came,' Agnes said. 'They wakened us.'

Kivrin looked enquiringly at Rosemund. 'Has your father come?'

'Nay,' she said. 'I know not who they are. I think they must be servants of the bishop's envoy.'

They were. There were four of them, monks, though not of the class of the Cistercian monk, and two laden donkeys, and they had obviously only now caught up with their master. They unloaded two large chests while Kivrin and the girls watched several wadmal bags and an enormous wine cask.

'They must be planning to stay a long while,' Agnes said.

'Yes,' Kivrin said. God has sent you to this place. He will not let

369

you be taken from it. 'Come,' she said cheerfully. 'I will comb your hair.'

She took Agnes inside and cleaned her up. The short nap hadn't improved Agnes' disposition, and she refused to stand still while Kivrin combed her hair. It took her till mass to get all the straw and most of the tangles out, and Agnes continued to whine the whole way to the church.

There had apparently been vestments as well as wine in the envoy's luggage. The bishop's envoy wore a black velvet chasuble over his dazzlingly white vestments, and the monk was resplendent in yards of samite and gilt embroidery. The clerk was nowhere to be seen, and neither was Father Roche, probably exiled because of his dirty robe. Kivrin looked towards the back of the church, hoping he'd been allowed to witness all this holiness, but she couldn't see him among the villagers.

They looked somewhat the worse for wear too, and some of them were obviously badly hungover. As was the bishop's envoy. He rattled through the words of the mass tonelessly and in an accent Kivrin could scarcely understand. It bore no resemblance to Father Roche's Latin. Nor to what Latimer and the priest at Holy Re-Formed had taught her. The vowels were all wrong and the 'c' in *excelsis* was almost a 'Z'. She thought of Latimer drilling her on the long vowels, of Holy Re-Formed's priest insisting on 'c as in eggshell', on 'the true Latin'.

And it was the true Latin, she thought. 'I will not leave you,' he had said. He had said, 'Be not afraid.' And I understood him.

As the mass progressed, the envoy chanted faster and faster, as if he were anxious to be done with it. Lady Imeyne didn't seem to notice. She looked smugly serene in the knowledge of doing good and nodded approvingly at the sermon, which seemed to be about forsaking worldly things.

As they were filing out, though, she stopped at the door of the church and looked towards the bell tower, her lips pursed in disapproval. Now what? Kivrin thought. A mote of dust on the bell?

'Saw you how the church looked, Lady Yvolde?' Imeyne said angrily to Sir Bloet's sister over the sound of the bell. 'He had set no candles in the chancel windows, but only cressets as a peasant

370

uses.' She stopped. 'I must stay behind to speak to him of this. He has disgraced our house before the bishop.'

She marched off towards the bell tower, her face set with righteous anger. And if he *had* set candles in the windows, Kivrin thought, they would have been the wrong kind or in the wrong place. Or he would have blown them out incorrectly. She wished there were some way to warn him, but Imeyne was already halfway to the tower and Agnes was tugging insistently on Kivrin's hand.

'I'm tired,' she said. 'I would go to bed.'

Kivrin took Agnes to the barn, dodging among the villagers who were starting in on a second round of merrymaking. Fresh wood had been thrown on the bonfire, and several of the young women had joined hands and were dancing around it. Agnes lay down willingly in the loft, but she was up again before Kivrin made it into the house, trotting across the courtyard after her.

'Agnes,' Kivrin said sternly, her hands on her hips. 'What are you doing up? You said you were tired.'

'Blackie is ill.'

'Ill?' Kivrin said. 'What's wrong with him?'

'He is ill,' Agnes repeated. She took hold of Kivrin's hand and led her back to the barn and up to the loft. Blackie lay in the straw, a lifeless bundle. 'Will you make him a poultice?'

Kivrin picked the puppy up and laid him back down gingerly. He was already stiff. 'Oh, Agnes, I'm afraid he's dead.'

Agnes squatted down and looked at him interestedly. 'Grandmother's chaplain died,' she said. 'Had Blackie a fever?'

Blackie had too much handling, Kivrin thought. He had been passed from hand to hand, squeezed, trodden on, half-choked. Killed with kindness. And on Christmas, though Agnes didn't seem particularly upset.

'Will there be a funeral?' she asked, putting out a tentative finger to Blackie's ear.

No, Kivrin thought. There hadn't been any shoe-box burials in the Middle Ages. The contemps had disposed of dead animals by tossing them into the undergrowth, by dumping them in a stream. 'We will bury him in the woods,' she said, though she had no idea how they would manage that with the ground frozen. 'Under a tree.'

For the first time, Agnes looked unhappy. 'Father Roche must bury Blackie in the churchyard,' she said.

Father Roche would do nearly anything for Agnes, but Kivrin couldn't imagine him agreeing to Christian burial for an animal. The idea of pets being creatures with souls hadn't become popular until the nineteenth century, and even the Victorians hadn't demanded Christian burial for their dogs and cats.

'I will say the prayers for the dead,' Kivrin said.

'Father Roche must bury him in the churchyard,' Agnes said, her face puckering. 'And then he must ring the bell.'

'We cannot bury him until after Christmas,' Kivrin said hastily. 'After Christmas I will ask Father Roche what to do.'

She wondered what she should do with the body for now. She couldn't leave him lying there where the girls slept. 'Come, we will take Blackie below,' she said. She picked up the puppy, trying not to grimace, and took him down the ladder.

She looked around for a box or a bag to put Blackie in, but she couldn't find anything. She finally laid him in a corner behind a scythe and had Agnes bring handfuls of straw to cover him with.

Agnes flung the straw on him. 'If Father Roche does not ring the bell for Blackie, he will not go to heaven,' she said, and burst into tears.

It took Kivrin half an hour to calm her down again. She rocked her in her arms, wiping her streaked face and saying 'Shh, shh.'

She could hear noise from the courtyard. She wondered if the Christmas merrymaking had moved into the courtyard. Or if the men were going hunting. She could hear the whinny of horses.

'Let's go see what's happening in the courtyard,' she said. 'Perhaps your father is here.'

Agnes sat up, wiping her nose. 'I would tell him of Blackie,' she said, and got off Kivrin's lap.

They went outside. The courtyard was full of people and horses. 'What are they doing?' Agnes asked.

'I don't know,' Kivrin said, but it was all too clear what they were doing. Cob was leading the envoy's white stallion out of the stable, and the servants were carrying out the bags and boxes they had carried in early that morning. Lady Eliwys stood at the door, looking anxiously into the courtyard.

'Are they leaving?' Agnes asked.

'No,' Kivrin said. No. They can't be leaving. I don't know where the drop is.

The monk came out, dressed in his white habit and his cloak. Cob went back into the stable and came out again, leading the roan Kivrin had ridden when they went to find the holly, and carrying a saddle.

'They *are* leaving,' Agnes said.

'I know,' Kivrin said. 'I can see that they are.'

CHAPTER TWENTY-THREE

Kivrin grabbed Agnes' hand and started back to the safety of the barn. She must hide until they were gone. 'Where are we going?' Agnes asked.

Kivrin darted around two of Sir Bloet's servants carrying a chest. 'To the loft.'

Agnes stopped dead. 'I do not wish to lie down!' she wailed. 'I am not tired!'

'Lady Katherine!' someone called from across the courtyard.

Kivrin scooped Agnes up and started rapidly for the barn. 'I am not tired!' Agnes shrieked. 'I am *not*!'

Rosemund ran up beside her. 'Lady Katherine! Did you not hear me? Mother wants you. The bishop's envoy is leaving.' She took hold of Kivrin's arm and turned her back towards the house.

Eliwys was still standing in the doorway, watching them now, and the bishop's envoy had come out and was standing beside her in his red cloak. Kivrin couldn't see Imeyne anywhere. She was probably inside, packing Kivrin's clothes.

'The bishop's envoy has urgent business at the priory at Bernecestre,' Rosemund said, leading Kivrin to the house, 'and Sir Bloet goes with them.' She smiled happily at Kivrin. 'Sir Bloet says he will accompany them to Courcy that they may lie there tonight and arrive in Bernecestre tomorrow.'

Bernecestre. Bicester. At least it wasn't Godstow. But Godstow was along the way. 'What business?'

'I know not,' Rosemund said, as if it were unimportant, and Kivrin supposed for her it was. Sir Bloet was leaving, and that was all that mattered. Rosemund plunged happily through the mêlée of servants and baggage and horses towards her mother.

The bishop's envoy was speaking to one of his servants, and Eliwys was watching him, frowning. Neither of them would see her if she turned and walked rapidly back behind the open doors of the stable, but Rosemund still had hold of her sleeve and was pulling her forward.

'Rosemund, I must go back to the barn. I have left my cloak—' she began.

'Mother!' Agnes cried and ran towards Eliwys and nearly into one of the horses. It whinnied and tossed its head, and a servant dived for its bridle.

'Agnes!' Rosemund shouted and let go of Kivrin's sleeve, but it was too late. Eliwys and the bishop's envoy had already seen them and started over to them.

'You must not run among the horses,' Eliwys said, catching Agnes against her.

'My hound is dead,' Agnes said.

'That is no reason to run,' Eliwys said, and Kivrin knew she hadn't even heard her. Eliwys turned back to the bishop's envoy.

'Tell your husband we are grateful for the loan of your horses, that ours may be rested for the journey to Bernecestre,' he said, and he sounded distracted, too. 'I will send them from Courcy with a servant.'

'Would you see my hound?' Agnes said, tugging on her mother's skirt.

'Hush,' Eliwys said.

'My clerk does not ride with us this afternoon,' he said. 'I fear he made too merry yestereve and feels now the pains of too much drink. I beg your indulgence, good lady, that he may stay and follow when he is recovered.'

'Of course he may stay,' Eliwys said. 'Is there aught we can do to help him? My husband's mother—'

'Nay. Leave him be. There is naught can help an aching head save sleep. He will be well by evening,' he said, looking like he had made too merry himself. He seemed nervous, inattentive, as if he had a splitting headache, and his aristocratic face was grey in the bright morning light. He shivered and pulled his cloak around him.

He hadn't so much as glanced at Kivrin, and she wondered if

he had forgotten his promise to Lady Imeyne in his haste. She looked anxiously towards the gate, hoping Imeyne was still chastising Roche and wouldn't suddenly appear to remind him of it.

'I regret that my husband is not here,' Eliwys said, 'and that we could not give you better welcome. My husband—'

'I must see to my servants,' he interrupted. He held out his hand and Eliwys dropped to one knee and kissed his ring. Before she could rise, he had stridden off towards the stable. Eliwys looked after him worriedly.

'Do you wish to see him?' Agnes said.

'Not now,' Eliwys said. 'Rosemund you must make your farewells to Sir Bloet and Lady Yvolde.'

'He is cold,' Agnes said.

Eliwys turned to Kivrin. 'Lady Katherine, know you where Lady Imeyne is?'

'She stayed behind in the church,' Rosemund said.

'Perhaps she is still at her prayers,' Eliwys said. She stood on tiptoe and scanned the crowded courtyard. '*Where* is Maisry?'

Hiding, Kivrin thought, which is what I should be doing.

'Would you have me seek for her?' Rosemund asked.

'Nay,' Eliwys said. 'You must bid Sir Bloet farewell. Lady Katherine, go and fetch Lady Imeyne from the church that she may bid the bishop's envoy goodbye. Rosemund, why do you still stand there? You must bid your betrothed farewell.'

'I will find Lady Imeyne,' Kivrin said, thinking, I'll go out through the passage, and if she's still in the church I'll duck behind the huts and go into the woods.

She turned to go. Two of Sir Bloet's servants were struggling with a heavy chest. They set it down with a thunk in front of her, and it tipped over on to its side. She backed up and started round them, trying to keep from walking behind the horses.

'Wait!' Rosemund said, catching up with her. She caught hold of her sleeve. 'You must come with me to bid Sir Bloet farewell.'

'Rosemund—' Kivrin said, looking towards the passage. Any second lady Imeyne would come through there, clutching her Book of Hours.

'Please,' Rosemund said. She looked pale and frightened.

'Rosemund—'

'It will but take a moment and then you can fetch Grandmother.' She pulled Kivrin over to the stable. 'Come. Now, while his sister-in-law is with him.'

Sir Bloet was standing watching his horse being saddled and talking to the lady with the amazing coif. It was no less enormous this morning, but had obviously been put on hastily. It listed sharply to one side.

'What is this urgent business of the bishop's envoy?' she was saying.

He shook his head, frowning, and then smiled at Rosemund and stepped forward. She stepped back, holding tightly to Kivrin's arm.

His sister-in-law bobbed her wimple at Rosemund and went on, 'Has he had news from Bath?'

'There has been no messenger last night or this morning,' he said.

'If there has been no message, why spoke he not of this urgent business when first he came?' the sister-in-law said.

'I know not,' he said impatiently. 'Hold. I must bid my betrothed farewell.' He reached for Rosemund's hand, and Kivrin could see the effort it took her not to pull it back.

'Farewell, Sir Bloet,' she said stiffly.

'Is that how you would part from your husband?' he asked. 'Will you not give him a farewell kiss?'

Rosemund stepped forward and kissed him rapidly on the cheek, then stepped immediately back and out of his reach. 'I thank you for your gift of the brooch,' she said.

Bloet dropped his gaze from her white face to the neck of her cloak. 'You are here in place of the friend I love,' he said, fingering it.

Agnes ran up, shouting, 'Sir Bloet! Sir Bloet!' and he caught her and swung her up into his arms.

'I have come to bid you goodbye,' she said. 'My hound died.'

'I will bring you a hound for a wedding gift,' he said, 'if you will give me a kiss.'

Agnes flung her arms around his neck and planted a noisy kiss on each red cheek.

'You are not so chary of your kisses as your sister,' he said, looking at Rosemund. He set Agnes down. 'Or will you give your husband two kisses as well?'

Rosemund didn't say anything.

He stepped forward and fingered the brooch. '*Io suiicien lui dami amo*,' he said. He put his hands on her shoulders. 'You must think of me whenever you wear my brooch.' He leaned forward and kissed her throat.

Rosemund didn't flinch away from him, but the colour drained out of her face.

He released her. 'I will come for you at Eastertide,' he said, and it sounded like a threat.

'Will you bring me a black hound?' Agnes said.

Lady Yvolde came up to them, demanding 'What have your servants done with my travelling cloak?'

'I will fetch it,' Rosemund said and darted off towards the house with Kivrin still in tow.

As soon as they were safely away from Sir Bloet, Kivrin said, 'I must find Lady Imeyne. Look, they are nearly ready to leave.'

It was true. The jumble of servants and boxes and horses had resolved itself into a procession, and Cob had opened the gate. The horses the three kings had ridden in on the night before were loaded with their chests and bags, their reins tied together. Sir Bloet's sister-in-law and her daughters were already mounted and the bishop's envoy was standing beside Eliwys' mare, tightening the cinch on the saddle.

Only a few more minutes, Kivrin thought, let her stay in the church a few more minutes, and they'll be gone.

'Your mother bade me find Lady Imeyne,' Kivrin said.

'You must come with me into the hall first,' Rosemund said. Her hand on Kivrin's arm was still trembling.

'Rosemund, there isn't any time—'

'Please,' she said. 'What if he comes into the hall and finds me?'

Kivrin thought of Sir Bloet kissing her on the throat. 'I will come with you,' she said, 'but we must hurry.'

They ran across the courtyard through the door and nearly into the fat monk. He was coming down the steps from the bower and looked angry or hungover. He went out through the screens without a glance at either of them.

There was no one else in the hall. The table was still covered with cups and platters of meat, and the fire was burning smokily, untended.

'Lady Yvolde's cloak is in the loft,' Rosemund said. 'Wait for me.' She scrambled up the ladder as though Sir Bloet were after her.

Kivrin went back to the screens and looked out. She couldn't see the passageway. The bishop's envoy was standing by Eliwys' mare with one hand on the pommel of its saddle, listening to the monk, who was leaning close as he spoke. Kivrin glanced up the stairs at the shut door of the bower, wondering if the clerk was truly hungover or had had some sort of falling out with his superior. The monk's gestures were obviously upset.

'Here it is,' Rosemund said, climbing down, clutching the cloak in one hand and the ladder in the other. 'I would have you take it to Lady Yvolde. It will take but a minute.'

It was the chance she'd been waiting for. 'I will,' she said, took the heavy cloak from Rosemund and started out. As soon as she was outside, she would give the cloak to the nearest servant to deliver to Bloet's sister and head straight for the passageway. Let her stay in the church a few more minutes, she prayed. Let me make it to the green. She stepped out of the door, into Lady Imeyne.

'Why are you not ready to leave?' Imeyne said, looking at the cloak in her arms. 'Where is *your* cloak?'

Kivrin shot a glance at the bishop's envoy. He had both hands on the pommel and was stepping on to Cob's linked hands. The friar was already mounted.

'My cloak is in the church,' Kivrin said. 'I will fetch it.'

'There is no time. They are departing.'

Kivrin looked desperately around the courtyard but they were all out of reach: Eliwys standing with Gawyn by the stable, Agnes talking animatedly to one of Sir Bloet's nieces, Rosemund nowhere to be seen, presumably still in the house, hiding.

'Lady Yvolde bade me to bring her her cloak,' Kivrin said.

'Maisry can take it to her,' Imeyne said. 'Maisry!'

Let her still be hiding, Kivrin prayed.

'*Maisry!*' Imeyne shouted, and Maisry came slinking out from the brewhouse door, holding her ear. Lady Imeyne snatched the cloak out of Kivrin's arms and dumped it on Maisry's. 'Stop snivelling and take this to Lady Yvolde,' she snapped.

She grabbed Kivrin by the wrist. 'Come,' she said, and started towards the bishop's envoy. 'Holy Father, you have forgotten Lady Katherine, whom you promised to take with you to Godstow.'

'We do not go to Godstow,' he said and swung himself into the saddle with an effort. 'We journey to Bernecestre.'

Gawyn had mounted Gringolet and was walking him towards the gate. He's going with them, she thought. Perhaps on the way to Courcy I can persuade him to take me to the drop. Perhaps I can persuade him to tell me where it is, and I can get away from them and find it myself.

'Can she not ride with you to Bernecestre then, and a monk escort her to Godstow? I would have her returned to her nunnery.'

'There is no time,' he said, picking up the reins.

Imeyne grabbed hold of his scarlet cope. 'Why do you leave so suddenly? Has aught offended you?'

He glanced at the friar, who was holding the reins of Kivrin's mare. 'Nay.' He made a vague sign of the cross over Imeyne. '*Dominus vobiscum, et cum spiritu tuo,*' he murmured, looking pointedly at her hand on his cope.

'What of a new chaplain?' Imeyne insisted.

'I am leaving my clerk behind to serve you as chaplain,' he said.

He's lying, Kivrin thought, and glanced up sharply at him. He exchanged another secretive glance with the monk, and Kivrin wondered if their urgent business was simply getting away from this complaining old woman.

'Your clerk?' Lady Imeyne said, pleased, and let go of the cope.

The bishop's envoy spurred his horse and galloped across the courtyard, nearly running down Agnes, who scurried out of the way and then ran to Kivrin and buried her head in her skirt. The monk mounted Kivrin's mare and rode after him.

'God go with you, Holy Father,' Lady Imeyne called after him, but he was already out the gate.

And then they were all gone, Gawyn riding out last at a flashy gallop to make Eliwys notice him, and they hadn't taken her off to Godstow and out of reach of the drop. Kivrin was so relieved she didn't even worry over Gawyn's having gone with them. It was less than a half-day's ride to Courcy. He might even be back by nightfall.

Everyone seemed relieved, or perhaps it was only the letdown of Christmas afternoon and the fact that they had all been up since yesterday morning. No one made any movement to clear the tables, which were still covered with dirty trenchers and half-full serving bowls. Eliwys sank into the high seat, her arms dangling over the side, and looked at the table uninterestedly. After a few minutes she called for Maisry, but when she didn't answer Eliwys didn't shout for her again. She leaned her head against the carved back and closed her eyes.

Rosemund went up to the loft to lie down, and Agnes sat down next to Kivrin by the hearth and put her head on her lap, playing absently with her bell.

Only Lady Imeyne refused to give in to the letdown of the afternoon. 'I would have my new chaplain say prayers,' she said, and went up to knock on the bower door.

Eliwys protested lazily, her eyes still closed, that the bishop's envoy had said the clerk should not be disturbed, but Imeyne knocked several times, loudly and without result. She waited a few minutes, knocked again, and then came down the steps and knelt at the foot of them to read her Book of Hours and keep an eye on the door so she could waylay the clerk as soon as he emerged.

Agnes batted at her bell with one finger, yawning broadly.

'Why don't you go up into the loft and lie down with your sister?' Kivrin suggested.

'I'm not *tired*,' Agnes said, sitting up. 'Tell me what happened to the naughty girl.'

'Only if you lie down,' Kivrin said, and began the story. Agnes didn't last two sentences.

In the late afternoon, Kivrin remembered Agnes' puppy. Everyone was asleep by then, even Lady Imeyne, who had given up on the clerk and gone up to the loft to lie down. Maisry had come in at some point and crawled under one of the tables. She was snoring loudly.

Kivrin eased her knees carefully out from under Agnes' head and went out to bury the puppy. There was no one in the courtyard. The remains of a bonfire still smouldered in the centre of the green, but there was no one round it. The villagers must be taking a Christmas afternoon nap, too.

Kivrin brought back Blackie's body and went into the stable for a wooden spade. Only Agnes' pony was there and Kivrin frowned at it, wondering how the clerk was supposed to follow the envoy to Courcy. Perhaps he hadn't been lying, after all, and the clerk was to be the new chaplain whether he liked it or not.

Kivrin carried the spade and Blackie's already stiffening body across to the church and round to the north side. She laid the puppy down and began chipping through the crusted snow.

The ground was literally as hard as stone. The wooden spade didn't even make a dent, even when she stood on it with both feet. She climbed the hill to the beginnings of the wood, dug through the snow at the base of an ash tree and buried the puppy in the loose leaf mould.

'*Requiescat in pace*,' she said so she could tell Agnes the puppy had had a Christian burial and went back down the hill.

She wished Gawyn would ride up now. She could ask him to take her to the drop while everyone was still asleep. She walked slowly across the green, listening for the horse. He would probably come by the main road. She propped the spade against the wattle fence of the pigsty and went round the outside of the manor wall to the gate, but she couldn't hear anything.

The afternoon light began to fade. If Gawyn didn't come soon, it would be too dark to ride out to the drop. Father Roche would be ringing vespers in another half-hour, and that would wake everyone up. Gawyn would have to tend his horse, though, no matter what time he got back, and she could sneak out to the stable and ask him to take her to the drop in the morning.

Or perhaps he could simply tell her where it was, draw her a map so she could find it herself. That way she wouldn't have to go into the woods alone with him, and if Lady Imeyne had him out on another errand the day of the rendezvous, she could take one of the horses and find it herself.

She stood in by the gate till she got cold and then went back along the wall to the pigsty and into the courtyard. There was still no one in the courtyard, but Rosemund was in the anteroom, with her cloak on.

'Where have you been?' she said. 'I've been looking everywhere for you. The clerk—'

Kivrin's heart jerked. 'What is it? Is he leaving?' He'd woken from his hangover and was ready to leave. And Lady Imeyne had persuaded him to take her to Godstow.

'Nay,' Rosemund said, going into the hall. It was empty. Eliwys and Imeyne must both be in the bower with him. She unfastened Sir Bloet's brooch and took her cloak off. 'He is ailing. Father Roche sent me to find you.' She started up the stairs.

'Ailing?' Kivrin said.

'Aye. Grandmother sent Maisry to the bower to take him somewhat to eat.'

And to put him to work, Kivrin thought, following her up the steps. 'And Maisry found him ill?'

'Aye. He has a fever.'

He has a hangover, Kivrin thought, frowning. But Roche would surely recognise the effects of drink, even if Lady Imeyne couldn't, or wouldn't.

A terrible thought occurred to her. He's been sleeping in my bed, Kivrin thought, and he's caught my virus.

'What symptoms does he have?' she asked.

Rosemund opened the door.

There was scarcely room for them all in the little room. Father Roche was by the bed, and Eliwys stood a little behind him, her hand on Agnes' head. Maisry cowered by the window. Lady Imeyne knelt at the foot of the bed next to her medicine casket, busy with one of her foul-smelling poultices, and there was another smell in the room, sickish and so strong it overpowered the mustard and leek smell of the poultice.

They all, except Agnes, looked frightened. Agnes looked interested, the way she had with Blackie, and Kivrin thought, he's dead, he's caught what I had, and he's died. But that was ridiculous. She had been here since the middle of December. That would mean an incubation period of nearly two weeks, and no one else had caught it, not even Father Roche, or Eliwys, and they had been with her constantly while she was ill.

She looked at the clerk. He lay uncovered in the bed, wearing a shift and no breeches. The rest of his clothes were draped over the foot of the bed, his purple cloak dragging on the floor. His shift was yellow silk, and the ties had come unfastened so that it was open halfway down his chest, but she wasn't noticing either his hairless skin or the ermine bands on the sleeves of his shift. He was ill. *I was never that ill*, Kivrin thought, *not even when I was dying.*

She went up to the bed. Her foot hit a half-empty earthenware wine bottle and sent it rolling under the bed. The clerk flinched. Another bottle, with the seal still on it, stood at the head of the bed.

'He has eaten too much rich food,' Lady Imeyne said, mashing something in her stone bowl, but it was clearly not food poisoning. Nor too much alcohol, in spite of the wine bottles. *He's ill*, Kivrin thought. *Terribly ill.*

He breathed rapidly in and out through his open mouth, panting like poor Blackie, his tongue sticking out. It was bright red and looked swollen. His face was an even darker red and his expression was distorted, as if he were terrified.

She wondered if he might have been poisoned. The bishop's envoy had been so anxious to leave he had nearly run Agnes down, and he had told Eliwys not to disturb him. The church had done things like that in the 1300s, hadn't they? Mysterious deaths in the monastery and the cathedral. Convenient deaths.

But that made no sense. The bishop's envoy and the monk would not have hurried off and given orders not to disturb the victim when the whole point of poison was to make it look like botulism or peritonitis or the dozen other unaccountable things people died of in the Middle Ages. And why would the bishop's envoy poison one of his own underlings when he could demote him, the way Lady Imeyne wanted to demote Father Roche.

'Is it the cholera?' Lady Eliwys said.

No, Kivrin thought, trying to remember its symptoms. Acute diarrhoea and vomiting with massive loss of body fluids. Pinched expression, dehydration, cyanosis, raging thirst.

'Are you thirsty?' she asked.

The clerk gave no sign that he had heard. His eyes were half-closed and they looked swollen, too.

Kivrin laid her hand on his forehead. He flinched a little, his reddened eyes flickering open and then closed.

'He's burning with fever,' Kivrin said, thinking, cholera doesn't produce this high a fever. 'Fetch me a cloth dipped in water.'

'Maisry!' Eliwys snapped, but Rosemund was already at her elbow with the same filthy rag they must have used on her.

At least it was cool. Kivrin folded it into a rectangle, watching the clerk's face. He was still panting, and his face contorted when she laid the rag across his forehead, as if he were in pain. He clutched his hand to his belly. Appendicitis? Kivrin thought. No, that usually was accompanied by a low-grade fever. Typhoid fever could produce temps as high as 40 degrees, though usually not at the onset. It produced enlargement of the spleen, as well, which frequently resulted in abdominal pain.

'Are you in pain?' she asked. 'Where does it hurt?'

His eyes flickered half-open again, and his hands moved restlessly on the coverlet. That was a symptom of typhoid fever, that restless plucking, but only in the last stages, eight or nine days into the progress of the disease. She wondered if the priest had already been ill when he came.

He had stumbled getting off his horse when they arrived, and the monk had had to catch him. But he had eaten and drunk more than a little at the feast, and grabbed at Maisry. He couldn't have been very ill, and typhoid came on gradually, beginning with a headache and an only slightly elevated temperature. It didn't reach 39 degrees until the third week.

Kivrin leaned closer, pulling his untied shift aside to look for typhoid's rose-coloured rash. There wasn't any. The side of his neck seemed slightly swollen, but swollen lymph glands went with most every infection. She pulled his sleeve up. There weren't any rose spots on his arm either, but his fingernails were a bluish-brown colour, which meant not enough oxygen. And cyanosis was a symptom of cholera.

'Has he vomited or had loosening of his bowels?' she asked.

'Nay,' Lady Imeyne said, smearing a greenish paste on a piece of stiff linen. 'He has eaten too much of sugars and spices, and it has fevered his blood.'

It couldn't be cholera without vomiting, and at any rate the fever was too high. Perhaps it was her virus after all, but she hadn't felt any stomach pain, and her tongue hadn't swollen like that.

The clerk raised his hand and pushed the rag off his forehead and on to the pillow, and then let his arm fall back to his side. Kivrin picked the rag up. It was completely dry. And what besides a virus could cause that high a fever? She couldn't think of anything but typhoid.

'Has he bled from the nose?' she asked Roche.

'Nay,' Rosemund said, stepping forward and taking the rag from Kivrin. 'I have seen no sign of bleeding.'

'Wet it with cold water but don't wring it out,' Kivrin said. 'Father Roche, help me to lift him.'

Roche put his hands to the priest's shoulders and raised him up. There was no blood on the linen under his head.

Roche laid him gently back down. 'Think you it is the typhoid fever?' he said, and there was something curious, almost hopeful in his tone.

'I know not,' Kivrin said.

Rosemund handed Kivrin the rag. She had taken Kivrin at her word. It was dripping with icy water.

Kivrin leaned forward and laid it across the clerk's forehead.

His arms came up suddenly, wildly, knocking the cloth backwards out of Kivrin's hand, and then he was sitting up, flailing at her with both his hands, kicking out with his feet. His fist caught her on the side of her leg, buckling her knees so that she almost toppled on to the bed.

'I'm sorry, I'm sorry,' Kivrin said, trying to get her balance, trying to clutch at his hands. 'I'm sorry.'

His bloodshot eyes were wide open now, staring straight ahead. *Gloriam tuam,* he bellowed in a strange high voice that was almost a scream.

'I'm sorry,' Kivrin said. She grabbed at his wrist and his other arm shot out, striking her full in the chest.

'*Requiem aeternum dona eis,*' he roared, rising up on his knees and then his feet to stand in the middle of the bed. '*Et lux perpetua luceat eis.*'

Kivrin realised suddenly that he was trying to chant the mass for the dead.

Father Roche clutched at his shift and the clerk lashed out, kicking himself free, and then went on kicking, spinning around as if he were dancing.

'*Miserere nobis.*'

He was too near the wall for them to reach him, hitting the timbers with his feet and flailing arms at every turn without even seeming to notice. 'When he comes within reach, we must grab his ankles and knock him down,' Kivrin said.

Father Roche nodded out of breath. The others stood transfixed, not even trying to stop him, Imeyne still on her knees. Maisry pushed herself completely into the window, her hands over her ears and her eyes squeezed shut. Rosemund had retrieved the sopping rag and held it in her outstretched hand as if she thought Kivrin might try to lay it on his head again. Agnes was staring open-mouthed at the clerk's half-exposed body.

The clerk spun back towards them, his hands pawing at the ties on the front of his shift, trying to rip them free.

'Now,' Kivrin said.

Father Roche and she reached for his ankles. The clerk went down on one knee and then, flinging his arms out wide, burst free and launched himself off the high bed straight at Rosemund. She put her hands up, still holding the rag, and he hit her full in the chest.

'*Miserere nobis,*' he said, and they went down together.

'Grab his arms before he hurts her,' Kivrin said, but the clerk had stopped flailing. He lay atop Rosemund, motionless, his mouth almost touching hers, his arms limply out at his sides.

Father Roche took hold of the clerk's unresisting arm and rolled him off Rosemund. He flopped on to his side, breathing shallowly but no longer panting.

'Is he dead?' Agnes asked, and, as if her voice had released the rest of them from a spell, they all moved forward, Lady Imeyne struggling to her feet, gripping the bedpost.

'Blackie died,' Agnes said, clutching at her mother's skirts.

'He is not dead,' Imeyne said, kneeling beside him, 'but the fever in his blood has gone to the brain. It is often thus.'

It's never thus, Kivrin thought. This isn't a symptom of any disease I've ever heard of. What could it be? Spinal meningitis? Epilepsy?

She bent down next to Rosemund. The girl lay rigidly on the floor, her eyes squeezed shut, her hands clenched into whitening fists. 'Did he hurt you?' Kivrin asked.

Rosemund opened her eyes. 'He pushed me down,' she said, her voice quivering a little.

'Can you stand?' Kivrin asked.

Rosemund nodded and Eliwys stepped forward, Agnes still clinging to her skirt. They helped Rosemund to her feet.

'My foot hurts,' she said, leaning on her mother, but in a minute she was able to stand on it. 'He . . . of a sudden . . .'

Eliwys supported her to the end of the bed and sat her down on the carved chest. Agnes clambered up next to her. 'The bishop's clerk jumped on top of you,' she said.

The clerk murmured something and Rosemund looked fearfully at him. 'Will he rise up again?' she asked Eliwys.

'Nay,' Eliwys said, but she helped Rosemund up and led her to the door. 'Take your sister down to the fire and sit with her,' she told Agnes.

Agnes took hold of Rosemund's arm and led her out. 'When the clerk dies, we will bury him in the churchyard,' Kivrin could hear her say going down the stairs. 'Like Blackie.'

The clerk looked already dead, his eyes half-open and unseeing. Father Roche knelt next to him and hoisted him easily over his shoulder, the clerk's head and arms hanging limply down, the way Kivrin had carried Agnes home from the midnight mass. Kivrin hastily pulled the coverlid off and Roche eased him down on to the bed.

'We must draw the fever from his head,' Lady Imeyne said, returning to her poultice. 'It is the spices that have fevered his brain.'

'No,' Kivrin whispered, looking at the priest. He lay on his back with his arms out at his sides, the palms up. The thin shift was ripped halfway down the front and had fallen completely off his left shoulder so his outstretched arm was exposed. Under the arm was a red swelling. 'No,' she breathed.

The swelling was bright red and nearly as large as an egg. High fever, swollen tongue, intoxication of the nervous system, buboes under the arms and in the groin.

Kivrin took a step back from the bed. 'It can't be,' she said. 'It's something else.' It had to be something else. A boil. Or an ulcer of some kind. She reached forward to pull the sleeve away from it.

The clerk's hands twitched. Roche stretched to grasp his wrists, pushing them down into the featherbed. The swelling was hard to the touch, and around it the skin was a mottled purplish-black.

'It can't be,' she said. 'It's only 1320.'

'This will draw the fever out,' Imeyne said. She stood up stiffly, holding the poultice out in front of her. 'Pull his shift away from his body that I may lay on the poultice.' She started towards the bed.

'No!' Kivrin said. She put her hands up to stop her. 'Stay away! You mustn't touch him!'

'You speak wildly,' Imeyne said. She looked at Roche. 'It is naught but a stomach fever.'

'It isn't a fever!' Kivrin said. She turned to Roche. 'Let go of his hands and get away from him. It isn't a fever. It's the plague.'

All of them, Roche and Imeyne and Eliwys, looked at her as stupidly as Maisry.

They don't even know what it is, she thought desperately, because it doesn't exist yet, there was no such thing as the Black Death yet. It didn't even begin in China until 1333. And it didn't reach England till 1348. 'But it is,' Kivrin said. 'He's got all the symptoms. The bubo and the swollen tongue and the haemorrhaging under the skin.'

'It is naught but a stomach fever,' Imeyne said and pushed past Kivrin to the bed.

'No—' Kivrin said, but Imeyne had already stopped, the poultice poised above his naked chest.

'Lord have mercy on us,' she said, and backed away, still holding the poultice.

'Is it the blue sickness?' Eliwys said frightenedly.

And suddenly Kivrin saw it all. They had not come here because of the trial, because Lord Guillaume was in trouble with the king. He had sent them here because the plague was in Bath.

'Our nurse died,' Agnes had said. And Lady Imeyne's chaplain, Brother Hubard. 'Rosemund said he died of the blue sickness,' Agnes had told her. And Sir Bloet had said that the trial had been delayed because the judge was ill. That was why Eliwys hadn't wanted to send word to Courcy and why she had been so angry when Imeyne sent Gawyn to the bishop. Because the plague was in Bath. But it couldn't be. The Black Death hadn't reached Bath until the autumn of 1348.

'What year is it?' Kivrin said.

The women looked at her dumbly, Imeyne still holding the forgotten poultice. Kivrin turned to Roche. 'What is the year?'

'Are you ill, Lady Katherine?' he said anxiously, reaching for her wrists as if he were afraid she was going to have one of the clerk's seizures.

She jerked her hands away. 'Tell me the year.'

'It is the twenty-first year of Edward the Third's reign,' Eliwys said.

Edward the Third, not the Second. In her panic she could not remember when he had reigned. 'Tell me the *year*,' she said.

'*Anno domini*,' the clerk said from the bed. He tried to lick his lips with his swollen tongue. 'One thousand three hundred and forty-eight.'

BOOK THREE

Buried with my own hands five of my children in a single grave . . . No bells. No tears. This is the end of the world.

Agniola di Tura
Siena, 1347

CHAPTER TWENTY-FOUR

Dunworthy spent the next two days ringing Finch's list of techs and Scottish fishing guides and setting up another ward in Bulkeley-Johnson. Fifteen more of his detainees were down with the flu, among them Ms Taylor, who had collapsed forty-nine strokes short of a full peal.

'Fainted dead away and let go her bell,' Finch reported. 'It swung right over with a noise like doom and the rope thrashed about like a live thing. Wrapped itself round my neck and nearly strangled me. Ms Taylor wanted to go on after she came to herself, but of course it was too late. I do wish you'd speak to her, Mr Dunworthy. She's very despondent. Says she'll never forgive herself for letting the others down. I told her it wasn't her fault, that sometimes things are simply out of one's control, aren't they?'

'Yes,' Dunworthy said.

He had not succeeded in reaching a tech, let alone persuading him to come to Oxford and he had not found Basingame. He and Finch had phoned every hotel in Scotland, and then every inn and rental cottage. William had got hold of Basingame's credit records, but there were no purchases of fishing lures or waders in some remote Scottish town, as he had hoped and no entries at all after the fifteenth of December.

The telephone system was becoming progressively disabled. The visual cut out again, and the recorded voice, announcing that due to the epidemic all circuits were busy, interrupted after only two digits on nearly every call he tried to put through.

He did not so much worry about Kivrin as carry her with him, a heavy weight, as he punched and repunched the numbers, waited for ambulances, listened to Mrs Gaddson's complaints. Andrews had not phoned back, or if he had, had not succeeded in getting through. Badri murmured endlessly of death, the nurses carefully transcribing his ramblings on slips of paper. While he waited for the techs, for the fishing guides, for someone to answer the telephone, he pored over Badri's words, searching for clues. 'Black', Badri had said, and 'laboratory', and 'Europe'.

The phone system grew worse. The recorded voice cut in as he punched the first number, and several times he couldn't raise a dial tone. He gave up for the moment and worked on the contacts charts. William had managed to get hold of the primaries' confidential NHS medical records, and he pored over them, searching for radiation treatments and visits to the dentist. One of the primaries had had his jaw X-rayed but on second look, he saw it had been on the twenty-fourth, after the epidemic began.

He went over to Infirmary to ask the primaries who weren't delirious whether they had any pets or had been duck hunting recently. The corridors were filled with stretcher trolleys, each one of them with a patient on it. They were jammed up against the doors of Casualties and crosswise in front of the lift. There was no way he could get past them to it. He took the stairs.

William's blonde student nurse met him at the door of Isolation. She was wearing a white cloth gown and mask. 'I'm afraid you can't go in,' she said, holding up a gloved hand.

Badri's dead, he thought. 'Is Mr Chaudhuri worse?' he asked.

'No. He seems actually to be resting a bit more quietly. But we've run out of SPGs. London's promised to send us a shipment tomorrow, and the staff's making do with cloth, but we haven't enough for visitors.' She fished in her pocket for a scrap of paper. 'I wrote down his words,' she said, handing it to him. 'I'm afraid most of it's unintelligible. He says your name and – Kivrin's? – is that right?'

He nodded, looking at the paper.

'And sometimes isolated words, but most of it's nonsense.'

She had tried to write it down phonetically, and when she understood a word, she underscored it. 'Can't', he had said, and 'rats', and 'so worried'.

Over half the detainees were down by Sunday morning, and

everyone not ill was nursing them. Dunworthy and Finch had given up all notion of putting them in wards, and at any rate they had run out of cots. They left them in their own beds, or moved them, bed and all, into rooms in Salvin to keep their makeshift nurses from running themselves ragged.

The bell ringers fell one by one, and Dunworthy helped put them to bed in the old library. Ms Taylor, who could still walk, insisted on going to visit them.

'It's the least I can do,' she said, panting after the exertion of walking across the corridor, 'after I let them down like that.'

Dunworthy helped her on to the air mattress William had carried over and covered her with a sheet. ' "The spirit is willing, but the flesh is weak," ' he said.

He felt weak himself, bone-tired from the lack of sleep and the constant defeats. He had finally managed, between boiling water for tea and washing bedpans, to get through to one of Magdalen's techs.

'She's in hospital,' her mother had said. She'd looked harried and tired.

'When did she fall ill?' Dunworthy'd asked her.

'Christmas Day.'

Hope had surged in him. Perhaps Magdalen's tech was the source. 'What symptoms does your daughter have?' he'd asked eagerly. 'Headache? Fever? Disorientation?'

'Ruptured appendix,' she'd said.

By Monday morning three-quarters of the detainees were ill. They ran out, as Finch had predicted, of clean linens and NHS masks and, more urgently, of temps, antimicrobials and aspirin. 'I tried to ring Infirmary to ask for more,' Finch said, handing Dunworthy a list, 'but the phones have all gone dead.'

Dunworthy walked to the Infirmary to fetch the supplies. The street in front of Casualties was jammed, a jumble of ambulance vans and taxis and protesters carrying a large sign that proclaimed 'The Prime Minister Has Left Us Here to Die'. As he squeezed past them and in the door, Colin came running out. He was wet, as usual, and red-faced and red-nosed from the cold. His jacket was unstripped.

'The telephones are out,' he said. 'There was an overload. I'm running messages.' He pulled an untidy clutch of folded papers from his jacket pocket. 'Is there anyone you'd like me to take a message to?'

Yes, he thought. To Andrews. To Basingame. To Kivrin.

'No,' he said.

Colin stuffed the already-wet messages back in his pocket. 'I'm off then. If you're looking for Great-aunt Mary, she's in Casualties. Five more cases just came in. A family. The baby was dead.' He darted off through the traffic jam.

Dunworthy pushed his way into Casualties and showed his list to the house officer, who directed him to Supplies. The corridors were still full of stretcher trolleys, though now they were lined lengthwise on both sides so there was a narrow passage between. Bending over one of the stretcher trolleys was a nurse in a pink mask and gown reading something to one of the patients.

' "The Lord shall make the pestilence cleave unto thee" ' she said, and he realised too late that it was Mrs Gaddson, but she was so intent on her reading she did not look up. ' "Until he have consumed thee from the land." '

The pestilence shall cleave unto thee, he said silently, and thought of Badri. 'It was the rats,' Badri had said. 'It killed them all. Half of Europe.'

She can't be in the Black Death, he thought, turning down the corridor to Supplies. Andrew had said the maximal slippage was five years. In 1325 the plague hadn't even begun in China. Andrews had said the only two things that would not have automatically aborted the drop were the slippage and the coordinates, and Badri, when he could answer Dunworthy's questions, insisted he had checked Puhalski's coordinates.

He went into Supplies. There was no one at the desk. He rang the bell.

Each time Dunworthy had asked him, Badri had said the apprentice's coordinates were correct, but his fingers moved nervously over the sheet, typing, typing in the fix. *That can't be right. There's something wrong.*

He rang the bell again, and a nurse emerged from among the shelves. She had obviously come out of retirement expressly for the epidemic. She was ninety at the least, and her white uniform was yellowed with age, but still stiff with starch. It crackled when she took his list.

'Have you a supply authorisation?'

'No,' he said.

She handed him back his list and a three-page form. 'All orders must be authorised by the ward matron.'

'We haven't any ward matron,' he said, his temper flaring. 'We haven't any ward. We have fifty detainees in two dormitories and no supplies.'

'In that case, authorisation must be obtained from the doctor in charge.'

'The doctor in charge has an infirmary full of patients to take care of. She doesn't have time to sign authorisations. There's an epidemic on!'

'I am well aware of that,' the nurse said frigidly. 'All orders must be signed by the doctor in charge,' and walked creakily back among the shelves.

He went back to Casualties. Mary was no longer there. The house officer sent him up to Isolation, but she wasn't there either. He toyed with the idea of forging Mary's signature, but he wanted to see her, wanted to tell her about his failure to reach the techs, his failure to find a way to bypass Gilchrist and open the net. He could not even get a simple aspirin, and it was already the third of January.

He finally ran Mary to ground in the laboratory. She was speaking into the telephone, which was apparently working again, though the visual was nothing but snow. She wasn't watching it. She was watching the console, which had the branching contacts chart on it. 'What exactly is the difficulty?' she was saying. 'You said it would be here two days ago.'

There was a pause while the person lost in the snow apparently made some sort of excuse.

'What do you mean it was turned back?' she said incredulously. 'I've got a thousand people with influenza here.'

There was another pause. Mary typed something into the console, and a different chart appeared.

'Well, send it again,' she shouted. 'I need it now! I've got people dying here! I want it here by – hullo? Are you there?' The screen

397

went dead. She turned to click the receiver and caught sight of Dunworthy.

She beckoned him into the office. 'Are you there?' she said into the telephone. 'Hullo?' She slammed the receiver down. 'The phones don't work, half my staff is down with the virus, and the analogues aren't here because some idiot wouldn't let them into the quarantine area!' she said angrily.

She sank down in front of the console and rubbed her fingers against her cheekbones. 'Sorry,' she said. 'It's been rather a bad day. I've had three DOA's this afternoon. One of them was six months old.'

She was still wearing the sprig of holly on her lab coat. Both it and the lab coat were much the worse for wear, and Mary looked impossibly tired, the lines around her mouth and eyes cutting deeply into her face. He wondered how long it had been since she had slept and whether, if he were to ask her, she would even know.

She rubbed two fingers along the lines above her eyes. 'One never gets used to the idea that there is nothing one can do,' she said.

'No.'

She looked up at him, almost as if she hadn't realised he was there. 'Was there something you needed James?'

She had had no sleep, and no help, and three DOAs, one of them a baby. She had enough on her mind without worrying about Kivrin.

'No,' he said, standing up. He handed her the form. 'Nothing but your signature.'

She signed it without looking at it. 'I went to see Gilchrist this morning,' she said, handing it back to him.

He looked at her, too surprised and touched to speak.

'I went to see if I could convince him to open the net earlier. I explained that there's no need to wait until there's been full immunisation. Immunisation of a critical percentage of the virus pool effectively eliminates the contagion vectors.'

'And none of your arguments had the slightest effect on him.'

'No. He's utterly convinced the virus came through from the past.' Mary sighed. 'He's drawn up charts of the cyclical mutation patterns of Type A myxoviruses. According to them, one of the

Type A myxoviruses extant in 1318–19 was an H9N2.' She rubbed at her forehead again. 'He won't open the laboratory until full immunisation's been completed and the quarantine's lifted.'

'And when will that be?' he asked, though he had a good idea.

'The quarantine has to remain in effect until seven days after full immunisation or fourteen days after final incidence,' she said as if she were giving him bad news.

Final incidence. Two weeks with no new cases. 'How long will nationwide immunisation take?'

'Once we get sufficient supplies of the vaccine, not long. The Pandemic only took eighteen days.'

Eighteen days. After sufficient supplies of the vaccine were manufactured. The end of January. 'That's not soon enough,' he said.

'I know. We must positively identify the source, that's all.' She turned to look at the console. 'The answer's in here, you know. We're simply looking in the wrong place.' She punched in a new chart. 'I've been running correlations, looking for veterinary students, primaries who live near zoos, rural addresses. This one's of secondaries listed in Debrett, grouse shooting and all that. But the closest any of them's come to a waterfowl is eating goose for Christmas.'

She punched up the contacts chart. Badri's name was still at the top of it. She sat and looked at it a long moment, as remote as Montoya staring at her bones.

'The first thing a doctor has to learn is not to be too hard on himself when he loses a patient,' she said, and he wondered if she meant Kivrin or Badri.

'I'm going to get the net open,' he said.

'I hope so,' she said.

The answer did not lie in the contacts charts or the commonalities. It lay in Badri, whose name was still in spite of all the questions they had asked the primaries, in spite of all the false leads, the source. Badri was the index case, and some time in the four to six days before the drop he had been in contact with a reservoir.

He went up to see him. There was a different nurse at the desk outside Badri's room, a tall, nervous youth who looked no more than seventeen.

'Where's . . .' Dunworthy began and realised he didn't know the blonde nurse's name.

'She's down with it,' the boy said. 'Yesterday. She's the twentieth of the nursing staff to catch it, and they're out of subs. They asked for third-year students to help. I'm actually only first-year, but I've had first-aid training.'

Yesterday. A whole day had passed, then, with no one recording what Badri said. 'Do you remember anything Badri might have said while you were in with him?' he said without hope. A first-year student. 'Any words or phrases you could understand?'

'You're Mr Dunworthy, aren't you?' the boy said. He handed him a set of SPGs. 'Eloise said you wanted to know everything the patient said.'

Dunworthy put on the newly arrived SPGs. They were white and marked with tiny black crosses along the back opening of the gown. He wondered where they'd resorted to borrowing them from.

'She was awfully ill and she kept saying over and over how important it was.'

The boy led Dunworthy into Badri's room, looked at the screens above the bed, and then down at Badri. At least he looks at the patient, Dunworthy thought.

Badri lay with his arms outside the sheet, plucking at it with hands that looked like those in Colin's illustration of the knight's tomb. His sunken eyes were open, but he did not look at the nurse or at Dunworthy, or at the sheet, which his ceaseless hands could not seem to grasp.

'I read about this in meds,' the boy said, 'but I've never actually seen it. It's a common terminal symptom in respiratory cases.' He went to the console, punched something up and pointed at the top left screen. 'I've written it all down.'

He had, even the gibberish. He had written that phonetically, with ellipses to represent pauses, and (sic) after questionable words. 'Half,' he had written, and 'backer (sic)' and 'Why doesn't he come?'

'This is mostly from yesterday,' he said. He moved a cursor to the lower third of the screen. 'He talked a bit this morning. Now, of course, he doesn't say anything.'

Dunworthy sat down beside Badri and took his hand. It was ice-cold even through the imperm glove. He glanced at the temp screen. Badri no longer had a fever or the dark flush that had gone with it. He seemed to have lost all colour. His skin was the colour of wet ashes.

'Badri,' he said. 'It's Mr Dunworthy. I need to ask you some questions.'

There was no response. His cold hand lay limply in Dunworthy's gloved one, and the other continued picking steadily, uselessly at the sheet.

'Dr Ahrens thinks you might have caught your illness from an animal, a wild duck or a goose.'

The nurse looked interestedly at Dunworthy and then back at Badri, as if he were hoping he would exhibit another yet-unobserved medical phenomenon.

'Badri, can you remember? Did you have any contact with ducks or geese the week before the drop?'

Badri's hand moved. Dunworthy frowned at it, wondering if he were trying to communicate, but when he loosened his grip a little, the thin, thin fingers were only trying to pluck at his palm, at his fingers, at his wrist.

He was suddenly ashamed that he was sitting here torturing Badri with questions, though he was past hearing, past even knowing Dunworthy was here, or caring.

He laid Badri's hand back on the sheet. 'Rest,' he said, patting it gently, 'try to rest.'

'I doubt if he can hear you,' the nurse said. 'When they're this far gone they're not really conscious.'

'No. I know,' Dunworthy said, but he went on sitting there.

The nurse adjusted a drip, peered nervously at it and adjusted it again. He looked anxiously at Badri, adjusted the drip a third time and finally went out. Dunworthy sat on, watching Badri's fingers plucking blindly at the sheet, trying to grasp it but unable to. Trying to hold on. Now and then he murmured something, too soft to hear. Dunworthy rubbed his arm gently, up and down.

After a while, the plucking grew slower, though Dunworthy didn't know if that was a good sign or not.

'Graveyard,' Badri said.

'No,' Dunworthy said. 'No.'

He sat on a bit longer, rubbing Badri's arm, but after a little it seemed to make his agitation worse. He stood up. 'Try to rest,' he said and went out.

The nurse was sitting at the desk, reading a copy of *Patient Care*.

'Please notify me when . . .' Dunworthy said, and realised he would not be able to finish the sentence. 'Please notify me.'

'Yes, sir,' the boy said. 'Where are you?'

He fumbled in his pocket for a scrap of paper to write on and came up with the list of supplies. He had nearly forgotten it. 'I'm at Balliol,' he said, 'send a messenger,' and went back down to Supplies.

'You haven't filled this in properly,' the crone said starchily when Dunworthy gave her the form.

'I've had it signed,' he said, handing her his list. 'You fill it out.'

She looked disapprovingly at the list. 'We haven't any masks or temps.' She reached down a small bottle of aspirin. 'We're out of synthamycin and AZI.'

The bottle of aspirin contained perhaps twenty tablets. He put them in his pocket and walked down to the High to the chemist's. A small crowd of protesters stood outside in the rain, holding pickets that said, 'UNFAIR!' and 'Price gouging!' He went inside. They were out of masks, and the temps and the aspirin were outrageously priced. He bought all they had.

He spent the night dispensing them and studying Badri's chart, looking for some clue to the virus' source. Badri had run an on-site for Nineteenth Century in Hungary on the tenth of December, but the chart did not say where in Hungary, and William, who was flirting with the detainees who were still on their feet, didn't know, and the phones were out again.

They were still out in the morning when Dunworthy tried to phone to check on Badri's condition. He could not even raise a dialling tone, but as soon as he put down the receiver, the telephone rang.

It was Andrews. Dunworthy could scarcely hear his voice

through the static. 'Sorry this took so long,' he said, and then something that was lost entirely.

'I can't hear you,' Dunworthy said.

'I said, I've had difficulty getting through. The phones . . .' More static. 'I did the parameter checks. I used three different L-and-Ls and triangulated the . . .' The rest was lost.

'What was the maximal slippage?' he shouted into the phone.

The line went momentarily clear. 'Six days. That was with an L-and-L of . . .' More static. 'I ran probabilities, and the possible maximal for any L-and-Ls within a circumference of fifty kilometres was still five years.' The static roared in again, and the line went dead.

Dunworthy put the receiver down. He should have felt reassured, but he could not seem to summon any feeling. Gilchrist had no intention of opening the net on January the sixth, whether Kivrin was there or not. He reached for the phone to phone the Scottish Tourism Bureau, and as he did it rang again.

'Dunworthy here,' he said, squinting at the screen, but the visuals were still nothing but snow.

'Who?' a woman's voice that sounded hoarse or groggy said. 'Sorry,' it murmured. 'I meant to ring—' and something else too blurred to make out, and the visual went blank.

He waited to see if it would ring again and then went back across to Salvin. Magdalen's bell was chiming the hour. It sounded like a funeral bell in the unceasing rain. Ms Piantini had apparently heard the bell, too. She was standing in the quad in her nightgown, solemnly raising her arms in an unheard rhythm. 'Middle, wrong, and into the hunt,' she said when Dunworthy tried to take her back inside.

Finch appeared looking distraught. 'It's the bells, sir,' he said, taking hold of her other arm. 'They upset her. I don't think they should ring them under the circumstances.'

Ms Piantini wrenched free of Dunworthy's restraining hand. 'Every man must stick to his bell *without* interruption,' she said furiously.

'I quite agree,' Finch said, clutching her arm as firmly as if it were a bell rope, and led her back to her cot.

Colin came skidding in, drenched as usual and nearly blue with cold. His jacket was open, and Mary's grey muffler dangled uselessly about his neck He handed Dunworthy a message. 'It's from Badri's nurse,' he said, opening a packet of soap tablets and popping a light blue one into his mouth.

The note was drenched, too. It read 'Badri asking for you', though the word 'Badri' was so blurred he couldn't make out more than the B.

'Did the nurse say whether Badri was worse?'

'No, just to give you the message. And Great-aunt Mary says when you come, you're to get your enhancement. She said she doesn't know when the analogue will get here.'

Dunworthy helped Finch wresde Ms Piantini into bed and hurried to Infirmary and up to Isolation. There was another new nurse, this one a middle-aged woman with swollen feet. She was sitting with them propped up on the screens, watching a pocket vidder, but she stood up immediately when he came in.

'Are you Mr Dunworthy?' she asked, blocking his way. 'Dr Ahrens said you're to meet her downstairs immediately.'

She said it quietly, even kindly, and he thought, she's trying to spare me. She doesn't want me to see what's in there. She wants Mary to tell me first.

'It's Badri, isn't it? He's dead?'

She looked genuinely surprised. 'Oh, no, he's much better this morning. Didn't you get my note? He's sitting up.'

'Sitting up?' he said, staring at her, wondering if she were delirious with fever.

'He's still very weak, of course, but his temp's normal and he's alert. You're to meet Dr Ahrens in Casualties. She said it was urgent.'

He looked wonderingly towards the door to Badri's room. 'Tell him I'll be in to see him as soon as I can,' he said and hurried out of the door.

He nearly collided with Colin, who was apparently coming in. 'What are you doing here?' he demanded. 'Did one of the techs telephone?'

'I've been assigned to you,' Colin said. 'Great-aunt Mary says she doesn't trust you to get your T-cell enhancement. I'm supposed to take you down to get it.'

'I can't. There's an emergency in Casualties,' he said, walking rapidly down the corridor.

Colin ran to keep up with him. 'Well, then, after the emergency. She said I wasn't to let you leave Infirmary without it.'

Mary was there to meet them when the lift opened. 'We have another case,' she said grimly. 'It's Montoya.' She started for Casualties. 'They're bringing her in from Witney.'

'Montoya?' Dunworthy said. 'That's impossible. She's been out at the dig alone.'

She pushed open the double doors. 'Apparently not.'

'But she said – are you certain it's the virus? She's been working in the rain. Perhaps it's some other disease.'

Mary shook her head. 'The ambulance team ran a prelim. It matches the virus.' She stopped at the admissions desk and asked the house officer, 'Are they here yet?'

He shook his head. 'They've just come through the perimeter.'

Mary walked over to the doors and looked out, as if she didn't believe him. 'We got a call from her this morning, very confused,' she said, turning back to them. 'I telephoned to Chipping Norton, which is the nearest hospital, told them to send an ambulance, but they said the dig was officially under quarantine. And I couldn't get one of ours out to her. I finally had to persuade the NHS to grant a dispensation to send an ambulance.' She peered out of the doors again. 'When did she go out to the dig?'

'I—' Dunworthy tried to remember. She had phoned to ask him about the Scottish fishing guides on Christmas Day and then phoned back that afternoon to say, 'Never mind,' because she had decided to forge Basingame's signature instead. 'Christmas Day,' he said. 'If the NHS offices were open. Or the twenty-sixth. No, that was Boxing Day. The twenty-seventh. And she hasn't seen anyone since then.'

'How do you know?'

'When I spoke to her, she was complaining that she couldn't keep the dig dry single-handed. She wanted me to phone to the NHS to ask for students to help her.'

'How long ago was that?'

'Two – no, three days ago,' he said, frowning. The days ran together when one never got to bed.

'Could she have found someone at the farm to help after she spoke to you?'

'There's no one there in the winter.'

'As I remember, Montoya recruits anyone who comes within reach. Perhaps she enlisted some passer-by.'

'She said there weren't any. The dig's very isolated.'

'Well, she must have found someone. She's been out at the dig for seven days, and the incubation period's only twelve to forty-eight hours.'

'The ambulance is here!' Colin said.

Mary pushed out the doors, Dunworthy and Colin on her heels. Two ambulance men in masks lifted a stretcher out and on to a trolley. Dunworthy recognised one of them. He had helped bring Badri in.

Colin was bending over the stretcher, looking interestedly at Montoya, who lay with her eyes closed. Her head was propped up with pillows and her face was flushed the same heavy red as Ms Breen's had been. Colin leaned further over her and she coughed directly in his face.

Dunworthy grabbed the collar of Colin's jacket and dragged him away from her. 'Come away from there. Are you trying to catch the virus? Why aren't you wearing your mask?'

'There aren't any.'

'You shouldn't be here at all. I want you to go straight back to Balliol and—'

'I can't. I'm assigned to make certain you get your enhance-ment.'

'Then sit down over there,' Dunworthy said, walking him over to a chair in the reception area, 'and stay away from the patients.'

'You'd better not try to sneak out on me,' Colin said warningly, but he sat down, pulled his gobstopper out of his pocket and wiped it on the sleeve of his jacket.

Dunworthy went back over to the stretcher trolley. 'Lupe,' Mary was saying, 'we need to ask you some questions. When did you fall ill?'

'This morning,' Montoya said. Her voice was hoarse, and Dunworthy realised suddenly that she must be the person who had telephoned him. 'Last night I had a terrible headache' – she raised a muddy hand and drew it across her eyebrows – 'but I thought it was because I was straining my eyes.'

'Who was with you out at the dig?'

'Nobody,' Montoya said, sounding surprised.

'What about deliveries? Did someone from Witney deliver supplies to you?'

She started to shake her head, but it apparently hurt, and she stopped. 'No. I took everything with me.'

'And you didn't have anyone with you to help you with the excavation?'

'No. I asked Mr Dunworthy to tell the NHS to send some help, but he didn't.' Mary looked across at Dunworthy, and Montoya followed her glance. 'Are they sending someone?' she asked him. 'They'll never find it if they don't get someone out there.'

'Find what?' he said, wondering if Montoya's answer could be trusted or if she were half-delirious.

'The dig is half underwater right now,' she said.

'Find what?'

'Kivrin's corder.'

He had a sudden image of Montoya standing by the tomb, sorting through the muddy box of stone-shaped bones. Wrist bones. They had been wrist bones, and she had been examining the uneven edges, looking for a bone spur that was actually a piece of recording equipment. Kivrin's corder.

'I haven't excavated all the graves yet,' Montoya said, 'and it's still raining. They have to send someone out immediately.'

'Graves?' Mary said, looking at him uncomprehendingly. 'What is she talking about?'

'She's been excavating a mediaeval churchyard looking for Kivrin's body,' he said bitterly, 'looking for the corder you implanted in Kivrin's wrist.'

Mary wasn't listening. 'I want the contacts charts,' she said to the house officer. She turned back to Dunworthy. 'Badri was out at the dig, wasn't he?'

'Yes.'

'When?'

'The eighteenth and nineteenth,' he said.

'In the churchyard?'

'Yes. He and Montoya were opening a knight's tomb.'

'A tomb,' Mary said as if it were the answer to a question. She bent over Montoya. 'How old was the tomb?'

'1318,' Montoya said.

'Did you work on the knight's tomb this week?' Mary asked.

Montoya tried to nod, stopped. 'I get so dizzy when I move my head,' she said apologetically. 'I had to move the skeleton. Water'd got into the tomb.'

'What day did you work on the tomb?'

Montoya frowned. 'I can't remember. The day before the bells, I think.'

'The thirty-first,' Dunworthy said. He leaned over her. 'Have you worked on it since?'

She tried to shake her head again.

'The contacts charts are up,' the house officer said.

Mary walked rapidly over to his desk and took the keyboard over from him. She tapped several keys, stared at the screen, tapped more keys.

'What is it?' Dunworthy said.

'What are the conditions at the churchyard?' Mary said.

'Conditions?' he said blankly. 'It's muddy. She's covered the churchyard with a tarp, but a good deal of rain was still getting in.'

'Warm?'

'Yes. She mentioned it was muggy. She had several electric fires hooked up. What *is* it?'

She drew her finger down the screen, looking for something. 'Viruses are exceptionally sturdy organisms,' she said. 'They can lie dormant for long periods of time and be revived. Living viruses have been taken from Egyptian mummies.' Her finger stopped at a date. 'I thought so. Badri was at the dig four days before he came down with the virus.'

She turned to the house officer. 'I want a team out at the dig immediately,' she told him. 'Get NHS clearance. Tell them we may have found the source of the virus.' She typed in a new screen, drew her finger down the names, typed in something else and leaned back, looking at the screen. 'We had four primaries with no positive connection to Badri. Two of them were at the dig four days before they came down with the virus. The other one was there three days before.'

'The virus is at the dig?' Dunworthy said.

'Yes.' She smiled ruefully at him. 'I'm afraid Gilchrist was right after all. The virus did come from the past. Out of the knight's tomb.'

'Kivrin was at the dig,' he said.

Now it was Mary who looked uncomprehending. 'When?'

'The Sunday afternoon before the drop. The nineteenth.'

'Are you certain?'

'She told me before she left. She wanted her hands to look authentic.'

'Oh, my God,' she said. 'If she was exposed four days before the drop, she hadn't had her T-cell enhancement. The virus might have had a chance to replicate and invade her system. She might have come down with it.'

Dunworthy grabbed her arm. 'But that can't have happened. The net wouldn't have let her through if there was a chance she'd infect the contemps.'

'There wouldn't have been anyone for her to infect,' Mary said, 'not if the virus came out of the knight's tomb. Not if he died of it in 1318. The contemps would already have had it. They'd be immune.' She walked rapidly over to Montoya. 'When Kivrin was out at the dig, did she work on the tomb?'

'I don't know,' Montoya said. 'I wasn't there. I had a meeting with Gilchrist.'

'Who would know? Who else was there that day?'

'No one. Everyone had gone home for vac.'

'How did she know what she was supposed to do?'

'The volunteers left notes to each other when they left.'

'Who was there that morning?' Mary asked.

'Badri,' Dunworthy said and took off for Isolation.

He walked straight into Badri's room. The nurse, caught off-guard with her swollen feet up on the displays, said, 'You can't go in without SPGs,' and started after him, but he was already inside.

Badri was lying propped against a pillow. He looked very pale, as if his illness had bleached all the colour from his skin, and weak, but he looked up when Dunworthy burst in and started to speak.

'Did Kivrin work on the knight's tomb?' Dunworthy demanded.

'Kivrin?' His voice was almost too weak to be heard.

The nurse banged in the door. 'Mr Dunworthy, you are *not* allowed in here—'

'On Sunday,' Dunworthy said. 'You were to have left her a message telling her what to do. Did you tell her to work on the tomb?'

'*Mr Dunworthy*, you're exposing yourself to the virus—' the nurse said.

Mary came in, pulling on a pair of imperm gloves. 'You're not supposed to be in here without SPGs, James,' she said.

'I *told* him, Dr Ahrens,' the nurse said, 'but he barged past me and—'

'Did you leave Kivrin a message at the dig that she was to work on the tomb?' Dunworthy insisted.

Badri nodded his head weakly.

'She was exposed to the virus,' Dunworthy said to Mary. 'On Sunday. Four days before she left.'

'Oh, no,' Mary breathed.

'What is it? What's happened?' Badri said trying to push himself up in the bed. 'Where's Kivrin?' He looked from Dunworthy to Mary. 'You pulled her out, didn't you? As soon as you realised what had happened? Didn't you pull her out?'

'What had happened—?' Mary echoed. 'What do you mean?'

'You have to have pulled her out,' Badri said. 'She's not in 1320. She's in 1348.'

CHAPTER TWENTY-FIVE

'That's impossible,' Dunworthy said.

'1348?' Mary said bewilderedly. 'But that can't be. That's the year of the Black Death.'

She can't be in 1348, Dunworthy thought. Andrews said the maximal slippage was only five years. Badri said Puhalski's coordinates were correct.

'1348?' Mary said again. He saw her glance at the screens on the wall behind Badri, as if hoping he were still delirious. 'Are you certain?'

Badri nodded. 'I knew something was wrong as soon as I saw the slippage—' he said, and sounded as bewildered as Mary.

'There couldn't have been enough slippage for her to be in 1348,' Dunworthy cut in. 'I had Andrews run parameter checks. He said the maximal slippage was only five years.'

Badri shook his head. 'It wasn't the slippage. That was only four hours. It was too small. Minimal slippage on a drop that far in the past should have been at least forty-eight hours.'

The slippage had not been too great. It had been too small. I didn't ask Andrews what the minimal slippage was, only the maximal.

'I don't know what happened,' Badri said. 'I had such a headache. The whole time I was setting the net, I had a headache.'

'That was the virus,' Mary said. She looked stunned. 'Headache and disorientation are the first symptoms.' She sank down in the chair beside the bed. '1348.'

1348. He could not seem to take this in. He had been worried about Kivrin catching the virus, he had been worried about there

411

being too much slippage, and all the time she was in 1348. The plague had hit Oxford in 1348. At Christmastime.

'As soon as I saw how small the slippage was, I knew there was something wrong,' Badri said, 'so I called up the coordinates—'

'You said you checked Puhalski's coordinates,' Dunworthy said accusingly.

'He was only a first-year apprentice. He'd never even done a remote. And Gilchrist didn't have the least idea what he was doing I tried to tell you. Wasn't she at the rendezvous?' He looked at Dunworthy. 'Why didn't you pull her out?'

'We didn't know,' Mary said, still sitting there stunned. 'You weren't able to tell us anything. You were delirious.'

'The plague killed fifty million people,' Dunworthy said. 'It killed half of Europe.'

'James,' Mary said.

'I tried to tell you,' Badri said. 'That's why I came to get you. So we could pull her out before she left the rendezvous.'

He had tried to tell him. He had run all the way to the pub. He had run out in the pouring rain without his coat to tell him, pushing his way between the Christmas shoppers and their shopping bags and umbrellas as if they weren't there, and arrived wet and half-frozen, his teeth chattering with the fever. *There's something wrong.*

I tried to tell you. He had. 'It killed half of Europe,' he had said, and 'It was the rats,' and 'What year is it?' He had tried to tell him.

'If it wasn't the slippage, it has to have been an error in the coordinates,' Dunworthy said, gripping the end of the bed.

Badri shrank back against the propped pillows like a cornered animal.

'You said Puhalski's coordinates were correct.'

'James,' Mary said warningly.

'The coordinates are the only other thing that could go wrong,' he shouted. 'Anything else would have aborted the drop. You said you checked them twice. You said you couldn't find any mistakes.'

'I couldn't,' Badri said. 'But I didn't trust them. I was afraid he'd made a mistake in the sidereal calculations that wouldn't show up.' His face went grey. 'I refed them myself. The morning of the drop.'

The morning of the drop. When he had had the terrific head-ache. When he was already feverish and disorientated. Dun-worthy remembered him typing at the console, frowning at the display screens. I watched him do it, he thought. I stood and watched him send Kivrin to the Black Death.

'I don't know what happened,' Badri said. 'I must have—'

'The plague wiped out whole villages,' Dunworthy said. 'So many people died, there was no one left to bury them.'

'Leave him alone, James,' Mary said. 'It's not his fault. He was ill.'

'Ill,' he said. 'Kivrin was exposed to your virus. She's in 1348.'

'James,' Mary said.

He didn't wait to hear it. He yanked the door open and plunged out.

Colin was balancing on a chair in the corridor, tipping it back so the front two legs were off the ground. 'There you are,' he said.

Dunworthy walked rapidly past him.

'Where are you going?' Colin said, tipping the chair forward with a crash. 'Great-aunt Mary said not to let you leave till you'd had your enhancement.' He lurched sideways, caught himself on his hands, and scrambled up. 'Why aren't you wearing your SPGs?'

Dunworthy shoved through the ward doors.

Colin came skidding through the doors. 'Great-aunt Mary said I was absolutely not to let you leave.'

'I don't have time for enhancements,' Dunworthy said. 'She's in 1348.'

'Great-aunt Mary?'

He started down the corridor.

'Kivrin?' Colin asked, running to catch up. 'She can't be. That's when the Black Death was, isn't it?'

Dunworthy shoved open the door to the stairs and started down them two at a time.

'I don't understand,' Colin said. 'How did she end up in 1348?'

Dunworthy pushed open the door at the foot of the stairs and started down the corridor to the call box, fishing in his overcoat for the pocket calendar Colin had given him.

'How are you going to pull her out?' Colin asked. 'The laboratory's locked.'

Dunworthy pulled out the pocket calendar and began turning pages. He'd written Andrews' number in the back.

'Mr Gilchrist won't let you in. How are you going to get into the laboratory? He said he wouldn't let you in.'

Andrews' number was on the last page. He picked up the receiver.

'If he does let you in, who's going to run the net? Mr Chaudhuri?'

'Andrews,' Dunworthy said shortly and began punching in the number.

'I thought he wouldn't come. Because of the virus.'

Dunworthy put the receiver to his ear. 'I'm not leaving her there.'

A woman answered. '24837 here,' she said. 'H. F. Shepherds', Limited.'

Dunworthy looked blankly at the pocket calendar in his hand. 'I'm trying to reach Ronald Andrews,' he said. 'What number is this?'

'24837,' she said impatiently. 'There's no one here by that name.'

He slammed the phone down. 'Idiot telephone service,' he said. He punched in the number again.

'Even if he agrees to come, how are you going to find her?' Colin asked, looking over his shoulder at the receiver. 'She won't be there, will she? The rendezvous isn't for three days.'

Dunworthy listened to the telephone's ringing, wondering what Kivrin had done when she realised where she was. Gone back to the rendezvous and waited there, no doubt. If she was able to. If she was not ill. If she had not been accused of bringing the plague to Skendgate.

'24837 here,' the same woman's voice said. 'H. F. Shepherds', Limited.'

'What number is this?' Dunworthy shouted.

'24837,' she said, exasperated.

'24837,' Dunworthy repeated. 'That's the number I'm trying to reach.'

'No, it's not,' Colin said, reaching across him to point to Andrews' number on the page. 'You've mixed the numbers.' He took the receiver away from Dunworthy. 'Here, let me try it for you.' He punched in the number and handed the receiver back to Dunworthy.

The ringing sounded different, further away. Dunworthy thought about Kivrin. The plague had not hit everywhere at once. It had been in Oxford at Christmas, but there was no way of knowing when it had reached Skendgate.

There was no answer. He let the phone ring ten times, eleven. He could not remember which way the plague had come from. It had come from France. Surely that meant from the east, across the Channel. And Skendgate was west of Oxford. It might not have reached there until after Christmas.

'Where's the book?' he asked Colin.

'What book? Your appointment calendar, you mean? It's right here.'

'The book I gave you for Christmas. Why don't you have it?'

'Here?' Colin said, bewildered. 'It weighs at least five stone.'

There was still no answer. Dunworthy hung up the receiver, snatched up the calendar and started towards the door. 'I expect you to keep it with you at all times. Don't you know there's an epidemic on?'

'Are you all right, Mr Dunworthy?'

'Go and get it,' Dunworthy said.

'What, right now?'

'Go back to Balliol and get it. I want to know when the plague reached Oxfordshire. Not the town. The villages. And which direction it came from.'

'Where are you going?' Colin asked, running alongside him.

'To make Gilchrist open the laboratory.'

'If he won't open it because of the flu, he'll never open it for the plague,' Colin said.

Dunworthy opened the door and went out. It was raining hard. The EC protesters were huddled under Infirmary's overhang. One of them started towards him, proffering a flyer. Colin was right. Telling Gilchrist the source would have no effect. He would remain convinced the virus had come through the net. He would be afraid to open it for fear the plague would come through.

'Give me a sheet of paper,' he said, fumbling for his pen.

'A sheet of paper?' Colin said. 'What for?'

Dunworthy snatched the flyer from the EC protester and began scribbling on the back. 'Mr Basingame is authorising the opening of the net,' he said.

Colin peered at the writing. 'He'll never believe that, Mr Dunworthy. On the back of a *flyer*?'

'Then fetch me a sheet of paper!' he shouted.

Colin's eyes widened. 'I will. You wait here, all right?' he said placatingly. 'Don't leave.'

He dashed back inside and reappeared immediately with several sheets of hardcopy paper. Dunworthy snatched it from him and scrawled the orders and Basingame's name. 'Go and fetch your book. I'll meet you at Brasenose.'

'What about your coat?'

'There's no time,' he said. He folded the paper in fourths and jammed it inside his jacket.

'It's raining. Shouldn't you take a taxi?' Colin said.

'There aren't any taxis.' He started off down the street.

'Great-aunt Mary's going to kill me, you know,' Colin called after him. 'She said it was my responsibility to see that you got your enhancement.'

He should have taken a taxi. It was pouring by the time he reached Brasenose, a hard slanting rain that would be sleet in another hour. Dunworthy felt chilled to the bone.

The rain had at least driven the picketers away. There was nothing in front of Brasenose but a few wet flyers they had dropped. An expandable metal gate had been pulled across the front of the entrance to Brasenose. The porter had retreated inside his lodge and the shutter was down.

'Open up!' Dunworthy shouted. He rattled the gate loudly. 'Open up immediately!'

The porter pulled the shutter up and looked out. When he saw it was Dunworthy he looked alarmed and then belligerent. 'Brasenose is under quarantine,' he said. 'It's restricted.'

'Open this gate immediately,' Dunworthy said.

'I'm afraid I can't do that, sir,' he said. 'Mr Gilchrist has given orders that no one be admitted to Brasenose until the source of the virus is discovered.'

'We know the source,' Dunworthy said. 'Open the gate.'

The porter let the shutter down, and in a minute he came out of the lodge and over to the gate. 'Was it the Christmas decorations?' he said. 'They said the ornaments were infected with it.'

'No,' Dunworthy said. 'Open the gate and let me in.'

'I don't know whether I should do that, sir,' he said, looking uncomfortable. 'Mr Gilchrist . . .'

'Mr Gilchrist isn't in charge any more,' he said. He pulled the folded paper out of his jacket and poked it through the metal gates at the porter.

He unfolded it and read it, standing there in the rain.

'Mr Gilchrist is no longer Acting Head,' Dunworthy said. 'Mr Basingame has authorised me to take charge of the drop. Open the gate.'

'Mr Basingame,' he said, peering at the already-blotted signature. 'I'll find the keys,' he said.

He went back in the lodge, taking the paper with him. Dunworthy huddled against the gate, trying to keep out of the freezing rain and shivering.

He had been worried about Kivrin sleeping on the cold ground and she was in the middle of a holocaust, where people froze to death because no one was left on their feet to chop wood, and the animals died in the fields because no one was left alive to bring them in. Eighty thousand dead in Siena, three hundred thousand in Rome, more than a hundred thousand in Florence. One half of Europe.

The porter finally emerged with a large ring of keys and came over to the gate. 'I'll have it open in a moment, sir,' he said, sorting through the keys.

Kivrin would surely have gone back to the drop as soon as she realised it was 1348. She would have been there all this time, waiting for the net to open, frantic that they hadn't come to get her.

If she had realised. She would have no way of knowing she was in 1348. Badri had told her the slippage would be several days. She would have checked the date against the Advent holy days and thought she was exactly where she was supposed to be. It would never have occurred to her to ask the year. She would think she was in 1320, and all the time the plague would be sweeping towards her.

The gate's lock clicked free and Dunworthy pushed the gate open far enough to squeeze through. 'Bring your keys,' he said. 'I need you to unlock the laboratory.'

'That key's not on here,' the porter said, and disappeared into the lodge again.

It was icy in the passage, and the rain came slanting in, colder still. Dunworthy huddled next to the door of the lodge, trying to catch some of the heat from inside, and jammed his hands hard against the bottoms of his jacket pockets to stop the shivering.

He had been worried about cut-throats and thieves, and all this time she had been in 1348, where they had piled the dead in the streets, where they had burned Jews and strangers at the stake in their panic.

He had been worried about Gilchrist not doing parameter checks, so worried that he had infected Badri with his anxiety, and Badri, already feverish, had refed the coordinates. *So worried.*

He realised suddenly that the porter had been gone too long, that he must be warning Gilchrist.

He moved towards the door, and as he did the porter emerged, carrying an umbrella and exclaiming over the cold. He offered half the umbrella to Dunworthy.

'I'm already wet through,' Dunworthy said and strode off ahead of him through the quad.

The door of the laboratory had a yellow plastic banner stretched across it. Dunworthy tore it off while the porter searched, through his pockets for the key to the alarm, switching the umbrella from hand to hand.

Dunworthy glanced up behind him at Gilchrist's rooms. They overlooked the laboratory and there was a light on in the sitting-room, but Dunworthy couldn't detect any movement.

The porter found the flat cardkey that switched off the alarm. He switched it off and began looking for the key to the door. 'I'm still not certain I should unlock the laboratory without Mr Gilchrist's authorisation,' he said.

'Mr Dunworthy!' Colin shouted from halfway across the quad. They both looked up. Colin came racing up, drenched to the skin, with the book under his arm, wrapped in the muffler. 'It – didn't – hit – parts of Oxfordshire – till – March,' he said, stopping between words to catch his breath 'Sorry. I – ran – all the way.'

'What parts?' Dunworthy asked.

Colin handed the book to him and bent over, his hands on his knees, taking deep, noisy breaths. 'It – doesn't – say.'

Dunworthy unwound the muffler and opened the book to the page Colin had turned down, but his spectacles were too spattered with rain to read it, and the open pages were promptly soaked.

'It says it started in Melcombe and moved north to Bath and east,' Colin said. 'It says it was in Oxford at Christmas and London the next October, but that parts of Oxfordshire didn't get it till late spring, and that a few individual villages were missed until July.'

Dunworthy stared blindly at the unreadable pages. 'That doesn't tell us anything,' he said.

'I know,' Colin said. He straightened up, still breathing hard, 'but at least it doesn't say the plague was all through Oxfordshire by Christmas. Perhaps she's in one of those villages it didn't come to till July.'

Dunworthy wiped the wet pages with the dangling muffler and shut the book. 'It moved east from Bath,' he said numbly. 'Skendgate's just south of the Oxford-Bath road.'

The porter had finally decided on a key. He pushed it into the lock.

'I rang up Andrews again, but there was still no answer.'

The porter opened the door.

'How are you going to run the net without a tech?' Colin said.

'Run the net?' the porter said, the key still in his hand. 'I understood that you wished to obtain data from the computer. Mr Gilchrist won't allow you to run the net without authorisation.' He took out Basingame's authorisation and looked at it.

'I'm authorising it,' Dunworthy said and swept past him into the laboratory.

The porter started in, caught his open umbrella on the door frame and fumbled on the handle for the catch.

Colin ducked under the umbrella and in after Dunworthy.

Gilchrist must have turned the heat off. The laboratory was

scarcely warmer than the outside, but Dunworthy's spectacles, wet as they were, steamed up. He took them off and tried to wipe them dry on his wet suit jacket.

'Here,' Colin said and handed him a wadded length of paper tissue. 'It's lavatory paper. I've been collecting it for Mr Finch. The thing is, it's going to be difficult enough to find her if we land in the proper place, and you said yourself that getting the exact time and place are awfully complicated.'

'We already have the exact time and place,' Dunworthy said, wiping his spectacles on the lavatory paper. He put them on again. They were still blurred.

'I'm afraid I shall have to ask you to leave,' the porter said. 'I cannot allow you in here without Mr Gilchrist's—' He stopped.

'Oh, blood,' Colin muttered, 'it's Mr Gilchrist.'

'What's the meaning of this?' Gilchrist said. 'What are you doing here?'

'I'm going to bring Kivrin through,' Dunworthy said.

'On whose authority?' Gilchrist said. 'This is Brasenose's net, and you are guilty of unlawful entry.' He turned on the porter. 'I gave you orders that Mr Dunworthy was not to be allowed on the premises.'

'Mr Basingame authorised it,' the porter said. He held the damp paper out.

Gilchrist snatched it from him. 'Basingame!' He stared down at it. 'This isn't Basingame's signature,' he said furiously. 'Unlawful entry, and now forgery. Mr Dunworthy, I intend to file charges. And when Mr Basingame returns, I intend to inform him of your—'

Dunworthy took a step towards him. 'And I intend to inform Mr Basingame how his Acting Head of Faculty refused to abort a drop, how he intentionally endangered an historian, how he refused to allow access to this laboratory, and how as a result the historian's temporal location could not be determined.' He waved his arm at the console. 'Do you know what this fix says? This fix that you wouldn't let my tech read for ten days because of a lot of imbeciles who don't understand time travel, including you? Do you *know* what it says? Kivrin's not in 1320. She's in 1348, in the middle of the Black Death.' He turned and gestured towards the screens. 'And she's been there two weeks. Because of your stupidity. Because of—' He stopped.

'You have no right to speak to me that way,' Gilchrist said. 'And no right to be in this laboratory. I demand that you leave immediately.'

Dunworthy didn't answer. He took a step towards the console.

'Call the proctor,' Gilchrist said to the porter. 'I want them thrown out.'

The screen was not only blank but also dark, and so were the function lights above it on the console. The power switch was turned to off. 'You've switched off the power,' Dunworthy said, and his voice sounded as old as Badri's had. 'You've shut down the net.'

'Yes,' Gilchrist said, 'and a good thing too, since you feel you have the right to barge in without authorisation.'

He put a hand out blindly towards the blank screen, staggering a little. 'You've shut down the net,' he repeated.

'Are you all right, Mr Dunworthy?' Colin said, taking a step forward.

'I thought you might attempt to break in and open the net,' Gilchrist said, 'since you seem to have no respect for Mediaeval's authority. I cut off the power to prevent that happening, and it appears I did the right thing.'

Dunworthy had heard of people being struck down by bad news. When Badri had told him Kivrin was in 1348, he had not been able to absorb what it meant, but this news seemed to strike him with a physical force. He couldn't catch his breath. 'You shut the net down,' he said. 'You've lost the fix.'

'Lost the fix?' Gilchrist said. 'Nonsense. There are backups and things, surely? When the power's switched on again—'

'Does that mean we don't know where Kivrin is?' Colin asked.

'Yes,' Dunworthy said, and thought as he fell, I am going to hit the console like Badri did but he didn't. He fell almost gently, like a man with the wind knocked out of him, and collapsed like a lover into Gilchrist's outstretched arms.

'I knew it,' he heard Colin say. 'This is because you didn't get your enhancement Great-aunt Mary's going to kill me.'

CHAPTER TWENTY-SIX

'That's impossible,' Kivrin said. 'It can't be 1348,' but it all made sense: Imeyne's chaplain dying, and their not having any servants, Eliwys' not wanting to send Gawyn to Oxford to find out who Kivrin was. 'There is much illness there,' Lady Yvolde had said, and the Black Death had hit Oxford at Christmas in 1348. 'What happened?' she said, and her voice rose out of control. 'What *happened*? I was supposed to go to 1320. 1320! Mr Dunworthy told me I shouldn't come, he said Mediaeval didn't know what they were doing, but they couldn't have sent me to the wrong *year*!' She stopped. 'You must get out of here! It's the Black Death!'

They all looked at her so uncomprehendingly that she thought the interpreter must have lapsed into English again. 'It's the Black Death,' she said again. 'The blue sickness!'

'Nay,' Eliwys said softly, and Kivrin said, 'Lady Eliwys, you must take Lady Imeyne and Maisry down to the hall.'

'It cannot be,' she said, but she took lady Imeyne's arm and led her out, Imeyne clutching the poultice as if it were her reliquary. Maisry darted after them, her hands clutched to her ears.

'You must go, too,' Kivrin said to Roche. 'I will stay with the clerk.'

'Thruuuu . . .' the clerk murmured from the bed, and Roche turned to look at him. The clerk struggled to rise and Roche started towards him.

'No!' Kivrin said, and grabbed his sleeve. 'You mustn't go near him.' She interposed herself between him and the bed. 'The clerk's illness is contagious,' she said, willing the interpreter to translate. 'Infectious. It is spread by fleas and by . . .' she hesitated, trying to think how to describe droplet infection, 'by the humours and exhalations of the ill. It is a deadly disease, which kills nearly all who come near it.'

She watched him anxiously, wondering if he had understood anything she'd said, if he *could* understand it. There had been no knowledge of germs in the 1300s, no knowledge of how diseases spread. The contemps had believed the Black Death was a judgment from God. They had thought it was spread by poisonous mists that floated across the countryside, by a dead person's glance, by magic.

'Father,' the clerk said, and Roche tried to step past Kivrin, but she barred his way.

'We cannot leave them to die,' he said.

They did, though, she thought. They ran away and left them. People abandoned their own children, and doctors refused to come, and all the priests fled.

She stooped and picked up one of the strips of cloth Lady Imeyne had torn for her poultice. 'You must cover your mouth and nose with this,' she said.

She handed it to him and he looked at it, frowning, and then folded it into a flat packet and held it to his face.

'Tie it,' Kivrin said, picking up another one. She folded it diagonally and put it over her nose and mouth like a bandit's mask and tied it in a knot at the back. 'Like this.'

Roche obeyed fumbling with the knot, and looked at Kivrin. She moved aside, and he bent over the clerk and put his hand on his chest.

'Don't—' she said, and he looked up at her. 'Don't touch him any more than you have to.'

She held her breath as Roche examined him, afraid that he would start up suddenly again and grab at Roche, but he didn't move at all. The bubo under his arm had begun to ooze blood and a slow greenish pus.

Kivrin put a restraining hand on Roche's arm. 'Don't touch it,' she said. 'He must have broken it when we were struggling with him.' She wiped the blood and pus away with one of Imeyne's cloth strips and bound up the wound with another, tying it tightly at the shoulder. The clerk did not wince or cry out, and when she looked at him she saw he was staring straight ahead, unmoving.

'Is he dead?' she asked.

'Nay,' Roche said, his hand on his chest again, and she could see the faint rise and fall. 'I must bring the sacraments,' he said through the mask, and his words were almost as blurred as the clerk's.

No, Kivrin thought, the panic rising again. Don't go. What if he dies? What if he rises up again?

Roche straightened. 'Do not fear,' he said. 'I will come again.'

He went out rapidly, without shutting the door, and Kivrin went over to close it. She could hear sounds from below – Eliwys' and Roche's voices. She should have told him not to speak to anyone. Agnes said, 'I wish to stay with Kivrin,' and began to howl and Rosemund answered her angrily, shouting over the crying.

'I will tell Kivrin,' Agnes said, outraged, and Kivrin shoved the door to and barred it.

Agnes must not come in here, nor Rosemund, nor anyone. They must not be exposed. There was no cure for the Black Death. The only way to protect them was to keep them from catching it. She tried frantically to remember what she knew about the plague. She had studied it in History of Meds, and Dr Ahrens had talked about it when she'd given Kivrin her inoculations.

There were two distinct types, no, three – one went directly into the bloodstream and killed the victim within hours. Bubonic plague was spread by rat fleas, and that was the kind that produced the buboes. The other kind was pneumonic, and it didn't have buboes. The victim coughed and vomited up blood, and that was spread by droplet infection and was horribly contagious. But the clerk had the bubonic, and that wasn't as contagious. Simply being near the patient wouldn't do it – the flea had to jump from one person to another.

She had a sudden vivid image of the clerk falling on Rosemund, bearing her down to the floor. What if she gets it? she thought. She can't, she can't get it. There isn't any cure.

The clerk stirred in the bed, and Kivrin went over to him.

'Thirsty,' he said, licking his lips with his swollen tongue. She brought him a cup of water, and he drank a few gulps greedily and then choked and spewed it over her.

She backed away, yanking off the drenched mask. It's the bubonic, she told herself, wiping frantically at her chest. This kind isn't spread by droplet. And you can't get the plague, you've had your inoculation. But she had had her antivirals and her T-cell enhancement, too. She should not have been able to get the virus either. She should not have landed in 1348.

'What *happened*?' she whispered.

It couldn't be the slippage. Mr Dunworthy had been upset that they hadn't run slippage checks, but even at its worst, the drop would only have been off by months, not years. Something must have gone wrong with the net.

Mr Dunworthy had said Mr Gilchrist didn't know what he was doing, and something had gone wrong, and she had come through in 1348, but why hadn't they aborted the drop as soon as they knew it was the wrong date? Mr Gilchrist might not have had the sense to pull her out, but Mr Dunworthy would have. He hadn't wanted her to come in the first place. Why hadn't he opened the net again?

Because I wasn't there, she thought. It would have taken at least two hours to get the fix. By then she had wandered off into the woods. But he would have held the net open. He wouldn't have closed it again and waited for the rendezvous. He'd hold it open for her.

She half ran to the door and pushed up on the bar. She must find Gawyn. She must make him tell her where the drop was.

The clerk sat up and flung his bare leg over the bed as if he would go with her. 'Help me,' he said, and tried to move his other leg.

'I can't help you,' she said angrily. 'I don't belong here.' She shoved the bar up out of its sockets. 'I must find Gawyn.' But as soon as she said it, she remembered that he wasn't there, that he had gone with the bishop's envoy and Sir Bloet to Courcy. With the bishop's envoy, who had been in such a hurry to leave he had nearly run down Agnes.

She dropped the bar and turned on him. 'Did the others have the plague?' she demanded. 'Did the bishop's envoy have it?' She remembered his grey face and the way he had shivered and pulled his cloak around him. He would infect all of them: Bloet and his haughty sister and the chattering girls. And Gawyn. 'You knew you had it when you came here, didn't you? Didn't you?'

The clerk held his arms out stiffly to her, like a child. 'Help me,' he said, and fell back, his head and shoulder nearly off the bed.

'You don't deserve to be helped. You brought the plague here.'

There was a knock.

'Who is it?' she said angrily.

'Roche,' he called through the door, and she felt a wave of relief, of joy that he had come, but she didn't move. She looked down at the clerk, still lying half off the bed. His mouth was open and his swollen tongue filled his entire mouth.

'Let me in,' Roche said. 'I must hear his confession.'

His confession. 'No,' Kivrin said.

He knocked again, louder.

'I can't let you in,' Kivrin said. 'It's contagious. You might catch it.'

'He is in peril of death,' Roche said. 'He must be shriven that he may enter into heaven.'

He's not going to heaven, Kivrin thought. He brought the plague here.

The clerk opened his eyes. They were bloodshot and swollen, and there was a faint hum to his breathing. He's dying, she thought.

'Katherine,' Roche said.

Dying, and far from home. Like I was. She had brought a disease with her, too, and if no one had succumbed to it, it was not because of anything she had done. They had all helped her, Eliwys and Imeyne and Roche. She might have infected all of them Roche had given her the last rites, he had held her hand.

Kivrin lifted the clerk's head gently and laid him straight in the bed. Then she went to the door.

'I'll let you give him the last rites,' she said, opening it a crack, 'but I must speak to you first.'

Roche had put on his vestments and taken off his mask He carried the holy oil and the viaticum in a basket. He set them on the chest at the foot of the bed, looking at the clerk, whose

426

breathing was becoming more laboured. 'I must hear his confession,' he said.

'No!' Kivrin said. 'Not until I've told you what I have to.' She took a deep breath. 'The clerk has the bubonic plague,' she said, listening carefully for the translation 'It is a terrible disease. Nearly all who catch it die. It is spread by rats and their fleas and by the breath of those who are ill, and their clothes and belongings.' She looked anxiously at him, willing him to understand. He looked anxious, too, and bewildered.

'It's a terrible disease,' she said. 'It's not like typhoid or cholera. It's already killed hundreds of thousands of people in Italy and France, so many in some places there's no one left to bury the dead.'

His expression was unreadable. 'You have remembered who you are and whence you came,' he said, and it wasn't a question.

He thinks I was fleeing the plague when Gawyn found me in the woods, she thought. If I say yes, he'll think I'm the one who brought it here. But there was nothing accusing in his look, and she had to make him understand.

'Yes,' she said, and waited.

'What must we do?' he said.

'You must keep the others from this room, and you must tell them they must stay in the house and let no one in. You must tell the villagers to stay in their houses, too, and if they see a dead rat not to go near it. There must be no more feasting or dancing on the green. The villagers mustn't come into the manor house or the courtyard or the church. They mustn't gather together anywhere.'

'I will bid Lady Eliwys keep Agnes and Rosemund inside,' he said, 'and tell the villagers to keep to their houses.'

The clerk made a strangled sound from the bed, and they both turned and looked at him.

'Is there naught we can do to help those who have caught this plague?' he said, pronouncing the word awkwardly.

She had tried to remember what remedies the contemps had tried while he was gone. They had carried nosegays of flowers and drunk powdered emeralds and applied leeches to the buboes, but all of those were worse than useless, and Dr Ahrens had said it wouldn't have mattered what they had tried, that nothing except antimicrobials like tetracycline and streptomycin would have worked, and those had not been discovered until the twentieth century.

'We must give him liquids and keep him warm,' she said.

Roche looted at the clerk. 'Surely God will help him,' he said.

He won't, she thought. He didn't. Half of Europe. 'God cannot help us against the Black Death,' she said.

Roche nodded and picked up the holy oil.

'You must put your mask on,' Kivrin said, kneeling to pick up the last cloth strip. She tied it over his mouth and nose. 'You must always wear it when you tend him,' she said, hoping he wouldn't notice she wasn't wearing hers.

'Is it God who has sent this upon us?' Roche said.

'No,' Kivrin said. 'No.'

'Has the Devil sent it then?'

It was tempting to say yes. Most of Europe had believed it was Satan who was responsible for the Black Death. And they had searched for the Devil's agents, tortured Jews and lepers, stoned old women, burned young girls at the stake.

'No one sent it,' Kivrin said. 'It's a disease. It's no one's fault. God would help us if He could, but He . . .' He what? Can't hear us? Has gone away? Doesn't exist?'

'He cannot come,' she finished lamely.

'And we must act in His stead?' Roche said.

'Yes.'

Roche knelt beside the bed. He bent his head over his hands and then raised it again. 'I knew that God had sent you among us for some good cause,' he said.

She knelt too, and folded her hands.

'*Mittere digneris sanctum Angelum,*' Roche prayed. 'Send us Thy holy angel from heaven to guard and protect all those that are assembled together in this house.'

'Don't let Roche catch it,' Kivrin said into the corder. 'Don't let Rosemund catch it. Let the clerk die before it reaches his lungs.'

Roche's voice chanting the rites was the same as it had been when she was ill, and she hoped it comforted the clerk as it had comforted her. She couldn't tell. He was unable to make his confession, and the anointing seemed to hurt him. He winced when the oil touched the palms of his hands, and his breathing seemed to grow louder as Roche prayed. Roche raised his head and looked at him. His arms were breaking out in the tiny purplish-blue bruises that meant the blood vessels under the skin were breaking, one by one.

Roche turned and looked at Kivrin. 'Are these the last days,' he asked, 'the end of the world that God's apostles have foretold?'

Yes, Kivrin thought. 'No,' she said. 'No. It's only a bad time. A terrible time, but not everyone will die. And there will be wonderful times after this. The Renaissance and class reforms and music. Wonderful times. There will be new medicines, and people won't have to die from this or smallpox or pneumonia. And everyone will have enough to eat, and their houses will be warm even in the winter.' She thought of Oxford, decorated for Christmas, the streets and shops lit. 'There will be lights everywhere, and bells that you don't have to ring.'

Her words had calmed the clerk. His breathing eased and he fell into a doze.

'You must come away from him now,' Kivrin said and led Roche over to the window. She brought the bowl to him. 'You must wash your hands after you have touched him,' she said.

There was scarcely any water in the bowl. 'We must wash the bowls and spoons we use to feed him,' she said, watching him wash his huge hands, 'and we must burn the cloths and bandages. The plague is in them.'

He wiped his hands on the tail of his robe and went down to tell Eliwys what she was to do. He brought back a length of linen and a bowl of fresh water. Kivrin tore the linen into wide strips and tied one over her mouth and nose.

The bowl of water did not last long. The clerk had come out of his doze and asked repeatedly for a drink. Kivrin held the cup for him, trying to keep Roche away from him as much as possible.

Roche went to say vespers and ring the bell. Kivrin closed the door after him, listening for sounds from below, but she couldn't hear anything. Perhaps they are asleep, she thought, or ill. She thought of Imeyne bending over the clerk with her poultice, of

Agnes standing at the end of the bed of Rosemund underneath him.

It's too late, she thought, pacing beside the bed, they've all been exposed. How long was the incubation period? Two weeks? No, that was how long the vaccine took to take effect. Three days? Two? She could not remember. And how long had the clerk been contagious? She tried to remember who he had sat next to at the Christmas feast, who he had talked to, but she hadn't been watching him. She'd been watching Gawyn. The only clear memory she had was of the clerk grabbing Maisry's skirt.

She went to the door again and opened it. 'Maisry!' she called.

There was no answer, and that didn't mean anything, Maisry was probably asleep or hiding, and the clerk had bubonic, not pneumonic, and it was spread by fleas. The chances were that he had not infected anyone, but as soon as Roche came back, she left him with the clerk and took the brazier downstairs to fetch hot coals. And to reassure herself that they were all right.

Rosemund and Eliwys were sitting by the fire, with sewing on their laps, with Lady Imeyne next to them, reading from her Book of Hours. Agnes was playing with her cart, pushing it back and forth over the stone flags and talking to it. Maisry was asleep on one of the benches near the high table, her face sulky even in sleep.

Agnes ran into Imeyne's foot with the cart, and the old woman looked down at her and said, 'I will take your toy from you if you cannot play meetly, Agnes,' and the sharpness of her reprimand, Rosemund's hastily suppressed smile, the healthy pinkness of their faces in the fire's light, were all inexpressibly reassuring to Kivrin. It could have been any night in the manor.

Eliwys was not sewing. She was cutting linen into long strips with her scissors, and she looked up constantly at the door. Imeyne's voice, reading from her Book of Hours, had an edge of worry, and Rosemund, tearing the linen, looked anxiously at her mother. Eliwys stood up and went out through the screens. Kivrin wondered if she had heard someone coming, but after a minute, she came back to her seat and took up the linen again.

Kivrin came on down the stairs quietly, but not quietly enough.

Agnes abandoned her cart and scrambled up. 'Kivrin!' she shouted, and launched herself at her.

'Careful!' Kivrin said, warding her off with her free hand. 'These are hot coals.'

They weren't hot, of course. If they were, she wouldn't have come down to replace them, but Agnes backed away a few steps.

'Why do you wear a mask?' she asked. 'Will you tell me a story?'

Eliwys had stood up, too, and Imeyne had turned to look at her. 'How does the bishop's clerk?' Eliwys asked.

He is in torment, she wanted to say. She settled for, 'His fever is down a little. You must keep well away from me. The infection may be in my clothes.'

They all got up, even Imeyne, closing her Book of Hours on her reliquary, and stepped back from the hearth, watching her.

The stump of the Yule log was still on the fire. Kivrin used her skirt to take the lid from the brazier and dumped the grey coals on the edge of the hearth. Ash roiled up, and one of the coals hit the stump and bounced and skittered along the floor.

Agnes laughed, and they all watched its progress across the floor and under a bench except Eliwys, who had turned back to watch the screens.

'Has Gawyn returned with the horses?' Kivrin asked, and then was sorry. She already knew the answer from Eliwys' strained face, and it made Imeyne turn and stare coldly at her.

'Nay,' Eliwys said without turning her head. 'Think you the others of the bishop's party were ill, too?'

Kivrin thought of the bishop's grey face, of the friar's haggard expression. 'I don't know,' she said.

'The weather grows cold,' Rosemund said. 'Mayhap Gawyn thought to stay the night.'

Eliwys didn't answer. Kivrin knelt by the fire and stirred the coals with the heavy poker, bringing the red coals to the top. She tried to manoeuvre them into the brazier, using the poker, and then gave up and scooped them up with the brazier lid.

'You have brought this upon us,' Imeyne said.

Kivrin looked up, her heart suddenly thumping, but Imeyne

was not looking at her. She was looking at Eliwys. 'It is your sins have brought this punishment to bear.'

Eliwys turned to look at Imeyne, and Kivrin expected shock or anger in her face, but there was neither. She looked at her mother-in-law uninterestedly, as if her mind were somewhere else.

'The Lord punishes adulterers and all their house,' Imeyne said, 'as now he punishes you.' She brandished the Book of Hours in her face. 'It is your sin that has brought the plague here.'

'It was you who sent for the bishop,' Eliwys said coldly. 'You were not satisfied with Father Roche. It was you who brought them here, and the plague with them.'

She turned on her heel and went out through the screens.

Imeyne stood stiffly, as though she had been struck, and went back to the bench where she had been sitting. She eased herself to her knees and took the reliquary from her book and ran the chain absently through her fingers.

'Would you tell me a story now?' Agnes asked Kivrin.

Imeyne propped her elbows on the bench and pressed her hands against her forehead.

'Tell me the tale of the wilful maiden,' Agnes said.

'Tomorrow,' Kivrin said, 'I will tell you a story tomorrow,' and took the brazier back upstairs.

The clerk's fever was back up. He raved shouting the lines from the mass for the dead as if they were obscenities. He asked for water repeatedly and Roche, and then Kivrin, went out to the courtyard for it.

Kivrin tiptoed down the stairs, carrying the bucket and a candle, hoping Agnes wouldn't see her, but they were all asleep except Lady Imeyne. She was on her knees praying, her back stiff and unforgiving. You have brought this upon us.

Kivrin went out into the dark courtyard. Two bells were ringing, slightly out of rhythm with each other, and she wondered if they were vespers bells or tolling a funeral. There was a half-filled bucket of water by the well, but she dumped it on to the cobbles and drew a fresh one. She set it by the kitchen door and went in to get something for them to eat. The heavy cloths used to cover the food when it was brought into the manor were lying on the end of the table. She piled bread and a chunk of cold meat on to one and tied it at the corners, and then grabbed up the rest of them and carried all of it upstairs. They ate sitting on the floor in front of the brazier and Kivrin felt better almost with the first bite.

The clerk seemed better, too. He dozed again, and then broke out in a hot sweat. Kivrin sponged him off with one of the coarse kitchen cloths, and he sighed as if it felt good, and slept. When he woke again, his fever was down. They pushed the chest over next to the bed and set a tallow lamp on it, and she and Roche took turns sitting beside him, and resting on the window seat. It was too cold to truly sleep, but Kivrin curled up against the stone sill and napped, and every time she woke he seemed to be improved.

She had read in History of Meds that lancing the buboes sometimes saved a patient. His had stopped draining, and the hum had gone from his chest. Perhaps he wouldn't die after all.

There were some historians who thought the Black Death had not killed as many people as the records indicated. Mr Gilchrist thought the statistics were grossly exaggerated by fear and lack of education, and even if the statistics were correct, the plague hadn't killed one half of every village. Some places had only had one or two cases. In some villages, no one had died at all.

They had isolated the clerk as soon as they'd realised what it was, and she had managed to keep Roche from getting close most of the time. They had taken every possible precaution. And it hadn't turned into pneumonic. Perhaps that was enough, and they had caught it in time. She must tell Roche they must close the village, keep anyone else from coming in, and perhaps the plague would just pass over them. It had done that. Whole villages had been left untouched, and there were parts of Scotland where the plague had never reached at all.

She must have dozed off. When she woke, it was growing light and Roche was gone. She looked over at the bed. The clerk lay perfectly still, his eyes wide and staring, and she thought, he's died and Roche has gone to dig his grave, but even as the thought formed, she could see the coverings over his chest rise and fall. She felt for his pulse. It was fast and so faint she could scarcely feel it.

The bell began to ring, and she realised Roche must have gone to say matins. She pulled her mask up over her nose and leaned over the bed. 'Father,' she said softly, but he gave no indication at all that he heard her. She put her hand on his forehead. His fever was down again, but his skin didn't feel normal. It was dry, papery, and the haemorrhages on his arms and legs had darkened and spread. His engorged tongue stuck out between his teeth, hideously purple.

He smelled terrible, a sickening odour she could smell through her mask. She climbed up on the window seat and untied the waxed linen. The fresh air smelled wonderful, cold and sharp, and she leaned out over the ledge and breathed deeply.

There was no one in the courtyard, but as she drank in the clean, cold air, Roche appeared in the doorway of the kitchen, carrying a bowl of something that steamed. He started across the cobbles to the door of the manor house, and as he did lady Eliwys appeared. She spoke to Roche, and he started towards her and then stopped short and pulled up his mask before he answered her. He's trying to keep clear of people at any rate, Kivrin thought. He passed on into the manor house, and Eliwys went out to the well.

Kivrin tied the linen to the side of the window and looked around for something to fan the air with. She jumped down, got one of the cloths she had taken from the kitchen, and clambered back up again.

Eliwys was still by the well, drawing up the bucket. She stopped holding the rope, and turned to look towards the gate. Gawyn came through it, leading his horse by the bridle.

He stopped when he saw her, and Gringolet stumbled into him and flung his head up, annoyed. The expression on Gawyn's face was the same as it had always been, full of hope and longing, and Kivrin felt a surge of anger that it hadn't changed, even now. He doesn't know, she thought. He's just returned from Courcy. She felt a pang of pity for him, that he had to find out, that Eliwys would have to tell him.

Eliwys hauled the bucket up even with the edge of the well, and Gawyn took one more step towards her, holding on to Gringolet's bridle, and then stopped.

He knows, Kivrin thought. He knows, after all. The bishop's envoy has come down with it, she thought, and he's ridden home to warn them. She realised suddenly he hadn't brought the horses back with him. The friar has it, she thought, and the rest of them have fled.

He watched Eliwys heave the heavy bucket up on to the stone edge of the well, not moving. He would do anything for her, Kivrin thought, anything at all, he would rescue her from a hundred cut-throats in the woods, but he can't rescue her from this.

Gringolet, impatient to be in the stable, shook his head. Gawyn put his hand up to his muzzle to steady him, but it was too late. Eliwys had already seen him.

She let go of the bucket. It landed with a splash Kivrin could hear, far above them, and then Eliwys was in his arms. Kivrin put her hand to her mouth.

There was a light knock on the door. Kivrin jumped down to open it. It was Agnes.

'Would you not tell me a story now?' she said. She was very bedraggled. No one had braided her hair since yesterday. It stuck out under her linen cap at all angles, and she had obviously slept by the hearth. One sleeve was filthy with ashes.

Kivrin resisted the urge to brush them off. 'You cannot come in,' she said, holding the door nearly shut. 'You will catch the sickness.'

'There is none to play with me,' Agnes said. 'Mother has gone and Rosemund still sleeps.'

'Your mother has only gone out for water,' she said firmly. 'Where is your grandmother?'

'Praying.' She reached for Kivrin's skirt, and Kivrin jerked back.

'You must not touch me,' she said sharply.

Agnes' face puckered into a pout. 'Why are you wroth with me?'

'I'm not angry with you,' Kivrin said more gently. 'But you can't come in. The clerk is very ill, and all who come close to him may' – there was no hope of explaining contagion to Agnes – 'may fall ill, too.'

'Will he die?' Agnes said, trying to see round the door.

'I fear so.'

'Will you?'

'No,' she said, and realised she was no longer frightened. 'Rosemund will waken soon. Ask her to tell you a story.'

'Will Father Roche die?'

'No. Go and play with your cart till Rosemund wakes.'

'Will you tell me a story after the clerk is dead?'

'Yes. Go *downstairs*.'

Agnes went reluctantly down three steps, holding on to the wall 'Will we all die?' she asked.

'No,' Kivrin said. Not if I can help it. She shut the door and leaned against it.

The clerk still lay unseeing and unaware, his whole being turned inward to the battle with an enemy his immune system had never seen before, and had no defences against.

The knocking came again. 'Go downstairs, Agnes,' Kivrin said, but it was Roche, carrying the bowl of broth he had brought from the kitchen and a hod of red coals. He dumped them into the brazier and knelt beside it, blowing on them.

He had handed the bowl to Kivrin. It was lukewarm and smelled terrible. She wondered what it had in it and if that had brought the fever down.

Roche stood up and took the bowl, and they tried to spoon the broth into the clerk, but it dribbled off his huge tongue and down the sides of his mouth.

Someone knocked.

'Agnes, I told you, you can't come in here,' Kivrin said impatiently, trying to mop up the bedclothes.

'Grandmother sent me to bid you come.'

'Is Lady Imeyne ill?' Roche said. He started for the door.

'Nay. It is Rosemund.'

Kivrin's heart began to pound.

Roche opened the door, but Agnes did not come in. She stood on the landing, staring at his mask.

'Is Rosemund ill?' Roche asked anxiously.

'She fell down.'

Kivrin darted past them and down the steps.

Rosemund was sitting on one of the benches by the hearth, and Lady Imeyne was standing over her.

'What's happened?' Kivrin demanded.

'I fell,' Rosemund said, sounding bewildered. 'I hit my arm '
She held it out to Kivrin, the elbow crooked.

Lady Imeyne murmured something.

'What?' Kivrin said, and realised the old lady was praying. She
looked round the hall for Eliwys. She wasn't there. Only Maisry
huddled frightenedly by the table, and the thought flickered
through Kivrin's mind that Rosemund must have tripped over
her.

'Did you fall over something?' she asked.

'Nay,' Rosemund said, still sounding dazed. 'My head hurts.'

'Did you hit your head?'

'Nay.' She pulled her sleeve back. 'I hit my elbow on the
stones.'

Kivrin pushed the loose sleeve up past her elbow. It was
scraped but there was no blood. Kivrin wondered if she could
have broken it. She was holding it at such an odd angle. 'Does this
hurt?' she asked moving it gently.

'Nay.'

She twisted the forearm gently. 'Does this?'

'Nay.'

'Can you move your fingers?' Kivrin said.

Rosemund waggled them each in turn, her arm still crooked
Kivrin frowned at it, puzzled. It might be sprained, but she didn't
think she'd be able to move it so easily. 'Lady Imeyne,' she said,
'would you fetch Father Roche?'

'He cannot help us,' Imeyne said contemptuously, but she
started for the stairs.

'I don't think it's broken,' Kivrin said to Rosemund.

Rosemund lowered her arm, gasped and jerked it up again.
The colour drained from her fece, and beads of sweat broke out
on her upper lip.

It *must* be broken, Kivrin thought, and reached for the arm
again. Rosemund pulled away and, before Kivrin even realised
what was happening, toppled off the bench and on to the floor.

She had hit her head this time. Kivrin heard it thunk against
the stone. Kivrin scrambled over the bench and knelt beside her.
'Rosemund, Rosemund,' she said. 'Can you hear me?'

She didn't move. She had flung her injured arm out when she

fell, as if to catch herself, and when Kivrin touched it, she flinched, but she didn't open her eyes. Kivrin looked round wildly for Imeyne, but the old woman was not on the stairs. She got to her knees.

Rosemund opened her eyes. 'Do not leave me,' she said.

'I must fetch help,' she said.

Rosemund shook her head.

'Father Roche!' Kivrin called, though she knew he could not hear her through the heavy door, and Lady Eliwys came through the screens and ran across the flagged floor.

'Has she the blue sickness?' she said.

No. 'She fell,' Kivrin said. She laid her hand on Rosemund's bare, outflung arm. It felt hot. Rosemund had closed her eyes again and was breathing slowly, evenly, as if she had fallen asleep.

Kivrin pushed the heavy sleeve up and over Rosemund's shoulder. She turned her arm up so she could see the armpit and Rosemund tried to jerk away, but Kivrin held her tightly.

It was not as large as the clerk's had been, but it was bright red and already hard to the touch. No, Kivrin thought. No. Rosemund moaned and tried to pull her arm away, and Kivrin laid it gently down, arranging the sleeve under it.

'What's happened?' Agnes said from halfway down the stairs. 'Is Rosemund ill?'

I can't let this happen, Kivrin thought. I must get help. They've all been exposed, even Agnes, and there's nothing here to help them. Antimicrobials won't be discovered for six hundred years.

'Your sins have brought this,' Imeyne said.

Kivrin looked up. Eliwys was looking at Imeyne, but absently, as if she hadn't heard her.

'Your sins and Gawyn's,' Imeyne said.

'Gawyn,' Kivrin said. He could show her where the drop was, and she could go get help. Dr Ahrens would know what to do. And Mr Dunworthy. Dr Ahrens would give her vaccine and streptomycin to bring back.

'Where is Gawyn?' Kivrin said.

Eliwys was looking at her now, and her face was full of longing, full of hope. He has finally got her attention, Kivrin thought. 'Gawyn,' Kivrin said. 'Where is he?'

'Gone,' Eliwys said.

'Gone where?' she said. 'I must speak with him. We must go fetch help.'

'There is no help,' Lady Imeyne said. She knelt beside Rosemund and folded her hands. 'It is God's punishment.'

Kivrin stood up. 'Gone where?'

'To Bath,' Eliwys said. 'To bring my husband.'

Transcript from the Domesday Book
(070114–070526)

I decided I'd better try to get this all down. Mr Gilchrist said he hoped with the opening of Mediaeval we'd be able to obtain a first-hand account of the Black Death, and I guess this is it.

The first case of plague here was the clerk who came with the bishop's envoy. I don't know if he was ill when they arrived or not. He could have been and that was why they came here instead of going on to Oxford, to get rid of him before he infected them. He was definitely ill on Christmas morning when they left, which means he was probably contagious the night before, when he had contact with at least half the village.

He has transmitted the disease to Lord Guillaume's daughter, Rosemund, who fell ill on . . . the twenty-sixth? I've lost all track of time. Both of them have the classic buboes. The clerk's bubo has broken and is draining. Rosemund's is hard and growing larger. It's nearly the size of a walnut. The area around it is inflamed. Both of them have high fevers and are intermittently delirious.

Father Roche and I have isolated them in the bower and have told everyone to stay in their houses and avoid all contact with each other, but I'm afraid it's too late. Nearly everyone in the village was at the Christmas feast, and the whole family was in here with the clerk.

I wish I knew whether the disease is contagious before the symptoms appear and how long the incubation period is. I know that the plague takes three forms: bubonic, pneumonic, and septicaemic, and I know the pneumonic form is the most contagious since it can be spread by coughing or breathing on people and by touch. The clerk and Rosemund both seem to have the bubonic.

I am so frightened I can't even think. It washes over me in waves. I'll be doing all right, and then suddenly the fear swamps me, and I have to take hold of the bed frame to keep from running out of the room, out of the house, out of the village, away from it!

I know I've had my plague inoculations, but I'd had my T-cells enhanced and my antivirals, and I still got whatever it was I got, and every time the clerk touches me, I cringe. Father Roche keeps forgetting to wear his mask, and I'm so afraid he's going to catch it, or Agnes. And I'm afraid the clerk is going to die. And Rosemund. And I'm afraid somebody in the village is going to get pneumonic, and Gawyn won't come back, and I won't find the drop before the rendezvous.

(Break)

I feel a bit calmer. It seems to help, talking to you, whether you can hear me or not.

Rosemund's young and strong And the plague didn't kill everyone. In some villages no one at all died.

———— ∞ ————

CHAPTER TWENTY-SEVEN

They took Rosemund up to the bower, making a pallet on the floor for her in the narrow space beside the bed. Roche covered it with a linen sheet and went out to the barn's loft to fetch bed coverings.

Kivrin had been afraid Rosemund would baulk at the sight of the clerk, with his grotesque tongue and blackening skin, but she scarcely glanced at him. She took her surcote and shoes off and lay down gratefully on the narrow pallet. Kivrin took the rabbit-skin coverlid from the bed and put it over her.

'Will I scream and run at people like the clerk?' Rosemund asked.

'Nay,' Kivrin said, and tried to smile. 'Try to rest. Does it hurt anywhere?'

'My stomach,' she said, putting her hand to her middle. 'And my head. Sir Bloet told me the fever makes men dance. I thought it was a tale to frighten me. He said they danced till blood came out of their mouths and they died. Where is Agnes?'

'In the loft with your mother,' Kivrin said. She had told Eliwys to take Agnes and Imeyne up to the loft and shut themselves in, and Eliwys had done it without even a backward glance at Rosemund.

'My father comes soon,' Rosemund said.

'You must be quiet now and rest.'

'Grandmother says it is a mortal sin to fear your husband, but I cannot help it. He touches me in ways that are not seemly and tells me tales of things that cannot be true.'

I hope he dies in agony, Kivrin thought. I hope he is infected already.

'My father is even now on his way,' Rosemund said.

'You must try to sleep.'

'If Sir Bloet were here now, he would not dare to touch me,' she said and closed her eyes. 'It would be he who was afraid.'

Roche came in, bearing an armload of bedclothes, and went out again. Kivrin piled them on top of Rosemund, tucked them in around her, and laid the fur she had taken from the clerk's bed back over him.

The clerk still lay quietly, but the hum in his breathing had begun again, and now and then he coughed. His mouth hung open, and the back of his tongue was coated with a white fur.

I can't let this happen to Rosemund, Kivrin thought, she's only twelve years old. There must be something she could do. Something. The plague bacillus was a bacteria. Streptomycin and the sulfa drugs could kill it, but she couldn't manufacture them herself, and she didn't know where the drop was.

And Gawyn had ridden off to Bath. Of course he had. Eliwys had run to him, she had thrown her arms around him, and he would have gone anywhere, done anything for her, even if it meant bringing home her husband.

She tried to think how long it would take Gawyn to ride to Bath and back. It was seventy kilometres. Riding hard he could make it there in a day and a half. Three days, there and back. If he were not delayed, if he could find Lord Guillaume, if he did not fall ill. Dr Ahrens had said untreated plague victims died within four or five days, but she did not see how the clerk could possibly last that long. His temp was up again.

She had pushed Lady Imeyne's casket under the bed when they brought Rosemund up. She pulled it out and looked through it at the dried herbs and powders. The contemps had used homegrown remedies like St John's wort and bittersweet during the plague, but they had been as useless as the powdered emeralds.

Fleabane might help, but she couldn't find any of the pink or purple flowers in the little linen bags.

When Roche came back, she sent him for willow branches from the stream, and steeped them into a bitter tea. 'What is this brew?' Roche asked, tasting it and making a face.

'Aspirin,' Kivrin said. 'I hope.'

Roche gave a cup to the clerk, who was past caring what it tasted like, and it seemed to bring his temp down a little, but Rosemund's rose steadily all afternoon, till she was shivering with chills. By the time Roche left to say vespers, she was almost too hot to touch.

Kivrin uncovered her and tried to bathe her arms and legs in cool water to bring the fever down, but Rosemund wrenched angrily away from her. 'It is not seemly you should touch me thus, sir,' she said through chattering teeth. 'Be sure I shall tell my father when he returns.'

Roche did not come back. Kivrin lit the tallow lamps and tucked the bed coverings around Rosemund, wondering what had become of him.

She looked worse in the smoky light, her face wan and pinched. She murmured to herself, repeating Agnes' name over and over, and once she asked fretfully, 'Where is he? He should have been here ere now.'

He should have been, Kivrin thought. The bell had tolled vespers half an hour ago. Roche is in the kitchen, she told herself, making us soup. Or he has gone to tell Eliwys how Rosemund is. He isn't ill. But she stood up and climbed on the window seat and looked out into the courtyard. It was getting colder, and the dark sky was overcast. There was no one in the courtyard, no light or sound anywhere.

Roche opened the door, and she jumped down, smiling. 'Where have you been? I was —' she said and stopped.

Roche was wearing his vestments and carrying the oil and viaticum. No, she thought, glancing at Rosemund. No.

'I have been with Ulf the Reeve,' he said. 'I heard his confession.' Thank God it's not Rosemund, she thought, and then realised what he was saying. The plague was in the village.

'Are you certain?' she asked. 'Does he have the plague boils?'

'Aye.'

'How many others are in the household?'

'His wife and two sons,' he said tiredly. 'I bade her wear a mask and sent her sons to cut willows.'

'Good,' she said. There was nothing good about it. No, that wasn't true. At least it was bubonic plague and not pneumonic, so

443

there was still a chance the wife and two sons wouldn't get it. But how many other people had Ulf infected, and who had infected him? Ulf would not have had any contact with the clerk. He must have caught it from one of the servants. 'Are any others ill?'

'Nay.'

It didn't mean anything. They only sent for Roche when they were very ill, when they were frightened. There might be three or four other cases already in the village. Or a dozen.

She sat down on the window seat, trying to think what to do. Nothing, she thought. There's nothing you can do. It swept through village after village, killing whole families, whole towns. One third to one half of Europe.

'No!' Rosemund screamed, and struggled to rise.

Kivrin and Roche both dived for her, but she had already lain back down. They covered her up, and she kicked the bedclothes off again. 'I will tell Mother, Agnes, you wicked child,' she murmured. 'Let me out.'

It grew colder in the night. Roche brought up more coals for the brazier, and Kivrin climbed up in the window again to fasten the waxed linen over the window, but it was still freezing. Kivrin and Roche huddled by the brazier in turn, trying to catch a little sleep, and woke shivering like Rosemund.

The clerk did not shiver, but he complained of the cold his words slurred and drunken-sounding. His feet and hands were cold and without feeling.

'They must have a fire,' Roche said. 'We must take them down to the hall.'

You don't understand, she thought. Their only hope lay in keeping the patients isolated, in not letting the infection spread. But it has already spread, she thought, and wondered if Ulf's extremities were growing cold and what he would do for a fire. She had sat in one of their huts by one of their fires. It would not warm a cat.

The cats died too, she thought and looked at Rosemund. The shivering racked her poor body, and she seemed already thinner, more wasted.

'The life is going out of them,' Roche said.

'I know,' she said, and began picking up the bedclothes. 'Tell Maisry to spread straw on the hall floor.'

The clerk was able to walk down the steps, Kivrin and Roche both supporting him, but Roche had to carry Rosemund in his arms. Eliwys and Maisry were spreading straw on the far side of the hall. Agnes was still asleep, and Imeyne knelt where she had the night before, her hands folded stiffly before her face.

Roche lay Rosemund down, and Eliwys began to cover her. 'Where is my father?' Rosemund demanded hoarsely. 'Why is he not here?'

Agnes stirred. She would be awake in a minute and clambering on Rosemund's pallet, gawking at the clerk. She must find some way to keep Agnes safely away from them. Kivrin looked up at the beams, but they were too high, even under the loft, to hang curtains from, and every available coverlid and fur was already being used. She began turning the benches on their sides and pulling them into a barricade. Roche and Eliwys came to help, and they tipped the trestle table over and propped it against the benches.

Eliwys went back over to Rosemund and sat down beside her. Rosemund was asleep, her face flushed with the reddish light from the fire.

'You must wear a mask,' Kivrin said.

Eliwys nodded but she didn't move. She smoothed Rosemund's tumbled hair back from her face. 'She was my husband's favourite,' she said.

Rosemund slept nearly half the morning. Kivrin pulled the Yule log off to the side of the hearth and piled cut logs on the fire. She uncovered the clerk's feet so they could feel the heat.

During the Black Death, the Pope's doctor had made him sit in a room between two huge bonfires, and he had not caught the plague. Some historians thought the heat had killed the plague bacillus. More likely his keeping away from his highly contagious flock was what had saved him, but it was worth trying. Anything was worth trying, she thought, watching Rosemund. She piled more wood on.

Father Roche went to say matins, though it was past midmorning. The bell woke Agnes up. 'Who tumbled the benches down?' she asked running over to the barricade.

'You must not come past this fence,' Kivrin said, standing well back from it. 'You must stay by your grandmother.'

Agnes clambered on to a bench and peered over the top of the tresde table. 'I see Rosemund,' she said. 'Is she dead?'

'She is very ill,' Kivrin said sternly. 'You must not come near us. Go and play with your cart.'

'I would see Rosemund,' she said, putting one leg over the table.

'No!' Kivrin shouted. 'Go and sit with your grandmother!'

Agnes looked astonished and then burst into tears. 'I would see Rosemund!' she wailed but she went over and sat sulkily beside Imeyne.

Roche came in. 'Ulf's elder son is ill,' he said. 'He has the swellings.'

There were two more cases during the morning and one in the afternoon, including the steward's wife. All of them had buboes or small seedlike growths on the lymph glands except the steward's wife.

Kivrin went with Roche to see her. She was nursing the baby, her thin, sharp face even sharper. She was not coughing or vomiting, and Kivrin hoped the buboes had simply not developed yet. 'Wear masks,' she told the steward. 'Give the baby milk from the cow. Keep the children from her,' she said hopelessly. Six children in two rooms. Don't let it be pneumonic plague, she prayed. Don't let them all get it.

At least Agnes was safe. She had not come near the barricade since Kivrin shouted at her. She had sat for a bit, glaring at Kivrin with an expression that was so fierce it would have been comical under other circumstances, and then gone up to the loft to fetch her cart. She had set a place for it at the high table, and they were having a feast.

Rosemund was awake. She asked Kivrin for a drink in a hoarse voice, and as soon as Kivrin had given it to her, she fell quietly asleep. Even the clerk dozed, the hum of his breathing less loud, and Kivrin sat down gratefully beside Rosemund.

She should go out and help Roche with the steward's children,

446

at least make sure he was wearing his mask and washing his hands, but she suddenly felt too tired to move. If I could just lie down for a minute, she thought, I might be able to think of something.

'I would go see Blackie,' Agnes said.

Kivrin jerked her head around, startled out of what had almost been sleep.

Agnes had put on her red cape and hood and was standing as close to the barricade as she dared. 'You vowed you would take me to see my hound's grave.'

'Hush, you will wake your sister,' Kivrin said.

Agnes started to cry, not the loud wail she used when she wanted her own way, but quiet sobs. She's reached her limit too, Kivrin thought. Left alone all day, Rosemund and Roche and I all off-limits, everyone busy and distracted and frightened. Poor thing.

'You vowed,' Agnes said, her lip quivering.

'I cannot take you to see your puppy now,' Kivrin said gently, 'but I will tell you a story. We must be very quiet, though.' She put her finger to her lips. 'We must not wake Rosemund or the clerk.'

Agnes wiped her runny nose with her hand. 'Will you tell me the story of the maiden in the woods?' she said in a stage whisper.

'Yes.'

'Can Cart listen?'

'Yes,' Kivrin whispered, and Agnes tore across the hall to fetch the little wagon, ran back with it and climbed up on the bench, ready to mount the barricade.

'You must sit down on the floor against the table,' Kivrin said, 'and I will sit here on the other side.'

'I will not be able to hear you,' Agnes said, her face clouding again.

'Of course you will, if you are very quiet.'

Agnes got down off the bench and sat down, scooting into position against the table. She set Cart on the floor beside her. 'You must be very quiet,' she said to it.

Kivrin went over and looked quickly at her patients and then sat down against the table and leaned back, feeling exhausted all over again.

'Once in a far land,' Agnes prompted.

'Once in a far land, there was a maiden. She lived by a great forest—'

'Her father said, "Go not into the woods," but she was wilful and did not listen,' Agnes said.

'She was wilful and did not listen,' Kivrin said. 'She put on her cloak—'

'Her red cloak with a hood,' Agnes said. 'And she went into the wood even though her father told her not to.'

Even though her father told her not to. 'I'll be perfectly all right,' she had told Mr Dunworthy. 'I can take care of myself.'

'She should not have gone into the woods, should she?' Agnes said.

'She wanted to see what was there. She thought she would go just a little way,' Kivrin said.

'She should not have,' Agnes said, passing judgment. '*I* would not. The woods are dark.'

'The woods are very dark, and full of frightening noises.'

'Wolves,' Agnes said, and Kivrin could hear her scooting closer to the table, trying to get as close to Kivrin as she could. Kivrin could imagine her huddled against the wood, her knees up, hugging the little wagon.

'The maiden said to herself, "I don't like it here," and she tried to go back, but she could not see the path, it was so dark, and suddenly, something jumped out at her!'

'A wolf,' Agnes breathed.

'No,' Kivrin said. 'It was a bear. And the bear said, "What are you doing in my forest?" '

'The maiden was frightened,' Agnes said in a small, frightened voice.

'Yes. "Oh, please don't eat me, Bear," the maiden said. "I am lost and cannot find my way home." Now the bear was a kindly bear, though he looked cruel, and he said, "I will help you find your way out of the woods," and the maiden said, "How? It is so dark." "We will ask the owl," the bear said. "He can see in the dark." '

She talked on, making up the tale as she went, oddly comforted by it. Agnes stopped interrupting, and after a while Kivrin raised herself up, still talking, and looked over the barricade. ' "Do you know the way out of the wood?" the bear asked the crow. "Yes," the crow said.'

Agnes was asleep against the table, the cape spilled out around her and the cart hugged to her chest.

She should be covered up, but Kivrin didn't dare. All the bedclothes were full of plague germs. She looked over at Lady Imeyne, praying in the corner, her face to the wall. 'Lady Imeyne,' she called softly, but the old lady gave no sign she had heard.

Kivrin put more wood on the fire and sat back down against the table, leaning her head back. ' "I know the way out of the woods," the crow said, "I will show you," ' Kivrin said softly, 'but he flew away over the treetops, so fast they could not follow.'

She must have slept, because the fire was down when she opened her eyes and her neck hurt. Rosemund and Agnes still slept, but the clerk was awake. He called to Kivrin, his words unrecognisable. The white fur covered his whole tongue, and his breath was so foul Kivrin had to turn her head away to take a breath. His bubo had begun to drain again, a thick, dark liquid that smelled like rotting meat. Kivrin put a new bandage on, clenching her teeth to keep from gagging, and carried the old one to the far corner of the hall, and then went out and washed her hands at the well, pouring the icy water from the bucket over one hand and then the other, taking in gulps of the cold air.

Roche came into the courtyard. 'Ulric, Hal's son,' he said, walking with her into the house, 'and one of the steward's sons, the eldest, Walthef.' He stumbled into the bench nearest the door.

'You're exhausted,' Kivrin said. 'You should lie down and rest.'

On the other side of the hall, Imeyne stood up, getting awkwardly to her feet, as though her legs had fallen asleep, and started across the hall towards them.

'I cannot stay. I came to fetch a knife to cut willows,' Roche said, but he sat down by the fire and stared blankly into it.

'Rest a minute at least,' Kivrin said. 'I will fetch you some ale.' She pushed the bench to the side and started out.

'You have brought this sickness,' Lady Imeyne said.

Kivrin turned. The old lady was standing in the middle of the hall, glaring at Roche. She held her book to her chest with both

449

hands. Her reliquary dangled from them. 'It is your sins have brought the sickness here.'

She turned to Kivrin. 'He said the litany for Martinmas on St Eusebius' Day. His alb is dirty.' She sounded as she had when she was complaining to Sir Bloet's sister, and her hands fumbled with the reliquary, counting off his sins on the links of the chain. 'He put the candles out by pinching them and broke the wicks.'

Kivrin watched her, thinking, she's trying to justify her own guilt. She wrote to the bishop asking for a new chaplain, she told him where they were. She can't bear the knowledge that she helped bring the plague here, Kivrin thought, but she couldn't summon up any pity. You have no right to blame Roche, she thought, he has done everything he can. And you've knelt in a corner and prayed.

'God has not sent this plague as a punishment,' she told Imeyne coldly. 'It's a disease.'

'He forgot the Confiteor Deo,' Imeyne said, but she hobbled back to her corner and lowered herself to her knees. 'He put the altar candles on the rood screen.'

Kivrin went over to Roche. 'No one is to blame,' she said.

He was staring into the fire. 'If God does punish us,' he said, 'it must be for some terrible sin.'

'No sin,' she said. 'It is not a punishment.'

'*Dominus!*' the clerk cried, trying to sit up. He coughed again, a racking, terrible cough that sounded like it would tear his chest apart, though nothing came up. The sound woke Rosemund and she began to whimper, and if it isn't a punishment, Kivrin thought, it certainly looks like one.

Rosemund's sleep had not helped her at all. Her temp was back up again, and her eyes had begun to look sunken. She jerked as if flogged at the slightest movement.

It's killing her, Kivrin thought. I have to do something.

When Roche came in again, she went up to the bower and brought down Imeyne's casket of medicines. Imeyne watched, her lips moving soundlessly, but when Kivrin set it in front of her and asked her what was in the linen bags, she put her folded hands up to her face and closed her eyes.

Kivrin recognised some of them. Dr Ahrens had made her

study medicinal herbs, and she recognised comfrey and lungwort and the crushed leaves of tansy. There was a little pouch of powdered mercury sulphide, which no one in their right mind would give anyone, and a packet of foxglove, which was almost as bad.

She boiled water and poured in every herb she recognised and steeped it. The fragrance was wonderful, like a breath of summer, and it tasted no worse than the willow-baric tea, but it didn't help either. By nightfall, the clerk was coughing continuously, and red blotches had begun to appear on Rosemund's stomach and arms. Her bubo was the size of an egg and as hard. When Kivrin touched it, she screamed with pain.

During the Black Death the doctors had put poultices on the buboes or lanced them. They had also bled people and dosed them with arsenic, she thought, though the clerk had seemed better after his buboes broke, and he was still alive. But lancing it might spread the infection or, worse, take it into the bloodstream.

She heated water and wet rags to lay on the bubo, but even though the water was lukewarm, Rosemund screamed at the first touch. Kivrin had to go back to cold water, which did no good. None of it's doing any good she thought, holding the wet cold cloth against Rosemund's armpit None of it.

I must find the drop, she thought. But the woods stretched on for miles, with hundreds of oak trees, dozens of clearings. She would never find it. And she couldn't leave Rosemund.

Perhaps Gawyn would turn back. They had closed the gates of some cities – perhaps he would not be able to get in, or perhaps he would talk to people on the roads and realise Lord Guillaume must be dead. Come back, she willed him, hurry. Come back.

Kivrin went through Imeyne's bag again, tasting the contents of the pouches. The yellow powder was sulphur. Doctors had used that during epidemics too, burning it to fumigate the air, and she remembered learning in History of Meds that sulphur killed certain bacteria, though whether that was only in the sulphur compounds she couldn't remember. It was safer than cutting the bubo open, though.

She sprinkled a little on the fire to test it, and it billowed into a yellow cloud that burned Kivrin's throat even through her mask.

The clerk gasped for breath and Imeyne, over in her corner, set up a continuous hacking.

Kivrin had expected the smell of bad eggs to disperse in a few minutes, but the yellow smoke hung in the air like a pall, burning their eyes. Maisry ran outside, coughing into her apron, and Eliwys took Imeyne and Agnes up to the loft to escape it.

Kivrin propped the manor door open and fanned the air with one of the kitchen cloths, and after a while the air cleared a little, though her throat still felt parched. The clerk continued to cough but Rosemund stopped, and her pulse slowed till Kivrin could scarcely feel it.

'I don't know what to do,' Kivrin said, holding her hot, dry wrist. 'I've tried everything.'

Roche came in, coughing.

'It is the sulphur,' she said. 'Rosemund is worse.'

He looked at her and felt her pulse and then went out again, and Kivrin took that as a good sign. He would not have left if Rosemund were truly bad.

He came back in a few minutes, wearing his vestments and carrying the oil and viaticum of the last rites.

'What is it?' Kivrin said. 'Has the steward's wife died, then?'

'Nay,' he said, and looked past her at Rosemund.

'No,' Kivrin said. She scrambled to her feet to stand between him and Rosemund. 'I won't let you.'

'She must not die unshriven,' he said, still looking at Rosemund.

'Rosemund isn't dying,' Kivrin said, and followed his gaze.

She looked already dead, her chapped lips half-open and her eyes blind and unblinking. Her skin had taken on a yellowish cast and was stretched tautly over her narrow face. No, Kivrin thought desperately. I must do something to stop this. She's twelve years old.

Roche moved forward with the chalice, and Rosemund raised her arm, as if in supplication, and then let it fall.

'We must open the plague boil,' Kivrin said. 'We must let the poison out.'

She thought he was going to refuse, to insist on hearing

Rosemund's confession first, but he did not. He set the chrism and chalice down on the stone floor and went to fetch a knife.

'A sharp one,' Kivrin called after him, 'and bring wine.' She set the pot of water on the fire again. When he came back with the knife, she washed it off with water from the bucket, scrubbing the encrusted dirt near the hilt with her fingernails. She held it in the fire, the hilt wrapped in the tad of her surcote, and then poured boiling water over it and then wine and then the water again.

They moved Rosemund closer to the fire, the side with the bubo facing it so they could have as much light as possible, and Roche knelt at Rosemund's head. Kivrin slipped her arm gently out of her shift and bunched the fabric under her for a pillow. Roche took hold of her arm, turning it so the swelling was exposed.

It was almost the size of an apple, and her whole shoulder joint was inflamed and swollen. The edges of the bubo were soft and almost gelatinous, but the centre was still hard.

Kivrin opened the bottle of wine Roche had brought, poured some on a cloth, and swabbed the bubo gently with it. It felt like a rock embedded in the skin. She was not sure the knife would even cut into it.

She picked up the knife and poised it above the swelling, afraid of cutting into an artery, of spreading the infection, of making it worse.

'She is past pain,' Roche said.

Kivrin looked down at her. She hadn't moved even when Kivrin pressed on the swelling. She stared past them both at something terrible. I can't make it worse, Kivrin thought. Even if I kill her, I can't make it worse.

'Hold her arm,' she said, and Roche pinned her wrist and halfway up the forearm, pressing her arm flat to the floor. Rosemund still didn't move.

Two quick, clean slices, Kivrin thought. She took a deep breath and touched the knife to the swelling.

Rosemund's arm spasmed, her shoulder twisting protectively away from the knife, her thin hand clenching into a claw. 'What do you do?' she said hoarsely. 'I will tell my father!'

Kivrin jerked the knife back. Roche caught at Rosemund's arm and pushed it back against the floor, and she hit weakly at him with her other hand.

'I am the daughter of Lord Guillaume D'Iverie,' she said. 'You cannot treat me thus.'

Kivrin scooted out of her reach and scrambled to her feet, trying to keep the knife from touching anything. Roche reached forward and caught both her wrists easily in one hand. Rosemund kicked out weakly at Kivrin. The chalice fell over and wine spilled out in a dark puddle.

'We must tie her,' Kivrin said, and realised she was holding the knife aloft, like a murderer. She wrapped it in one of the cloths Eliwys had torn, and ripped another into strips.

Roche bound Rosemund's wrists above her head while Kivrin tied her ankles to the leg of one of the upturned benches. Rosemund didn't struggle, but when Roche pulled her shift up over her exposed chest, she said, 'I know you. You are the cut-throat who waylaid the Lady Katherine.'

Roche leaned forward, pressing his full weight down on her forearm, and Kivrin cut across the swelling.

Blood oozed and then gushed, and Kivrin thought, I've hit an artery. She and Roche both lunged for the pile of cloths, and she grabbed a thick wad of them and pressed them against the wound. They soaked through immediately, and when she released her hand to take the one Roche handed her, blood spurted out of the tiny cut. She jammed the tail of her surcote against it, and Rosemund whimpered, a small, helpless sound like Agnes' puppy, and seemed to collapse, though there was nowhere for her to fall.

I've killed her, Kivrin thought.

'I can't stop the bleeding,' she said, but it had already stopped. She held the skirt of her surcote against it, counting to a hundred and then two hundred, and carefully lifted a corner of it away from the wound.

Blood still welled from the cut, but it was mixed with a thick yellow-grey pus. Roche leaned forward to dab at it, but Kivrin stopped him. 'No, it's full of plague germs,' she said, taking the cloth away from him. 'Don't touch it.'

She wiped the sickening-looking pus away. It oozed up again, followed by a watery serum. 'That's all of it, I think,' she said to Roche. 'Hand me the wine.' She looked round for a clean cloth to pour it on.

There weren't any. They had used them all, trying to stop the bleeding. She tipped the wine bottle carefully and let the dark liquid dribble into the cut. Rosemund didn't move. Her face was grey, as if all the blood had been drained out of her. As it had been. And I don't have a transfusion to give her. I don't even have a clean rag.

Roche was untying Rosemund's hands. He took her limp hand in his huge one. 'Her heart beats strongly now,' he said.

'We must have more linen,' Kivrin said, and burst into tears.

'My father will see you hanged for this,' Rosemund said.

<hr />

Transcript from the Domesday Book
(071145–071862)

Rosemund is unconscious. I tried to lance her bubo last night to drain out the infection, and I'm afraid I only made things worse. She lost a great deal of blood. She's very pale and her pulse is so faint I can't find it in her wrist at all.

The clerk is worse, too. His skin continues to haemorrhage, and it's clear he's near the end. I remember Dr Ahrens saying untreated bubonic plague kills people in four or five days, but he can't possibly last that long.

Lady Eliwys, Lady Imeyne, and Agnes are still well, though Lady Imeyne seems to have gone almost insane in her search for someone to blame. She boxed Maisry's ears this morning and told her God was punishing us all for her laziness and stupidity.

Maisry *is* lazy and stupid. She cannot be trusted to watch Agnes for five minutes at a time, and when I sent her for water to wash Rosemund's wound this morning, she was gone over half an hour and came back without it.

I didn't say anything. I didn't want Lady Imeyne hitting her again, and it is only a matter of time before Lady Imeyne gets round to blaming me. I saw her watching me over her

Book of Hours when I went out for the water Maisry forgot, and I can well imagine what she's thinking – that I know too much about the plague not to have been fleeing it, that I am supposed to have lost my memory, that I was not injured but ill.

If she makes those accusations, I'm afraid she'll convince Lady Eliwys that I'm the cause of the plague and that she shouldn't listen to me, that they should take the barricade down and pray together for God to deliver them.

And how will I defend myself? By saying, I'm from the future, where we know everything about the Black Death except how to cure it without streptomycin and how to get back there?

Gawyn still isn't back. Eliwys is frantic with worry. When Roche went to say vespers she was standing at the gate, no cloak, no coif, watching the road. I wonder if it has occurred to her that he might already have been infected when he left for Bath. He rode to Courcy with the bishop's envoy, and when he came back he already knew about the plague.

(Break)

Ulf, the reeve, is near death, and his wife and one of his sons have it. No buboes, but the woman has several small lumps like seeds inside her thigh. Roche constantly has to be reminded to wear his mask and to not touch the patients more than he has to.

The history vids say the contemps were panic-stricken and cowardly during the Black Death, that they ran away and wouldn't tend the sick, and that the priests were the worst of all, but it isn't like that at all.

Everyone's frightened, but they're all doing the best they can, and Roche is wonderful. He sat and held the reeve's wife's hand the whole time I examined her, and he doesn't flinch at the most disgusting jobs – bathing Rosemund's wound, emptying chamber pots, cleaning up after the clerk. He never seems afraid. I don't know where he gets his courage.

He continues to say matins and vespers and to pray,

456

telling God about Rosemund and who has it now, reporting their symptoms and telling what we're doing for them, as if He could actually hear him. The way I talk to you.

Is God there, too, I wonder, but shut off from us by something worse than time, unable to get through, unable to find us?

(Break)

We can hear the plague. The villages toll the death knell after a burial, nine strokes for a man, three for a woman, one for a baby, and then an hour of steady tolling. Esthcote had two this morning, and Osney has tolled continuously since yesterday. The bell in the south-west that I told you I could hear when I first came through has stopped. I don't know whether that means the plague is finished there or whether there's no one left alive to ring the bell.

(Break)

Please don't let Rosemund die. Please don't let Agnes get it. Send Gawyn back.

⌘

CHAPTER TWENTY-EIGHT

The boy who had run from Kivrin the day she tried to find the drop came down with the plague in the night. His mother was standing waiting for Father Roche when he went to matins. The boy had a bubo on his back, and Kivrin lanced it while Roche and the mother held him.

She didn't want to do it. The scurvy had left him already weak, and Kivrin had no idea whether there were any arteries below the shoulder blades. Rosemund did not seem at all improved, though Roche claimed her pulse was stronger. She was so white, as if she had been utterly drained of blood, and so still. And the boy didn't look as if he could stand to lose any blood.

But he bled hardly at all, and the colour was already coming back into his cheeks before Kivrin finished washing the knife.

'Give him tea made from rose hips,' Kivrin said, thinking that at least that would help the scurvy. 'And willow bark.' She held the blade of the knife over the fire. The fire was no bigger than the day she had sat by it, too weak to find the drop. It would never keep the boy warm, and if she told the woman to go gather firewood, she might expose someone else. 'We will bring you some wood,' she said, and then wondered how.

There was still food left over from the Christmas feast, but they were fast running out of everything else. They had used most of the wood that was already cut trying to keep Rosemund and the clerk warm, and there was no one to ask to chop the logs that lay piled against the kitchen. The reeve was ill, the steward was tending his wife and son.

Kivrin gathered up an armful of the already-split wood and some pieces of loose bark for kindling and took it back to the hut, wishing she could move the boy into the manor house, but Eliwys had the clerk and Rosemund to tend, and she looked ready to collapse herself.

Eliwys had sat with Rosemund all night, giving her sips of willow tea and rebandaging the wound. They had run out of cloths, and she had taken off her coif and torn it into strips. She sat where she could see the screens, and every few minutes she had stood up and gone over to the door, as if she heard someone coming. With her dark hair down over her shoulders, she looked no older than Rosemund.

Kivrin took the firewood to the woman, dumping it on the dirt floor next to the rat cage. The rat was gone, killed, no doubt, and not even guilty. 'The Lord blesses us,' the woman said to her. She knelt by the fire and began carefully adding the wood to it.

Kivrin checked the boy again. His bubo was still draining a clear watery fluid, which was good. Rosemund's had bled half the night and then begun to swell and grow hard again. And I can't lance it again, Kivrin thought. She can't lose any more blood.

She started back to the hall, wondering if she should relieve Eliwys or try to chop some wood. Roche, coming out of the steward's house, met her with the news that two more of the steward's children were ill.

It was the two youngest boys, and it was clearly the pneumonic. Both were coughing, and the mother intermittently retched a watery sputum. The Lord blesses us.

Kivrin went back to the hall. It was still hazy from the sulphur, and the clerk's arms looked almost black in the yellowish light. The fire was no better than the one in the woman's hut. Kivrin brought in the last of the cut wood and then told Eliwys to lie down, that she would tend Rosemund.

'Nay,' Eliwys said, glancing towards the door. She added, almost to herself, 'He has been three days on the road.'

It was seventy kilometres to Bath, a day and a half at least on horseback and the same amount of time back, if he had been able to get a fresh horse in Bath. He might be back today, if he had found Lord Guillaume immediately. If he comes back, Kivrin thought.

Eliwys glanced at the door again, as if she heard something, but

459

the only sound was Agnes, crooning softly to her cart. She had put a kerchief over it like a blanket and was spooning make-believe food into it. 'He has the blue sickness,' she told Kivrin.

Kivrin spent the rest of the day doing household chores – bringing in water, making broth from the roast joint, emptying the chamber pots. The steward's cow, its udders swollen in spite of Kivrin's orders, came lowing into the courtyard and followed her, nudging her with its horns till Kivrin gave in and milked it. Roche chopped wood in between visits to the steward and the boy, and Kivrin, wishing she had learned how to split wood, hacked clumsily at the big logs.

The steward came to fetch them again just before dark to his younger daughter. That's eight cases so far, Kivrin thought. There were only forty people in the village. One third to one half of Europe was supposed to have caught the plague and died and Mr Gilchrist thought that was exaggerated. One third would be thirteen cases, only five more. Even at 50 per cent only twelve more would get it, and the steward's children had all already been exposed.

She looked at them, the older daughter stocky and dark like her father, the youngest boy sharp-faced like his mother, the scrawny baby. You'll all get it, she thought and that will leave eight.

She couldn't seem to feel anything, even when the baby began to cry and the girl took it on her knee and stuck her filthy finger in its mouth. Thirteen, she prayed. Twenty at the most.

She couldn't feel anything for the clerk either, even though it was clear he could not last the night. His lips and tongue were covered with a brown slime, and he was coughing up a watery spittle that was streaked with blood. She tended him automatically, without feeling.

It's the lack of sleep, she thought, it's making us all numb. She lay down by the fire and tried to sleep, but she seemed beyond sleep, beyond tiredness. Eight more people, she thought, adding them up in her mind. The mother will catch it, and the reeve's wife and children. That leaves four. Don't let one of them be Agnes or Eliwys. Or Roche.

In the morning Roche found the cook lying in the snow in front of her hut, half-frozen and coughing blood. Nine, Kivrin thought.

460

The cook was a widow, with no one to take care of her, so they brought her into the hall and laid her next to the clerk, who was, amazingly, horribly, still alive. The haemorrhaging had spread all over his body now, his chest crisscrossed with bluish-purple marks, his arms and legs nearly solid black. His cheeks were covered with a black stubble that seemed somehow a symptom too, and under it his face was darkening.

Rosemund still lay white and silent, balanced between life and death, and Eliwys tended her quietly, carefully, as if the slightest movement, the slightest sound, might tip her into death. Kivrin tiptoed among the pallets, and Agnes, sensing the need for silence, fell completely apart.

She whined, she hung on the barricade, she asked Kivrin half a dozen times to take her to see her hound, her pony, to get her something to eat, to finish telling her the story of the naughty girl in the woods.

'How does it end?' she whined in a tone that set Kivrin's teeth on edge. 'Do the wolves eat the girl?'

'I don't know,' Kivrin snapped after the fourth time. 'Go and sit by your grandmother.'

Agnes looked contemptuously at Lady Imeyne, who still knelt in the corner, her back to all of them. She had been there all night. 'Grandmother will not play with me.'

'Well, then, play with Maisry.'

She did, for five minutes, pestering her so mercilessly she retaliated and Agnes came screaming back, shrieking that Maisry had pinched her.

'I don't blame her,' Kivrin said, and sent both of them to the loft.

She went to check on the boy, who was so improved he was sitting up, and when she came back, Maisry was hunched in the high seat, sound asleep.

'Where's Agnes?' Kivrin said.

Eliwys looked around blankly. 'I know not. They were in the loft.'

'Maisry,' Kivrin said, crossing to the dais. 'Wake up. Where is Agnes?'

Maisry blinked stupidly at her.

461

'You should not have left her alone,' Kivrin said. She climbed up into the loft, but Agnes wasn't there, so she checked the bower. She wasn't there either.

Maisry had got out of the high seat and was huddled against the wall, looking terrified. 'Where is she?' Kivrin demanded.

Maisry put a hand up defensively to her ear and gaped at her.

'That's right,' Kivrin said. 'I *will* box your ears unless you tell me where she is.'

Maisry buried her face in her skirts.

'Where *is* she?' Kivrin said, and jerked her up, by her arm. 'You were supposed to watch her. She was your responsibility!'

Maisry began to howl, a high-pitched sound like an animal.

'Stop that!' Kivrin said. 'Show me where she went!' She pushed her towards the screens.

'What is it?' Roche said, coming in.

'It's Agnes,' Kivrin said. 'We must find her. She may have gone out into the village.'

Roche shook his head. 'I did not see her. She is likely in one of the outbuildings.'

'The stables,' Kivrin said, relieved. 'She said she wanted to go see her pony.'

She was not in the stables. 'Agnes!' she called into the manure-smelling darkness, 'Agnes!' Agnes' pony whinnied and tried to push its way out of its stall, and Kivrin wondered when it had last been fed, and where the hounds were. 'Agnes.' She looked in each of the boxes and behind the manger, anywhere a little girl might hide. Or fall asleep.

She might be in the barn, Kivrin thought, and came out of the stable, shielding her eyes from the sudden brightness. Roche was just emerging from the kitchen. 'Did you find her?' Kivrin asked, but he didn't hear her. He was looking towards the gate, his head cocked as if he were listening.

Kivrin listened, but she couldn't hear anything. 'What is it?' she asked. 'Can you hear her crying?'

'It is the Lord,' he said and ran towards the gate.

Oh, no, not Roche, Kivrin thought, and ran after him. He had stopped and was opening the gate. 'Father Roche,' Kivrin said, and heard the horse.

It was galloping towards them, the sound of the hoofs loud on the frozen ground Kivrin thought, Roche meant the lord of the manor. He thinks Eliwys' husband has finally come, and then, with a shock of hope, it's Mr Dunworthy.

Roche lifted the heavy bar and slid it to the side.

We need streptomycin and disinfectant, and he's got to take Rosemund back to hospital with him. She'll have to have a transfusion.

Roche had the bar off. He pushed on the gate.

And vaccine, she thought wildly. He'd better bring back the oral. Where's Agnes? He must get Agnes safely away from here.

The horse was nearly at the gate before she came to her senses. 'No!' she said, but it was too late. Roche already had the gate open.

'He can't come here,' Kivrin shouted, looking about wildly for something to warn him off with. 'He'll catch the plague.'

She'd left the spade by the empty pigsty after she buried Blackie. She ran to get it. 'Don't let him through the gate,' she called, and Roche flung his arms up in warning, but he had already ridden into the courtyard.

Roche dropped his arms. 'Gawyn!' he said, and the black stallion looked like Gawyn's, but a boy was riding it. He could not have been older than Rosemund, and his face and clothes were streaked with mud. The stallion was muddy too, breathing hard and spattering foam, and the boy looked as winded. His nose and ears were brightened with the cold. He started to dismount, staring at them.

'You must not come here,' Kivrin said, speaking carefully so she wouldn't lapse into English. 'There is plague in this village.' She raised her spade, pointing it like a gun at him.

The boy stopped halfway off the horse, and sat down in the saddle again.

'The blue sickness,' she added in case he didn't understand, but he was already nodding.

'It is everywhere,' he said, turning to take something from the pouch behind his saddle. 'I bear a message.' He held out a leather wallet towards Roche, and Roche stepped forward for it.

'No!' Kivrin said and took a step forward, jabbing the spade at the air in front of him. 'Drop it on the ground!' she said. 'You must not touch us.'

The boy took a tied roll of vellum from the wallet and threw it at Roche's feet.

Roche picked it up off the flagstones and unrolled it. 'What says the message?' he asked the boy, and Kivrin thought, of course, he can't read.

'I know not,' the boy said. 'It is from the Bishop of Bath. I am to take it to all the parishes.'

'Would you have me read it?' Kivrin asked.

'Mayhap it is from the lord,' Roche said. 'Mayhap he sends word that he has been delayed.'

'Yes,' Kivrin said, taking it from him, but she knew it wasn't.

It was in Latin, printed in letters so elaborate they were hard to read, but it didn't matter. She had read it before. In the Bodleian.

She leaned the spade against her shoulder and read the message, translating the Latin: 'The contagious pestilence of the present day, which is spreading far and wide, has left many parish churches and other livings in our diocese without parson or priest to care for their parishioners.'

She looked at Roche. No, she thought. Not here. I won't let that happen here.

'Since no priests can be found who are willing—' The priests were dead or had run away, and no one could be persuaded to take their place, and the people were dying 'without the Sacrament of Penance'.

She read on, seeing not the black letters but the faded brown ones she had deciphered in the Bodleian. She had thought the letter was pompous and ridiculous. 'People were dying right and left,' she had told Mr Dunworthy indignantly, 'and all the bishop was concerned about was church protocol!' But now, reading it to the exhausted boy and Father Roche, it sounded exhausted, too. And desperate.

'If they are on the point of death and cannot secure the services of a priest,' she read, 'then they should make confession to each other. We urge you, by these present letters, in the bowels of Jesus Christ, to do this.'

Neither the boy nor Roche said anything when she had

finished reading. She wondered if the boy had known what he was carrying. She rolled the vellum up and handed it back to him.

'I have been riding three days,' the boy said, slumping forward tiredly in the saddle. 'Can I not rest here a while?'

'It is not safe,' Kivrin said, feeling sorry for him. 'We will give you and your horse food to take with you.'

Roche turned to go into the kitchen, and Kivrin suddenly remembered Agnes. 'Did you see a little girl on the road?' she asked. 'A five-year-old child, with a red cloak and hood?'

'Nay,' the boy said, 'but there are many on the roads. They flee the pestilence.'

Roche was bringing out a wadmal sack. Kivrin turned to fetch some oats for the stallion and Eliwys shot past them both, her skirts tangling between her legs, her loose hair flying out behind her.

'Don't—' Kivrin shouted, but Eliwys had already caught hold of the stallion's bridle.

'Where do you come from?' she asked, grabbing at the boy's sleeve. 'Have you seen aught of my husband's *privé*, Gawyn?'

The boy looked frightened. 'I come from Bath, with a message from the bishop,' he said, pulling back on the reins. The horse whinnied and tossed its head.

'What message?' Eliwys said hysterically. 'Is it from Gawyn?'

'I do not know the man of whom you speak,' the boy said.

'Lady Eliwys—' Kivrin said, stepping forward.

'Gawyn rides a black steed with a saddle chased in silver,' Eliwys persisted, pulling on the stallion's bridle. 'He has gone to Bath to fetch my husband, who witnesses at the Assizes.'

'None go to Bath,' the boy said. 'All who can flee it.'

Eliwys stumbled, as though the stallion had reared, and seemed to fall against its side.

'There is no court, nor any law,' the boy said. 'The dead lie in the streets, and all who but look on them die, too. Some say it is the end of the world.'

Eliwys let go of the bridle and took a step back. She turned and looked hopefully at Kivrin and Roche. 'They will surely be home soon, then. Is it certain you did not see them on the road? He rides a black steed.'

'There were many steeds.' He kicked the horse forward towards Roche, but Eliwys didn't move.

Roche stepped forward with the sack of food. The boy leaned
down, grabbed it and wheeled the stallion around, nearly running
Eliwys down. She didn't try to get out of the way.

Kivrin stepped forward and caught hold of one of the reins.
'Don't go back to the bishop,' she said.

He jerked up on the reins, looking more frightened of her than
of Eliwys.

She didn't let go. 'Go north,' she said. 'The plague isn't there
yet.'

He wrenched the reins free, kicked the stallion forward and
galloped out of the courtyard.

'Stay off the main roads,' Kivrin called after him. 'Speak to no
one.'

Eliwys still stood where she was.

'Come,' Kivrin said to her. 'We must find Agnes.'

'My husband and Gawyn will have ridden first to Courcy to
warn Sir Bloet,' she said, and let Kivrin lead her back to the
house.

Kivrin left her by the fire and went to look in the barn. Agnes
wasn't there, but she found her own cloak, left there on Christmas
Eve. She flung it around her and went up into the loft. She looked
in the brewhouse and Roche searched the other buildings, but
they didn't find her. A cold wind had sprung up while they stood
talking to the messenger, and it smelled like snow.

'Perhaps she is in the house,' Roche said. 'Looked you behind
the high seat?'

She searched the house again, looking behind the high seat and
under the bed in the bower. Maisry still lay whimpering where
Kivrin had left her, and she had to resist the temptation to kick
her. She asked Lady Imeyne, kneeling to the wall, if she had seen
Agnes or not.

The old woman ignored her, moving her links of chain and her
lips silently.

Kivrin shook her shoulder. 'Did you see her go out?'

Lady Imeyne turned and looked at her, her eyes glittering. 'She
is to blame,' she said.

'Agnes?' Kivrin said, outraged. 'How could it be *her* fault?'

Imeyne shook her head and looked past Kivrin at Maisry. 'God punishes us for Maisry's wickedness.'

'Agnes is missing and it grows dark,' Kivrin said. 'We must find her. Did you not see where she went?'

'To blame,' she whispered and turned back to the wall.

It was getting late now, and the wind was whistling round the screens. Kivrin ran out to the passage and on to the green.

It was like the day she had tried to find the drop on her own. There was no one on the snow-covered green, and the wind whipped and tore at her clothes as she ran. A bell was ringing somewhere far off to the north-east, slowly, a funeral toll.

Agnes had loved the bell tower. Kivrin went in and shouted Agnes' name even though she could see up to the bellrope. She went out and stood looking at the huts, trying to think where Agnes would have gone.

Not the huts, unless she had got cold. Her puppy. She had wanted to go and see her puppy's grave. Kivrin hadn't told her she'd buried it in the woods. Agnes had told her it had to be buried in the churchyard. Kivrin could see she wasn't there, but she went through the lychgate.

Agnes had been there. The prints of her little boots led from grave to grave and then off to the north side of the church. Kivrin looked up the hill at the beginning of the woods, thinking, what if she went into the woods? We'll never find her.

She ran round the side of the church. The prints stopped and circled back to the church. Kivrin opened the door. It was nearly dark inside and colder than the wind-whipped churchyard. 'Agnes!' she called.

There was no answer, but there was a faint sound up by the altar, like a rat scurrying out of sight. 'Agnes?' Kivrin said, peering into the gloom behind the tomb in the side aisles. 'Are you here?' she said.

'Kivrin?' a quavering little voice said.

'Agnes?' she said, and ran in its direction. 'Where are you?'

She was by the statue of St Catherine, huddled among the candles at its base in her red cape and hood. She had pressed herself against the rough stone skirts of the statue, eyes wide and frightened. Her face was red and damp with tears. 'Kivrin?' she cried and flung herself into her arms.

'What are you doing here, Agnes?' Kivrin said, angry with relief. She hugged her tightly. 'We've been looking everywhere for you.'

She buried her wet face against Kivrin's neck. 'Hiding,' she said. 'I took Cart to see my hound, and I fell down.' She wiped at her nose with her hand. 'I called and called for you, but you didn't come.'

'I didn't know where you were, honey,' Kivrin said, stroking her hair. 'Why did you come in the church?'

'I was hiding from the wicked man.'

'What wicked man?' Kivrin said, frowning.

The heavy church door opened, and Agnes clasped her little arms in a stranglehold around Kivrin's neck 'It is the wicked man,' she whispered hysterically.

'Father Roche!' Kivrin called. 'I've found her. She's here.' The door shut, and she could hear his footsteps. 'It's Father Roche,' she said to Agnes. 'He's been looking for you, too. We didn't know where you'd gone.'

She loosened her grip a little. 'Maisry said the wicked man would come and get me.'

Roche came up panting, and Agnes buried her head against Kivrin again. 'Is she ill?' he asked anxiously.

'I don't think so,' Kivrin said. 'She's half-frozen. Put my cloak over her.'

Roche clumsily unfastened Kivrin's cloak and wrapped it around Agnes.

'I hid from the wicked man,' Agnes said to him, turning in Kivrin's arms.

'What wicked man?' Roche said.

'The wicked man who chased you in the church,' she said. 'Maisry said he comes and gets you and gives you the blue sickness.'

'There isn't any wicked man,' Kivrin said, thinking, I'll shake Maisry till her teeth rattle when I get home. She stood up. Agnes' grip tightened.

Roche groped along the wall to the priest's door and opened it Bluish light flooded in.

'Maisry said he got my hound,' Agnes said, shivering. 'But he didn't get me. I hid.'

Kivrin thought of the black puppy, limp in her hands, blood around its mouth. No, she thought, and started rapidly across the snow. She was shivering because she'd been in the icy church so long. Her face felt hot against Kivrin's neck. It's only from crying, Kivrin told herself, and asked her if her head ached.

Agnes shook or nodded her head against Kivrin and wouldn't answer. No, Kivrin thought, and walked faster, Roche close behind her, past the steward's house and into the courtyard.

'I did not go in the woods,' Agnes said when they got to the house. 'The naughty girl did, didn't she?'

'Yes,' Kivrin said, carrying her over to the fire. 'But it was all right. The father found her and took her home. And they lived happily ever after.' She sat Agnes down on the bench and untied her cape.

'And she never went in the woods again,' she said.

'She never did.' Kivrin pulled her wet shoes and hose off. 'You must lie down,' she said, spreading her cloak next to the fire. 'I will bring you some hot soup.' Agnes lay down obediently, and Kivrin pulled the sides of the cloak up over her.

She brought her soup but Agnes didn't want any, and she fell asleep almost immediately.

'She's caught a chill,' she told Eliwys and Roche almost fiercely. 'She was outside all afternoon. She's caught cold,' but after Roche left to say vespers, she uncovered Agnes and felt under her arms, in her groin. She even turned her over, looking for a lump between the shoulder blades like the boy's.

Roche didn't ring the bell. He came back with a ragged quilt that was obviously from his own bed, made it into a pallet and moved Agnes on to it.

The other vespers bells were ringing. Oxford and Godstow and the bell from the south-west. Kivrin couldn't hear Courcy's double bell. She looked at Eliwys anxiously, but she didn't seem to be listening. She was looking across Rosemund at the screens.

The bells stopped and Courcy's started up. They sounded odd, muffled and slow. Kivrin looked at Roche. 'Is it a funeral bell?'

'Nay,' he said, looking at Agnes. 'It is a holy day.'

She had lost track of the days. The bishop's envoy had left on Christmas morning and in the afternoon she had found out it was the plague, and after that it seemed like an endless day. Four days, she thought, it's been four days.

She had wanted to come at Christmas because there were so many holy days even the peasants would know what day it was, and she couldn't possibly miss the rendezvous. Gawyn went to Bath for help, Mr Dunworthy, she thought, and the bishop took all the horses, and I didn't know where it was.

Eliwys had stood up and was listening to the bells. 'Are those Courcy's bells?' she asked Roche.

'Yes,' he said. 'Fear not. It is the Slaughter of the Innocents.'

The slaughter of the innocents, Kivrin thought, looking at Agnes. She was asleep, and she had stopped shivering, though she still felt hot.

The cook cried out something, and Kivrin went around the barricade to her. She was crouched on her pallet, struggling to get up. 'Must go home,' she said.

Kivrin coaxed her down again and fetched her a drink of water. The bucket was nearly empty, and she picked it up and started out with it.

'Tell Kivrin I would have her come to me,' Agnes said. She was sitting up.

Kivrin put the bucket down. 'I'm here,' Kivrin said, kneeling down beside her. 'I'm right here.'

Agnes looked at her, her face red and distorted with rage. 'The wicked man will get me if Kivrin does not come,' she said. 'Bid her come *now*.'

<hr />

Transcript from the Domesday Book
(073453–074912)

I've missed the rendezvous. I lost count of the days, taking care of Rosemund, and I couldn't find Agnes, and I didn't know where the drop was.

You must be worried sick, Mr Dunworthy. You probably

think I've fallen among cut-throats and murderers. Well, I have. And now they've got Agnes.

She has a fever but no buboes, and she isn't coughing or vomiting. Just the fever. It's very high – she doesn't know me and keeps calling me to come. Roche and I tried to bring it down by sponging her with cold compresses, but it keeps going back up.

(Break)

Lady Imeyne has it. Father Roche found her this morning on the floor in the corner. She may have been there all night. The last two nights she has refused to go to bed and has stayed on her knees, praying to God to protect her and the rest of the godly from the plague.

He hasn't. She has the pneumonic. She's coughing and vomiting mucus streaked with blood.

She won't let Roche or me tend her. 'She is to blame for this,' she told Roche, pointing at me. 'Look at her hair. She is no maid. Look at her clothes.'

My clothes are a boy's jerkin and leather hose I found in one of the chests in the loft. My kirtle got ruined when Lady Imeyne vomited on me, and I had to tear my shift up for cloths and bandages.

Roche tried to give Imeyne some of the willow-bark tea, but she spat it out. She said, 'She lied when she said she was waylaid in the woods. She was sent here to kill us.'

Bloody spittle dribbled down her chin as she spoke and Roche wiped it off. 'It is the disease that makes you believe these things,' he said gently.

'She was sent here to poison us,' Imeyne said. 'See how she has poisoned my son's children. And now she would poison me, but I will not let her give me aught to eat or drink.'

'Hush,' Roche said sternly. 'You must not speak ill of one who seeks to help you.'

She shook her head, turning it wildly from side to side. 'She seeks to kill us all. You must burn her. She is the Devil's servant.'

471

I've never seen him angry before. He looked almost like a cut-throat again. 'You know not whereof you speak,' he said. 'It is God who has sent her to help us.'

I wish it were true, that I were of any help at all, but I'm not. Agnes screams for me to come and Rosemund lies there as if she were under a spell and the clerk is turning black, and there's nothing I can do to help any of them. Nothing.

(Break)

All the steward's family have it. The youngest boy, Lefric, was the only one with a bubo, and I've brought him in here and lanced it. There's nothing I can do for the others. They all have pneumonic.

(Break)

The steward's baby is dead.

(Break)

The Courcy bells are tolling. Nine strokes. Which one of them is it? The bishop's envoy? The fat monk who helped steal our horses? Or Sir Bloet? I hope so.

(Break)

Terrible day. The steward's wife and the boy who ran from me when I went to find the drop both died this afternoon. The steward is digging both their graves, though the ground is so frozen I don't see how he can even make a dent in it. Rosemund and Lefric are both worse. Rosemund can scarcely swallow and her pulse is thready and irregular. Agnes is not as bad, but I can't get her fever down. Roche said vespers in here tonight.

After the set prayers, he said, 'Good Jesus, I know you have sent what help you can, but I fear it cannot prevail against this dark plague. Thy holy servant Katherine says this terror is a disease, but how can it be? For it does not move from man to man, but is everywhere at once.'

It is.

(Break)

Ulf, the reeve, is dead.
Also Sibbe, daughter of the steward.
Joan, daughter of the steward.
The cook (I don't know her name).
Walthef, oldest son of the steward.

(Break)

Over 50 per cent of the village has it. Please don't let Eliwys get it. Or Roche.

———⚬⚬⚬———

CHAPTER TWENTY-NINE

He called for help, but no one came, and he thought that every-one else had died and he was the only one left, like the monk, John Clyn, in the monastery of the Friars Minor. 'I, waiting for death till it come . . .'

He tried to press the button to call the nurse, but he couldn't find it. There was a hand-bell on the bed-stand next to the bed, and he reached for it, but there was no strength in his fingers and it clattered to the floor. It made a horrible, endless sound, like some nightmarish Great Tom, but nobody came.

The next time he woke, though, the bell was on the bed-stand again, so they must have come while he was asleep. He squinted blurrily at the bell and wondered how long he had been asleep. A long time.

There was no way to tell from the room. It was light but there was no angle to the light, no shadows. It might be afternoon or midmorning. There was no digital on the bed-stand or the wall, and he didn't have the strength to turn and look at the screens on the wall behind him. There was a window, though he could not raise himself up enough to see properly out of it, but he could see it was raining. It had been raining when he went to Brasenose – it could be the same afternoon. Perhaps he had only fainted, and they had brought him here for observation.

' "I also will do this unto you," ' someone said.

Dunworthy opened his eyes and reached for his spectacles, but they weren't there. ' "I will even appoint over you terror, con-sumption, and burning ague." '

It was Mrs Gaddson. She was sitting in the chair beside his bed, reading from the Bible. She was not wearing her mask and gown, though the Bible still seemed to be swathed in plastene. Dunworthy squinted at it.

' "And when ye are gathered together within your cities, I will send the pestilence among you." '

'What day is it?' Dunworthy asked.

She paused looked curiously at him and then went on placidly. ' "And ye shall be delivered into the hand of the enemy." '

He could not have been here very long. Mrs Gaddson had been reading to the patients when he went to see Badri. Perhaps it was still the same afternoon, and Mary had not come in to throw Mrs Gaddson out yet.

'Can you swallow?' the nurse said. It was the ancient sister from Supplies. 'I need to give you a temp,' she croaked. 'Can you swallow?'

He opened his mouth and she put the temp capsule on his tongue. She tipped his head forward so he could drink, her apron crackling.

'Did you get it down?' she asked letting him lean back a bit.

The capsule was lodged halfway down his throat, but he nodded. The effort made his head ache.

'Good. Then I can remove this.' She stripped something from his upper arm.

'What time is it?' he asked trying not to cough up the capsule.

'Time for you to rest,' she said, peering farsightedly at the screens behind his head.

'What day is it?' he said, but she had already hobbled out. 'What day is it?' he asked Mrs Gaddson, but she was gone, too.

He could not have been here long. He still had a headache and a fever, which were early symptoms of influenza. Perhaps he had only been ill a few hours. Perhaps it was still the same afternoon, and he had awakened when they moved him into the room, before they had had time to connect a call button or give him a temp.

'Time for your temp,' the nurse said. It was a different one, the pretty blonde nurse who had asked him all the questions about William Gaddson.

'I've already had one.'

'That was yesterday,' she said. 'Come now, let's have it down.'

475

The first-year student in Badri's room had told him she was down with the virus. 'I thought you had the virus,' he said.

'I did but I'm well again, and so shall you be.' She put her hand behind his head and raised him up so he could take a sip of water.

'What day is it?' he asked.

'The eleventh,' she said. 'I had to think a bit. There at the end things got a bit hectic. Nearly all the staff were down with it, and everyone working double shifts. I quite lost track of the days.' She typed something into the console and looked up at the screens, frowning.

He had already known it before she told him, before he tried to reach the bell to call for help. The fever had made one endless rainy afternoon out of all the delirious nights and drugged mornings he could not remember, but his body had kept clear track of the time, tolling off the hours, the days, so that he had known even before she'd told him. He had missed the rendezvous.

There was no rendezvous, he told himself bitterly. Gilchrist shut down the net. It would not have mattered if he had been there, if he had not been ill. The net was closed and there was nothing he could have done.

January the eleventh. How long had Kivrin waited at the drop? A day? Two days? Three before she began to think she had the date wrong, or the place? Had she waited all night by the Oxford-Bath road, huddled in her useless white cloak, afraid to build a fire for fear the light would attract wolves or thieves? Or peasants fleeing from the plague? And when had it come to her finally that no one was coming to get her?

'Is there anything I can fetch for you?' the nurse asked. She pushed a syringe into the cannula.

'Is that something to make me sleep?' he asked.

'Yes.'

'Good,' he said and closed his eyes gratefully.

He slept either a few minutes or a day or a month. The light, the rain, the lack of shadows, were the same when he woke. Colin was sitting in the chair beside the bed reading the book Dunworthy had given him for Christmas and sucking on something. It can't have been that long, Dunworthy thought, squinting at him, the gobstopper is still with us.

'Oh, good,' Colin said, shutting the book with a clap. 'That horrid sister said I could only stay if I promised not to wake you up, and I didn't, did I? You'll tell her you woke all on your own, won't you?'

He took the gobstopper out, examined it and stuck it in his pocket. 'Have you *seen* her? She must have been alive during the Middle Ages. She's nearly as necrotic as Mrs Gaddson.'

Dunworthy squinted at him. The jacket whose pocket he had stuck the gobstopper in was a new one, green, the grey plaid muffler round his neck even grimmer against the verdure, and Colin looked older in it, as if he had grown while Dunworthy was asleep.

Colin frowned. 'It's me, Colin. Do you know me?'

'Yes, of course I know you. Why aren't you wearing your mask?'

Colin grinned. 'I don't have to. And at any rate, you're not contagious any more. Do you want your spectacles?'

Dunworthy nodded, carefully, so the aching wouldn't begin again.

'When you woke up the other times, you didn't know me at all.' He rummaged in the drawer of the bedstand and handed Dunworthy his spectacles. 'You were awfully bad. I thought you were going to pack it in. You kept calling me Kivrin.'

'What day is it?' Dunworthy asked.

'The twelfth,' Colin said impatiently. 'You asked me that this morning. Don't you remember?'

Dunworthy put on his spectacles. 'No.'

'Don't you remember anything that's happened?'

I remember how I failed Kivrin, he thought. I remember leaving her in 1348.

Colin scooted the chair closer and laid the book on the bed. 'The sister told me you wouldn't because of the fever,' Colin said, but he sounded faintly angry at Dunworthy, as if it were his fault. 'She wouldn't let me in to see you and she wouldn't tell me anything. I think that's completely unfair. They make you sit in a waiting-room, and they keep telling you to go home, there's nothing you can do here, and when you ask questions, they say. "The doctor will be with you in a moment," and won't tell you anything. They treat you like a child. I mean, you have to find out some time, don't you? Do you know what Sister did this morning? She chucked me out. She said, "Mr Dunworthy's been very ill. I don't want you to upset him." As if I would.'

He looked indignant, but at the same time tired, worried. Dunworthy thought of him haunting the corridors and sitting in the waiting-room, waiting for news. No wonder he looked older.

'And just now Mrs Gaddson said I was only to tell you good news because bad news would very likely make you have a relapse and die and it would be my fault.'

'Mrs Gaddson's still keeping up morale, I see,' Dunworthy said. He smiled at Colin. 'I don't suppose there's any chance of her coming down with the virus?'

Colin looked astonished. 'The epidemic's stopped,' he said. 'They're lifting the quarantine next week.'

The analogue had arrived, then, after all Mary's pleading. He wondered if it had come in time to help Badri, and then wondered if that was the bad news Mrs Gaddson didn't want told. I have already been told the bad news, he thought. The fix is lost, and Kivrin is in 1348.

'Tell me some good news,' he said.

'Well, nobody's fallen ill for two days,' Colin said, 'and the supplies finally came through, so we've something decent to eat.'

'You've got some new clothes as well, I see.'

Colin glanced down at the green jacket. 'This is one of the Christmas presents from my mother. She sent them after—' He stopped and frowned. 'She sent me some vids, and a set of face plasters as well.'

Dunworthy wondered if she had waited till after the epidemic was effectively over before bothering to ship Colin's gifts, and what Mary had had to say about it.

'See,' Colin said, standing up. 'The jacket strips up automatically. You just touch the button, like this. You won't have to tell me to strip it up any more.'

The sister came rustling in. 'Did he wake you up?' she demanded.

'I told you so,' Colin muttered. 'I didn't, Sister. I was so quiet you couldn't even hear me turn the pages.'

'He didn't wake me up, and he's not bothering me,' Dunworthy said before she could ask her next question. 'He's telling me only good news.'

'You shouldn't be telling Mr Dunworthy anything. He must rest,' she said and hung a bag of clear liquid on the drip. 'Mr Dunworthy is still too ill to be bothered with visitors.' She hustled Colin out of the room.

'If you're so worried about visitors, why don't you stop Mrs Gaddson reading Scripture to him?' Colin protested. 'She'd make anybody ill.' He stopped short at the door, glaring at the sister. 'I'll be back tomorrow. Is there anything you'd like?'

'How is Badri?' Dunworthy asked and braced himself for the answer.

'Better,' Colin said. 'He was almost well, but he had a relapse. He's a good deal better now, though. He wants to see you.'

'No,' Dunworthy said, but the sister had already shut the door.

'It's not Badri's fault,' Mary had said, and of course it wasn't. Disorientation was one of the early symptoms. He thought of himself, unable to punch in Andrews' number, of Ms Piantini making mistake after mistake on the handbells, murmuring 'Sorry', over and over.

'Sorry,' he murmured. It had not been Badri's fault. It was his. He had been so worried about the apprentice's calculations that he had infected Badri with his fears, so worried that Badri had decided to refeed the coordinates.

Colin had left his book lying on the bed. Dunworthy pulled it towards him. It seemed impossibly heavy, so heavy his arm shook with the effort of holding it open, but he propped that side against the rail and turned the pages, almost unreadable from the angle he was lying at, till he found what he was looking for.

The Black Death had hit Oxford at Christmas, shutting down the universities and causing those who were able to flee to the surrounding villages, carrying the plague with them. Those who couldn't died in their thousands, so many there were 'none left to keep possession or make up a competent number to bury the dead'. And the few who were left barricaded themselves inside the colleges, hiding and looking for someone to blame.

He fell asleep with his spectacles on, but when the nurse

removed them he woke. It was William's nurse, and she smiled at him.

'Sorry,' she said, putting them in the drawer. 'I didn't mean to wake you.'

Dunworthy squinted at her. 'Colin says the epidemic's over.'

'Yes,' she said, looking at the screens behind him. 'They found the source of the virus and got the analogue all at the same time, and only just in time. Probability was projecting an 85 per cent morbidity rate with 32 per cent mortality even with antimicrobials and T-cell enhancement and that was without adding in the supply shortages and so many of the staff being down. As it was, we had nearly 19 per cent mortality and a good number of the cases are still critical.'

She picked up his wrist and looked at the screen behind his head. 'Your fever's down a bit,' she said. 'You're very lucky, you know. The analogue didn't work on anyone already infected. Dr Ahrens—' she said, and then stopped. He wondered what Mary had said. That he would pack it in. 'You're very lucky,' she said again. 'Now try to sleep.'

He slept, and when he woke again Mrs Gaddson was standing over him, poised for attack with her Bible.

' "He will bring upon thee all the diseases of Egypt," ' she said as soon as he had opened his eyes. ' "Also every sickness and every plague, until thou be destroyed." '

' "And ye shall be delivered into the hand of the enemy," ' Dunworthy murmured.

'What?' Mrs Gaddson demanded.

'Nothing.'

She had lost her place. She flipped back and forth through the pages, searching for pestilences, and began reading. ' ". . . Because that God sent his only begotten Son into the world." '

God would never have sent him if He'd known what would happen, Dunworthy thought. Herod and the slaughter of the innocents and Gedisemane.

'Read to me from St Matthew,' he said. 'Chapter 26, verse 39.'

Mrs Gaddson stopped, looking irritated, and then leafed through the pages to Matthew. ' "And he went a little farther, and fell on his face, and prayed, saying, O my Father, if it be possible, let this cup pass from me."'

God didn't know where His Son was, Dunworthy thought. He had sent his only begotten Son into the world and something had gone wrong with the fix, someone had turned off the net, so that He couldn't get to him, and they had arrested him and put a crown of thorns on his head and nailed him to a cross.

'Chapter 27,' he said. 'Verse 46.'

She pursed her lips and turned the page. 'I really do not feel these are appropriate Scriptures for—'

'Read it,' he said.

' "And about the ninth hour Jesus cried with a loud voice, saying, *Eli, Eli, lama sabachthani?* that is to say, My God, my God, why hast thou forsaken me?"'

Kivrin would have no idea what had happened. She would think she had the wrong place or the wrong time, that she had lost count of the days somehow during the plague, that something had gone wrong with the drop. She would think they had forsaken her.

'Well?' Mrs Gaddson said. 'Any other requests?'

'No.'

Mrs Gaddson flipped back to the Old Testament. ' "For they shall fall by the sword, by the famine, and by the pestilence,"' she read. ' "He that is far off shall die of the pestilence."'

In spite of everything, he slept, waking finally to something that was not endless afternoon. It was still raining, but now there were shadows in the room and the bells were chiming four o'clock. William's nurse helped him to the lavatory. The book had gone, and he wondered if Colin had come back without his remembering, but when the nurse opened the door of the bedstand for his slippers, he saw it lying there. He asked the nurse to crank his bed to sitting, and when she had gone he put on his spectacles and took the book out again.

The plague had spread so randomly, so viciously, the contemps had been unable to believe it was a natural disease. They had accused lepers and old women and the mentally impaired of poisoning wells and putting curses on them. Anyone strange, anyone foreign was immediately suspected. In Sussex they had stoned two travellers to death. In Yorkshire they had burnt a young woman at the stake.

'So that's where it got to,' Colin said, coming into the room. 'I thought I'd lost it.'

He was wearing his green jacket and was very wet. 'I had to carry the handbell cases over to Holy Re-Formed for Ms Taylor, and it's absolutely pouring.'

Relief washed over him at the mention of Ms Taylor's name, and he realised he had not asked after any of the detainees for fear it would be bad news.

'Is Ms Taylor all right, then?'

Colin touched the bottom of his jacket and it sprang open, spraying water everywhere. 'Yes. They're doing some bell thing at Holy Re-Formed on the fifteenth.' He leaned round so he could see what Dunworthy was reading.

Dunworthy shut the book and handed it to him. 'And the rest of the bell ringers? Ms Piantini?'

Colin nodded. 'She's still in hospital. She's so thin you wouldn't know her.' He opened the book. 'You were reading about the Black Death, weren't you?'

'Yes,' Dunworthy said. 'Mr Finch didn't come down with the virus, did he?'

'No. He's been filling in as tenor for Ms Piantini. He's very upset. We didn't get any lavatory paper in the shipment from London, and he says we're nearly out. He had a fight with the Gallstone over it.' He laid the book back on the bed. 'What's going to happen to your girl?'

'I don't know,' Dunworthy said.

'Isn't there anything you can do to get her out?'

'No.'

'The Black Death was terrible,' Colin said. 'So many people died they didn't even bury them. They just left them lying in big heaps.'

'I can't get to her, Colin. We lost the fix when Gilchrist shut the net down.'

'I know, but isn't there something we can do?'

'No.'

'But—'

482

'I intend to speak to your doctor about restricting your visitors,' the sister said sternly, removing Colin by the collar of his jacket.

'Then begin by restricting Mrs Gaddson,' Dunworthy said, 'and tell Mary I want to see her.'

Mary did not come but Montoya did, obviously fresh from the dig. She was mud to the knees, and her dark curly hair was grey with it. Colin came with her, and his green jacket was thoroughly bespattered.

'We had to sneak in when *she* wasn't looking,' Colin said.

Montoya had lost a good deal of weight. Her hands on the bed rail were very thin, and the digital on her wrist was loose.

'How are you feeling?' she asked.

'Better,' he lied, looking at her hands. There was mud under her fingernails. 'How are *you* feeling?'

'Better,' she said.

She must have gone directly to the dig to look for the corder as soon as they released her from hospital. And now she had come directly here.

'She's dead isn't she?' he said.

Her hands took hold of the rail, let go of it. 'Yes.'

Kivrin had been in the right place, after all. The locationals had been shifted by only a few kilometres, a few metres, and she had managed to find the Oxford-Bath road, she had found Skendgate. And died in it, a victim of the influenza she had caught before she went. Or of starvation after the plague, or of despair. She had been dead seven hundred years.

'You found it then,' he said, and it was not a question.

'Found what?' Colin said.

'Kivrin's corder.'

'No,' Montoya said.

He felt no relief. 'But you will,' he said.

Her hands shook a little, holding the rail. 'Kivrin asked me to,' she said. 'The day of the drop. She was the one who suggested the corder look like a bone spur, so the record would survive even if she didn't "Mr Dunworthy's worried about nothing," she said, "but if something should go wrong, I'll try to be buried in the churchyard so you,"' her voice faltered, '"so you won't have to dig up half of England."'

Dunworthy closed his eyes.

'But you don't *know* that she's dead, if you haven't found the corder,' Colin burst out. 'You said you didn't even know where she was. How can you be sure she's dead?'

'We've been conducting experiments with laboratory rats at the dig. Only a quarter of an hour's exposure to the virus is required for infection. Kivrin was directly exposed to the tomb for over three hours. There's a 75 per cent chance she contracted the virus, and with the limited med support available in the fourteenth century, she's almost certain to have developed complications.'

Limited med support. It was a century that had dosed people with leeches and strychnine, that had never heard of sterilisation or germs or T-cells. They would have stuck filthy poultices on her and muttered prayers and opened her veins. 'And the doctors bled them,' Gilchrist's book had said, 'but many died in despite.'

'Without antimicrobials and T-cell enhancement,' Montoya said, 'the virus' mortality rate is 49 per cent. Probability—'

'Probability,' Dunworthy said bitterly. 'Are these Gilchrist's figures?'

Montoya glanced at Colin and frowned. 'There is a 75 per cent chance Kivrin contracted the virus, and a 68 per cent chance she was exposed to the plague. Morbidity for bubonic plague is 91 per cent, and the mortality rate is—'

'She didn't get the plague,' Dunworthy said. 'She'd had her plague immunisation. Didn't Dr Ahrens or Gilchrist tell you that?'

Montoya glanced at Colin again.

'They said I wasn't allowed to tell him,' Colin said, looking defiantly at her.

'Tell me what? Is Gilchrist ill?' He remembered looking at the screens and then collapsing forward into Gilchrist's arms. He wondered if he had infected him when he fell.

Montoya said, 'Mr Gilchrist died of the flu three days ago.'

Dunworthy looked at Colin. 'What else did they instruct you to keep from me?' Dunworthy demanded. 'Who else died while I was ill?'

Montoya put up her thin hand as if to stop Colin, but it was too late.

'Great-aunt Mary,' Colin said.

Maisry's run away. Roche and I looked everywhere for her, afraid she'd fallen ill and crawled into some corner, but the steward said he saw her starting into the woods while he was digging Walthef's grave. She was riding Agnes' pony.

She will only spread it, or make it as far as some village that already has it. It's all around us now. The bells sound like vespers, only out of rhythm, as if the ringers had gone mad. It's impossible to make out whether it is nine strokes or three. Courcy's double bells tolled a single stroke this morning. I wonder if it is the baby. Or one of the chattering girls.

Rosemund is still unconscious, and her pulse is very weak. Agnes screams and struggles in her delirium. She keeps shrieking for me to come, but she won't let me near her. When I try to talk to her, she kicks and screams as if she were having a tantrum.

Eliwys is wearing herself out trying to tend Agnes and Lady Imeyne, who screams 'Devil!' at me when I tend her and nearly gave me a black eye this morning. The only one who lets me near him is the clerk, who is beyond caring. He cannot possibly last the day. He smells so bad we've had to move him to the far end of the room. His bubo has started to suppurate again.

(Break)

Gunni, second son of the steward.
The woman with the scrofula scars on her neck.
Maisry's father.
Roche's altar boy, Cob.

(Break)

Lady Imeyne is very bad. Roche tried to give her the last rites, but she refused to make her confession.

485

'You must make your peace with God ere you die,' Roche said, but she turned her face to the wall and said, 'He is to blame for this.'

(Break)

Thirty-one cases. Over 75 per cent. Roche consecrated part of the green this morning because the churchyard is nearly full.

Maisry hasn't come back. She's probably sleeping in the high seat of some manor house the inhabitants have fled and when this is all over she'll become the ancestor of some noble old family.

Perhaps that's what's wrong with our time, Mr Dunworthy, it was founded by Maisry and the bishop's envoy and Sir Bloet. And all the people who stayed and tried to help, like Roche, caught the plague and died.

(Break)

Lady Imeyne is unconscious and Roche is giving her the last rites. I told him to.

'It is the disease that speaks. Her soul has not turned against God,' I said, which isn't true, and perhaps she does not deserve forgiveness, but she does not deserve this either, her body poisoned, rotting, and I can scarcely condemn her for blaming God when I blame her. And neither is responsible. It's a disease.

The consecrated wine has run out, and there is no more olive oil. Roche is using cooking oil from the kitchen. It smells rancid. Where he touches her temples and the palms of her hands, the skin turns black.

It's a disease.

(Break)

Agnes is worse. It's terrible to watch her, lying there panting like her poor puppy and screaming, 'Tell Kivrin to come and get me. I do not like it here!'

Even Roche can't stand it. 'Why does God punish us thus?' he asked me.

486

'He doesn't. It's a disease,' I said, which is no answer, and he knows it.

All of Europe knows it, and the Church knows it, too. It will hang on for a few more centuries, making excuses, but it can't overcome the essential fact – that He let this happen. That He comes to no one's rescue.

(Break)

The bells have stopped. Roche asked me if I thought it was a sign the plague had stopped. 'Perhaps God has been able to come to help us after all,' he said.

I don't think so. In Tournai church officials sent out an order stopping the bells because the sound frightened the people. Perhaps the Bishop of Bath has sent one out as well.

The sound *was* frightening, but the silence is worse. It's like the end of world.

———

CHAPTER THIRTY

Mary had been dead almost the entire time he had been ill. She had come down with it the day the analogue arrived. She had developed pneumonia almost immediately, and on the second day her heart had stopped. The sixth of January. Epiphany.

'You should have told me,' Dunworthy had said.

'I *did* tell you,' Colin had protested. 'Don't you remember?'

He had no memory of it at all, had had no warning even when Mrs Gaddson was allowed free access to his room, when Colin had said, 'They won't tell you anything.' It had not even struck him as odd that she hadn't come to see him.

'I told you when she got ill,' Colin had said, 'and I told you when she died, but you were too ill to care.'

He thought of Colin waiting outside her room for news and then coming and standing by his bedside, trying to tell him. 'I'm sorry, Colin.'

'You couldn't help it that you were ill,' Colin said. 'It wasn't your fault.'

Dunworthy had told Ms Taylor that, and she had not believed him any more than he believed Colin now. He did not think that Colin believed it either.

'It was all right,' Colin said. 'Everyone was very nice except Sister. She wouldn't let me tell you even after you started getting better, but everyone else was nice except the Gallstone. She kept reading me Scriptures about how God strikes down the un-righteous. Mr Finch rang my mother, but she couldn't come, and so he made all the funeral arrangements. He was very nice. The Americans were nice, too. They kept giving me sweets.'

'I'm sorry,' Dunworthy had said then, and after Colin had gone, expelled by the ancient sister. 'I'm sorry.'

Colin had not been back, and Dunworthy didn't know whether the nurse had barred him from the Infirmary or whether, in spite of what he said, Colin would not forgive him.

He had abandoned Colin, gone off and left him at the mercy of Mrs Gaddson and the sister and doctors who would not tell him anything. He had gone where he could not be reached, as incommunicado as Basingame, salmon fishing on some river in Scotland. And no matter what Colin said, he believed that if Dunworthy had truly wanted to, illness or no, he could have been there to help him.

'You think Kivrin's dead, too, don't you?' Colin had asked him after Montoya left. 'Like Ms Montoya does?'

'I'm afraid so.'

'But you said she couldn't get the plague. What if she's not dead? What if she's at the rendezvous right now, waiting for you?'

'She'd been infected with influenza, Colin.'

'But so were you, and you didn't die. Maybe she didn't die either. I think you should go see Badri and see if he has any ideas. Maybe he could turn the machine on again or something.'

'You don't understand,' he'd said. 'It's not like a pocket torch. The fix can't be switched on again.'

'Well, but maybe he could do another one. A new fix. To the same time.'

To the same time. A drop, even with the coordinates already known, took days to set up. And Badri didn't have the coordinates. He only had the date. He could 'make' a new set of coordinates based on the date, if the locationals had stayed the same, if Badri in his fever hadn't scrambled them as well and if the paradoxes would allow a second drop at all.

There was no way to explain it all to Colin, no way to tell him Kivrin could not possibly have survived influenza in a century where the standard treatment was bloodletting. 'It won't work, Colin,' he'd said, suddenly too tired to explain anything 'I'm sorry.'

'So you're just going to leave her there? Whether she's dead or not? You're not even going to ask Badri?'

'Colin—'

'Great-aunt Mary did everything for you. She didn't give up!'

'*What* is going on in here?' the sister had demanded, creaking in. 'I'm going to have to ask you to leave if you persist in upsetting the patient.'

'I was leaving anyway,' Colin had said and flung himself out.

He hadn't come back that afternoon or all evening or the next morning.

'Am I being allowed visitors?' Dunworthy asked William's nurse when she came on duty.

'Yes,' she said, looking at the screens. 'There's someone waiting to see you now.'

It was Mrs Gaddson. She already had her Bible open.

'Luke chapter 23, verse 33,' she said, glaring pestilentially at him. 'Since you're so interested in the Crucifixion. "And when they were come to the place, which is called Calvary, there they crucified him." '

If God had known where His Son was, He would never have let them do that to him, Dunworthy thought. He would have pulled him out, He would have come and rescued him.

During the Black Death, the contemps believed God had abandoned them. 'Why do you turn your face from us?' they had written. 'Why do you ignore our cries?' But perhaps He hadn't heard them. Perhaps He had been unconscious, lying ill in heaven, helpless Himself and unable to come.

' "And there was a darkness over all the earth until the ninth hour," ' Mrs Gaddson read, ' "and the sun was darkened . . ." '

The contemps had believed it was the end of the world, that Armageddon had come, that Satan had triumphed at last. He had, Dunworthy thought. He had closed the net. He had lost the fix.

He thought about Gilchrist. He wondered if he had realised what he had done before he died or if he had lain unconscious and oblivious, unaware that he had murdered Kivrin.

' "And Jesus led them out as far as to Bethany," ' Mrs Gaddson read, ' "and he lifted up his hands, and blessed them. And it came to pass, while he blessed them, he was parted from them, and carried up into heaven." '

He was parted from them, and was carried up into heaven. God did come to get him, Dunworthy thought. But too late. Too late.

She went on reading until William's nurse came on duty. 'Naptime,' she said briskly, shoving Mrs Gaddson out. She came over to the bed, snatched his pillow from under his head and gave it several sharp whacks.

'Has Colin come?' he asked.

'I haven't seen him since yesterday,' she said, pushing the pillow back under his head. 'I want you to try to go to sleep now.'

'Ms Montoya hasn't been here?'

'Not since yesterday.' She handed him a capsule and a paper cup.

'Have there been any messages?'

'No messages,' she said. She took the empty cup from him. 'Try to sleep.'

No messages. 'I'll try to be buried in the churchyard,' Kivrin had told Montoya, but they'd run out of room in the churchyards. They had buried the plague victims in trenches, in ditches. They had thrown them in the river. Towards the end they hadn't buried them at all. They had piled them in heaps and set fire to them.

Montoya would never find the corder. And if she did, what would the message be? 'I went to the drop, but it didn't open. What happened?' Kivrin's voice rising in panic, in reproach, crying, '*Eli, eli*, why hast thou forsaken me?'

William's nurse made him sit up in a chair to eat his lunch. While he was finishing his stewed prunes, Finch came in.

'We're nearly out of tinned fruit,' he said, pointing at Dunworthy's tray. '*And* lavatory paper. I have no idea how they expect us to start term.' He sat down on the end of the bed. 'The University's set the start of term for the twenty-fifth, but we simply can't be ready by then. We still have fifteen patients in Salvin, the mass immunisations have scarcely started, and I'm not at all convinced we've seen the last of the flu cases.'

'What about Colin?' Dunworthy said. 'Is he all right?'

'Yes, sir. He was a bit melancholy after Dr Ahrens passed away, but he's cheered up a good deal since you've been on the mend.'

'I want to thank you for helping him,' Dunworthy said. 'Colin told me you'd arranged for the funeral.'

'Oh, I was glad to help, sir. He'd no one else, you know. I was certain his mother would come now that the danger's past, but she said it was too difficult to make arrangements at such short notice. She did send lovely flowers. Lilies and laser blossoms. We held the service in Balliol's chapel.' He shifted on the bed. 'Oh, and speaking of the chapel, I do hope you don't mind, but I've given permission to Holy Re-Formed to use it for a handbell concert on the fifteenth. The American bell ringers are going to perform Rimbaud's 'When at Last My Saviour Cometh', and Holy Re-Formed's been requisitioned by the NHS as an immunisation centre. I do hope that's all right.'

'Yes,' Dunworthy said, thinking about Mary. He wondered when they had had the funeral, and if they had rung the bell afterwards.

'I can tell them you'd rather they used St Mary's,' Finch said anxiously.

'No, of course not,' Dunworthy said. 'The chapel's perfectly all right. You've obviously been doing a fine job in my absence.'

'Well, I try, sir. It's difficult, with Mrs Gaddson.' He stood up. 'I don't want to keep you from your rest. If there's anything I can bring you, anything I can do?'

'No,' Dunworthy said, 'there's nothing you can do.'

He started for the door and then stopped. 'I hope you'll accept my condolences, Mr Dunworthy,' he said, looking uncomfortable. 'I know how close you and Dr Ahrens were.'

Close, he thought after Finch was gone. I wasn't close at all. He tried to remember Mary leaning over him, giving him his temp, looking up anxiously at the screens, to remember Colin standing by his bed in his new jacket and his muffler, saying, 'Great-aunt Mary's dead. Dead. Can't you hear me?' but there was no memory there at all. Nothing.

The sister came in and hooked up another drip that put him out, and when he woke he felt abruptly better.

'It's your T-cell enhancement taking hold,' William's nurse told him. 'We've been seeing it in a good number of cases. Some of them make miraculous recoveries.'

She made him walk to the toilet and, after lunch, down the corridor. 'The further you can go, the better,' she said, kneeling to put his slippers on.

I'm not going anywhere, he thought. Gilchrist shut down the net.

She strapped his drip bag to his shoulder, hooked the portable motor to it and helped him on with his robe. 'You mustn't worry about the depression,' she said, helping him out of bed. 'It's a common symptom after influenza. It will fade as soon as your chemical balance is restored.'

She walked him out into the corridor. 'You might want to visit some of your friends,' she said. 'There are two patients from Balliol in the ward at the end of the corridor. Ms Piantini's in the fourth bed. She could do with a bit of cheering.'

'Did Mr Latimer—' he said, and stopped. 'Is Mr Latimer still a patient?'

'Yes,' she said, and he could tell from her voice that Latimer hadn't recovered from his stroke. 'He's two doors down.'

He shuffled down the corridor to Latimer's room. He hadn't gone to see Latimer after he fell ill, first because of having to wait for Andrews' call and then because the Infirmary had run out of SPGs. Mary had said he had suffered complete paralysis and loss of function.

He pushed open the door to Latimer's room. Latimer lay with his arms at his sides, the left one crooked slightly to accommodate the hookups and the drip. There were tubes in his nose and down his throat, and op-fibres leading from his head and chest to the screens above the bed. His face was half-obscured by them, but he gave no sign that they bothered him.

'Latimer?' he said, going to stand beside the bed.

There was no indication he'd heard. His eyes were open, but they didn't shift at the sound, and his face under the tangle of tubes didn't change. He looked vague, distant, as if he were trying to remember a line from Chaucer.

'Mr Latimer,' he said more loudly, and looked up at the screens. They didn't change either.

He's not aware of anything, Dunworthy thought. He put his hand on the back of the chair. 'You don't know anything that's happened, do you?' he said. 'Mary's dead. Kivrin's in 1348,' he said, watching the screens, 'and you don't even know. Gilchrist shut down the *net*.'

The screens didn't change. The lines continued to move steadily, unconcernedly across the displays.

'You and Gilchrist sent her into the Black Death,' he shouted, 'and you lie there—' He stopped and sank down in the chair.

'I tried to tell you Great-aunt Mary was dead,' Colin had said, 'but you were too ill.' Colin had tried to tell him, but he had lain there, like Latimer, unconcerned, oblivious.

Colin will never forgive me, he thought. Any more than he'll forgive his mother for not coming to the funeral. What had Finch said, that it was too difficult to make arrangements at such short notice? He thought of Colin alone at the funeral, looking at the lilies and laser blossoms his mother had sent, at the mercy of Mrs Gaddson and the bell ringers.

'My mother couldn't come,' Colin had said, but he didn't believe that. Of course she could have come, if she had truly wanted to.

He will never forgive me, he thought. And neither will Kivrin. She's older than Colin, she'll imagine all sorts of extenuating circumstances, perhaps even the true one. But in her heart, left to the mercy of who knows what cut-throats and thieves and pestilences, she will not believe I could not have come to get her. If I had truly wanted to.

Dunworthy stood up with difficulty, holding on to the seat and the back of the chair and not looking at Latimer or the displays, and went back out into the corridor. There was an empty stretcher trolley against the wall, and he leaned against it for a moment.

Mrs Gaddson came out of the ward. 'There you are, Mr Dunworthy,' she said. 'I was just coming to read to you.' She opened her Bible. 'Should you be up?'

'Yes,' he said.

'Well, I must say, I'm glad you're recovering at last. Things have simply fallen apart while you've been ill.'

'Yes,' he said.

'You really must do something about Mr Finch, you know. He

allows the Americans to practise their bells at all hours of the day and night, and when I complained to him about it he was quite rude. And he assigned my Willy nursing duties. Nursing duties! When Willy's always been susceptible to illness. It's been a miracle that he didn't come down with the virus before this.'

It very definitely has been, thought Dunworthy, considering the number of very probably infectious young women he had had contact with during the epidemic. He wondered what odds Probability would give on his having remained unscathed.

'And then for Mr Finch to assign him nursing duties!' Mrs Gaddson was saying 'I didn't allow it, of course. "I refuse to let you endanger Willy's health in this irresponsible manner," I told him. "I cannot stand idly by when my child is in mortal danger," I said.'

Mortal danger. 'I must go and see Ms Piantini,' Dunworthy said.

'You should go back to bed. You look quite dreadful.' She shook the Bible at him. 'It's scandalous the way they run this Infirmary. Allowing their patients to go gadding about. You'll have a relapse and die, and you'll have no one but yourself to blame.'

'No,' Dunworthy said, pushed open the door into the ward and went inside.

He had expected the ward to be nearly empty, the patients all sent home, but every bed was full. Most of the patients were sitting up, reading or watching portable vidders, and one was sitting in a wheelchair beside his bed looking out at the rain.

It took Dunworthy a moment to recognise him. Colin had said he'd had a relapse, but he had not expected this. He looked like an old man, his dark face pinched to whiteness under the eyes and in long lines down the sides of the mouth. His hair had gone completely white. 'Badri,' he said.

Badri turned round. 'Mr Dunworthy.'

'I didn't know that you were in this ward,' Dunworthy said.

'They moved me here after—' he stopped. 'I heard that you were better.'

'Yes.'

I can't bear this, Dunworthy thought. How are you feeling?

495

Better, thank you. And you? Much improved. Of course there is the depression, but that is a normal post-viral symptom.

Badri wheeled his chair round to face the window, and Dunworthy wondered if he could not bear it either.

'I made an error in the coordinates when I refed them,' Badri said, looking out at the rain. 'I fed in the wrong data.'

He should say, 'You were ill, you had a fever.' He should tell him mental confusion was an Early Symptom. He should say, 'It was not your fault.'

'I didn't realise I was ill,' Badri said, picking at his robe as he had plucked at the sheet in his delirium. 'I'd had a headache all morning, but I put it down to working the net. I should have realised something was wrong and aborted the drop.'

And I should have refused to tutor her, I should have insisted Gilchrist run parameter checks, I should have made him open the net as soon as you said there was something wrong.

'I should have opened the net the day you fell ill and not waited for the rendezvous,' Badri said, twisting the sash between his fingers. 'I should have opened it immediately.'

Dunworthy glanced automatically at the wall above Badri's head, but there were no screens above the bed. Badri was not even wearing a temp patch. He wondered if it was possible that Badri didn't know Gilchrist had shut down the net, if in their concern for his recovery they had kept it from Badri as they had kept the news of Mary's death from him.

'They refused to discharge me from hospital,' Badri said. 'I should have forced them to let me go.'

I will have to tell him, Dunworthy thought, but he didn't. He stood there silently, watching Badri torture the sash into wrinkles, and feeling infinitely sorry for him.

'Ms Montoya showed me the Probability statistics,' Badri said. 'Do you think Kivrin's dead?'

I hope so, he thought I hope she died of the virus before she realised where she was. Before she realised we had left her there. 'It was not your fault,' he said.

'I was only two days late opening the net. I was certain she'd be there waiting. I was only two days late.'

'What?' Dunworthy said.

'I tried to get permission to leave hospital on the sixth, but they refused to discharge me until the eighth. I got the net open as soon as I could but she wasn't there.'

'What are you talking about?' Dunworthy said. 'How could you open the net? Gilchrist shut it down.'

Badri looked up at him. 'We used the backup.'

'What backup?'

'The fix I did on our net,' Badri said, sounding bewildered. 'You were so worried about the way Mediaeval was running the drop, I decided I'd better put on a backup, in case something went wrong. I came to Balliol to ask you about it on Tuesday afternoon, but you weren't there. I left you a note saying I needed to talk to you.'

'A note,' Dunworthy said.

'The laboratory was open. I ran a redundant fix through Balliol's net,' Badri said. 'You were so worried.'

The strength seemed suddenly to go out of Dunworthy's legs. He sat down on the bed.

'I tried to tell you,' Badri said, 'but I was too ill to make myself understood.'

There had been a backup all along. He had wasted days and days trying to force Gilchrist to unlock the laboratory, searching for Basingame, waiting for Polly Wilson to contrive a way into the University's computer, and all the while the fix had been in the net at Balliol. 'So worried,' Badri had said through his delirium. 'Is the laboratory open?' 'Back up,' he had said. Backup.

'Can you open the net again?'

'Of course, but even if she hasn't contracted the plague—'

'She hasn't,' Dunworthy cut in. 'She was immunised.'

'—she wouldn't still be there. It's been eight days since the rendezvous. She couldn't have waited there all this time.'

'Can someone else go through?'

'Someone else?' Badri said blankly.

'To look for her. Could someone else use the same drop to go through?'

'I don't know.'

'How long would it take you to set it up so we could try it?'

'Two hours at the most. The temporals and locationals are already set, but I don't know how much slippage there'd be.'

The door to the ward burst open and Colin came in. 'There you are,' he said. 'The nurse said you'd taken a walk, but I couldn't find you anywhere. I thought you'd got lost.'

'No,' Dunworthy said, looking at Badri.

'She said I'm to bring you back,' Colin said, taking hold of Dunworthy's arm and helping him up, 'that you're not to overdo it.' He herded him towards the door.

Dunworthy stopped at the door. 'Which net did you use when you opened the net on the eighth?' he said to Badri.

'Balliol's,' he said. 'I was afraid part of the permanent memory had been erased when Brasenose's was shut down, and there was no time to run a damage assessment routine.'

Colin backed the door open. 'The sister comes on duty in half an hour. You don't want *her* to find you up.' He let the door swing shut. 'I'm sorry I wasn't back sooner, but I had to take immunisation schedules out to Godstow.'

Dunworthy leaned against the door. There might be too much slippage, and the tech was in a wheelchair, and he was not sure he could walk as far as the end of the corridor, let alone back to his room. So worried. He had thought Badri meant 'You were so worried I decided to refeed the coordinates,' but he had meant 'I put on a backup.' A backup.

'Are you all right?' Colin asked. 'You're not having a relapse or anything, are you?'

'No,' he said.

'Did you ask Mr Chaudhuri if he could redo the fix?'

'No,' he said. 'There was a backup.'

'A backup?' he said excitedly. 'You mean, another fix?'

'Yes.'

'Does that mean you can rescue her?'

He stopped and leaned against the stretcher trolley. 'I don't know.'

'I'll help you,' Colin said. 'What do you want me to do? I'll do anything you say. I can run errands and fetch things for you. You won't have to do a thing.'

'It might not work,' Dunworthy said. 'The slippage . . .'

'But you're going to try, aren't you? Aren't you?'

A band tightened round his chest with every step, and Badri had already had one relapse, and even if they managed it, the net might not send him through.

'Yes,' he said. 'I'm going to try.'

'Apocalyptic!' Colin said.

Transcript from the Domesday Book
(078926–079064)

Lady Imeyne, mother of Guillaume D'Iverie.

(Break)

Rosemund is sinking. I can't feel the pulse in her wrist at all, and her skin looks yellow and waxen, which I know is a bad sign. Agnes is fighting hard. She still doesn't have any buboes or vomiting, which is a good sign, I think. Eliwys had to cut off her hair. She kept pulling at it, screaming for me to come and braid it.

(Break)

Roche has anointed Rosemund. She couldn't make a confession, of course. Agnes seems better, though she had a nosebleed a little while ago. She asked for her bell.

(Break)

You bastard! I will not let you take her. She's only a child. But that's your speciality, isn't it? Slaughtering the innocents? You've already killed the steward's baby and Agnes' puppy and the boy who went for help when I was in the hut, and that's enough. I won't let you kill her, too, you son of a bitch! I won't *let* you!

CHAPTER THIRTY-ONE

Agnes died the day after New Year's, still screaming for Kivrin to come.

'She is here,' Eliwys said, squeezing her hand. 'Lady Katherine is here.'

'She is *not*,' Agnes wailed her voice hoarse but still strong. 'Tell her to come!'

'I will,' Eliwys promised, and then looked up at Kivrin, her expression faintly puzzled. 'Go and fetch Father Roche,' she said.

'What is it?' Kivrin asked. He had administered the last rites that first night, Agnes flailing and kicking at him as if she were having a tantrum, and since then she had refused to let him near her. 'Are you ill, lady?'

Eliwys shook her head still looking at Kivrin. 'What will I tell my husband when he comes?' she said, and laid Agnes' hand along her side, and it was only then that Kivrin realised she was dead.

Kivrin washed her little body, which was nearly covered with purplish-blue bruises. Where Eliwys had held her hand, the skin was completely black. She looked like she had been beaten. As she has been, Kivrin thought, beaten and tortured. And murdered. The slaughter of the innocents.

Agnes' surcote and shift were ruined, a stiffened mass of blood and vomit, and her everyday linen shift had long since been torn into strips. Kivrin wrapped her body in her own white cloak, and Roche and the steward buried her.

Eliwys did not come. 'I must stay with Rosemund,' she said when Kivrin told her it was time. There was nothing Eliwys could do for Rosemund – the girl lay as still as if she were under a spell, and Kivrin thought the fever must have caused some brain damage. 'And Gawyn may come,' Eliwys said.

It was very cold. Roche and the steward puffed out great clouds of condensation as they lowered Agnes into the grave, and the sight of their white breath infuriated Kivrin. She doesn't weigh anything, she thought bitterly, you could carry her in one hand.

The sight of all the graves angered her, too. The churchyard was filled, and nearly all the rest of the green that Roche had consecrated. Lady Imeyne's grave was almost in the path to the lychgate, and the steward's baby did not have one – Father Roche had let it be buried at its mother's feet though it had not been baptised – and the churchyard was still full.

What about the steward's youngest son, Kivrin thought angrily, and the clerk? Where do you plan to put them? The Black Death was only supposed to have killed one third to one half of Europe. Not all of it.

'*Requiescat in pace*. Amen,' Roche said, and the steward began shovelling the frozen earth on to the little bundle.

You were right, Mr Dunworthy, she thought bitterly. White only gets dirty. You're right about everything, aren't you? You told me not to come, that terrible things would happen. Well, they have. And you can't wait to tell me I told you so. But you won't have that satisfaction because I don't know where the drop is, and the only person who does is probably dead.

She didn't wait for the steward to finish shovelling earth down on Agnes or for Father Roche to complete his chummy little chat with God. She started across the green, furious with all of them: with the steward for standing there with his spade, eager to dig more graves, with Eliwys for not coming, with Gawyn for not coming. No one's coming, she thought No one.

'Katherine,' Roche called.

She turned, and he half-ran up to her, his breath like a cloud around him.

'What is it?' she demanded.

He looked at her solemnly. 'We must not give up hope,' he said.

'Why not?' she burst out. 'We're up to 85 per cent, and we

haven't even got started. The clerk is dying, Rosemund's dying, you've all been exposed. Why shouldn't I give up hope?'

'God has not abandoned us utterly,' he said. 'Agnes is safe in His arms.'

Safe, she thought bitterly. In the ground. In the cold. In the dark. She put her hands up to her face.

'She is in heaven, where the plague cannot reach her. And God's love is ever with us,' he said, 'and naught can separate us from it, neither death, nor life, nor angels, nor things present—'

'Nor things to come,' Kivrin said.

'Nor height, nor depth, nor any other creature,' he said. He put his hand on her shoulder, gently, as if he were anointing her. 'It was His love that sent you to help us.'

She put her hand up to his where it rested on her shoulder and held it tightly. 'We must help each other,' she said.

They stood there like that for a long minute, and then Roche said, 'I must go and ring the bell that Agnes' soul may have safe passage.'

She nodded and took her hand away. 'I'll go check on Rosemund and the others,' she said and went into the courtyard.

Eliwys had said she needed to stay with Rosemund, but when Kivrin got back to the manor house she was nowhere near her. She lay curled up on Agnes' pallet, wrapped in her cloak, watching the door. 'Perhaps his horse was stolen by those that would flee the pestilence,' she said, 'and that is why he is so long in coming.'

'Agnes is buried,' Kivrin said coldly, and went to check on Rosemund.

She was awake. She looked up solemnly at Kivrin when she knelt by her and reached for Kivrin's hand.

'Oh, Rosemund,' Kivrin said, tears stinging her nose and eyes. 'Sweetheart, how do you feel?'

'Hungry,' Rosemund said. 'Has my father come?'

'Not yet,' Kivrin said, and it even seemed possible that he might. 'I will fetch you some broth. You must rest until I come back. You have been very ill.'

Rosemund obediently closed her eyes. They looked less sunken, though they still had dark bruises under them. 'Where is Agnes?' she asked.

Kivrin smoothed her dark, tangled hair back from her face. 'She is sleeping.'

'Good,' Rosemund said. 'I would not have her shouting and playing. She is too noisy.'

'I will fetch you the broth,' Kivrin said. She went over to Eliwys. 'Lady Eliwys, I have good news,' she said eagerly. 'Rosemund is awake.'

Eliwys raised herself up on one elbow and looked at Rosemund, but apathetically, as if she were thinking of something else, and presently she lay down again.

Kivrin, alarmed, put her hand to Eliwys' forehead. It seemed warm, but Kivrin's hands were still cold from outside and she couldn't tell for certain. 'Are you ill?' she asked.

'No,' Eliwys said, but still as if her mind were on something else. 'What shall I tell him?'

'You can tell him that Rosemund is better,' she said, and this time it seemed to get through to her. Eliwys got up and went over to Rosemund and sat down beside her. But by the time Kivrin came back from the kitchen with the broth, she had gone back to Agnes' pallet and lay curled up under her fur-trimmed cloak.

Rosemund was asleep, but it was not the frightening deathlike sleep of before. Her colour was better, though her skin was still drawn tightly over her cheekbones.

Eliwys was asleep too, or feigning sleep, and it was just as well. While she had been in the kitchen the clerk had crawled off his pallet and halfway over the barricade, and when Kivrin tried to haul him back, he struck out at her wildly. She had to go fetch Father Roche to help subdue him.

His right eye had ulcerated, the plague eating its way out from inside, and the clerk clawed at it viciously with his hands. '*Domine Jesu Christe*,' he swore, '*fidelium defunctorium de poenis infermis.*' Save the souls of the faithful departed from the pains of hell.

Yes, Kivrin prayed, wrestling with his clawed hands, save him now.

She rummaged through Imeyne's medical kit again, searching for something to kill the pain. There was no opium powder, and was the opium poppy even in England yet in 1348? She found a few papery orange scraps that looked a little like poppy petals and steeped them in hot water, but the clerk couldn't drink it. His mouth was a horror of open sores, his teeth and tongue caked with dried blood.

He doesn't deserve this, Kivrin thought. Even if he did bring the plague here. Nobody deserves this. 'Please,' she prayed, and wasn't sure what she asked.

Whatever it was, it was not granted. The clerk began to vomit a dark bile, streaked with blood, and it snowed for two days, and Eliwys grew steadily worse. It did not seem to be the plague. She had no buboes and she didn't cough or vomit, and Kivrin wondered if it were illness or simply grief or guilt. 'What shall I tell him?' Eliwys said over and over again. 'He sent us here to keep us safe.'

Kivrin felt her forehead. It was warm. They're all going to get it, she thought. Lord Guillaume sent them here to keep them safe, but they're all going to get it, one by one. I have to do something. But she couldn't think of anything. The only protection from the plague was flight, but they had already fled here, and it had not protected them, and they couldn't flee with Rosemund and Eliwys ill.

But Rosemund's getting stronger every day, Kivrin thought, and Eliwys doesn't have the plague. It's only a fever. Perhaps they have another estate where we could go. In the north.

The plague was not in Yorkshire yet. She could see to it that they kept away from the other people on the roads, that they weren't exposed.

She asked Rosemund if they had a manor in Yorkshire. 'Nay,' Rosemund said, sitting up against one of the benches. 'In Dorset,' but that was of no use. The plague was already there. And Rosemund, though she was better, was still too weak to sit up for more than a few minutes. She could never ride a horse. If we had horses, Kivrin thought.

'My father had a living in Surrey, also,' Rosemund said. 'We stayed there when Agnes was born.' She looked at Kivrin. 'Did Agnes die?'

'Yes,' Kivrin said.

She nodded as if she were not surprised. 'I heard her screaming.'

Kivrin couldn't think of anything to say to that.

'My father is dead, isn't he?'

There was nothing to say to that either. He was almost certainly dead, and Gawyn, too. It had been eight days since he had left for Bath. Eliwys, still feverish, had said this morning, 'He will come now that the storm is over,' but even she had not seemed to believe it.

'He may yet come,' Kivrin said. 'The snow may have delayed him.'

The steward came in, carrying his spade, and stopped at the barricade in front of them. He had been coming in every day to look at his son, staring at him dumbly over the upturned table, but now he only glanced at him and then turned to stare at Kivrin and Rosemund, leaning on his spade.

His cap and shoulders were covered with snow, and the blade of the spade was wet with it. He has been digging another grave, Kivrin thought. Whose?

'Has someone died?' she asked.

'Nay,' he said, and went on looking almost speculatively at Rosemund.

Kivrin stood up. 'Did you want something?'

He looked at her blankly, as if he could not comprehend the question, and then back at Rosemund. 'No,' he said, and picked up the spade and went out.

'Goes he to dig Agnes' grave?' Rosemund asked looking after him.

'No,' Kivrin said gently. 'She is already buried in the churchyard.'

'Goes he then to dig mine?'

'No,' Kivrin said, appalled. 'No! You're not going to die. You're getting better. You were very ill, but the worst is over. Now you must rest and try to sleep so you can get well.'

Rosemund lay down obediently and closed her eyes, but after a minute she opened them again. 'My father being dead, the crown will dispose of my dowry,' she said. 'Think you Sir Bloet still lives?'

I hope not, Kivrin thought, and then, poor child, has she been worrying about her marriage all this time? Poor little thing. His being dead is the only good to come out of the plague. If he is dead. 'You mustn't worry about him now. You must rest and get your strength back.'

'The king will sometimes honour a previous betrothal,' Rosemund said, her thin hands plucking at the blanket, 'if both parties be agreed.'

You don't have to agree to anything, Kivrin thought. He's dead. The bishop killed them.

'If they are not agreed, the king will bid me marry who he will,' Rosemund said, 'and Sir Bloet at least is known to me.'

No, Kivrin thought, and knew it was probably the best thing. Rosemund had been conjuring worse horrors than Sir Bloet, monsters and cut-throats, and Kivrin knew they existed.

Rosemund would be sold off to some nobleman the king owed a debt to or whose allegiance he was trying to buy, one of the troublesome supporters of the Black Prince, perhaps, and taken God knew where to God knew what situation.

There were worse things than a leering old man and a shrewish sister-in-law. Baron Garnier had kept his wife in chains for twenty years. The Count of Anjou had burned his alive. And Rosemund would have no family, no friends, to protect her, to tend her when she was ill.

I'll take her away, Kivrin thought suddenly, to somewhere where Bloet can't find her and we'll be safe from the plague.

There was no such place. It was already in Bath and Oxford, and moving south and east to London, and then Kent, north through the Midlands to Yorkshire and back across the Channel to Germany and the Low Countries. It had even gone to Norway, floating in on a ship of dead men. There was nowhere that was safe.

'Is Gawyn here?' Rosemund asked, and she sounded like her mother, her grandmother. 'I would have him ride to Courcy and tell Sir Bloet that I would come to him.'

'Gawyn?' Eliwys said from her pallet. 'Is he coming?'

No, Kivrin thought. No one's coming. Not even Mr Dunworthy.

It didn't matter that she had missed the rendezvous. There would have been no one there. Because they didn't know she was in 1348. If they knew, they would never have left her here.

Something must have gone wrong with the net. Mr Dunworthy had been worried about sending her so far back without parameter checks. 'There could be unforeseen complications at that distance,' he'd said. Perhaps an unforeseen complication had garbled the fix or made them lose it, and they were looking for her in 1320. I've missed the rendezvous by nearly thirty years, she thought.

'Gawyn?' Eliwys said again and tried to rise from her pallet.

She could not. She was growing steadily worse, though she still had none of the marks of the plague. When it began to snow, she had said, relieved, 'He will not come now until the storm is over,' and got up and gone to sit with Rosemund but by the afternoon she had to lie down again, and her fever went steadily higher.

Roche heard her confession, looking worn out. They were all worn out. If they sat down to rest, they were asleep in seconds. The steward, coming in to look at his son Lefric, had stood at the barricade, snoring, and Kivrin had dozed off while tending the fire and burned her hand badly.

We can't go on like this, she thought, watching Father Roche making the sign of the cross over Eliwys. He'll die of exhaustion. He'll come down with the plague.

I have to get them away, she thought again. The plague didn't reach everywhere. There were villages that were completely untouched. It had skipped over Poland and Bohemia, and there were parts of northern Scotland it had never reached.

'*Agnus dei, qui tollis peccata mundi, miserere nobis,*' Father Roche said, his voice as comforting as it had been when she was dying, and she knew it was hopeless.

He would never leave his parishioners. The history of the Black Death was full of stories of priests who had abandoned their people, who had refused to perform burials, who had locked themselves in their churches and monasteries or run away. She wondered now if those statistics were inaccurate, too.

And even if she found some way to take them all, Eliwys, turning even now as she made her confession to look at the door, would insist on waiting for Gawyn, for her husband to come, as she was convinced they would now that the snow had stopped.

'Has Father Roche gone to meet him?' she asked Kivrin when

Roche left to take the sacraments back to the church. 'He will be here soon. He has no doubt gone first to Courcy to warn them of the plague, and it is only half a day's journey from there.' She insisted that Kivrin move her pallet in front of the door.

While Kivrin was rearranging the barricade to keep the draft from the door off her, the clerk cried out suddenly and went into convulsions. His whole body spasmed, as if he were being shocked, and his face become a terrible rictus, his ulcerated eye staring upward.

'Don't *do* this to him,' Kivrin shouted, trying to wedge the spoon from Rosemund's broth between his teeth. 'Hasn't he been through enough?'

His body jerked. 'Stop it!' Kivrin sobbed. 'Stop it!'

His body abruptly slackened. She jammed the spoon between his teeth and a little trickle of black slime came out of the side of his mouth.

He's dead she thought, and could not believe it. She looked at him, his ulcerated eye half-open, his face swollen and blackened under the stubble of his beard. His fists were clenched at his sides. He did not look human, lying there, and Kivrin covered his face with a rough blanket, afraid that Rosemund might see him.

'Is he dead?' Rosemund asked sitting up curiously.

'Yes,' Kivrin said. 'Thank God.' She stood up. 'I must go and tell Father Roche.'

'I would not have you leave me here alone,' Rosemund said,

'Your mother is here,' Kivrin said, 'and the steward's son, and I will only be a few minutes.'

'I am afraid,' Rosemund said.

So am I, Kivrin thought, looking down at the coarse blanket. He was dead, but even that had not relieved his suffering. He looked still in anguish, still in terror, though his face no longer looked even human. The pains of hell.

'Please do not leave me,' Rosemund said.

'I must tell Father Roche,' Kivrin said, but she sat down between the clerk and Rosemund and waited until she was asleep before she went to find him.

He wasn't in the courtyard or the kitchen. The steward's cow was in the passage, eating the hay from the bottom of the pigsty, and it ambled after her out on to the green.

The steward was in the churchyard digging a grave, his chest level with the snowy ground. He already knows, she thought, but that was impossible. Her heart began to pound.

'Where is Father Roche?' she called, but the steward didn't answer or look up. The cow came up beside her and lowed at her.

'Go away,' she said, and ran across to the steward.

The grave was not in the churchyard. It lay on the green, past the lychgate, and there were two other graves in a line next to it, the iron-hard earth piled on the snow beside each one.

'What are you doing?' she demanded. 'Whose graves are these?'

The steward flung a spadeful of dirt on to the mound. The frozen clods made a clattering sound like stones.

'Why do you dig three graves?' she said. 'Who has died?' The cow nudged her shoulder with its horn. She twisted away from it. 'Who has died?'

The steward jabbed the spade into the iron-hard ground. 'It is the last days, boy,' he said, stepping down hard on the blade, and Kivrin felt a jerk of fear, and then realised he hadn't recognised her in her boy's clothes.

'It's me, Katherine,' she said.

He looked up and nodded. 'It is the end of time,' he said. 'Those who have not died, will.' He leaned forward, putting his whole weight on the spade.

The cow tried to dig its head in under her arm.

'Go *away*!' she said, and hit it on the nose. It backed away gingerly, skirting the graves, and Kivrin noticed they were not all the same size.

The first was large, but the one next to it was no bigger than Agnes' had been, and the one he stood in did not look much longer. I told Rosemund he wasn't digging her grave, she thought, but he was.

'You have no right to do this!' she said. 'Your son and Rosemund are getting better. And Lady Eliwys is only tired and ill with grief. They aren't going to die.'

The steward looked up at her, his face as expressionless as

509

when he had stood at the barricade, measuring Rosemund for her grave. 'Father Roche says you were sent to help us, but how can you avail against the end of the world?' He stood down on the spade again. 'You will have need of these graves. All, all will die.'

The cow trotted over to the opposite side of the grave, its face on a level with the steward's, and lowed in his face, but he did not seem to notice it.

'You must not dig any more graves,' she said. 'I forbid it.'

He went on digging, as if he had not noticed her either.

'They're not going to die,' she said. 'The Black Death only killed one third to one half of the contemps. We've already had our quota.' He went on digging.

Eliwys died in the night. The steward had to lengthen Rosemund's grave for Eliwys, and when they buried her, Kivrin saw he had started another for Rosemund.

I must get them away from here, she thought, looking at the steward. He stood with the spade cradled against his shoulder, and as soon as he had filled in Eliwys' grave, he started in on Rosemund's grave again. I must get them away before they catch it.

Because they were going to catch it. It lay in wait for them, in the bacilli on their clothes, on the bedding, in the very air they breathed. And if by some miracle they didn't catch it from that, the plague would sweep through all of Oxfordshire in the spring, messengers and villagers and bishop's envoys. They could not stay here.

Scotland, she thought, and started for the manor. I could take them to northern Scotland. The plague didn't reach that far. The steward's son could ride the donkey, and they could make a litter for Rosemund.

Rosemund was sitting up on her pallet. 'The steward's son has been crying out for you,' she said as soon as Kivrin came in.

He had vomited a bloody mucus. His pallet was filthy with it, and when Kivrin cleaned him up, he was too weak to raise his head. Even if Rosemund can ride, he can't, she thought despairingly. We're not going anywhere.

In the night, she thought of the wagon that had been at the rendezvous. Perhaps the steward could help her repair it, and

Rosemund could ride in that. She lit a rushlight from the coals of the fire and crept out to the stable to look at it. Roche's donkey brayed at her when she opened the door, and there was a rustling sound of sudden scattering as she held the smoky light up.

The smashed boxes lay piled against the wagon like a barricade, and she knew as soon as she pulled them away that it wouldn't work. It was too big. The donkey could not pull it, and the wooden axle was missing, carried off by some enterprising contemp to mend a hedge with or burn for firewood. Or to stave off the plague with, Kivrin thought.

It was pitch-black in the courtyard when she came out, and the stars were sharp and bright, as they had been on Christmas Eve. She thought of Agnes asleep against her shoulder, the bell on her little wrist, and the sound of the bells, tolling the Devil's knell. Prematurely, Kivrin thought. The Devil isn't dead yet. He's loose on the world.

She lay awake a long time, trying to think of another plan. Perhaps they could make some sort of litter the donkey could drag if the snow wasn't too deep. Or perhaps they could put both children on the donkey and carry the baggage in packs on their backs.

She fell asleep finally and was awakened again almost immediately, or so it seemed to her. It was still dark, and Roche was bending over her. The dying fire lit his face from below so that he looked as he had in the clearing when she had thought he was a cut-throat, and still partly asleep, she reached out and put her hand gently to his cheek.

'Lady Katherine,' he said, and she came awake.

It's Rosemund, she thought, and twisted round to look at her, but she was sleeping easily, her thin hand under her cheek.

'What is it?' she said. 'Are you ill?'

He shook his head. He opened his mouth and then closed it again.

'Has someone come?' she said, scrambling to her feet.

He shook his head again.

It can't be someone ill, she thought. There's no one left. She looked at the pile of blankets by the door where the steward slept, but he wasn't there. 'Is the steward ill?'

'The steward's son is dead,' he said in an odd stunned voice, and she saw that Lefric was gone, too. 'I went to the church to say matins—' Roche said, and his voice faltered. 'You must come with me,' he said and strode out.

Kivrin snatched up her ragged blanket and hurried out into the courtyard after him.

It could not be later than six. The sun was only just above the horizon, staining the overcast sky and the snow with pink. Roche was already disappearing through the narrow passage to the green. Kivrin flung the blanket over her shoulders and ran after him.

The steward's cow was standing in the passage, its head through a break in the fence of the pigsty, pulling at the straw. It raised its head and mooed at Kivrin.

'Shoo!' she said, flapping her hands at it, but it only pulled its head out of the wattle fence and started towards her, lowing.

'I don't have time to milk you,' she said, and shoved its hindquarters out of the way and squeezed past.

Father Roche was halfway across the green before she caught up with him. 'What is it? Can't you tell me?' she asked, but he didn't stop or even look at her. He turned towards the line of graves on the green, and she thought, feeling suddenly relieved, the steward's tried to bury his son himself, without a priest.

The small grave was filled in, the snowy earth mounded over it, and he had finished Rosemund's grave and dug another, larger one. The spade was sticking out of it, its handle leaning against the end.

Roche didn't go to Lefric's grave. He stopped at the newest one, and said, in that same stunned voice, 'I went to the church to say matins—' and Kivrin looked into the grave.

The steward had apparently tried to bury himself with the shovel, but it had proved unwieldy in the narrow space, and he had propped it against the end of the grave and begun pulling the earth down with his hands. He held a large clod in his frozen hand.

His legs were nearly covered, and it gave him an indecent look, as if he were lying in his bath. 'We must bury him properly,' she said, and reached for the shovel.

Roche shook his head. 'It is holy ground,' he said numbly, and she realised that he thought the steward had killed himself.

It doesn't matter, she thought, and realised in spite of everything, horror after horror, Roche still believed in God. He had been going to the church to say matins when he found the steward and if they all died, he would go on saying them and not find anything incongruous in his prayers.

'It's the disease,' Kivrin said, though she had no idea whether it was or not. 'The septicaemic plague. It infects the blood.'

Roche looked at her uncomprehendingly.

'He must have fallen ill while he was digging,' she said. 'Septicaemic plague poisons the brain. He was not in his right mind.'

'Like Lady Imeyne,' he said, sounding almost glad.

He didn't want to have to bury him outside the pale, Kivrin thought, in spite of what he believes.

She helped Roche straighten the steward's body a little, though he was already stiff. They did not attempt to move him or wrap him in a shroud. Roche laid a black cloth over his face, and they took turns shovelling the soil in on him. The frozen earth clattered like stones.

Roche did not go to the church for his vestments or the missal. He stood first beside Lefric's grave and then the steward's and said the prayers for the dead. Kivrin, standing beside him, her hands folded, thought, he wasn't in his right mind. He had buried his wife and six children, he had buried almost everyone he knew, and even if he hadn't been feverish, if he had crawled into the grave and waited to freeze to death, the plague had still killed him.

He did not deserve a suicide's grave. He doesn't deserve any grave, Kivrin thought. He was supposed to go to Scotland with us, and was horrified at the sudden shock of delight she felt.

We can go to Scotland now, she thought, looking at the grave he had dug for Rosemund. Rosemund can ride the donkey, and Roche and I can carry the food and blankets. She opened her eyes and looked at the sky, but now that the sun was up, the clouds looked lighter, as if they might break up by midmorning. If they left this morning, they could be out of the forest by noon and on to the Oxford – Bath road. By night they could be on the highway to York.

'*Agnus dei, qui tollis peccata mundi,*' Roche said, '*dona, eis requiem.*'

We must take oats for the donkey, she thought, and the axe for cutting firewood. And blankets.

Roche finished the prayers. '*Dominus vobiscum et cum spiritu tuo,*' he said. '*Requiescat in pace.* Amen.' He started off to ring the bell.

There isn't time for that, Kivrin thought, and then took off towards the manor. She could be half-packed by the time Roche had tolled the death knell, and she could tell him her plan, and he could load the donkey, and they could go. She ran across the courtyard and into the manor. They would have to take coals to start the fire with. They could use Imeyne's medicine casket.

She went into the hall. Rosemund was still asleep. That was good. There was no point in waking her until they were ready to leave. She tiptoed past her and got the casket and emptied it out. She laid it next to the fire and started out to the kitchen.

'I woke and you were not here,' Rosemund said. She sat up on her pallet. 'I was afraid you had gone.'

'We're all going,' Kivrin said. 'We're going to go to Scotland.' She went over to her. 'You must rest for the journey, I will be back in a bit.'

'Where are you going?' Rosemund said.

'Only to the kitchen. Are you hungry? I will bring you some porridge. Now lie down and rest.'

'I do not like to be alone,' Rosemund said. 'Can you not stay with me a little?'

I don't have *time* for this, Kivrin thought. 'I'm only going to the kitchen. And Father Roche is here. Can't you hear him? He's ringing the bell. I'll only be a few minutes. All right?' She smiled cheerfully at Rosemund, and she nodded reluctantly. 'I'll be back soon.'

She nearly ran outside. Roche was still ringing the death knell, slowly, steadily. Hurry, she thought, we don't have much time. She searched the kitchen, setting the food on the table. There was a round of cheese and plenty of manchets left – she stacked them like plates in a wadmal sack, put in the cheese and carried it out to the well.

Rosemund was standing in the doorway of the manor, holding on to the frame. 'Can I not sit in the kitchen with you?' she asked. She had put on her kirtle and her shoes, but she was already shivering in the cold air.

'It is too cold,' Kivrin said, hurrying over to her. 'And you must rest.'

'When you are gone, I fear you will not come back,' she said.

'I'm right here,' Kivrin said, but she went inside and fetched Rosemund's cloak and an armful of furs.

'You can sit here on the doorstep,' she said, 'and watch me pack.' She put the cloak over Rosemund's shoulders and sat her down, piling the furs about her like a nest. 'All right?'

The brooch that Sir Bloet had given Rosemund was still at the neck of the cloak. She fumbled with the fastening, her thin hands trembling a little. 'Do we go to Courcy?' she asked.

'No,' Kivrin said, and pinned the brooch for her. *Io suiicien lui dami amo.* You are here in place of the friend I love. 'We're going to Scotland. We will be safe from the plague there.'

'Think you my father died from the plague?'

Kivrin hesitated.

'My mother said he was only delayed or unable to come. She said perhaps my brothers were ill, and he would come when they were recovered.'

'And so he may,' Kivrin said, tucking a fur around Rosemund's feet. 'We'll leave a letter for him so he'll know where we went.'

Rosemund shook her head. 'If he lived, he would have come for me.'

Kivrin wrapped a coverlet around Rosemund's thin shoulders. 'I must fetch food for us to take,' Kivrin said gently.

Rosemund nodded, and Kivrin went across to the kitchen. There was a sack of onions against the wall and another of apples. They were wizened, and most of them had brown spots, but Kivrin lugged the sack outside. They would not need to be cooked and they would all be in need of vitamins before spring.

'Would you like an apple?' she asked Rosemund.

'Yes,' Rosemund said, and Kivrin searched through the sack, trying to find one that was still firm and unwrinkled. She unearthed a reddish-green one, polished it on her leather hose and took it to her, smiling at the memory of how good an apple would have tasted when she was ill.

But after the first bite, Rosemund seemed to lose interest. She leaned back against the doorjamb and looked quietly up at the sky, listening to the steady toll of Roche's bell.

Kivrin went back to sorting the apples, picking out the ones worth taking and wondering how much the donkey could carry. They would need to take oats for the donkey. There would be no grass, though when they reached Scotland there might be heather that it could eat. They shouldn't have to take water. There were plenty of streams. But they would need to take a pot to boil it in.

'Your people never came for you,' Rosemund said.

Kivrin looked up. She was still sitting against the door with the apple.

They did come, Kivrin thought, but I wasn't there. 'No,' Kivrin said.

'Think you the plague has killed them?'

'No,' Kivrin said, and thought, at least I don't have to think of them dead or helpless somewhere. At least I know they're all right.

'When I go to Sir Bloet, I will tell him how you helped us,' Rosemund said. 'I will ask that I might keep you and Father Roche by me.' Her head went up proudly. 'I am allowed my own attendants and chaplain.'

'Thank you,' Kivrin said solemnly.

She set the sack of good apples next to the one of cheese and bread. The bell stopped, its overtones still echoing in the cold air. She picked up the bucket and lowered it into the well. She would cook some porridge and chop the bruised apples into it. It would make a filling meal for the trip.

Rosemund's apple rolled past her feet to the base of the well and stopped. Kivrin stooped to pick it up. It had only a little bite out of it, white against the shrivelled red. Kivrin wiped it against her jerkin. 'You dropped your apple,' she said, and turned to give it back to her.

Her hand was still open, as if she had leaned forward to catch it when it fell. 'Oh, Rosemund,' Kivrin said.

Transcript from the Domesday Book
(079110–079239)

Father Roche and I are going to Scotland. There really isn't any point in telling you that, I suppose, since you'll never hear what's on this corder, but perhaps someone will stumble across it on a moor someday or Ms Montoya will do a dig in northern Scotland when she's finished with Skendgate, and if that happens, I wanted you to know what happened to us.

I know flight is probably the worst thing to do, but I have to get Father Roche away from here. The whole manor is contaminated with the plague – bedding, clothes, the air – and the rats are everywhere. I saw one in the church when I went to get Roche's alb and stole for Rosemund's funeral. And even if he doesn't catch it from them, the plague is all around us and I will never be able to convince him to stay here. He will want to go and help.

We'll keep off the roads and away from the villages. We've got food enough for a week, and then we'll be far enough north that I should be able to buy food in a town. The clerk had a sack of silver with him. And don't worry. We'll be all right. As Mr Gilchrist would say, 'I've taken every possible precaution.'

CHAPTER THIRTY-TWO

Apocalyptic was very likely the correct term for his even thinking he could rescue Kivrin, Dunworthy thought. He was worn out by the time Colin got him back to his room, and his temp was back up. 'You rest,' Colin said, helping him into bed. 'You can't have a relapse if you're going to rescue Kivrin.'

'I need to see Badri,' he said, 'and Finch.'

'I'll take care of everything,' Colin said, and darted out.

He would need to arrange his and Badri's discharge and med support for the pickup, in case Kivrin was ill. He would need a plague inoculation. He wondered how long would be required for it to take effect. Mary had said she'd immunized Kivrin while she was in hospital for her corder implant. That had been two weeks before the drop but perhaps it didn't take that long to confer immunity.

The nurse came in to check his temp. 'I'm just going off-duty,' she said, reading his patch.

'How soon can I be discharged?' he asked.

'Discharged?' she said, sounding surprised. 'My, you must be feeling better.'

'I am,' he said. 'How long?'

She frowned. 'There's a good deal of difference between being ready for a bit of a walk and being ready to go home.' She adjusted the drip. 'You don't want to overdo it.'

She went out, and after a few minutes Colin came in with Finch and the Middle Ages book 'I thought perhaps you'd need this for costumes and things.' He dumped it on Dunworthy's legs. 'I'll just go fetch Badri.' He dashed out.

'You're looking a good deal better, sir,' Finch said. 'I'm so glad

I'm afraid you're badly needed at Balliol. It's Mrs Gaddson. She's accused Balliol of undermining William's health. She says the combined strain of the epidemic and reading Petrarch has broken his health. She's threatening to go to the Head of the History Faculty with it.'

'Tell her she's more than welcome to try. Basingame's in Scotland somewhere,' Dunworthy said. 'I need you to find how long in advance of exposure an inoculation against bubonic plague needs to be given, and I need the laboratory readied for a drop.'

'We're using it for storage just now,' Finch said. 'We've had several shipments of supplies from London, though none of lavatory paper, even though I specifically requested—'

'Move them into the hall,' Dunworthy said. 'I want the net ready as soon as possible.'

Colin opened the door with his elbow and wheeled Badri in, using his other arm and a knee to hold it open. 'I had to sneak him past the ward sister,' he said breathlessly. He pushed the wheel-chair up to the bed.

'I want—' Dunworthy said, and stopped, looking at Badri. The thing was impossible. Badri was in no condition to run the net. He looked exhausted by the mere effort of having been brought from the ward, and he was fumbling at the pocket of his robe as he had at his sash.

'We'll need two RTNs, a light measure and a gateway,' Badri said, and his voice sounded exhausted too, but the despair had gone out of it. 'And we'll need authorisations for both drop and pickup.'

'What about the protesters who were at Brasenose?' Dunworthy asked. 'Will they try to prevent the drop?'

'No,' Colin said. 'They're over at the National Trust Head-quarters. They're trying to shut down the dig.'

Good, Dunworthy thought. Montoya will be too occupied with trying to defend her churchyard against picketers to interfere. Too occupied to look for Kivrin's corder.

'What else will you need?' he asked Badri.

'An insular memory and redundant for the backup.' He pulled

a sheet of paper from the pocket and looked at it. 'And a remote hookup so I can run parameter checks.'

He handed the list to Dunworthy, who handed it to Finch. 'We'll also need med support for Kivrin,' Dunworthy said, 'and I want a telephone installed in this room.'

Finch was frowning at the list.

'And don't tell me we're out of any of these,' Dunworthy said before he could protest. 'Beg, borrow, or steal them.' He turned back to Badri. 'Will you need anything else?'

'To be discharged,' Badri said, 'which, I'm afraid will be the greatest obstacle.'

'He's right,' Colin said. 'Sister will never let him out. I had to sneak him in here.'

'Who's your doctor?' Dunworthy asked.

'Dr Gates,' Badri said, 'but—'

'Surely we can explain the situation,' Dunworthy interrupted, 'explain that it's an emergency.'

Badri shook his head. 'The last thing we can do is tell him the circumstances. I persuaded him to discharge me to open the net while you were ill. He didn't think I was well enough, but he allowed it, and then when I had the relapse . . .'

Dunworthy looked anxiously at him. 'Are you certain you're capable of running the net? Perhaps I can get Andrews now that the epidemic's under control.'

'There isn't time,' Badri said. 'And it was my fault. I want to run the net. Perhaps Mr Finch can find another doctor.'

'Yes,' Dunworthy said. 'And tell mine I need to speak with him.' He reached for Colin's book.

'I'll need a costume.' He flipped through the pages, looking for an illustration of mediaeval clothing. 'No strips, no zippers, no buttons.' He found a picture of Boccaccio and showed it to Finch. 'I doubt if Twentieth Century has anything. Telephone the Dramatic Society and see if they've got something.'

'I'll do my best, sir,' Finch said, frowning doubtfully at the illustration.

The door crashed open and the sister rattled in, enraged. 'Mr Dunworthy, this is utterly irresponsible,' she said in a tone that had no doubt caused casualties from the Second Falklands War terrors. 'If you will not take care of your own health, you might at the least not endanger that of the other patients.' She fixed her gaze on Finch. 'Mr Dunworthy is to have no more visitors.'

She glared at Colin and then snatched the wheelchair handles from him. 'What can you have been thinking of, Mr Chaudhuri?' she said, whipping the wheelchair around so smartly Badri's head snapped back. 'You have already had one relapse. I have no intention of allowing you to have another.' She pushed him out.

'I told you we'd never get him out,' Colin said.

She flung the door open again. '*No* visitors,' she said to Colin.

'I'll be back,' Colin whispered and ducked past her.

She fixed him with her ancient eye. 'Not if I have anything to say about it.'

She apparently had something to say about it. Colin didn't return till after she'd gone off-duty, and then only to bring the remote hookup to Badri and report to Dunworthy on plague inoculations. Finch had telephoned the NHS. It took two weeks for the inoculation to confer full immunity, and seven days before partial. 'And Mr Finch wants to know if you shouldn't also be inoculated against cholera and typhoid.'

'There isn't time,' he said. There wasn't time for a plague inoculation either. Kivrin had already been there over three weeks, and every day lowered her chances of survival. And he was no closer to being discharged.

As soon as Colin left, he rang William's nurse and told her he wanted to see his doctor 'I'm ready to be discharged,' he said.

She laughed.

'I'm completely recovered,' he said. 'I did ten laps in the corridor this morning.'

She shook her head. 'The incidence of relapse in this virus has been extremely high. I simply can't take the risk.' She smiled at him. 'Where is it you're so determined to go? Surely whatever it is can survive another week without you.'

'It's the start of term,' he said, and realised that was true. 'Please tell my doctor I wish to see him.'

'Dr Warden will only tell you what I've told you,' she said, but she apparently relayed the message because he tottered in after tea.

He had obviously been hauled out of a senile retirement to help with the epidemic. He told a long and pointless story about medical conditions during the Pandemic and then pronounced creakily, 'In my day we kept people in hospital till they were fully recovered.'

Dunworthy didn't try to argue with him. He waited until he and the sister had hobbled down the corridor, sharing reminiscences from the Hundred Years War, and then strapped on his portable drip and walked to the public phone near Casualties to get a progress report from Finch.

'The sister won't allow a phone in your room,' Finch said, 'but I've good news about the plague. A course of streptomycin injections along with gamma globulin and T-cell enhancement will confer temporary immunity and can be started as little as twelve hours before exposure.'

'Good,' Dunworthy said, 'find me a doctor who'll give them and authorise my discharge. A young doctor. And send Colin over. Is the net ready?'

'Very nearly, sir. I've obtained the necessary drop and pickup authorisations and I've located a remote hookup. I was just going to fetch it now.'

He rang off and Dunworthy walked back to the room. He hadn't lied to the nurse. He was feeling stronger with each passing moment, though there was a tightness around his lower ribs by the time he made it back to his room. Mrs Gaddson was there, searching eagerly through her Bible for murrains and agues and emerods.

'Read me Luke 11, verse 9,' Dunworthy said.

She looked it up. ' "And I say unto you, Ask, and it shall be given you," ' she read, glaring at him suspiciously. ' "Seek, and ye shall find, knock, and it shall be opened unto you." '

Ms Taylor came at the very end of visiting hours, carrying a measuring tape. 'Colin sent me to get your measurements,' she said. 'The old crone out there won't let him on the floor.' She draped the tape around his waist. 'I had to tell her I was visiting Ms Piantini. Hold your arm out straight.' She stretched the tape along his arm. 'She's feeling a lot better. She may even get to ring Rimbaud's "When at Last My Saviour Cometh" with us on the fifteenth. We're doing it for Holy Re-Formed you know, but the NHS has taken over their church so Mr Finch has very kindly let us use Balliol's chapel. What size shoe do you wear?'

She jotted down his various measurements, told him Colin would be in the next day and not to worry, the net was nearly ready. She went out presumably to visit Ms Piantini, and came back a few minutes later with a message from Badri.

'Mr Dunworthy, I've run twenty-four parameter checks,' it read. 'All twenty-four show minimal slippage, eleven show slippage of less than an hour, five slippage of less than five minutes. I'm running divergence checks and DARs to try to find out what it is.'

I know what it is, Dunworthy thought. It's the Black Death. The function of the slippage was to prevent interactions that might affect history. Five minutes' slippage meant there were no anachronisms, no critical meetings the continuum must keep from happening. It meant the drop was to an uninhabited area. It meant the plague had been there. And all the contemps were dead.

Colin didn't come in the morning, and after lunch Dunworthy walked to the public phone again and rang Finch. 'I haven't been able to find a doctor willing to take on new cases,' Finch said. 'I've telephoned every doctor and medic within the perimeter. A good many of them are still down with flu,' he apologised, 'and several of them—'

He stopped but Dunworthy knew what he had intended to say. Several of them had died, including the one who would certainly have helped, who would have given him the inoculations and discharged Badri.

'Great-aunt Mary wouldn't have given up,' Colin had said. She wouldn't have, he thought, in spite of the sister and Mrs Gaddson and a band of pain below the ribs. If she were here, she would have helped him however she could.

He walked back to his room. The sister had posted a large placard reading 'Absolutely No Visitors Allowed' on his door, but she was not at her desk or in his room. Colin was, carrying a large damp parcel.

'The sister's in the ward,' Colin said, grinning 'Ms Piantini very conveniently fainted. You should have seen her. She's very good at it.' He fumbled with the string. 'The nurse just came on duty, but you needn't worry about her either. She's in the linen room with William Gaddson.' He opened the parcel. It was full of clothing: a long black doublet and black breeches, neither of them remotely mediaeval, and a pair of women's black tights.

'Where did you get this?' Dunworthy said. 'A production of *Hamlet*?'

'*Richard III*,' Colin said. 'Keble did it last term. I took the hump out.'

'Is there a cloak?' Dunworthy said, sorting through the clothing. 'Tell Finch to find me a cloak A long cloak that will cover everything.'

'I will,' Colin said absently. He was fumbling intently with the band on his green jacket. It sprang open, and Colin threw it off his shoulders. 'Well? What do you think?'

He had done considerably better than Finch. The boots were wrong – they looked like a pair of gardener's Wellingtons – but the brown burlap smock and shapeless grey-brown trousers looked like the illustration of a serf in Colin's book.

'The trousers have a strip,' Colin said, 'but you can't see it under the shirt. I copied it out of the book. I'm supposed to be your squire.'

He should have anticipated this. 'Colin,' he said, 'you can't go with me.'

'Why not?' Colin said. 'I can help you find her. I'm good at finding things.'

'It's impossible. The—'

'Oh, now you're going to tell me how dangerous it is in the Middle Ages, aren't you? Well, it's rather dangerous here, isn't it? What about Great-aunt Mary? She'd have been safer in the Middle Ages, wouldn't she? I've been doing lots of dangerous things. Taking medicine to people and putting up placards in the wards. While you were ill, I did all sorts of dangerous things you don't even know about—'

'Colin—'

'You're too *old* to go alone. And Great-aunt Mary told me to take care of you. What if you have a relapse?'

'Colin—'

'My mother doesn't care if I go.'

'But I do. I can't take you with me.'

'So I'm to sit here and wait,' he said bitterly, 'and nobody will tell me anything, and I won't know whether you're alive or dead.' He picked up his jacket. 'It's not fair.'

'I know.'

'Can I come to the laboratory, at least?'

'Yes.'

'I still think you should let me go,' he said. He began folding the tights. 'Shall I leave your costume here?'

'Better not. The sister might confiscate it.'

'What's all this, Mr Dunworthy?' Mrs Gaddson said.

They both jumped. She came into the room, bearing her Bible.

'Colin's been collecting for the clothing drive,' Dunworthy said, helping him wad the clothing into a bundle. 'For the detainees.'

'Passing clothes from one person to another is an excellent way of spreading infection,' she said to Dunworthy.

Colin scooped up the bundle and ducked out.

'And allowing a child to come here and risk catching something! He offered to come and walk me home from the Infirmary last night, and I said, "I won't have you risking your health for me!"'

She sat down next to the bed and opened her Bible. 'It's pure negligence, allowing that boy to visit you. But I suppose it's no more than what I should have expected from the way you run your college. Mr Finch has become a complete tyrant in your absence. He simply flew at me in a rage yesterday when I requested an extra roll of lavatory paper—'

'I want to see William,' Dunworthy said.

'Here!' she sputtered. 'In hospital?' She shut her Bible with a snap. 'I simply won't allow it. There are still a great many infectious cases and poor Willy—'

Is in the linen room with my nurse, he thought. 'Tell him I wish to see him as soon as possible,' he said.

She brandished the Bible at him like Moses bringing down the plagues on Egypt. 'I intend to report your callous indifference to your students' well-being to the Head of the History Faculty,' she said and stormed out.

He could hear her complaining loudly in the corridor to someone, presumably the nurse, because William appeared almost immediately, smoothing down his hair.

'I need injections of streptomycin and gamma globulin,' Dunworthy said. 'I also need to be discharged from hospital, as does Badri Chaudhuri.'

He nodded. 'I know. Colin told me you're going to try to retrieve your historian.' He looked thoughtful. 'I know this nurse . . .'

'A nurse can't give an injection without authorisation by a doctor, and the discharges will require authorisation as well.'

'I know a girl up in Records. When do you want this by?'

'As soon as possible.'

'I'll get right on it. It might take two or three days,' he said, and started out. 'I met Kivrin once. She was at Balliol to see you. She's very pretty, isn't she?'

I must remember to warn her about him, Dunworthy thought, and realised he had actually begun to believe he might be able to rescue her in spite of everything. Hold on, he thought, I'm coming. Two or three days.

He spent the afternoon walking up and down the corridor, trying to build his strength up. Badri's ward had an 'Absolutely No Visitors Allowed' placard on each of the doors, and the sister fixed him with a watery blue eye each time he approached them.

Colin came in, wet and breathless, with a pair of boots for Dunworthy. 'She has guards everywhere,' he said. Mr Finch says to tell you the net's ready except he can't find anyone to do med support.'

'Tell William to arrange it,' he said. 'He's taking care of the discharges and the streptomycin injection.'

'I know. I've got to deliver a message to Badri from him. I'll be back.'

He did not come back, and neither did William. When Dunworthy walked to the phone to ring Balliol, the sister caught him halfway and escorted him back to his room. Either her tightened defences included Mrs Gaddson as well, or Mrs Gaddson was still angry over William. She did not come all afternoon.

Just after tea a pretty nurse he hadn't seen before came in with a syringe. 'Sister's been called away on an emergency,' she said.

'What's that?' he asked, pointing to the syringe.

She tapped the console keyboard with one finger of her free hand. She looked at the screen, tapped in a few more characters, and came around to inject him. 'Streptomycin,' she said.

She did not seem nervous or furtive, which meant William must have managed the authorisation somehow. She infected the largish syringe into the cannula, smiled at him and went out. She had left the console on. He got out of bed and went round to read what was on the screen.

It was his chart. He recognised it because it looked like Badri's and was as unreadable. The last entry read 'ICU15802691 14–1–55 1805 150/RPT 1800 CRS IMSTMC 4ML/q6h NHS40–211–7 M AHRENS.'

He sat down on the bed. Oh, Mary.

William must have obtained her access code, perhaps from his friend in Records, and fed it into the computer. Records was no doubt far behind, swamped by the paperwork of the epidemic, and had not yet got to Mary's death. They would catch the error some day, though the resourceful William had no doubt already arranged for its erasure.

He scrolled the screen back through his chart. There were M. AHRENS entries up to 8–1–55, the day she had died. She must have nursed him until she could no longer stand. No wonder her heart had stopped.

He switched the console off so that the sister wouldn't spot the entry and got into bed. He wondered if William planned to sign her name to the discharges as well. He hoped so. She would have wanted to help.

No one came in all evening. The sister hobbled in to check his tach bracelet and give him his temp at eight o'clock, and she entered them in the console but didn't appear to notice anything. At ten a second nurse, also pretty, came in, repeated the streptomycin injection, and gave him one of gamma globulin.

She left the screen on, and Dunworthy lay down so he could

see Mary's name. He didn't think he would be able to sleep, but he did. He dreamed of Egypt and the Valley of the Kings.

'Mr Dunworthy, wake up,' Colin whispered. He was shining a pocket torch in his face.

'What is it?' Dunworthy said, blinking against the light. He groped for his spectacles. 'What's happened?'

'It's me, Colin,' he whispered. He turned the torch on himself. He was wearing, for some unknown reason, a large white lab coat, and his face looked strained, sinister in the upturned light of the torch.

'What's wrong?' Dunworthy asked.

'Nothing,' Colin whispered. 'You're being discharged.'

Dunworthy hooked his spectacles over his ears. He still couldn't see anything. 'What time is it?' he whispered.

'Four o'clock.' He thrust his slippers at him and turned the torch on the closet. 'Do hurry.' He took Dunworthy's robe off the hook and handed it to him. 'She's likely to come back any moment.'

Dunworthy fumbled with the robe and slippers, trying to wake up, wondering why they were being discharged at this odd hour and where the sister was.

Colin went to the door and peeked out. He switched the torch off, stuck it in the pocket of the too-large lab coat and eased the door shut. After a long, breath-holding moment, he opened it a crack and looked out. 'All clear,' he said, motioning to Dunworthy. 'William's taken her into the linen room.'

'Who, the nurse?' Dunworthy asked, still groggy. 'Why is she on duty?'

'Not the *nurse*. The *sister*. William's keeping her in there till we're gone.'

'What about Mrs Gaddson?'

Colin looked sheepish. 'She's reading to Mr Latimer,' he said defensively. 'I had to do *something* with her, and Mr Latimer can't hear her.' He opened the door all the way. There was a wheelchair just outside. He took hold of the handles.

'I can walk,' Dunworthy said.

'There isn't time,' Colin whispered. 'And if anyone sees us I can tell them I'm taking you up to Scanning.'

Dunworthy sat down and let Colin push him down the corridor and past the linen room and Latimer's room. He could hear Mrs Gaddson's voice dimly through the door, reading from Exodus.

Colin continued on tiptoe to the end of the corridor and then took off at a rate that could not possibly be mistaken for taking a patient to Scanning, down another corridor, round a corner, and out of the side door where they had been accosted by the 'The End of Time Is Near' sandwich board.

It was pitch-black in the alley and raining hard. He could only dimly make out the ambulance parked at the street end. Colin knocked on the back of it with his fist, and an ambulance attendant jumped down. It was the medic who had helped bring Badri in. And had picketed Brasenose. 'Can you climb up?' she asked, blushing.

Dunworthy nodded and stood up.

'Pull the doors to,' she told Colin and went round to get in the front.

'Don't tell me, she's a friend of William's,' Dunworthy said, looking after her.

'Of course,' Colin said. 'She asked me what sort of mother-in-law I thought Mrs Gaddson would be.' He helped him up the step and into the ambulance.

'Where's Badri?' Dunworthy asked, wiping the rain off his spectacles.

Colin pulled the doors to. 'At Balliol. We took him first, so he could set up the net.' He looked anxiously out of the back window. 'I do hope Sister doesn't sound the alarm before we're gone.'

'I shouldn't worry about it,' Dunworthy said. He had clearly underestimated William's powers. The ancient sister was probably on William's lap in the linen room, embroidering their intertwined initials on the towels.

Colin switched on the torch and shone it on the stretcher. 'I brought your costume,' he said, handing Dunworthy the black doublet.

Dunworthy took off his robe and put it on. The ambulance started up, nearly knocking him over. He sat down on the side bench, bracing himself against the swaying side, and pulled on the black tights.

William's medic had not switched on the siren, but she was going at such a rate she should have. Dunworthy clung to the strap with one hand and pulled on the breeches with the other, and Colin, reaching for the boots, nearly went over on his head.

'We found you a cloak,' Colin said. 'Mr Finch borrowed it off the Classical Theatre Society.' He shook it out. It was Victorian, black and lined in red silk. He draped it over Dunworthy's shoulders.

'What production did *they* put on? *Dracula*?'

The ambulance lurched to a stop and the medic yanked open the doors. Colin helped Dunworthy down, holding up the train of the voluminous cloak like a page boy. They ducked in under the gate. The rain pattered loudly on the stones overhead and under the sound of the rain was a clanging sound.

'What's that?' Dunworthy asked, peering out into the dark quad.

' "When at Last My Saviour Cometh",' Colin said. 'The Americans are practising it for some church thing. Necrotic, isn't it?'

'Mrs Gaddson said they were practising at all hours, but I'd no idea she meant five in the morning.'

'The concert's tonight,' Colin said.

'Tonight?' Dunworthy said, and realised it was the fifteenth. The sixth on the Julian calendar. Epiphany. The Arrival of the Wise Men.

Finch hurried towards them with an umbrella. 'Sorry I'm late,' he said, holding it over Dunworthy, 'but I couldn't find an umbrella. You've no idea how many of the detainees go off and forget them. Especially the Americans—'

Dunworthy started across the quad. 'Is everything ready?'

'The med support's not here yet,' Finch said, attempting to keep the umbrella over Dunworthy's head, 'but William Gaddson just telephoned to say it was all arranged and she'd be here shortly.'

Dunworthy would not have been surprised if he had said the sister had volunteered for the job. 'I do hope William never decides to take to a life of crime,' he said.

'Oh, I don't think he would, sir. His mother would never allow it.' He ran a few steps, trying to keep up. 'Mr Chaudhuri's running the preliminary coordinates. And Ms Montoya's here.'

He stopped. 'Montoya? What is it?'

'I don't know, sir. She said she had information for you.'

Not now, he thought. Not when we're this close.

He went into the laboratory. Badri was at the console, and Montoya, wearing her terrorist jacket and muddy jeans, was leaning over him, watching the screen. Badri said something to her, and she shook her head and looked at her digital. She glanced up and saw Dunworthy, and an expression of compassion came into her face. She stood up and reached in to the pocket of her shirt.

No, Dunworthy thought.

She walked over to him. 'I didn't know you were planning this,' she said, pulling out a folded sheet of paper. 'I want to help.' She handed him the paper. 'This is what information Kivrin had to work with when she went through.'

He looked at the paper in his hand. It was a map.

'This is the drop.' She pointed to a cross on a black line. 'And this is Skendgate. You'll recognise it by the church. It's Norman, with murals above the rood screen and a statue of St Anthony.' She smiled at him. 'The patron saint of lost objects. I found the statue yesterday.'

She pointed to several other crosses. 'If by some chance she didn't go to Skendgate, the most likely villages are Esthcote, Henefelde and Shrivendun. I've listed their distinguishing landmarks on the back.'

Badri stood up and came over. He looked even frailer than he had in the ward, if that were possible, and he moved slowly, like the old man he had become. 'I'm still getting minimal slippage, no matter what variables I feed in,' he said. He put his hand under his ribs. 'I'm running an intermittent, opening for five minutes at two-hour intervals. That way we can hold the net open for up to twenty-four hours, thirty-six if we're lucky.'

Dunworthy wondered how many of those two-hour intervals Badri would hold up for. He looked done in already.

'When you see the shimmer or the beginnings of moisture condensation, move into the rendezvous area,' Badri said.

'What if it's dark?' Colin asked. He had taken off the lab coat, and Dunworthy saw that he was in his squire's costume.

'You should still be able to see the shimmer, and we'll call out to you,' Badri said. He grunted softly and put his hand to his side again. 'You've been immunised?'

'Yes.'

'Good. All we're waiting for then is the med support.' He looked hard at Dunworthy. 'Are you sure you're well enough to do this?'

'Are you?' Dunworthy asked.

The door opened and William's nurse came in, wearing a slick. She blushed when she saw Dunworthy. 'William said you needed med support. Where would you like me to set up?'

I *must* remember to warn Kivrin about him, Dunworthy thought. Badri showed her where he wanted her, and Colin ran out for her equipment.

Montoya led Dunworthy over to a chalked circle under the shields. 'Are you going to wear your spectacles?'

'Yes,' he said. 'You can dig them up in your churchyard.'

'I'm certain they won't be there,' she said solemnly. 'Do you want to sit or lie down?'

He thought of Kivrin, lying with her arm across her face, helpless and blind. 'I'll stand,' he said.

Colin came back in with a steamer trunk. He set it down by the console and came over to the net. 'You've no business going by yourself,' he said.

'I must go by myself, Colin.'

'Why?'

'It's too dangerous. You can't imagine what it was like during the Black Death.'

'Yes, I can. I read the book through twice, and I've had my—' He stopped. 'I know all about the Black Death. Besides, if it's as bad as all that, you shouldn't go by yourself. I wouldn't get in the way, I promise.'

'Colin,' he said helplessly, 'you're my responsibility. I can't take the risk.'

Badri came over to the net, carrying a light measure. 'The nurse needs help with the rest of her equipment,' he said.

'If you don't come back, I'll never know what happened to you,' Colin said. He turned and ran out.

Badri made a slow circuit of Dunworthy, taking measurements. He frowned, took hold of his elbow, took more measurements. The nurse came over with a syringe. Dunworthy rolled up the sleeve of his doublet.

'I want you to know I don't approve of this at all,' she said, swabbing Dunworthy's arm. 'Both of you properly belong in hospital.' She plunged the syringe in and walked back to her steamer trunk.

Badri waited while Dunworthy rolled down his sleeve and then moved his arm, took more measurements, moved it again. Colin carried a scan unit in and went back out without looking at Dunworthy.

Dunworthy watched the display screens change and change again. He could hear the bell ringers, an almost-musical sound with the door shut. Colin opened the door, and they clanged wildly for a moment while he manoeuvered a second steamer trunk through the door.

Colin dragged it over to where the nurse was setting up, and then went over to the console and stood beside Montoya, watching the screens generate numbers. He wished he had told them he would go through sitting down. The stiff boots pinched his feet, and he felt tired from the effort of standing still.

Badri spoke into the ear again and the shields came down, touched the floor, draped a bit. Colin said something to Montoya and she glanced up, frowned and then nodded, and turned back to the screen. Colin walked over to the net.

'What are you doing?' Dunworthy said.

'One of the curtain things is caught,' Colin said. He walked to the far side and tugged on the fold.

'Ready ' Badri said.

'Yes,' Colin said and backed away towards the prep door. 'No, wait.' He came back up to the shields. 'Shouldn't you take your spectacles off? In case somebody sees you come through?'

Dunworthy removed his spectacles and tucked them inside his doublet.

'If you don't come back, I'm coming after you,' Colin said, and backed away. 'Ready,' he called.

Dunworthy looked at the screens. They were nothing but a blur. So was Montoya, who had leaned forward over Badri's shoulder. She glanced at her digital. Badri spoke into the ear.

Dunworthy closed his eyes. He could hear the bell ringers banging away at 'When at Last My Saviour Cometh'. He opened them again.

'Now,' Badri said. He pushed a button, and Colin darted towards the shields and under, straight into Dunworthy's arms.

CHAPTER THIRTY-THREE

They buried Rosemund in the grave the steward had dug for her. 'You will have need of these graves,' the steward had said, and he was right. They would never have managed to dig it themselves. It was all they could do to carry her out to the green.

They laid her on the ground beside the grave. She looked impossibly thin lying there in her cloak, wasted almost to nothing. The fingers of her right hand, still half-curved around the apple she had let drop, were nothing but bones.

'Heard you her confession?' Roche asked.

'Yes,' Kivrin said, and it seemed to her that she had. Rosemund had confessed to being afraid of the dark and the plague and being alone, to loving her father and to knowing she would never see him again. All the things that she herself could not bring herself to confess.

Kivrin unfastened the loveknot pin Sir Bloet had given Rosemund and wrapped the cloak around her, covering her head, and Roche picked her up in his arms like a sleeping child and stepped down into the grave.

He had trouble climbing out, and Kivrin had to take hold of his huge hands and pull him out. And when he began the prayers for the dead he said, '*Domine, ad adjuvandum me festina.*'

Kivrin looked anxiously at him. We must get away from here before he catches it too, she thought, and didn't correct him. We don't have a moment to lose.

'*Dormiunt in somno pacis,*' Roche said, and picked up the shovel and began filling in the grave.

It seemed to take for ever. Kivrin spelled him, chipping at the mound that had frozen into a solid mass and trying to think how far they could get before nightfall. It wasn't noon yet. If they left soon, they could get through the Wychwood and across the Oxford-Bath road on to the Midland Plain. They could be in Scotland within the week, near Invercassley or Dornoch, where the plague never came.

'Father Roche,' she said as soon as he began tamping down the earth with the flat of the shovel. 'We must go to Scotland.'

'Scotland?' he said, as if he had never heard of it.

'Yes,' she said. 'We must go away from here. We must take the donkey and go to Scotland.'

He nodded. 'We must carry the sacraments with us. And ere we go I must ring the bell for Rosemund, that her soul may pass safely unto heaven.'

She wanted to tell him no, that there wasn't time, they must leave now, immediately, but she nodded. 'I will fetch Balaam,' she said.

Roche started for the bell tower, and she took off running for the barn before he had even reached it. She wanted them to be gone now, now, before anything else happened, as if the plague were waiting to leap out at them like the bogeyman from the church or the brewhouse or the barn.

She ran across the courtyard and into the stable and led the donkey out. She began to strap his panniers on.

The bell tolled once, and then was silent, and Kivrin stopped, the girth strap in her hand, and listened, waiting for it to ring again. Three strokes for a woman, she thought, and knew why he had stopped. One for a child. Oh, Rosemund.

She tied the girth strap and began to fill the panniers. They were too small to hold everything. She would have to tie the sacks on. She filled a coarse bag with oats for the donkey, scooping it out of the grain bin with both hands and spilling whole handfuls on the filthy floor, and knotted it with a rough rope that hung on Agnes' pony's stall The rope was tied to the stall with a heavy knot she couldn't untie. She ended by having to run to the kitchen for a knife and back again, bringing the sacks of food she had gathered up earlier.

She cut the rope free and sliced it into shorter sections, threw down the knife and went out to the donkey. He was trying to gnaw a hole in the sack of oats. She tied it and the other bags to his back with the pieces of rope and led him out of the courtyard and across the green to the church.

Roche was nowhere in sight. Kivrin still needed to fetch the blankets and the candles, but she wanted to put the sacraments in the panniers first. Food, oats, blankets, candles. What else had she forgotten?

Roche appeared at the door. He was not carrying anything.

'Where are the sacraments?' she called to him.

He didn't answer. He leaned for a moment against the church door, staring at her, and the look on his face was the same as when he had come to tell her about the steward. But they've all died, she thought, there's nobody left to die.

'I must ring the bell,' he said and started across the churchyard towards the bell tower.

'You've already rung it,' she said. 'There's no time for the funeral knell. We must start for Scotland.' She tied the donkey to the gate, her cold fingers fumbling with the rough rope, and hurried after him, catching him by the sleeve. 'What is it?'

He turned, almost violently, towards her, and the expression on his face frightened her. He looked like a cut-throat, a murderer. 'I must ring the bell for vespers,' he said and shook himself violently free of her hand.

Oh, no, Kivrin thought.

'It is only midday,' she said. 'It isn't time for vespers yet.' He's just tired, she thought. We're both so tired we can't think straight. She took hold of his sleeve again. 'Come, Father. We must go if we're to get through the woods by nightfall.'

'It is past time,' he said, 'and I have not yet rung them. Lady Imeyne will be angry.'

Oh, no, she thought, oh no oh no.

'I will ring it,' she said, stepping in front of him to stop him. 'You must go into the house and rest.'

'It grows dark,' he said angrily. He opened his mouth as if to shout at her, and a great gout of vomit and blood heaved up out of him and on to Kivrin's jerkin.

Oh no oh no oh no.

He looked bewilderedly at her drenched jerkin, the violence gone out of his face.

'Come, you must lie down,' she said, thinking, we will never make it to the manor house.

'Am I ill?' he said, still staring at her blood-covered jerkin.

'No,' she said. 'You are but tired and must rest.'

She led him towards the church. He stumbled and she thought, if he falls, I will never get him up. She helped him inside, bracing the heavy door open with her back, and sat him down against the wall.

'I fear the work has tired me,' he said, leaning his head against the stones. 'I would sleep a little.'

'Yes, sleep,' Kivrin said. As soon as he had closed his eyes she ran back to the manor house for blankets and a bolster to make him a pallet. When she skidded in with them, he was no longer there.

'Roche!' she cried, trying to see up the dark nave. 'Where are you?'

There was no answer. She darted out again, still clutching the bedding to her chest, but he wasn't in the bell tower or the churchyard, and he could not possibly have made it to the house. She ran back in the church and up the nave and he was there, on his knees in front of the statue of St Catherine.

'You must lie down,' she said, spreading the blankets on the floor.

He lay down obediently, and she put the bolster behind his head. 'It is the plague, is it not?' he asked looking up at her.

'No,' she said, pulling the coverlid up over him. 'You're tired that's all. Try to sleep.'

He turned on his side, away from her, but in a few minutes he sat up, the murderous expression back, and threw the covers off. 'I must ring the vespers bell,' he said accusingly, and it was all Kivrin could do to keep him from standing up. When he dozed again, she tore strips from the frayed bottom of her jerkin and tied his hands to the rood screen.

'Don't do this to him,' Kivrin murmured over and over without knowing it. 'Please! Please! Don't do this to him.'

He opened his eyes. 'Surely God must hear such fervent prayers,' he said, and sank into a deeper, quieter sleep.

Kivrin ran out and unloaded the donkey and untied him, gathered up the sacks of food and the lantern and brought them inside the church. He was still sleeping. She crept out again and ran across to the courtyard and drew a bucket of water from the well.

He still did not appear to have wakened, but when Kivrin wrung out a strip torn from the altar cloth and bathed his forehead with it, he said, without opening his eyes, 'I feared that you had gone.'

She wiped the crusted blood by his mouth. 'I would not go to Scotland without you.'

'Not Scotland,' he said. 'To heaven.'

She ate a little of the stale manchet and cheese from the food sack and tried to sleep a little, but it was too cold. When Roche turned and sighed in his sleep, she could see his breath.

She built a fire, pulling up the stick fence around one of the huts and piling the sticks in front of the rood screen, but it filled the church with smoke, even with the doors propped open. Roche coughed and vomited again. This time it was nearly all blood. She put the fire out and made two more hurried trips for as many furs and blankets as she could find and made a sort of nest of them.

Roche's fever went up in the night. He kicked at the covers and raged at Kivrin, mostly in words she couldn't understand, though once he said clearly, '*Go*, curse you!' and over and over, furiously, 'It grows dark!'

Kivrin brought the candles from the altar and the top of the rood screen and set them in front of St Catherine's statue. When his ravings about the dark got bad, she lit them all and covered him up again, and it seemed to help a little.

His fever rose higher, and his teeth chattered in spite of the rugs heaped over him. It seemed to Kivrin that his skin was already darkening, the blood vessels haemorrhaging under the skin. Don't do this. Please.

In the morning he was better. His skin had not blackened after all; it was only the uncertain light of the candles that had made it seem mottled. His fever had come down a little and he slept soundly through the morning and most of the afternoon, not vomiting at all. She went out for more water before it got dark.

Some people recovered spontaneously and some were saved by

prayers. Not everyone died who was infected. The death rate for pneumonic plague was only 90 per cent.

He was awake when she went in, lying in a shaft of smoky light. She knelt and held a cup of water under his mouth, tilting his head up so he could drink.

'It is the blue sickness,' he said when she let his head back down.

'You're not going to die,' she said. Ninety per cent. Ninety per cent.

'You must hear my confession.'

No. He could not die. She would be left here all alone. She shook her head unable to speak.

'Bless me, Father, for I have sinned,' he began in Latin.

He hadn't sinned. He had tended the sick, shriven the dying, buried the dead. It was God who should have to beg forgiveness.

'—in thought, word, deed and omission. I was angry with Lady Imeyne. I shouted at Maisry.' He swallowed. 'I had carnal thoughts of a saint of the Lord.'

Carnal thoughts.

'I humbly ask pardon of God, and absolution of you, Father, if you think me worthy.'

There is nothing to forgive, she wanted to say. Your sins are no sins. Carnal thoughts. We held down Rosemund and barricaded the village against a harmless boy and buried a six-month-old baby. It is the end of the world. Surely you are to be allowed a few carnal thoughts.

She raised her hand helplessly, unable to speak the words of absolution, but he did not seem to notice. 'Oh, my God,' he said, 'I am heartily sorry for having offended Thee.'

Offended Thee. You're the saint of the Lord, she wanted to tell him, and where the hell is He? Why doesn't He come and save you?

There was no oil. She dipped her fingers in the bucket and made the sign of the cross over his eyes and ears, his nose and mouth, his hands that had held her hand when she was dying.

'*Quid quid deliquiste*,' he said, and she dipped her hand in the water again and marked the cross on the soles of his feet.

'*Libera nos, quaesumus, Domine*,' he prompted.

'*Ah omnibus malis,*' Kivrin said, '*praeteritis, praesentibus, et futuris.*' Deliver us, we beseech Thee, O Lord from all evils, past, present, and to come.

'*Perducat te ad vitam aeternam,*' he murmured.

And bring thee unto life everlasting. 'Amen,' Kivrin said, and leaned forward to catch the blood that came pouring out of him.

He vomited the rest of the night and most of the next day, and then sank into unconsciousness in the afternoon, his breathing shallow and unsteady. Kivrin sat beside him, bathing his hot forehead. 'Don't die,' she said when his breathing caught and struggled on, more laboured. 'Don't die,' she said softly. 'What will I do without you? I will be all alone.'

'You must not stay here,' he said. He opened his eyes a little. They were red and swollen.

'I thought you were asleep,' she said regretfully. 'I didn't mean to wake you.'

'You must go again to heaven,' he said, 'and pray for my soul in purgatory, that my time there may be short.'

Purgatory. As if God would make him suffer any longer than he was already.

'You will not need my prayers,' she said.

'You must return to that place whence you came,' he said, and his hand came up in a vague drifting motion in front of his face, as if he were trying to ward off a blow.

Kivrin caught his hand and held it, but gently, so as not to bruise the skin, and laid it against her cheek.

You must return to that place whence you came. Would that I could, she thought. She wondered how long they had held the drop open before they gave up. Four days? A week? Perhaps it was still open. Mr Dunworthy wouldn't have let them close it while there was any hope at all. But there isn't, she thought. I'm not in 1320. I'm here, at the end of the world.

'I can't,' she said. 'I don't know the way.'

'You must try to remember,' Roche said, freeing his hand and waving it. 'Agnes, pass the fork.'

He was delirious. Kivrin got up on her knees, afraid he might try to rise again.

'Where you fell,' he said, putting his hand under the elbow of the waving arm to brace it, and Kivrin realised he was trying to point. 'Pass the fork.'

Past the fork.

'What is past the fork?' she asked.

'The place where first I found you when you fell from heaven,' he said and let his arms fall.

'I thought that Gawyn had found me.'

'Aye,' he said as if he saw no contradiction in what she said. 'I met him on the road while I was bringing you to the manor.'

He had met Gawyn on the road.

'The place where Agnes fell,' he said, trying to help her remember. 'The day we went for the holly.'

Why didn't you tell me when we were *there*? Kivrin thought, but she knew that, too. He had had his hands full with the donkey, which had baulked at the top of the hill and refused to go any further.

Because it saw me come through, she thought, and knew that he had stood over her, in the glade, looking down at her as she lay there with her arm over her face. I heard him, she thought. I saw his footprint.

'You must return to that place, and thence again to heaven,' he said and closed his eyes.

He had seen her come through, had come and stood over her as she lay there with her eyes closed, had put her on his donkey when she was ill. And she had never guessed, not even when she saw him in the church, not even when Agnes told her he thought she was a saint.

Because Gawyn had told her he had found her. Gawyn, who was 'like to boast', and who had wanted more than anything to impress Lady Eliwys. 'I found you and brought you hence,' he had told her, and perhaps he didn't even consider it to be a lie. The village priest was no one, after all. And all the time, when Rosemund was ill and Gawyn had ridden off to Bath and the drop opened and then closed again for ever, Roche had known where it was.

'There is no need to wait for me,' he said. 'No doubt they long for your return.'

'Hush,' she said gently. 'Try to sleep.'

He sank into a troubled doze again, his hands still moving

restlessly, trying to point, and plucking at the coverings. He pushed the covers off and reached for his groin again. Poor man, Kivrin thought, he was not to be spared any indignities.

She placed his hands back on his chest and covered him, but he pushed the covering down again and pulled the tail of his tunic up over his breeches. He grabbed at his groin and then shuddered and let go, and something in the movement made Kivrin think of Rosemund.

She frowned. He had vomited blood. That and the stage the epidemic had reached had made her think he had the pneumonic plague, and she hadn't seen any buboes under his arms when she took his coat off. She pulled the tail of his robe aside, exposing his coarsely woven woollen hose. They were tight round his middle and entangled with the tail of his alb. She would never be able to pull them off without lifting him, and there was so much wadded cloth she couldn't see anything.

She laid her hand gently on his thigh, remembering how sensitive Rosemund's arm had been. He flinched but did not waken, and she slid her hand to the inside and up, only just touching the cloth. It was hot. 'Forgive me,' she said and slid her hand between his legs.

He screamed and made a convulsive movement, his knees coming up sharply, but Kivrin had already jerked back out of the way, her hand over her mouth. The bubo was gigantic and red hot to the touch. She should have lanced it hours ago.

Roche had not awakened, even when he screamed. His face was mottled, and his breath came steadily, noisily. His spasmodic movement had sent his coverings flying again. She stopped and covered him. His knees came up, but less violently, and she pulled the coverings up round him and then took the last candle from the top of the rood screen, put it in the lantern and lit it from one of St Catherine's.

'I'll be back in just a moment,' she said, and went down the nave and out.

The light outside made her blink, though it was nearly evening. The sky was overcast, but there was little wind and it seemed warmer outside than in the church. She ran across the green, shielding the open part of the lantern with her hand.

There was a sharp knife in the barn. She had used it to cut the rope when she was packing the wagon. She would have to sterilise it before she lanced the bubo. She had to open the swollen lymph node before it ruptured. When the buboes were in the groin, they were perilously close to the femoral artery. Even if Roche didn't bleed to death immediately when it ruptured, all that poison would go straight into his bloodstream. It should have been lanced hours ago.

She ran between the barn and the empty pigsty and into the courtyard. The stable door stood open, and she could hear someone inside. Her heart jerked. 'Who is there?' she said, holding the lantern up.

The steward's cow was standing in one of the stalls, eating the spilled oats. It raised its head and lowed at Kivrin, and started towards her at a stumbling run.

'I don't have time,' Kivrin said. She snatched up the knife from where it lay on the tangle of ropes and ran out. The cow followed, lumbering awkwardly because of its overfull udder and mooing piteously.

'Go *away*,' Kivrin said, near tears. 'I have to help him or he'll die.' She looked at the knife. It was filthy. When she had found it in the kitchen it had been dirty, and she had laid it down in the manure and dirt of the barn floor between times while she was cutting the ropes.

She went over to the well and picked up the bucket. There was no more than an inch of water in the bottom, and it had a skin of ice on it. There was not enough even to cover the knife, and it would take for ever to start a fire and bring it to a boil. There was no time for that. The bubo might already have ruptured. What she needed was alcohol, but they had used all the wine lancing the buboes and giving sacraments to all the dying. She thought of the bottle the clerk had had in Rosemund's bower.

The cow shoved against her. 'No,' she said firmly, and pushed open the door of the manor house, carrying the lantern.

It was dark in the anteroom, but the sunlight streamed into the hall through narrow windows, making long, smoky, golden shafts that lit the cold hearth and the high table and the wadmal sack of apples Kivrin had spilled out across it.

The rats didn't run. They looked up at her when she came in, their small black ears twitching, and then went back to the apples. There were nearly a dozen of them on the table, and one sat on Agnes' three-legged stool, its delicate paws up to its face as if it were praying.

She set down the lantern on the floor. 'Get out,' she said.

The rats on the table didn't even look up. The one who was praying did, across its folded paws, a cold, appraising look, as if she were an intruder.

'Get out of here!' she shouted and ran towards them.

They still didn't run. Two of them moved behind the saltcellar, and one of them dropped the apple it was holding with a thunk on to the table. It rolled off the edge and on to the rush-strewn floor.

Kivrin raised her knife. 'Get.' She brought it down on the table, and the rats scattered. 'Out.' She raised it again. She swept the apples off the table and on to the floor. They bounced and rolled on to the rushes. In its surprise or fright, the rat that had been on Agnes' stool ran straight towards Kivrin. 'Of. Here.' She threw the knife at it and it sprinted back under the stool and disappeared in the rushes.

'Get out of here,' Kivrin said and buried her face in her hands.

'Mwaa,' the cow said from the anteroom.

'It's a disease ' Kivrin whispered shakily, her hands still over her mouth. 'It's nobody's fault.'

She went and retrieved the knife and the lantern. The cow had wedged itself halfway through the manor door and got stuck. It lowed at her piteously.

She left it there and went up to the bower ignoring the sounds of skittering above her. The room was icy cold. The linen that Eliwys had fastened over the window had torn loose and was hanging by one corner. The bed hangings were down at one side too, where the clerk had tried to pull himself up on them, and the flock mattress lay half off the bed. There were small sounds from under the bed, but she didn't try to see where they were coming from. The chest was still open, its carved lid propped against the foot of the bed, and the clerk's heavy purple cloak lay folded in it.

The bottle of wine had rolled under the bed. Kivrin flung herself down on the floor and reached under the bed for it. It rolled away from her touch, and she had to crawl halfway under the bed before she could get hold of it.

The stopper had come out, probably when she had kicked it under the bed. A little wine clung stickily to the mouth.

'No,' she said hopelessly, and sat there for a long minute, holding the empty bottle.

There wasn't any wine in the church. Roche had used it all for the last rites.

She suddenly remembered the bottle he had given her to use on Agnes' knee. She wriggled under the bed and swept her arm carefully along the bedboard, afraid of knocking it over. She couldn't remember how much had been in it, but she didn't think she'd used it all.

She nearly knocked it over, in spite of her carefulness, and grabbed for the wide neck as it tilted. She backed out from under the bed and shook it gently. It was nearly half-full. She stuck her knife in the waistband of her jerkin, tucked the bottle under her arm, grabbed up the clerk's cloak and went downstairs. The rats were back, working on the apples, but this time they ran when she started down the stone steps, and she did not try to see where they'd gone.

The cow had worked over half of its body through the anteroom door and was now hopelessly blocking the way. Kivrin set everything down inside the screens, sweeping a space clear of rushes so she could stand the bottle upright on the stone floor, and pushed the cow back out, the cow lowing unhappily the whole time.

Once out, it promptly tried to come back in to Kivrin. 'No,' she said, 'there's no time,' but she went back into the barn and up into the loft and threw down a forkful of hay. Then she scooped up everything and ran back to the church.

Roche had lapsed into unconsciousness. His body had relaxed. His big legs sprawled out in front of him, wide apart, and his hands lay out at his sides, palms up. He looked like a man knocked out by a blow. His breathing was heavy and tremulous, as if he were shivering.

Kivrin covered him with the heavy purple cloak. 'I'm back, Roche,' she said, and patted his outflung arm, but he didn't give any indication that he had heard.

546

She took the guard off the lantern and used the flame to light all the candles. There were only three of Lady Imeyne's candles left, all of them over half-burned. She lit the rushlights, too, and the fat tallow candle in the niche of the statue of St Catherine, and moved them closer to Roche's legs, so she would be able to see.

'I'm going to have to take your hose off,' she said, folding back the coverlid. 'I have to lance the bubo.' She untied the ragged points on the hose and he didn't flinch at her touch, but he moaned a little, and it sounded liquid.

She pulled at the hose, trying to get them down over his hips, and then yanked at the legs, but they were too tight. She would have to cut them off.

'I'm going to cut your hose off,' she said, crawling back to where she'd left the knife and the bottle of wine. 'I'll try not to cut you.' She sniffed at the bottle and then took a little swig and choked. Good. It was old and full of alcohol. She poured it over the blade of the knife, wiped the edge on her leg, poured some more, careful to leave enough to pour over the wound when she had it opened.

'*Beata*,' Roche murmured. His hand groped for his groin.

'It's all right,' Kivrin said. She took hold of one of the legs of his hose and slit the wool. 'I know it hurts now, but I'm going to lance the bubo.' She pulled the rough fabric apart with both hands and blessedly it tore, making a loud ripping sound. Roche's knees contracted. 'No, no, leave your legs down,' Kivrin said, trying to push on his knees. 'I have to lance the bubo.'

She couldn't get them down. She left them for the moment and finished tearing the leg of his hose, reaching under his leg to split the rough cloth the rest of the way up, so she could see the bubo. It was twice as big as Rosemund's and completely black. It should have been lanced hours ago, days ago.

'Roche, please put your legs down,' she said, leaning on them with all her weight. 'I have to open the plague boil.'

There was no response. She was not sure he could respond, that his muscles were not somehow contracting on their own, the way the clerk's had, but she couldn't wait until the spasm, if that was what it was, had passed. It might rupture at any minute.

She stepped away a minute and then knelt down by his feet,

and reached up under his folded legs, gripping the knife. Roche moaned, and she pulled the knife down a little and then moved it forward slowly, carefully, till it touched the bubo.

His kick caught her full in the ribs, sending her sprawling. She let go of the knife and it skittered loudly across the stone floor. The kick had knocked the wind out of Kivrin and she lay there, gasping for air, taking long, wheezing breaths. She tried to sit up. Pain stabbed at her right side and she fell back, clutching at her ribs.

Roche was still screaming, a long, impossible sound, like a tortured animal. Kivrin rolled slowly on to her left side, holding her hand tightly against her ribs, so she could see him. He rocked back and forth like a child, screaming all the while, his legs drawn up protectively to his chest. She could not see the bubo.

Kivrin tried to raise herself, bracing her hand against the stone floor until she was half-sitting, and then edging her hand towards her till she could put both hands down and get on to her knees. She cried out, little whimpering screams that were lost in Roche's. He must have broken some ribs. She spat on her hand, afraid of seeing blood.

When she was finally on her knees, she sat back on her feet a minute, huddling against the pain. 'I'm sorry,' she whispered, 'I didn't mean to hurt you.' She half-crawled towards him on her knees, using her right hand as a crutch. The effort made her breathe more deeply, and every breath stabbed into her side. 'It's all right, Roche,' she whispered. 'I'm coming. I'm coming.'

He pulled his legs up spasmodically at the sound of her voice, and she moved round to his side, between him and the side wall, well out of his reach. When he kicked her, he had knocked over one of St Catherine's candles, and it lay in a yellow puddle beside him, still burning Kivrin set it upright and laid her hand on his shoulder. 'Shh, Roche,' she said. 'It's all right. I'm here now.'

He stopped screaming. 'I'm sorry,' she said, leaning over him. 'I didn't mean to hurt you. I was only trying to lance the bubo.'

His knees pulled up even tighter than before. Kivrin picked up the red candle and held it above his naked backside. She could see the bubo, black and hard in the candle's light. She had not even pierced it. She raised the candle higher, trying to see where the knife had gone. It had clattered away in the direction of the tomb.

She held the candle out in that direction, hoping to catch a glint of metal. She couldn't see anything.

She started to stand up, moving carefully to guard against the pain, but halfway to her feet it caught at her, and she cried out and bent forward.

'What is it?' Roche said. His eyes were open, and there was a little blood at the corner of his mouth. She wondered if he had bitten through his tongue when he was screaming. 'Have I done hurt to you?'

'No,' she said, kneeling back down beside him. 'No. You have done no hurt.' She blotted at his mouth with the sleeve of her jerkin.

'You must,' he said, and when he opened his mouth, more blood leaked out. He swallowed. 'You must say the prayers for the dying.'

'No,' she said. 'You will not die.' She wiped at his mouth again. 'But I must lance your bubo before it ruptures.'

'Do not,' he said, and she did not know whether he meant don't lance the bubo or don't leave. His teeth were gritted, and blood was leaking between them. She sank into a sitting position, careful not to cry out, and took his head on to her lap.

'*Requiem aeternam dona eis,*' he said and made a gurgling sound, '*et lux perpetua.*'

The blood was seeping from the roof of his mouth. She propped his head up higher, wadding the purple coverlet under it, wiping his mouth and chin with her jerkin. It was sodden with blood. She reached off to the side for his alb. 'Do not,' he said.

'I won't,' she said. 'I'm right here.'

'Pray for me,' he said and tried to bring his hands together on his chest. 'Wreck—' He choked on the word he was trying to say, and it ended in a gurgling sound.

'*Requiem aeternam,*' Kivrin said. She folded her own hands. '*Requiem aeternam dona eis, Domine,*' she said.

'*Et lux*—' he said.

The red candle beside Kivrin flickered out, and the church was filled with the sharp smell of smoke. She glanced round at the other candles. There was only one left, the last of lady Imeyne's wax candles, and it was burnt nearly down to the lip of its holder.

'*Et lux perpetua,*' Kivrin said.

'*Luceat eis,*' Roche said. He stopped and tried to lick his bloody lips. His tongue was swollen and stiff. '*Dies irae, dies illa.*' He swallowed again and tried to close his eyes.

'Don't put him through any more of this,' she whispered in English. 'Please. It's not fair.'

'*Beata,*' she thought he said and tried to think of the next line, but it didn't begin with 'blessed'.

'What?' she said, leaning over him.

'In the last days,' he said, his voice blurred by his swollen tongue.

She leaned closer.

'I feared that God would forsake us utterly,' he said.

And He has, she thought. She wiped at his mouth and chin with the tail of her jerkin. He has.

'But in His great mercy He did not,' he swallowed again, 'but sent His saint unto us.'

He raised his head and coughed, and blood rushed out over both of them, saturating his chest and her knees. She wiped at it frantically, trying to stop it, trying to keep his head up, and she couldn't see through her tears to wipe the blood away.

'And I'm no use,' she said, wiping at her tears.

'Why do you weep?' he said.

'You saved my life,' she said, and her voice caught in a sob, 'and I can't save yours.'

'All men must die,' Roche said, 'and none, nor even Christ, can save them.'

'I know,' she said. She cupped her hand under her face, trying to catch her tears. They collected on her hand and fell dripping on to Roche's neck.

'Yet have you saved me,' he said, and his voice sounded clearer. 'From fear.' He took a gurgling breath. 'And unbelief.'

She wiped at her tears with the back of her hand and took hold of Roche's hand. It felt cold and already stiff.

'I am most blessed of all men to have you here with me,' he said and closed his eyes.

Kivrin shifted a little so her back was against the wall. It was dark outside, no light at all coming in through the narrow windows. Lady Imeyne's candle sputtered and then flamed again. She moved Roche's head so it didn't push against her ribs. He groaned and his hand jerked as if to free itself of hers, but she held on. The candle flickered into sudden brightness and left them in darkness.

***

Transcript from the Domesday Book
(082808–083108)

I don't think I'm going to make it back, Mr Dunworthy. Roche told me where the drop is, but I've broken some ribs, I think, and all the horses are gone. I don't think I can get up on Roche's donkey without a saddle.

I'm going to try to see to it that Ms Montoya finds this. Tell Mr Latimer adjectival inflection was still prominent in 1348. And tell Mr Gilchrist he was wrong. The statistics weren't exaggerated.

(Break)

I don't want you to blame yourself for what happened. I know you would have come to get me if you could, but I couldn't have gone anyway, not with Agnes ill.

I wanted to come, and if I hadn't, they would have been all alone, and nobody would have ever known how frightened and brave and irreplaceable they were.

(Break)

It's strange. When I couldn't find the drop and the plague came, you seemed so far away I would not ever be able to find you again. But I know now that you were here all along, and that nothing, not the Black Death nor seven hundred years, nor death, nor things to come, nor any other creature could ever separate me from your caring and concern. It was with me every minute.

***

CHAPTER THIRTY-FOUR

'Colin!' Dunworthy shouted, grabbing Colin's arm as he dived under the drape and into the net, head down. 'What in God's name do you think you're doing?'

Colin twisted free of his grasp. 'I don't think you should go alone!'

'You can't just break through the net! This isn't a quarantine perimeter. What if the net had opened? You could have been killed!' He took hold of Colin's arm again and started towards the console. 'Badri! Hold the drop!'

Badri was not there. Dunworthy squinted nearsightedly at where the console had been. They were in a forest, surrounded by trees. There was snow on the ground and the air sparkled with crystals.

'If you go alone, who'll take care of you?' Colin said. 'What if you have a relapse?' He looked past Dunworthy and his mouth fell open. 'Are we there?'

Dunworthy let go of Colin's arm and grabbed in his jerkin for his spectacles.

'Badri!' he shouted. 'Open the drop!' He put on his spectacles. They were covered with frost. He yanked them off again and scraped at the lenses. 'Badri!'

'Where are we?' Colin asked.

Dunworthy hooked his spectacles over his ears and looked around at the trees. They were ancient, the ivy twining their trunks silver with frost. There was no sign of Kivrin.

He had expected her to be here, which was ridiculous. They had already opened the drop and not found her, but he had hoped that when she realised where she was, she would come back to the drop and wait. But she wasn't here, and there was no sign she had ever been.

The snow they were standing in was smooth and free of footprints. It was deep enough to hide any she might have left before it fell, but it wasn't deep enough to have hidden the smashed cart and the scattered boxes. And there was no sign of the Oxford-Bath road.

'I don't know where we are,' he said.

'Well, I know it's not Oxford,' Colin said, stamping through the snow. 'Because it's not raining.'

Dunworthy looked up through the trees at the pale, clear sky. If there had been the same amount of slippage as in Kivrin's drop, it would be midmorning.

Colin darted off through the snow towards a thicket of reddish willows.

'Where are you going?' Dunworthy said.

'To find a road. The drop's supposed to be near a road, isn't it?' He plunged into the thicket and disappeared.

'Colin!' he shouted, starting after him. 'Come back here.'

'Here it is!' Colin called from somewhere beyond the willows. 'The road's here!'

'Come back here!' Dunworthy shouted.

Colin reappeared, holding the willows apart.

'Come here,' he said more calmly.

'It goes up a hill,' Colin said, squeezing through the willows into the clearing. 'We can climb it and see where we are.'

He was already wet, his brown coat covered with snow from the willows, and he looked wary, braced for bad news.

'You're sending me back, aren't you?'

'I must,' Dunworthy said, but his heart sank at the prospect. Badri would not have the drop open for at least two hours, and he was not certain how long it would stay open. He didn't have two hours to spare, waiting here to send Colin through, and he couldn't leave him behind. 'You're my responsibility.'

'And you're mine,' Colin said stubbornly. 'Great-aunt Mary told me to take care of you. What if you have a relapse?'

'You don't understand. The Black Death—'

'It's all right. Really. I've had the streptomycin and all that. I made William have his nurse give them to me. You can't send me back now, the drop isn't open, and it's too cold to just stay here and wait for an hour. If we go and look for Kivrin now, we might have found her by then.'

He was right about their not being able to remain here. The cold was already seeping through the outlandish Victorian cape, and Colin's burlap coat was even less protection than his old jacket and as wet.

'We'll go to the top of the hill,' he said, 'but first we must mark the clearing so we can find it again. And you can't go running off like that. I want you in sight at all times. I don't have time to go looking for you as well.'

'I won't get lost,' Colin said, rummaging in his pack. He held up a flat rectangle. 'I brought a locator. It's already set to home in on the clearing.'

He held the willows apart for Dunworthy, and they went out to the road. It was scarcely a cow path and was covered with snow unmarked except by the tracks of squirrels and a dog, or possibly a wolf. Colin walked obediently at Dunworthy's side till they were halfway up the hill and then couldn't restrain himself and took off running.

Dunworthy trudged after him, fighting the tightness already in his chest. The trees stopped halfway up the hill, and the wind began where they left off. It was bitingly cold.

'I can see the village,' Colin shouted down to him.

He came up beside Colin. The wind was worse here, cutting straight through the cape, lining or no lining, and pushing long streamers of cloud across the pale sky. Far off to the south a plume of smoke climbed straight into the sky, and then, caught by the wind, veered off sharply to the east.

'See?' Colin said, pointing.

A rolling plain lay below them, covered in snow almost too bright to look at. The bare trees and the roads stood out darkly against it, like markings on a map. The Oxford–Bath road was a straight black line, bisecting the snowy plain, and Oxford a pencil drawing. He could see the snowy roofs and the square tower of St Michael's above the dark walls.

'It doesn't look like the Black Death is here yet, does it?' Colin said.

Colin was right. It looked serene, untouched, the ancient Oxford of legend. It was impossible to imagine it overrun with the plague, the dead carts full of bodies being pulled through the narrow streets, the colleges boarded up and abandoned and everywhere the dying and the already dead. Impossible to imagine Kivrin out there somewhere, in one of those villages he could not see.

'Can't you see it?' Colin said, pointing south. 'Behind those trees.'

He squinted trying to make out buildings among the cluster of trees. He could see a darker shape among the grey branches, the tower of a church, perhaps, or the angle of a barn.

'There's the road that leads to it,' Colin said, pointing to a narrow grey line that began somewhere below them.

Dunworthy examined the map Montoya had given him. There was no way to tell which village it was, even with her notes, without knowing how far they were from the intended drop site. If they were directly south of it, the village was too far east to be Skendgate, but where he thought it should be there were no trees, nothing, only a flat field of snow.

'Well?' Colin said. 'Are we going to it?'

It was the only village visible, if it was a village, and it looked to be no more than a kilometre away. If it was not Skendgate, it was at least in the proper direction, and if it had one of Montoya's 'distinguishing characteristics', they could use it to get their bearings.

'You must keep with me at all times and speak to no one, do you understand?'

Colin nodded, clearly not listening. 'I think the road is this way,' he said and ran down the far side of the hill.

Dunworthy followed, trying not to think how many villages there were, how little time there was, how tired he was after only one hill.

'How did you talk William into the streptomycin inoculations?' he asked when he caught up with Colin.

'He wanted Great-aunt Mary's med number so he could forge the authorisations. It was in the kit in her shopping bag.'

'And you refused to give it to him unless he agreed?'

'Yes, and I told him I'd tell his mother about all his girls,' he said and ran off ahead again.

The road he'd seen was a hedge. Dunworthy refused to set off through the field it bordered. 'We must keep to the roads,' he said.

'This is quicker,' Colin protested. 'It isn't as if we can get lost. We've got the locator.'

Dunworthy refused to argue. He continued along the road, looking for a turning. The narrow fields gave way to woods and the road turned back to the north.

'What if there isn't a road that leads to the village?' Colin said after half a kilometre, but at the next turning there was one.

It was narrower than the one past the drop, and no one had travelled along it since the snow. They waded into it, their feet breaking through the frozen crust at every step. Dunworthy looked anxiously ahead for a glimpse of the village, but the woods were too thick to see through.

The snow made it slow going, and he was already out of breath, the tightness in his chest like an iron band.

'What do we do when we get there?' Colin asked striding effortlessly through the snow.

'*You* stay out of sight and wait for me,' Dunworthy said. 'Is that perfectly clear?'

'Yes,' Colin said. 'Are you certain this is the right road?'

He was not certain at all. It had been curving west, away from the direction Dunworthy thought the village lay in, and just ahead it bent north again. He peered anxiously through the trees, trying to catch a glimpse of stone or thatch.

'The village wasn't this far, I'm sure of it,' Colin said, rubbing his arms. 'We've been walking for hours.'

It had not been hours, but it had been at least an hour, and they had not come to so much as a cottar's hut, let alone a village. There were a score of villages here, but where?

Colin took out his locator. 'See,' he said, showing Dunworthy the readout. 'We've come too far south. I think we should go back to the other road.'

Dunworthy looked at the readout and then at the map. They were nearly due south of the drop and over three kilometres from it. They would have to retrace their steps nearly all the way, with no hope of finding Kivrin in that time, and at the end of it, he was not certain he would be able to go any further. He already felt done in, the band tightening round his chest with every step, and he had a sharp pain midway up his ribs. He turned and looked at the curve ahead, trying to think what to do.

'My feet are freezing,' Colin said. He stamped his feet in the snow and a bird flew up, startled and flapped away. Dunworthy looked up, frowning. The sky was becoming overcast.

'We should have followed the hedge,' Colin said. 'It would have been much—'

'Hush,' Dunworthy said.

'What is it?' Colin whispered. 'Is someone coming?'

'Shh,' Dunworthy whispered. He backed Colin to the edge of the road and listened again. He'd thought he'd heard a horse, but now he couldn't hear anything. It might only have been the bird.

He motioned Colin behind a tree. 'Stay here,' he whispered and crept forward till he could see round the curve.

The black stallion was tied to a thorn bush. Dunworthy backed hastily behind a spruce tree and stood still, trying to see the rider. There was no one in the road. He waited trying to quiet his own breathing so he could hear, but no one came and he could hear nothing but the stallion's pacing.

It was saddled and its bridle was chased with silver, but it looked thin, its ribs standing out sharply against the girth. The girth itself was loose, and the saddle slipped a little to the side as the stallion stepped backward. It tossed its head pulling hard against the reins. It was obviously trying to free itself, and as Dunworthy moved closer he could see it was not tied but tangled in the brambles.

He stepped into the road. The stallion turned its head towards him and began to whinny wildly.

'There, there, it's all right,' he said, coming up carefully on its left side. He put his hand on its neck, and it stopped whinnying and began nosing at Dunworthy, looking for food.

He looked for some grass sticking up through the snow to feed it, but the area around the thornbush was nearly bare.

'How long have you been trapped here, old boy?' he asked. Had the stallion's owner been stricken with the plague as he rode, or had he died and the panicked horse bolted running until its flying reins got tangled in the bush?

He walked a little way into the woods, looking for footprints, but there weren't any. The stallion began to whinny again, and he went back to free it, snatching up stalks of grass that stuck up through the snow as he went.

'A horse! Apocalyptic!' Colin said, racing up. 'Where did you find it?'

'I told you to stay where you were.'

'I know, but I heard the horse whinnying and I thought you'd run into trouble.'

'All the more reason for you to have obeyed me.' He handed the grass to Colin. 'Feed him these.'

He bent over the bush and pulled out the reins. The stallion, in its efforts to extricate itself, had twisted the rein hopelessly round the spiked brambles. Dunworthy had to hold the branches back with one hand and reach in with the other to unwind it. He was covered with scratches within seconds.

'Whose horse is it?' Colin asked, offering the horse a piece of grass from a distance of several feet. The starving animal lunged at it and Colin jumped back, dropping it. 'Are you sure it's tame?'

Dunworthy had incurred a near-fatal injury when the stallion jerked its head down for the grass, but he had the rein free. He wrapped it round his bleeding hand and took up the other one.

'Yes,' he said.

'Whose horse is it?' Colin said, stroking its nose timidly.

'Ours.' He tightened the girth and helped Colin, protesting up behind the saddle, and mounted.

The stallion, not yet realising it was free, turned its head accusingly when he kicked it gently in the sides but then cantered off back down the snow-packed road, delighted at its freedom.

Colin clutched frantically at Dunworthy's middle, just at the spot where the pain was, but by the time they had gone a hundred metres, he was sitting up straight and asking 'How do you steer it?' and 'What if you want it to go faster?'

It took them no time at all to return to the main road. Colin wanted to go back to the hedge and strike out across country, but Dunworthy turned the stallion the other way. The road forked in half a kilometre and he took the left-hand road.

It was a good deal more travelled than the first one, though the woods it led through were even thicker. The sky was completely overcast now, and the wind was picking up.

'I see it!' Colin said, and let go with one hand to point past a stand of ash trees to a glimpse of dark grey stone roof against the grey sky. A church, perhaps, or a manor house. It lay off to the east, and almost immediately a narrow track branched from the road over a rickety wooden plank bridging a stream, and across a narrow meadow.

The stallion did not prick up its ears or attempt to speed its pace, and Dunworthy concluded it must not be from this village. And a good thing, too, or we'd be hanged for horse stealing before we could ask where Kivrin is, he thought, and saw the sheep.

They lay on their sides, mounds of dirty grey wool, though some of them had huddled near the trees, trying to keep out of the wind and the snow.

Colin hadn't seen. 'What do we do when we get there?' he asked Dunworthy's back. 'Do we sneak in or just ride up and ask somebody if they've seen her?'

There will be no one to ask, Dunworthy thought. He kicked the stallion into a canter, and they rode through the ash trees and into the village.

It was not at all like the illustrations in Colin's book, buildings round a central clearing. They were scattered in among the trees, almost out of sight of one another. He glimpsed thatched roofs, and further off, in a grove of ash trees, the church, but here, in a clearing as small as that of the drop, was only a timbered house and a low shed.

It was too small to be a manor house – the steward's perhaps, or the reeve's. The wooden door of the shed stood open, and snow had drifted in. There was no smoke from the roof, and no sound.

'Perhaps they've fled,' Colin said. 'Lots of people fled when they heard the plague was coming. That's how it spread.'

Perhaps they had fled. The snow in front of the house was packed flat and hard, as if many people and horses had been in the yard.

'Stay here with the horse,' he said, and went up to the house. The door here was not shut either, though it had been pulled nearly to. He ducked in the little door.

It was icy inside and so dark after the bright snow that he could see nothing except the red after-image. He pushed the door open all the way, but there was still scarcely any light, and everything seemed tinged with red.

It must be the steward's house. There were two rooms, separated by a timbered partition, and matting on the floor. The table was bare, and the fire on the hearth had been out for days. The little room was filled with the smell of cold ashes. The steward and his family had fled, and perhaps the rest of the villagers too, no doubt taking the plague with them. And Kivrin.

He leaned against the doorjamb, the tightness in his chest suddenly a pain again. Of all his worries over Kivrin, this one had never occurred to him, that she would have gone.

He looked into the other room.

Colin ducked his head in the door. 'The horse keeps trying to drink out of a bucket that's out here. Should I let it?'

'Yes,' Dunworthy said, standing so Colin couldn't see round the partition. 'But don't let him drink too much. He hasn't had any water for days.'

'There isn't all that much in the bucket.' He looked round the room interestedly. 'This is one of the serf's huts, right? They really were poor, weren't they? Did you find anything?'

'No,' he said. 'Go and watch the horse. And don't let him wander off.'

Colin went out, brushing his head against the top of the door.

The baby lay on a bag of flocking in the corner. It had apparently still been alive when the mother died; she lay on the mud floor, her hands stretched out towards it. Both bodies were dark, almost black, and the baby's swaddling clothes were stiff with darkened blood.

'Mr Dunworthy!' Colin called, sounding alarmed, and Dunworthy jerked round afraid he had come in again, but he was still out with the stallion, whose nose was deep in the bucket.

'What is it?' he asked.

'There's something over there on the ground.' Colin pointed towards the huts. 'I think it's a body.' He yanked on the stallion's reins, so hard the bucket fell over and a thin puddle of water spilled out on the snow.

'Wait,' Dunworthy said, but Colin was already running forward into the trees, the stallion following.

'It is a b—' Colin said, and his voice cut off sharply. Dunworthy ran up, holding his side.

It was a body, a young man's. He lay sprawled face-up in the snow in a frozen puddle of black liquid. There was a dusting of snow on his face. His buboes must have burst, Dunworthy thought, and looked at Colin, but Colin was not looking at the body, but at the clearing.

It was larger than the one in front of the steward's house. At its edges lay half a dozen huts, at the far end the Norman church. And in the centre, on the trampled snow, lay the bodies.

They had made no attempt at burying them, though by the church there was a shallow trench, a mound of snow-covered earth piled beside it. Some of them seemed to have been dragged to the churchyard – there were long, sledlike marks in the snow – and one at least had crawled to the door of his hut. He lay half in, half out.

' "Fear God," ' Dunworthy murmured, ' "for the hour of His judgment is come." '

'It looks like there was a battle here,' Colin said.

'There was,' Dunworthy said.

Colin stepped forward, peering down at the body. 'Do you think they're all dead?'

'Don't touch them,' Dunworthy said. 'Don't even go near them.'

'I've had the gamma globulin,' he said, but he stepped back from the body, swallowing.

'Take deep breaths,' Dunworthy said, putting his hand on Colin's shoulder. 'And look at something else.'

561

'They said in the book it was like this,' he said, staring determinedly at an oak tree. 'Actually, I was afraid it might be a good deal worse. I mean, it doesn't smell or anything.'

'Yes.'

He swallowed again. 'I'm all right now.' He looked round the clearing. 'Where do you think Kivrin's likely to be?'

Not here, Dunworthy prayed.

'She might be in the church,' Colin said, starting forward with the stallion again, 'and we need to see if the tomb's there. This might not be the right village.' The stallion took two steps forward and reared its head its ears back. It whinnied frightenedly.

'Go and put him in the shed,' Dunworthy said, taking hold of the reins. 'He can smell the blood, and he's frightened. Tie him up.'

He led the stallion back out of sight of the body and handed the reins to Colin, who took them, looking worried. 'It's all right,' he said, leading it towards the steward's house. 'I know just how you feel.'

Dunworthy walked rapidly across the clearing to the churchyard. There were four bodies in the shallow pit and two graves next to it, covered with snow, the first to die perhaps, when there were still such things as funerals. He went round to the front of the church.

There were two more bodies in front of the door. They lay face-down, on top of one another, the one on top an old man. The body underneath was a woman's. He could see the skirts of her rough cloak and one of her hands. The man's arms were flung across the woman's head and shoulders.

Dunworthy lifted the man's arm gingerly, and his body shifted slightly sideways, pulling the cloak with it. The kirtle underneath was dirty and smeared with blood, but he could see that it had been bright blue. He pulled the hood back. There was a rope round the woman's neck. Her long blonde hair was tangled in the rough fibres.

They hanged her, he thought with no surprise at all.

Colin ran up. 'I figured out what these marks on the ground are,' he said. 'They're where they dragged the bodies. There's a little boy behind the barn with a rope round his neck.'

Dunworthy looked at the rope, at the tangle of hair. It was so dirty it was scarcely blonde.

'They dragged them to the churchyard because they couldn't carry them, I bet,' Colin said.

'Did you put the stallion in the shed?'

'Yes. I tied it to a beam thing,' he said. 'It wanted to come with me.'

'He's hungry,' Dunworthy said. 'Go back to the shed and give him some hay.'

'Did something happen?' Colin asked. 'You're not having a relapse, are you?'

Dunworthy didn't think Colin could see her dress from where he stood. 'No,' he said. 'There should be some hay in the shed. Or some oats. Go and feed the stallion.'

'All right,' Colin said defensively, and ran towards the shed. He stopped halfway across the green. 'I don't have to give it the hay, do I?' he shouted. 'Can I just lay it down in front of it?'

'Yes,' Dunworthy said, looking at her hand. There was blood on her hand too, and down the inside of her wrist. Her arm was bent, as though she had tried to break her fall. He could take hold of her elbow and turn her on to her back quite easily. All it required was to take hold of her elbow.

He picked up her hand. It was stiff and cold. Under the dirt it was red and chapped, the skin split in a dozen places. It could not possibly be Kivrin's, and if it were, what had she gone through these past two weeks to bring her to this state?

It would all be on the corder. He turned her hand gently over, looking for the implant scar, but her wrist was too caked with dirt for him to be able to see it, if it was there.

And if it was, what then? Call Colin back and send him for an axe in the steward's kitchen and chop it out of her dead hand so they could listen to her voice reciting the horrors that had happened to her? He could not do it, of course, any more than he could turn her body over and know once and for all that it was Kivrin.

He laid the hand gently back next to the body and took hold of her elbow and turned her over.

She had died of the bubonic variety. There was a foul yellow stain down the side of her blue kirtle where the bubo under her arm had split and run. Her tongue was black and so swollen it filled her entire mouth, like some ghastly, obscene object thrust between her teeth to choke her, and her pale face was swollen and distorted.

It was not Kivrin. He tried to stand, staggering a little, and then thought, too late, that he should have covered the woman's face.

'Mr Dunworthy!' Colin shouted, coming at a dead run, and he looked up blindly, helplessly at him.

'What's *happened*?' Colin said accusingly. 'Did you find her?'

'No,' he said, blocking Colin's way. 'We're not going to find her.'

Colin was looking past him at the woman. Her face was bluish-white against the white snow, the bright blue dress. 'You found her, didn't you? Is that her?'

'No,' Dunworthy said. But it could be. It could be. And I cannot turn over any more bodies, thinking it might be. His knees felt watery, as though they would not support him. 'Help me back to the shed,' he said.

Colin stood stubbornly where he was. 'If it's her, you can tell me. I can bear it.'

But I can't, Dunworthy thought. I can't bear it if she's dead.

He started back towards the steward's house, keeping one hand on the cold stone wall of the church and wondering what he would do when he came to open space.

Colin leaped beside him, taking his arm, looking anxiously at him. 'What's the matter? Are you having a relapse?'

'I just need to rest a bit,' he said and went on, almost without meaning to, 'Kivrin wore a blue dress when she went.' When she went, when she lay down on the ground and closed her eyes, helpless and trusting, and disappeared for ever into this chamber of horrors.

Colin pushed the door of the shed open and helped Dunworthy inside, holding him up with both hands on his arm. The stallion looked up from a sack of oats.

'I couldn't find any hay,' Colin said, 'so I gave it some grain. Horses eat grain, don't they?'

564

'Yes,' Dunworthy said, leaning into the sacks. 'Don't let him eat them all. He'll gorge himself and burst.'

Colin went over to the sack and began dragging it out of the stallion's reach. 'Why did you think it was Kivrin?' he said.

'I saw the blue dress,' Dunworthy said. 'Kivrin's dress was that colour.'

The bag was too heavy for Colin. He yanked on it with both hands, and the side split, spilling oats on the straw. The stallion nibbled eagerly at them. 'No, I mean all those people died of the plague, didn't they? And she's been immunised. So she couldn't get the plague. And what else would she die of?'

Of this, Dunworthy thought. No one could have lived through this, watching children and infants die like animals, piling them in pits and shovelling earth over them, dragging them along with a rope round their dead necks. How could she have survived this?

Colin had manoeuvred the sack out of reach. He let it fall next to a small chest and came over and stood in front of Dunworthy, a little breathless. 'Are you sure you're not having a relapse?'

'No,' he said, but he was already beginning to shiver.

'Perhaps you're just tired,' Colin said. 'You rest, and I'll be back in a moment.'

He went out, pushing the shed's door shut behind him. The stallion was nibbling the oats Colin had spilled, taking noisy, chomping bites. Dunworthy stood up, holding on to the rough beam, and went over to the little casket. The brass bindings had tarnished and the leather on the lid had a small gouge in it, but otherwise it looked brand-new.

He sat down beside it and opened the lid. The steward had used it for his tools. There was a coil of leather rope in it and a rusty mattock head. The blue cloth lining Gilchrist had talked about in the pub was torn where the mattock had lain against it.

Colin came back in, carrying the bucket. 'I brought you some water,' he said. 'I got it out of the stream.' He set the bucket down and fumbled in his pockets for a bottle. 'I've only got ten aspirin, so you can't have much of a relapse. I stole them from Mr Finch.'

He shook two into his hands. 'I stole some synthomycin too, but I was afraid it hadn't been invented yet. I figured they had to have had aspirin.' He handed the aspirin tablets to Dunworthy

565

and brought the bucket over. 'You'll have to use your hand. I thought the contemps' bowls and things were probably full of plague germs.'

Dunworthy swallowed the aspirin and scooped a handful of water out of the bucket to wash it down. 'Colin,' he said.

Colin took the bucket over to the stallion. 'I don't think this is the right village. I went in the church and the only tomb in there was of some lady.' He pulled the map and the locator out of another pocket. 'We're still too far east. I think we're here' – he pointed at one of Montoya's notes – 'so if we go back to that other road and then cut straight east—'

'We're going back to the drop,' Dunworthy said. He stood up carefully, not touching the wall or the trunk.

'Why? Badri said we had a day at least, and we've only checked one village. There are lots of villages. She could be in any of them.'

Dunworthy untied the stallion.

'I could take the horse and go look for her,' Colin said. 'I could ride really fast and look in all these villages and then come back and tell you as soon as I find her. Or we could split up the villages and each take half, and whoever finds her first could send some kind of signal. We could light a fire or something and then the other one would see it and come.'

'She's dead Colin. We're not going to find her.'

'Don't *say* that!' Colin said, and his voice sounded high and childish. 'She *isn't* dead! She had her inoculations!'

Dunworthy pointed at the leather casket. 'This is the casket she brought through.'

'Well, what if it is?' Colin said. 'There could be lots of chests like it. Or she could have run away, when the plague came. We can't go back and just leave her here! What if it was me that was lost and I waited and waited for somebody to come and nobody did?' His nose had begun to run.

'Colin,' Dunworthy said helplessly, 'sometimes you do everything you can, and you still can't save them.'

'Like Great-aunt Mary,' Colin said. He swiped at his tears with the back of his hand. 'But not always.'

Always, Dunworthy thought. 'No,' he said. 'Not always.'

'Sometimes you can save them,' Colin said stubbornly.

'Yes,' he said. 'All right.' He tied the stallion up again. 'We'll go and look for her. Give me two more aspirin, and let me rest a bit till they take effect, and we'll go and look for her.'

'Apocalyptic,' Colin said. He grabbed the bucket away from the stallion, who had gone back to slurping it. 'I'll fetch some more water.'

He went running out, and Dunworthy eased himself to sitting against the wall. 'Please,' he said. 'Please let us find her.'

The door opened slowly. Colin, standing in the light, was outlined in radiance. 'Did you hear it?' he demanded. 'Listen.'

It was a faint sound, muffled by the walls of the shed. And there was a long pause between peals, but he could hear it. He stood up and went outside.

'It's coming from over there,' Colin said, pointing towards the south-west.

'Get the stallion,' Dunworthy said.

'Are you certain it's Kivrin?' Colin said. 'It's the wrong direction.'

'It's Kivrin,' he said.

CHAPTER THIRTY-FIVE

The bell stopped before they even got the stallion saddled. 'Hurry!' Dunworthy said, cinching the girth strap.

'It's all right,' Colin said, looking at the map. 'It rang three times. I've got a fix on it. It's due south-west, right? And this is Henefelde, right?' He held it in front of Dunworthy, pointing to each place in turn. 'Then it's got to be this village here.'

Dunworthy glanced at it and then towards the south-west again, trying to keep the direction of the bell clear in his mind. He was already unsure of it, though he could still feel the throbbing of its tolling. He wished the aspirin would take effect soon.

'Come on, then,' Colin said, pulling the stallion over to the door of the shed. 'Get on, and let's go.'

Dunworthy put his foot in the stirrup and swung the other leg over. He was instantly dizzy. Colin looked speculatively at him, and then said, 'I think I'd better drive,' and swung himself up in front of Dunworthy.

Colin's kick on the stallion's flanks was too gentle and his yanking on the reins too violent but the stallion, amazingly, moved off docilely across the green and on to the lane.

'We know where the village is,' Colin said confidently. 'All we need to find is a road that goes in that direction,' and almost immediately declared that they had found it. It was a fairly wide path, and it led down a slope and into a stand of pines, but only a few yards into the trees it split in two, and Colin looked questioningly back at Dunworthy.

The stallion didn't hesitate. It started off down the right-hand path. 'Look, it knows where it's going,' Colin said delightedly.

I'm glad one of us does, Dunworthy thought, pressing his eyes

568

shut against the jouncing landscape and the throbbing. The stallion, given its head, was obviously going home, and he knew he should tell Colin that, but the illness was closing in on him again, and he was afraid to let go of Colin's waist for even a moment, for fear the fever would get away from him. He was so cold. That was the fever, of course, the throbbing, the dizziness, they were all the fever, and a fever was a good sign, the body marshalling its forces to fight off the virus, assembling the troops. The chill was only a side effect of the fever.

'Blood, it's getting colder,' Colin said, pulling his coat closed with one hand. 'I hope it doesn't snow.' He let go of the reins altogether and pulled his muffler up round his mouth and nose. The stallion didn't even notice. It plodded steadily ahead through deeper and deeper woods. They came to another fork and then another, and each time Colin consulted the map and the locator, but Dunworthy couldn't tell which fork he chose or whether the horse had simply kept on in the direction it had set.

It began to snow, or they rode into it. All at once it was snowing, small steady flakes that obscured the path and melted on Dunworthy's spectacles.

The aspirin began to take effect Dunworthy sat up straighter and pulled his own cloak about him. He wiped his spectacles on the tail of it. His fingers were numb and bright red. He rubbed his hands together and blew on them. They were still in the woods, and the path was narrower than when they started.

'The map says Skendgate is five kilometres from Henefelde,' Colin said, wiping snow off the locator, 'and we've come at least four, so we're nearly there.'

They were not nearly anywhere. They were in the middle of the Wychwood, on a cow path or a deer trail. It would end at a cottar's hut or a salt lick, or a berry bush the horse had fond memories of.

'See, I told you,' Colin said, and there, past the trees, was the top of a bell tower. The stallion broke into a canter. 'Stop,' Colin said to the stallion, pulling on the reins. 'Wait a minute.'

Dunworthy took the reins and slowed the horse to a reluctant walk as they came out of the woods, past a snow-covered meadow, and to the top of the hill.

The village lay below them, past a stand of ash trees, obscured by the snow so that they could only make out grey outlines: manor house, huts, church, bell tower. It wasn't the right village – Skendgate didn't have a bell tower – but if Colin had noticed, he didn't say anything. He kicked the stallion ineffectually a few times, and they rode slowly down the hill, Dunworthy still holding on to the reins.

There were no bodies Dunworthy could see, but there were no people either, and no smoke from the huts. The bell tower looked silent and deserted, and there were no footprints around it.

Halfway down the hill, Colin said, 'I saw something.' Dunworthy had seen it, too. A flicker of movement that could have been a bird or a moving branch. 'Just over there,' Colin said, pointing towards the second hut. A cow wandered out from between the huts, untied, its teats bulging, and Dunworthy was certain of what he'd feared, that the plague had been here, too.

'It's a cow,' Colin said disgustedly. The cow looked up at the sound of Colin's voice and began to walk towards them, lowing.

'Where is everybody?' Colin said. 'Somebody had to ring the bell.'

They're all dead, Dunworthy thought, looking towards the churchyard. There were new graves there, the earth mounded up over them and the snow still not completely covering them. Hopefully, they're all buried in that churchyard, he thought, and saw the first body. It was a young boy. He was sitting with his back to a tombstone, as if he were resting.

'Look, there's somebody,' Colin said, yanking back on the reins and pointing at the body. 'Hello there!'

He twisted round to look at Dunworthy. 'Will they understand what we say, do you think?'

'He's—' Dunworthy said.

The boy stood up, hauling himself painfully to his feet, one hand on the tombstone for support, looking around as if for a weapon.

'We won't hurt you,' Dunworthy called, trying to think what the Middle English would be. He slid down from the stallion, clinging to the back of the saddle at the abrupt dizziness. He straightened and extended his hand, palm outward, towards the boy.

The boy's face was filthy, streaked and smeared with dirt and blood, and the front of his smock and rolled-up trousers were soaked and stiff with it. He bent down, holding his side as if the movement hurt him, picked up a stick that had been lying covered with snow, and stepped forward, barring his way. '*Kepe from baire. Der fevreblau hast bifallen us.*'

'Kivrin,' Dunworthy said, and started towards her.

'Don't come any closer,' she said in English, holding the stick out in front of her like a spear. Its end was broken off jaggedly.

'It's me, Kivrin, Mr Dunworthy,' he said, still walking towards her.

'No!' she said and backed away, jabbing the broken spade at him. 'You don't understand. It's the plague.'

'It's all right, Kivrin. We've been inoculated.'

'Inoculated,' she said as if she didn't know what the word meant. 'It was the bishop's clerk. He had it when they came.'

Colin ran up, and she raised the stick again.

'It's all right,' Dunworthy said again. 'This is Colin. He's been inoculated as well. We've come to take you home.'

She looked at him steadily for a long minute, the snow falling around them 'To take me home,' she said, no expression in her voice, and looked down at the grave at her feet. It was shorter than the others, and narrower, as if it held a child.

After a minute she looked up at Dunworthy, and there was no expression in her face either. I am too late, he thought despairingly, looking at her standing there in her bloody smock, surrounded by graves. They have already crucified her. 'Kivrin,' he said.

She let the spade fall. 'You must help me,' she said, and turned and walked away from them towards the church.

'Are you sure it's her?' Colin whispered.

'Yes,' he said.

'What's the matter with her?'

I'm too late, he thought, and put his hand on Colin's shoulder for support. She will never forgive me.

'What's wrong?' Colin asked. 'Are you feeling ill again?'

571

'No,' he said, but he waited a moment before he took his hand away.

Kivrin had stopped at the church door and was holding her side again. A chill went through him. She has it, he thought. She has the plague. 'Are you ill?' he asked.

'No,' she said. She took her hand away and looked at it as if she expected it to be covered with blood. 'He kicked – me.' She tried to push the church door open, winced, and let Colin. 'I think he broke some ribs.'

Colin got the heavy wooden door open and they went inside. Dunworthy blinked against the darkness, willing his eyes to adjust to it. There was no light at all from the narrow windows, though he could tell where they were. He could make out a low, heavy shape ahead on the left – a body? – and the darker masses of the first pillars, but beyond them it was completely dark. Beside him, Colin was fumbling in his baggy pockets.

Far ahead, a flame flickered illuminating nothing but itself. It went out. Dunworthy started towards it.

'Hold on a minute,' Colin said, and flashed on a pocket torch. It blinded Dunworthy, making everything outside its diffused beam as black as when they first came in. Colin shone it round the church, on the painted walls, the heavy pillars, the uneven floor. The light caught on the shape Dunworthy had thought was a body. It was a stone tomb.

'She's up there,' Dunworthy said, pointing towards the altar, and Colin obligingly aimed the torch in that direction.

Kivrin was kneeling by someone who lay on the floor in front of the rood screen. It was a man, Dunworthy saw as they came closer. His legs and lower body were covered with a purple blanket, and his large hands were crossed on his chest. Kivrin was trying to light a candle with a coal, but the candle had burned down into a misshapen stub of wax and would not stay lit. She seemed grateful when Colin came up with his torch. He shone it full on them.

'You must help me with Roche,' she said, squinting into the light. She leaned towards the man and reached for his hand.

She thinks he's still alive, Dunworthy thought, but she said, in that flat matter-of-fact voice, 'He died this morning.'

Colin shone the pocket torch on the body. The crossed hands were nearly as purple as the blanket in the harsh light of the torch, but the man's face was pale and utterly at peace.

'What was he, a knight?' Colin said wonderingly.

'No,' Kivrin said. 'A saint.'

She laid her hand on his stiff one. Her hand was calloused and bloody, the fingernails black with dirt. 'You must help me,' she said.

'Help you what?' Colin asked.

She wants us to help her bury him, Dunworthy thought, and we can't. The man she had called Roche was huge. He must have towered over Kivrin when he was alive. Even if they could dig a grave, the three of them together could not carry him, and Kivrin would never let them put a rope round his neck and drag him out to the churchyard.

'Help you what?' Colin said. 'We don't have much time.'

They hadn't any time. It was already late afternoon, and they would never find their way through the forest after dark, and there was no telling how long Badri could keep the intermittent going. He had said twenty-four hours, but he had not looked strong enough to last two, and it had already been nearly eight. And the ground was frozen, and Kivrin's ribs were broken, and the effects of the aspirin were wearing off. He was beginning to shiver again here in the cold church.

We can't bury him, he thought, looking at her kneeling there, and how can I tell her that when I have arrived too late for anything else?

'Kivrin,' he said.

She patted the stiff hand gently. 'We won't be able to bury him,' she said in that calm, expressionless voice. 'We had to put Rosemund in his grave, after the steward—' She looked up at Dunworthy. 'I tried to dig another one this morning, but the ground's too hard I broke the spade.' She looked up at Dunworthy. 'I said the mass for the dead for him. And I tried to ring the bell.'

'We heard you,' Colin said. 'That's how we found you.'

'It should have been nine strokes,' she said, 'but I had to stop.'

She put her hand to her side, as if remembering pain. 'You must help me ring the rest.'

'Why?' Colin said. 'I don't think there's anybody left alive to hear it.'

'It doesn't matter,' Kivrin said, looking at Dunworthy.

'We haven't time,' Colin said. 'It'll be dark soon, and the drop is—'

'I'll ring it,' Dunworthy said. He stood up. 'You stay there,' he said, though she had made no move to get up. 'I'll ring the bell.' He started back down the nave.

'It's getting *dark*,' Colin said, trotting to catch up with him, the light from his torch dancing crazily over the pillars and the floor as he ran, 'and you said you didn't know how long they could hold the net open. *Wait* a minute.'

Dunworthy pushed open the door, squinting against the expected glare of the snow, but it had grown darker while they were in the church, the sky heavy and smelling of snow. He walked rapidly across the churchyard to the bell tower. The cow that Colin had seen when they rode in the village ducked through the lychgate and ambled across the graves towards them, its hooves sinking in the snow.

'What's the use of ringing it when there's no one to hear it?' Colin said, stopping to switch off his torch and then running to catch up again.

Dunworthy went in the tower. It was as dark and cold as the church and smelled of rats. The cow poked its head in, and Colin squeezed past it and stood against the curving wall.

'You're the one who keeps saying we have to get back to the drop, that it's going to close and leave us here,' Colin said. 'You're the one who said we didn't have time even to find Kivrin.'

Dunworthy stood there a moment, letting his eyes adjust and trying to catch his breath. He had walked too fast, and the tightness in his chest was worse. He looked up at the rope. It hung above their heads in the darkness, a greasy-looking knot a foot from the frayed end.

'Can I ring it?' Colin said, staring up at it.

'You're too small,' Dunworthy said.

'I'm *not*,' he said and jumped up at the rope. He caught the end, below the knot, and hung on for several moments before dropping, but the rope scarcely moved, and the bell only clanged faintly and out of tune, as if someone had hit the side of it with a rock. 'It's *heavy*,' he said.

Dunworthy raised his arms and took hold of the rough rope. It was cold and bristly. He yanked sharply down, not sure he could do any better than Colin, and the rope cut into his hands. *Bong*.

'It's loud!' Colin said, clapping his hands over his ears and gazing delightedly up at it.

'One,' Dunworthy said. One and up. Remembering the Americans, he bent his knees and pulled straight down on the rope. Two. And up. And three.

He wondered how Kivrin had been able to ring any strokes at all with her hurt ribs. The bell was far heavier, far louder than he had imagined, and it seemed to reverberate in his head, his tightening chest. *Bong*.

He thought of Ms Piantini, bending her chubby knees and counting to herself. Five. He had not appreciated what difficult work it was. Each pull seemed to yank the breath out of his lungs. Six.

He wanted to stop and rest, but he didn't want Kivrin, listening inside the church, to think he had quit, that he had only intended to finish the strokes she had begun. He tightened his grip above the knot and leaned against the stone wall for a moment, trying to ease the tightness in his chest.

'Are you all right, Mr Dunworthy?' Colin said.

'Yes,' he said, and pulled down so hard it seemed to tear his lungs open. Seven.

He should not have leaned against the wall. The stones were cold as ice. They had set him shivering again. He thought of Ms Taylor, trying to finish the Chicago Surprise Minor, counting how many strokes were left, trying not to give in to the pounding in her head.

'I can finish it,' Colin said, and Dunworthy could scarcely hear him. 'I can go get Kivrin, and we can do the last two strokes. We can both pull on it.'

Dunworthy shook his head. 'Every man must stick to his bell,' he said breathlessly and yanked down on the rope. Eight. He must not let go of the rope. Ms Taylor had fainted and let it go, and the bell had swung right over, the rope whipping like a live thing. It had wrapped itself around Finch's neck and nearly strangled him. He must hold to it, in spite of everything.

He pulled down on the rope and hung on to it till he was certain he could stand and then let it rise. 'Nine,' he said.

Colin was frowning at him. 'You're having a relapse, aren't you?' he said suspiciously.

'No,' Dunworthy said, and let go of the rope.

The cow had its head in the door. Dunworthy pushed it roughly aside and walked back to the church and went inside.

Kivrin was still kneeling beside Roche, her hand still holding his stiff one.

He stopped in front of her. 'I rang the bell,' he said.

She looked up without nodding.

'Don't you think we'd better go now?' Colin said. 'It's getting dark.'

'Yes,' Dunworthy said. 'I think we'd best—' The dizziness caught him completely unaware, and he staggered and nearly fell on to Roche's body.

Kivrin put out her hand and Colin dived for him, the torch flashing erratically across the beamed ceiling as he grabbed Dunworthy's arm. He caught himself on one knee and the flat of his hand and reached out with the other for Kivrin, but she was on her feet and backing away.

'You're ill!' It was an accusation, an indictment. 'You've caught the plague, haven't you?' she said, her voice showing emotion for the first time. '*Haven't* you?'

'No,' Dunworthy said, 'it's—'

'He's having a relapse,' Colin said, sticking the torch in the crook of the statue's arm so he could help Dunworthy to a sitting position. 'He didn't pay any attention to my placards.'

'It's a virus,' Dunworthy said, sitting down with his back to the statue. 'It's not the plague. Both of us have had streptomycin and gamma globulin. We can't get the plague.'

He leaned his head back against the statue. 'It's a virus. I'll be all right. I only need to rest a moment.'

'I told him he shouldn't have rung the bell,' Colin said,

emptying the burlap sack on to the stone floor. He wrapped the empty sack round Dunworthy's shoulders.

'Are there any aspirin left?' Dunworthy asked.

'You're only supposed to take them every three hours,' Colin said, 'and you're not supposed to take them without water.'

'Then fetch me some water,' he snapped.

Colin looked to Kivrin for support, but she was still standing on the other side of Roche's body, watching Dunworthy warily.

'Now,' Dunworthy said, and Colin ran out, his boots echoing on the stone floor. Dunworthy looked across at Kivrin, and she took a step back.

'It isn't the plague,' he said. 'It's a virus. We were afraid you had been exposed to it before you came through and had come down with it. Did you?'

'Yes,' she said, and knelt beside Roche. 'He saved my life.'

She smoothed the purple blanket, and Dunworthy realised it was a velvet cloak. It had a large silk cross sewn in the centre of it.

'He told me not to be afraid,' she said. She pulled the cloak up over his chest, over his crossed hands, but the action left his feet, in thick, incongruous sandals, uncovered. Dunworthy took the burlap bag from round his shoulders and spread it gently over the feet and then stood up, carefully, holding on to the statue so he wouldn't fall again.

Kivrin patted Roche's hands under the cloak. 'He didn't mean to hurt me,' she said.

Colin came back in with a bucket half-full of water he must have found in a puddle. He was breathing hard. 'The cow attacked me!' he said, scooping a filthy dipper out of the bucket. He emptied the aspirin into Dunworthy's hand. There were five tablets.

Dunworthy took two of them, swallowing as little of the water as he could, and handed the others to Kivrin. She took them from him solemnly, still kneeling on the floor.

'I couldn't find any horses,' Colin said, handing Kivrin the dipper. 'Just a mule.'

'Donkey,' Kivrin said. 'Maisry stole Agnes' pony.' She gave Colin the dipper and took hold of Roche's hand again. 'He rang the bell for everyone, so their souls could go safely to heaven.'

'Don't you think we'd better be going?' Colin whispered. 'It's almost dark out.'

'Even Rosemund,' Kivrin said as if she hadn't heard. 'He was already ill. I told him there wasn't time, that we had to leave for Scotland.'

'We must go now,' Dunworthy said, 'before the light fails.'

She didn't move or let go of Roche's hand. 'He held my hand when I was dying.'

'Kivrin,' he said gently.

She laid her hand on Roche's cheek and got to her knees. Dunworthy offered her his hand but she stood up by herself, her hand pressed to her side, and walked down the nave.

At the door she turned and looked back into the darkness. 'He told me where the drop was when he was dying, so I could go back to heaven. He told me he wanted me to leave him there and go, so that when he came I would already be there,' she said, and went out into the snow.

CHAPTER THIRTY-SIX

The snow fell silently, peacefully on the stallion and the donkey waiting by the lychgate. Dunworthy helped Kivrin on to the stallion, and she did not flinch away from his touch as he had been afraid she would, but as soon as she was up, she leaned away from his grasp and took hold of the reins. As soon as he removed his hands, she slumped back against the saddle, her hand against her side.

Dunworthy was shivering now, clenching his teeth against it so Colin wouldn't see. It took three tries to get him on to the donkey, and he thought he might slip off at any minute.

'I think I'd better lead your mule,' Colin said, looking disapprovingly at him.

'There isn't time,' Dunworthy said. 'It's getting dark. You ride behind Kivrin.'

Colin led the stallion over to the lychgate, climbed up on the lintel, and scrambled up behind Kivrin.

'Do you have the locator?' Dunworthy said, trying to kick the donkey without falling off.

'I know the way,' Kivrin said.

'Yes,' Colin said. He held up the locator. 'And the pocket torch.' He flicked it on and then shone it all round the churchyard, as if looking for something they might have left behind. He seemed to notice the graves for the first time.

Is that where you buried everybody?' he said, holding the light steady on the smooth white mounds.

Yes,' Kivrin said.

'Did they die a long time ago?'

She turned the stallion and started it up the hill. 'No,' she said.

The cow followed them partway up the hill, its swollen udders swinging, and then stopped and began lowing pitifully. Dunworthy looked back at it. It mooed uncertainly at him, and then ambled back down the road towards the village. They were nearly to the top of the hill, and the snow was letting up, but below, in the village, it was still snowing hard. The graves were covered completely, and the church was obscured the bell tower scarcely visible at all.

Kivrin did not so much as glance back. She rode steadily forward sitting very straight, with Colin on behind her, holding not to Kivrin's waist but to the high back of the saddle. The snow came down fitfully, and then in single flakes, and by the time they were in thick woods again, it had nearly stopped.

Dunworthy followed the horse, trying to keep up with its steady gait, trying, not to give way to the fever. The aspirin was not working – he had taken it with too little water – and he could feel the fever beginning to overtake him, beginning to shut out the woods and the donkey's bony back and Colin's voice.

He was talking cheerfully to Kivrin, telling her about the epidemic, and the way he told it, it sounded like an adventure. 'They said there was a quarantine and we'd have to go back to London, but I didn't want to do that. I wanted to see Great-aunt Mary. So I sneaked through the barrier, and the guard saw me and said, "You there! Stop!" and started to chase me, and I ran down the street and into this alley.'

They stopped, and Colin and Kivrin dismounted. Colin took off his muffler and she pulled up her blood-stiff smock and tied it round her ribs. Dunworthy knew the pain must be even worse than he'd thought, that he should try at least to help her, but he was afraid that if he got down off the donkey, he would not be able to get back on.

Kivrin and Colin mounted again, she helping him up, and they set off again, slowing at every turning and side path to check their direction, Colin hunching over the locator's screen and pointing, Kivrin nodding in confirmation.

'This was where I fell off the donkey,' Kivrin said when they stopped at a fork. 'That first night I was so ill. I thought he was a cut-throat.'

They came to another fork. It had stopped snowing but the

clouds above the trees were dark and heavy. Colin had to shine his torch on the locator to read it. He pointed down the right-hand path and got on behind Kivrin again, telling her his adventures.

'Mr Dunworthy said, "You've lost the fix," and then he went straight over into Mr Gilchrist and they both fell down,' Colin said. 'Mr Gilchrist was acting like he'd done it on purpose, he wouldn't even help me cover him up. He was shivering like blood, and he had a fever, and I kept shouting, "Mr Dunworthy! Mr Dunworthy!" but he couldn't hear me. And Mr Gilchrist kept saying, "I'm holding you personally responsible."'

It began to spit snow again and the wind picked up. Dunworthy clung to the donkey's stiff mane, shivering.

'They wouldn't tell me *anything*,' Colin was saying, 'and when I tried to get in to see Great-aunt Mary, they said, "We don't allow children."'

They were riding into the wind, the snow blowing against Dunworthy's cloak in freezing gusts. He leaned forward till he was nearly lying on the donkey's neck.

'The doctor came out,' Colin said, 'and he started whispering to this nurse, and I knew she was dead,' and Dunworthy felt a sudden stab of grief, as if he were hearing it for the first time. Oh, Mary, he thought.

'I didn't know what to do,' Colin said, 'so I just sat there, and Mrs Gaddson, she's this *necrotic* person, came up and started reading to me out of the Bible how it was God's will. I hate Mrs Gaddson!' he said violently. 'She's the one who deserved to get the flu!'

Their voices began to ring, the overtones echoing against and round the woods so that he shouldn't have been able to understand them, but oddly they rang clearer and clearer in the cold air, and he thought they must be able to hear them all the way to Oxford, seven hundred years away.

It came to Dunworthy suddenly that Mary wasn't dead, that here in this terrible year, in this century that was worse than a ten, she had not yet died, and it seemed to him a blessing beyond any he had any right to expect.

'And that was when we heard the bell,' Colin said. 'Mr Dunworthy said it was you calling for help.'

'It was,' Kivrin said. 'This won't work. He'll fall off.'

'You're right,' Colin said, and Dunworthy realised that they had dismounted again and were standing next to the donkey, Kivrin holding the rope bridle.

'We have to put you on the horse,' Kivrin said, taking hold of Dunworthy's waist. 'You're going to fall off the donkey. Come on. Get down. I'll help you.'

They both had to help him down, Kivrin reaching round him in a way he knew had to hurt her ribs, Colin almost holding him up.

'If I could just sit down for a moment,' Dunworthy said through chattering teeth.

'There isn't *time*,' Colin said, but they helped him to the side of the path and eased him down against a rock.

Kivrin reached up under her smock and brought out three aspirin. 'Here. Take these,' she said, holding them out to him on her open palm.

'Those were for you,' he said. 'Your ribs—'

She looked at him steadily, unsmilingly. 'I'll be all right,' she said, and went to tie the stallion to a bush.

'Do you want some water?' Colin said. 'I could build a fire and melt some snow.'

'I'll be all right,' Dunworthy said. He put the aspirin in his mouth and swallowed them.

Kivrin was adjusting the stirrups, untying the leather straps with practised skill. She knotted them and came back over to Dunworthy to help him up. 'Ready?' she said, putting her hand under his arm.

'Yes,' Dunworthy said, and tried to stand up.

'This was a mistake,' Colin said. 'We'll never get him on,' but they did, putting his foot in the stirrups and his hands round the pommel and hoisting him up, and at the end he was even able to help them a little, offering a hand so Colin could clamber up the side of the stallion in front of him.

He had stopped shivering, but he was not sure whether that was a good sign or not, and when they started off again, Kivrin ahead on the jolting donkey, Colin already talking, he leaned into Colin's back and closed his eyes.

'So I decided that when I get out of school, I'm going to come to Oxford and be an historian like you,' Colin was saying. 'I don't want to come to the Black Death, though, I want to go to the Crusades.'

He listened to them, leaning against Colin. It was getting dark, and they were in the Middle Ages in the woods, two cripples and a child, and Badri, another cripple, trying to hold the net open and susceptible to relapse himself. But he could not seem to summon any panic or even any worry. Colin had the locator and Kivrin knew where the drop was. They would be all right.

Even if they could not find the drop and they were trapped here for ever, even if Kivrin could not forgive him, she would be all right. She would take them to Scotland, where the plague never went, and Colin would pull fishhooks and a frying pan out of his bag of tricks and they would catch trout and salmon to eat. They might even find Basingame.

'I've watched sword fighting on the vids, and I know how to drive a horse,' Colin said, and then, '*Stop!*'

Colin jerked the reins back and up, and the stallion stopped, its nose against the donkey's tail. The donkey had stopped short. They were at the top of a little hill. At its bottom was a frozen puddle and a line of willows.

'Kick it,' Colin said, but Kivrin was already dismounting.

'He won't go any further,' she said. 'He did this before. He saw me come through. I thought it was Gawyn, but it was Roche all along.' She pulled the rope bridle off over the donkey's head, and it immediately bolted back along the narrow path.

'Do you want to ride?' Colin asked her, already scrambling down. She shook her head. 'It hurts more mounting and dismounting than walking.' She was looking across at the farther hill. The trees went only halfway up, and above them the hill was white with snow. It must have stopped snowing, though Dunworthy hadn't been aware of it. The clouds were breaking up, and between them the sky was a pale, clear lavender.

'He thought I was St Catherine,' she said. 'He saw me come through, like you were afraid would happen. He thought I had been sent from God to help them in their hour of need.'

'Well, and you did, didn't you?' Colin said. He jerked the reins awkwardly, and the stallion started down the hill, Kivrin walking beside it. 'You should have seen the mess in the other place we were. Bodies everywhere, and I don't think anybody helped them.'

He handed the reins to Kivrin. 'I'll go and see if the net's open,' he said and ran ahead. 'Badri was going to open it every two hours.' He crashed into the thicket and disappeared.

Kivrin brought the stallion to a stop at the bottom of the hill and helped Dunworthy down.

'We'd best take his saddle and bridle off,' Dunworthy said. 'When we found him, he was tangled in a bush.'

Together they got the girth uncinched and the saddle off. Kivrin unhooked the bridle and reached up to stroke the stallion's head.

'He'll be all right,' Dunworthy said.

'Maybe,' she said.

Colin burst through the willows, scattering snow everywhere. 'It's not there.'

'It'll open soon,' Dunworthy said.

'Are we taking the horse with us?' Colin asked. 'I thought historians weren't allowed to take anything into the future. But it'd be great if we could take him. I could ride him when I go to the Crusades.'

He exploded back through the thicket, spraying snow. 'Come on, it could open any time.'

Kivrin nodded. She smacked the stallion on its flank. It walked a few paces and then stopped and looked back at them questioningly.

'Come *on*,' Colin said from somewhere inside the thicket, but Kivrin didn't move.

She put her hand against her side.

'Kivrin,' Dunworthy said, moving to help her.

'I'll be all right,' she said and turned away from him to push aside the tangled branches of the thicket.

It was already twilight under the trees. The sky between the black branches of the oak was lavender-blue. Colin was dragging a fallen log into the middle of the clearing. 'In case we just missed it and have to wait a whole two hours,' he said. Dunworthy sat down gratefully.

'How do we know where to stand when the net opens?' Colin asked Kivrin.

'We'll be able to see the condensation,' she said. She went over to the oak tree and bent down to brush the snow away from its base.

'What if it gets dark?' Colin asked.

She sat down against the tree, biting her lips as she eased herself on to the roots.

Colin squatted down between them. 'I didn't bring any matches or I'd start a fire,' he said.

'It's all right,' Dunworthy said.

Colin switched on his pocket torch and then switched it off again. 'I think I'd better save this in case something goes wrong.'

There was a movement in the willows. Colin leaped up. 'I think it's starting,' he said.

'It's the stallion,' Dunworthy said. 'He's eating.'

'Oh.' Colin sat back down. 'You don't think the net already opened and we didn't see it because it was dark?'

'No,' Dunworthy said.

'Perhaps Badri had another relapse and couldn't keep the net open,' he said, sounding more excited than scared.

They waited. The sky darkened to purple-blue, and stars began to come out in the branches of the oak. Colin sat on the log beside Dunworthy and talked about the Crusades.

'You know all about the Middle Ages,' he said to Kivrin, 'so I thought perhaps you'd help me get ready, you know, teach me things.'

'You're not old enough,' she said. 'It's very dangerous.'

'I know,' Colin said. 'But I really want to go. You have to help me. Please?'

'It won't be anything like you expect,' she said.

'Is the food necrotic? I read in this book Mr Dunworthy gave me how they ate spoiled meat and swans and things.'

Kivrin looked down at her hands for a long minute. 'Most of it was terrible,' she said softly, 'but there were some wonderful things.'

Wonderful things. He thought of Mary, leaning against Balliol's gate, talking about the Valley of the Kings, saying, 'I'll never forget it.' Wonderful things.

'What about Brussels sprouts?' Colin asked. 'Did they eat Brussels sprouts in the Middle Ages?'

Kivrin almost smiled. 'I don't think they were invented yet.'

'Good!' He jumped up. 'Did you hear that? I think it's starting. It sounds like a bell.'

Kivrin raised her head, listening. 'A bell was ringing when I came through,' she said.

'Come on,' Colin said, and yanked Dunworthy to his feet. 'Can't you hear it?'

It was a bell, faint and far away.

'It's coming from over here,' Colin said. He darted to the edge of the clearing 'Come on!'

Kivrin put her hand on the ground for support and got to her knees. Her free hand went involuntarily to her side.

Dunworthy reached his hand out to her, but she didn't take it. 'I'll be all right,' she said quietly.

'I know,' he said, and let his hand drop.

She stood up carefully, holding on to the rough trunk of the oak, and then straightened and stood free of it.

'I got it all on the corder,' she said. 'Everything that happened.'

Like John Clyn, he thought, looking at her ragged hair, her dirty face. A true historian, writing in the empty church, surrounded by graves. *I, seeing so many evils, have put into writing all the things that I have witnessed. Lest things which should be remembered perish with time.*

Kivrin turned her palms up and looked at her wrists in the twilight. 'Father Roche and Agnes and Rosemund and all of them,' she said. 'I got it all down.'

She traced a line down the side of her wrist with her finger. '*Io suiicien lui damo amo,*' she said softly. 'You are here in place of the friends I love.'

'Kivrin,' Dunworthy said.

'Come on!' Colin said. 'It's starting. Can't you hear the bell?'

'Yes,' Dunworthy said. It was Ms Piantini on the tenor, ringing the lead-in to 'When at Last My Saviour Cometh.'

Kivrin came and stood next to Dunworthy. She placed her hands together, as if she were praying.

'I can see Badri!' Colin said. He cupped his hands round his mouth. 'She's all right!' he shouted. 'We saved her!'

Ms Piantini's tenor clanged and the other bells chimed in joyously. The air began to glitter, like snowflakes.

'Apocalyptic!' Colin said, his face alight.

Kivrin reached out for Dunworthy's hand and clasped it tightly in her own.

'I knew you'd come,' she said, and the net opened.

Connie Willis was born in Colorado and graduated from university there. Her first story was published in 1971 and she began full-time writing in the early 80s. Her novels and short stories have won multiple Hugo and Nebula Awards. She lives in Colorado.

A full list of SF Masterworks can be found at

www.gollancz.co.uk